Journey of the Shield·Brethren

LAKE BAIKAL

GHATAI ANATE

Karakorum

Dzungarian Gate

EMPIRE OF THE GREAT KHANS

YELLOW RIVER

CHINA

HIMALAYAN MOUNTAINS

YANGTZI RIVER

NATE HI

BAY OF BENGAL

KHMER EMPIRE

The Mongoliad

BOOK THREE

INCLUDES *SEER*,
A PREQUEL TO THE MONGOLIAD TRILOGY

The Mongoliad

BOOK THREE

INCLUDES *SEER*, A
PREQUEL TO THE MONGOLIAD TRILOGY

NEAL STEPHENSON, GREG BEAR,
MARK TEPPO, NICOLE GALLAND, ERIK BEAR,
JOSEPH BRASSEY, COOPER MOO

IILLUSTRATIONS BY MIKE GRELL

47N●RTH

The characters and events portrayed in this book are
fictitious. Any similarity to real persons, living or dead, is
coincidental and not intended by the author.

Published by 47North
PO Box 400818
Las Vegas, NV 89140

ISBN-13: 9781612187242
ISBN-10: 1612187242

To Erik Artzt, Fraser Mendel, Andrew Somlyo, and Brandon Uttech. A journey is always more entertaining when in the company of these gentlemen.

CONTENTS

seer

MARK TEPPO

1

Their morning training was interrupted by the unexpected arrival of a plainly dressed man. Lugo, the youngest initiate at the chapter house, noticed him first and nearly received a blow to the head as a result of his inattention. Shouting at the rest of the men to stop their drill, Andreas glared at the man who was standing inside the chapter house gate. "How might we assist you?" he called across the yard, more than a little annoyed at the interruption.

"I have a proposition for your quartermaster," the man said.

The half dozen Shield-Brethren in the yard looked back and forth at Andreas, their training master, and Saluador, the most senior of the men at the chapter house; in many of their sweat-streaked faces, Andreas could read an eagerness to be done with training. With a sigh, he rested his longsword against his shoulder and waved a hand, dismissing the group to fetch the quartermaster.

"Bring wine," Saluador called after them.

"What sort of proposition?" Andreas inquired.

A fringe of yellow hair ran along the man's jaw, and he stared, unblinking, at Andreas and Saluador as he thought. Andreas was reminded of the owls he had seen in the northern forests, silent watchers that would sit on branches and do nothing but stare as the dark veil of night was lowered over the trees.

"I'll speak of it with your quartermaster," the stranger said finally.

Andreas chewed on the inside of his cheek and glanced at Saluador, who shrugged. They were dressed in simple shirts and pants, damp with sweat and dirt from their training. It was easy to mistake them for mere soldiers; they were not offended by such assumptions.

They were spared further insightful conversation by Lugo, who returned with a bottle of wine and two cups. Saluador led the man over to a small table in the shade along the southern wall, and he poured wine into the cups as the man settled stiffly on a nearby stool.

Domingo emerged from the main house, trailed by Harald and Guillén. While Domingo was as simply attired as the rest, he had thrown a blue cloak over his shoulders to give the nominal impression that he was in charge. He was a burly man, with a worn face that had been hardened over the years like a sunbaked brick. He was missing his left arm; it had been lost while crusading in the Holy Land, during an assault on a watchtower outside the Egyptian city of Damietta. Cut off in a single stroke by a Muslim saber and then claimed by the Nile. The end of the stump had taken a long time to heal, and it was a tangled mess of scar tissue.

"Domingo Ramon de Sargantas," the Shield-Brethren quartermaster said, offering his hand. "I am in charge of this chapter house."

The man had been staring at the scarred knob of Domingo's left arm. "Jacobi de Reyns," he said suddenly when he realized what he was doing. He clasped Domingo's offered hand.

Reyns was a city north of Paris, and Andreas wondered what the man was doing in Catalonia. He had come alone to the chapter house, and his clothes were not very ostentatious. Jacobi looked to be a dozen or more years older than Andreas, well past the age when sons broke away from their families and went off to strange lands to find their fortunes. *What fortune had he lost?* Andreas wondered. *Or did it elude him still?*

Of course, he was far from home as well. Farther, in fact, as Lund was a week's travel beyond Reyns. But he hadn't looked on the cold and gray water of the Baltic Sea for many years. For him, it was a matter of wanderlust. *That is why I never stay long,* he would tell those who asked, *I want to see the world.* He had been to the northernmost and southernmost shores of Christendom; as far east as Petraathen, the ancient citadel of the Shield-Brethren; and as far west as a dingy tavern not a mile from this chapter house, just beyond the ruins of the Roman walls that marked the center of Barcelona.

"I am told you have a proposition for us," Domingo said, picking up one of the two cups as he sat down opposite the merchant.

"Yes," Jacobi said, blinking several times. "I have several wagons of goods that need to arrive safely at their destination, and I seek to hire a small company of your men to accompany them."

Domingo regarded the man for a moment before answering. "The *Ordo Militum Vindicis Intactae* do not hire themselves out as caravan guards," he said finally. "There are several hundred men-at-arms in Barcelona who would satisfy your needs."

"I know none of them," Jacobi replied. "Nor their reputations."

Domingo made a noise in his chest and idly reached over to scratch the end of his shortened arm. Andreas had only been at the Shield-Brethren chapter house for a few months, but he had been there long enough to notice a connection between the quartermaster's mood and the presence of a nagging itch in the scarred knob of Domingo's arm.

The trader's comment was a bit clumsy in its inference, but not surprising. The *Ordo Militum Vindicis Intactae*—the Shield-Brethren, as they were more commonly known—were famed throughout Christendom for their martial prowess. The few victories the West could claim in the crusades, for instance, came about because of the presence of the Shield-Brethren in the Holy Land. What merchant wouldn't want men of this caliber guarding his caravan?

"You don't know us, either," Domingo pointed out.

"You have a reputation for trustworthiness," the trader said finally, reaching for his cup. "It is a simple proposition. I do not understand your reticence." He took a small sip, staring over the rim at Domingo with his wide eyes. "Do you think I cannot afford you?"

Domingo waved the question away. "I am not as concerned about the cost as I am the reason why you seek to incur it."

"My cargo is valuable," Jacobi said. "Why would I not pay to keep it safe?"

"From whom?"

"I am traveling into the Pyrenees," Jacobi said. "There is much unrest on the other side of those mountains. The Inquisition is still in Toulouse. Who knows what manner of ruffian and fugitive is fleeing the Church, heading south into the mountains." He tilted his head to one side. "Heading this way."

"They'll be unorganized, scattered," Domingo countered. "Easily put off by an organized host of armed men."

"Exactly my point," Jacobi countered. "Why wouldn't I want the most organized—the most effective—host guarding my goods? Why wouldn't I want the order that was worthy enough for Eleanor of Aquitaine?"

"That was a long time ago," Domingo said quietly.

"It wasn't," the trader argued with a slight wave of his hand. "I was a child when King Richard was ransomed. I remember the songs." He leaned forward, his eyes wide. "I expect you do too."

"Regardless, I do not have any men I can spare," Domingo said.

Jacobi de Reyns turned his head and looked at the loitering Shield-Brethren. "Yes," he said slowly, blinking twice, "they look very busy."

Domingo scowled at the indolent Shield-Brethren. Andreas stared back at the quartermaster and the merchant, arms crossed over his chest. He wasn't about to be cowed by the owlish trader. How any of them spent their time was none of the man's business.

Domingo shook his head very slightly as he reached for his cup of wine. "I'll give your proposal some thought," he said.

"Excellent," Jacobi said, taking a tiny sip from his cup. "I am staying at the Inn of the Ram's Head. Do you know it?" When Domingo nodded, the trader stood, smoothing the front of his robe. "I hope to leave before midday the day after the next," he said.

"You'll know my decision well before then," Domingo said.

"Very good," Jacobi said. He offered the quartermaster a curt nod before he departed.

Domingo waited until the trader had passed through the narrow gate of the chapter house before he banged his fist on the table. Lugo, who had been toying with his sword, started, and Andreas saw him wince and raise his thumb to his mouth. Saluador scratched his chin and appeared to find an interesting pattern in the white clouds scattered across the sky.

Andreas ambled over to the table, and without being asked, refilled Domingo's cup. He tossed out the remnants of the wine in the trader's cup, and refilled it as well. He sat down in the empty chair and drank heavily from the warm and sweet liquid.

"Weren't there some drills you should be doing?" Domingo asked.

"We did them," Andreas said.

"No man can ever drill too much," Domingo said.

"Perhaps, but it is important to take a break every now and then," Andreas said. "Otherwise accidents can happen."

Domingo glanced over at Lugo, who snatched his thumb away from his mouth. "I can see that," Domingo noted drily.

"They could use some real exercise," Andreas said, "and a change of scenery."

"Are you volunteering to lead them?" Domingo inquired.

"Me?" Andreas shook his head as he drank more of the wine. "I don't have the right temperament for command," he said.

"Then why do you make such a suggestion?" Domingo asked. He wiggled his stump at Andreas. "Do you expect me to take this commission and lead them?"

Andreas eyed the scarred knob. "It isn't as simple as it seems," he said.

Domingo grunted, and his face shifted into a more thoughtful expression. "Of course it isn't. He wants more than our reputation."

"It should cost him more," Andreas said. When Domingo glared at him, he shrugged. "Coin is coin. It puts food in our bellies more readily than reputation."

"Aye, that it does." Domingo sighed. "Visit him at the inn after sundown. Ask for double his price. If he agrees, take the commission."

Andreas said nothing as he stared across the narrow yard. It had been a year since he had appeared at any Shield-Brethren chapter house, and he knew such negligence on his part was unbecoming of the vows he had sworn. But the spirit of those vows could only be fulfilled by actively aiding the less fortunate in Christendom. Too many of his Brothers never left the confines of the Shield-Brethren chapter houses, inculcated by old habits passed down from the *Electi* in Petraathen. He was not so blind as to be unaware of the influence his training at Týrshammar had on his attitude, nor had he ever found himself regretting that education. It made him difficult, he knew; his upbringing made him rebellious and untrustworthy among his own Brothers—the only family he had.

So he had wandered far—north, south, east, and now west. Perhaps it was time to put aside the childish notion that it was a desire to see Christendom that drove him, and acknowledge that what drove him was some other emotion entirely. He thought of

Raphael, the Shield-Brethren knight he had met a few years ago, not far from Marzburg, in Germany. Raphael had trusted Andreas with his life—even though they had met but a day prior—and Andreas had not forgotten what that trust felt like. That sense of belonging.

"I'll lead them," he said. For a fleeting moment, he felt an inordinate panic threaten to overwhelm him, but he held on to the responsibility being offered. A tiny part of him squirmed, that endless restlessness that had plagued him for so many years fighting against being so constrained, and then it was still. It wasn't gone—just held in abeyance by something stronger.

* * *

In a number of French territories, the Inn of the Ram's Head would have been considered unfit conditions for a person of decent birth. Even riding a horse along the street where the inn sat would call into question a respectable person's reputation, but as it was, Jacobi de Reyns was a long way from anywhere that mattered and well out of sight of anyone who might know him or his family. The inn was dark and squalid and anonymous. The beer was cold and the food—while heavy on the oil, and mostly fish—was hot. The serving staff was comely as well—not too old, not too young, and certainly willing to offer him a salacious wink when they refilled his tankard.

It had been a while since he had enjoyed any female companionship, and he appreciated the suggestion—as aloof and impersonal as it was—that he might end his lengthy dry spell if he had the right amount of coin.

Though, if he had the right amount of coin, he'd be in Paris, sleeping with French whores. Where he should be, instead of godforsaken Catalonia.

Everything had been working fine two years ago; he and his partners had established a trade route between Carcassonne and

Bourges, with stops in Toulouse, Albi, and Clermont. Goods were moving readily back and forth. They were doubling their cargo with every circuit.

And then one of his partners had been detained by the Inquisition. Tomas had confessed, though Jacobi knew not quite what it was that Tomas had *to* confess. It didn't matter, though; in an instant, all of their merchandise and wagons were seized. He had only managed to avoid capture by virtue of not being in his house in Albi when the soldiers of the Inquisition came. He had been several miles south, in a nameless inn, having a clandestine affair with a delightful girl named Giselle.

Giselle's uncle had interrupted his afternoon tryst, arriving quite unexpectedly. Jacobi had tried to flee through the room's window, minus some of his clothing. He had dashed to the stable for his horse, where he had met the innkeeper, who was, it turned out, the one who had ratted him out to Giselle's uncle. Jacobi would have given the man a good thrashing, but was rebuffed—quite readily—by the pitchfork the innkeeper was waving about.

Bleeding from the thigh—and other nether regions—Jacobi had fled back to Albi, arriving in time to watch his house be put to the torch. The Inquisition's men took what property he had worth seizing, including his very frightened and very angry wife, Secile.

It had been her murderous expression, as she had caught sight of him skulking in the back of the crowd, that had convinced him it was time to leave France.

He hadn't gotten very far before his injuries became infected, starting with a certain portion of his anatomy. *It is God's justice*, several doctors had said when he tried to find someone who would treat him. He didn't have enough money to change their minds, and without any hope, he had wandered into the mountains along the southern border of France. Feverish and afraid that the diagnosis was coming true, he had stumbled into a tiny village high in the mountains, somewhere between Toulouse and Catalonia, where he had found a healer who was not as worried about God and His justice. She was part of a community of women—widows of crusaders, estranged daughters, and wild mystics who still believed the tenets of Catharism.

God's justice, indeed.

When he had recovered from the festering illness of his wounds, he had pledged himself to the village. It was remote, and while the community was mostly self-sufficient, there was some need for trade. He had no other expertise to offer, and he felt there was a debt to be paid. It took him a little while to convince them they needed a trader—someone who could arrange for a tiny trickle of goods to flow through their village. There were other villages scattered throughout the mountains; in time, perhaps he could build a new trade route. It wouldn't be nearly as bountiful as what he had had in France, but it might be enough.

That was, until the arrival of Captain Folquets de Vilapros, another displaced refugee from the crusade against the Cathars in Toulouse. Like him, the captain had lost his lands and his fortune during the Inquisition's expurgation of Albi; unlike Jacobi, though, he had managed to hang on to some of his retainers—the loyal sort who did not quibble about the source of their master's income...

A bustle of voices near the inn's door drew Jacobi out of his reverie, and he looked up to spy one of the Shield-Brethren moving through the crowded room with an enviable ease. The local toughs gave ground without even being aware of doing so, the merchants and traders nodded and spoke conversationally with the man as he passed, and one of the serving girls pressed herself and a tankard of beer against him with robust enthusiasm. He was the blond one who had been listening in on his conversation with the quartermaster. He looked more Frisian than Spanish, and he carried himself with a grace that teetered on the edge of swaggering arrogance but never quite spilled over. He caught sight of Jacobi and sat down opposite the trader, his back to the door.

"A fine evening in a fine establishment, good sir," the man said, a genuinely warm smile on his face.

"The weather is too warm and this is a shithole," Jacobi groused, put off by the man's strong presence. Normally, he would have been more contrite—more polite—but his mood had darkened during the last few minutes as he had started to brood about Vilapros.

The Shield-Brethren knight paused in the process of quaffing a large portion of his tankard and lowered it, foam dripping from his ruddy beard. "Aye," he said agreeably. "Both of those things are most certainly true. I am glad to see you are a man who prefers to speak plainly." He put his tankard down. "I am Andreas, knight initiate of the *Ordo Militum Vindicis Intactae*. Our quartermaster asked me to inform you of his decision." Jacobi was somewhat taken aback by Andreas's frankness, and he stared at him for a moment, blinking slowly. "And what was his decision?" he asked finally when it was clear that Andreas wasn't going to provide it without being prompted.

"How much were you willing to pay?" Andreas asked.

Jacobi frowned. He had told Domingo how much he had been willing to pay. Why was this man asking him again? With a tiny sigh, he repeated the number, glancing around as he did.

Andreas leaned forward. "Are you afraid one of those mercenaries Domingo told you about would hear what you are offering us?" he asked.

"No," Jacobi sputtered. "I just...This is hardly the place to talk about money."

"Then why did you ask us to come here?" Andreas asked.

Jacobi felt his face flush, and Andreas laughed.

"Did you think we were just going to wander in here and say, 'Why, yes, sir trader, we'd be happy to risk life and limb for a paltry sum such as you are willing to offer'?" Andreas asked. He shook his head and raised his tankard.

"Are you trying to bully me into paying more?" Jacobi snapped.

Andreas belched and shook his head. "How can an honest man be frightened if he is not confronted with a weapon?" He put his hands on the table. "Have I brought a knife to this table?"

"No," Jacobi said.

"Then I think you are using the wrong word," Andreas said. He raised his empty tankard and waggled it, trying to catch the eye of one of the serving girls.

"What do you want, then?" Jacobi said.

"Triple," Andreas replied.

"What?"

"I want triple the price you offered," Andreas said, smiling.

"That's outrageous," Jacobi sputtered.

"So is the original number you offered," Andreas pointed out. He smiled as the dark-haired girl swept over, pouring herself into his lap. "I seem to have emptied this one already," he said, showing her the inside of his tankard. "Might you be so kind as to bring another?"

She laughed, found an excuse to touch his chest several times as she got up, and disappeared into the crowd with his empty vessel.

Andreas turned back to Jacobi, and his face lost some of its easy charm. Jacobi swallowed, seeing for an instant a different man entirely sitting across from him. "You came to us," Andreas said quietly, "knowing full well our order does not do mercenary work, and then you remind us that we are not above doing such work for kings and queens, as if to say that our honor has a price that only the very wealthy and powerful can afford. Now, some of my brethren might take that as a slight, comparing us to the Templars like that, but I am a well-traveled man. I have been to France. I understand that, on occasion, the French have a tendency to be brusque—rude, even—and

I do not fault you or your family or your fellow countrymen for such gracelessness." He smiled—a cold, hard smile of a man who had seen much worse things than *mere* gracelessness...and done such things as well. "I too have my own moments of clumsiness. Like now, perhaps, when I tell you that if I were to take this commission, I would gladly gut you and leave you behind at the first sign that you had lied to us about the dangers of this journey."

Jacobi nodded slowly. "I understand," he said. His throat was tight, and he forced himself to swallow, fighting the bilious anger rising from his gut. *Just like the rest*, he thought. *So quick to make threats. So quick to push others around.* He considered rejecting Andreas's offer. He could get double the number of mercenaries for the original price he had offered.

But what of Vilapros? There was no doubt in his mind that the captain's men would intercept him on the way back to the village. The captain's man might couch his terms in pleasant language, but the ugliness was the same. The road was there. Jacobi owed for using it.

Just like the rest, he thought bitterly. Did it matter who he paid?

But this was different, wasn't it? *Hire them*, he reminded himself; *do what you were asked to do.*

"Double," he said with a light cough.

Andreas smiled, and it was as if a shadow had fled from the room. "I like you, Jacobi de Reyns," he announced. "You are not easily cowed." He slapped the table with his hand. "Double it is," he said. "But I want half before we leave."

* * *

Late in the afternoon, clouds had billowed over the mountains, straining to bring water to the many valleys hidden within the Pyrenees. The rain shower had been brief, a narrow curtain of warm water that moved slowly across the mountain lake before falling on the tiny village of Estartyol that lay along the western shore of the lake. The storm dragged warm air in its wake, and when the sun fell behind the mountains, the evening was cool but not crisp. A sure sign that the season was turning. Spring was coming.

A shawl loosely wrapped about her shoulders, Gaucelis strode toward the chapel of San Berenguer. The sky above was still streaked with clouds, white threads across an indigo canvas, and candlelight leaked out from many of the doors and windows of the small village. She could hear the sound of raucous voices from the one-roomed shack the villagers called a tavern, and judging by the cadence of the one voice that rose above the rest and the sporadic laughter that accompanied it, Míro was telling one of his ribald stories. A new one, she suspected, judging by the wealth of laugher.

She did not join the rest of the villagers very often for Míro's performances. While the village did not suffer much in the way of leadership, both she, in her role as healer, and Alice, the old dowager from Catalonian nobility, suffered the weight and responsibility of the villagers' safety. As such, she knew it was best to be more concerned about the well-being of Estartyol than the ribald witticisms of Míro's plays.

The chapel was the only building in Estartyol that was made from stone, and its walls were old when it had housed a pagan temple. Charlemagne had brought Christianity with him when he had scaled the Pyrenees during his efforts to conquer Spain. He had driven out the old religions, converting many of the temples into churches celebrating the Christian God. Some, however, were in remote locations, more readily forgotten than transformed. His armies had pillaged them and left them in ruin, the fallen walls waiting to be rediscovered by those who needed sanctuary, those who the Church and the Inquisition—its instrument of forceful conversion—deemed dangerous. Heretical.

The chapel was never locked. Gaucelis pushed open the broad door and entered the tiny church. When she closed the door behind her, the sounds from the tavern vanished. The chapel was still and quiet. A single candle burned at the far end, and judging from its height, it had been recently lit. There were a dozen rough benches scattered around the chamber, haphazardly arranged in a broad arc in front of the raised altar. As Gaucelis walked toward the altar, she spotted a huddled shape lying near one of the frontmost benches.

She rushed toward the body, half dreading and half knowing who it was. She knelt and carefully turned the prostrate person over. "Constansa." She sighed when she saw the young face.

The woman lying on the floor was still breathing, a slow but steady rhythm of exhausted slumber. Gaucelis had felt an urge to come to the chapel this evening—the nervous twinge in her heart that she had long learned not to ignore—and she was relieved to find her apprehension was misplaced. "Rest, my child," she whispered to Constansa as she arranged the young woman more comfortably on the floor. As she did, she noticed a piece of pale parchment trapped beneath Constansa's body. Pulling the parchment free, Gaucelis held it up to better examine it in the weak candlelight.

Constansa had drawn a half circle along the bottom edge of the parchment. Above it, following the curve, was a dense wall of hard charcoal slashes that marched across the sheet like spear tips. On the other half of the sheet, descending from the top, were splotches of red—some bright and shiny, while most were dark and hard. It looked like a rain of rose petals, and Gaucelis's breath caught in her throat as she realized the source of the paint. She dropped the parchment and grabbed at Constansa's limp hands, searching for signs of violence.

Constansa's pale wrists were unmarked, but the tips of several fingers on her right hand were smeared with dried blood. A jagged cut, still oozing blood, lay across her left palm. *Brush, palette, and paint. The artist using her own body as tools.*

Gaucelis let out a try cry of fright when she realized Constansa's eyes had opened. The young woman was not awake, but her eyes were large and dark, holes in her head like the empty eye sockets of a skull. Constansa's lips moved, and Gaucelis leaned closer, trying to make out the words being whispered over and over again.

"They're coming..."

11

Andreas had been trying to remember the words to a ribald drinking song he had heard a few weeks ago when Saluador rode up next to him. The Spaniard's horse was a hand or so taller than his own, and in keeping with the man himself, much more spirited. Andreas was tall enough to see over most crowds, but Saluador eclipsed him readily. The Spaniard kept his beard and hair short, cropped close to his head, and when he smiled, his cheeks dimpled in a way that was very disarming to the ladies. Unfortunately, Saluador had not managed how to make his ready charm extend to his eyes. The ladies found this contrast exciting and dangerous, but Andreas thought that a man who couldn't smile naturally was a man who harbored a deep and long-standing grudge. Probably against something he could never change, like God or the weather or the color purple. Which made him unpredictable.

Still, he bore the scars of brotherhood on his forearms. He had been to Petraathen. He had been found worthy by the *Electi*, the aged fathers of the Shield-Brethren order, and he had survived the Trial of the Shield. Andreas's reservations meant little.

"What do you think our cargo is?" Saluador asked, letting his horse match the ambling gate of Andreas's mount.

Andreas sat up in his saddle and glanced over his shoulder at the caravan of four wagons following him. Each wagon was heavily loaded with a variety of chests and crates. "Are you collecting wagers?" he asked, squinting at Saluador, the sun in the sky behind the taller Shield-Brethren.

"Aye." Saluador laughed. "Though, if the trader told you, then your wager is no good. It would not be fair to the rest of us."

"Jacobi did not tell me," Andreas said, knowing that was part of what the others had sent Saluador to find out.

"Did you peek?"

"How?" Andreas asked. "I haven't seen chests sealed that tight since the last time I was aboard a Venetian trade ship."

Saluador smacked his hand on his thigh. "So you tried to peek!"

"Aye, I did," he said with a laugh. He leaned toward Saluador, his humor shifting to a more serious tone. "Before I accepted the commission, I asked around. Jacobi de Reyns has a reputation for being an honest man, and he's been running goods through Catalonia for a few years. I found a number of men who had worked as caravan guards. They all said he paid without issue and the job was easy work. Three days ago, he arrived in Barcelona, coming from someplace farther south—Xàtiva was what some heard. On arrival, he paid off his existing guards, and then he came directly to our chapter house."

"So what changed?" Saluador wondered.

"I don't know," Andreas said with a shrug. "He's hired us for six days, to take him to some village we won't have heard of, he says. Up in the mountains. It can't be that far."

"Could be farther than you think," Saluador said. "Six days means we could be in France. Near Toulouse." He shook his head. "The Inquisition is still chasing Cathars over there. Not a good time to be hauling secret goods."

Andreas nodded, his gaze flicking back to the lead wagon. Jacobi drove it himself, sitting awkwardly on the wooden bench, his legs splayed out against the edge of the wagon. Andreas found it curious that the trader had eschewed a horse for the much less comfortable plank on the wagon, though perhaps there was a story behind Jacobi's stiff-legged posture.

"I warned him," Andreas said. "I told him that if he was using us as a shield to hide what he was transporting, I'd gut him and leave him by the side of the road."

"I'd help," Saluador said.

Aye, Andreas thought, *I'm sure you would.*

They hadn't been on the road a full day and already he was having second thoughts on accepting Domingo's request to lead this mission.

* * *

Gaucelis unrolled the parchment and laid it on the knife-scarred table, using several of the tavern's cups to hold the sheet flat. The other three—Míro, Alice, and Tibal—gathered around to inspect the illustration Gaucelis had discovered with Constansa.

"Is that blood?" Tibal asked, scratching at one of the hardened lumps with a fingernail. He squinted, showing his teeth, peering closely at what was now caught under his nail.

"It is," Gaucelis said. "She cut her palm and used her blood to make the...these petals."

Alice hung back, ostensibly to grant Tibal and Míro space to pore over the illustration. Gaucelis knew Tibal's eyesight wasn't what it had once been, and Míro made little effort to hide his fascination with Constansa's illustration. But Gaucelis knew there was a deeper reason for Alice's reticence. It had been nearly two years since Constansa's last *creative outburst*—as Alice was wont to describe it—and Gaucelis knew the dowager had prayed heavily that the previous incident had been the last. That the young woman was of sound mind and spirit. That she was safe.

That they all were safe.

"It is oddly beautiful," Míro said, clearing his throat nervously when he caught sight of Alice's hard glare. "Rose petals falling from the sky, like tears from God. The fact that they are red tells us that God is looking down this hill of spears—this battlefield—and is saddened by what He sees." He gestured at the sheet. "She tells a sad story with much brevity and clarity. As a poet, I find it marvelous."

"As a man who has been in the mud and muck of more than one battle, I think you're a fucking idiot," Tibal muttered.

Míro did not take umbrage to the veteran's comments. Their tempestuous relationship provided the grist for more than one night's worth of fanciful tales that had made the dark winter nights less bleak. Gaucelis knew that Tibal rarely missed one of Míro's performances, even when he was the subject of the poet's ribald mockery.

"What else?" Alice asked, prompting Gaucelis to tell the others what she had confessed to the dowager not an hour before. Míro, who had been about to reply to Tibal, closed his mouth and looked expectantly at Gaucelis.

"She spoke to me," Gaucelis said. "Even though she was still asleep, she said, 'They're coming.'"

"Who are?" Tibal demanded. When Gaucelis didn't answer, he pounded his fist against the table, making the tankards jump. "Who is coming?" His eyes were wide, and his jaw worked heavily, like a hound worrying a piece of gristly meat.

"I...I don't know," Gaucelis said. She felt a softness in her eyes, tears threatening to come, and she lowered her head so the others would not see her despair. How could she protect these women?

"What am I supposed to do?" Tibal demanded, first to her and then to Alice. "Huh? I have half a dozen men who know how to wield a sword. We have no walls. We can't stop that bastard Vilapros and his men from coming here whenever they want. We have no hope against a real army."

"We don't know anyone is coming," Alice said in a quiet voice. "We don't know for certain."

"Waiting until we know *for certain* is too late," Tibal spat. He stabbed a finger at the charcoal lines across the bottom of the sheet. "If the Inquisition is pushing its crusade into the mountains, none of us are safe. Who knows where Vilapros is hiding in the mountains, but I'm sure he won't go to ground and hope they won't find him. He'll run at the first sign of an armed host, and his band of ruffians will run with him. The Church stripped him of everything—his pride too. He won't stand up to them. Everyone else is worthless. We'll all be dead." He banged his hand on the table once more, swearing heavily, and then he stormed out of the inn, slamming the door behind him.

"And you think I am the overly dramatic one," Míro noted in the silence that followed. "Maybe this is nothing more than a bad dream. We all have them once in a while, don't we?"

Gaucelis shook her head, and Míro raised his eyes toward the room of the inn and sighed. "How long has she been having the dreams this time?" he asked.

"She never stopped," Gaucelis admitted, drawing an outraged gasp from Alice. "I burned them," she continued, letting go of the secret she had held for the last two years. "I gave her scraps of paper. It calmed her. It made it easier for her to sleep. If she could draw what was in her head, then it went away. It was the only thing that seemed to ease her suffering. And when she slept, I took the pictures away and burned them. That way no one would ever know. It was our secret—hers and mine."

"So why didn't you burn this one?" Míro asked.

Gaucelis gestured at the sheet. "Because she hurt herself. I couldn't hide what she did to her hand. I think she doesn't want our secret to be secret anymore."

* * *

The small caravan reached the base of Montserrat in the late afternoon, several hours earlier than Jacobi had anticipated. There was an inn—marked by a black sheep painted on a warped plank of wood—at the break in the road. The main road continued north, following the winding course of the Llobregat River. Beside the inn, another track went west, heading up into the rocky embrace of the multi-peaked massif. Santa Maria de Montserrat, a Benedictine monastery, lay at the end of the road. Pilgrims who were unprepared for the austere hospitality of the monastery stayed at the inn before embarking on the final leg of their journey.

Jacobi walked painfully about the yard of the inn, trying to loosen the knotted muscles of his left leg. The pitchfork and subsequent infection had left a stiffness in his leg he could never quite get rid of. As he worked out the tension in his leg, the five Shield-Brethren helped his three-man crew with securing the wagons and unhitching the horses. He was mildly surprised by the Shield-Brethren's assistance—normally the hired guards made it very clear that their jobs started and ended with protecting the wagons. Everything else was Jacobi's problem.

The Shield-Brethren had the wagons arranged in a neat formation, two by two, and, along with their own mounts, arranged the horses in a tidy picket line along a swath of tall grasses. Watching them work, Jacobi noted the efficiency of the operation: a pair of men could easily defend all four wagons with bows; the horses were all connected to the same length of rope, but each individual horse could quickly be set free.

The ache in his leg subsiding, Jacobi wandered over to the cluster of wagons. The Shield-Brethren were unrolling their bedrolls—one beneath each wagon—and Jacobi was impressed by their devotion to the commission. The tall one, Saluador, must have read his surprise in his expression. "We don't get paid if the cargo wanders off," he said. "It's hard to keep an eye on it while sleeping inside." He thrust his chin toward the inn behind Jacobi.

"That is very true," Jacobi said. "But surely you don't expect bandits here."

"I expect them everywhere," Saluador said. "Because if I were a bandit, this would be where I'd steal your wagons." He laughed at Jacobi's expression, and several of the other Shield-Brethren joined in his merriment.

"Don't scare the man with the money," Andreas said, coming up behind Jacobi. His tone belied his words, though, and Saluador threw him a mock salute. Having finished their preparations, he and the other Shield-Brethren set off for the inn, leaving Andreas and Jacobi with the wagons.

"They follow orders, at least," Andreas said. "Beyond that, you get what you pay for, I suppose."

"That would appear to be the case," Jacobi said. His mood shifted as he realized he had been harboring a bit of a grudge with the lanky Shield-Brethren leader after their conversation the previous night. He had been taken in by Andreas's jovial nature and had been caught off guard by the sudden negotiation. There was also the nagging suspicion that he had caved to exactly the amount Andreas had wanted, and given the efficiency of the Shield-Brethren and the seriousness with which they approached their commission, it was not an unwarranted amount. He should be more pleased with what he was getting for his money.

But there was the issue of the remaining payment he had to make before reaching Estartyol, and therein lay the true source of his displeasure. Would he pay the toll, or would he hide behind the Shield-Brethren?

Andreas seemed oblivious to Jacobi's internal conflict. "After they've had a meal, several of the men are going up to Santa Maria de Montserrat to pay their respects to the Virgin," he said. "Do you wish to join us?"

Jacobi almost laughed, the sound dying in his throat with a strangled sigh. "No," he said, then coughed. "It has been a long day. I will take my rest in the inn."

"As you wish," Andreas said. He examined Jacobi's face for a moment, trying to read something in the trader's expression. "I will probably remain here," he decided. "Someone should watch the wagons."

Jacobi made an agreeable noise. "I will have a plate of food sent out," he offered, hoping such munificence would smooth over the current awkwardness.

Andreas inclined his head. "That is kind of you, Master Jacobi."

Jacobi waved his hand. "It is the least I could do," he scoffed. As he took his leave and walked toward the inn, he fought the urge to shake his head in frustration.

I am being tested, he thought. *She made this happen. What am I going to do?*

III

There were several tiny cells attached to the back of the chapel of San Berenguer. Originally, there had been an external door—the arch was still visible from the outside—but it had been blocked up at some point so as to make the chapel more secure. There was only one way in or out now, which was part of the reason why the front door was never locked. The cells were narrow rooms, barely wide or deep enough for a person to lie flat, and their ceilings sloped down to the outside wall. There were six altogether, and each had a pair of narrow slits that allowed air and light; though, during the summer months, they tended to get rather stifling.

Constansa slept in the leftmost cell, performed all of her prayers in the next one, and ate her meals and entertained guests in the third one. The other three, the cells to the right of the door from the chapel proper, remained empty and unused, though Gaucelis had slept in the first one on the right more than once. Especially when Constansa was in the grip of one of the many fevers that had assailed her during the winter months.

The young woman was not in the first cell on the left, and Gaucelis set the tray of food she was carrying down on the small table that was pushed up against the outside wall. Constansa was not in the next cell, either, and Gaucelis found her lying on her back in the last cell, staring up at the two slashes of light that broke through the rough canopy of the ceiling.

She was a thin woman, perpetually undernourished, and she had a tendency to seem even tinier in her voluminous robe. She had high and prominent cheekbones, a narrow nose too long for her face, a high forehead, and pale green eyes that tended to wander. Her hair had been brown once, but in the past few years, it had lost its color. She had cut it herself late in the previous year, and most of the gaps and jagged spots had grown back. But it was still pale. Her hands were narrow, like her face, and her fingers were nimble. They moved constantly and the few times Gaucelis saw them still were when Constansa gripped a piece of charcoal or a brush. The only time she was still enough to listen to the voices inside her head.

"Good morning, Constansa," Gaucelis said, hovering in the doorway of the cell. "How are you this morning?"

Constansa tilted her head. "Well, thank you," she said quietly. Her hands were clasped over her stomach, but then she held up her left. "I appear to have had an accident."

"Yes," Gaucelis said carefully. "I found you last night, asleep beside the altar. You must have caught your hand on a rough edge of stone. It is a shallow cut, and I have cleaned it for you. It should heal well."

"It is odd that I did not cry out," Constansa said.

"Yes, that same thought occurred to me too. Perhaps your sleep was troubled enough that you moved about, but you never woke up."

"Like a ghost," Constansa exclaimed. She raised her head and looked at the cloth wrapped around her hand. "But ghosts cannot be harmed by stone, or anything real."

"It was merely an idea," Gaucelis said with a shrug. "I brought some food. Are you hungry?"

"Not yet," Constansa said, sitting up. "Alice is frightened."

Gaucelis hesitated, reaching out to lightly touch the stone wall. In the wake of one of her exceptionally vivid dreams, Constansa might—on occasion—exhibit startling prescience and awareness of what others in the village were thinking, as if whatever divine mystery that overcame her lingered, like the way a room smelled of fresh flowers even after the flowers had been removed.

"She is," Gaucelis said finally. "So is Tibal."

"I am sorry to have caused them distress," Constansa said. "Though, they have cause to be frightened. We all do." She paused, playing with the cloth wrapped around her hand. "I asked Jacobi to do something for me," she said.

"What?" Gaucelis asked. "When?"

"Shortly before he left," Constansa said. She looked up, and Gaucelis was struck by how young and how innocent her face was. How desperately she wanted Gaucelis to not be angry with her. "I have never felt this before," Constansa said, a desperate breathlessness in her voice. "I knew I was going to dream something terrible. It was as if I dreamed of my future, without knowing what my future was going to be. How can I dream of the dream of what might be?" She shook her head. "But I know Alice is frightened; I know that Tibal and that you are too." She plucked at the cloth around her hand again. "I dreamed of this," she whispered. "And...and I couldn't..."

"What did you do?" Gaucelis asked, her throat constricting.

"I asked Jacobi to find the Rose Knights," Constansa said.

* * *

Andreas heard the trader's draft horses shuffle and nicker softly to one another when the Shield-Brethren returned from their pilgrimage to the Virgin of Montserrat. He remained still, lying on his back under one of the wagons. The moon had risen shortly after nightfall, round and fat, and its light kept many shadows at bay. The air was crisp, with a hint of winter's bite still lingering, but he had wrapped himself in both his cloak and several blankets. He was comfortable and there was no reason to get up to talk with the others. There would be time enough over the next few days to hear all about their trip.

The people of Catalonia had a much richer relationship with the Virgin Mary than other parts of Christendom, which made it easier for the Shield-Brethren to pay homage to their Virgin—the one who had been with them since the founders of the order had come north from Greece. Some of the Shield-Brethren did not bother to maintain the illusion, and simply spoke of Mary as their patron. Others remained true to the old ways, their hearts forever bound to a goddess who had been forgotten by nearly everyone else.

Did that make the Shield-Brethren heretics or liars? It was a difficult question to answer, and Andreas simply preferred not to think about it too much. It didn't matter whom he prayed to, did it? What mattered were his actions and his intent. The rest was beyond him.

He heard the men talk quietly, and as he watched, two shadows split off toward the dark shape of the inn. The other two crawled under other wagons and were noisy in their preparations for sleep. He lay quietly, his fingers idly tracing the raised pattern on the silver brooch he wore on his cloak. He had had it made in Venice, after returning from crusading in the Holy Land, when he had decided to let his feet guide him. He didn't wear a tabard with the colors and the sigil of the Shield-Brethren. His only concession to his order was the brooch.

He had passed the trial and taken the vows. He did not need to trumpet these facts to everyone he met. They were his secrets. His strength.

He rolled over, settling against the ground. Trying to get comfortable. *Did she speak to them?* he wondered, trying to clear his mind for sleep. There were stories about members of the order being granted visions, illuminating visits from the Virgin. Those who kept their spirits pure and focused would be blessed with guidance, and Andreas knew several members of the order who thought they had been granted such visions. But he remained skeptical, giving little credence to these claims. They felt too much like the delusions of frightened men, and such fear was unbecoming of a Shield-Brethren knight.

I will ask them about the Virgin in the morning, he thought. As much as he wanted to put aside such nonsense, he knew it mattered to them. *I am their leader,* he reminded himself; *therefore it matters to me too.*

He sighed and closed his eyes.

10

They followed the Llobregat for the next two days, dancing with the river like young lovers. The weather remained pleasant, high clouds billowing overhead in the afternoon—occasionally releasing rain but never for very long—and so they made camp in the most convenient places they could find when the sun started to graze the western horizon. They saw one or two other caravans—Jacobi recognized one of the traders traveling in the other direction—a few farmers, traveling monks, and other itinerants, but very little that caused the Shield-Brethren any concern.

As the days were slow—hour after hour of sitting idly on the wagon bench, trying to find a good position that wouldn't cause his leg to cramp—Jacobi found himself striking up conversations with each of the Shield-Brethren.

It was easy to talk with Saluador. In fact, by midday after they had left Montserrat, he began to worry that he might not be able to get Saluador to *stop* talking. Andreas came to his rescue, though, sending the tall Spaniard ahead to ride point for a few hours, a decision that seemed to make everyone relax a bit.

Lugo was the youngest of the group, and Jacobi learned that he had recently returned from the Shield-Brethren's mountain fortress far to the east, where he had undergone a secret initiation ritual. The lad was reticent to say more, and Jacobi did not pry. He remembered—all too well—the Inquisition's predilection for damning by association. It wasn't enough to seek out Cathars; Cathars' sympathizers were subject to scrutiny as well. He had been scrutinized once; he wasn't in a rush to have it happen again.

Though, if it did, it wouldn't be because of his association with the Shield-Brethren...

Harald, like Andreas, hailed from the Low Countries; though, judging by the young man's dark hair, one of his parents was from somewhere east and south. Italy, perhaps. Harald was the quiet one, stoic when not being addressed and curt with his answers when Jacobi posed a few innocent questions. The knight seemed distressed by Jacobi's interest, and after a few tries, the trader gave up. *Harald the Silent*, he had dubbed the man.

The last one was named Guillén, and he was broad through the chest and neck. The others were stocky as well, but Guillén looked as if he could pull one of the wagons by himself. Which could be useful should they encounter bandits.

Jacobi put his hands together and silently sent a prayer to the Virgin Mary. *Let there be no bandits*, he begged. *Let the remainder of this trip be as dull as this afternoon.*

"Praying for rain, eh?" Guillén asked. "Inquire if there might be a breeze in our future as well."

Jacobi dropped his hands, idly rubbing the tight muscles in his left thigh. "I am sure a light rain would be accompanied by a pleasing zephyr," he said. "I suppose you insist on wearing your maille for reasons not dissimilar to those Saluador spoke of the other night regarding the defense of the wagons."

"We do." Guillén nodded. "It does me no good packed away in my bags. But I might as well have left it at our chapter house. My horse would have thanked me. I take it your previous escorts were not as prudent in their dress?"

They never had any reason to be, Jacobi thought, keeping the words to himself. "No, they did not," he said.

"Andreas says our destination is a village in the mountains," Guillén said. "Some little village we've never heard of?"

"That is correct," Jacobi said.

"I have been across these mountains a few times," Guillén said. "I have family that live along the Loire." He laughed. "My uncle—he fancies himself a winemaker."

"You wouldn't know of this village," Jacobi said, anticipating the true focus of Guillén's thoughts.

Guillén sucked on a tooth as he let his gaze run over the covered wagon. "There are a lot of little villages in the mountains," he said. "A couple of houses, some garden plots, maybe a flock of sheep or two. Sometimes there is even a church."

"That sounds about right," Jacobi said.

"Sometimes the church is older than the surrounding houses," Guillén said. "Sometimes the people who live there do so because they prefer the god in the temple rather than the Christian God."

"I suppose some do."

"The last time I visited my uncle, I saw many armored men on the roads around Toulouse. They were in the midst of a crusade—in France, if you can imagine! The Languedoc was suffering from a plague of heretics. Many whom, I suspect, would have fled into the mountains between Toulouse and Catalonia were they able. They might take refuge in tiny valleys, in fact, finding sanctuary in old churches that had been forgotten."

"Do you think I am taking you to such a place?" Jacobi inquired, attempting to affect an offended tone of voice.

Guillén laughed. "Of course you are," he said. "That much has been obvious since you hired us. I'm just wondering what sort of heretics live there." He leaned forward in his saddle. "Do they worship tree spirits or something darker?"

"They are all God-fearing folk," Jacobi retorted.

"Even the foulest demon fears God," Guillén pointed out.

"I am offended at your suggestion," Jacobi snapped.

Guillén raised a hand in supplication. "I meant no offense," he said. "I am but a mere soldier. Truly, it is not my place to question one person's—or an entire village's—relationship with God."

"What of yours?" Jacobi said, biting back. "What is your relationship with God?"

"Mine?" Guillén touched his chest. "The same as yours, Master Jacobi. Are we all not part of the same Church? Is our order not sanctified by the Pope in Rome?"

"Are you like them, then?"

"Who?"

"The knights you met in Toulouse. Are you just like them in that you maintain the True Faith?" He knew he was asking too many questions, that he was pushing the knight unnecessarily, and it would undoubtedly cause more grief than it would assuage any *feelings* he had on the subject.

"We are not tools of the Inquisition," Guillén said sharply.

"Nor do I serve Hell," Jacobi replied.

Guillén regarded him for a long moment; Jacobi noticed that the man's hand was resting lightly on the hilt of the knife in his belt.

"Estartyol," he said suddenly. "The village is called Estartyol. There is a tiny lake nearby."

"Well," Guillén said finally, offering Jacobi a tight smile. He moved his hand off his knife. "I look forward to meeting these villagers," he said. "Perhaps one of them could take me fishing on this lake." He shook his reins and his horse picked up its pace.

Jacobi watched him ride away, once more caught in the web of his confusion and frustration. The more time he spent with these men, the more he feared that, in doing what Constansa had asked of him, he had put his soul in jeopardy. Perhaps he should have made the pilgrimage to the Virgin of Montserrat and thrown himself upon her mercy instead of continuing to believe the words of the witch-woman of Estartyol.

* * *

Constansa watched the rectangles of light crawl across the stone floor of her cell. Dimly, she knew that the sun—whose light was coming in through the narrow slits in the ceiling of her cell—could not move that fast across the sky, and she knew that she was in the grip of the divine presence. She would not need to blink or draw breath; she was suspended, held apart from the world that moved around her.

The shafts of light were filled with tiny figures, golden angels twisting slowly as if they were falling through water and not the air. She reached out, her hand pushing them aside, and she felt their tiny kisses. The flutter of their silken wings against her rough flesh. To them, her skin must feel like the stony wall of the cell felt beneath her touch.

There was a piece of parchment on the table. She was not bothered by the fact she could not remember putting it there. Objects appeared and disappeared all the time when she was held apart. The angels in the light pulled her toward the table, and she drifted across the room, sinking onto the stool with a sigh. There was a lump of charcoal on the table, and it glittered in the sunlight, tiny diamonds winking from shallow crevices. She picked it up, letting her fingers explore the shape, and after a few moments, she found how its contours fit best in her hand.

The light drifted across the sheet of parchment, and she laughed at the tiny footprints the angel left on the page. She daubed after some of them, leaving black tracks, and soon she saw the picture she was meant to draw. Her hand began to move faster, connecting the marks.

The shafts of light crawled up the wall, and the shadows that had been hiding in the corners of the room swam back out, gliding along the floor. She closed her eyes, as there was nothing more to see.

Her hand knew what to do.

She felt the divine grip lessening, and her breath caught in her chest. Something akin to a sob bubbled up in her throat, but she pressed her lips closed. She was not quite ready to let it out.

Not until she finished.

Her hand moved faster. The parchment was not very large, and she filled it quickly with her illustration. The top of the sheet was filled with a profusion of lines—a rain of arrows, perhaps, or a storm threatening from heavy clouds. Below, a man knelt. His head was bare, and his frame was covered in tiny circles—as many as there were jagged lines across the top of the sheet.

The man's eyes were open, and he stared out of the sheet as if he were watching Constansa draw him. Only when she was satisfied with his expression did she start to sketch in the shadow behind him.

ᴗ

Harald was waiting for them at the second switchback on the long and winding road up the mountainside. The horses laboriously plodded past the tiny shelf where Harald waited, and once they were all on the next loop of the road, Andreas drew his horse up next to Harald's.

"What is it?" he asked.

Harald had been the advance scout. Harald pointed across the valley, and Andreas looked over at the ridge. The road climbed up the northern slope from the valley, wound along the top of the flat peak, crossed a sprightly mountain stream, and then wrapped around the other side of the valley before disappearing over the top of the southern ridge. There was a group of horsemen coming through the gap in the southern ridge. Sunlight glinted off metal helmets and shields.

"Do you think they mean us harm?" Andreas asked.

"I think this hill is a bad place to be caught in the open," Harald said, listing off his concerns. "I think the river is a natural place for an ambush. And I think we were hired because something like this might happen."

Andreas nodded, counting riders. "Twelve," he said. It was hard to tell from this distance, but several looked as if they were wearing maille. Shirts, at least. He couldn't be sure if they were more armored than that.

"More than I care for," Harald said.

"Aye," Andreas agreed. He clapped the other man on the shoulder. "Let's assume they have bad intentions, shall we?"

Harald nodded grimly. "The worst sort of intentions," he said.

*＊＊

The bridge was only wide enough for one wagon at a time, and there were no guide rails, so each horse had to be carefully led across so none of the wagon wheels slipped off. As the other Shield-Brethren helped Jacobi and his men with the delicate task, Andreas took Saluador and rode on ahead. The man's size alone would be a useful deterrent.

On the other side of the bridge, the road widened slightly, allowing them to ride abreast. Andreas rode on the outside, and he kept an eye on the slope beyond the road. Close to the bridge, the ridge was well-defined by a rocky spur; as they rode, the land lost its rugged shape and became a tree-covered slope that was too steep for horses. There were breaks in the forest, sections of the road abutted by clusters of boulders and rocky outcroppings.

The sun was warmer and the air was colder, sure signs they had left the lowlands behind. Their horses raised a little dust as they rode; most of the afternoon cloudbursts had dumped their rain before they had reached the mountains.

Andreas and Saluador both carried shields along with rid-ing swords—the shorter one-handed blade more suited to fight-ing from horseback—and longswords. Saluador had a bow as well, strung but attached to his saddle. It was one thing to be prepared; it was another to ride up to a group of unknown men with an arrow laid across a bow. They both wore maille under their plain habits;

their shields were marked with the seal of the *Ordo Militum Vindicis Intactae*, though they wore no tabards proclaiming the same.

The approaching group of horsemen became less of an organized troop and more of a motley collective the closer Andreas and Saluador got. They carried no standard, and only half the men had shields. Some of the shields sported rampant lions of various sizes, and they were still too far away to make out other heraldic details. They were strung out in a loose pack, which told Andreas that some of them had been in organized cavalry once or twice. "Mercenaries or deserters?" he asked Saluador. "They're too well equipped to be outlaws."

"Too organized for mercenaries," Saluador noted. "If they are, what's their commission?"

He had a good point. There was no sign of a wagon train or the sense that the company was guarding any one individual within their ranks.

A trio split off from the rest, galloping toward Andreas and Saluador, and the Shield-Brethren slowed their horses. By letting the riders come to them, they were allowing a little more distance between this group and the remainder of the company.

Andreas loosened his sword in its sheath, and Saluador plucked an arrow from his quiver and laid it and his bow across his thighs.

Up close, Andreas's evaluation of the riders didn't improve. Two of the three wore maille shirts, and in both cases, the chain was dull and stained. The other man wore a simple leather vest with no protection on the arms. Several swords, a hatchet, and a couple of knives between the three of them. They all wore unkempt beards, streaked with dirt and sweat.

"Ho, travelers," Andreas called out in the *linga franca* when the trio came into earshot.

The riders came to a halt, two falling in behind the one in the vest. "A good afternoon to you," the one in the leather said. "This is a somewhat out-of-the-way place to meet other travelers, especially those who appear to be hauling goods over the mountains."

"That we are," Andreas said.

"This is not the road to Toulouse," the man said. "Are you lost, perhaps?"

"No, our man knows where he is going."

"And where is that?"

Andreas said nothing, and after a moment, the man nodded. "This is a narrow road," he pointed out. "One of us should yield to the other."

"Agreed," Andreas said. "It would be easier for your company to divert their course temporarily."

The man smiled, revealing stained teeth. "Would it be?" he said. "Is that what you think?"

Andreas nodded. "It is, which is why I suggested it. Our wagons are much less nimble than horses." He glanced at Saluador. "It seems very rude of me to suggest an improbable solution, don't you think? Especially to some gentlemen I have just met."

Saluador nodded. "Yes, that does seem rude."

Andreas returned his attention to the three men, sparing a quick glance at the rest of the approaching company, gauging their distance. "I was not attempting to be rude, good man," he said, "and yet you find my suggestion impertinent."

"Impertinent?" The man looked at his fellows, repeating the word again as if he found its sound to be humorous. "What is in those wagons, friend?" he asked, turning back to Andreas.

"You presume much with that question," Andreas replied, the levity gone from his voice.

The man nodded slowly, stroking his chin. "I guess I do."

Andreas sighed. "I had hoped for more civility," he said. He was about to say something else when he heard the sound of a horse coming up from behind him, and quickly too.

"Wait!" Jacobi pulled hard on the reins of his horse, bringing the animal to a dust-stirring halt beside the Shield-Brethren. The trader's face was pinched heavily, and he sat at an angle in the saddle, his left hip canted upward.

"Aah, Jacobi de Reyns," the leather-clad man said. "I thought it might be you." His eyes flickered toward Andreas. "Your escort is a bit...discourteous."

Jacobi held up his hands. "They are overprotective, Martis. That is all."

"You know this man?" Andreas asked.

"Of course he does," Saluador snorted, reading the situation more clearly than Andreas. "This is a regular assignation. It would appear that this road has a *toll* associated with it."

Martis screwed up his face at Saluador's words, but he didn't disagree with what had been said.

"Is this true?" Andreas asked Jacobi. "Do you pay this man on every trip?"

"No...not every trip," the trader sputtered.

Martis laughed. "Only because sometimes he sneaks along a different road, but the captain keeps track, doesn't he, Jacobi? He knows how often you come and go."

"It's not like that," Jacobi said to Andreas.

"No?" Andreas said, trying to keep his anger in check. "Why didn't you say something when you hired us? Why didn't you tell me of this arrangement when we reached the bridge? Why did you let me ride ahead and meet these men without foreknowledge of your relationship?" He didn't expect Jacobi to answer, for he knew the trader's reasons. Jacobi had hoped he and the other Shield-Brethren would either scare these men off or get drawn into a battle with them—one that Jacobi hoped the Shield-Brethren would win, thereby ridding this route of its pernicious toll collectors.

All without having to reveal his own culpability in the matter.

"I can explain," Jacobi started. "Please, this is all a mis-understanding."

"Aye," Andreas answered. "It most certainly is." He nodded to Saluador. "We should have never taken this commission." He jerked his reins. "Good luck, Jacobi de Reyns. My men and I are going to return to Barcelona. We will not be accompanying you any farther."

Saluador held his tongue until they were out of earshot of the trader and the trio of horsemen. "We're going to walk away?" he said to Andreas. His horse was close and he loomed over Andreas.

"We don't fight because someone pays us to," Andreas said. "Did he pay us less than he typically pays those men? Were we a bargain? Even at double what he offered?"

"Of course we are," Saluador pointed out. "Once those men are dead, he doesn't have to pay the toll anymore. If he paid more for us on this trip, he'll make it up on the next one."

"We're not hired killers," Andreas snapped.

Saluador leaned over and grabbed at Andreas's reins, pulling both horses to a halt. "No, we're not," the tall Spaniard said. "But who are we?"

Andreas stared at him, fuming. He did not care for the other man's tone or words, but they could not be easily dismissed. Saluador was right. The Shield-Brethren had taken money from Jacobi in return for protection on the road. To not give aid when it was needed was to be as villainous as the men who sought to extort money from Jacobi.

"Domingo put you in charge," Saluador said, "even though you have no ties to this region. You are a Brother to us, Andreas, even though you are not kin, and though we are not *your* kin, I ask you to think of these lands as yours."

Andreas shaded his eyes and peered at the other man. "Would I suffer bandits such as these in my lands?" he said. "Is that what you are asking me?"

"Aye," Saluador said. "Would you?"

Andreas lowered his hand and looked down the road at the wagons crossing the bridge. The last one was halfway across the narrow span. Saluador was right, of course, but the manner in which the Shield-Brethren had been taken advantage of bothered him. Their own pedigree had been leveraged against them, forcing them into a course of action that—while well-intentioned—was not one of their choosing.

Such courses of action had a tendency to be deadly.

But then an idea blossomed in his mind, and he smiled at Saluador. "My pride has muddled my thinking," he said. "I told Jacobi we would not be accompanying him on the remainder of his journey, but by my accounting, Jacobi owes us the other half of our commission. I think we should hold on to these wagons as collateral until he can pay us."

"I fear your thinking is still muddled," Saluador said.

"Patience, good Saluador." Andreas patted the other man on the shoulder. "Ready yourself and wait for my signal. All will become clear in time."

* * *

When Harald had pulled Andreas aside, Jacobi had suspected it was because Martis's band had been spotted, and while the wagons continued their torturous crawl up the switchbacks, he had conducted a lengthy conversation with himself about what was going to happen when the two groups met. He suspected it would happen after the bridge, and when Andreas and Saluador rode ahead, he let them go without a word. But his decision did not sit well, and when one of the wagon wheels slipped off the bridge and it was Guillén who scrambled beneath the wagon to bolster it until the wheel could be guided back on the bridge, he realized he could not stomach his own cowardice. As soon as the wagon reached solid ground again, he spurred his horse toward Andreas and Saluador.

He arrived in the nick of time, inserting himself between Martis and the Shield-Brethren. Doing so, he knew he would reveal his intentions to be entirely what Andreas and the rest thought they had been. And he had deserved the scathing glance Andreas had given him when the Shield-Brethren had abandoned him. *Yes,* he had thought, *I am that sort of man. I lied to you. I brought you here under false pretenses. I expected you to kill these men because I was too weak to stand up to them.*

But what could he have done otherwise? When caught in the midst of a tryst with an unmarried girl, he had fled. When faced with losing his livelihood, he had run away. When his wife had been taken, he had stood by and watched. How was this any different?

And the thought that made him consider driving his horse over the nearby cliff was the sad realization that he had let Constansa down. She had asked him to bring the Rose Knights to Estartyol, and he had failed to do that too.

"Well," Martis said, scratching at his thin beard. "I don't entirely know what you were hoping to accomplish there, Jacobi, but it seems like it didn't work out so well for you."

"No," Jacobi said quietly, his eyes still on the cliff edge. "Very little has."

"Now, I suspect the captain won't take too kindly that you were trying to upset our little arrangement."

"I suspect he won't," Jacobi said.

"Maybe I won't tell him," Martis said. "What do you think about that?"

"I suspect you'll do whatever you want," Jacobi said, finally turning his gaze toward Martis.

"That I shall." Martis grinned.

One of the other men said something, calling Martis's attention toward the road, and when Martis's grin slipped off his face, Jacobi finally pulled himself out of his misery and looked as well.

His wagons were coming down the road. As were the Shield-Brethren. In fact, Andreas was sitting on the front wagon's bench, leading the caravan.

"What's this?" Martis snapped when the caravan slowed to a halt in front of them. "I thought you said you were going back to Barcelona."

"We are," Andreas said. "After we visit Estartyol. One of my companions, Guillén, says there is decent fishing in the lake there." He waved a hand at Martis. "You and your men are blocking the road, sir."

Jacobi turned his head and noted that the remainder of Martis's party had ridden up behind the trio of riders. They milled about; having missed the earlier exchange, they were unsure of what was transpiring.

He was confused too. Andreas's pronouncement had seemed rather final.

"It is those wagons," Martis pointed out. "If you were not encumbered with them, we would not be having this confusion."

"These wagons?" Andreas looked behind him. "Oh, yes, these. Well, we found them back at the bridge there, sadly abandoned by their owner. He even left several drivers behind—is that not a travesty? They tell us that we could probably sell these wagons—and their goods—at a reasonable price in Estartyol."

"These are your wagons?" Martis asked in a slightly strangled voice.

"Yes, they are," Andreas said without a trace of guile in his voice.

"What is going on?" Martis snapped at Jacobi.

Jacobi had raised a hand to his mouth to hide the fact that his lips kept trying to quirk into a smile, but he lowered his hand now. "I appear to have lost my wagons," he said as contritely as possible. "I had no idea these men I had hired would turn out to be such ruffians. Frankly, I am shocked to discover—"

"Shut up," Martis snapped. He glowered at Jacobi for a second, as if trying to understand the trader's role in this confusion. Still fingering the hilt of his sword, he swung his head toward Andreas. "There is a toll on this road," he said.

"There is?" Andreas seemed surprised. "Alas," he continued, "my companions and I are part of an order that stresses poverty and humility. We have no money, which is why we were taking these wagons to the village. A reasonable exchange would be quite a boon for our—"

"Shut up!" Martis screamed, rising in his saddle. "This is—" He jerked backward, falling against the rear of his horse. An arrow protruded from his open mouth. He gurgled, blood spurting around the shaft of the arrow, and then he slowly slid off his horse and fell on the ground. Everyone stared as he flopped about for a few moments, spitting blood and choking to death, and finally he stopped, his body relaxing.

"Now," Andreas said quietly in the silence that followed, and there was no mistaking the tone of his voice. It was the voice of the man Jacobi had glimpsed briefly in the inn in Barcelona. The one with no remorse or doubt. "The rest of you have a choice," Andreas said, speaking to the remainder of Martis's band. "Join him, or clear the fucking road."

Behind Andreas, Saluador sat perfectly still in his saddle, his bow ready with another arrow nocked and drawn. The other Shield-Brethren had drawn their swords. Only Andreas appeared to be unready for combat, but Jacobi knew that such indifference was a ruse.

01

Since Constansa had drawn the bloody picture, a dread had settled over the valley. Only a few knew the source of the despair that had wormed its way into the hearts and hearths of the village, and they found themselves shunning the others. At first, Gaucelis had found the chapel to be stifling and too small when she and Alice both found excuses to spend hours within the sanctuary. She knew little of Alice's history—as was true for many of the older women who lived in the village—but Alice was comfortable with silence, suggesting that Alice might have been at a nunnery before coming to Estartyol.

When the Inquisition had come, many of the minor orders had found their rules questioned, their beliefs called into doubt. It did not matter how remote their location was or the size of their community. They were leading lives outside the proscribed order. They could not be tolerated.

Gaucelis had found herself dwelling on the existence they had built for themselves at Estartyol. Many of them had come here from the county of Toulouse, fleeing the Inquisition's persecution of Catharism. The crusaders had taken land and holdings indiscriminately; some had used the Church as an excuse to settle other disputes—the losers having had no choice but to flee France. Men like Folquets de Vilapros, who had once been a landowner near

Carcassonne. Now reduced to being a self-titled "captain" of a small band of roving mercenaries. He had claimed to offer protection to Estartyol and a few other nearby villages, but she suspected—and as Tibal had recently confirmed—de Vilapros's protection was thinly veiled tyranny.

Did they tolerate it because it was less painful than the alternative? And, in the dark of night, when sleep evaded each of them, did they gaze into their hearts and see how deeply entrenched their fear was?

She had been newly married when her husband, a forgotten son of a minor branch of the Counts of Comminges, had answered the call put forth by Boniface of Montferrat and, taking much of their household with him, had departed for Venice to fight for the Church. He did not return, and after a few years of fighting, the chilly disposition of her husband's extended family grew to be too wearying, so she had left Muret and drifted south and east. She was accepted by a community of Cathars, unaware and uncaring about their divisive religious beliefs, and when the crusaders had come, she had found herself cast out once more.

When she had come to Estartyol, she had fallen in love with the solitude offered by the high mountains. She adored the whisper of the wind on the lake, and unlike the rest of the villagers, she did not mind the bitterness of the winters. The cold air reminded her that life was precious. She had no intention of ever leaving Estartyol.

When the door of the chapel banged open and Míro rushed in, she met his arrival with a wearied acceptance. *This, then, was the end*, she thought, but she caught sight of the wild elation on his face, and her heart beat more quickly. "What is it?" she asked.

"It's Jacobi," he said. "Come and see. It's not what we thought at all."

* * *

Of the group, Guillén was the most prone to romantic fancy, but Andreas had to admit that the village seemed as idyllic as Guillén had imagined it to be. The lake—a pale blue mirror nestled between forested peaks—dominated the narrow valley. The village lay on the far side of the valley, a cluster of several dozen tiny houses around a block of dark stone that was undoubtedly an old church. When they reached the valley floor, Jacobi rode ahead to alert the villagers of their arrival, and Andreas let the horses find their own pace as they followed the track around the shore of the lake.

The Shield-Brethren rode quietly, listening to the wind and the birds. There had been little talk after the ruffians had fled the mountain trail. They all had their own thoughts on the encounter, and Andreas knew to let them alone until they were ready to discuss it.

Saluador had fired the arrow without receiving a signal from Andreas. On one hand, he had been disappointed by the other man's error, but it had been a decisive move, one that had, in fact, spared them all from further bloodshed.

He had been thinking of making an example of Martis anyway, so did he have to say anything to Saluador? He would, eventually, because Saluador knew he had loosed the arrow without real provocation.

Did that make it murder?

Andreas hadn't decided what he was going to do, and as the horses came within sight of the village, he set aside the conundrum. There would be time later to think about it.

The horses pricked up their ears as they realized they were nearly home, and trotted faster.

A small crowd had gathered in front of the tiny church, milling about in an open field that passed for the village green. Jacobi had already dismounted from his horse, and Andreas caught only a brief glimpse of the trader in the cluster of villagers, eager to hear his news. They were asking him about his wagons, his escort, and

Andreas caught a name here and there. *Vilapros—was that Martis*, he wondered, *or the man Martis reported to?*

As the wagons approached, rattling over the hard ground, the crowd turned toward him and his men. He drew back the reins, bringing the horses and wagon to a halt. He stared at the villagers, looking at their faces and taking note of the three people who had just come out of the chapel. They were older than many of the others and their clothes were no finer, but they seemed to be important persons in the village hierarchy. "Greetings, good people of Estartyol," he said, standing up on the wagon's board. "I am Andreas. My companions and I have been asked to deliver these wagons to you."

Everyone began asking questions, and Andreas made no move to quell the noise, knowing that it would run itself out in time. There was no need to hurry the villagers. As he waited, a bent man with broad shoulders shoved his way through the crowd and approached Saluador's horse. Even though the man walked with a limp, Andreas recognized the rolling precision of his step—the way a swordsman walked, always aware of his surroundings. The old man pointed at Saluador's shield. "Who are you?" he asked, looking at Andreas.

"We are members of the *Ordo Militum Vindicis Intactae*," Saluador said.

"They're Rose Knights," Jacobi said, and it was his words that stirred the crowd.

Andreas eyed the villagers with some suspicion, wondering what he and the others had stumbled into.

"Was there trouble on the road?" the old fighter asked, looking back and forth between Andreas and Saluador. Andreas found it curious that the old man did not ask the question of the trader.

"Aye," he said, being honest with the old soldier, "there was. And it was taken care of."

"Casualties?"

"Just one."

"Theirs?"

Andreas nodded. "A man named Martis."

The name caused some reaction among the villagers. The old man hawked and spit. "Damn it," he said, pointing a finger at Jacobi. "You brought this upon us," he snapped, and then he turned his ire to the group standing on the chapel's porch. "She brought this upon us."

Andreas realized there was a fourth person standing at the chapel door. Her body was wreathed in a shapeless brown robe and her hood was pulled up to hide her face. If the old man hadn't said *she*, he wouldn't have been sure the person was female. The crowd began to shout and holler more than before, and like he had done, the person waited for their ire to run out. Finally, when the crowd had fallen mostly silent, she raised her arms—revealing pale and slender hands—and pushed back her hood.

She was younger than Andreas had expected. She looked at everyone, pausing briefly as she gazed at each face. She finished where she'd started—staring at the old soldier. When she spoke, her voice was soft, and in a crowded room, it would have never been heard. But outside in the sunny silence of the valley, her words carried. "What are you afraid of?" she asked.

She did not wait for any answer, turning almost immediately, and disappearing back into the church, leaving only the echo of her words ringing in Andreas's ears.

ᴜ11

Constansa's question unsettled the crowd, and its jovial mood began to wane. Villagers wandered off, the cold dread starting to seep into their bones again. Alice's face remained pinched as she watched Jacobi direct the men to unload the wagons. Míro and Tibal made gestures to help, but mostly stood by and watched the work be done by the others. The Rose Knight who had spoken with Tibal extricated himself from the work and approached the chapel porch. His skin had been darkened and his hair lightened by years of sun, and Gaucelis suspected he was from the north.

The Rose Knight stopped at the foot of the porch and bowed— proficiently enough for a man more accustomed to martial affairs. "I am Andreas," he said, "the leader of these men. I sense that our arrival is both cause for celebration and dismay, and I wish to impress upon you that our intention was to provoke neither reaction. We were meant to be invisible."

Gaucelis eyed the broad-shouldered man critically. "I am Gaucelis," she said, "and my companions are Alice and Míro. You have already met Tibal."

"And the young woman who briefly appeared?" he asked.

Alice made a noise in her throat and shook her head slightly. Míro looked at his shoes. Gaucelis frowned at both of them, but said nothing.

"Aah," Andreas said. "Well, yes, that explains a great deal." He bowed again. "For a moment, I had thought the young woman was directing her question at me, but now I see that she was, in fact, speaking to you. It sounds like a conversation that has been going on for some time, and I do not see any reason to intrude upon it. My men and I will be departing shortly." He bowed again and began walking back to the wagons.

Gaucelis glared at Alice and Míro. The knight's words stung, all the more so because there was a great deal of truth to them. But Constansa was right. They were afraid, and when she looked in her heart, Gaucelis realized she had been living with fear for a long time.

"Wait," she called out, chasing after the knight. She heard Alice call out her name, but she ignored the older woman. *Too long,* she thought as she strode across the field. *I have been frightened for too long.*

"Her name is Constansa," she said as Andreas turned back. "She is a...fragile girl, but she..."

"Why did Tibal say what he did about her?"

"There is a man who *protects* us," Gaucelis said, adding emphasis on the distasteful word. "Martis was his man."

"Aah, and because Martis is dead, you fear this man—"

"De Vilapros," Gaucelis interrupted. "*Captain* Folquets de Vilapros."

"This de Vilapros," Andreas continued. "You fear he will seek restitution for his loss?"

"I do," Gaucelis said. "*We* do."

"And what does this have to do with Constansa?"

"Because she asked me to bring you here," Jacobi replied. He had come up behind Andreas during their conversation, and having interrupted it now, he walked around until he stood beside both of them.

"By name?" Andreas asked, somewhat skeptical.

"She told me to find the Rose Knights," Jacobi said. He pointed at the brooch on Andreas's shirt.

Andreas glanced down at the silver brooch, staring at it as though he had never seen it before. "Perhaps you might start at the beginning," he said, raising his head.

Gaucelis was taken aback to see something not unlike fear in his eyes. Seized by an impulse, she reached out and touched the knight's arm. "Come with me," she said. "Let her tell you." Ignoring Jacobi's wide-eyed expression, she led the knight toward the chapel.

* * *

The chapel was simple and unadorned—the sort of house of worship that Andreas found comfortable. No hideous pageantry. No profusion of iconography. No ostentatious ornamentation. Just a simple room—quiet and dim—filled with plain benches and a plain wooden altar. A sanctuary where one could commune with God as he or she saw fit.

The young woman, Constansa, was kneeling at the front of chapel, and the headwoman, Gaucelis, indicated he should sit on one of the benches. He did, and she knelt beside Constansa, leaning over to whisper quietly. Constansa gave no sign she had heard the other woman, and Gaucelis rose to her feet. She glanced at Andreas fleetingly and then crossed the altar to a narrow arch set along the back wall. She went through the wooden door, leaving Andreas and Constansa alone, and when the door rattled lightly against the frame, Constansa stirred from her prayers.

She had a plain face—pleasing enough, but not so striking that he would recall it with much clarity in time. Her eyes were dark and still, but there was a restlessness to their motion, as if she were a deer in the brush, hoping that no one would spot her, but ready to flee in an instant. She had a makeshift bandage tied around her left hand.

"Jacobi told you that I asked him to bring you here, didn't he?" She was soft-spoken, but direct—a quality that Andreas liked.

"Aye, he did," he said. "And I am curious as to how you know of my order by that name."

"It is the only name I knew," Constansa replied. "I told Jacobi, and he seemed to know who I was talking about."

"And where did this idea come from?" Andreas asked.

"From this," Gaucelis said, and Andreas looked up to see that the headwoman had returned. She had a sheath of parchment in her hands, and the pages were covered with heavy illustrations. The one on top—the one she was showing him—depicted a line of spears flying before a rising sun across the bottom of the sheet and a heavy rain of dark petals falling from above.

Andreas swallowed heavily. He was glad the others weren't with him. *It's just a drawing*, he told himself, but he couldn't shake the impact the illustration had had on him. He knew the falling petals represented his order—there was no doubt in his mind—and the spears and the half circle filled him with an enormous sense of dread.

"That is an interesting picture," he heard himself saying. "But I do not understand what it is supposed to represent."

Gaucelis set the first illustration down on a nearby bench and showed him another. The same line of spears—though across the top this time—and a portrait of a kneeling man.

"Is that supposed to be me?" he asked, his throat tight.

Constansa sighed. "I do not know," she said. "Do you think it is?"

Andreas's response was cut short by the sound of the chapel door opening, and he was happy to look away from the picture. Jacobi was leading several of the Shield-Brethren, who were carrying one of the chests from the wagons. Jacobi indicated where the chest should be put down, and Saluador and Lugo complied. As Jacobi fussed with the lock, the two Shield-Brethren stood nearby.

"Is that you?" Lugo asked, pointing at the picture in Gaucelis's hand.

"No," Andreas said quickly—too quickly—and he saw Saluador's eyes widen slightly as the tall man leaped to a conclusion of his own. Saluador sank to one knee and bowed his head in prayer. Lugo stared at the other man for a moment, his face screwed up in confusion, and then he too reached a similar conclusion.

"This isn't what you think it is," Andreas said. He stood, intending on shooing the other men out.

Jacobi opened the chest and stood back.

Andreas drew up short, staring at the contents. "What is that?" The chest was filled with neat stacks of pristine sheets. They didn't have the rough texture of parchment.

"Paper," Jacobi supplied. "There is a mill in Xàtiva."

Gaucelis pushed roughly past Andreas and slammed the lid of the chest shut. "How could you?" she scolded Jacobi.

"It's what she wanted," Jacobi said with a shrug, as if to say the decision had not been his. He was merely serving someone else, and Andreas shivered at the man's abasement to the desires of another. His men were listening. Could they be swayed so readily?

"I asked him to bring me the paper, Gaucelis," Constansa said, her hand on Andreas's arm. "I don't want you destroying my pictures anymore. I want them to be shared with everyone."

"Dear child," Gaucelis said, her face fighting to hold back tears, "we can't tell anyone. They won't understand. They'll be frightened."

"They already are," Constansa said. "But that is because they don't understand. I want to ease their suffering."

Tears tracked down Gaucelis's cheeks. "Not this way."

"Then what way?" Constansa asked. She held up her left hand. "Am I supposed to hurt myself again? Should I cut my face next time so that you can't hide it?"

Gaucelis shook her head.

"We can't be afraid of who we are," Constansa said. "We can't be afraid of what we believe." She looked at Jacobi, who ducked his head and refused to look at her. "Fear is poisonous. It will kill us just as readily."

And Andreas surprised himself by turning and putting his hand over Constansa's mouth. She started, and when she reached up to move his hand, he intercepted it with his other hand. He shook his head and spoke over his shoulder. "I think it is best if Constansa and I have a private conversation." He listened for any sign of movement, and hearing nothing, he spoke again, his voice harder. "Saluador, Lugo, that is an order. Take Gaucelis and Jacobi with you."

He heard Saluador mutter something, but the tall man complied. Andreas remained still, staring at Constansa. She made no move to extricate herself from his grip, staring at him with her green eyes. He found himself thinking about the lake nearby, wondering how deep the water was, and he shook himself free of those thoughts. He closed his eyes, and he didn't let go of Constansa until he heard the chapel door shut.

"I don't believe in visions," he said, forestalling any other discussion. As if he could, through sheer force of his will, undo anything that his men might have seen, any thoughts that they might, even now, be having.

"It does not matter if you do," she replied. "I will still have them."

"They mean nothing," he tried to argue, waving a hand at the scattered pieces of parchment. She had pierced his defenses already, but he would not relent so quickly. In battle, being stabbed or cut did not mean immediate defeat. You kept fighting until your heart stopped. Until your spirit was broken.

"They mean whatever you think they mean," she replied.

"That is nonsense," he snapped. "You interpret them. You suggest meaning. People act differently because of your suggestions. Jacobi wouldn't have hired us if you hadn't told him to."

"And what harm came from that?" she asked.

Andreas stared at her, his mind tangled with too many thoughts. They had killed Martis, a man who was nothing more than a bandit. They had broken a long-standing illicit toll being levied against the trader. Indeed, what *harm* lay in those actions? In fact, the encounter with Martis and his men could have been much worse. Some of the Shield-Brethren could have died. The wagons could have been lost. Had they, in fact, done more good than harm by accepting Jacobi's commission? Would the money not benefit the Shield-Brethren chapter house?

"Do your men not respect you?" she asked, as if reading his thoughts. "Have you not led them well? Are they all safe and without injury?"

"That is not the point," Andreas growled.

"Were you not afraid of leadership?" she continued, ignoring him. "Have you not been running from your responsibility to your order?"

"That's enough," Andreas snapped, raising his hand as if to strike her before she could say anything more. She stared at him, unafraid, and he dropped his hand, ashamed of what he had been about to do.

He heard the rustling sound of the parchment as she retrieved the large sheet. She held it out so that he could see the rose petals falling upon the thick line of spears.

"They're coming," she said. "And you've been running the wrong way."

Beneath the spears, the half circle rose from the bottom of the page. *The sun*, he realized, *rising in the east.*

* * *

Jacobi had been keeping an eye on the chapel door while the rest of the cargo was being distributed, and when Andreas quietly slipped out of the church, he was the only one who witnessed the knight's return. Andreas seemed distant, a thoughtful expression on his face, and Jacobi hesitated briefly before approaching the knight.

"There is a final matter," Jacobi said, clearing his throat. He held up the small purse he was holding. "The other half of your commission—or should I call it the proceeds from selling the contents of *your* wagons?"

A tiny smile flitted across Andreas's mouth. "What sort of trader am I that I allowed you and the others to dictate prices to me?" he asked.

"Not a very good one," Jacobi pointed out.

Andreas nodded as he accepted the pouch. "Then I will accept this as our commission. And I apologize for stealing your wagons."

"No need," Jacobi said. "It all worked out."

"I suppose it did." The distant stare returned to Andreas's face. "What of de Vilapros?" he asked. "After we leave, will he demand restitution from Estartyol for Martis's death?"

"He might," Jacobi said. "But no one will miss Martis, and it is time for us to stand up to men like de Vilapros."

Andreas looked past Jacobi. "Your man, Tibal—he seems like an old dog that has a little bite in him still."

Jacobi looked over his shoulder to where the old soldier was barking orders at his reluctant volunteers, who were apparently unloading cargo in the most inefficient manner possible. "He might."

"If I see de Vilapros, I will warn him about the old dog," Andreas said.

Jacobi caught the use of the singular in Andreas's words. "You're not returning to Barcelona with the others?"

Andreas shook his head. "No, I have been remiss in my duties," he said. "I have wandered too far west."

"Did she...?"

"Constansa?" Andreas shook his head. "She is a confused young woman who draws interesting pictures, Jacobi. Do not see too much in them. Nor listen too intently to her words." He touched the trader lightly on the chest. "Though, she was right about one thing," he said. "Don't be afraid, especially of what lies in here."

Jacobi clasped Andreas's hand. "Good-bye, Andreas," he said. "Go without fear."

Andreas gripped his hand tight. "You too, Jacobi de Reyns."

* * *

The Shield-Brethren were not surprised by his announcement that he would not be returning to Barcelona with them. They stood about awkwardly for a few minutes, pretending to fuss with their gear and their horses, until it became clear they were all avoiding saying good-bye.

Saluador broached the subject in the only way he knew. He strode up to Andreas and embraced him in an enormous bear hug. "May the Virgin watch over you," he said when he finally released Andreas.

"I believe she does," Andreas said, a thoughtful note in his voice. "The men are yours, Saluador. Take care of them."

"I will," Saluador replied.

"And stay out of de Vilapros's path."

"Who?" Saluador asked, mock confusion on his face.

Andreas slapped him on the chest. "It was a well-shot arrow, my friend," he said. "It may have saved all of us."

Saluador nodded. "Thank you, my friend. I will continue to pray for forgiveness, but I do not regret my action."

"That is all any of us can do," Andreas said.

Lugo couldn't crush Andreas as readily as Saluador, so he didn't try. Instead, he offered Andreas the leather purse Andreas had given him earlier. It was lighter, but there was still a weight of silver in it. "We're not that poor of an order," Lugo said. "Not as poor as you are, that's for certain."

Andreas inclined his head, accepting the gift. "I will spend it foolishly," he said.

Lugo grinned. "I am sure you will."

Harald said little, as was his wont, but his embrace was just as strong as Saluador's.

That left Guillén.

"Have a safe journey," Andreas said, offering his hand. "You should be back in Barcelona in a few days."

Guillén snorted as he clasped Andreas's forearm. "I'm not going anywhere," he said. "Not for a few days, at least." He jerked a thumb in the direction of the lake. "I still want to go fishing. These three are just going to have to wait."

"And if de Vilapros shows up?"

"Who?" Guillén asked.

Andreas laughed. "I hope I meet him first. He definitely needs to be warned off."

"You wouldn't dare," Saluador protested. Lugo, though, looked as if he hoped Andreas would.

Andreas gazed at the four men who had been briefly under his command, and the tightness that had been gripping his chest since he had spoken with Constansa loosened. He laughed, letting go of numerous things: the responsibility of command, a nagging trepidation about what lay ahead of him, and an old fear that he had been carrying for a long time. Longer than he had realized.

These were his Brothers. His kin. They would die for him, and he would do the same.

There was no reason to be afraid anymore.

He knew his place in the world.

The Mongoliad

BOOK THREE

CAST OF CHARACTERS

In Hünern

Andreas: Shield-Brethren knight initiate

Rutger: Shield-Brethren knight master, quartermaster of the Rock

Styg: Shield-Brethren initiate

Eilif: Shield-Brethren initiate

Maks: Shield-Brethren initiate

Knútr: Shield-Brethren knight initiate

Hans: orphan of Legnica, member of the local gang known as the "Rats"

Ernust: itinerant brewmaster, Hans's adopted uncle

Father Pius: Roman Catholic priest

Dietrich von Grüningen: *Heermeister* of the Livonian Order

Sigeberht: the *Heermeister*'s bodyguard

Burchard: the *Heermeister*'s bodyguard

Kristaps: the First Sword of Fellin, Livonian knight

Leuthere de Montfont: Templar master

Emmeran: Hospitaller master

Onghwe Khan: Ögedei Khan's dissolute son

Tegusgal: captain of Onghwe Khan's personal guard

Ashiq Temür: second in command of Onghwe Khan's personal guard

Zugaikotsu No Yama: Nipponese *ronin*

Kim Alcheon: Korean Flower Knight

Lakshaman: Malay knife fighter

In Rome

Father Rodrigo Bendrito: a priest of the Roman Catholic Church

Ferenc: a young Magyar hunter

Ocyrhoe: orphan of Rome

Robert of Somercotes: English Cardinal of the Roman Catholic Church

Matteo Rosso Orsini: Senator of Rome

Sinibaldo Fieschi: Cardinal of the Roman Catholic Church

Rainiero Capocci: Cardinal of the Roman Catholic Church

Giovanni Colonna: Cardinal of the Roman Catholic Church

Rinaldo de Segni: Cardinal of the Roman Catholic Church

Tommaso da Capua: Cardinal of the Roman Catholic Church

Romano Bonaventura: Cardinal of the Roman Catholic Church

Gil Torres: Cardinal of the Roman Catholic Church

Goffredo Castiglione: Cardinal of the Roman Catholic Church

Stefano de Normandis dei Conti: Cardinal of the Roman Catholic Church

Riccardo Annibaldi: Cardinal of the Roman Catholic Church

Master Constable Alatrinus: keeper of the Septizodium

Giacomo da Pecorara: Cardinal Bishop of the Roman Catholic Church

Oddone de Monferrato: Cardinal of the Roman Catholic Church

Frederick II: Holy Roman Emperor

Léna: Binder, presently attached to the emperor's court

In the East

Feronantus: Shield-Brethren knight master, the Old Man of the Rock

Percival: Shield-Brethren knight initiate
Raphael: Shield-Brethren knight initiate
Yasper: Dutch alchemist, Shield-Brethren companion
Istvan: Hungarian horse rider, Shield-Brethren companion
Cnán: Binder, Shield-Brethren guide
Eleázar: *Matamoros*, Shield-Brethren initiate
Rædwulf: English longbowman, Shield-Brethren initiate
Vera: leader of the Shield-Maidens
Haakon: Shield-Brethren initiate
Benjamin: Jewish trader
Krasniy: Ruthenian gladiator

Ögedei Khan: *Khagan* of the Mongol Empire
Yelu Chucai: Kitayan advisor to the *Khagan*
Gansukh: Mongolian hunter, emissary of Chagatai Khan
Munokhoi: *Torguud* captain
Namkhai: *Torguud* wrestling champion
Lian: Chinese slave and tutor
Jachin: Ögedei Khan's second wife
Alchiq: *jaghun* commander, known as Graymane to the Shield-Brethren
Tarbagatai: Mongolian hunter
Sübegei: Mongolian hunter

1241

veturnætur

Leaving Finn

THE SHIELD-BRETHREN BURIED Finn on the hill where they had set up camp. "It is not as grand as one of those burial mounds—the *kurgans*—we have seen," Raphael pointed out to Feronantus, "but it has a view of where we came from, and the sun will always warm the ground." Given the choice, Finn had always preferred to sleep outside, where the sun could find him and warm his bones in the morning. Finn may not have been a sworn member of the Shield-Brethren, but he was a feral brother to many of them.

One by one the members of the Shield-Brethren attacked the rocky ground of the hilltop. Without coming out and saying as much, they all wanted to be the one to dig Finn's grave, as if the backbreaking labor would somehow assuage their individual guilt. It was not that they valued Finn above their other fallen comrades—the loss of any brother was equally horrific—but each was racked with a sense of responsibility for the circumstances of the hunter's death.

As he prepared Finn's body for burial, Raphael tried not to let his thoughts dwell on other members of their company whom they had lost. Or even his own role in the deaths of those dear friends. With Vera's assistance, he laid the small man's body on Percival's cloak—the knight refused to hear otherwise—and arranged Finn's limbs as best he could. The stiffness that creeps into a man's body in the wake of death had filled Finn, and one of his arms resisted Raphael's efforts. His face, once it had been tenderly washed by Vera, was surprisingly boyish. Raphael felt the weight of his years when he saw the delicate lashes and the unlined swath of forehead clearly for the first time. *Too young*, he thought, *to die so far from home.*

And he realized how little he knew of Finn. How little any of them knew.

"Wait," he said to Vera as she made to cover Finn's face with Percival's cloak. He strode to his bags and dug out his worn journal and his writing instruments. With the sun peering over his shoulder, he sat and carefully sketched Finn's face on a blank page. *There will be a record*, he promised his dead friend. *You will not be forgotten.*

As Raphael painstakingly tried to capture the essence of Finn's character—an amalgamation of the peaceful features before him and those memories he had of more exuberant expressions—Vera busied herself with washing Finn's feet and hands. The leather of his boots had been soft and supple once, but months and months of being in the wilderness had hardened the material into a second skin over Finn's feet. She tugged at them briefly, and then gave up, opting to run a knife along the thin seams instead.

"Strangely fastidious," she noted when she got to his hands. Raphael looked up from his sketching as she showed him Finn's palms. Calloused, as expected, but surprisingly clean. The nails were long, but there was no dirt or filth beneath them.

The Binder, Cnán, approached, and with some interest examined Finn's hands. "Like a cat," she said, and Raphael nodded in agreement.

"They're done with the grave," Cnán reported. "Though," she snorted, "I think Percival would like to keep digging."

Raphael nodded. "Yes, I can imagine he would."

There had been very little conversation among the company since Alchiq's attack on Finn; the sudden shock of the Mongol's assault had left them all wordless. But no words were necessary to comprehend Percival's grief at having fallen asleep at the watch.

Privately, Raphael thought it was more likely that the Frank had been captivated by an ecstatic vision—much like the one that had come over him in the forest shortly after the death of Taran and the knight's horse. He tried to push the idea out of his thoughts though, because he did not want to face the dreadful conclusion that followed: illumination brought death to those nearby. What price was being exacted for the guidance the knight was receiving?

Vera indicated to Cnán that she should help with the wrapping of the dead. "It is time," the Shield-Maiden said to Raphael, her stern eyes unusually soft. "No amount of drawing will bring life back to this face."

"Aye," Raphael agreed, and he set aside his tools. He lent a hand, and soon Finn was nothing more than a squat bundle.

The other Shield-Brethren came down from the hill and carefully carried the body to its final resting place. Without speaking, they lowered Finn's corpse into the deep trough they had hacked out of the rocky hilltop. *It was deep*, Raphael noted. Deep enough that the body might never be disturbed by the carrion eaters.

Feronantus waved them off, and even Percival relented, letting their aged leader undertake the task of filling the hole by himself. They stood around awkwardly for a little while, watching Feronantus scoop and pack handfuls of sand and rock into the hole. Once a thick layer had been carefully laid over the body to protect it from being crushed during the burial process, Feronantus would shovel dirt in more readily. A cairn would be raised and words would be spoken, but until then, they had little to do but wait.

Death itself was always quick, Raphael reflected, staring off at the distant horizon. *It is the survivors who feel pain the longest.*

"Where's Istvan?" Vera asked.

Raphael blinked away from his thoughts and scanned the surrounding countryside. "I don't know," he said.

"Chasing Graymane," Cnán offered, pointing toward the west.

Raphael vaguely recalled their pursuit of the Mongol commander after Finn's death, the long line of horses strung out across the plain. One by one, their steeds had faltered, until only Istvan and Alchiq remained, two tiny dots dancing in the midmorning heat. "He hasn't returned?" he asked, caught between surprise and apprehension.

Cnán shook her head. "I find myself hoping that he doesn't. At least, not today." She looked at Raphael and Vera, and they both saw their own pain mirrored in the Binder's eyes. "If he is still hunting, then he might still catch him. If he comes back, we'll know if he was successful or not."

Vera nodded. "I don't want him to return empty-handed either. Better he not return at all."

None of us are going to return, Raphael thought as he turned and looked back at Finn's slowly filling grave.

* * *

That night the company made no fire, and the stars wheeled dizzyingly overhead. The air grew cold quickly after the sun vanished in a burning haze of gold and red in the west. They hobbled their horses near a band of scraggly brush that the animals appeared to be interested in eating, and then they wandered off to make their respective prepartions for sleep.

Raphael tried to make himself comfortable. The lush grasslands surrounding the river had given way to flatter terrain, and he found the sere landscape to be oddly distressing. The muscles in his lower back and thighs kept twitching, phantom fears that the ground would suddenly tilt and he would slide away. But slide away into what? They had passed beyond the edge of the world that he— or any of the Shield-Brethren—knew. His hands pressed against the blanket beneath him, pressing the wool against the hard ground.

His reaction was not a sign of madness; it was simply a reaction to the unfamiliar. Men were drawn to civilization; only the most severe ascetic among them relished isolation. Penitent hermits craved seclusion. Being away from the squalor of humanity was an integral part of their spiritual monasticism. They could talk more readily to God in the silence of their mountaintop cave or their desert isolation. It was easier to believe that the voice you heard responding to your queries issued from a divine trumpet if there were no other souls nearby.

But he was a soldier. He slept more soundly when surrounded by the sounds of men preparing for war. His mind was less prone to fearful speculation when he rested behind a stout battlement. Even the sounds of domesticated animals were a welcome lullaby: cows calling to one another in the pasture; the nervous clucking of chickens as they scratched in the yard; dogs, barking at shadows.

On the steppes, there was nothing but the sound of the wind through the grasses; when there was no grass, the wind had no voice, and the silence was unsettling.

He heard her bones creak as she lay down next to him. A blanket fluttered like the wing of a large bird, and he shivered slightly as the cloth descended upon his chest and legs. Her breath hummed against the skin of his neck as she pressed her head against his. Their hands found one another beneath the blanket. Beneath the stars.

Her skin was hot. Pressed against her, his mouth seeking hers, he thought they could stay warm enough to survive the night.

In the morning, there was only a fading blush of heat in the base of his throat. A lingering memento of Vera's kiss.

* * *

"This emptiness does not go on forever," Cnán said. "We have ridden off your maps, but we are barely at the edge of ones I have seen that show the boundaries of the Mongolian Empire."

"No wonder it is so huge," Yasper complained. "Do you really control the land if there is nothing there?"

The lithe alchemist slouched in his saddle, his jaw working absently on a piece of salted meat. In the days since they had crossed the river—since they had left Finn behind—Yasper was typically one of the first to break camp, and more often than not, volunteered to take point. At first, Cnán had found it odd that Feronantus usually acquiesced to the Dutchman's request. While Yasper was not his to command, typically Feronantus would set one of the more proficient scouts riding before the company. Cnán soon realized Feronantus's strategy: the alchemist was looking for something—a natural deposit of some alchemical treasure. As long as Yasper was keeping an eye out for anything unusual, then he would be a satisfactory scout and Feronantus could allow the other riders some rest.

Though, recently, he had been afflicted with the same malaise as the more experienced Shield-Brethren.

Graymane's trail had led them toward Saray-Jük—not surprising, given the presence of more Mongol troops there—and with some caution they had found the place where Benjamin had instructed them to meet him. The caravanserai was deserted—nothing more than a scattering of fire pits near a stand of scrawny trees and a tiny trickle of a stream. The ashes were cold and there were too many tracks of Mongol ponies—it was dangerous for them to stay in the area. Before they left, Cnán found the cryptic message left by the trader, a series of marks carved into the bark of one of the trees—almost as if she had known to look for them. *South and east for six days*, the message had read, *look for the rock*.

Which rock? Feronantus had asked.

It will probably be the only *rock*, Raphael had pointed out.

Given how Yasper tended to focus so tightly on his own little projects, Cnán suspected he might ride right into the rock before he noticed it.

While Raphael's comment was all too accurate and would likely be the only guidance the company needed, she knew the rock. It was one of the landmarks the Binders used as they passed from the east to the west. A station in the wilderness where messages could be coded and left for others to pick up.

Some Binders, like her, traveled widely, but others stayed within a few days' travel of where they had been born and raised. At the verge of their domain, they would receive messages and instructions from other kin-sisters, and being more qualified to navigate the dense locality, they would complete the assignment for the foreign Binder. In this way, messages could be carried across the known world and delivery could be readily assured, because the kin-sisters were never dependent upon one messenger.

Such a landmark was used by the Silk Road traders as well.

Cnán glanced over her shoulder at the string of horses and riders behind her. While she was accustomed to traveling across wastelands such as this, she could tell the tedium of riding from daybreak to sunset was beginning to wear on the rest of the company.

And they have no idea how many more days await them, she thought.

"What are you smiling about?" Yasper inquired.

"Nothing," she replied, setting her face aright. "What could I possibly see that would provoke some humor in me?"

"That's why I asked," Yasper said. He sat up and tapped his horse lightly with his stick, edging closer to her. "You've been this way before," he noted. "Tell me, have you seen deposits of salt?"

"Salt?"

"Yes." He spread his hand out flat and moved it across the landscape. "Like a dry lake. A place where the wind plays."

Cnán laughed. "All of this land is like that."

"No, no. Not like this. Perfectly flat. Alchemists call it a *sabkha*."

Cnán shrugged. "I do not know that word," she said, though she had a dim recollection of a Turkic word that might mean the same thing. She tried to dredge up the word, but nothing felt quite right on her tongue. "Nor have I seen one," she admitted.

"A pity," Yasper said. "Neither have I."

Cnán smiled again. "There's still time," she said.

"I know, I know." Yasper flapped his hands and blew out, puffing up his cheeks. "This...*wasteland*...wears on me. I've been trying to find some solace in my recipes, but my supplies are terribly meager, especially after..." He trailed off, and Cnán knew he was thinking about the loss of his horse in Kiev.

When he had fled from the fight with the Shield-Brethren, the Livonian commander Kristaps had returned through the same stinking tunnels they had used to reach the Shield-Maiden sanctuary. Upon emerging from the well house, the Livonian had stumbled upon her, Yasper's, and Finn's horses. He had taken all three—a smart ploy to reduce their ability to pursue him. Yasper hadn't been so distraught about the lack of his horse as he had been about the loss of his numerous satchels and jars and powders.

All of his alchemical supplies, gone.

Since then he had been trying to replenish his stores, with some mixed success. The market in the border town had supplied him with the firecrackers they had used so effectively against the Mongol war party, as well as a number of other basic ingredients. Yasper had been excited when they had first stumbled across the wormwood—the hearty plant native to these lands—but after days and days of seeing clumps of it everywhere, Yasper's enthusiasm had diminished drastically. Cnán knew little about the alchemist's recipes (and wanted to know very little, actually), but what she had gleaned was that all of his potions, unguents, powders, and salves were built from a carefully measured base of two or three simple ingredients.

Salt being one of those basic ingredients.

"What is it that you hope to create?" she asked, out of boredom more than any concerted interest.

Yasper offered her a wolfish grin. "Why, nothing more than the secrets of the universe, of course," he laughed. "Every alchemist seeks to unlock the riddle of existence by discerning the secret methods by which God constructed the world. All of this," he gestured around them, "though this is not much, but all of the world was created through a complex set of instructions. Men have spent their entire lives trying to enumerate the multitudinous mystery of creation. Pliny—do you know Pliny? No, of course you don't—Pliny wrote thirty-seven volumes on the natural history of the world. Thirty-seven!" He sat up in his saddle, his mood improving as he spoke. "Can you imagine how complicated this world is that God has created? Don't you want to understand how all the various pieces fit together?"

"I hadn't really thought about it," Cnán admitted. "But why do you want to understand it? So that you can become a god too?"

Yasper shook his head. "That would be heresy," he clucked his tongue at her, a grin stretching his mouth. "No, we seek to understand who we truly are, and what our true purpose is. If we can comprehend how the world was made, and learn the power of transmutation—the art of changing one thing into another—could we not give ourselves that same gift?"

"Which gift?"

"Transmutation."

"Trans-what?"

"Becoming something new."

Cnán scratched her nose. "What's wrong with what we are?"

Yasper closed one eye and stared critically at her. "What's *right* about what we are?" he asked.

Cnán, now somewhat sorry she had even asked her initial question, shook her head and stared out at the horizon in the vain hope of finding something to distract the alchemist. He was warming to this one-sided conversation, and she feared it was only going to get more confusing. "Look," she said, sitting up in her saddle and pointing. She was not embarrassed to hear a note of elation in her voice. "There!"

Ahead of them, a thin black shape reached up from the flat ground, a finger stretching to poke the empty dome of the heavens. It wiggled, like a worm struggling to pull itself from rain-softened mud.

"Rider!" Cnán called out to the others while Yasper stood in his saddle, shading his eyes. After peering through the heat haze for a moment, he sank back down into his saddle, and the slope of his shoulders told her everything.

"It's Istvan," he said bitterly.

As the Hungarian drew closer, she could confirm what the alchemist had noticed as well. The Hungarian was alone.

But what chilled her was the fact that he was in *front* of them.

Where had Graymane gone?

FACTUS SUM TAMQUAM UAS PERDITUM

2

E NEEDED TO make a dramatic entrance. Not far from the secret door he used to come and go from the Septizodium, there was a crack in the wall that opened into a narrow slot. Previously, Fieschi had used it as a makeshift dressing room, exchanging the vestments of his station for a plain wool robe. Now, as the tunnels beneath the Septizodium began to fill with smoke and the cries of the panicked cardinals, he waited patiently in his hiding spot.

Before squeezing into his secret *sanctum*, he had gone ahead to the secret door and released the hidden latch. He had pushed it open slightly, just enough for a little air to get in, and for a little smoke to get out. The young messengers had used the door, and while he suspected the two jesters—Colonna and Capocci—had known of its existence prior to the arrival of the intruders, he didn't want to leave it to Providence that it would be found: he needed witnesses, an audience that would flock to his miraculous appearance.

Fieschi set his shoulders against the back of his niche to get more comfortable. He opened and closed his right hand slowly, keeping the aching paralysis of his recent exertion at bay. *Quoniam fortitudo mea et refugium meum es tu*, he prayed, *et propter nomen tuum deduces me et enutries me.*

7 7

Fieschi recalled a sermon St. Augustine had delivered on the thirty-first Psalm—in particular, a portion of the homily concerning Abraham. The patriarch was justified by the virtue of his faith; his good works came second. God is my rock and my fortress, and I am unshakeable in my faith. *"Exsultabo, et laetabor in misericordia tua,"* he whispered, knowing that God would hear him, *"quoniam respexisti humilitatem meam; salvasti de necessitatibus animam meum."*

By destroying Somercotes, he had saved the Church. Were such trials not part of God's love and kindness? Surely God would forgive him of his transgression.

* * *

The fire, incendiary agent of Satan, eagerly devoured the combustibles in the narrow room. It had licked the walls and found them wanting, and so it had fallen upon the dead body. Fueled by the cloth and the flesh, it had grown larger, sending out creeping tendrils of fire that wormed their way through the cracks in the walls. It was no longer a single blaze by the time Capocci approached Somercotes's room, but a string of fires, prancing with unholy glee, in a number of the tiny rooms the cardinals had been using.

Most of the smoke came from Somercotes's room, rolling off the huddled mass that popped and crackled as the fire joyfully burned fat and flesh off bone. Capocci ducked his head, breathing through his mouth; he knew that smell. Years ago, when he still believed in Gregory IX, he had led Papal troops into Viterbo and besieged the citadel of Rispampano. The Roman troops resisted for a few days, hurling everything they could haul up to the battlements down upon his troops, including burning pitch. The screams of dying men and the smell of their burning flesh had only hardened the resolve of his soldiers.

Somercotes's body lay curled near the center of his room. Not on his bed and not near the door—two places that Capocci would have expected to find the body had the fire been an accident. He pushed aside the inquisitive thoughts that crowed his brain, and waddled slowly into the hot room. His beard crackled as strands of his capacious whiskers began to curl and burn from the heat. Blinking heavily to clear the smoke from his eyes, he reached out with his gloved hand.

Somercotes couldn't still be alive. The fire danced too merrily along his frame, and the crackling, sizzling sound of burning meat was so loud. And the smell...Capocci grabbed something—an elbow, perhaps—and clenched his teeth as the fire gnawed through the heavy leather of his gloves. He pulled, intending to drag the body out of the inferno, but there was no resistance, and he fell back on the floor.

Clutched in his hand, covered in writhing tendrils of fire, was a spitting piece of charred meat. The entire arm.

Spitting out an oath that he would have to beg forgiveness for later, Capocci tried to hurl Somercotes's arm away, but the fire had fused the meat to the leather of his glove. Orange tongues of flame licked at the cuff of his sleeve. Using his other hand, he stripped the glove off—both of them, in the end—and scrambling backward, he fled from the room and its grisly pyre.

Capocci leaned against the hallway wall, coughing and choking as he tried to catch his breath without inhaling the fouled air. He knew he should check the other rooms. Hopefully they were empty, but what if they weren't? Would their occupants be any more alive than Somercotes?

He wanted to run away. He wasn't such a prideful man that he couldn't admit when he was afraid. Fear was a powerful emotion, and giving himself up to God meant letting go of the fear. But such a sacrifice did not make him invulnerable or fireproof.

It made him cautious.

He had to be sure, though. He had to be sure there was no one else. Only then could he listen to the voice in his head—the one that telling him that Somercotes's death was not an accident.

* * *

Rodrigo had dreamed of a dragon once. It was sinuous and long, and covered in red and brown scales. When it roared, a great billow of black smoke issued from its mouth. There were great furnaces in its belly, stoked by infernal spirits, and in the wake of that smoke came the fire. The brilliant, burning fire.

He ran from that fire. To stand his ground would be to be burned, and while he had faith in God—while he *believed* that God watched over him and that God's love was enough to protect him from any such foul denizen of Hell—another part of him was broken and fearful. That part of him fled, dragging the rest of his spirit with him. The rest of his body and mind. Running from the fire...

Rodrigo bashed his hands against rough rock as he tripped. The smoke surrounded him—it was in his mouth, his nose, his eyes—but there was less of it down here next to the rock. He wanted to press his face against the rocky ground, and let the smoke pass over him. Let the dragon's fire burn the sky overhead. Down here, nestled against the ground, he would escape notice. He could still breathe.

"Get up." Someone grabbed his robes and dragged him upright. He fought back, his body racked with heaving coughs, but he had no real strength in his arms. He let himself be dragged along until it became clear that whoever was carrying him would continue to do so—*more roughly, in fact*, he realized as his knees bounced painfully off the ground.

When he had his feet beneath him again, the hand released its hold, and he was free to continue staggering down the endless passage.

As if he were running up the dragon's throat, trying to escape the burning churn of the infernal fires in its belly.

Then, without warning, he was free. The smoke went upward, a curling black finger rising into the pure serenity of the blue sky, and the walls of the tunnel fell away. He had escaped.

And with the freedom came a sudden rush of clarity, as if much more than smoke was wiped clear of his eyes and throat. He had been in the grips of the fever again, the persistent heat that plagued his soul. It was such a heavy weight to carry that the brief moments when he felt God's eyes upon him were such a momentous blessing. He felt so...*elevated*.

He looked behind him at the unadorned outer walls of the Septizodium. He stood in an alley, one of the many unmarked and unmemorable gaps between buildings in Rome. The door through which he had stumbled wasn't a real door, but a clever panel of stone. Any other time, he would never have noticed it against the mottled background of the surrounding stone, but it hung open now, and a column of black smoke spiraled up from it. There were other spires of smoke rising over the rooftop; clearly, there were other exits from the Septizodium. They might not have been plain to those who were sequestered inside, but smoke had a talent for finding a way out.

The tall, elderly cardinal—Colonna, Rodrigo could remember his name effortlessly now—stood nearby, his chest heaving with a great cough. He spat something foul on the ground and wiped the back of his hand across his mouth. "Are you all right?" he asked, and Rodrigo recognized his voice as the one that had kept shouting at him during his long exodus from the fire-laden darkness.

"Yes," Rodrigo replied. "Well enough."

Colonna nodded and made the sign of the cross. "Watch for others," he said, "I am going to see if anyone...is waiting for us to... *escape*." He took a step up the alley, and then seemed to realize he was still cradling a small earthenware jar in his hands. "Hold on to this," he said, thrusting it toward Rodrigo.

"What is it?"

Colonna cocked his head to one side. "Just...hold it." Shaking his head, he headed up the alley, leaving Rodrigo to wonder what was on the cardinal's mind.

Rodrigo peered at the jar, cradling it tentatively. The stopper was a thick wooden plug surrounded by a layer of wax, and the seal was so tight that if he turned it upside down—like so—the stopper did not come out. He held the jar close to his ear, cautiously listening, but he heard nothing over the groaning rumble of the fire burning deep within the Septizodium.

I am being a fool, he thought. *If it is the one thing that Colonna brought out of this prison, then it must be important. That is enough for me.* He glanced in the direction the tall cardinal had gone. *We all have our secrets.*

Unburdened by the fever, he dispassionately recalled what he had seen at the abandoned farm near Mohi: the slaughtered horses in the barn; the children hiding in the hayloft; their mother, lying on the hearth in the house, her body burned and defiled; the old man pinned to the wall with arrows, forced to watch. He could remember it all clearly, unburdened by the horror and dread he had felt at the time. It was as if he were looking at the pages of an illuminated manuscript, and no matter how badly he desired to close this book and hide these pictures forever, he could not. They were an indelible part of him now, burned into his memory by the fever. By the vision.

He could also remember what Brother Albertus had taught him many years prior. He had been so young, so eager to learn how to worship God, and the older monk had been equally eager to share his newfound knowledge with a bright student. The *Ars Notoria*, a means by which he would be able to more readily explore his relationship with God. By understanding the *language* of God, by learning how the tongue and the mind were connected.

Brother Albertus had taught him a prayer. *Te quaeso Domine mî illumina conscientiam meam splendore luminis tui.* To call upon God to illuminate him with his light so that he would remember what he had seen and heard. *Adorna animam meum ut audiendo audiam et audita memoriter teneam.*

Bless me, God, so that I may remember.

And he did. He remembered all of it, as clearly as if he were experiencing it for the first time. Was this God's love? Or, by invoking those names that Brother Albertus had taught him, had he transgressed against the glory of God? *Algaros, Theomiros...*the names of angels, according to Brother Albertus, aspects of God that would fill him with the celestial majesty.

He had tried to forget. After covering and burying the dead, he had knelt in prayer before the hearth where the woman had been killed. He had asked God to undo all that had been done to him. He did not want to remember anymore. He wanted to open his eyes and be innocent again.

But God never answered his prayer. His knees aching, the wound in his abdomen slowly weeping down his side, he had refused to quit praying. He would pray until God heard him, or until his soul went to God directly. He wouldn't stop.

And then the angels had come. First, they were nothing more than beams of light, streaming through the holes in the rough walls of the house. They came swirling and combining into a winged figure that floated over the hearth.

Aperi mititissime animam meam. Mercifully open the dullness of my soul...

Rodrigo clenched Colonna's earthenware jar tight to this chest. *Our secrets,* he thought, imagining a great door closing over the part of his memory that refused to fade.

A clatter of metal and the chatter of voices drew him away from that memory and cast him into another. Soldiers, wearing purple and white, were coming toward him and the smoking hole of the secret entrance of the Septizodium. Rodrigo saw them coming, but he also saw—with equal clarity—a sweltering afternoon in a market-place. Ferenc was there, riding beside him, and there was a girl too. Behind them. Watching them. He had seen her again. Where? In the darkness of the dragon's belly, before it had been woken from its slumber. Like a tiny bird that had been swallowed, she had fluttered down into their prison. She had brought him something...the ring! Archbishop Csák's signet ring.

"Father Rodrigo."

He started, blinking heavily. His vision blurred, swimming with too many distinct images, too many layers overlapping. Eventually, cleared away by a minute wash of tears, all that remained was the concerned faces of Cardinal Colonna and another man whom he recognized but did not know. "Yes?" he said.

Colonna indicated the other man. "This is Master Constable Alatrinus." His voice was flat. "He and his men are here to ensure our *safety*..."

The Master Constable nodded. "Please, Father. Let my men escort you."

"Where?" Rodrigo managed. He was still clenching the jar, and he lowered his arms, though he did not relinquish his burden. He caught sight of a ring on his right thumb, and he stared at the ornate band. The Archbishop had been a large man, much heavier and taller than Rodrigo, and his hands had been enormous.

But that wasn't why he stared at the ring. He stared because he had no memory of putting it there.

"A safe distance," the Master Constable said. He put a hand on Rodrigo's shoulder and squeezed slightly, misinterpreting the priest's confusion as being caused by inhaling too much smoke.

One of the guards called for the Master Constable's attention, and the hand disappeared from Rodrigo's shoulder. Someone else was coming out of the tunnel, a soot-blackened apparition with white hair.

"It's Capocci," Colonna breathed with a sigh of relief.

Confusion grew as more guards arrived, overfilling the narrow terminus of the alley. The Master Constable shoved his way through the crowd to Capocci's side as the white-bearded cardinal sank to the ground. Rodrigo could not hear the cardinal's response to the Master Constable's question, but the answer was plain to read on the latter's face as he stood.

"Find out how many they're pulling out of the courtyard," he said to one of his men. "Tell them I have three. Get an accurate count." The man nodded, and brushing past Colonna and Rodrigo, he ran to deliver his message.

As several other soldiers knelt to help Capocci to his feet, the Master Constable gingerly approached the smoking mouth of the tunnel entrance. *Was he going to go in?* Rodrigo felt a shout rising in his throat; he wanted to warn the Master Constable. *How could the man not see that no one could still be alive in there?*

"Ho!" the Master Constable shouted. "Is anyone there?"

Rodrigo choked on his words as something moved in the darkness of the door. The Master Constable jumped back, startled by the sudden appearance of a figure. What had he summoned with his words?

A man staggered out of the tunnel, his face and clothes streaked with soot. He fell to the ground at the Master Constable's feet, gasping for air. With a shaky hand, he grabbed at the soldier's boot, clutching the leather like a drowning man grabbing a piece of driftwood.

Rodrigo stared, and as the man raised his face, he remembered something else: the last time he had seen Somercotes alive, they had been interrupted by a visitor, who had taken Somercotes away. The hawk-faced man. This man on the ground before him.

Cardinal Fieschi.

chinese fire

3

O Haakon, the only difference between the previous few weeks and this last week was the pace at which the caravan traveled. Since they had arrived at the capital city of the Mongol Empire—*Karakorum*, he could pronounce it better now—little had changed for him and the other men who had survived the rough journey across the steppes, and within a day or so it had become apparent that Karakorum was not to be their final destination. He had watched, with great fascination, the preparations that had gone on for the departure of the *Khagan*. He had even caught a fleeting glimpse of the man himself shortly before the caravan had departed once again. This time, however, the pace of the wagons was indolent in comparison, and there was little reason to wedge himself between the bars of the cage in order to minimize the buffeting and shaking he received from the hard track. The rocking motion of the cart reminded him of the gentle motion of the longboats at sea—a motion that was as familiar to every Northern boy as the warm embrace of his own mother. Throughout the day, he had dozed numerous times.

As a result, Haakon had been awake when the attack had started.

Raphael, one of the well-traveled Shield-Brethren he had met at the chapter house outside of Legnica, would—when properly coaxed by the others—tell stories to the trainees. Like Feronantus, he was prone to being short and gruff with the young men, but when he spoke of other places and other times, he became bewitchingly eloquent. Raphael had spoken of the siege of Córdoba, and he had likened the bombardment of fiery arrows and flaming balls of pitch to the sun being shattered by the angry fist of God. You could not flee from such a disaster, he told them, you could only stand witness as the sky was blotted out by fiery rain. If one of those shards of the sun was meant for you, then that was your fate.

When Haakon saw the tiny lights rise from the horizon, he thought of them more as a flight of startled birds than as falling pieces of the sun, but he watched them nonetheless, no less fascinated. As the arrows fell on the camp, the stillness of the night was disturbed by the rushing thrum they made through the air. The burning arrows scattered throughout the sea of tents and wagons, and each one, as it landed, became a flickering beacon that called out to its companions. Within the camp, Haakon could hear the rising commotion of the Mongolian response: voices shouting orders to protect the *Khagan*, screams of pain, and cries of bewilderment. The entire camp was not unlike an anthill that had been poked with a stick. At first, it would be a writhing, chaotic mass; but then, an organization would emerge. Some of the ants would start attacking the stick; others would fall to rebuilding the nest, or carrying the food and the young to safety.

Haakon watched as another wave of fire arrows took flight. They rose and fell, spreading themselves throughout an area closer to the cages. One thwacked into the ground not far from him, and Haakon stared at the burning strip of cloth wrapped around the shaft of the arrow.

Krasniy, the red-haired giant who was squeezed into his own cage nearby, hissed at Haakon. When he saw that he had the young man's attention, the giant hunched his back, finding a better position within the confinement of his prison, and jerked a thumb at the roof of his cage. He strained, muscles standing out in his thick neck, as he tried to snap the heavy cords that bound the roof to the bars. Haakon watched Krasniy for a moment, and then returned his attention to the fires and chaos around them. No one seemed to be paying much attention; for the moment, the giant could try to escape.

Krasniy let out a huge rush of air, a noisy exhalation that bordered on a cry of frustration and despair. Haakon didn't have to look to know what the sound meant. The cage was stronger than it looked. Or the giant was weaker than he had thought. The cords held.

Haakon wedged his shoulder against the bars of his cage, and stretched his arm as far as he could manage. The arrow was just out of reach, and the flames licked at the tips of his fingers. Another inch or so. That was all he needed. He pressed his feet against the floor of the cage, trying to gain a little more leverage, trying to squeeze a little more of his arm through the bars. The flames danced merrily, capering in delight at his efforts. He opened his hand wider, ignoring the searing pain that followed, and wrapped several fingers around the arrow. With a gasp, he shoved himself away from the bars, closing his hand into a fist.

He rolled over, twisting his wrist so that the arrow fit through the bars. He threw it to the floor of his cage and beat at it rapidly with both hands. Slapping hard to put out the flame, to not feel the pain as the fire fought back.

The orange flames flickered and vanished, leaving only a thin strand of white smoke and a stinging pain in his palms. Gingerly, he picked up the arrow. The fire had devoured the cloth that had been wrapped around the shaft, and the shaft itself was charred enough that he thought it would break if he flexed it at all. But that wasn't what he was interested in.

It was a heavy war arrow, and the metal arrowhead was hot to the touch. Its edge was still sharp.

He snapped the head and a few inches of wood off the charred shaft and shifted around in his cage until he was closer to Krasniy's cage. The giant was watching him, and when Haakon tossed the arrowhead over to his cage, he grinned at the young Northerner.

Just as Krasniy was twisting himself in his cage to get at the ropes, a group of Mongol warriors sprinted out of the line of *ger*. Krasniy froze, but the men were not interested in what the prisoners were doing. As quickly as they appeared, they were gone, and both of the prisoners relaxed. Krasniy stared at the piece of arrow in his hands—it appeared almost like a child's toy in his thick fingers—and then he shook his head.

Haakon nodded. When the attack had first started, the confusion had seemed like a perfect opportunity for them to try to escape, but the chaos also meant guards could wander by at any time. It would take time to saw through the ropes, and without knowing they would be undisturbed, it would be a risk. As frustrating as it was, it was better to wait.

Cradling his hand in his lap, Haakon arranged himself as comfortably as he could in his cage. In the weeks he had had to watch his captors, there had been almost no opportunities to see them in combat. He had learned a great deal by watching how they rode their horses, how they organized their patrols, and the type of armor and weapons they carried, but he hadn't actually seen them fight.

The flights of flaming arrows had stopped, and Haakon suspected this meant the attackers were launching their ground offensive. The rain of fire was meant to disorient and confuse the *Khagan*'s men, a tactic that would reduce their effectiveness. Perhaps this meant the attackers did not have so many numbers that they were going to overwhelm the camp. While it was likely that most of the fighting would happen near the perimeter of the camp, Haakon sat near the bars of his cage and watched. He saw men and women running about in a chaotic effort to put out fires, and occasionally he would spot the glint of firelight off steel as armed warriors moved through the *ger*, intent on finding invaders.

Stories of Feronantus's insight into battlefield tactics were told and retold among the initiates at Týrshammar, and here was an opportunity for Haakon to *observe*—to learn something of his enemy that might be useful knowledge. Yet he could see so very little.

As he strained to get a better glimpse of the fighting, he wondered if there was any leader in the West that could command such willing sacrifice—not just from his soldiers, but from all of his subjects. Soldiers would fight to protect their lord—that was their commission, after all—but civilians, for the most part, suffered whatever rule was impressed upon them. Some kings did manage to instill some devotion in their subjects, and the landed nobility might be inclined to take up arms for their ruler out of a similar devotion, but the wholesale fixation of a people on their leader on the scale that was the Mongol Empire dwarfed any kingdom Haakon had ever heard of in the West. Not even the Pope enjoyed this kind of fervor from his flock.

The Mongolian devotion to their *Khagan* was... daunting.

But he does have enemies, Haakon thought. He could hear men fighting. He flexed his singed fingers, wishing he had a real weapon.

* * *

Munokhoi paid little attention to the wild faces that rushed at him from the gloom. The night was filled with twisting strands of smoke, which disgorged screaming Chinese men at random intervals. Some of them had weapons—swords and spears he brushed aside like seedpods floating on a breeze—and others were wide-mouthed phantoms that he silenced with a quick thrust of his blood-drenched sword. They came and went, and their deaths were but tiny sparks that vanished instantly in the raging fire of his bloodlust. He wanted the Chinese fire thrower.

He had seen its fiery exhalation a moment ago, a spurt of purple flame that had appeared like a tear in the night. The men fighting near him had been knocked down, and when he raised his right arm, he felt jagged jolts of pain run down his side. Tiny bits of metal hissed and steamed in his armor, and his elbow gleamed with fresh blood. But he didn't stop. He couldn't stop. Not now.

He was so close.

There were two of them—Chinese alchemists—hunched together like two whores tittering to one another. One held a tiny covered lantern that let slip tiny shards of firelight; the other was frantically trying to wipe down a long misshapen tube. There were a number of pots and satchels scattered around them, the cumbersome tools of the nefarious device.

With a shout, Munokhoi dashed toward them. The one carrying the lantern looked up, and light from his lantern glinted off Munokhoi's upraised sword. He brought his arm down, felt the blade bite into flesh, and then he yanked the sword toward him, pulling the Chinese man off balance.

The first alchemist dropped the lantern, and its cover was knocked askew. The other alchemist froze, the whites of his eyes glowing in the dim light.

Munokhoi twisted his blade and pulled it free. The first alchemist made a wet coughing sound, and fell to his knees, vainly trying to stem the steady stream of blood coming from a mortal wound in his neck. Munokhoi kicked him out of the way and pointed his dripping blade at the second alchemist.

"Show me how it works," Munokhoi snapped, speaking Chinese.

The alchemist shook his head, trying to pretend he didn't understand Munokhoi's words. The tube in his hands looked like a piece of swollen bamboo, though it was made from iron; one end was dark with soot. The alchemist's hands were stained black as well, and he was missing two fingers from his left hand.

Munokhoi flicked the point of his sword, letting it ring off the tube, and then he flicked it up. The man jerked his head back, but not quickly enough, and the sword point opened up a line on his cheek from which blood immediately started to well.

"Show me," Munokhoi said again, all trace of humor gone from his voice.

His body shaking, the Chinese alchemist lowered himself to his knees and started to comply. Munokhoi watched closely as the man loaded the ingredients from the pouches and pots into the mouth of the tube, trying to keep them straight in his mind. A thick plug with a thin tail went first, the tail emerging from the back side of the tube. Then, two handfuls of black powder. Shards of metal went next, and Munokhoi felt the muscles in his side and lower back twitch as he heard them rattle into the dark mouth of the weapon. He knew that when he had his wounds examined later, similar pieces of ragged metal would be found embedded in his armor and skin. Last was another piece of flat metal, almost like a cap, that the Chinese man lowered carefully so that it filled the mouth of the barrel before sliding in.

Munokhoi nodded, his tongue flicking over his dry lips. Yes, he could remember that sequence. Eagerly, he gestured with his empty hand for the Chinese alchemist to give him the loaded weapon, and to his surprise, the man flung the tube directly at his face.

Caught off guard, Munokhoi reared back instead of intercepting the clumsily hurled missile. He found his pulse racing at the thought that the weapon was going to explode in his face, but the tube struck him in the chest—nothing more than an inert, heavy object—and then fell to the ground.

The Chinese alchemist was gone, having taken that split-second opportunity to flee.

Munokhoi stared into the night for a moment, idly rubbing his chest where the weapon had hit him, and then he retrieved the tube from the ground. Peering at it carefully, he decided it was unharmed. The man had distracted him with it long enough to make his own escape, and Munokhoi couldn't help but chuckle at the man's well-timed cowardice.

He had been planning on using the weapon on the man anyway.

He examined the string hanging from its back, and determined that it was a fuse. He retrieved the discarded lantern, checked on the tiny stub of a candle that provided its illumination, and looked about for a suitable target.

The first alchemist was still alive. He was hunched over on his knees, choking and struggling to staunch the flow of blood from his neck. Munokhoi held the candle up to the end of the fuse until the tiny string caught fire. Sparking and hissing, the fuse crinkled, rolling itself up into the back of the tube.

Munokhoi pointed the tube at the choking man and whistled lightly, catching his attention. The alchemist looked up, startled by the noise, and his eyes focused on the mouth of the tube. He dropped his hands from his bloody throat, and started to curse Munokhoi. One of those long Chinese curses that went on forever.

Fortunately, the man's last breath was cut short by the detonation of the weapon. It jerked in Munokhoi's hands, belching a tongue of blue flame with a mighty roar, and the alchemist was smashed against the ground as if he had been swatted by the hand of a giant. The air was filled with the reeking stench of the fire powder, and the tube was so hot in his hands that he almost dropped it.

The alchemist's body looked as if it had been set upon by wolves, hungry beasts that had stolen its head and part of an arm, shredding the rest to a mess of bloody strips.

Cackling with delight, Munokhoi set the tube down on the ground and began to investigate the pots and leather bags.

the orphan's tale

CYRHOE THOUGHT THE watchful eyes of the Holy Roman Empire would be closer to the walls of Rome. As they trudged away from the city, she tried to explain to Ferenc what she expected to find. Those leaving Rome would move freely, most likely, and it would only be city-bound travelers who would attract attention. The soldiers of the Holy Roman Empire had been charged with detaining men of the cloth—ecclesiastical officials, presumably cardinals—who were traveling to Rome in order to participate in the Papal conclave. After a lengthy session of *Rankalba* she thought he understood the *what* of the empire's obstruction, though she was not sure he understood the *why*.

In her imagination, the road would be blocked by a gate, much like the gates in the Aurelian Wall, and soldiers of the empire would be checking all pilgrims bound for Rome, seeking some sign or symbol of their Papal importance. Such was the imagination of a city-bound child; she realized her ignorance as soon as they were outside the city, for the roads were lightly traveled and surrounded by open countryside.

She understood Ferenc's confusion as she realized the approach to Rome was not as well guarded as she had anticipated. Ferenc had tried to tell her something about how the priest's vision had protected them on their approach to the city, but he wasn't fluent enough with *Rankalba*—the secret language of knots and finger touching—to express himself plainly. *And was such protection even necessary?* she wondered.

He was frustrated with their lack of a truly common language, as was she, and she tried to reassure him. *I will teach you more,* she told him. He had shrugged—*When?*—and since she had no answer, they let their hands drop. They walked in silence, and her fingers ached to reach out and try to soothe him.

It took them until the early afternoon to find men who wore the colors of the Holy Roman Empire. A brace of them stood at either side of the road, watching for Rome-bound traffic, and they were able to get within shouting distance before the men noticed their approach. Ocyrhoe squeezed Ferenc's arm one last time, and then presented herself to the ruddy-faced, pale-haired soldier who seemed to be in charge of the group. She put her curled fist over her heart and bowed, wishing she knew the precise ritual address for seeking audience. Cardinal Somercotes had known more about Binder etiquette than she did...

The soldier's disdainful expression softened when she began to speak in slow, clear Italian. "I am bound with a message to the Emperor," she began. "Robert of Somercotes, Cardinal of the Church, sends greetings and words." Beyond that, she had no idea what to do next.

Neither did the soldier. He blinked at her a few times. "Do you want money?" he finally asked. His accent was thick, and Ocyrhoe thought for a moment that he was speaking Latin, but then she understood the emphasis he was putting on his vowels and realized he was speaking a dialect so estranged from her Roman Italian that it was almost a different language.

Despite her best effort, she could not hide her righteous indignation at being mistaken for a wandering orphan, and her expression was so intense that the ruddy-faced soldier jerked back in surprise.

"I do not want money," she retorted. "I am *bound* with a *message* to the Emperor. A *cardinal* has sent me. I must speak with your officer. Now."

The other men clustered around them, and the ruddy-faced soldier, not quite sure what to do with this strange and intense girl, glanced back and forth between Ocyrhoe and Ferenc. Ferenc stared back at him for a moment, then smiled wanly. Ocyrhoe checked the urge to stamp on his foot; he was not helping her credibility.

Resolute in her need, she remained standing in front of the soldier, staring at him, until he turned to one of the other soldiers and sent him running to fetch someone who would know what to do. Ocyrhoe knew she did not have exactly the right salute, or exactly the right greeting, but she was sure the words *bound* and *message*—especially in conjunction with the words *Emperor* and *cardinal*—would catch someone's attention.

It was a hot, sticky afternoon, and she and Ferenc wandered over to the shade of a nearby tree. Several of the other soldiers were amused by her indifference to them, and they took it upon themselves to join her and Ferenc in the shade. They remained standing, while she and Ferenc sat, maintaining the illusion that the pair were under guard.

Ocyrhoe didn't much care what they thought, as long as they left her alone. She found a comfortable crook in the roots of the tree. Someone would come from the soldiers' camp soon enough. And as Ferenc and the soldiers watched over her, she fell into a light slumber. What else could she do at this point?

* * *

The sun had softened, and the shade of the tree was much longer when she woke. There were more people gathered around the tree—additional soldiers and a young man no older than Ferenc who, in much better Italian, asked them to follow him. Accompanied by a group of soldiers, she and Ferenc let themselves be led across the sparse countryside to a covert village of canvas tents that were hidden behind a narrow wood of dense trees.

A full-fledged Binder would not stare. A full-fledged Binder would not even appear to be interested in what was around her, Ocyrhoe told herself, so focused would she be on completing her task. But the tent village of the Holy Roman Empire was the strangest environment she had ever seen.

She saw almost no women; most of the men and boys were coiffed, shod, and dressed alike; and although the village appeared to be a mobile community—with livestock, ovens, latrines, even a chapel—the sounds and sights were all wrong: there were no cries of street peddlers, no shouting children, no banners advertising wares, no open stalls of a marketplace. It was a stolid, unfriendly place.

But she did not ogle. And neither, she was pleased to see, did Ferenc. The moment they'd gotten out of the city, he had relaxed in a way she had not seen before, and even now, he seemed far more at home than she felt.

The two youths to whom they had been entrusted—one before them, one behind—marched them between two rows of low-slung sleeping tents, and then turned left directly into a much larger, higher tent. Ocyrhoe squinted in the diminished light.

Despite the heat, the walls of the tent were pegged down, preventing any breeze from cooling the stuffy air within. There were three-legged stools scattered at one end of the enclosed space, around a low table with an unlit lamp on it. The soldier behind them tied back the tent flap, which let in sunlight but very little air. He saluted his fellow soldier and then departed.

Ocyrhoe and Ferenc exchanged looks. Ferenc, probably intending to show her that he trusted her, smiled again and shrugged. She wished he would not do that; it made him look doltish in front of the soldiers.

His smile faded suddenly and his head moved slightly toward the open tent flap. He held up three fingers, and then he imitated the stance of the young man guarding them. Reflexively, Ocyrhoe did likewise.

A moment later, three silhouettes appeared at the tent flap. Ocyrhoe tried to look at them with respectful casual confidence—but then she saw one of them was a slender dark-haired woman with familiar knots tied into one lock of her hair. Ocyrhoe felt her eyes open wide and her jaw drop, despite herself. *Stop that*, she ordered her facial muscles, refusing to let them break out into a smile of relief.

A Binder.

The woman was older than any of the kin-sisters Ocyrhoe knew, maybe older, even, than Auntie. She was with two men—the second youth who had led them here, and a man who must be the commander of the soldiers' unit. The commander's face looked chiseled out of marble; his eyes were so pale Ocyrhoe wondered how he could bear the Roman sunlight. He stared at her unblinkingly. "Yes?" he said, expectantly.

The woman made a subtle noise, which immediately commanded his attention. She had a stateliness to her that suggested a noble upbringing, but she was dressed almost like a servant, and she was barefoot. "We understand you are bound to us with a message," she said, directing the words *at* the man as much as *to* Ocyrhoe. She spoke Italian with a lilting accent, as if her own tongue were much more fluid. She looked concerned, though, and almost as humorless as the commander.

Of course: most people in power, or who served power, knew about the Binders, but few ever had occasion to interact with them directly; they were not common messengers for hire. It made sense that the Emperor would have Binders in his service, but of course not all of his military commanders would know what to do with them.

"We understand...you are bound to us *with a message*," she repeated, more forcefully.

Ocyrhoe gaped at the woman, then, not knowing what else to do, put her fist over her heart. "I am bound to you with a message," she echoed hurriedly. "From Robert of Somercotes, Cardinal of the Church, to His Imperial Majesty Frederick."

The Binder gave her a strange, perhaps even an accusing look, and Ocyrhoe felt her face flushing. "I am the only sister left in the city," she added. "This message would have come sooner, and...more correctly, if there were anyone else...more experienced...to bring it."

The woman's dark eyes opened wide, briefly, like a cat just before it pounces. Then they narrowed, and the woman turned with barely hidden disdain to the commander, then back to Ocyrhoe. Her expression softened. "Our mother receives one of her children most gladly. You may give your message to this man, and he will carry it to its final destination. Then, relieved of your burden, you and I may talk."

Ocyrhoe felt her entire body sag with relief. "Thank you," she said, her throat tight.

She turned her attention back to the man. The words tumbled out: "Robert of Somercotes, Catholic cardinal, greets His Imperial Majesty Frederick and summons him or his men to the Septizodium within the walls of Rome, where all of the cardinals are being held against their will by Senator Orsini until they have selected the new Pope. I will lead your men to the Septizodium."

She glanced nervously at the woman. There was a pause.

The woman closed her right hand and moved it slightly toward her heart. Ocyrhoe picked up on the hint and slammed her fist against her sternum, eyes still on the Binder.

"Thus delivered of your message, you are as the fox, unbound and unencumbered," the woman said. Ocyrhoe sucked in a breath and almost recited the confirming phrase after her, then realized this would only make her look more foolish. Instead she nodded, once.

During this exchange, the commander and both soldiers had exchanged concerned looks, and now the commander spoke rapidly to the woman in that same dialect spoken by the ruddy-faced soldier. She could not quite follow what was being said, and she could sense Ferenc's frustration as well.

The woman replied briefly, and Ocyrhoe heard the cardinal's name and a reference to the Emperor; the commander responded with a brusque nod and left, the two young guards following him.

Left alone with the newcomers, the Binder cast a questioning eye at Ferenc—who returned her look just as quizzically as before.

"He is with me," Ocyrhoe said quickly. "He knows *Rankalba*."

The woman blinked and pursed her lips. "You have taught him?" she demanded accusingly.

"No," Ocyrhoe said quickly. She tried to think how best to explain their strange fellowship, but the Binder had already turned her attention to Ferenc. She moved to him swiftly, took his arm, and signed something onto it. He glanced, startled, at Ocyrhoe, then made the sign for *Mother* on the woman's arm.

The woman shook her head angrily and pushed his fingers from her arm.

"He is from Buda. I think his mother was a Binder," Ocyrhoe interjected, trying to mediate between the woman's anger and Ferenc's confusion. "He does not sign quickly and we have not had time for long explanations. He must be completely confused by what is happening."

The woman searched Ferenc's face for a long moment before answering. "There may be men in this camp who speak his language. I will have someone explain everything to him," she said.

Ocyrhoe let slip a tired laugh. "*Everything?* You do not know how long that will take," she said. The woman turned her attention to Ocyrhoe, and under the brunt of that gaze, Ocyrhoe wondered how much the woman actually *knew*.

"I am Léna," the Binder said as she gestured toward the camp stools at the other end of the tent. "Please, let us sit and talk."

Her name alone revealed nothing of who she might be or from where she may have come. Were they not kin-sisters? Ocyrhoe wondered. Why did she not share more of her identity? The delight she had been relishing at meeting another Binder threatened to slip away, and she hid her panic beneath the stoic mask she had worn when they had first reached the camp. "I am Ocyrhoe," she replied guardedly, and with a gesture toward her companion, "He is Ferenc."

"Tell me what is happening in Rome," Léna directed as they sat down on the stools.

"Did you send the dove?" Ocyrhoe asked.

"What dove?"

"The dove on the statue of Minerva," Ocyrhoe said, and as the panic threatened to overwhelm her, she let her tongue go. "Are you the Bind-Mother?"

Léna gave her another long, questioning stare. "I see," she sighed at last. "You are an *orba matre*."

Ocyrhoe didn't know what to do with her hands, and so she clutched the rim of the stool. Holding tight. "I am...I don't understand."

"A child, born of a Binder mother"—Léna glanced at Ferenc—"a *girl* child, would know more than you do, for your age."

"I was *chosen*," Ocyrhoe said, a little hotly.

Léna smiled reassuringly. "Do not be insulted by my words, child. I am trying to determine what you are. We both know you are not a Binder, not fully."

With nothing but their expressions and body language to read, Ferenc had stiffened when Ocyrhoe got defensive, and now he reached out a protective hand toward her. She took a deep breath and stroked his forearm without looking at him. In this tent, in this company, she realized she was treating the boy like a dog…a faithful dog. He did not seem to notice, or to care.

"About three months ago, a messenger came from Rome with word that Senator Orsini was moving against our sisters," Léna explained. "Since then, we have had no other news from the city. And then, with the death of the Pope, and this *sede vacante*, it has been a most troubling—"

"The Emperor is here, in this camp?" Ocyrhoe interrupted.

Léna inclined her head and stared over her long nose at Ocyrhoe. "No, I did not say—"

"He is," Ocyrhoe offered a tiny smile. Léna's explanation and Ferenc's reassurance had calmed her, dispelling the desire for flight, and in its wake, her awareness was coming back. It wasn't the same as the way the city spoke to her, but other subtle suggestions were there, if she simply took the time to read them. "A Binder's duty is to deliver her message," she said. "If the commander had to leave this camp in order to relay my message, then I would not have truly delivered it and you would not have released me from that duty. If you are discharging your duty properly, then wherever you are, he must be as well."

Léna looked strangely satisfied at Ocyrhoe's response. "Your arrival is timely, child; he has stayed overlong away from his court in Palermo and had planned to return soon. Your message will, I suspect, change his mind. There is more afoot, however. Why have our kin-sisters been taken? It would be helpful if you could tell me everything you can about what has transpired in Rome."

SEEKING REVENGE

HE CHANGE THAT came over Luo Xi was as dramatic as if a mask had been removed, revealing a face pitted and harsh beneath a delicately painted facade. Lines appeared in his face, deep striations etched in his forehead and cheeks. Such lines were not unusual—every Chinese person who had suffered under the yoke of Mongolian oppression was similarly burdened—but he secretly cultivated his suffering. His grip on Lian's arm was tight, his fingers digging into her flesh as if he would squeeze down to her bones.

"These dogs ravage our homeland," he snarled at her, all pretense of geniality gone. "They loot our cities. Kill our children." He shoved her again, driving her ahead of him. "They rape our women."

She wanted to run, wanted to flee the lash of his words. Moments ago, she had wanted his eyes on her, wanted him to be distracted from his surroundings, but now she didn't want his attention.

One of the soldiers slapped Gansukh on the legs with the shaft of his spear, and the Mongol warrior rolled away from the blow, getting his legs under him. Even though Gansukh didn't understand a word of what was being said, the message was clear. Clenching his teeth, Gansukh wobbled to his feet, and as he stood upright, one of the other soldiers whacked him across the back, causing him to stumble and nearly fall.

She couldn't help herself, and she darted toward Gansukh. A Chinese soldier reached for her, and she slowed, pulling her arm out of his reach. He grinned, revealing a wide gap between his upper front teeth; lowering his spear so that the point hovered near her breast, he shook his head.

Beyond him, Gansukh stared at her. One of his eyes was swollen partially shut, dark shadows already discoloring his flesh. Dirt and ash and blood streaked his face, and a chill ran across her arms as she met his one-eyed gaze.

The Chinese soldier clucked his tongue, flicking the tip of his spear toward the unruly mass of her unbound hair, which fell across her breasts. She looked away from Gansukh, met the Chinese man's eyes for a second, and then demurely dropped her gaze toward the ground.

She caught sight of a dagger shoved negligently through the man's belt, and she sucked in her breath. *Her dagger!*

A man staggered toward the group, and Luo Xi drew his sword. It wasn't a Mongol, and Luo Xi relaxed his guard enough to slam his helmet back on his head as the wounded man came closer.

Lian recognized him as the other commander, the one who had argued with Luo earlier. The one who had argued against taking hostages. He had worn a helmet too, but it was gone now, and his head was covered with blood, some of it still wet.

"We have failed," he gasped to Luo. "We had the banner—" He caught sight of Lian, and stared owlishly at her. Slowly, as if he were having a great deal of trouble remembering something of vital import, he looked at the four men surrounding Gansukh. "My men are dead," he said, and he swung his gaze back to Luo. "We are all dead."

Luo's face was ashen. "Idiot," he hissed. "We only needed the sprout. Why didn't you take it?"

"It wasn't there." Seeing Luo's expression, he shook his head. "It had been harvested already," he explained. "We had no choice but to take the banner. Otherwise—"

Luo cut him off with a wordless hiss. "Do not think you know what is best. The banner is too old to sustain life. What we need—"

"Commander," one of the soldiers interrupted Luo. He pointed toward the rise that blocked the caravan from view. The light was softer now, no longer the harsh radiance of hungry fires. White plumes of smoke hung in the night air. "The Mongols are putting out the fires," he said.

Luo's companion swayed unsteadily. "If they know why we are here, they will not negotiate." He pointed toward Gansukh. "Your hostage will not save you."

The soldiers guarding Gansukh shuffled uneasily.

"I cannot run," the man said softly, indicating the dried blood on his head. "I can barely walk..."

Luo lowered his head briefly in acknowledgment; then, with a swift jab, he ran his sword into the belly of the wounded Chinese man. The look of confusion on the other man's face faded, and the tension in his face eased. His gaze remained locked on Luo, and he grunted lightly as Luo pulled the sword free. Something akin to a smile came to his lips.

All the air had fled from Lian's lungs. She couldn't move; she couldn't scream. She could only stare in horror as the dying Chinese man tried to speak, failed, and crumpled to the ground.

Luo whirled, his face twisted into a demonic mask. "Kill them both," he snarled. "And then run. Run as fast as you can, for the Mongol dogs will be at your heels."

His sword was red with blood, and as he strode toward them, the paralysis that had held Lian vanished. "Wait," she cried.

Luo didn't slow down. He raised his sword.

"Let me do it." Lian was as surprised as Luo to hear the words come out of her mouth.

Luo hesitated. "What?"

"If I kill him," she said, letting the words run out of her mouth of their own accord. She didn't think about where they were coming from or what they meant. All she knew was that if she wavered, if she showed any fear or hesitation, this sudden resolve would vanish. "If I kill him, will you take me with you?"

Luo's mouth twisted, finally shaping itself into a nasty leer. "You want revenge on this dog?"

Lian stood firm, pushing her chin out and throwing her shoulders back. "*This one*. All of them."

Luo examined her, letting his eyes roam over her body. His sword dipped slightly, but his body was still rigid.

"Commander," one of the guards interrupted.

"Go," Luo shouted, the muscles in his neck standing out. "Run, you cowards!" His eyes remained locked on Lian.

Two of the four guards took him at his word, dropping their spears and sprinting away into the darkness. One of the remaining pair lingered, unwilling to turn his back on Gansukh or leave his weapon. The gap-toothed one stayed, and Lian's gaze fell on the dagger in his belt again.

"Let me do it," she said again, and pointed at the dagger. "That's his dagger. I want to kill him with it."

Luo laughed, and Lian tried to not flinch at the sound, though it made her skin crawl. He nodded to his man, who pulled the blade free of his belt and tossed it to the ground. "Go," Luo said to the remaining pair. "I...*we*," he amended with a curt nod at Lian, "will meet you at the second camp."

The soldiers needed no other prompting, and they too fled.

"Pick it up," Luo said, indicating the knife as he walked toward the captive Mongol.

Gansukh hadn't understood any of their conversation, but the look on Luo's face was plain enough, as was the bloody sword. As the Chinese commander approached him, Gansukh strained at his bonds while moving slowly backward, giving himself some room to maneuver. He wouldn't be able to dodge Luo's attack, but his expression said he wasn't going to make it easy for the Chinese man.

Lian crouched, and with a shaking hand, reached for her dagger. Was she going to go through with this? Could she actually kill a man? In his own way, Gansukh had tried to warn her at the feast. He had said she would be punished if she were caught with the weapon, which was true, but there was another message behind his admonition. *Why carry it*, he had implied, *if you aren't willing to use it?* She slipped the blade from its sheath, and wrapped her fingers tightly about the handle.

She had no choice.

Luo feinted with his sword, and when Gansukh dodged away, the Chinese man leaped forward with a savage side kick that connected with Gansukh's stomach. Gansukh doubled over, gasping and retching, and Luo brought a knee up sharply to Gansukh's lowered face. Gansukh's head snapped back, and he toppled over. His hands, bound behind his back, prevented him from lying prone, and he flopped onto his side. He curled forward, retching and shaking. Trying to protect the parts of his body that had been traumatized.

Luo looked over at Lian, and nodded at the sight of the dagger in her hands. "Do it quickly," he sneered, "and I won't leave your corpse with his."

"Pull the dog's head back," she instructed with more confidence than she felt. She couldn't dwell on what was going to happen after the next few moments. She couldn't let herself wonder if she was doing the right thing. She had to focus on what had to be done, on what was required in order for her to survive.

Luo put his sword down, and crouched next to Gansukh's contorted body. He hauled the semi-conscious man upright, and positioning himself behind Gansukh, he grabbed the Mongol's hair. "Do it," he hissed at Lian, exposing Gansukh's throat.

Gansukh shuddered, his one eye rolling in its socket. Luo's strike had bloodied his nose, and his lower face was smeared with blood and dirt. His mouth hung open. He was unrecognizable to Lian, just another Mongolian warrior—indistinguishable from the men who had taken her from her family years ago. They were all alike. It was as Luo had said: the Mongols destroyed everything; they burned countless villages; they had raped generations of Chinese women; they had plundered the great cities. So much had been lost to Mongolian rapaciousness, wiped from existence.

Gansukh was one of them. Had he not demonstrated that fact when he chose his brutal Khan over her? Had he not denied her the ability to defend herself by stealing the very dagger she now held in her hand? Had he not wanted to keep her as a slave? It didn't matter how much she taught him about how to speak, how to dress, how to be *civilized*; he was still a barbarian, a dog with blood on his face and hands.

She gripped the dagger tight, the way Gansukh had taught her.

She looked at Luo's sweat-slicked face, and her stomach twisted as she realized his expression was just as alien. His eager anticipation of Gansukh's death sickened her.

But he was one of her own countrymen—her rescuer. He was going to help her get back to China. Back to her family. She was going to be free. All she had to do was kill one man. One *Mongol*.

"Kill him," Luo barked. He jerked Gansukh back, leaning forward as he did so. His face was so close to Gansukh's, his mouth nearly touching the Mongol's ear. "Watch her," he laughed in Gansukh's ear. "I want you to see your death."

Gansukh surged against Luo, but he had little strength and less leverage. The Chinese man held Gansukh tight, his knee in the middle of Gansukh's back. Gansukh snorted, blowing blood and snot out of his impacted nose; his open eye stared wildly at Lian.

She licked her dry lips and stepped forward, swinging the dagger from left to right. Her swing was slow and weak, and Luo grimaced as he watched her halfhearted attack. She was too far away, and the blade missed Gansukh's neck.

Luo was starting to say something, his lips curled in an ugly snarl, when he realized she wasn't finished. Having come as close as she dared to the Chinese commander, she stabbed savagely upward, the way Gansukh had taught her, driving the dagger deep into Luo's neck.

a colorful tongue

"**Y**OU ARE YOUNG to have gone through so much loss," Léna said when Ocyrhoe finished telling her story. "I hope you know how strong you are."

Ocyrhoe shook her head. "I am not strong. I am small and weak, and that is why they didn't come for me. I don't know anything. I was not worth hunting."

"You were the only one left, dear child, and you managed not only to survive but to bring a message out." Léna stared intently at Ocyrhoe. "You taught yourself to hear within the silence. While you lack an understanding of certain rituals and the signs we use to identify ourselves to one another, you have innate and remarkable skills." She laughed gently. "They should be frightened of you. Not the other way around."

Ocyrhoe should have been pleased by such compliments, but the only thing she felt was deep exhaustion. It seemed ironic now, how eager she'd been to tell her story to a kin-sister, but it was so tiring. She had wanted to find out what was going on in Rome, but she actually had more information than anyone else. The more she learned, it seemed, the less she understood.

Léna wasn't finished with her questions. "What happened when it was only you?"

Ocyrhoe exhaled, letting the words run out of her in a tumbling rush to be done. She knew she was babbling, but she didn't care. "I don't even remember what happened next. I don't know what I ate, or where I slept, or if it was too hot or cold. The days were a blur. The Bear—" she stopped, flustered at her use of the nickname. How would this woman know who she meant? "The *Senator*," she corrected. "Senator Matteo Orsini. His men had a list, I knew it as plainly as I knew I was the last one, and I couldn't go anywhere I had been before. All I could do was practice my lessons. Learn the faces. Listen to the city. Stay out of sight. Stay alive.

"I would visit the statue of Minerva, because I remembered that Varinia had said that she watched over us. I didn't know what else to do; maybe if I prayed..." She shrugged, summarizing her frustration and helplessness in that simple motion. "But why did I do that?" she continued. "I don't really know. One day there was a pigeon with a message that said, *Where are my eyes in Rome?* Had one of my other sisters made it to Palermo? I didn't know. And so I kept watch. I kept waiting until—"

Until the priest and Ferenc had arrived, and in the few days since—*how many days? One? Two?*—everything had changed.

"Enough," Léna said. "I have asked too much of you already, I can tell. Let me send in some food, and then I shall inquire about someone who speaks your friend's language. I have questions for him."

* * *

When Léna left, Ocyrhoe sat with Ferenc on the cool and dry ground. They leaned against one another, their fingers tapping on the other's skin. She told him as much as she could: the woman was a friend, another *like her*, and they had been talking about what had happened to others like them; she had gone to fetch them food and someone who spoke his tongue; afterward, they would return to Rome, probably with armed soldiers, to rescue Father Rodrigo from the Septizodium. Ferenc was remarkably patient throughout the lengthy process of Ocyrhoe telling him all this. If he were a tracker or a hunter, she assumed he should have been more intent on knowing what the goal was, but he appeared quite placid. He only showed some urgency when the food arrived; he ate quickly, as if he feared the hovering page boys might try to snatch the plates away before he was finished. He kept a protective eye on her too; otherwise he may as well have been one of the camp stools, so quiet and still he was.

She realized her affection for him went deeper than the simple love one had for an attentive pet.

When they finished eating, the page boys took away all the dishes, and they were left alone with a guard standing outside the tent. Dimly Ocyrhoe could hear the joyless sounds of camp life going on around them, and the light outside the open tent flap finally softened to an amber tint. A page boy came in and lit the lantern, and a hint of cool air began to circulate through the tent.

"Léna?" Ferenc asked and Ocyrhoe almost jumped; he had been silent so long.

"She wanted to find a Magyar speaker," she said, and then signed on his arm. "She wants to *talk* to you."

"About my mother," Ferenc signed back, and gave her a questioning look. When she nodded, he signed, "My mother is dead."

Ocyrhoe grimaced and patted the back of his hand. "Mine too," she sighed.

"She was killed by the invaders," Ferenc added.

Ocyrhoe snapped out of her maudlin remembrance of Auntie coaching her on how to use the needle and thread. "The invaders," she signed. "The invaders who also made your priest body-sick and mind-sick."

Ferenc nodded.

Her life, her focus, had always been about the city of Rome. She knew there were lands beyond; Auntie had taken her to another woman's house on occasion to look at maps, and Auntie had wanted her to memorize them, but she had always found it so hard to make sense of the jagged lines. She knew that Binders were sent to other places, like the ones named on these maps, but she was a child of Rome, and there was always so much happening there. Her attention had never had occasion to wander far, and recent events seemed so enormously significant: the death of the Pope, the incarceration of the cardinals, the destruction of the Binder network, the Emperor's blockade of the city. What could possibly be more significant? Even the worried murmurs in the marketplaces about vicious, keen-eyed invaders from the East seemed so distant and so...*unimportant*. The threat of these *Mongols* was only something that strangers visiting from far-off places concerned themselves with.

But the Mongols had destroyed Ferenc's life, and Ferenc was not a stranger.

Ferenc touched her cheek, and she started. "You are staring at me," he signed, a self-conscious, slightly lopsided smile tugging at his mouth.

"Sorry," she signed hurriedly. "I am sad for you."

At that moment, there was a movement by the tent flap, and they both scrambled to their feet. Ferenc looked embarrassed, and she thought it was not entirely because he hadn't noticed the approach of all the people who were streaming into the tent.

First two heavily armed young men entered, wearing livery that featured a black eagle with widespread wings on the chest. After them came Léna and the commander. They were followed by a striking-looking man who was pale skinned, pale eyed, and nearly bald. The hair he did have—which covered much of his face and his bare arms—was a vivid reddish color. His tunic was far more ornate than those of the other men, and the entire front of it was covered with an image of the same black eagle, which gleamed with iridescence. After him came several more well-dressed men, all ruddy and tall, and all with the eagle insignia somewhere on their person; these were followed by two more armed guards.

The group, a dozen in all, entered formally, and took a seemingly ceremonial stance just inside the tent flap. Léna stepped forward and gestured for them to come closer. Ocyrhoe stepped forward cautiously, Ferenc behind her, a protective and reassuring hand resting on her narrow shoulder.

Ocyrhoe wondered who the man with the red hair was. He was ugly, in part because he was squinting, as if he could not see well. He looked stern, but not cruel. She had already met the commander; perhaps he was a general? Would he be leading the soldiers back to the Septizodium when they went?

"Ocyrhoe," Léna said, "I have the honor of presenting you to the Wonder of the World, Frederick Hohenstaufen, the Emperor of the Holy Roman Empire, and King of Germany, Burgundy, and Sicily."

Ocyrhoe recovered from her surprise, and gazed upon the man with respect, which she was sure he could tell from her gaze. But Léna said sharply, "You are to bow to him."

Ocyrhoe hurriedly did so, and felt Ferenc do likewise behind her. "Your Majesty," Ocyrhoe said. Ferenc made an earnest attempt to imitate the sounds of her address, but ended up mumbling nonsense syllables.

Frederick chuckled. "You are the first goddamned Roman who has bowed to me in months," he said to the top of Ocyrhoe's head; he spoke with a heavy accent, but she could understand him clearly. There was a pause, during which nobody spoke or moved. "It's all right, you may stand up now," he said at last, still to the top of her head.

Ocyrhoe straightened. "It is an honor to meet Your Majesty," she said, wondering if his cursing was intended to frighten or intimidate her. Ferenc, behind her, had straightened as well; she was grateful that he made no attempt to imitate her words again.

"I have heard Somercotes's message," Frederick said.

Wanting to demonstrate her professionalism, Ocyrhoe quickly put her hand to her heart and declared, "Thus delivered of my message, I am like the fox, here unbound and unencumbered."

Léna's lips tugged back in an almost motherly smile. Frederick, as if he had not heard her, continued on, "Léna has informed me of what has transpired in your city, and it saddens me that Senator Orsini—what did you call him? *The Bear?* Yes, it saddens me that the Bear has treated his innocent people so monstrously. Whatever grievance you have with the Senator, I too share."

Binders bear no grudges, she heard Varinia's voice recite in her mind. *Binders bear nothing but messages and knowledge.* She opened her mouth to say it aloud, but Frederick seemed to not require a response from her. "Jesus Christ. I am sure you'd take as much satisfaction as I would in my men destroying that goddamned Orsini and tearing down his whole goddamned palace, but I cannot indulge the impulse. Why are you gaping at me?"

Ocyrhoe blinked, and looked at the ground to recover her composure. He spoke like the other children who ran wild in the alleys and tumbledown hovels of Rome. She'd never heard anyone in good clothing use such foul language—and he did it so casually. She had never wasted much imagination anticipating how an Emperor might behave, but she assumed his demeanor should resemble the Pope's, and Frederick's most certainly did not.

"Forgive me, Your Majesty," she said, and looked up again. "I am to return with your response to my message, and I am uncertain of..." She found herself struggling to find the right words. *He isn't a street rat; think of the ways Auntie and Melia taught you to speak.* "I only wish to be certain of your reply."

"Oh, I'll reply," Frederick said with a huff of bitter laughter. "You better damn well believe I'll reply. But not the way he asked me to. If I send soldiers in there to storm the Septizodium, the Church will accuse me of all sorts of goddamned abominations, and as soon as they've gotten their new false idol on the throne of Saint Peter, he'll only continue to blather at me the same way his predecessor did. Perhaps, instead of simply excommunicating me, they'll put my entire empire under interdiction." He started to pace about the tent, and his attendants shuffled closer to the canvas walls to give him space. "Not that I give a shit about that, of course, but my nobles tend to twist their hands like frantic ladies when the subject of eternal damnation comes up. They are like pustules on my ass, even when things are going well."

Ocyrhoe bit the inside of her cheek to keep herself quiet; she was absolutely astounded at the man's language and attitude. She herself had never felt any particular interest or attraction to the Church—the few times she had been inside any of the churches in Rome had been as part of her lessons with Varinia—but she knew enough to be respectful. She had been to several public events outside the Lateran Palace and St. Peter's Basilica, and had watched in wonder at the reverence with which each person approached the Pope. Even from those whom she later learned did not like the Pope. And excommunication. It had to be a horrible thing, the way people in Rome spoke of it, but the Emperor seemed to think it was less troubling than a mild ailment of the stomach.

"No, my child," Frederick continued in the same offhand tone, "I must take a different tack altogether. The Church rages against me because I am preventing some of its cardinals from returning to Rome. They wish to elect a new Pontiff, but their own rules have forced them into a deadlock. I knew Orsini had hidden them, so as to better prevent my spies from influencing their decision, but the decision to remain in that fucking nightmare hellhole of a ruin is theirs. Not mine.

"So, rather than leaping to take up this role they wish me to play—the part of the villain—and *assaulting* their precious conclave, I will opt to be the hero and *salvage* their byzantine procedure instead. I will not send troops into Rome; I will release one of the cardinals instead. I will allow him to accompany you to the Septizodium, where he may join the others in damnable discomfort and imprisonment. May his vote end their tedious torture."

He offered her a dazzling smile, clearly very pleased with his decision. "He will probably vote for the wrong man, but"—he threw up his hands and looked toward the roof of the tent—"there is no right man. Attempting to control the outcome has been a misguided waste of my goddamned time, frankly. It doesn't matter who the hell they choose, he isn't likely to approve of me. Let's just get the damn thing settled; let the new puppet dance on his throne, let him waggle his finger at me and write his endless bulls and tracts, castigating me and telling me how to run the empire. I will ignore him much like the man before him; life will go on."

Ocyrhoe did not know if she was supposed to respond to this diatribe (though she suspected a response was neither necessary nor required), and so she stood there mutely, a pleasant smile plastered to her face. How would she tell all of this to Ferenc? For all his patience, she knew he was eager to return to Rome with a complement of soldiers and stage a dashing rescue of his beloved Father Rodrigo. She glanced at Léna, wondering if the Binder had found someone who spoke Ferenc's native Magyar.

Léna was staring at her, a thoughtful yet distracted expression on her face. She had seen similar expressions on the faces of artisans in the marketplace crafting something out of raw material. It was an expression of concentration; simultaneously assessing the half-crafted state of the object in front of them and comparing it to their mental image of what that thing was meant to become.

Having finished his proclamation, Frederick turned and said something to one of his officials in a guttural tongue that she did not know. The man responded tentatively, and at a nod from Frederick, bowed and scurried out of the tent. Frederick said something to Léna—in the same tongue—and she stirred from her reverie, her reply precipitating a rapid conversation. Frederick's face lost some of its ready humor, but he eventually agreed to whatever she was suggesting. Even though she did not understand what they were saying, Ocyrhoe was fascinated by the brief insight into the working relationship between them—they seemed to be conversing as equals. Then, very abruptly but cheerfully, the Emperor bid good afternoon to Ocyrhoe and Ferenc, and strode out of the tent while they were still bowing to him. The entire retinue, except for Léna, followed.

"If I ever used half as much gutter-speak, Auntie would have whipped me," Ocyrhoe declared when the entourage was well outside the tent.

Léna—very briefly—smirked. "His Majesty is renowned for his colorful and often blasphemous language. He grew up in Sicily," she said, as if that somehow either explained or excused his language. "I hope you understood the import of his words?"

Ocyrhoe nodded, turning toward Ferenc and taking his arm to start the lengthy process of relaying Frederick's decision.

"You will stay here in the camp until His Majesty has determined which cardinal it will be. His *guests*, as he describes them, are staying at the castles of men he trusts. When the one he has selected arrives, we will return to Rome."

Ocyrhoe paused, her fingers resting on the back of Ferenc's hand. "*We?*" she asked.

"Yes," Léna said. "I will be going with you."

LIAN'S DAGGER

IAN STABBED LUO in the neck, and she had only a moment to be shocked by the volume of blood spurting over the blade and her hand before the Chinese commander violently clawed at her. He caught some of her hair with a wild grab, and clutching the black strands tightly, he yanked her head forward. The hilt of the dagger was slippery, but she tightened her grip and sawed the blade back and forth. More blood gushed out, and Luo gurgled and coughed, and blood spattered from his yawning mouth.

Gansukh, having ducked aside during Lian's stab, planted his feet more firmly against the ground and shoved. Luo, a dead man's grip on Lian's hair, stumbled back.

The dagger came out of Luo's neck, and Lian, her resolve failing, swung it again and again at Luo's hand and arm. She wasn't trying to cut him; she just wanted him to let go. She just wanted to get away. Luo—covered in blood, mouth gasping wordlessly, eyes rolling back in his head—no longer seemed alive. He was a shambling apparition, already claimed by death but whose body was still animate. Would death claim her as well, bound as they were by Luo's frightful grip? She felt the blade of the dagger bite into flesh, and holding the hilt tight, she cut again.

Finally, Luo's hand let go. His legs gave out, and he fell down. His body jerked, legs kicking as if they were still trying to walk. He lay on his side, one arm reaching out. He stared at her, though his eyesight had already fled, and his mouth tried to form a word, but he never finished. His legs stopped, and his frame relaxed. The fingers of his outstretched hand folded in, and his gaze fell to her feet.

"Lian."

She started, dropping the dagger. When Gansukh whispered her name again, she finally managed to tear her gaze away from the dead Chinese commander.

Gansukh was sitting up, half turned toward her. He raised his shoulders, trying to draw her attention toward his bound hands. "The dagger," he whispered, blinking and nodding toward her feet. "Cut me free."

Nodding dumbly, she bent to pick up the dagger. She recoiled at how much blood was on the blade and the handle, unwilling to touch the bloodied weapon, but then she saw her own hand and arm. She froze, staring at the stain.

"Lian," Gansukh hissed. "Don't panic."

I've killed a man. The thought swelled in her head, and she could hear the individual words growing louder and louder inside her skull. She couldn't make them stop. A terrible voice—hers, hoarse and ragged with utter despair—was shouting the words, and a multitude of echoes answered, chirping and shrieking the words in response, *kill kill kill* killed *a man...*

"Drop it," Gansukh barked, and her hand opened of its own accord like a startled bird taking wing from a bush. Then, freed from the dagger, she recoiled from the sticky *thing* lying on the ground, stumbling and tripping over her own feet.

Clumsily, Gansukh dragged himself toward the dagger, falling onto his side and blocking her view of it. He stared at her, moonlight making his swollen and pulpy face a hideously grinning mask.

His shoulders moved as he struggled to pick up the dagger with his bound hands and orient the blade so that it could cut his bonds, but he didn't give up. With dogged, unblinking persistence he kept trying to free himself, all the while without saying a word—without admonishing her to help him in any way.

She regarded him with fascination as if she were watching a wild animal try to chew its way out of a snare. A tiny part of her still wept and shrieked within, but mostly she found herself fixated on Gansukh, staring uncomprehendingly at this being who fought with every iota of his body to live. Who would kill in order to live. He had done so, and would again. And it wouldn't bother him. It was part of who he was, a real part of the world in which he lived.

It wasn't her world. She had strayed into it. He had warned her. He had tried to protect her, but she had gone anyway. Was she like him now? Would she fight and claw for her own life? Would she kill again in order to survive?

She shivered, not wanting to know the answer to those questions, but as the voices in her head fell silent, there was no avoiding the knowledge.

* * *

Gansukh could barely see. One eye was swollen shut, the result of a brutal clubbing from one of the Chinese guards, and his nose was broken. His other eye was nearly glued shut with sand and blood and tears. His lower back ached—he was sure he would be pissing blood in the morning—and his shoulders shook as he tried to move his hands up and down. He gasped heavily, breathing through his mouth, and his tongue pressed against his lower teeth. He could still feel pain. *It is enough*, Gansukh thought.

It had been enough at Kozelsk, when he had been pinned down behind a barn with arrows in his gut and his leg. He hadn't died then. Narrow-faced Jebe, an old boyhood rival, laid out in the city street, pinned to the mud by arrows. Still alive, each breath a gasping torment. He had sat there, hiding behind the worn barrels, and watched Jebe die, ashamed that he was hoping that his death would be quicker. That he'd never see it coming.

But as long as could still feel pain, death wasn't coming for him at all.

His hands slipped, and he thought he had missed the blade of the dagger, but as he tried to reseat the cloth that bound his hands behind his back against the sharp blade, he realized his work was done. The cloth had separated, sawed through by his dogged determination. By his denial of death.

His shoulders quivering with exhaustion and strain, he tried to pull his hands apart. Slowly, he felt the rope stretch and come apart around his wrists, and with a last, shuddering tug, he split his bonds. His hands flopped around, his shoulders sighing with relief at no longer being restrained. The skin along his upper arms and across the top of his back prickled fiercely, a thousand needles being shoved under his skin. Grimacing, he rolled over.

Behind him lay the crumpled corpse of the Chinese commander. The earth around the man's head was darkened with blood. There was no movement of his chest, and his gaze remained fixed and unblinking. *Just like Jebe.*

Gansukh struggled to sit up. "Lian?"

Unlike the Chinese commander, she was still breathing, though judging from the manner in which each breath rattled out of her body, she was deep in shock. She could hear him, but she wasn't present.

The ground vibrated, the sound of hooves against the packed earth. Gansukh recognized the rhythmic beat, the noise of steppe ponies. Friendly riders. With a lingering glance at Lian, he struggled to his feet so as to not be mistaken for a Chinese raider, trying to flee.

He brushed the last few strands of rope from his wrists and tried to summon the breath—and presence of mind—to speak.

Lian. He walked, his legs stiff and slow to respond, over to her. He made no effort to touch her; he just positioned himself between her and where he thought the approaching riders were coming from.

Short-legged horses emerged from the gloom, and they quickly shifted their course to converge on Gansukh and Lian. The man on the lead horse was much too large for the frame of the horse, making him seem all that much more like a giant in comparison, and Gansukh felt his throat relax when he recognized the man. The wrestler, Namkhai.

Namkhai pulled his horse up short—deliberately blocking the advance of the riders behind him—and Gansukh stood still as other riders flowed around Namkhai like a stream diverting around a large stone. Out of the corner of his field of vision, Gansukh saw a pale flicker as moonlight glanced off a rider's naked head. *Munokhoi.* He inclined his head toward Namkhai, acknowledging what the wrestler had just done for him.

Respect. Hard won and easily lost. But still very much the coin of the realm among the true men of the steppes.

Horses continued to flow around them, and by the time the *Torguud* captain managed to bring his horse around, a ring of Mongolian riders had formed. Freezing the tableau of recent events into an image that would now be assessed.

Gansukh. Lian. The dagger. The dead Chinese commander.

Munokhoi pushed his mount through the throng, his sword raised above his head. "I said to cut down anyone on foot," he shouted, his voice breaking. "Why are these dogs still standing?" He refused to look at Gansukh and Lian, staring at his men with a wild ferocity, daring any of them to question his order. His face was streaked with soot and blood, which made his bulging eyes only that much more deranged.

"Because they are not dogs," replied Namkhai evenly.

Munokhoi jerked his horse's head back, and the animal nearly reared. Its nostrils flared and it showed its teeth. "They are dogs if I say they are dogs," he retorted, still not looking at Gansukh or Lian.

Namkhai stared at the aggravated *Torguud* captain with the same calm mien that Gansukh had seen when they had wrestled. Appraising. Waiting. Confident. Unafraid.

Munokhoi knew the gaze as well, and he looked away. He finally looked down at Gansukh and Lian, his lips curling into a sneer. "She's Chinese," he pointed out as if no one had ever noticed. "The Chinese attacked us. They are her people. She must have told them where to find us."

"Was the *Khagan* hiding?" Gansukh found his voice, and in the silence that followed his words, he cleared his throat and explained his question. "If she had to tell them where we were, that would suggest that they couldn't have found us with their own eyes." He rolled his shoulders and straightened his back. "Are you saying that the Khan of Khans was traveling in stealth? That he was afra—"

Munokhoi kicked his horse, and it lunged forward while simultaneously trying to avoid running into Gansukh. Gansukh shuffled to his right, but not so much that he abandoned Lian, and the horse's shoulder bumped into his chest. He stepped back, not out of fear of being hurt by the horse, but to get out of range of Munokhoi's sword. His hand, reaching back, brushed Lian's arm, and he felt her shiver.

"They are no danger to us, Munokhoi," Namkhai said. "There is no danger to the *Khagan* here." Namkhai's voice was clipped and tight, somewhat impatient. With a hint of a challenge. "We should be guarding the *Khagan*. Not riding around in the dark, chasing ghosts."

"You will go where I tell you to go," Munokhoi raged.

Gansukh took another step back, directing Lian to move with him. He knew that physical contact with her would clearly link them together, but what could be gained by denying their connection? Munokhoi was out of control. He was dangerous when he was soft-spoken and calculating, but that was only because everyone knew that calm facade hid a much more monstrous aspect of the man. They were all seeing it now, and glancing around at the faces of the other men, Gansukh saw that he was not the only one who was concerned.

Namkhai remained unruffled, as if he had seen this facet of Munokhoi before and was not concerned. Gansukh looked at Namkhai's expression and knew the wrestler had looked upon something much more terrifying than the enraged *Torguud* captain and had found that thing wanting. Namkhai was still waiting to find a reason to be truly *afraid*, and judging by the placid arrangement of his features he was prepared to wait a long time.

"Namkhai's right," Gansukh said. "There are no more Chinese. They've all fled. Back south."

A few heads turned toward the south, but most eyes were still roving back and forth between Munokhoi, Namkhai, and Gansukh. Munokhoi had gone icily quiet. His hand rested on the hard rim of his saddle, and Gansukh noticed the shape of his saddlebags. They were full. *But of what?*

"Escaped, you mean. Escaped with the help of their Chinese spy." Munokhoi had control of his voice again, and Gansukh felt a chill touch his spine. "She may be no danger to the *Khagan* now, but she'll bring her murderous brothers back for another attack."

Lian stirred at Gansukh's side. Words tumbled from her mouth, but they were so softly spoken that only Gansukh heard them. He tried not to react. She was speaking Chinese.

"She brought them to us; she betrayed our *Khagan*," Munokhoi repeated, still holding on to his previous accusation. "Your *whore* is a traitor. Protect her, and *you* are a traitor." His hand twitched, and almost imperceptibly, he turned toward the pair of bags thrown across his horse's back.

"You are a liar." Gansukh stared up at the *Torguud* captain, keeping his gaze away from the bulging saddlebags. "Lian killed the Chinese commander." He pointed in the direction of the body. "He lies over there. There is her dagger." He grasped for her hand, found it, and raised it up for the throng to see. "Here is his blood."

Munokhoi spat on the ground, refusing to look at the dead Chinese man. "Look at my face," Gansukh demanded, letting go of Lian's hand. "I was their captive. They were going to interrogate me, but she came to my rescue."

Namkhai locked eyes with the two men nearest the dead man, and they dismounted to examine the corpse. Namkhai jerked his head, and the two Mongols flipped the body over. Grabbing the corpse by the hands, they dragged it around Munokhoi's horse and deposited it on the ground next to Lian and Gansukh. She shied away from the body, stepping more closely to Gansukh, her hands lightly touching his arm. The Chinese man lay on his back, the dark ruin of his throat plainly visible.

"Anyone could have killed this dog." Munokhoi spat on the body.

Gansukh felt Lian go rigid and then relax. When she spoke, her voice was clear and precise. "I killed him," she said. She wasn't looking at Munokhoi. She held Namkhai's gaze. "And when I killed their leader, the rest fled. Like the broken dogs they were. We've stopped their attack."

"*We?*" Munokhoi's voice dripped with scorn and disbelief.

"We," Gansukh said simply. "Following them would be a mistake. We do not know this terrain. We do not know if they even have a camp. Those who are still alive are scattered, running for their lives. What would we gain by chasing lost dogs in the dark? It is better for us to return to the Khan's side."

Namkhai nodded in agreement, but he made no move to do that. He only looked at Munokhoi with that same flat expression. Waiting.

Munokhoi had two options as Gansukh read the situation: agree with him and return to the Mongol camp, or insist on continuing the hunt. If they continued and found little trace of the Chinese raiders—which seemed likely—then Munokhoi risked losing face with the *Khagan* for making a foolish decision. If he returned to camp now, he only lost face with the current group of men by standing down from his challenge to Gansukh. It was an infuriating choice, Gansukh knew, but as he watched the *Torguud* captain weigh these choices, he realized Munokhoi was considering a third choice. Killing both him and Lian now before anyone could intervene.

Lian sensed the conflict in Munokhoi as well, and she took a step back and to the left, putting some distance between herself and Gansukh. Making two separate targets. Gansukh, surprising himself, took a step to his right, preparing to flank his enemy.

Munokhoi growled deep in his throat, and his eyes betrayed him, flicking down to the saddlebags.

What secret did he have in there? Gansukh wondered.

"Captain," Namkhai said, breaking the tension. "What are your orders?" What saved them was not the question, but the deference in Namkhai's voice. The submissive request for direction from a superior.

"We head back to camp," Munokhoi snapped. "Take them with us." Without another word, he pushed his horse through the rank of men and the sound of its hooves trailed after it in the night.

Singly and in pairs, the other riders followed their captain until only Namkhai and two other riders remained.

"We'll follow you," Gansukh said. "Somewhat more slowly."

Namkhai shook his head. "Ride with them," he said, indicating the other horsemen. "We are to bring you back *with* us." The expression on his face made it quite clear he was not interested in any more discussion.

AN AUSPICIOUS OUTING

NDREAS AWOKE TO the sound of the initiates battering one another in the training yard. He lay quietly
on his cot for a few minutes, listening to the rhythmic
clacking noise of their training weapons. His back and
shoulders were cold and stiff, a reminder of a bruising hit he'd
taken during his last qualifying bout. He'd endured worse, he
reminded himself as he rolled to his side. *I am a knight initiate. As
long as I can stand—even if only on one leg—I will carry on.* A grim smile
played itself across his lips as he climbed to his feet and stretched,
the muscles in his back and legs complaining. *Just as long as I can
still hold a sword.*

Shuffling slowly, he wandered from his alcove—a tiny cell once
used by a lay brother as a quiet sanctum for prayer—through the
ruined monastery, and to the heavy cloth masquerading as a door
over the ragged threshold of the hall. Squinting, even though the
outside light was diffused by the pale morning fog and the tall trees
surrounding their chapter house, he pushed through the cloth and
tottered outside. A barrel had been placed next to the door, and
rain from the last few days had topped it off. He dipped his hands in
and, splashing his face, drove away the last clinging vestiges of sleep.
Warm, we sleep. Cold, we wake.

No longer bleary-eyed and befuddled by the dawn light, he straightened and looked for the source of the clacking noise—the young men, sparring with training blades.

Since the Shield-Brethren had made this place their temporary home, the overall deterioration of the buildings had been arrested, and the unkempt grounds had been transformed. The training yard, in particular, had been nothing but a swath of open ground covered with pale grass and a few fiercely determined shrubs. But after many hours of men trampling back and forth, the ground had been scoured of plant life and pounded flat.

The trainees roamed freely across the yard, working in pairs and in teams of three under the watchful eye of Knútr, one of the other knight initiates. Andreas wandered toward the trainees—watching their technique, eyeing their form. He was no *oplo*—not like Taran had been—to see at a glance where a man faltered, but he knew his way around instruction at arms all the same. Maks, for example, had a tendency to favor striking on the right side more than the left, and this morning he seemed to be trying the reverse. Without much success. *He's thinking about it too much*, Andreas thought, *his mind is getting in the way of what he wants to do.*

Beyond the yard, others were practicing archery, putting arrows into a line of straw men that had been erected close to the tree line. The penalty for missing the target was to scour the underbrush for the missing arrow, and the trainees had all quickly learned to hit some part of their target. Now, they were improving their precision.

Doing drills was a continuous facet of life—for the knights as well as the trainees—and their Spartan existence in this makeshift chapter house meant an opportunity for more drills. Training for war was much different from training for duels in the lists, and while a part of what they prepared for was combat in the Khan's arena, most of their preparations were for war. As Andreas watched the young men train, it was clear to him that they were no longer mere boys. Some laughed and joked with one another as they awaited their turns—exuding confidence in their body language; the faces of others were fixed resolutely—not with fear or apprehension, but stern focus. *The Virgin watch over them*, Andreas silently implored. *They are still so young.*

Styg was sitting next to one of the cookeries with two other trainees, idly prodding the flames with a long stick. He looked up as Andreas approached, as did the other two, and Andreas was jarred by their expressions. He'd had that same look once, when he had worn training leather of his own. That imploring look of adoration and admiration the student has for his *oplo*. The look that said, *There is a hero.*

Andreas couldn't help but think of his teachers over the years. And of his fellow students, both at Petraathen and elsewhere. *How many of them were still alive?* he wondered. *How many of them had died with that look still on their faces?*

"I can't promise the hare is well cooked," Styg said, a grin on his broad face, "but at least it isn't badly burned."

Andreas eyed the logs on which the young men were sitting. After years of traveling, he was accustomed to the often rough-hewn quality of the furnishings at camps and chapter houses, but the muscles in his lower back were tight as he considered sitting down. He needed to move around more, to get his blood moving, to shake off the stiffness that had crept into his body during sleep. However, eyeing the three faces around the cook pit, he indulged their desire to talk, and lowered himself to the log. Even though the wood had been softened by the rain, his buttocks complained slightly as he sat. How long had it been since he had sat on a plush silk pillow?

"Anything that hasn't been heavily salted will taste like *manna* just now," he said as Styg pulled the hare from its spit and cut it into pieces. "*Panis Dominus*," Andreas explained to the other young men, answering the question clearly written on their faces. When the

Latin elicited no sign of understanding in their eyes, he shrugged and reached for the offered food. He juggled the charred pieces lightly, blowing on them, before tossing several into his mouth.

Styg had overestimated his abilities. The hare was overcooked.

"There's going to be a fight today," one of the pair said. "At the arena."

Andreas chewed his food slowly, nodding for the young man to continue. He had gathered as much from the activity in the wrecked city the last time he had been there, but he was curious what sort of rumors made their way back to the boys who remained at the chapter house.

"One of the Livonians is fighting."

Andreas swallowed heavily, pushing the partially masticated food down his throat. "Indeed," he offered, trying to recall the names on the lists. "Do you know who his opponent is?"

"One of the Khan's privileged fighters."

Which one? Andreas wondered. The messages that Hans eked out of the Mongol compound were appropriately cryptic, and there had been few sightings of the Khan's coterie of exotic fighters, but Andreas had managed to glean several names: Kim Alcheon, the Flower Knight; the crazily named demon who had fought Haakon, the one the crowd called "Zug"; Madhukar, the stone-shouldered wrestler whose cudgel had caved in a Templar's helm early in the matches, before the arena had been closed. According to Hans, the Flower Knight was still gathering accomplices, men who could be trusted to fight in an uprising. He hoped, and not just because his opponent was a Livonian Knight—as ungracious as that thought was—that the Khan's man survived today's fight.

"I would like to see this fight," Andreas said. He let that sink in with the three of them as he chewed another tough piece of hare. "I am still on the lists, and it will be my turn to fight in that arena soon. It would be good to scout out the terrain, don't you think?"

Styg nodded happily. "It is always good to take your enemy's measure before actually engaging him."

"I don't expect to encounter any trouble in Hünern, but it is like a hive that has been stuck more than once with a stick, don't you think? Its residents will be restless, prone to reacting at the slightest hint of provocation."

"It would be foolish to expose yourself to such danger," one of the others piped up, eagerly grasping at the opportunity being dangled in front of him.

Andreas nodded as he tossed the rest of his portion of the overcooked meat into his mouth. There was something about the threat of conflict—of the looming possibility of a violent death—that enriched a man's senses. Food, even when burned, became more flavorful. The sun was brighter, its light searing through the recalcitrant fog. The crisp morning air, inhaled through his nose, had a faint scent of distant rain.

As he took his leave of the threesome, Andreas couldn't help but look on the trainees with new eyes, noting that the same bracing enthusiasm that filled him was present in them as well. Death instilled a vitality for living. Detractors of the Shield-Brethren were quick to call them bloodthirsty monsters who thrived on violence, but the opposite was true. It was a foreign mind-set for those who had never carried a sword or walked across a field of battle, and Andreas had long ago given up on trying to explain it to those who did not already understand. The horrors of war—of a life filled with violence—could only be balanced by cherishing each moment of that life with a resolute assuredness and a sharp awareness of what beauty it did have.

His well-used panoply awaited him back in his tiny chamber. His longsword was notched, his maille patched, and gambeson stained. Cleanliness was a part of the Shield-Brethren vows, and he did his best to maintain what he owned in that spirit, but over time, his harness and weapons became more and more permanently marked by the travails of his life.

He had spent many years wandering Christendom, and he could not recall the origin of all the scrapes and nicks in his maille. While the masters of Petraathen had been displeased with him, they had not stripped him of his privilege. He could have returned to Týrshammar or gone to one of the other chapter houses of the Brethren, but he had opted to travel the known world instead. His journey had been lonely more often than not, but it had been one of his choosing. The decision to join his brothers at Legnica had, at first, been born out of curiosity, and in the first few weeks, he had felt—on more than one occasion—the gentle whisper of the wanderlust that had guided him for so many years. But that was akin to the temptation offered Christ during his exile in the wilderness. The promise of illicit freedom was a strong pull on a man who feared the true path he knew he had to walk.

* * *

The long alley behind the alehouse was drenched in sunlight, and the three men and the boy stood awkwardly close in the narrow space. Each but the child held a mug of ale, and the man who was not wearing the blue cloak of the Shield-Brethren was a short, stocky fellow going bald across the top of his head. His name was Ernust, and he had a quick smile and a sharp laugh, which Andreas found refreshingly infectious.

Of course, the ale helped.

"I will not accept your money," Ernust said, setting his mug down upon the wooden lid of a nearby cask. "There is little else to do in this city but brew ale and swap stories." He grinned at Andreas and Styg. "The Livonian Brothers of the Sword are cheap bastards; they've taken advantage of more than a few of the poor people who come into my alehouse. Anyone who gives them—or any of the

Khan's thugs, for that matter—a good thumping will never want for drink in my establishment."

"Your kindness is matched only by the quality of your drink, brewmaster," Andreas said. "However, I do have two more men with me. They are keeping an eye on our horses." He nodded toward the entrance of the alley. "Arvid and Sakse are their names, and while their cheeks are still as soft as rabbit's fur, they are men enough to be thirsty. While I will accept your gracious hospitality for myself and Styg, I would not presume to assume that—"

Ernust scoffed, brushing aside Andreas's concern with a wave of his burly hand. "Hans," he said to the boy hovering nearby, "fetch two more mugs for the knight's companions." The boy nodded and ducked through the heavy curtain on the back wall of the alehouse.

"I fear that we are an unfortunate influence on your young charge," Andreas said when Hans was gone. "He puts himself in danger for a cause that is not his. My heart is heavy with the thought that I might bring pain and suffering to your family." He raised his mug and examined its content. "Especially in light of your generosity."

"The lad makes his own choices. Has since his mother died," the brewmaster explained. "She was my sister, and she died a year before the Mongols came—thank God for that simple blessing—and the lad's been living—" He chuckled. "Well, he was always welcome in my house, though he visited but once before running off again. Back to the streets he knew. A bit of a wild one, he is, and if you don't mind my saying so, your attention has had an impact on him. But, I suppose you knights get that all the time, don't you? The boys do love men in armor. And the swords—"

Andreas gave the man such a stern glance that the brewmaster's voice died in his throat. The portly man dropped his eyes and fidgeted with his mug. "My apologies, Sir Knight. I meant no harm..."

"None was taken," Andreas said. "Your ward has become much loved by me and mine, and his aid has strengthened our cause in a way that can never be fully repaid. Though, I wish to try." He cleared his throat, considered what he wanted to say next, and then raised his mug to his lips. "When this unfortunate business is finished," he continued after a long drink, "I would like to take Hans with us. I would like to make him my squire. I would protect him, and would pay for his education and training in the *Ordo Militum Vindicis Intactae*—"

A small noise caught their attention. The edge of the heavy curtain was raised, and Hans was staring at them with bright eyes. His mouth moved, trying to summon words, and after a few feeble attempts, he gave up and launched himself out of the doorway. He impacted Andreas in a tight hug that caught the big man off guard, but he smiled awkwardly and returned the youth's affectionate embrace. He ruffled Hans's hair and gently disengaged the boy's arms. "You've done us a great service," he said, somewhat gruffly. "What I offer is a hard life, and is in no way proper compensation for the risks you have undertaken on our behalf, but it is all that I have to offer you."

"You...you offer me much," Hans said shyly, wiping his tear-stained face. "I just tell the other boys where to go, and listen to their messages when they return. They're the ones taking all the risks..." He looked at his uncle. "I worry about what they face when I send them out, and I am ashamed that I have not gone myself."

Andreas looked at the boy, seeing him not for the first time with fresh eyes. "Hans, when I asked you to find a way for us to communicate, I knew the dangerous task to which I was assigning you. What you feel is what I have felt—what any commander of men has felt when he has given an order that has sent one of his companions into danger. You must always remember this feeling, and use it to temper your judgment and your compassion, lest you become careless with the lives you hold in your charge. That you can do what you have done—and that you feel what you do—tells me that my order would be honored to have a boy—nay, a *man* like you in our ranks." He smiled. "That is, if you would join us..."

Hans raised his eyes, and the fear seemed to ease, at least a little. The guilt remained, but Andreas knew that that would never flee. A part of him felt the same, knowing what the boy would inevitably face, if he took this path. "I won't let you down," Hans said after a long moment. "Now, or in the future." His eyes grew hard and resolute. "I promise."

Ernust pressed a palm of one hand against an eye and squinted up at the sun. "I wish you'd not begged off on a single drink today, sir," he said in a proud voice. "I'd like to give you an entire cask. 'Tis truly a moment to celebrate."

Laying down his mug, Andreas put a hand on the brewer's shoulder. "I wish I could," he chuckled. "But we've less pleasant business to attend to."

* * *

Andreas was not unfamiliar with the reputation garnered by champions—he had won more than a few competitions in his time—and he had been party to the affection showered upon a victorious host as it enters a newly liberated city. But none of those experiences truly prepared him for the celebrity bestowed by the dissolute Khan's tournament. He and his three companions had managed to slip into the outskirts of Hünern without much notice, enabling him to detour to the unmarked alley where Hans's uncle operated his brewery. However, as they left the alley and made their way toward the arena, they were beset by a sea of wide-eyed citizens. They were shouting his name, and their hands clutched at his legs, at the hem of his cloak, at his saddle and gear. It did not seem to matter to them that he had lost to the Flower Knight at First Field; all they seemed to remember were his other bouts, the ones he could barely recall the details of. Andreas shifted uneasily in his saddle; his horse, sensing his discomfort at the press of bodies, stamped and tossed its head nervously.

The immense blossom of the Circus rose like a fungus flower from the carcass of the rotting city. Unable to do much else in the madding crowd, he examined the tumbledown structure. Its timbers had all been sourced from nearby ruins—even as far away as Legnica proper—and it was a testament to the Mongol engineers that they were able to erect such an impressive structure from such a hodgepodge of materials. It was not a particularly attractive building, yet the row of banners snapping in the wind that blew across the top of the bulbous shape and the persistent roar of voices from within stirred him in a manner not unlike the way in which a suitor is transfixed by the woman he desires.

"I never know," Styg said quietly, "whether I should stare in awe at that thing, or be scared out of my wits."

"Aye," Andreas murmured in response. Death was close, infecting his body and brain with a rich reminder of life. Making him overly aware of the inherent beauty of God's touch in the world that surrounded them.

He dug his heels into his horse's side, urging the nervous animal through the surging crowd. If they dawdled too long, they would be late.

The most direct path was filled with spectators and adoring fans, and so Andreas directed his horse off the main road and onto the alleys and paths between the ruins and the shanties in an attempt to shake some of the crowd. Some of the lanes were so narrow that he could touch walls and tents on either side of his horse as they passed. Circuitously, the Shield-Brethren made their way toward the arena.

As they approached, the grandiose impression of the arena faded, revealing the true fragility of the structure. Wood slats and tall beams were haphazardly slapped one atop another in an intricate creation that was no more or less than barely organized chaos. *It is a death trap*, Andreas thought grimly. *Few exits—easily sealed. It's nothing more than kindling, waiting for a torch.*

A sudden chill made him shudder, and he turned away from the looming edifice and raised his face toward the warm sun overhead. Pushing aside a vision of fire, he set his focus on the task at hand: watching the fights, learning about his opponents, and preparing for when it would be his turn to walk on the sand of the arena. Fear was only of use insofar as it taught a man what was dangerous and what was not, and Andreas had lived through worse things than one-on-one duels for the entertainment of bloodthirsty crowds. As he rode, the taste of the brewer's beer was a balm on his tongue, still fresh on the palate of memory.

Nearby, a horn called on the morning air and an ocean of voices rose from inside the arena. Sunlight danced across ramshackle rooftops, glinting off the tiny spires of adornments and fragmented curios the locals had mounted over their heads. The city's rooftops had a gleaming newness strangely at odds with the muck and ash that layered the ground. Hünern was a ruin where the survivors of the horrors of war made do with what they could, scrounging for hope amid the ashes, and yet there was beauty here as well. Andreas guided his horse absently while he took the time to examine the tiny efforts the people had made to make the city livable again.

When the bone-heavy weariness of his oath and his duties threatened to overwhelm him, he only had to look to these unfortunates to be reminded of why he had taken up both oath and arms. Their plight fortified his spirit, regardless of the deep-seated knowledge that there would be no end of injustice and despair in the known world from which to draw strength.

The shadow of the stands and their waving banners fell over Andreas and his companions as they reached the open ground surrounding the arena proper. He shook off the last of his apprehension, squaring his shoulders and sitting tall in his saddle. Several young men, eager to earn some pittance, approached the riders. Andreas waved them off. The horses of the Shield-Brethren would not be tended to by local boys, even ones as eager as these.

Arvid and Sakse were clearly disappointed when told they were going to stay with the horses, and Andreas tried to explain why without going into too many details. There was some history with the Livonians concerning the disposition of some horses, he told the pair. It was important to be wary of Livonians who might take it upon themselves to thieve their horses, given the opportunity that insufficiently guarded horses might present.

Styg nodded sagely during this explanation, though Andreas could tell the younger man was fighting to hold back his laughter.

Leaving the horses with the two younger men, Andreas and Styg entered the arena through one of the narrow gates. They walked through a short tunnel that terminated in a short series of steps that brought them up to the first level of the audience. As they emerged from the unpleasant dimness of the tunnel, they were afforded their first glimpse of the sandy pit that was the arena proper, surrounded by the tall walls at whose crest began the stands in which the crowds sat.

Styg drew in a sharp breath at the sight of the filled stands, and Andreas felt a similar awe clutch his chest as he gazed upon so many different peoples clustered together for the singular purpose of watching men fight. The Colosseum in Rome had served a similar purpose once, and Andreas had heard his share of stories about the gladiators of old, but the sheer diversity of the audience here was much more *worldly* than the bloodthirsty crowd that gathered in Old Rome. His heart skipped a beat as he looked upon Saracens, Slavs, Germans, Franks, Mongols, Persians, Turks, and those of a number of other races he couldn't readily identify; he saw the same rapt expression on all their faces. They were here to watch someone bleed. It would help them forget their own woes, Andreas knew; it was one of the ugly truths of the world. Steeling himself, he took a few more steps forward so that he could look down upon the killing field.

The sand had been raked, but there was still a shadow that resided in it, a ghostly smear of the blood shed in the last fight. The hint of blood in the sand had a tangible effect on the audience, and there was a pressing hunger in the air. The back of his throat constricted, and his tongue was numb in his mouth. It was not unlike battlefield nerves, but it felt so much more vile and wrong for the place and manner in which it crept into his blood.

"Remember why we have come today," Andreas said to Styg. He swallowed heavily, pushing his revulsion back down into his stomach where it roiled angrily.

Styg pressed his lips together and gave Andreas a jerky nod. Andreas laid a hand on the younger man's shoulder and gave it a reassuring squeeze.

QUONIAM
FORTIDUO MEA

IN THE LONG, flat valley between the Palatine and the Aventine hills lay the overgrown ruins of the Circus Maximus. It had been hundreds of years since chariots had churned across the sand, and the ground had slowly been reclaimed by wild grass and narrow stands of trees. The only reminders that the ground had once been trampled by frenzied horses were a squat tower and a series of low stables at the southern end. The stables themselves were vacant of horses now, but the largest stall was filled with a confused collection of dirty and agitated cardinals.

Fieschi remained on the periphery of the bare room. The chamber was not unlike many of the rooms they had so recently inhabited not far from here; the main difference was the large opening at the north end that looked out upon the empty expanse of the Circus Maximus.

And the guards. A line of a dozen of Orsini's men stood between the cardinals and the open field, just to remind them that they were still prisoners of the Senator of Rome.

The Bear was on his way, they had been told, though Fieschi surmised that the delay had more to do with Orsini playing to their fear and confusion than any real conflicting activity. *What else could be more exciting in Rome this afternoon than a fire in an abandoned temple?* he thought with a wry smile.

The other cardinals milled about in the empty stable, still congratulating themselves on their narrow escapes. Bonaventura, especially, seemed particularly enlivened by the experience. His cheeks were ruddy with excitement, and he was deep in his fourth or fifth retelling of the experience of having been lifted out of the Septizodium by a brace of soldiers. Da Capua, who had heard the story at least twice already, hung on every word like an eager sycophant, and announced that he would write a ballad about the ordeal. Dei Conti, meanwhile, kept his annoyance off his face as he listened to Bonaventura's rambling story—he had been, from what he had muttered to Fieschi earlier, standing next to Bonaventura during the rescue. Torres, inscrutable as ever, held council with Annibaldi and Castiglione, while de Segni tried—yet again—to open negotiation with the guards, who remained unmoved by the tall cardinal's exhortations. Colonna fussed over his friend, Capocci, who was seated as comfortably as possible in this Spartan environment.

Capocci's hands had been badly burned, and the Master Constable had found some cloth that had been soaked in water and wrapped around them, to provide some relief from the pain while a healer was found. Colonna kept wanting to check the bandages but, realizing he was being a fussy nursemaid, would catch himself. Capocci ignored the other man's fluttering presence, his gaze steady and unwavering.

Fieschi did not shy away from that gaze. Whenever he glanced over, Capocci's expression was the same, and he found no reason to give the man any satisfaction. He met Capocci's glare with a calm and untroubled expression of his own. *He knows nothing*, he thought. *He might have seen Somercotes's body, but he cannot know what happened.*

He wants to believe that I am responsible; it would fit his impression of me—a simple solution that would ease his mind.

Fieschi looked away from the wounded cardinal, returning his attention to the line of guards and the open field beyond. His mind drifting, wondering about the races that had once been held in the valley. Thousands of citizens had once clustered around the raked sands while charioteers beat their horses bloody in an effort to gain glory for their leaders. The pagan rituals of the gods of Imperial Rome had been brutal, savage rites of a weaker age, but they had had their place in that world. It did not surprise Fieschi that a place like the Circus had fallen into disuse; Christianity was, after all, *civilized*. Love for Christ had brought them all out of darkness, and—with proper guidance—that love would bring them all to salvation. It was much as Augustine said: Rome loved Romulus and made him a god; the devout believed Christ to be God, and therefore loved Him.

Yet he could not help but wonder about the *power* of that crowd's love. The roar of their voices, chanting and screaming the names of their champions. The orgiastic surge of delight when their man won a race. Or the tumultuous rage when a favorite son fell, his body most likely crushed beneath the wheels of another's chariot. To control that energy, to know that these men raced for your pleasure, to soak in the emotional exultation of the crowd that had come to *worship* at this barbaric temple of your creation. Such power was an aphrodisiac to the Roman Emperors, surely, as it would be to any ruler. It was an earthly love, a devotion to the materials of the flesh and the world; while it felt fierce and all-consuming, it was not the same love one could have for Christ, for God.

He had, in fact, had this argument with Frederick once. Years ago, before the Holy Roman Emperor drifted from his allegiance to the Pope. Frederick, reveling too much perhaps in his delight at playing the fool, had taken the side of Imperial Rome. *It was better to have the love and respect of your subjects,* he had argued, *than to persist in frightening them with the threat of losing the love of a Supreme Being they will never know.*

He had quoted Scripture in response. Fieschi caught himself smiling at the memory. The thirty-first Psalm. *Diligite Dominum, omnes sancti eius, quoniam veritatem requiret Dominus, et retribuet abundantur facientibus superbiam.*

God rewards the faithful, and His rewards were abundant to the proud believer.

The Rome of Romulus was gone, sacked and pillaged as it grew too decrepit to protect itself. Rome belonged to Christ now, and he was going to make it the heavenly city that Augustine had posited.

"*Ego autem in te speravi, Domine,*" he whispered, lightly touching his forehead with a trembling finger. "*Deus meus es tu.*"

Fieschi caught sight of the mad priest, standing in the far corner of the stable like a forgotten child. He clutched a plain jar in his hands, holding it tightly as if it contained a sacred relic. Much like he had clung to his satchel when he had been first lowered into the Septizodium.

Fieschi finished making the sign of the cross before letting his hand drift toward his satchel. He still had the priest's parchment, the page covered with the frenzied scribbling of a heretical prophecy. For an instant, Fieschi almost felt some empathy for the deluded priest. To be so bereft of God's love that he could be snared by the heretical vision of those words, to be so *lost* that he could *believe* that he had been the recipient of a divine visitation. To feel the Serpent's tongue and mistake it for the whispering voice of an angel.

He sent a silent prayer of gratitude to God. *Quoniam fortiduo mea at refugium meum es tu.* His purpose was clear; his path was like a ribbon of shining white stones, laid before him.

* * *

They called him the Bear, a nickname that Rodrigo assumed was nothing more than a childish play on the Senator's name, but when he saw the man approaching the stables, he realized how true the appellation was.

Matteo Rosso Orsini wore his hair long, in a style reminiscent of the sculpted faces of Roman Emperors that peered down at the citizen of Rome from every building and temple. His hair had lost some of its youthful luster, but it was still a rich brown color that reminded Rodrigo of the dirt in freshly plowed fields. The Senator was tall and wide, though not so tall that he was a giant among his men, nor so wide that his detractors would call him fat. The wind toyed with his hair and flung his cape about his shoulders. The light of the sun inflamed a tracery of gold thread in his tunic, making his clothes appear to be made from a wealth of golden leaves, all stitched together in a seamless pattern. When he reached the stables, he stood silently at the doors, waiting for the cardinals to acknowledge his arrival.

Eventually, their conversations trickled to an end, though Bonaventura seemed hesitant to let go of the audience he had been enjoying.

Rodrigo had been watching Cardinal Colonna. The feud between the Colonnas and the Orsinis had been so long-standing that it was a persistent part of his memories of growing up in Rome, like the Colosseum or the ruins of the Circus Maximus. Judging by the cardinal's expression, nothing had been settled between their families.

"Look what has dragged itself out of bed," Colonna muttered, a little too loudly in the near silence.

"Good afternoon, Your Eminences." Orsini ignored the cardinal's comment, and his voice was naturally loud and commanding, rising from the barrel-like vault of his chest. "I deeply regret the occasion of our meeting. I have just come from the Septizodium, where Master Constable Alatrinus has informed me of the tragic death of Cardinal Somercotes." He paused, his eyes on de Segni, who appeared to be on the verge of speaking. The cardinal, who was nearly the tallest among the group (other than Cardinal Colonna, who was taller even than the Bear), squirmed under the Bear's gaze and finally looked down at the ground.

"There will be opportunity later for discussion as to how this tragedy came about, and I will hear all of your recriminations and accusations in time. However, this tragedy does not alter the critical task which is your duty—"

"He would not be dead if you hadn't imprisoned us!"

They were all surprised at the source of the voice. Mild-tempered Castiglione, who was prone to disappear in any given gathering of the cardinals, was flushed and animated. Spurred on by the echo of his voice in the chamber, the cardinal strode toward Orsini, one hand raised to point dramatically at the Senator. "You will bear the mark of the cardinal's death, Senator," Castiglione continued. "When your soul is released, God will reject it. You will not be afforded a place in Heaven; your soul, weighed down by *your* actions, will be cast into endless perdition."

"Is that so?" Orsini asked, raising one eyebrow. Rodrigo thought he was remarkably calm for a man who had just been condemned by a cardinal of the Church. His own stomach was tied in a knot at the very idea of being subjugated to such an accusation, and the Bear seemed nonplussed by Castiglione's accusatory finger. "I am wounded by your words, Your Eminence," he said. "I fear your temper and exhaustion do you a disservice; your head is filled with words you do not mean to say. How, pray tell, do you find me responsible for Cardinal Somercotes's untimely death? I was not in the Septizodium. I have been at my estate all afternoon. In fact, the Master Constable tells me that the halls beneath the Septizodium are still filled with fire and smoke. It would be a miracle if the cardinal were still alive down there, but, alas, I must confess that I have no hope that such a thing is true." He brought his hands together and bowed his head. "May God receive his soul with all alacrity."

The Bear's reaction threw Castiglione, and the cardinal's outrage faltered for a moment. "Our imprisonment is unjust, as is your insistence that we immediately vote on a successor to the late Pope. This is a matter of the Church. We do not elect a new Bishop of Rome at *your command*. You serve at our—"

"I serve Rome," Orsini thundered. "Have you forgotten your *late* Pope's concessions to the city when *we* allowed him to return from his inglorious exile? Have you forgotten the insults laid against the Church by that jackanape of an Emperor? Frederick wants—"

"Neither you nor Frederick have any authority over us," Castiglione interrupted. He stepped closer to the Senator. "God sees the willful blasphemy of your pride. He has marked how your words and actions have injured those of His flock who are close to Him. *Deus iudex iustus, fortis, et patiens; numquid irascitur per singulos dies*. Have care, Senator Orsini, your soul is in peril."

Something flickered across the Bear's eyes—a shadow of fear, perhaps—but it fled so quickly, Rodrigo had nothing more than a fleeting impression of the Senator's reaction. The Bear's face was otherwise impassive as he considered the cardinal's heated words.

"What would you have me do, Your Eminence?" the Bear finally asked.

"Release us," Castiglione snapped.

"I cannot do that," Orsini said, and Rodrigo heard a surprising weariness in his voice. "You have a sacred task to accomplish, and I cannot allow you to shirk that responsibility."

Castiglione drew himself up, puffing out his chest. "We shall never cast a vote," he replied. "One by one, we shall all die of exposure or *accidents*, and God will condemn you again for each of us."

An ugly sneer twisted Orsini's mouth. "No," he replied, rejecting Castiglione's defiance. "You *will* vote, and you will vote tonight." He stepped close to the Cardinal, towering over him. "By sunrise, you *will* have elected a new Pope." The sneer spread across his face. "You have all had enough time to bicker amongst yourselves and select a candidate you can all live with. Let God strike me down— *right now*—if He thinks I am asking too much of Your Eminences."

Rodrigo held his breath, as did everyone else in the room. Everyone except for the hawk-faced man, Cardinal Fieschi, who seemed to be watching all of this with barely concealed delight. Orsini did not waver; he stood his ground before Castiglione and met the cardinal's gaze without a shred of fear in his broad features.

A burning sensation started in Rodrigo's belly, a bloom of fire that spread to his ribs and chest. It was the fever, assaulting him again. He clutched the jar tightly to his chest, and fell back against the wall of the stables. His teeth began to chatter. Bright lights began to spark in the corners of his vision. Was this the presence of God coming over him? Was a thunderbolt about to split the brick roof of the stables? Rodrigo shivered, unwilling to watch what came next, but unable to close his eyes or look away.

Castiglione took a step back, and he passed a hand in front of his face, making the sign of the cross.

"Master Constable," Orsini barked, his gaze unwavering.

"Sir!" The Master Constable stepped up behind the Senator.

"Prepare some transportation for these eminent persons. This location is hardly suitable for the task before them. They need food and shelter that more reflects their station." He raised his shoulders slightly. "Perhaps your previous lodgings were ill-considered. I see no reason to repeat those conditions..."

Castiglione, realizing he was being addressed, shook his head. "No," he said. "The Lateran Palace will be fine."

The Master Constable bobbed his head in acknowledgment and made to leave, but the Senator stopped him with a word.

"They go to the Basilica of Saint Peter," Orsini corrected. Castiglione thought to argue the point, but Orsini cut him off. "You will be under my guard until morning. Unless you prefer to allow my men complete access to the Papal residence... ?"

"Saint Peter's is fine," Fieschi spoke up from the edge of the room. The hawk-faced man glanced at the other cardinals. "It is one more night, my friends, and it will be more comfortable than the Septizodium. Let us not forget what it is that we are supposed to accomplish. And how little time we have left."

* * *

Rodrigo did not recall the particulars of the wagon ride. The soldiers procured two rickety wagons and several equally aged and withered mules readily enough. It was hardly a suitable procession, but the events of the day had taken their toll, and the cardinals submitted meekly enough to the ignominy of a bumpy wagon ride across Rome.

He lay against the front of the cart, still holding on to the jar given to him by Colonna, who was in the other cart with Capocci. When he turned his head to the side and peered through the uneven spaces in the slats, he could see the other wagon, but he could not tell which of the slumped shapes were either of the two men. He still felt isolated, and while such a feeling was not unusual, he felt it with newfound clarity. Some of the men he had met in the Septizodium had given him hope. Soon, he hoped, the new Pope would be elected, and then he could finally divest himself of his message.

The wagon jumped sharply, and several of the cardinals voiced their annoyance at the bumpy ride. The jar popped out of Rodrigo's grip and bounced on the wooden floor of the cart. He got his hands on it quickly enough, but as he checked it, he realized the stopper had come loose.

He sat up hurriedly, his eyes frantically scanning the wagon bed for the narrow plug. He caught sight of it on his left, near the wall of the wagon. As he reached for it, the wagon hit another bump, and the stopper jumped out of reach. It slid across the wooden floor, bounced against the lowest slat on the side, and then slipped through the gap. Rodrigo stared, and then whipped his head around to fixate on the jar.

It was open! What had Colonna said was inside? Rodrigo tilted the jar up to see its contents, and as he did so, he saw with utter clarity what was going to happen next. When it happened, he was not surprised; he simply accepted the Hand of God as it reached down and jostled the cart one last time.

The jar spun out of his hand, scattering its contents all over him. He closed his eyes, accepting the squirming offerings that God was giving to him. *Scorpions.*

He remembered waking from a horrible dream while trapped underground. There had been a scorpion on him—one much smaller than the specimens that crawled all over him now—and he had wondered if it had stung him. If the return of his fever could be attributed to the poisonous sting of the tiny creature.

There were so many more of them now. They were in his hair. One crawled across his forehead, and several more had already found their way into his robe.

This is God's Will, he thought, spreading his arms and accepting his destiny. He had not delivered his message; God would not let him die. Not until he had completed the task He had set for him.

One of the cardinals noticed the pale shapes crawling all over him and started screaming.

the khaçan's banner

N CATCHING SIGHT of the Spirit Banner, the *Khagan*'s warriors instinctively flocked toward it, and as he strode through the camp, Master Chucai found himself acquiring an entourage of bloodstained soldiers. At first he had waved them off, shouting at them to continue hunting for Chinese rebels who might still be skulking among the tents, but as his survey of the caravan continued, the soldiers began to show up in greater numbers.

They knew he was going to end up at the *Khagan*'s *ger* eventually, and they wanted to be there when he arrived. They followed the banner, and Chucai's practical examination of the damage and status of the caravan took on an air of a celebratory parade.

Chucai ignored the soldiers. They had been ambushed by an unknown force, and had reacted well. It was still too early to make an accurate assessment of how many had been killed or the extent of the destruction to the wagons and livestock, but as far as his eye could see, it looked like the damage was minimal. A few isolated fires still burned, but most of them were tiny patches of flame that were trying to creep off into the night and were slowly being starved of readily accessible fuel.

The *Khagan*'s wheeled *ger* had been spared, and while some of the men following him were beginning to spin tales about the *Khagan*'s invincibility, Chucai knew there was a more practical reason. The *Khagan* had not been the target of the Chinese raid. What they had wanted was the Spirit Banner.

His thumb unconsciously strayed to the rough scab on the pole.

He had fruitlessly searched the bodies of the three Chinese men who had tried to steal the banner. They hadn't been wearing any insignia or common markings on their armor, and other than a short string of glass beads in the pocket of one man, they had been carrying nothing. Which in itself was interesting, and had he been less distracted by the mystery of the banner, Chucai might have wondered more where these men had come from. But they were dead and their corpses offered him no useful clue. As he roamed through the camp, he was also keeping an eye out for any prisoners—living men who could answer the question burning in his mind.

A cheer rose from the men surrounding the *Khagan*'s *ger*, and it was answered by the host trailing behind him. Chucai grimaced, and beat the butt of the staff against the ground a few times as he slowed his relentless pace through the maze of tents. The soldiers of the Imperial Guard who had been left to watch over the *Khagan* had seen the Spirit Banner. Their shout was a roar of recognition, but it held an inquisitive note: *Those who return, tell us of your victory!*

Chucai sighed, and using both hands, raised the banner overhead. The string of soldiers behind him cheered as he waved it back and forth. When the Imperial Guard responded with another cheer, he angled toward the *Khagan*'s *ger*, leading his ragtag column of combatants to the celebration of their victory.

The *Khagan*, summoned from within his tent by the shouting, appeared at the flaps of his *ger*. The crowd, spotting him, began cheering even louder, and the noise became a tumult as men—wanting to be more boisterous than their voices would allow—began to beat their swords against the shields and to stomp their feet. By the time Chucai reached the base of the steps that led up to Ögedei's *ger*, the noise was so loud he wondered if it could be heard in Karakorum.

Ögedei waved at him to come up the stairs, indicating that he wanted to hold the Spirit Banner. Chucai nodded, and with some gravity, ascended a few of the steps so that he could hand over Genghis's legacy. Ögedei, his eyes startlingly clear, reached down and gripped the banner firmly. His brow furrowed slightly when Chucai did not immediately release the staff, and with some reluctance Chucai removed his hand from the banner.

The *Khagan* stood up straight and tall, raising the banner over his head. The crowd of warriors shouted in unison, their voices rising and falling in concert with the motion of Ögedei's arm as he shook the staff with exaggerated slowness. The horsehair braids undulated, and staring up at them, Chucai saw—for a split second—the manes and tails of an endless procession of wild horses, so many of them that he could not see the ground over which they ran.

Chucai thought of himself as an educated man, one well versed in the esoteric reaches of Chinese philosophy and mysticism, as well as the shamanistic legacy that underlay the Mongolian reverence for the Great Blue Sky. Intellectually, he knew the spirit trances that the Mongolian shamans sought for their enlightenment were—in all likelihood—a combination of wakeful dreaming and overactive imaginations, but that had never prevented a part of him from wondering about the experience of ecstatic vision. It would require more than a modicum of faith to accept. It was not a lack of spirituality; it was simply that he preferred to believe what he could *see* and *touch*.

He fell to one knee, his hands clutching at the wooden step of the *Khagan*'s wheeled *ger*. The thundering noise of the crowd overwhelmed him, echoing in his head like the roaring sound of a flash flood as it rushed through a narrow defile. He gasped, struggling to breathe, feeling like he was a small tree that had been uprooted by this flood. He was being hurled at the foaming crest of this wave.

Horses. Thousands and thousands and thousands of them. Running from one end of the world to the other.

"I am the Khan of Khans," Ögedei shouted, his voice cutting through the storm of noise. "My empire will cover the world."

With a great deal of difficulty, Chucai raised his head and stared up at Ögedei. The *Khagan's* face was glowing with sweat, and his teeth were bared in a feral grin. A wind tugged at his hair and the horsehair braids. Wisps of smoke swirled overhead, shapes like late summer thunderheads that were pulled into long streaks stretching out across the star-dappled sky.

The manes of horses, streaming behind them as they ran.

* * *

Following the *Khagan's* appearance, and with the rout of the Chinese raiders, most of the dignitaries and courtiers milled around for a little while before returning to their interrupted feast. A pall of smoke hung over the tents and wagons, and the air stank of scorched leather, fabric, flesh, and wood. *And yet, they fall to gorging themselves again, as if nothing has happened.* Master Chucai shook his head in disgust as he passed the banquet area. Having completed a tour of the sprawled camp, he was returning to the *Khagan's ger.*

An accurate assessment of the damage done by the raid and the fire would have to wait until daylight. Making an inspection of the camp had been his excuse for leaving the *Khagan's ger* so soon after returning the Spirit Banner, and he had performed this duty during his perambulation. Balancing the *Khagan's* desire to move swiftly with the need to provide properly for both the *Khagan*, his retinue, and the soldiers had been a tricky business, and Chucai was already making calculations in his head as to how he was going to manage the loss of supplies.

Mostly, he had wanted to clear his head after the confusing experience of the vision.

Where had it come from? He was exhausted, his mind dulled by the endless preparation for the *Khagan*'s trip, and he was more susceptible to the mental confusion produced by a powerful oratory. But the *Khagan*'s speech had not been very *elaborate*, nor terribly arousing in its content. Not the sort of rhetoric that should have been able to move him, even in his sleep-deprived state.

He had heard the *Khagan* make similar speeches in the past, in fact, and while he had seen how they impacted the warriors, he had never been impressed in the same way as he had been earlier. He had been able to watch the *Khagan* stir up his troops with a bemused detachment, much like the way he had observed Lian manipulating Gansukh. It was a simple skill every leader—and most women, for that matter—learned instinctively, and as an educated man he was somewhat inured to such manipulation.

And yet, he had been caught up in the fervor, like some fresh recruit eager to spill blood for the empire. An addled fool, hanging on each word.

He paused at the foot of the wooden stairs that led up to the immense platform of the *Khagan*'s mobile *ger*. *Had it been the Spirit Banner?* The thought had been nagging at him during his examination of the camp. He had tried to shake it loose, but it remained, a barbed porcupine quill caught in the spongy depth of his brain.

The Chinese had launched a foolhardy raid on the caravan in an effort to steal the banner. Given the Khan's dramatic appearance before his men, he couldn't dismiss the power that such a *symbol* as the banner had had on the warriors, but if all the Chinese had wanted to accomplish was a *symbolic assault* then why hadn't they simply destroyed the banner? It would have been easy enough to throw it in any one of a number of fires that their archers had started. Why steal it?

Because it had power.

Chucai snorted, rejecting that answer. He waved at the guards outside the *ger*, indicating that he wanted to see the *Khagan*, and when they acknowledged his presence, he mounted the steps. "My Khan," he called through the opening at the top of the tent flaps. "May I have a word?"

He listened for a response, and hearing little more than a single grunt of an answer, he glanced at the nearest guard and raised an eyebrow. The guard shrugged, and pulled back the flaps of the *ger*. Chucai ducked and entered.

The Khan was sitting in a cypress yokeback chair, a recent gift from a provincial sub-administrator from Ningxia, facing away from the *ger* flaps. He stared at the wall, lost in the roseate light provided by a nearby brazier of orange and red coals. His large cup—the one provided by Gansukh and later dented by the young man's skull—dangled perilously in his slack hands.

There were white feathers scattered all over the floor. Chucai frowned, wondering about the source of the down, and his gaze roamed across the chamber. He hoped the *Khagan* hadn't slaughtered a live bird in here...

The roof of the *ger* was low enough that Chucai had to duck slightly to avoid hitting his head on the support poles. He walked around (still keeping an eye out for any sign of a mangled bird), until the *Khagan* could see him. "My Khan," he said, sweeping into a deep bow. "I wish to report on the Chinese raid."

The *Khagan* stiffened slightly, drawing in breath, though he still appeared lost in thought. Chucai hesitated, watching the *Khagan* intently. Was Ögedei in some sort of trance, a passing vegetative state in the wake of channeling the vision? Traveling to the spirit realms exacted a harsh toll on shamans, and he had heard stories of seekers who had been so moved by their experiences that they never fully returned to their bodies. Their spirits, loosened in their flesh, eventually drifted away. One day, the body would just stop breathing.

Chucai cleared his throat noisily. *Such foolishness*, he thought sourly. *I am behaving like a superstitious herdsman.*

Ögedei stirred, blinking heavily. His hands closed more firmly around his cup, and he came back to himself. "Master Chucai," he mumbled. "What news have you for me?"

"The Chinese rebels have been defeated, my Khan. Their efforts to destroy your magnificent caravan were futile, and—"

"Any prisoners?"

"No, my Khan." Chucai ground his teeth. He had given strict orders, but he had been too late.

"What did they want?" Ögedei asked. "They did not fire on my *ger*." He raised the cup to his lips. "I have had much time to reflect on their strategies," he continued after drinking. "They were not idiots, I presume. Fools, but not idiots."

Chucai nodded. "No, My Khan. They were not idiots."

"How many were there?"

"Forty, perhaps. I have sent out a number of *arban* to ensure there are no more of them hiding nearby."

"How many of my Imperial Guard did we lose?"

"About the same number. Plus a number of—" Chucai waved a hand to indicate the inconsequence of having lost some of the non-essential members of the *Khagan's* retinue.

"What was their mission?"

"I suspect they were after the Spirit Banner," Chucai confessed. "Though I do not know why."

Ögedei's eyes twitched toward the wall of the tent, and as carelessly as possible, Chucai glanced over to see what Ögedei had been looking at. There was nothing on the wall, nothing but a vague shadow—a misshapen circle with tiny strands descending from it. A shadow of a head with long hair, he interpreted.

"Do they think I am that weak?" Ögedei asked. "If they stole my father's banner, would the empire fall apart instantly? Would I wake in the morning to find that every clan had deserted me?" He snorted, answering his own questions.

"I doubt it, my Khan," Chucai said. He wet his lips, suddenly disturbed by the shadow on the wall. Glancing around the room, he could not figure out how it was being projected on the wall. And when he looked at the wall again, the shadow had changed into an amorphous streak, as if the previous shape had started to run, like ink staining a page.

"What did your father tell you of the banner?" he asked curtly. The shadow was unsettling. The more he tried to ignore it, the more it crept into the periphery of his vision. "Where did he get it?"

Ögedei shrugged. He peered into his cup, seeming to have lost interest in Chucai's questions. "It's just a stick," he muttered. "Father made it."

He didn't, Chucai realized with an absolute certainty. He wanted to look at the wall once more, but the shadow was gone. All that remained was a blur in his mind, a shape that flowed and wavered. Like a horse's tail. Or the tassels of the Spirit Banner.

Why had the Chinese sought the banner? He recalled the rough spot on the wood, and wondered if he was asking the wrong question.

* * *

Chucai had meant to retire to his own *ger* to reflect more on the puzzle of the Spirit Banner, but he had been accosted almost immediately by Jachin, Ögedei's second wife, who had decided to place the blame of the Chinese attack on him. While he had been trying to extricate himself from the tiresome woman's ranting, they had been interrupted by Munokhoi. The *Torguud* captain had swept back into the camp, demanding an audience with the *Khagan.* Chucai, welcoming the opportunity to escape Jachin's tirade, had directed Munokhoi to his *ger,* knowing that Ögedei was in no shape to listen to the headstrong warrior. A decision which, in retrospect, might not have been the wisest. Out of sight of his underlings, Munokhoi unleashed a raging torrent of invective that appeared to have no end in sight. *It was as if the man has kept a tally of every perceived slight against him since Gansukh arrived at court,* he thought, *and now they are all being counted.*

"Enough," he snapped, waving his hands to get Munokhoi to stop.

Munokhoi came up short, caught in midsentence and midstep. He glared at the *Khagan*'s advisor, his eyes glittering with a copious amount of still untapped rage.

"Captain Munokhoi," Chucai said after a moment, "I appreciate your concern about young Gansukh and Mistress Lian. I will..." He was torn between several responses, and with a sign, decided to address the underlying matter directly by responding in a way that would further enrage the *Torguud* captain. "I will take it under consideration."

Munokhoi quivered. "Under consideration?" he hissed. "You will imprison—"

"You will do well to remember who is in charge of the *Khagan*'s court," Chucai snapped. The *Torguud* captain hadn't been able to contain himself, as Chucai had anticipated. His own frustration had an outlet now. "And wherever the *Khagan* is, wherever he takes an audience, that is his court. We are not at war, *Captain*. This is not the battlefield. Your concerns are noted."

Munokhoi did not say anything, but he refused to budge, staring daggers at Chucai. The fingers of his right hand twitched. He was not wearing his sword—Chucai had smartly requested that he leave his blade with one of the servants standing outside the *ger*—but the *Torguud* captain still had his knife.

For a long moment, Chucai held his stare, examining Munokhoi's eyes for some sign that the man was foolish enough to draw the blade. *Are you such a fool?* he projected. *What do you think will happen to you if you draw that knife? If you kill me, what will the* Khagan *think of you?*

Munokhoi seemed to be having similar thoughts. His hand relaxed and he looked away. He exhaled, and it was as if a storm cloud fled his body with his released breath.

"Gansukh and Lian are surrounded by the entire caravan. They know they are under scrutiny," Chucai explained, knowing that Munokhoi was actually listening to him now. "They know you are watching them. Whatever Gansukh and Lian may be, they are not fools. Even if Gansukh wanted to leave the *Khagan*'s service—*and I don't believe he does*—he's too smart to attempt it on this pilgrimage to Burqan-qaldun. And even if Lian wants to escape—which I grant you is something she desperately wants to do—she's too smart to attempt it without Gansukh's help. Now, consider the needs of someone *other than yourself.*"

Munokhoi blinked, and then slowly nodded as he realized Chucai was not going to continue until he had physically acknowledged Chucai's words.

"What drives the empire? Is it not an awareness of a grander destiny for *all* Mongol people? And in whom does this awareness reside?" Chucai paused, as if to give Munokhoi a moment to realize the answer to his question—a moment both he and the *Torguud* captain knew was unnecessary. "You live to serve the *Khagan*, *Captain*, just as I do. As do Gansukh and Lian, in their own ways. The empire is too vast for one man to handle. It has a singular vision, yes, but managing the myriad of people and clans and resources is well beyond the ability of *one* man. The *Khagan*, then, has to rely on people he can trust. People he knows will act *as he would act* if he were doing the job he has given them.

"Now, consider recent events. The *Khagan* has fallen into a malaise—which happens every year at this time. In the past, he drank to excess so as to forget the pain of his brother's death. This year, however, he has been convinced to make a spiritual pilgrimage to Burqan-qaldun."

Convinced, in no small part, by Gansukh, which Chucai decided to not say aloud.

"During his journey, the *Khagan* has been attacked by a motley force of disgruntled Chinese rebels," Chucai continued, "of which there are thousands and thousands scattered across his magnificent empire. This attack has been ably repulsed by his hand-picked *Torguud* captain. Your swift and decisive martial response not only ensures his safety, but validates his decision to make you the commander of the whole of his escort."

Chucai leaned forward. "Think carefully, Munokhoi. Do you really want to disturb the *Khagan*'s goodwill by *whining* to him about Gansukh and Lian? Especially when all that you are really talking about is the relationship between a warrior the *Khagan* admires and a Chinese *whore*?"

Munokhoi lowered his eyes. "No, Master Chucai." The muscles in his jaw flexed.

Chucai nodded and sank back into the embrace of his chair. "Thank you, *Captain*," he said, stressing Munokhoi's title to remind him how new it was—and still so easy to remove. "As I said earlier, I have heard your concerns. I will let you know if there is any assistance I might require."

Munokhoi bowed, albeit shortly and stiffly, and retired from the *ger*. One of Chucai's attendants poked his head into the tent as Chucai returned his attention to the scattered documents on his desk. "Master?" the man inquired.

"Find out where Master Gansukh is," Chucai said without looking up. "Do not disturb him. I simply want to know what he is doing."

The attendant nodded his understanding and vanished from the entrance of the *ger*, leaving Chucai to some long overdue privacy. He pressed the palms of both hands against his eyes. His head was pounding and he realized he hadn't eaten or drunk anything since before the Chinese attack.

He was still waiting to hear reports from the war parties that had been sent out to ensure that the Chinese force had been decimated and that there was no sign of another group waiting to strike. It would be dawn soon, and the caravan needed to move, despite the fire damage and those incapacitated. He didn't want to present too opportune a target, and as long as the caravan was moving he didn't have to consider the more troubling issue.

Munokhoi's patrols had failed to anticipate the Chinese attack. For all that he had just said to Munokhoi, the *Torguud* should have been better prepared.

He could insist that Munokhoi double the size of the patrols, but that was a game that the Chinese could play as well. At Karakorum, they had had the advantage of the walls and the city as well as the entirety of the Imperial Guard to provide adequate protection for the *Khagan*. But the Imperial Guard was not used to being mobile, nor did its leadership have the right experience.

Chucai drummed his fingers on the desk. *What of the young pony?* he reflected. *Would Gansukh be a better choice to lead the* Khagan's *guards?*

An attendant pushed his way into the *ger*, a cup of steaming tea in his hands. Without a word, he placed it on the desk and backed out of the tent. The cup was warm and the tea was a pale yellow color, with tiny white streaks that reflected back the light. Chucai held the cup, inhaling the aroma of the white tea and letting his mind go blank. Letting all the tumbling concerns in his head slip free.

The Khagan. Shortly after his audience with Ögedei, Chucai had been accosted by Jachin, who accused *him* of making Ögedei despondent and distracted. The *Khagan* was ignoring her, mumbling on about hunting a great bear at Burqan-qaldun, about recovering his warrior spirit. This was Chucai's fault: he had fostered this idea in the *Khagan*'s head; he had organized the caravan; he had allowed that whelp of Chagatai's to whisper in the *Khagan*'s ear. It was his doing, and she would have no more of it.

As much as Munokhoi's arrival had spared him further recriminations from Jachin, he had to admit there was some credence to her accusations. Ögedei was suffering from a lack of self-confidence, a lack of faith in his own ability to lead the empire.

For the most part, Chucai knew Ögedei's concerns were unfounded. Genghis had chosen Ögedei as his successor for good reasons, and for many years, he had been pleased to watch Ögedei grow into a role most thought him incapable of filling. He had watched Ögedei deftly manage the lesser khans and their inane territorial squabbles; he had seen the Khan handle delicate diplomatic situations with both the Chinese and the Koreans with aplomb. He had witnessed Ögedei's prowess in battle, a much different—yet equally critical—aspect of leadership.

In the end, it was something as simple and ludicrous as wine that threatened to destroy the empire.

Gansukh. What he had said to Munokhoi was entirely true: an empire could not be managed by one man. But it was true that some men wielded more influence than others. For some, their influence was obvious. Him, for example. Others, like Gansukh, might never be recognized by history, but their part in the overall success of the empire was paramount. Chagatai had chosen wisely.

It could have been ten; it could have been a thousand men sent by Chagatai to watch over the *Khagan* and keep him from drinking himself to death. But Chagatai had sent *one* man, and Chucai dared to allow himself the thought that Gansukh might actually succeed in saving the *Khagan*.

Which made this issue of Munokhoi's report that Lian had been trying to escape all the more infuriating. He could insist that she remain in his *ger*, and Gansukh would take his lessons under his watchful eye, but he sensed that a great deal of the success of their lessons lay in Lian's *unfettered* access to him. Doing so had its drawbacks though, and it was becoming more and more evident that he would, eventually, have to address Lian's influence over the young warrior.

There was also the issue of the Spirit Banner and why the Chinese had tried to steal it. *For what purpose?* he wondered. And the cut in the wood, the scab where something had been trimmed off the banner? The scab was too much like a living tree's effort to cover a wound, or like flesh healing after a cut from a knife. How could that be possible on a piece of wood that had been harvested and shaped many years ago?

His mind traced a complicated path through recent events. *If the cut had not been made on the banner tonight, then when? And by whom?* His mind returned to the female assassin who had fled the palace. When she had been spotted on the roof of the *Khagan's* palace, he had—like everyone else—assumed she had not yet entered the building. But what if that was the wrong conclusion? What if she had been spotted as she was *leaving?* What if, much like the Chinese raid, her target hadn't been the *Khagan*, but the Spirit Banner? If so, then this raid was a desperate—and much less subtle—attempt to accomplish what had failed earlier.

Chucai picked up his tea and sipped it carefully. *They didn't know,* he mused. The Chinese had attacked because they thought their agent had failed. But what if she hadn't? What if she had been successful in her theft and—had it not been for Gansukh and Munokhoi—escaped completely?

After the fruitless interrogation, the thief's clothing had been searched, and nothing had been found.

Which meant either Gansukh or Munokhoi had taken something from her before she had been delivered to the Khan's throne room. The fact that neither had admitted to having such a prize in their possession was—

"Master Chucai."

Chucai looked up, still lost in thought, and he dimly recognized the attendant standing inside the *ger*. The one he had sent to check on Gansukh.

"Master Gansukh is in his tent," the attendant reported.

Chucai grunted, and then as the attendant remained, he pulled himself out of his thoughts and cocked his head. "Yes?"

"Master Gansukh is not alone."

"Mistress Lian." It was a statement, not a question, and the attendant nodded in affirmation.

"Thank you," Chucai dismissed the attendant with a nod and leaned back in his seat, cradling the tea cup in his hands, an idea starting to form in his mind.

Gansukh and Lian, together. Confirmation of what he had suspected for some time. Their affection for each other was obvious even if they both denied it. In Karakorum, it had been difficult to distinguish between teacher and student and lovers, and Lian had always been very good at guarding her thoughts and feelings. Evidently, now, they were no longer concerned about hiding.

What should he do about it? According to Munokhoi's somewhat fragmented story, they had been discovered together on the steppes during the attack. Gansukh had been a prisoner of the Chinese and Lian had claimed to have killed one of their commanders in order to rescue Gansukh.

If true, this would help deny the charge that Gansukh had abandoned his duties during the attack to help Lian, but it would not dispel Munokhoi's accusations entirely.

Munokhoi saw both Lian and Gansukh as threats, and he had tried to convince Chucai the pair was a threat to the *Khagan* and not to his own personal advancement. The *Torguud* captain clearly hated the Chinese teacher, and it did not take much imagination to see why he hated Gansukh. A hatred that would only increase as it became obvious to others that Gansukh's knowledge of steppe fighting might be more useful than Munokhoi's own experience. Regardless of what Chucai commanded of him, Munokhoi would continue to look for opportunities to do both of them harm.

Knowing that, it was foolish for Lian to sleep alone. *In fact,* Chucai concluded, *it might be safer for both of them to stick together.*

And that was not entirely a bad situation. In fact, if Gansukh knew something about the Spirit Banner—if he had whatever had been cut from the wood—then Lian might be the only one who could get it from him.

ROUGH BEASTS

*L*AKSHAMAN LIVED BECAUSE other men bled. His world, the gilded prison of Onghwe Khan's menagerie, had been reduced to this axiomatic definition. He could no longer recall a life before the Khan's arena—not that such a life mattered to him anymore, anyway. He had seen the light go out of a man's eyes more than a hundred times, and each time, the cessation of the other's breath and heartbeat simply validated the primal truth of Lakshaman's existence.

Did he secretly yearn for something else? Some life that was not filled with the torpid stickiness of blood or the putrefying stench of fear? Did he look at his hands and wonder if they were meant to hold something other than his cruel knives? When he was led into the dark tunnel that led to the arena, did he gaze into the darkness and wonder if, perhaps, there was no end to this tunnel? Maybe it went on forever, and eventually, he would stop and look back and not be able to see where he came from. There would be no point in continuing, and so he would sit down in the darkness. Maybe he would even lie down and rest. If the fundamental truth of his existence was no longer valid, would he close his eyes and simply stop breathing?

The islander had asked him questions like those, recently. The one who called himself *Mountain of Skulls*. After Zug's defeat in the Circus, he had become oddly reflective and was prone to fits of introspection like this. As much as Zug's questions seemed to be the addled nonsense spewed by an idiot, Lakshaman had found himself unable to simply ignore them, and so he said they were silly questions. *There was always an end to the tunnel*, he told Zug, *and at the end, there would be a man waiting to die.*

The Khan's stickmen surrounded him as he strode through the tunnel. They stank of fear, even though they were many and Lakshaman's hands were bound. They walked stiffly, the tension in their arms and legs announcing their discomfort more loudly than a hungry baby's wail. Lakshaman gave them as little thought as he had Zug's philosophical questions. They were like the flies that swarmed horse shit.

He may even have said as much to the Flower Knight, Kim Alcheon, when the Korean had come to talk of rebellion. *They are flies on shit*, he may have said.

Does that make us the shit? Kim had enquired. He had been amused by Lakshaman's words, and for a moment, Lakshaman had felt a twinge of something deep within his brain, an unfamiliar emotional response.

If you wish to think of yourself that way—certainly, he may have said to Kim, ignoring the man's humorous query. The Korean had been spending too much time with Zug, and had picked up some of the Nipponese man's annoying habits. *They're just flies. I can swat flies.*

The gate at the end of the tunnel opened as it always did, and the channeled sound of the audience swept over him. Several of his Mongol guards hesitated, and Lakshaman found himself idly thinking about pulling the wings and legs off some flies as he stepped out of the dim tunnel. He blinked in the sunlight, and took a deep breath, inhaling the fecund aroma of the arena's sand, the sweat of his guards, and the stink of the massed audience. The familiar smells.

Soon there would be the scent of blood too.

One of the guards stepped forward to undo the bindings on his hands, and Lakshaman stared unblinkingly at the top of the man's head. The guard fumbled with the knots when he saw another of the guards placing Lakshaman's knives in the dirt—just out of reach, but still too close for the man's comfort. The Mongol nervously licked his lips and tugged hard on the last knot, trying not to be distracted by the presence of the knives.

Lakshaman didn't move; he didn't even blink. As soon as the final knot was loosened, he flexed the fingers of his right hand, and the Mongol guard fled.

The gate banged shut behind him, leaving Lakshaman alone in the arena, surrounded by the thunderous noise of the eager crowd. Slowly—Zug would have accused him of playing to the crowd slightly—Lakshaman stripped the loose bindings from his wrists and hands, tossing the rope aside. He flexed his hands, bending each of the joints of his fingers.

His knives waited for him. Unadorned, hilts wrapped with stained leather, blades marred with age and use, they were not fancy weapons. Lakshaman scooped them up, the hilts slapping comfortably against his palms, and finally turned his attention to his opponent.

The man was by now waiting for him in the center of the sandy arena, swathed in a coating of maille from neck to knees. A white coat covered his midsection, stained with dirt and stitched with a red sword beneath a Christian cross of the same color. The man's helmet was an unadorned metal can that offered only a thin slit in the front. While it made the man's face a difficult target, it also reduced his field of vision. He held a short hatchet in one hand, a horseman's hammer in the other.

A frown crossed Lakshaman's face. He was wearing mismatched leathers, a sleeved jerkin, and pants he had acquired from a dead man a long time ago. Though his blades were long, each roughly the same length as the span from his elbow to his fingertip, they were made for cutting. Against this man, they would not be very effective. Lakshaman glanced up at the colorful silk hangings of the Khan's pavilion. He would not be able to see the Khan very well if at all—the sun was high overhead and most of the pavilion was clothed in shadow—but the Khan could see him.

He would kill this man—he could imagine no other outcome. But the Khan's dismissal of his value was like an itch in a spot he could not easily reach. He was under-armed and underprotected to fight this man. Either the Khan was supremely confident of his ability, or Onghwe simply wanted a spectacle, a passing bloody fancy to occupy an otherwise indolent afternoon.

Like flies, he thought, and spat in the dirt. If he survived, he would speak with the Flower Knight. He did not care what Kim's plan was, as long as it allowed him an opportunity to kill Mongols.

Tightening his grip on his knives, he approached the knight. As he closed, the knight fell into an easy stance, hatchet held ready in front of him, hammer raised behind his head. Lakshaman adjusted his step, circling to his right—just outside the reach of the knight's hammer swing.

The knight shuffled, shifting to keep Lakshaman in front of him. He held himself with an easy confidence, assured in the superiority of his weapons and armor. His reach was longer; he had no reason to attack first. Lakshaman would have to get in closer to use his knives, and during that time, the knight would have a chance to use the hammer and hatchet.

Arrogance is good, Lakshaman thought. *It will make him slow.*

He continued to drift around the man, maintaining the same distance and letting the tips of his knives dance hypnotically. As if he were mentally assessing the knight's armament and trying—vainly—to ascertain a weak spot in the man's maille. He stopped being aware of breathing as his mind unconsciously focused on the subtle changes in the knight's posture and position.

The sun beat down, and Lakshaman felt sweat bead up on his neck and drip down the inside of his arms within his leather bracers. The knight's white coat would keep him somewhat cool, but his arms and head did not have the same protection. It had to be getting hot in that armor. How much patience did the knight have?

Having completed two complete circuits of the man's stationary position, Lakshaman settled into a low stance, knives ready, and waited. *How long?*

The Westerner leaped forward, the hatchet lashing out at Lakshaman's neck. It was a marvelously delivered blow, the weight of his opponent trailing behind the ax head as it whirled toward him. Waiting behind it was the hammer, held high in preparation to swing down and shatter bone. A less experienced fighter would have expected the hammer to come first, but Lakshaman had never doubted that the first strike would come from the hatchet. For all the swiftness of the knight's attack, signs of his intent had been readily clear to Lakshaman. The hatchet was in his enemy's left hand, and as it snapped toward him, Lakshaman stepped forward and to the outside. He slammed the pommel of one of his knives and his other forearm against the Westerner's arm, blocking the blow before it could even be fully extended.

He was close enough now for the knives.

The knight reacted quickly, folding his arm back to make his elbow a blunt object. His momentum carried him forward, and his elbow hit Lakshaman hard at the base of his rib cage. With a concussive *whuff*, the less-armored man felt half his breath abandon his body. It was only an instinctive tightening of his abdomen that prevented him from being left gasping for breath.

He felt the hammer coming. If he stood still and looked for it, his upraised face would be a natural target the knight could not miss. He could not step back quickly enough to avoid the strike either. He had to stay in close.

Lakshaman had a choice to move right or left, behind or in front of the knight's body. Moving in front meant that he was exposed to the man's weapons, but it also meant his own could come into play. Moving behind the knight would put his own back to the man. As the hammer came hurtling down, Lakshaman darted to his left.

As he moved, his left hand came up, and his blade slashed across the gap between the base of the man's helm and his neck, on the off chance that the armor was weaker there. Metal rang off metal with no sign of blood, and Lakshaman had no other opportunity to investigate his blow as the knight's hatchet blade came whirling past his nose.

The only reason the hatchet missed was because the move was one that Lakshaman himself knew—the whirling arm-over-arm assault that seemed, to an untrained eye, to be an impossible tangle of limbs. That the Westerner knew it was a surprise to Lakshaman—even more so that he would attempt it with disparate weapons like the hammer and hatchet—and it was only pure instinct that had warned him to pull back. As it was, the blade of the hatchet passed less than a finger's width in front of his face.

Lakshaman did not wait around to see if the knight was capable of continuing the whirlwind. The angle was bad, and his knives were not meant for stabbing, but he jabbed the one in his right hand up into the knight's left armpit anyway. He put as much strength as he could in the attack, and the knight collapsed around his weapon, a muffled grunt of pain coming from inside his helmet.

The knight jerked backward, and the knife was torn out of Lakshaman's grip. Instead of trying to retrieve it, Lakshaman grabbed for the shoulder of the man's coat, getting a fistful of cloth and maille. The knight was off balance. It would be easy to throw him now. Once the man was on the ground, the superiority of his weapons would be negated and it would be much easier to cut him.

Fire exploded across his back. The knight had managed to twist the hatchet and plant it into Lakshaman's back. His legs and arms still worked, so the hatchet had missed his spine, but the strike had split his leathers. Snarling like a wounded beast, Lakshaman drove his right knee into his enemy's groin, sending the man reeling. His back muscles shrieked in agony as the knight tried to hang on to the hatchet; finally, Lakshaman managed to twist away and pull the handle from his opponent's fingers.

The crowd roared with delight as they separated, each now missing one of their weapons. Lakshaman's knife lay in the dirt somewhere, and he tried to reach around and grasp the haft of the hatchet caught in his back. More pain lanced up his back and into the base of his skull as he twisted his body. His fingers slipped on the bloody handle.

The knight wobbled, his legs struggling to hold him upright. He grasped the lower edge of his helmet with one hand, adjusting it, and Lakshaman caught sight of a shadow at the base of his neck. His knife had cut the man after all. Not fatally, but he had drawn blood.

The crowd was on its feet, shouting and screaming a war cry of its own, as the knight gripped his hammer with both hands and charged. A bold attack. The man hadn't learned caution from their first exchange.

His teeth bared in a feral grin, Lakshaman's hand found the haft of the hatchet and pulled it free. Now he had a more suitable weapon.

The hammer swept down, and Lakshaman darted to his left, sweeping the bloody hatchet up to slam its handle against the shaft of the knight's hammer. Even before the shock of the contact rippled all the way up to his shoulder, he was already turning his wrist, letting the momentum of the hammer carry it past him. He was inside the knight's guard again.

The knight snapped his right hand out, and his metal-shod fist drove into Lakshaman's throat. He'd taken worse, but the blow made his throat close. Gagging, he felt his grip on the hatchet loosen. The knight hit him again, and he barely managed to tuck his chin down. The knight's fist scrapped across his jaw—once, twice.

Lakshaman stumbled back. The knight pressed his advantage, pounding Lakshaman with short jabs. They weren't terribly powerful hits, but the flurry of punches kept him off balance, forcing him to retreat.

He saw his opening: his opponent was covered from head to foot with the tightly linked maille, but it did not cover the entirety of the palms. At the base of the hand there was a patch of exposed skin. As long as the knight held a weapon, it wasn't vulnerable, but without one...

As the knight punched him again, Lakshaman jabbed upward with the knife in his left hand. He shoved the point into the base of the man's hand with all of his strength, and the knight's fist cocked at a strange angle. He felt the knife grind against bone, and he shoved and twisted the blade.

The knight screamed, and Lakshaman caught a flash of the whites of the man's eyes through the narrow slit of the helmet.

Letting go of both his knife and the nearly forgotten hatchet, Lakshaman grappled with his enemy. He looped his left arm around the knight's right, pinning the man's elbow against his side. The knight, moaning and spitting, threw his weight against Lakshaman in a desperate attempt to overwhelm the lesser-armored man and regain control of the grapple. Lakshaman dropped his hips—*the one whose hips are lower is the one who wins*—and twisted his body around as he swept his right leg back.

The knight tried to stop the throw, but he was too off-balance, and his armor gave him too much mass. He flew off his feet, and Lakshaman, still holding onto his arm, came tumbling with him. They crashed to the ground, and there was a bone-snapping crunch as his elbow twisted too far in the wrong direction.

Lakshaman rolled off his opponent, the roar of the crowd filling his head. Crouching, he warily regarded his downed opponent while his right hand tried to explore the painful gash in his back. His hand came away red with blood, but he could still move. He could still fight.

Unlike his opponent.

The knight was struggling to turn over, but his brain hadn't quite realized how useless his right arm was. The hand had been punctured by Lakshaman's knife, and the elbow was bent at a hideous angle. The maille sleeve was already dark with blood. If he was spared the ignominy of death in the arena, he would be maimed for the rest of his life.

Lakshaman was reminded of something he had seen as a boy, an odd memory of a time before he had become a fighter. One spring morning, he had stumbled upon a butterfly as it struggled to emerge from its chrysalis. He had watched it wriggle out of its sheath and tumble to the ground. Its wings never opened properly, and the fall had caused its crumpled wings to harden stiff in a wrinkled mass that would never carry it aloft. He remembered crouching over it, staring intently at this tiny creature whose life was over a scant minute after it had been born.

The knight flopped onto his back, clawing at his helmet with his good hand. He was screaming and crying inside the metal cap; he couldn't get a good look at what was wrong with his arm. He knew something was wrong, but the pain had to be so intense that his martial resolve had been swept away. He was like the butterfly, lying on the ground, struggling to fly but unable to understand why it couldn't.

Lakshaman retrieved his other knife from the sand and knelt beside the downed knight. With a grunt, he shoved his blade through the eye slit of the man's helmet. The man thrashed for a moment and then his limbs stilled.

Just like the butterfly when he had crushed it with his thumb.

SEQUESTERED

THERE HAD BEEN so much confusion when they had arrived at the Basilica of St. Peter. The second wagon, the one carrying the mad priest, had disgorged its passengers in a frenzied rush. Bonaventura had been screaming something about the *Devil's handiwork* and da Capua had climbed down as if transfixed by a heavenly vision. By the time Fieschi had joined the others, the wagon was empty of all its passengers but Father Rodrigo.

The priest sat in the back of the wagon, arms splayed loosely at his sides. His attention was on the shapes crawling on him, and shouldering his way past de Segni, Fieschi had seen that they were scorpions. Rodrigo was covered with them, and appeared to be unharmed.

"It is a miracle," da Capua offered, and Fieschi whirled to the incessantly romantic cardinal to quiet him, but paused as he caught sight of the expressions on the faces of the two mischief-makers, Colonna and Capocci.

"Yes," Colonna said, putting his large hands together in front of his quirking lips. Capocci had the benefit of his bandages, making it much easier to hide his own smile.

The Master Constable, unmoved by the sudden presence of divine intervention, hollered at the guards to rescue the bescorpioned priest. "The rest of them," the Master Constable said, pointing at the chapel behind them, "will be sequestered in the Chapel of the Crucifixion until morning."

"No." Castiglione placed himself in front of the Master Constable. He swayed slightly, and his face was flushed. *All of this excitement is taking its toll,* Fieschi mused.

In the cart, several guards were trying to figure out if they could use the tips of their swords to pick the scorpions off without accidentally cutting the dazed priest. One guard leaned forward, flicking a scorpion off the priest's robe, and the flung arachnid nearly struck one of the other guards, who yelped in fear and nearly stumbled off the back of the cart.

"The Senator has decreed that we will cast our vote by morning," Castiglione continued, oblivious to what was happening in the cart. "And while I do not condone his authority or this egregious manner in which he forces *the Church,* I will acquiesce to the point that God has not chosen to show His displeasure at the Senator's demands."

"I beg your pardon, Your Eminence?" The Master Constable asked, his attention distracted by the guards in the cart.

"We have been treated like rough animals. If the Senator wishes our *obedience*—however temporary—he would do well to seek it from us as *men.*" Castiglione pointed to the tall building—the Castel Sant'Angelo—behind the Master Constable. "Food and shelter," he said, "that is what we require now more than prayer and incarceration. If the Senator wants us to vote, then we will only do so after a meal that we do not have to eat out of a trough, and a night of slumber on a bed that is softer than the old bones of Rome herself."

Colonna and Capocci applauded Castiglione's mettle immediately, with an eagerness—Fieschi noted—that masked the delight with which they had been watching the cart. The other cardinals joined in, and the Master Constable—swiftly assessing the shift in the cardinals' mood—acquiesced.

After the guards managed to extricate Father Rodrigo from the cart and the cardinals were led toward Castel Sant'Angelo and a night of more humane conditions, Fieschi tarried by the now-empty cart. A pale shape squirmed along the boards, and he inspected it carefully.

The scorpion lacked a stinger.

The priest had never been in any danger. *However,* Fieschi mused, as he strolled after the others, *that did not make the incident any less a miracle.*

It was a matter of convincing the right individuals.

* * *

In the morning—an hour or so before dawn—it took two dozen of Orsini's men to roust the cardinals from the rooms the Master Constable had found for them. Like herding sheep back to their pen, the guards drove the cardinals into the Chapel of the Crucifixion. Colonna and Capocci cheerfully stepped into the round chamber and took their seats; Fieschi, stiff from a night of sleep on a real bed, strode in after them and sat on the opposite side of the chamber. Rinaldo and Stefano, the two de Segni cardinals, stumbled in next, Rinaldo still whispering to his younger cousin; while Bonaventura and Castiglione, the two candidates for the Pontiff's chair, both appeared unsettled and vaguely disturbed by what might come to pass in the vote. Torres and Annibaldi were unruffled, especially in comparison to the younger da Capua, who had all the appearance of a spooked child.

Fieschi had spoken to him briefly in the hallway outside their rooms. A few earnest words, a bit of quoted Scripture, and a conspiratorial air was all it took to lay the seed of an idea in the younger cardinal's mind. What had happened the day before in the cart was a demonstration of God's Grace—an incident that could, given a proper poetic treatment, turn into the basis of...

Of a miracle, da Capua had breathed.

In the voting chamber, there were ten chairs set up, backs against the walls, equidistant and too far apart for any prelate to communicate with any other during the voting process.

A priest followed the cardinals in while some of them were still deciding where to sit; he carried a tray on which sat a chalice, paten, several quills, a horn of ink, and strips of paper. He set these on the altar, bowed deeply to the cardinals, then left the room.

There was a thudding sound as a bolt slid home outside the door.

"This is much more comfortable than the Septizodium," said Colonna, into the sudden silence. "We really must thank the Bear for this...*indulgence.*" His friend Capocci smiled at the ecclesiastical pun, but the other cardinals looked uncomfortable. Some glanced around the room, staring at one another, as if seeking some kind of omniscient paternal reassurance.

"Where is our friend?" asked Capocci. "Did he survive his trial with the scorpions only to be lost to us in the night?"

"He is not a cardinal," said Fieschi dismissively. "He has no right to vote. I asked the Master Constable to take him to the Church of the Holy Sepulchre. He is to wait for us there."

"But is it safe for him to be wandering about the basilica on his own?" asked Annibaldi reasonably.

"It is the holiest spot outside of Jerusalem," Fieschi said impatiently. "And there are priests, clerics, and guards everywhere. He made quite a spectacle of himself yesterday; people will keep an eye on him." He paused, casting a glance toward da Capua. "I thought it best to keep one of God's chosen ones close to Him."

"Amen," da Capua said eagerly.

Colonna glanced at Capocci, who was staring at Fieschi quietly, chewing on a strand of his long beard. "Amen," the bearded cardinal echoed, his voice muffled by the thick strand of beard in his mouth.

Was that not your plan? Fieschi wondered, staring back at the cardinal. *Why else would you have kept those maimed scorpions?*

"Let us take a moment to pray," said Torres, rising and walking to the altar. He held up the papers, and then with ceremonial dourness, he began to walk around the circle, and offered a wide slip of the paper to each of his fellow cardinals. "And once we have reached our fill of prayer, let us begin."

* * *

The church was calm and cool, and everything was made of marble. The marble was beautiful, and echoed the sounds of things happening nearby, and this was comforting, for it kept the other sounds, the sounds inside his head, at bay. Rodrigo had slept poorly the previous night, the memory of the men screaming in the wagon with him haunting his nocturnal thoughts. The screaming reminded him of the horrible battle, the horrible war, the horrible soldiers, both foreign and familiar, and he did not want to be reminded of any of that. He was a poor simple priest, and he wanted to be left alone to worship. He could not keep track of where he was, or in what company. But they were all gone now, locked in the smaller chapel, leaving him alone. At last.

He still had not delivered the message, and he found it sulking in the back of his head, waiting for attention. He did not want to give it attention. But he could feel the message he was to deliver to the Pope, he could feel it dancing in his skull, around his brain, stamping its feet, and now demanding, no longer waiting for, his attention. Distracted and almost distressed, he dragged his eyes from the vein of marble and looked around him. He was in the transept of a church, a huge and magnificent cathedral that seemed familiar but distant, as if from another lifetime.

A young priest, even younger than he himself, and so innocent looking, was walking down the center aisle.

"Where am I?" Rodrigo asked plaintively.

The priest approached him, hand held up in smiling assurance. "You are in the Church of the Holy Sepulchre," the priest said. "Saint Peter's Basilica. I have been asked to assist you...if you need anything."

"Saint Peter?" Rodrigo cried out. "May I see him?"

The young man hesitated, then smiled again. "Certainly, Father. His tomb is directly below the altar. Follow me, please."

"I want to go alone," said Rodrigo. The young man looked innocent enough, but there were spies everywhere, and he needed to speak to the Pontiff in absolutely secrecy.

"I will show you where to descend," the young man said and held out his hand toward the altar.

* * *

Ferenc was relieved and grateful that they had found somebody to speak Magyar with him. The soldier—Helmuth—was not a native speaker, and his accent was very thick, but to have any kind of conversation at all nourished Ferenc's heart—even Father Rodrigo had been nearly silent through most of their harrowing journey from Mohi to Rome.

They were breaking their fast together, the soldier speaking and Ferenc listening. Perhaps it was an accident of birth, but Helmuth had a permanent sneer on his face; he radiated disdain toward the young hunter. It was clear to Ferenc that the man was judging him critically, and finding him unworthy—but of what he had no idea. He was so grateful to hear his native language spoken that he would have smiled to have abuses hurled at him.

Ocyrhoe and the other Binder woman were huddled together near them, talking quickly in words Ferenc could not follow. This bothered Ferenc, who felt protective toward Ocyrhoe, but unable to protect her. Several times during her long conversation with the woman the afternoon before, Ocyrhoe had been reduced nearly to tears, and he blamed Léna for this.

"When do we go back to the city?" Ferenc asked the man.

"We are waiting for the cardinals," Helmuth responded sullenly.

This made no sense. "But the cardinals are in the city! We are going back *to* the cardinals," he protested.

Helmuth shook his head. "Not all the cardinals. Some of them are being held as guests by His Majesty, the Emperor. They are his guests in Tivoli."

Ferenc found this even more confusing. "He is here; why are his guests not with him?"

Helmuth grinned in a superior way. "They are in Tivoli. They are guests of the empire, not of the Emperor personally."

Ferenc shook his head. "What does that mean, guests of the empire?"

Helmuth's grin faded. "It means they are prisoners," he said.

The young hunter would have given anything at that moment to turn back time, and to prevent Father Rodrigo from coming to Rome. This was a land of madness. "So all of the Church's cardinals are being held prisoner somewhere," he said. "Either in the Septizodium or in Tivoli. Then doesn't your Emperor sin as much as whoever holds the cardinals hostage in Rome?"

"It's not that simple," said Helmuth impatiently. "Anyhow, the Emperor is now releasing a cardinal, who will go into Rome with you."

"There are already plenty of cardinals in Rome," protested Ferenc. "What good will another cardinal do us?"

"The cardinals in Rome are being held hostage until they vote for a new Pope. They cannot make a choice. His Majesty hopes that if a cardinal is allowed to join them now, that cardinal might swing the vote one way or another."

"And then they will be released?"

"And then they will be released."

Ferenc mused on this. As a hunter he appreciated the use of strategy over brute force, but he had been very pleased with the notion of leading an army into the city to liberate Father Rodrigo.

"Where is Tivoli?" he asked at last.

"It is half a day's march away," said the soldier. "It is a well-traveled road and a carriage was sent for the cardinal overnight, so I imagine he will arrive here soon. In the meantime, you may bathe and have fresh clothes."

What a strange offer. "Is there something wrong with my clothes?" Ferenc asked.

Helmuth smiled condescendingly. "You are filthy, and so are your clothes. We make the offer to be hospitable and considerate. I have no time to educate you about basic human decency, so either take the offer or leave it—it is all one to me."

Ferenc wanted to speak to Ocyrhoe, but then realized she would be even less educated on these issues than himself. It was exhausting, being the eternally ignorant outsider. "I appreciate your hospitality," he said, restraining his true emotions, "and humbly accept your offer."

pickinc flowers 13

It WAS CUSTOMARY for Tegusgal—as captain of Onghwe Khan's guards—to attend the fights in the Circus. Many of the guards went as well, both to attend to the safety of the Khan but also to participate in the furious betting. Without Tegusgal around, the guards who remained at the Mongol compound had a tendency to let their displeasure at being left behind turn to laziness, which presented an opportunity for Kim and Zug to plan somewhat openly. The Mongols were typically loath to allow any group of fighters to enjoy true seclusion in numbers greater than two, but this afternoon they—and some of the men who they had approached previously—were allowed to gather in the training yard, where the relative absence of supervision permitted them to stand about and speak. So long as they periodically made a show of moving through patterns or drills, the bored guards would not be overly suspicious.

They made for a strange assortment of mismatched and dangerous individuals, a patchwork of potential violence that would alarm Tegusgal if he were ever to see them assembled. *Will it be enough?* That was the worry that gnawed at Kim as he surveyed his motley band.

Madhukar's shoulders rippled as he uttered a sound of dissatisfaction. The wrestler's grasp of the Mongol tongue was not exceptional, but Siyavash, a Persian with a face that looked like it had been carved from marble, understood some of the big man's native tongue. Enough to offer better translations.

"Too much waiting, Madhukar says," Siyavash murmured. "And standing around talking like this is dangerous."

"A little longer," Zug murmured where he stood, leaning against a stave of white wood. The *bushi* was already sharper than Kim had ever seen him, his focus honed like the edge of his skull-maker and set inexorably upon the task at hand. And yet, he exuded such patience. "Unless the Rose Knight has been killed by Lakshaman." The cheers from the arena had occasionally reached them, and judging by the ebb and flow of the noise, the fight was finished.

"We don't know to which of the fighting orders Lakshaman's opponent belonged," Kim said. "'Tis better to concern ourselves with what we know, and what we can accomplish."

"With or without him, what is your plan, Kim?" Siyavash intoned. The man's eyes held him steadily, hungry for freedom, suspicious of hope. These men had all entertained dreams of escape once upon a time, but the relentless yoke of their imprisonment had destroyed most of those ambitions. They were prisoners, surely, but they were not broken men, not like some of the others who were so filled with bitterness and resentment that the very idea of rebellion was violently loathsome. But they were wary of being hopeful. It was a dangerous emotion, the kind that could get them killed.

And yet, here they were. Gathered in the training yard, holding wooden weapons. Listening to the impossible plan as if it were an idea with the slightest possibility of success.

"Kill the Khan," Zug said with a jarring, blunt sobriety. "How, we are not certain. When? When the moment is right. How? That is part of why we are here."

"We are closest to him when we fight in the arena." Kim said, spinning a stave as though he were at his drills. "All we need to is put one of our own in the ring with one of theirs, and there will be an opportunity. If the Khan is killed, the Circus will crumble around him. Even Tegusgal cannot keep order at such a time."

Silence hung palpably on the field between them, broken only by the rise and fall of the wind. The cheers from the arena had died down, as a wave recedes from the pounded sand. Madhukar's face had been stoic as he listened, but now the wide mouth cracked into a broad grin that Kim suspected would have sent every child of Hünern running in terror.

"Good plan," he said in his halting grasp of the Mongol tongue. He thumped his wooden cudgel against the ground. Kim could easily imagine a skull bursting apart beneath it.

"That is not a plan," Siyavash said. "It is madness." Nevertheless, Madhukar's smile was contagious, and as much as the Persian wanted to keep himself free of the infectious gleam of hope, he couldn't help himself. "But I agree with Madhukar," he said finally.

"We will have to get word to the Rose Knight," Zug said. "Using the boys."

"Agreed," Kim said.

"A simple plan it is, then." Zug said with an air of finality. "Often, those are the best. The less we must argue about information, and the more we can act with weapons in hand, the better. A word is all that will be needed, and the understanding that those who stand in the arena will not live long after they make the kill."

There was the wild look in Zug's eyes once more as he spoke, and Kim was reminded again that a part of his friend longed for death. Given what Zug had been through, it was difficult for Kim to begrudge him his wish. He simply hoped that the burning desire did not kill them all. One by one, the others nodded their agreement.

And like that, the planning was done. They stood in silence awhile, listening to the wind of voices that blew over their heads from the distant structure of the arena that controlled all their destinies.

"Are there many flowers today?" A nervous young voice asked. Kim turned sharply, lowering his eyes to find one of the very boys they had been speaking of looking up nervously at him. So many children came and went from the camp, conscripted to bring everything from wine to drugs, that the Mongols seldom paid attention. These children had a courage that any man worth his strength could admire.

"I would hear of the fighting first," Kim said, kneeling down to bring himself eye level with the youth. Behind him, he could feel the attention of the others. "Who has won in the arena?"

"The red-cross knight is dead," the boy said simply.

Kim breathed a tangible sigh of relief. It had not been Andreas in the ring, as he had feared. He looked behind him, catching Zug's eye. "The one with the knives was wounded," the boy continued. "But he will live."

"The task falls to one of us then," Zug laughed.

Kim couldn't help but smile, and to quell the boy's confusion at their words, he rested a hand on the lad's shoulder. "Lakshaman— the man with the knives—will not fight again so soon," he said. "Therefore it will be one of us who goes to the arena. To fight the Rose Knight." He squeezed the boy's shoulder gently and leaned forward. "There are no more flowers to be picked here," he said quietly. "This is the message I want you to carry. We are done picking flowers, but two will bloom in the bloody sand. Can you remember that? The two will bloom together."

the paten and the chalice

ODRIGO WAS GRATEFUL the young priest had allowed him to descend into the crypt alone. He had approached the high altar in the middle of the church, its towering canopy dwarfed by the almost incomprehensible height of the cathedral's ceiling. A balustrade descended into the sacred pit below the altar, the walls lit by oil lamps. *Those lamps have burned unceasingly since I was last in Rome*, he thought, not sure how many days or hours or lifetimes that had been.

He followed the steps into a cavelike chamber, feeling as if Mother Earth herself was preparing to take him into her bosom and relieve him of his burden. At the far end of the lamplit space stood a wall of red and white marble with a low, arching doorway in the middle. On the other side, he knew, lay St. Peter, Christ's greatest disciple, in a repose more peaceful by far than anything Rodrigo himself had ever, would ever, know. The silence was absolute, as if the world had stopped, paused to breathe in the holy air of such a holy man. Even the lamps burned in ghostly silence—with none of that serpentlike hissing they made in the upper world.

Carefully, worshipfully, Rodrigo walked in callused bare feet toward the archway. He was only half convinced the father of Catholicism would awaken to hear his prophecy...but if he didn't, if Peter were too close to God to care now what became of the minions left on earth, it would still be restful to spend a moment by the crypt and pray to the saint for guidance.

Rodrigo lowered his head and entered the crypt. This too was lit by an eternal flame, an oil lamp suspended from the ceiling just above the coffin. For a long moment, too long, he tracked a tendril of soot rising from the flame, studied it as he had studied the marble.

That is the reward and the way of sacred repose, the blessed freedom to think such thoughts, make such observations undisturbed, alone, forever and ever.

Resting on top of the coffin were a chalice and paten, as if the tomb itself were an altar and somebody had been in the middle of preparing for mass but was suddenly called away. He walked to the coffin, touched the cool stone, and felt reassured by its simplicity amid the glamour that entombed it. He reached toward the paten and chalice, then paused, hand wavering slowly in the still, cool air, and picked up the paten. There were no communion wafers on it, and it was burnished gold, unsmudged by any fingers but his own. The chalice likewise looked freshly polished, pristine. He set the paten down on top of the tomb, and reached with both hands now toward the chalice. He cupped it between his palms, lifted it high, then brought it closer to his body. He looked inside.

It was not empty.

* * *

The cardinals had arrived; Ocyrhoe and Ferenc had been washed and dressed in cleaner clothes that did not quite fit them—especially Ocyrhoe, who was wearing a spare shift and stockings given to her by Léna; both had been shortened and the shift belted like a tunic, but she still seemed to float in it.

They stood now with Léna and Helmuth to the left of the Emperor. Frederick was dressed exactly as he had been the day before, except now he also wore a crown. As lofty as his clothing appeared, he himself did not look regal, nor did he speak at all the way Ocyrhoe thought an Emperor should. *The wonder of the world indeed*, she thought. *It is a wonder he is king of anywhere.* Then she chastised herself; Binders must be above such prejudices.

The tent flap opened, and all of them stood at attention, even the Emperor.

"Cardinal Bishop Giacomo da Pecorara," said a young servant standing by the tent flap. A tall, elegant, obviously irritated older man strode into the tent. He was dressed in a much finer red robe than any of the Cardinals Ocyrhoe had seen in the Septizodium; in all ways he was better kempt than they were too. Head held high, he walked with long, slow strides toward His Majesty. Behind him followed another man, shorter and wide-eyed and a few years younger, dressed just like him. The second cardinal had tucked a bulky object under each arm and walked with both arms out in front of him: one hand held a burning candle, the other hand cupped protectively in front to keep the flame from spluttering as he walked. *Why on earth would anyone waste the wax of a lit candle in broad daylight?* Ocyrhoe wondered.

"And cardinal Oddone de Monferrato," added the page boy hurriedly, abashedly, as if he had not expected the second cardinal.

"Why have you summoned me hither, my son?" asked Pecorara in a voice as cold as winter stone. The tall man named Helmuth began to murmur quietly to Ferenc, who nodded, his eyes glued to the cardinals. Ocyrhoe was glad her friend was finally able to understand what was going on around him, in full, while it was actually happening. She had never met anyone with so much patience.

Frederick's eyes glanced toward Monferrato and the candle. He let out a disgusted sigh, rolled his eyes, and cursed. "I'm setting you free, Your Eminence," he said tartly to Pecorara. Pecorara must have already known this was the cause of the summons; his face showed no surprise or even pleasure. "You are no longer required to remain a guest of the empire. You are at liberty to go into Rome immediately and take part in the election. In fact, I would be most obliged if you would do just that, so we can get the *fucking* charade over with and I can return home. If, God forbid, the goddamned Mongols get as far as my empire, and I cannot protect my people because the Church insists on squabbling with me, then the Church is sin made manifest. So thank you for not trying to escape—well, not trying too hard, at least—and you are now free to go. These folk to my left"—and here he gestured to Ocyrhoe, Ferenc, and Léna—"will take you straight to the palace."

The cardinal looked thoughtful for a moment. Then he pursed his lips. "I appreciate my liberty, but I am not the only one of God's chosen whom you have imprisoned. You have interfered with the smooth functioning of the Church at a time when it is needed most. For such a sacrilege, there is but one response." He looked over his right shoulder toward Monferrato. "Cardinal, if you please?" He held his hand out toward the junior cardinal.

"Oh for the love of *Christ*," Frederick said, annoyed. "Not this *again*."

Imperturbable and solemn, Pecorara received from Monferrato a small handbell. He took the handle, turned back toward the Emperor, and with a flick of his wrist, rang the bell twice, sharply. "You have spread division and confusion among the faithful," said the cardinal severely. "By your own willful acts, you have separated yourself from the Church and may no longer receive the sacraments. You are not a person to be followed."

Helmuth blanched. Ferenc tugged his sleeve politely for a translation, but the German soldier seemed too spooked to even notice.

Pecorara handed the bell back to Monferrato, who clumsily attempted to receive the bell, hand Pecorara the other object under his arm, and still hold the candle upright. The transfer accomplished, Pecorara returned his attention to the Emperor, and Ocyrhoe saw he held an enormous book. She guessed it was a Bible, since she could imagine no other modern book requiring so many words. The cardinal opened the book, held it out in the direction of the scowling Emperor, and then portentously slapped the left-hand side closed over the right-hand side, as if he had just captured an insect with it. Helmuth looked very uncomfortable, but Frederick himself only shook his head as if in derisive amusement.

Pecorara now returned the book to Monferrato, and received the candle. Again turning toward the Emperor, he very gravely raised the candle level with his face, and blew out the flame. Helmuth shifted nervously; Ferenc was frowning in confusion; Léna's face was unreadable; King Frederick looked, more than anything, peeved.

"Frederick Hohenstaufen, you are hereby excommunicated," Pecorara declared. "It has been signified by bell, book, and candle."

* * *

For Cardinal Rinaldo de Segni, the world was an uncomplicated place. That is not to say that God's creation was not incredibly complex; he knew his role, which was to devote his life to the message offered by God. Other men, like the Holy Roman Emperor, sought physical rewards: power, money, prestige. The Emperor, for all his learnedness, was nothing more than a greedy man who wanted to exert his dominion over the entire Italian peninsula. De Segni loved his Church and he would not suffer a Pontiff who was willing to submit the Church to the Emperor's power; clearly, it should be the other way around.

Which made writing *Bonaventura* on a slip of paper very easy.

He folded the paper, rose, and walked to the altar. The paten was lying atop the chalice. According to ritual tradition, he set his piece of paper on the paten and then lifted one side of it, drawing it aside so that the paper tumbled down into the chalice. He replaced the paten on top of the chalice. The first of ten votes had been cast.

* * *

With an explosion of bright light and trumpets, Rodrigo left the crypt of St. Peter far behind. A wind caught him, spun him about, pushed his head back on his neck, as if it might break him in two. He struggled, fighting the grip of the vision, but he was held fast in an ecstasy of cracking bone and sacred paralysis. As he feared his flesh would tear, the wind subsided. It puffed lightly against his cheek—a gentle, almost friendly slap—and he found himself on a mountain slope.

His dirty robes were gone, replaced by a thin white gown, and he stood barefoot on the verge of a grove of towering cedars, the aroma of them so thick and strong he could almost swallow it like nectar. He could not see the horizon beyond the trees, but the cedars were swaying wildly, erratically, as if they were trying to warn him of an approaching storm.

As a furious darkness spread like ink across the sky, a whip of lightning snapped the roots of a nearby cedar. The tree let out a groan as the sizzling bolt—like none he had ever seen—solidified into hot, bright silver where it struck the earth, then burrowed into the soil like an auger. The soil blackened and glistened and retreated, then fled from around the cedar's roots. The tree screamed, it was human, surely it was human—it sounded human—and looking up he could make out in the shadows of the branches a human face, neither male nor female but simply human, very human, and wise, a being who had ancestors and descendants and was being severed from both by the roots. The molten silver bolt, zinging and slicing, grabbed hold of the great tree's roots like a hand around a baby's throat, and shook it, shook it right out of the earth until the tree, screeching, horrified and uncomprehending, toppled, and fell with a groan and an earth-shaking *thud*. Its leaves and branches thrashed just inches from Rodrigo's head.

He wanted to comfort the tree, but he was afraid to touch it lest the lightning sense his presence and likewise fell him.

The remaining trees were wailing, branches flailing, trunks swaying, as if they would all bend over, reach down and touch the fallen cedar. Then the heavens shattered, split open by many streaks of lightning. Each tree was snatched and twisted by its topmost branches, as a hand might grab a woman's hair, and each began to tremble as if possessed. Shaking and screaming with one voice, all at once they were sucked out of the ground. They rose a few dozen feet into the air, bare roots shivering off the damp dirt that had sustained them, and then immediately, and in total silence—

They leaned over and collapsed on top of Rodrigo. Trunks crushed him, branches thrust out to pin his arms, and twigs descended to poke out his eyes.

Screaming in horror, Rodrigo lay across the tomb, feeling the cold stone beneath his fingers—but also the press of the dying trees, and he could not break free of either the dream—the vision—or the pain.

* * *

Cardinal Giovanni Colonna's family had feuded with the Orisinis for so many years that the genesis of the hatred had been forgotten.

But that did not prevent each successive generation from clinging to the long-standing rivalry. Colonna, not a man to hate easily, hated Orsini, and Orsini wanted Bonaventura on St. Peter's throne; therefore Bonaventura would never receive Colonna's vote. In all the previous elections, he had voted for Castiglione...but it seemed to him now that *all* the cardinals would be so enraged at Orsini that Castiglione would certainly get all their votes, especially after the magnificent way he had stood up to the Senator. So there was no danger that Bonaventura would win the election.

In which case, Colonna decided, he wanted to cast a vote that would remind everyone of the Church's humble and mystical beginnings. *For the Supreme Pontiff, I elect*—he wrote on his slip of paper—*Father Rodrigo Bendrito.* He grinned, stood up, and walked toward the altar.

* * *

Ocyrhoe could hardly believe what she was watching. Nothing in her training had prepared her for the petty, irrational tension between secular and holy powers. Raised as she was to be fairly indifferent to the sanctity of either, the intensity with which both Emperor and cardinal took themselves so very seriously seemed maddeningly bizarre. Surely men of such importance had greater concerns than this affected posturing to one another?

In response to the news of his excommunication, Frederick had simply sighed like a long-suffering parent. Then he smiled tightly at the cardinal. "Excuse me, Your Eminence, I believe I have made a mistake. You are not the cardinal I intended to liberate. Sorry for the long overnight journey, but I'm sure you'll find the trip back to my castle in Tivoli quite a pleasant one on this lovely autumn day." The cardinal's eyes blazed, but he said nothing.

"cardinal Monferrato," the Emperor continued, in an indulgent, conversational tone. "Seeing that you had the audacity to accompany your friend here without my permission, please step forward, ahead of your unsporting brother there."

Monferrato's eyes, already quite wide, showed full rims of white. He delicately took a step forward and stood beside Pecorara. "Yes, Your Majesty?" he said.

Frederick smiled briefly at the title, and again when he caught sight of Pecorara scowling at the other cardinal. "I asked you to step *ahead* of your brother. You are merely alongside him. Get the hell in *front* of him, man, *you* are the one I am talking to now."

Looking like a rabbit wondering which way to flee from two dogs, Monferrato took another careful step forward. Ocyrhoe could see Pecorara bristle. *What silly games*, she thought. Ferenc was still tugging Helmuth's sleeve, hoping for a translation of what was happening. Ocyrhoe reached over and started to spell out the Latin word for what had just happened, but changed her mind at the last moment. *Cast out*, she signed. *Surely he would understand that much*, she thought. The youth glanced uncertainly at Frederick and then at Ocyrhoe. Ferenc shrugged, letting her know that he understood what she was telling him—this was something *very bad* that churchmen could do to other people—but he was not sure what it meant, exactly.

Frederick didn't seem at all perturbed.

"Your Eminence," said Frederick to Monferrato. "If you will give me your solemn oath that *you* will not perform this same heathenish ritual against me, I will liberate you, instead, and my young scouts here will take you to the Papal enclave. Do not look behind you at Pecorara; this is your decision, and you must make it on your own."

There followed an eternal period of perhaps five heartbeats, as the cardinal struggled internally with all sorts of demons whose power over him Ocyrhoe could not comprehend. It was transparently obvious that he would agree, so when at last he did so, with a single mute nod, Frederick's smile of relief seemed exaggerated to her.

"Very well," the Emperor said, his smile vanishing. "Let us not let this moment of enthusiasm escape. Horses are waiting for you. Get yourself to Rome and end this wearying *sede vacante.*"

* * *

Rodrigo struggled to rise, but the weight of the vision—of the dying trees, fallen all around him—held him fast. He tried to draw breath, tried to call out to God to ease his suffering—surely he had carried this weight long enough?—but his plea was cut short by a fresh, blinding flash. The ground was hard as stone, yet it shattered and gave way beneath him, and he fell a thousand freezing years through blackness, until suddenly he landed.

Was this Hell? It was hot enough—but no, the air was bright and sunny, dusty even. This was some place on earth, perhaps in the Levant.

He felt and then heard a low, melodic rhythm and looked around to see he was surrounded by a thousand men, wearing only loincloths and sandals, sweat glinting from the ribs clearly visible beneath their sun-baked skins, groaning in pained protest against their burden: lined up in long rows pulling at a heavy rope, whipped by cruel slave-drivers wearing hardly more than they were, toiling away at the *something* that loomed over them.

Rodrigo looked up to see what he had already guessed would be there: a half-built pyramid. These driven men were tugging the next huge block into place, and he knew them, he knew them all: these were the sons of Israel, enslaved in Egypt.

The clouds rolled on overhead, tempering the heat of the day, and several men looked up in hopeful anticipation of a drizzle. But with a cough of thunder, the clouds darkened, opened great rents in the heavens—and the rain plummeted in sheets, but this rain was red and warm and sticky-slick: with shrieks of horror and disgust, the men held their hands over their heads and began to run around aimlessly, dragging their fetters and their overseers after them—all desperate for a shelter that was not there.

Rodrigo watched once more as if he stood before a stage spectacle; no blood fell on him, but he could hear it spatter on the ground and on men's skin; the air reeked of it, a foulness that made him choke and gag. As the screams grew louder and the panicked raced about more frantically still, the rain of blood gave way to a slimy cascade of frogs—live frogs, landing in heaps below the angry green sky, their croaking glugs of fear and confusion almost as loud as the cacophony of the men on whom they fell. Many that did not split open and spill their innards were instantly trampled on and smashed flat; others hopped about and added to the bedlam, as Rodrigo watched, knowing with a sick feeling exactly what had to come next.

For as the frogs ceased to fall, the entire dark cloud above descended upon the panicked men and proved to be an enormous swarm of flies, their buzzing louder than everything below com-bined—a ripping, whirring, cutting sound, as if their wings and jaws were made of metal and they had come to saw through every living thing they touched. They bit the men wherever they found flesh, and sharp cries from this stinging pain were added to the overwhelming din, like water dripping on cymbals above an avalanche of grinding boulders.

As Rodrigo watched, there followed in quick, awful succes-sion the plague of lice, the plague of boils, the murrain of cattle, the plague of locusts—a new, striped yellow and black cloud, fascinating to watch—and then, all-consuming darkness. And finally, of course, death everywhere, every first-born son throughout the land falling at the whim of the steel-winged, pock-faced angel of death.

And again the scene shifted dramatically. Rodrigo felt the earth disappear beneath his feet, and he was airborne, high above the catastrophe, the crisis, sailing in the darkness, until he saw below him water that stretched out as if forever...and he knew what this was too: the Red Sea, parting for Moses and the Jews, and behind them, in chariots and armed on foot, came the teeming armies of Egypt ...but the sea closed over them, and with a final scream of defiance, Egypt gave up its possession of the Jewish race.

And the people of Israel, free from captivity, turned their faces toward a barren desert, and set out on a journey that Rodrigo knew would last for forty years.

* * *

Gil Torres, the aging Spanish cardinal, stared balefully at the slip of paper in his hand. He had hated Gregory for keeping him in Rome when both he and the Emperor Frederick had wished his presence as imperial legate.

"But you are so useful to me," Gregory had crooned, "I must keep you here beside me; I cannot imagine how the daily life of the Papacy would function without you."

The flattery had disgusted Cardinal Torres. He knew it wasn't true, but he could not gainsay the Pontiff's wishes. And so his vote had been, throughout this process, for Castiglione—not because he cared so much for Castiglione, but because he knew that Bonaventura would have been Gregory's choice, and he had been determined to vote against Gregory's choice, period. However, after Castiglione's defiance of Orsini, it was obvious that all the cardinals would vote for Castiglione—possibly even Sinibaldo Fieschi, who had been Gregory's most devoted sycophant. Castiglione had even won Torres's own regard. Castiglione, clearly, would be Pope. Even if Gil Torres did not vote for him.

Which was a relief, because it freed Torres to think about what kind of man he'd actually *want* as Bishop of Rome. Somebody as different from Gregory as possible. Somebody without any political ties or machinations. Somebody with the hardiness to survive the stress of the throne of St. Peter. He thought of the befuddled but earnest priest who had somehow—he did not know or care how—survived the scorpion attack. That man had also survived a brutal battlefield, although Torres did not know the details. He had been shaken by his experience, but his faith had not been shaken, and faith—despite the reality of necessary politics—faith was, after all, important in a Pope.

Nobody else would think to do something as radical as vote for the distraught priest, but Torres thought it would be a good slap in the face to all the cynics and politicians in the room, if they heard his name called out once as a potential candidate.

Cardinal Torres wrote *Father Rodrigo Bendrito* on the form, and rose to cast his ballot.

* * *

In the heat and dust and the burning sun, the children of Israel wandered without rest, and Rodrigo wandered with them, a wisp, a spirit, unseen and unsensed by them, but suffering with them.

Moses was long dead. This was some other exodus, some other journey, he did not know whither.

He watched them under the blazing, punishing brilliance of the sun, and realized they had been traveling forever, were eternally traveling, in tents, with livestock, raising children as they went, and they would never, ever have a home. They were an endless caravan, this lost tribe of Israel, destined to wander forever. The king of this tribe was far distant, and they were moving away from the kingdom, not toward it. This tribe did not ride donkeys, nor did they ride camels. Instead they rode stocky, short-legged ponies. And they were no longer wandering around the deserts to the east, but coming directly toward Rodrigo and his flock and his home, determined to overtake everything he held dear.

At the same moment he knew that, he was terrified to realize he was becoming visible to them, they were aware of his existence, some could already see him, even seemed to hear him, and these wary few approached on their short horses and raised broad brown faces and sniffed the air around him. Sniffed, then smiled like wolves, and nodded to each other.

Rodrigo writhed on the tomb, consumed in a sweating, knotting horror beyond anything induced by the other visions, for he knew that this vision was real.

"Clergy!" one of the soldiers spat in derision, and reached out to grab his collar. Rodrigo was no longer a ghost among them, a silent observer; he had become all too solid, and even as he pulled away, the man pulled him down, so that he sat kneeling upright by the man's hip. "Beg for your life," the soldier said in a nasty, mocking voice. Other soldiers nearby in the throng turned their attention to him and laughed with him.

"I will not," Rodrigo retorted in a shaky voice. "I entrust my life to the Lord and His angels, and surely they will come to save me."

As he said the words, the bright blue sky above them cracked wide open and brilliant celestial light shone through, impossible to look at directly, it was so glorious and proud. Rodrigo, with a cry of relief, held up his arms toward the light, averted his eyes, and thanked the Lord for his salvation.

A large, beautiful angel, wings the size of tomb covers, came beating down upon these dangerous, swarthy enemies. Rodrigo's outstretched fingers reached for the angel's powerful hands, and he took in a breath in anticipation of being lifted bodily above these dangerous enemies.

But a sound like hissing filled the air, and the angel, rattled with arrows, shuddered and fell like a beautiful statue to the ground right before Rodrigo's feet. His body cracked and fell into pieces

as if he were made of glass. The enemy screamed in delight and triumph, and Rodrigo, beyond all help mortal or holy, felt alien hands
grabbing him, tugging, intent on tearing him apart.

* * *

Cardinal Goffredo da Castiglione wrote the *C* of his name, hesitated, then stopped. He glanced at the other cardinals who had not
yet voted. They were either writing or deep in prayer, or meditating, or pretending to do any combination of the three. While the
buzzing excitement of standing up to Orsini had passed, he could
still remember what the moment felt like: his heartbeat loud in his
ears; his cheeks warm with the rich flush of blood; the dampness
of his palms. It had been so invigorating in the moment, but this
morning, he was exhausted. He knew he had impressed every man in
that room—several had glanced knowingly at him as they returned
to their seats after casting their votes—but he also knew he could
not possibly behave like that on a regular basis without having some
kind of breakdown.

He did not want the job. It was that simple. Here it was, in his
hand, the time was right and he had earned it, but given the choice
between the throne of St. Peter or a comfortable bedroll, at this
moment he would choose the bedroll.

We need somebody younger, he thought. *To save and serve Christendom
in this dark hour, we need somebody full of piss and vinegar, somebody for
whom such staggering feats of righteousness are as natural as breathing.* It
would take a kind of fanaticism to wrest the Church away from the
dangerous extremes Gregory had brought it to, to return it to a path
of service and spirituality, from a path of power and control.

Happily, he realized, he had just recently met a fanatic, and a
Rome-born one to boot.

He raised the stylus and began to write a name.

* * *

Rodrigo writhed on the tomb of St. Peter, both senseless and fully—hideously—aware of the world around him. The phantom hands still grappled with him—pulling his limbs, yanking his hair, fingers digging into his mouth. He saw other lands being burned and ravaged by strange warriors, other people driven from their homes by savage invaders. The world was full of bloodshed and cries of annihilation. The tomb vanished beneath him, and he lay on the ground in some place he could not recognize, it was so ravaged by war—perhaps a plain that had once been fertile, or a desert that had once been pristine, or a mountain valley, perhaps even a city in which all the buildings had been razed. He could not tell. He did not know if he writhed in calcined dirt or the dust of human bones.

He had lost all sense of time and place, nor did he recognize any of those who raged across his vision. He did not know who belonged to what side, who was good or who was bad, who was in power and who was not, who was a Christian and who was not, who had done evil and who had done good. There were men fighting each other, nameless, faceless, faithless, one human being determined to kill another, with whatever means they had, each set on hearing the death throes of their fellow human beings. No other living thing was of value to them—and no doubt they would turn and kill their allies when they had finished killing their enemies.

To be alive and to be human meant to want to kill, maim, hurt, destroy. It did not matter what a man believed, or how he conducted his affairs, or where he lived. His merely being human meant he was the target of another's wrath, another's fury.

The most base animals do not turn on their own kind so, Rodrigo thought miserably as he watched men slaughter men, and women, and children. It hardly mattered who fought, who defended, who died—no one was to be spared the wrath of the others, and the world tumbled on with terrifying disinterest.

This was the past and the future, and Rodrigo was seeing all of it *now*.

* * *

All of the cardinals had voted except Cardinal Sinibaldo Fieschi. No doubt they assumed he was waiting until the end to make some kind of dramatic flourish, since it went without saying that he would vote for Bonaventura.

But he could count as well as Castiglione, and read men's faces better than anyone else in the room. If Somercotes were still alive, the Englishman would have translated Castiglione's grandstanding into a guaranteed victory. But Somercotes, thank Heaven, had gone to his reward, and Fieschi had no illusions about the impact of Castiglione's brief flare of leadership.

He thought about the demented priest, wandering around somewhere inside the basilica. Somercotes had taken the man by the collar so easily. *If I had gotten to him first*, he thought, *he would have been my puppet. I would have hidden the ring, passed him off for a cardinal, told him who to vote for...and then that fortuitous accident with the scorpions would have made everything so much easier. Idiots like da Capua—so easily swayed by the most puerile of mummery—would have taken the priest's word as gold, and voted as he told them—the candidate I would have already suggested to him! It would have been an easy victory for Bonaventura.*

Of course, Bonaventura had never been his favorite. He was a necessary tool, that was all. A mediocre instrument with which to accomplish a task of tremendous significance: to keep the Church away from the influence of Frederick, who was at best agnostic and quite possibly an atheist. Bonaventura was not especially smart, but he was doggedly good at keeping his eye on the prize: total emancipation from secular power. Beyond that, when it came to all the details of shepherding the masses, Bonaventura was not somebody Fieschi would have chosen to work with, in large part because he was too obstinate. Fieschi would have preferred somebody weak-willed, even feeble-minded, whom he could manipulate with the skill of a puppet master.

That is why he wrote *Father Rodrigo Bendrito* on the piece of paper. He could read men's faces, and he knew—he *knew*—that he was casting the seventh vote for the crazed priest; and he further knew that it had not occurred to any one of them that Rodrigo might actually be chosen.

Fieschi finished writing the name, underlined it for emphasis, and rose. He walked to the altar, placed the piece of paper on the paten, tilted it so that it slid into the chalice, and returned to his seat.

As Gil Torres and Colonna rose to count the votes, Fieschi relaxed in his seat. He reached for his satchel and took out the piece of paper he'd found in Rodrigo's satchel. His eyes skimmed over the words, not for the first time, and he took pleasure in the inanity of Rodrigo's prophecy.

The high Cedar of Lebanon will be felled. The stars will tumble from the heaven, and within eleven years, there will be but one god and one king. The second son will vanish, and the children of God will be freed. Wanderers will come, bearing a head. Woe to the priests! A new order rises; if it falls, woe to the Church! Battle will be joined, many times over, and faith will be broken. Law will be lost, and kingdoms will fail. The land of the infidels will be destroyed.

Yes, Fieschi thought, repressing a smile. *Yes, this man will serve us very nicely.*

UNDER THE NIGHT SKY

AFTER REUNITING WITH Istvan, Feronantus called for a *kinyen*. "For all of our company," he said, "both present and fallen." Cnán felt both honored and troubled by the elder knight's words. Nor was she alone in her feelings, judging by the expressions on the faces of some of the others. But they all fell to preparations nonetheless, building the illusion of a communal feast hall on the open plain.

She found a shallow depression, deep enough to provide some shelter from the wind. From its center, she could almost pretend the horizon was hidden beyond a gentle ridge. It must have held water once, as there was more wormwood clustered within the bowl than the surrounding area. The brush would burn after a fashion, sticky and smoldering until it dried out, and then it would flash with heat and light. Eleázar set to cutting down a supply of fuel for the fire.

Two hunting parties ranged north and south from the depression, engaged in an unspoken contest to see who could provide the best meat for the evening meal. Cnán privately thought neither team would find much, and her stomach grumbled noisily when Vera and Percival returned a few hours later with a pair of scrawny rabbits. However, when she spotted Rædwulf and Yasper a while later, her excited shouts brought the rest of the company running.

Rædwulf was walking beside his horse, who had been conscripted into pulling a makeshift travois that had been assembled from cloaks, rope, and one of Finn's hunting spears. Sprawled on the makeshift frame was a deer with a spread of velvet-covered antlers. Cnán's mouth watered at the sight.

"There are more out there," Yasper announced with a grin, "but figuring out how to carry *one* back to camp was hard enough."

"One is more than sufficient to best our paltry rabbits," Percival said.

"I like rabbit," Istvan pointed out.

Everyone ignored the Hungarian. Very little of what he had said since he returned had made much sense, and they could all see that he was lost in the throes of a freebutton mushroom madness. Though, how he had found them on the plain was a mystery no one had been able to explain.

"There's a herd about an hour north of here," Yasper explained. "And water too, I think. We could smell it, but didn't have a chance to find it. These deer spooked at the sight of us, but didn't run far."

Feronantus grunted slightly at the unspoken details of Yasper's report. A wild herd that knew enough of mounted riders to be wary, but not so much that they would abandon the sanctuary offered by running water.

Yasper slapped the side of the dead animal. "*Tarandos,*" he pronounced, winking at Raphael. "Aristotle's stag. We must be at the edge of the world when we start finding the beasts of legend."

Cnán guffawed at the lunacy of this statement, but the alchemist's mood was too infectious to be deterred.

* * *

Fresh vegetables were in short supply. Most of what the company carried was dried or salted—the meager rations a soldier ate without noticing taste or texture—but Yasper, once he had convinced Feronantus that he wasn't going to make the deer burn with witchfire, managed to blend together a paste that he threw on the fire at regular intervals as the deer cooked. It should have been slow-roasted, cut steaks buried in a bed of white coals, but their stomachs all growled so loudly—and so constantly—as Rædwulf was skinning the deer, that they decided to erect a makeshift spit and cook the meat as quickly as possible.

The fire was going to be visible for many miles, and the smell of cooking meat would spread for a similar distance. They couldn't hide on the steppes, and given everyone's exhaustion, Raphael didn't think such obscurity was high on anyone's mind. Better to fight with a full belly than to be denied one final, solid meal.

They gathered around the fire as Feronantus cut heavy chunks of steaming meat from the cooked deer. Squatting, lying, standing, kneeling—none of them went far—they fell upon the meat with the appetites of doomed men. Even Cnán, who typically ate very sparingly, like a tiny bird pecking at seeds, attacked a piece of meat with both hands, eagerly licking at the juices as they ran down her arms.

We needed this, Raphael thought, his belly groaning as it stretched around the weight of deer meat. Yasper had produced a pair of skins filled with the Mongolian liquor—*arkhi*—and Raphael intercepted one as it came past him. He had not gotten any more used to the pale liquid, but he drank it readily enough. He coughed, his nose and eyes watering, and he passed the skin on to a laughing Rædwulf.

"Breathe in more slowly," the big Welshman chuckled as he tipped back a portion nearly double the size Raphael had taken. Rædwulf grimaced and belched, eliciting a cheer from Eleázar on the other side of the fire. The Spaniard raised the other skin of *arkhi* in salute.

"I have drunk many strange things in my travels," Raphael admitted, "but this drink of the Mongols is difficult to acquire a taste for."

"I've had worse." Rædwulf offered the skin, but Raphael begged off. "That tree sap in Greece, for instance."

"*Retsina*," Yasper moaned. "Oh, the Greeks know many things, but it is a pity that they could not apply the same rigor to the crafting of wines as they do to the natural sciences and philosophy."

"Philosophy cannot solve every riddle, my friend," Rædwulf said.

"Making a decent spirit is not that hard of a riddle," Yasper countered. He received the second skin from Eleázar. "Do you know how the Mongols make this? They prepare the ingredients and attach it to their saddles. As they ride, the heat of the sun and the movement of their horse create a perfect environment for the spirits to arise."

"It sounds like you admire them," Istvan slurred from his semi-supine position next to Rædwulf.

Yasper shrugged. "Each of them is entirely self-reliant. They carry food and drink. Tools to mend their clothes and their weapons. Furs to sleep on. They can shoot from horseback, without any care as to the direction they face. A single Mongol could ride from one edge of the world to the other, and never suffer from any want. One man is dangerous, but when you field thousands of men like this, they become unstoppable."

Raphael glanced around the fire, and based on the expressions on the faces of the others, judged that few of the company shared the alchemist's admiration. Yasper, becoming aware of the silence in which the crackling shift of fire-glazed wood was overloud, lowered his eyes and struggled to find the words to repair the damage he had done to the mood.

"A woman's touch," Istvan croaked.

"I beg your pardon?" Raphael asked, eager to welcome the distraction.

"That's what they're missing." The Hungarian waved a hand toward the shadowy shapes of their hobbled horses. "Where would you put a whore?" He shrugged, the answer seemingly self-evident—even in his demented state. "They can't ride forever," he said. "A man can eat and sleep in his saddle, take a piss, and shit, even. Eventually he's going to have to stop." His head lolled back and he stared, unseeingly, at the night sky.

Eleázar guffawed, and when Raphael realized the Spaniard was looking at him, he felt his face redden. He tried very hard not to steal a glance at Vera, who sat between Yasper and Percival. Separate from him, but not *that* far away.

"Finally, something you and I agree on," Eleázar said, nodding toward Istvan. "What is the point of riding across the world if you don't get to enjoy the array of riches it has to offer you?"

Vera spat a hunk of gristle into the fire, where it snapped and sizzled. Percival shifted awkwardly and leaned forward as if to come to her aid in the conversation, but Vera stilled him with a steely glance. "No," she said, "the man with the huge *sword* speaks true. Were I as *well-endowed* as he, I would make sure to *sheath* such a weapon in every town I conquered. 'Tis only the basic rule of rapine, is it not? Take what isn't yours. At *sword point* no less."

"Eh," Eleázar blanched, refusing to meet Vera's intense gaze. "That is not what I meant. I only—"

"My Shield-Maidens and I were in Kiev when the Mongols came," Vera snapped. "It had been more than ten years since rumors of this invincible army had reached the city—*ten years* of waiting, of living in fear that the stories we had heard from the Cumans about the battle at the Kalka River were true. The Ruthenian nobility dismissed these stories, lying to themselves that they had been *victorious* at Kalka, that they had driven the horde away. They fought among themselves, ignorant children squabbling over lies of their own making, and when the horde came back—and it most certainly did—none of them were prepared.

"Refugees from the cities conquered by the Mongols streamed into Kiev. Our wards filled with wounded, women and children who had not been so badly maimed that they couldn't still walk tens and hundreds of miles to our citadel. These were the *lucky* ones, and though we did what we could for their physical wounds, each was deeply scarred by what they had seen, by what had been done to them. We could not help them. We could only offer prayers that their suffering would be eased."

Tossing her gnawed bone into the fire, Vera got to her feet. "By the time the Mongol army actually appeared outside the gates of Kiev, we were numb from the stories we had heard. From our citadel, we can see beyond each of the gates, and we watched the plains fill with enemy soldiers. Kiev had been besieged before; it was a jewel each of the Ruthenian princes longed to possess. But this army was different. The Khan—Batu—did not want to take Kiev as a treasure; he wanted to destroy it. Utterly."

Tears streamed down her face, and she angrily swiped them off her cheeks. Her eyes were bright with firelight. "I would submit that Kiev was one of the grandest cities in the world. I had watched it welcome all of the lost refugees from the surrounding principalities. It clasped all of these frightened people to its bosom and found places for them within its walls. It was a haven. It was home. And the Mongols burned it all, simply because they could."

After a long silence, Eleázar shifted awkwardly and opened his mouth to speak, but Vera cut him off with a savage slash of her hand. "They are monsters," she said, her voice hard. "Just as the men of the West have been monsters as well to those who they strive to subjugate, and I am not such a fool to think that *all* men are monsters, but by the blood of the Virgin, I will not ride with men who cannot remember the sanctity of their oaths or how to honor those whom they have sworn to protect."

Eleázar lowered his gaze. "I have erred greatly by insulting you, lady of the *skjalddis*," he said. His face was flushed, ruddy even, in the firelight. "It burdens my heart greatly to think that you might remember me by the ill-formed speech, and I hope that the words I have spoken this evening may, someday, be erased from your memory."

A wry smile tugged at the corner of Vera's mouth as she nodded, her hands unclenching. "I have heard tales from some of my more traveled sisters of the sweet-tongued men from Iberia," she said. "Though your speech is rough-hewn, Eleázar, I know it to be from your heart, unlike the words you spoke earlier, and for that I am thankful."

She turned her attention to the other side of the fire where Istvan lay, his head still thrown back. His mouth was open, and he shuddered and gurgled when Rædwulf kicked his leg. The Hungarian raised his head, closing his mouth and working his tongue against his teeth. "What?" he asked, blinking like a surprised doe.

"The lady finds you offensive," Percival said quietly.

Istvan stared up at Vera for a second, and then idly waved a hand in her direction. "Of course she does," he muttered. "She's one of *you*." He let his head slip back, and his attention wandered back up to the scattered stars across the wide night sky.

Yasper was the first to laugh, a dry chuckle that slowly worked its way around the fire, increasing in volume as each member of the company joined in, allowing a little levity to escape.

Vera threw a small stone at Istvan, who flinched as it bounced off his chest, flapping a hand as if he were brushing away a fly. She sat back down, and as she did so she met Raphael's gaze.

He returned it, having gotten much better about not looking away when she looked at him, and he found himself inordinately pleased that she appeared to be comforted by his presence.

* * *

While Rædwulf was telling a war story that seemed as if it would last longer than it would take for a man to fetch back one of the Englishman's longest arrow flights, Raphael excused himself and wandered off to piss. He walked downwind until he was at the edge of the fire's light, and after kicking the scraggly bush in front of him to make sure there was no nocturnal creature hiding in it, he stood and watered the plant.

As he finished, he heard the soft slap of a leather boot against the hard ground, and a hand fell on his shoulder. "A moment, brother," Percival said. Raphael nodded, and kept his gaze directed outward as Percival watered the next bush over.

"Tarry with me a while," the tall knight suggested as he finished. He pointed to his left. "Let us make the night circle," he said, referring to an old technique of nighttime patrolling. Two men would walk widdershins around a camp—one directing his attention to the ground before them, the other keeping his eyes trained outward. The outward-looking man would not have his vision spoiled by firelight from the camp, knowing that his companion was keeping him on the correct path.

"I have been troubled as of late," Percival said after they had walked awhile. Raphael grunted at this, but kept his eyes turned toward the emptiness beyond the camp. It was no mystery that the Frank shouldered a weight none of the rest of them wanted to—or could, for that matter—carry. It was not just Finn's death, or the fact that Percival had had the watch when Graymane had approached. It went back further than that. Roger had fallen in Kiev, a stop they had made at Percival's insistence.

"I know the others are disturbed by my visions," Percival said. "But you have been in the presence of those who have been recipients of the Virgin's Grace; you know how it changes a man. We cannot refuse what she gives us, even if we do not understand what it means."

"We rarely do," Raphael murmured, thinking of Eptor, the young brother in Damietta. Wounded in the horrific assault to take the city's guard tower in the Nile, Eptor had been shaken to the core of his being by the Virgin's Grace. He had seen ghosts—both companions who had fallen during the endless siege and other apparitions. The legate, Pelagius of Albano, had tried to turn Eptor's visions to his own end, even though he had no power over the Shield-Brethren. Conditions were horrendous at the camp, and most of the men were so sick they could barely stand, which was the only reason the Shield-Brethren had not abandoned the crusaders. They would not leave behind those who could not defend themselves, no matter how contrary to their Christian virtues they acted.

Knowing that Eptor trusted Raphael, the legate had demanded Raphael make the boy acknowledge the vision the Church wanted. Raphael had refused and been flogged for his insubordination. Pelagius tried to coerce Eptor during Raphael's punishment, and the legate's brutish insistence only frightened the sensitive boy.

By the time Raphael recovered from his punishment, Eptor had become lost in a squalid terror in his own mind. He had seen something while mentally fleeing the legate's demands, and this dreadful vision devoured his spirit. The end came quickly. He was feverish in the morning, his condition worsening with each hour; by nightfall, he was raving. He screamed most of the night, and shortly before dawn, he died.

Raphael had been with him during the last hour, waiting for sunrise. Waiting for the life to leave the tortured knight's body. His throat raw from screaming, he could only make tiny rasping noises like the sound of a knife being drawn against a leather strop. Raphael had sat as close as he dared, his head lowered toward the other man's lips, listening to Eptor's prayers. He only wanted to understand why the Virgin had chosen him.

"I have seen wheels in the sky," Percival was saying. "Circles of flame and smoke that are not really there. I saw them in the woods when I laid *Tonnerre* to rest, and though I did not realize it at the time, I saw them again the morning Finn died. I was on watch, Raphael, my eyes did not stray. I am a knight initiate of the Shield-Brethren. We do not shirk from our duties. We do not fail to protect our brothers-in-arms."

"We were tired," Raphael interjected. "None of us would have been any more alert that morning."

"I would have been," Percival insisted, and the conviction in his voice stilled Raphael's further comment. Percival laid a hand on Raphael's arm, and Raphael turned his head slightly, trying to see the Frank's face without spoiling his night vision. "I would have been," Percival repeated. "And I *was*. I watched the sun come up. I watched Finn leave our camp to go fetch water. I saw him find the ravine and climb down. I waited for him to come back." Percival's grip tightened. "The next thing I knew the sky had been blotted out by the spinning wheels, and Vera was shouting at me. I wanted to look away; I wanted to know what had caused her alarm. But I could not tear my eyes away from the wheels."

"What are they?" Raphael asked.

Percival dropped his hand and continued his slow course around the camp. "I do not know. They are both terrifying and beautiful. I find myself yearning to see them again, and I have never felt such desire as this before. Not even—no, I have never felt such conviction. And what is it that I desire? The sight of these wheels accompanies the death of those whom I love. What does the Virgin want of me? Am I to become a monster that puts his friends in danger so that he may receive a glimpse of Heaven?"

"No," Raphael countered. "That is not what she wants of you. You simply don't—" He paused. What could he tell Percival? What did he truly know of visions, of what they meant?

"But that is not all," Percival said. "When we were in the tomb of Saint Ilya, I had a different vision. One I felt I had had before. In the woods. It was not the wheels that drove me to Kiev, it was the other vision. The one of the cup."

Raphael inhaled sharply, but kept his tongue silent. *The true vision*, he feared.

"I saw a grave, a tomb of a great man. Resting on top of it was a flat plate and a gold cup. I saw my hands reach out and touch the plate, but I knew that was not what I sought. As soon as I had that thought, I felt myself put the plate back, and I reached for the cup instead. I used both hands, and they were not *these* hands..."

Raphael risked a glance over his shoulder, blinking as the firelight filled his left eye. Percival had raised his hands, staring at them as if he did not recognize them.

"...but they were *my* hands," Percival continued. "I picked up the cup, and I thought it was empty until I looked inside. And that is when I saw the wheels."

He stopped walking. Forgoing his night vision, Raphael stopped as well, turning to face the other man. "What is it?" he asked, sensing Percival had not yet spoken what was truly on his mind.

Percival raised his head and stared off into the night. He looked with such intensity that Raphael turned his head and tried to spy what Percival saw in the night. There was nothing but darkness beyond the camp, and Raphael shivered.

Percival was staring at *something*. It was not visible, and Raphael had a suspicion that even were the sun to be overhead, driving every shadow into hiding for a thousand miles, he would still not see what Percival saw.

"I'm going the wrong way," Percival said softly.

god's plan

NDREAS AND STYG stood in the heart of the raucous audience, watching as the dead Livonian was dragged away. The Khan's man, a ferocious fighter who had beaten considerable odds, had been driven out of the stadium by men with padded sticks. Men who were clearly terrified of the man, even though he was wounded. He had heard stories from the others about the riot that had followed Haakon's fight, about the demon warrior with the pole-arm who had slain a number of Mongol guards before they had subdued him. Clearly, this man was of the same ilk, and Andreas found it fascinating that the Mongols were so cowed by their prisoner.

But it was more than just the guards' trepidation toward the captive warrior. There was a restless uneasiness among them as well. Looking at the seething mass that filled the arena, Andreas began to understand the source of the Mongolian unease. They were mobile warriors, used to fighting their wars on horseback, skilled at covering great distances and making war as far away from their homeland as their great mobility permitted them.

Horses were more of a liability than an asset within the confines of a city, or even the close-knit environs of a forest. He recalled his own ride to the arena, through the throngs of the crowds and the narrow alleys. The Mongols were not weak, but they were not in their place of strength. On some level, they were aware of their reduced capabilities, but they couldn't do anything about it. Onghwe Khan's degenerate obsession with blood sports kept them here; but every day they remained, their confidence waned a little more. He could see it—plainly now—in how they handled the volatile assets that were at the heart of their leader's diversion. *They're as much a prisoner as the men they keep caged*, Andreas thought, *and it's starting to become apparent to them that they've locked themselves inside the cage with those who have every reason to want to do them harm.*

Even as this realization struck Andreas, so too did the urgency of this knowledge. While the Mongols still ran the Circus, their control was less absolute. Order in Hünern was precarious now, and the tiniest nudge was probably all that was required to make it slip, to let chaos in, and then devastation would visit Hünern again.

If I've noticed this, then others must have as well. Moving quickly through the crowd, Andreas forced his way out of the stands, Styg at his side. He had shown himself at the arena, letting the people take note of his presence, and he had witnessed for himself the type of fighters that the Khan had at his disposal, and now it was time to report back to Rutger.

To say that the situation had ever truly been under control was to lie, but the calm that had settled over Hünern in the wake of this seeming return to routine was a sham. Violence simmered beneath the surface of the city, waiting for the slightest provocation. Waiting to erupt.

"That man," Styg said, "was amazing. Call it luck, or call it fortune, but I've never seen such odds so quickly reversed."

"He wanted to live," Andreas said as they reached the stairs and began to descend into the dim tunnel beneath the stands. "The Livonian didn't understand what happens when you corner a wild beast, no matter how strong his advantage might have seemed." He paused, and with a touch, brought Styg to a halt as well. "Remember that, Styg. There are few advantages that can't be tipped when your opponent wants victory more than you do."

Styg nodded. The implications seemed to chill him.

Arvid and Sakse were waiting with the horses, and with the eagerness of unblooded youth, they wanted to hear about the fight. Andreas let Styg tell the tale, falling slightly behind the three men as they rode out of town. He prayed—fervently and silently—that the Virgin would hold back the waiting deluge of violence just a little longer. Once it started, it would not be controlled or stopped. At best, it could be channeled; if they were lucky, they might be able to turn it in the right direction.

Otherwise, he feared, the Shield-Brethren would be its first victims.

* * *

Dietrich punished the pell until the rope suspending the wooden block from the rafters snapped. The wood thudded to the earthen floor, and Dietrich stared at it for a long moment, furious that it had the audacity to lie down on him. Breathing more heavily than his pride wanted to acknowledge, he sheathed his sword and glanced around for something to quench his overwhelming thirst. Something to drown the fury still within him.

His man should have won the fight today. The Khan's man should have been the one bleeding out in the sand, not his knight. Yet another embarrassing incident for the Livonian order. His knight had been better armed and had worn maille that protected him from the other man's inferior weapons. But it hadn't been enough. It hadn't been nearly enough.

To make matters worse, the fight came on the heels of the meetings with the other militant orders—meetings that had ranged from frostily standoffish to downright disastrous. The other Grandmasters had, as a whole, been indifferent to his charges and his concerns. They all had been circumspect in their language and demeanor, but Dietrich had spent enough time at royal courts to read the unspoken distain and dismissal in their carriages.

No wonder they think I am a fool, he thought. *The best man I can field for the arena turns out to be an incompetent corpse.*

He had seen the fight from his usual place at the top of the stands, watching his man stumble instead of seizing opportunities. The hatchet in the back should have ended the fight, but instead the heathen bastard had plucked the weapon free and used it against his Livonian opponent. *His man had given the enemy his weapon!* The whole fight could have only been more embarrassing if the knight had fallen on his weapon and killed himself.

Moreover, he had seen the two Shield-Brethren knights in the audience, and with a creeping, seething certainly, he knew the audience was imagining how the fight would have gone if one of *them* had been down on the sand. The knights of Petraathen would have been victorious.

The rotting timbers of the old barn did little to keep out the noise of the Livonian compound, and he could hear the din of his soldiers doing their drills. Gritting his teeth, he cursed his current accommodations and how they denied him the slightest solitude. The echo of steel against steel sounded so *timorous* that each clash fouled his mood even more.

He cast about for the wineskin he had brought along. Drinking hadn't cured his mood, and he had thought that some physical activity might assuage his temper, but the rope had failed him—*like so much of this godforsaken place*, he thought—and it was time to return to the solace of the wine. There were times when he envied the common man and the ease of his vices. The callings of the just and the righteous could make taking one's pleasures far more complicated than it needed to be, especially when one was a man of position, tenuous though that might be.

He found the skin and took a long swallow. Staring absently at the far wall, he tried to put aside his frustration and concentrate on what he could accomplish.

An isolated *thud* interrupted his musing, and he glanced about, listening. The din of training had lessened, and there was a hum of voices growing nearer. One pleaded, and the other responded in clipped tones, swatting the first man's words aside like they were nothing more than an annoying fly. Dietrich smiled, the wineskin suddenly forgotten in his hands, as recognition of that second voice took hold of him swiftly, pulling his attention away from his frustrated ruminations and into the here and now.

The door to the barn banged open, and two men walked through. One, the pleader, was a new recruit, his spurs freshly earned and his courage not proven. The pale fuzz of his young beard didn't quite hide the lack of a chin, and his voice grated on Dietrich's ears even as he profusely apologized.

"Forgive me, *Heermeister*," the young knight babbled. "I told him that you were busy at your drills, and that he should take a moment to eat or drink after his lengthy ride—"

The other man brushed aside the complaints with a dismissive cut of his hand that struck the pleader across the mouth. Dietrich knew this one well, and much of his exhaustion and dismal mood were swept away by the sight of those cold and merciless blue eyes.

"Apologies, *Heermeister*," Kristaps said. "As this knave says, I have ridden long, but my news is of greater import than the needs of my belly." He was soaked through, his maille damaged and his tabard stained with blood. He could easily be mistaken for a battlefield wretch, a man-at-arms who had miraculously survived an enemy's charge by hiding beneath the fallen bodies of his comrades, but one only had to stare at those eyes for a moment to realize that such craven behavior would be incomprehensible to this man.

God has heard my prayers, Dietrich thought. *In my hour of need, he grants me salvation.*

Sir Kristaps of Steiermark, the First Sword of Fellin. Known to his enemies as Kristaps Red-Hilt and as Volquin's Dragon. One of the few who survived Schaulen; had it not been for Kristaps, none of them would have lived.

"It is a long ride from Rus," Dietrich said, coming out of his shock and remembering where Kristaps had been. "You came alone?"

Kristaps nodded, his face suffusing with an intense anger. "Overall, our errand was a success," he said in a tightly controlled voice. "Later, I will report of what we learned of the land's defenses. It was in the matter of the Lavra that our efforts were blunted by an ambush on the part of the Shield-Brethren." His eyes flashed. "Feronantus was there, *Heermeister*." He spat the name, and those that followed. "As well as Percival, Raphael, and Eleázar, and several others. Twelve all told, I think. Many of their finest."

Suddenly, it all made sense to Dietrich. The Shield-Brethren had broken their oath to the Pope: their best were *not* at the Circus of Swords, minding their duty. Instead, Feronantus had taken a party of his best knights on some errand that had them crossing paths with his own scouts in Rus. What were they doing out there? Did they know what the Livonian order was planning? Were they after some secret of their own? Why had they abandoned Christendom?

There were too many questions, and they tumbled noisily in his head, banging against a gleeful thought that threatened to crush them entirely—a way in which his honor, his order's honor—could be restored.

He held up his hand, more to silence his own flurry of thinking than to cut Kristaps off. There was nothing he could do about the

Shield-Brethren's betrayal at the moment. There was a more critical *opportunity* that needed to be seized.

"We have both endured sufferings at the hands of the Shield-Brethren, sufferings that have as yet been unavenged," he said. "I will hear more of your mission in the Rus, and what you know of these scurrilous Shield-Brethren, but first, I must ask: can you fight?"

Kristaps stared at him, his eyes even colder than before, and for a second Dietrich wondered if he had mistakenly spoken too plainly. It was, ultimately, a foolish question to ask Kristaps; if the man could breathe, he could fight. To question that dedication was rather impolitic of the *Heermeister* of the order to whom Kristaps had sworn his life and his sword.

Kristaps's face lost some of its ruddy color, and the hint of a smile curled his cruel mouth. "Of course, *Heermeister*," he said. "I slew one of their number with my dagger, and God did not strike me down. In fact, He spared me so that I could return and perform more work for Him."

There was the fervor and the passion that his current company of men lacked. If Dietrich could have had even fifty men like Kristaps, Schaulen would never have happened, and the pagans of the North would still know their place. He flicked a hand at the foppish knight who had tried to prevent Kristaps's entrance. "Food and wine," he commanded.

As the younger warrior scurried away, Dietrich offered his wineskin to Kristaps. "Oh, yes," he said. "God has a plan, and I think you will find it very satisfying."

THE STONE RING

HE *KHAGAN*'S CARAVAN failed to move the next morning, and did not appear to be inclined to move the following morning either. As the day wore on and Gansukh watched preparations for yet another feast, he wondered if the *Khagan* and his retinue would ever reach the Place of the Cliff.

He had spent too many summers and winters in the saddle, and his spirit was restless. This inactivity chaffed at him. The Chinese raiders had been routed, and what few survivors remained had scattered. The scouts had found little evidence that any raider remained within a half day's ride, but to stay in this valley was the foolhardy decision of a provincial administrator, not a warrior.

In addition, such inactivity meant too many opportunities for the *Khagan* to slide into a drunken stupor. Any decisive action would be slow in coming.

They had left Karakorum, but too much of the palace had come with them, which is why the routing of the Chinese had to be celebrated. Such idleness was typical of the way courtiers thought: *the Mongol Empire is brave and strong; we must have a feast!* After as many months as he had spent at court, Gansukh wasn't sure why he was still surprised at such a ridiculous decision.

Wandering around—*waiting*—darkened his mood, and on the few occasions when he caught sight of Master Chucai, he could tell the Khan's advisor was similarly concerned about the delays. Gansukh suspected Chucai would join him if he started whipping each and every ox and draft horse, until every wagon, *ger*, and lazy courtier was dragged toward Burqan-qaldun.

To keep his gnawing frustration at bay, Gansukh tried to stay alert to Munokhoi's movements. He knew how brittle his safety was, and even more so, Lian's. Gansukh continued to haunt the circle of tents near the *Khagan*'s *ger*, performing whatever odd job he could find so as to keep an eye and ear turned toward Munokhoi's comings and goings.

If the *Torguud* captain was aware of his silent shadow, he did not acknowledge it.

Now, as the sun began to slip toward the horizon, tickling the bellies of the white clouds with orange feathers, a crowd started to gather about the stones that had been laid in a large ring near the feasting area. Gansukh had participated in the gathering of the rocks from the surrounding hills, a boring and laborious task that had taken up a goodly portion of the morning, and as the rock haulers had been directed as to where to deposit their stones, Gansukh had gleaned a pretty good idea as to the eventual use of the circle.

An arena.

Much of the growing audience's attention was on the two cages facing each other on opposite sides of the circle. In one cage, on the northern side of the arena, a burly man with a body patched in thick black hair, a great bushy beard, a hooked nose—broken more than once and never set right—and dark eyes nearly lost in a perpetual squinting scowl. In the opposite cage, a tall blond ghost of a man, sitting more often than standing. While his attitude was quite passive, his cold blue eyes carefully and exactingly watched everything. Two guards stood beside each cage, and more guards circled the ring, keeping back the growing throng of spectators. People in the mob jostled each other for a better view as they jeered at the captives and loudly proclaimed their bets on the fight's outcome. The *Khagan*'s mighty *ger* had been moved a few hours ago so that it loomed over the circle of stones, and Munokhoi, Master Chucai, and a few other people—including one of Ögedei's wives—milled about on the raised platform near the *ger*'s entrance.

On the western side of the arena—not far from where Gansukh stood, watching the spectacle unfold—enterprising gamblers kept tallies in the dirt and with bundles of sticks as bettors huddled around them, shouting to make themselves heard.

"Three oxen on the wild ape-man from the West!"

"Ten goats on the fair one!"

"Put me down for six copper pieces on the big fellow!"

Up on the platform, Munokhoi strutted back and forth, pleased with the attention being given to the proceedings. Gansukh was fairly certain the fights had been Munokhoi's idea. It was the sort of demeaning spectacle that the *Torguud* captain would relish, and while he had little desire to watch, Gansukh stayed.

The crowd was getting noisier. Sporadic chants for the *Khagan* sprang up, but they had little strength and quickly petered out. Munokhoi's pace became more agitated, and with a last glance at the closed flaps of the *Khagan*'s *ger*, he sprang off the platform. Stalking over to the hairy man's cage, the *Torguud* captain sized up the fighter. Stroking his chin, he took his time examining the big man, circling the cage to study him while the prisoner watched him cautiously. Munokhoi abruptly grabbed the cage and rattled it hard, shouting like a demon right in the prisoner's face. The prisoner did not startle; he stared at Munokhoi, and the lines of his face creased deeper as his scowl intensified.

Munokhoi laughed boisterously and turned away. With long, quick strides, he walked over to the gathering of gamblers. "Put me in for twenty oxen on that man!" he ordered.

It was the other man however, the pale man, who intrigued Gansukh. Though captive and caged, he was fascinatingly tranquil. He did not hang his head in despair, nor did he glower and rage at his captors. He sat still in the center of his cage with his legs crossed. If he was waiting for some future opening, some chance at escape, he betrayed no sign of it, but Gansukh was certain there were depths beneath that placid surface. A great warrior must always search for the enemy's intentions and guard his own.

The dark-haired man was savagely strong. He growled at his captors like a dog trying to establish dominance. Gansukh could see why Munokhoi favored him. Strength, however, was not always a guarantee of victory. If the pale man was swift and clever, he could win the fight handily.

Waiting, Gansukh thought, and without realizing it, he had shoved away from the tent wall that he had been leaning against. "Twenty-five cows on the fair one," he said, loudly and clearly enough to be heard.

Munokhoi whirled to see who had called out, and catching sight of Gansukh, his entire body went rigid. His grin was malformed, uneven and showing too many teeth.

Gansukh did not react in any way. "Twenty-five," he repeated, his eyes flicking toward the gamblers.

Munokhoi was more than an annoyance; he was a very real danger. Gansukh couldn't kill him outright, nor could he continue to ignore him. Lian would argue otherwise—at least she would have previously. After killing the Chinese commander, she had gotten very hard to read. Perhaps she might condone the death of Munokhoi now.

If he asked her. But he wasn't going to. He didn't need to. Munokhoi was *his* problem, a problem that wasn't going to go away. And since he couldn't just stick a knife in him and be done with it, he had to come up with some excuse.

Judging by the *Torguud* captain's tension, it would not take much to provoke him, and if Munokhoi became openly hostile, then wasn't lethal self-defense justified? What better way to provoke him than by injuring his pride? And here was a convenient way to do just that: by publicly backing the pale man against Munokhoi's favorite.

"The scrawny one?"

The crowd fell silent at the voice, and everyone's attention turned to the *Khagan's* ger. Ögedei stood—swaying slightly, cup in hand—on the platform. "You favor the scrawny one?" he said, waving an arm at the pale warrior's cage.

"I wager what he lacks in muscle he makes up for in skill, my Khan," said Gansukh. "Even the superior force can be defeated through speed and tactics." The last was unnecessary, but he saw the effect his words had on Munokhoi.

"I remember your fight with Namkhai," the *Khagan* laughed. "I do not recall you being that swift, nor your tactics very effective, young pony." He let his gaze wander about the assembled throng. "Namkhai," he shouted, looking for his favorite wrestler. "Which do you prefer?"

Namkhai emerged from a clump of warriors not far from the platform. "I prefer to regard both men as equally dangerous," he offered diplomatically.

Ögedei waved his cup back and forth, and wine slopped out, staining both his and Master Chucai's robes. "That is the sort of answer I expect from my spineless administrators. Not from my champion wrestler."

Namkhai bowed his head briefly, acknowledging the *Khagan's* insight into his reply. "If I were to fight one of them," he said, "I would be more wary of the pale-haired one."

The *Khagan* stroked his beard expansively. "Perhaps I will offer you that chance," he mused as he raised his cup toward his lips. Namkhai tipped his head deferentially once more.

Munokhoi spat in the dirt, and several of the gamblers looked nervously between the *Torguud* captain and Gansukh.

Still drinking, Ögedei waved his hand at the guards surrounding the cages, indicating that he was done waiting for the fighting to begin. Cautiously, the cage doors were opened and the two contestants were offered crude wooden sticks approximating swords. The crowd yipped and yelled in frenzied bloodlust as the two men were directed at spear point toward one another.

"The winner," the *Khagan* decided with a glance at the cup in his hand, "receives one cup of *arkhi*." He languidly raised a hand, and when he let it fall, the spearmen withdrew their weapons, leaving the two men, sword-sticks in hand, to face off against one another in the ring of stones.

* * *

Haakon had never learned the other man's name, or even where he hailed from. Now, he might not need to. While the crudely carved shape in his hand implied this fight was not intended to be deadly, his opponent's expression suggested otherwise. The man stood still, solid as a boulder, both feet firmly planted, unmoving save for the steady rise and fall of his hairy chest. He held his stick directly in front of him instead of keeping it to his shoulder or some place where it could not be knocked aside.

Haakon figured him to be untrained in the finer arts of wielding a sword, but the man held his sword-stick firmly and resolutely, as if he had some knowledge of what a hilt felt like in his hand.

He will come quickly, when he does, Haakon thought as he slowly circled his opponent, prowling just out of easy reach. *He will seek to capitalize on his strength.* Haakon tried to calm his brain, but now that he was out of the cage, his brain was a whirling confusion of thoughts. Part of him focused on the fight, but other parts of his mind were reflecting on his situation. Was this not unlike the arena in Legnica? From violence to captivity to violence again, here he was, forced to be a fighting dog for the amusement of these barbarians. And when he ceased to be amusing? What then?

It's what they want you to think. It is the fear that will make you fight. It is the fear that will make you do something stupid.

Impatient, the big man lunged at Haakon's chest. The thrust was quick and dangerous, but it lacked any real strength. Haakon—anticipating this very attack—sidestepped easily, and whipped his own stick out to knock the big man's weapon aside. The first defense every student learned, drilled into them until it was an instinctive reaction. When Haakon tried to snap his stick back for a quick blow to his opponent's face, the man simply raised his arm and ducked his head. Haakon felt a momentary flare of anger at having made such a foolish mistake: these pieces of wood did not have sharp edges like real swords, and a blow on the upper arm and shoulder would sting, but it wouldn't do any real damage.

Growling, his opponent rushed him, using his own bent arm and sword as a makeshift battering ram. Haakon couldn't get his own sword back into play quickly enough, and all he had time to do was brace himself before the burly man smashed into him.

He tumbled back, letting the momentum of the push take him into a roll, and he heard the other man's sword slam down into the ground. Dirt pelted his legs. He came out of the roll into a crouch, looking up to see the big man standing with his legs spread, the sword rising up for another two-handed swing. Without rising, Haakon snapped his sword up, striking the big man's knee with a violent crack.

His opponent howled. He wobbled as he tried to complete his downward swing, but the stroke was slow and clumsy. Haakon scurried aside, and as he regained his feet, he slammed his sword down on the other man's extended hands, feeling the satisfying thwack of wood against bone, and then he followed through with a backhanded swipe. The tip slammed into the man's face, crunching cartilage, and a crimson torrent of blood gushed out of the man's nose.

Unlike the strike to the knee, the blow to his wrist and the broken nose appeared to only enrage the man, and with a roar, he retaliated with a jab of his thick fist. Haakon had closed after the strike to the wrist, and he pulled his head back to avoid the punch. The man's hard knuckles scraped across the side of his face, and out of the corner of his eye, he caught sight of the big man's other hand. *He had dropped his sword!* The second punch caught him squarely on the cheek. His vision blurred and doubled as pain lanced through his jaw.

The big man pawed at him, trying to get a grappling hold; blinking through a film of tears, Haakon fought to extricate himself. His wooden sword was heavy, stuck on something, and the more he pulled on it, the more resistance he felt. The big man clouted him on the side of the head once more, and Haakon's vision split even further. His sword was moving of its own volition now, and he dimly realized that his opponent had seized his weapon.

His arms were yanked upward, and he felt a blast of heavy breath on his neck. The wooden sword slammed against his chest, and he struggled against the big man's sudden leverage. He had gotten behind Haakon, and with a firm grip on the stick, was trying to choke him.

His field of vision was filled with yellow starbursts and streaks of shining light. He had managed to get his hand between the stick and his throat, but even still, he could barely pull any breath. The big man grunted and heaved, his sweaty frame braced against Haakon's back.

He was not going to last much longer. He needed air. His opponent was too strong.

Desperately, Haakon kicked backward. His first attempt missed, but he felt the big man shift his weight. *The knee!* His vision starting to darken, Haakon tried again, and this time he connected, the heel of his foot smashing against the knee he had hit previously.

There wasn't much strength in his blow—the angle was all wrong—but it was enough to make the other man stumble.

Haakon dropped down to his knees, leaning forward a tiny bit as he did so. The pressure against his throat increased as—for a second or two—he was straining against all of the other man's weight, but then he felt the balance tip in his favor. From his kneeling position he then bent forward, and the big man tumbled over his shoulder.

The other man landed heavily, the air forced from his lungs with a sickly gasp. He still had Haakon's sword, though his grip on it was loose.

His vision clearing as he greedily sucked in air, Haakon threw himself toward the supine man, reaching for the sword. Sensing Haakon's approach, the big man struggled to sit up, but Haakon punched his broken and bloody nose. Wrenching the sword out of the man's slack fingers, Haakon jabbed the short hilt into his opponent's throat, and then clumsily scuttled away before the big man could grab him.

There was no need. The combination of being hit again on the nose and the blow to the windpipe had taken all of his opponent's will to fight. The big man was curled into a ball, his body shaking as he tried to draw breath.

Still somewhat unsteady himself, Haakon used the wooden sword as a crutch and got to his feet. Suddenly aware of the crowd around him, he started to raise his hands—and the sword—into the air, but when he spied the warriors with spears approaching, he dropped the sword.

But he still raised his arms in victory, a signal the crowd responded to with an enthusiastic roar of approval. The men with spears indicated he should return to his cage, and with a final glance at his downed opponent, he staggered across the sandy field to his tiny cell. His vision still suffered, but he could see well enough, and he threw a salute to the tall Mongolian standing on the raised platform.

The tall man wasn't quite as imposing as General Subutai, but his clothing was much finer and more ostentatious than anyone else's. And he had a way of looking down on everyone around him that reminded Haakon of the liege lord who controlled the land on which Haakon's village had been located.

Khagan, he thought, recalling the name he had heard from the guards during the long trip to Karakorum. *The Khan of Khans.*

Waiting at his cage was a man holding a wooden bowl filled with an eggshell-white fluid. Before he ducked back into his prison, Haakon took the offered bowl and quaffed it in three gulps. It was sour and vile, but he knew it would numb the pain that was going to visit him soon.

He glanced at the man he suspected was the supreme ruler of the Mongols, and raised the empty bowl.

A humorless smile playing across his lips, the *Khagan* lifted his own cup in return.

* * *

Gansukh did not join the crowd in their noisy exclamations. Half were cheering the bravery of the pale youth, while others shouted insults at the burly, black-haired man. He started to smile, and as soon as he realized he was doing so, he twisted his lips into a frown and turned away from the spectacle.

It did not matter that they were prisoners taken from foreign lands conquered by the Mongols. They were still men, and no man should be forced to fight for the entertainment of others. If they had refused to fight, they would have been killed. And what galled him further was a recollection of the wrestling match with Namkhai. He had challenged Namkhai, in fact, and not because he wanted to demonstrate his martial prowess, but because he wanted to get the *Khagan*'s attention. He was a free man, a warrior of the steppes, and yet, he too had fought for the pleasure of the *Khagan*. How different was he from those men in their cages?

He had sought to anger Munokhoi—and, judging by the *Torguud* captain's clenched fists and stormy expression, he had accomplished as much—but this method was not to his liking.

"Young pony," the *Khagan*'s voice drew his attention away from Munokhoi and the gamblers. Gansukh tilted his chin up and looked toward the *Khagan*'s *ger*. "The pale-haired one is very fierce. You were right."

Gansukh inclined his head in acknowledgment.

"Would you fight him?"

Gansukh froze. His guts churned, and with a great deal of caution, he raised his head. "My Khan?" he asked, attempting to keep his face calm.

Ögedei stared at him, his eyes unblinking. "Namkhai said he would, and I wonder if you have the same desire."

"My desire is whatever my *Khagan* desires," Gansukh said, his tongue thick in his mouth. He hated saying the words, but he knew they were what Lian would have wanted him to say. It was the *safe* response, and here—in the midst of a crowd of warriors and courtiers, it was best to stick to the safe answers. Judging by the expression on a few of the faces in the crowd, he had disappointed them. They had been hoping for another replay of the night where he had challenged the *Khagan* and given him the cup.

Not tonight.

Ögedei grimaced, and raised his cup, draining the last few gulps of wine within. Ögedei too had hoped for a different answer.

As the *Khagan*'s attention drifted, Gansukh took several steps to his left. He glanced over his shoulder as he slipped into the crowd's embrace.

Munokhoi was watching him, a feral smile on his lips.

Gansukh hesitated. *I am not a coward*, he thought. This spectacle wasn't to his liking. He was tired. He was simply opting to retire early. He wasn't running away.

"Bring out more fighters," the *Khagan* shouted, and the crowd lustily roared its approval.

Gansukh fled, unable—and unwilling—to enjoy the gladiatorial bloodlust of the crowd. As he hurried through the sea of tents, he imagined he could hear Munokhoi's mocking laughter ringing in his ears.

He fled back to his *ger*. And Lian.

THE ROOTS OF
OUR STORIES

I AM GOING THE wrong way.

Percival's words echoed in Raphael's mind as they completed their widdershins circuit of the company's camp. The night circle watch had been an excuse on Percival's part to unburden himself of a portion of the mental weight that he carried, and Raphael struggled with the import of what the Frank had told him. Percival had said *I*, implying that the vision he had received was his alone. What did that mean for the company? Would Percival depart in the morning, heading back toward the West?

That was the direction he had looked when he had said those words to Raphael. The endless sky of the steppes was disorienting, and it was hard to gauge one's facing, but Raphael knew—with a shivering realization that made him hug himself—that Percival could feel the Grail. He could point to it the way a lodestone pointed north. As the company continued to ride east, Percival got farther and farther away.

Would his visions become more chaotic—more distracting—the farther he got from the source? Would the wheels—the images that Percival feared were signs of impending death—become more forceful in their apparition? Was his continued presence dooming every member of the company on *its* quest?

Raphael's mind fled back to Damietta, to Eptor's anguish. The boy had suffered greatly, and to what end? Raphael had wondered, in the years since, what would have happened if Eptor had simply died during the assault on the stone tower in the Nile. Would the legate have realized sooner the futility of their crusade? Would Francis of Assisi been able to reach a better accord between Christian and Muslim? How many less would have died during the Fifth Crusade?

And Francis himself, sequestered in the ragged shack at the peak of La Verna, receiving the stigmata. It had happened soon after Raphael's visit to the Franciscan hermitage, and the venerable priest had died a few years later. But had those marks—those symbols of being marked by God—given Francis any solace in his lifelong quest for compassion and unity?

What good had ever come from listening to visions?

The annals of the *Ordo Militum Vindicis Intactae* were filled with stories of men receiving divine insight. He had, himself, told more than one fable to eager trainees about the blessings offered to the devoted and the pure-hearted by their patron goddess in whatever guise she wore. Athena. Freya. Mary. The name did not matter as long as the men believed their prayers were heard. Those who asked for guidance would be given it. Their mission—as hard and as unforgiving as it was—was not a fool's errand. They would be rewarded for their diligence. Their lives—and their deaths, especially—would have meaning.

But what of Finn? Of Roger? Of Taran? Of Eptor, and so many others? Victories were won upon the sacrifices of these men, but was the world ever changed for the better?

* * *

Cnán quietly listened as the men told their stories. When she had first joined the company, she had sat apart from them during the evening meals and had ignored the way their conversations stuttered to a halt when she wandered into earshot. After a few months, they had grudgingly accepted her presence and no longer treated her as a complete pariah. She was no longer a stranger at their gatherings, and, more often than not, they ignored her completely. She had become invisible, and she was not bothered by their idle dismissal; in fact, such camouflage was part of her Binder training, though she had not had much opportunity to practice it over the last few years. She was, unlike many of the other kin-sisters she had met, a wanderer.

She knew enough to know that she might never fully comprehend the vastness of her sisterhood, but she also realized that *knowing* was not required in order to fully participate. Wherever she went, she could find signs of other sisters, and that they would welcome her and whatever news she carried. It was comforting, in her isolation, to know that she was part of an extended family. Over time, in the company of these men, she had come to realize she and they had more in common than she had thought.

The men of the *Ordo Militum Vindicis Intactae* were both knights and vagabonds. Independent, fiercely loyal, and surprisingly intelligent, they were bound by a set of principles that remained unspoken and mysterious to her. Not like the tenets espoused by the zealous Christian missionaries or the mumbled riddles clung to by starved ascetics she had encountered in her travels. The Shield-Brethren, like her kin-sisters, appeared to believe in a grand design, even if each of them, singularly, did not know the full extent of its shape or plan.

They are messengers too, she realized.

Shortly after completing her first assignment as a Binder, she had given up on the idea of family, hurling herself completely into the roles offered to her as a roaming messenger. She made no attachments, avoided falling in love with any boy, and never let herself be drawn into local politics. She delivered her messages and kept moving. She had seen a great deal of the world, and every once in a while wondered if there was a Binder who had traveled farther than she. She had chosen this life, and had reveled in the freedom such a decision had granted her.

And yet, listening to the Shield-Brethren, she began to realize how lonely her life truly was. Few of these men knew each other well before they had begun this journey, but now, they were tightly bound. Even Istvan, as much as the others expressed a near constant dislike of the mad Hungarian. They were—for lack of a better word—*family*.

Yasper was telling the story of the fight in the tunnels at Kiev again, though no one seemed to mind. Cnán smiled as he pulled at his face and waved his arms, imitating the gibbering priest with the flaming staff. He was exaggerating, of course; the alchemist had a natural penchant for embellishing details that made even the most mundane aspect of an event seem exceptionally heroic. She recalled slipping in the corridor and nearly dropping her knife, but in Yasper's version, her clumsiness became a clever tuck-and-roll that saved all of them.

And Finn. Yasper lingered long on Finn's valiant spear work. The hunter, more terrified than any of being caught underground and burned alive, held off a dozen of the crazed and raggedy monks with graceful precision. His spear, a serpentine extension of his hand, darted back and forth—piercing throats, slashing cheeks and hands. The filthy monks were forced to climb over their dead, and for all their efforts, each man only added to the pile of bodies choking the narrow tunnel.

Somewhat drunkenly, his words disjointed and slurred, Istvan told them of Finn's bloody work in the Mongol camp. The

Hungarian was not as good a storyteller as Yasper, and his memory of the raid was spotty at best, but he spoke with some admiration of the hunter's swift knife and sure hand among the sleeping Mongols. *Six*, Istvan claimed. Finn slew six, before any of the enemy even realized death was among them.

Feronantus told them the story of how he met Finn. Following the Livonian defeat at Schaulen, the commander of the Livonian presence on the island of Saaremaa sought to be named the new *Heermeister*. He thought the best way to rally support for his claim was to keep the island under Livonian rule, thereby enabling his decimated order a safe haven from which to rebuild. The islanders resisted, and since a fair number of sons of the island's gentry were apprenticed at the Týrshammar, the Shield-Brethren were pressed to take a side in the conflict. Feronantus resisted, stating such involvement was akin to allowing the Shield-Brethren to be nothing more than hired mercenaries. The men of Týrshammar must remain aloof from this local conflict.

However, small raiding parties began to whittle down the Livonian ranks. These guerilla-style attacks were successful for two reasons: the islanders were intimately familiar with the local terrain; and, given the relatively wild nature of the landscape, a number of men used to such conditions proved to be exceptionally useful. They wore no insignia that could connect them to Týrshammar, of course, and in the end, their presence was overshadowed by the exploits of a single man. A hunter, who was neither one of the Shield-Brethren nor a native of the island. His prowess and zeal were so great that his exploits were already immortalized in song and drunken tale-telling before the last Livonian had fled the island.

The hunter's name was Finn, and he never spoke of why he had devoted himself to the islanders' cause, and Feronantus never asked. When the Shield-Brethren longboat returned to Týrshammer, Finn had been seated on the oar bench with the other men. He pulled an oar as an equal, stayed for a fortnight at the Rock as a guest, and then vanished one foggy night.

When Feronantus and the rest of the Shield-Brethren landed at Stralsund to come to Legnica, Finn had been waiting for them. Without a word, he had joined the company as if no time had passed.

"You always leave out the best parts," Yasper groaned when Feronantus finished his story. "Who was the woman?"

Eleázar lowered the satchel of *arkhi*. "What woman?" he asked, wondering what part of the story he had missed.

"The whole reason he was on Saaremaa in the first place." Yasper smacked his forehead with one hand. "You don't think he was up there because the hunting was good!"

Cnán glanced at Feronantus, who met her gaze briefly, his lined face giving nothing away. Then he leaned back, and the firelight no longer reached his eyes.

"It's not always about a woman, Yasper," Raphael observed as he returned to the circle, Percival not far behind him.

"Is that so?" Yasper retorted, making a big show of leaning forward and glancing in Vera's direction. He had drunk more *arkhi* than the rest of them, and even though he wasn't standing, he nearly toppled over. Eleázar reached out a large hand to steady the slight alchemist. When Yasper had recovered, Eleázar shoved him, knocking the Dutchman sprawling on his ass.

"Excuse the wretch," Eleázar said to the circle at large. "His tongue has come loose in his head. Hopefully, he'll get it tightened before he joins us again."

From his supine position, Yasper raised a hand and made a rude gesture in the Spaniard's general direction. The company laughed, forgiving the Dutchman's momentary enthusiasm; and as Raphael and Percival sat back down, Cnán caught the glance that went back and forth between Raphael and Vera.

Vera noticed her watching, and suddenly embarrassed to have been caught spying on a private exchange, Cnán leaped to her feet. Waving everyone to silence, she launched into her own story about Finn. She was flustered at first, stumbling over the tale, but after a few seconds, she stopped thinking about Vera and Raphael—and Percival too; *how had he managed to get in her thoughts like that?*—and sank into her role as bard.

It was a simple story. One that had little room for embellishment the way Yasper would have told it, and none of the romantic gravitas of Feronantus's, but it was *her* story. She prided herself on her woodcraft: on her ability to read the trails; to know where water and fruit-bearing plants could be found; to move so silently through the woods that the birds never betrayed her position with warning calls to another. Yet, compared to Finn, she was a large cow, blundering through the heavy brush.

No matter how far she ranged ahead or behind the company during their journey, she invariably found sign that Finn had already been there. At first, she thought he was clumsy in how he hid his passage, and then she allowed herself to think she was actually sharp-eyed enough to notice the tiny marks of the hunter's trail. When they had been traveling in the forests of Poland and Rus, she would find tufts of hair from the pelts he wore caught on the unruly bark of the black alders. She would find the occasional boot print—usually only a partial print, at that—on boggy ground. His marks, tiny chips cut out of tree bark high above ground, indicated the presence of water, wildlife, and possible ambush sites; over time, she deciphered them all.

"I thought I was being clever," she admitted to the company, "but I was only learning to see the signs Finn was leaving for me. I know he understood Latin better than he ever admitted, but out in the woods, it didn't matter. He told me everything I needed to know without saying a word."

One day, a few weeks after they had left Legnica, she had spotted Finn near a tiny stream and had decided to shadow him. Moving as carefully as she knew how, she tried to keep the wary hunter in sight. Several times she thought she had lost him, only to have him reappear in a different direction from where she had thought he had been traveling. After a few hours of this cat-and-mouse game, she realized he knew she was behind him. He had known all along, and when he vanished again, she gave up, feeling very foolish for having indulged in such a whimsical distraction.

When she had turned around, Finn jumped back. He had been standing right behind her. Grinning wildly, he had scampered off as she had chased him, only to vanish in thick woods again. "He was a ghost," she said. "I would catch a glimpse of him out of the corner of my eye, but when I looked, he was gone. The only sign that I wasn't imagining things was how the branches shook, as if the trees were laughing at me. They knew where he was, but they would never tell me."

They were smiling at her story, and she felt a warmth suffuse her that had little to do with the fire. She sat down quickly, suddenly very self-conscious, leaving her story somewhat unfinished. But she had said enough.

Feronantus had called this gathering a *kinyen*, and she suddenly recalled what that meant. This was the private mess of the fully initiated members of the order. She had stood up and spoken about one of their fallen companions as an equal, and none of them had objected on the grounds that neither she nor Finn were sworn members of the order.

They accepted her. She was part of the family now.

* * *

As the night wore on, the Shield-Brethren honored their fallen comrades. After they spoke of Finn, they remembered Roger: his perpetual scowl, the endless supply of hand axes, knives, and other sharp implements that seemed to grow on him like fruit; his steadfastness in battle, regardless of his disgruntlement at being forced to fight. They talked of Taran as well—their eternal *oplo*—who, even in death, still reminded them of their bad form when holding a sword, of how often they failed to close the line, and how they consistently neglected to ready themselves for their next opponent as their first was still dying. Even Istvan joined in, though his tales were intermittently interrupted by disjointed conversations held with phantoms only he could see. After a while, the others would take these asides as opportunities to pass the *arkhi* or to wander off to relieve themselves, confident they would miss little of the Hungarian's story.

Feronantus, however, listened intently to Istvan's ramblings.

What secrets do you hope to hear? Raphael wondered, his curiosity aroused. His interest lay, partially, in having something to distract him from Percival's confession, but their leader's enigmatic relationship with the Hungarian had always puzzled the others. His eyes half-closed, Raphael watched Feronantus, trying to read something in the older man's features.

Life on Týrshammar had changed the elder knight. The wind and rain of the north left their mark on a man's features, but Feronantus had been more than *weathered* by his exile. His face had become like rough stone, making it very difficult to ascertain his thoughts and emotions.

One of the failings of the Shield-Brethren's hidden fortress was its very inaccessibility; too often, in the absence of real news, the boys of Petraathen would turn to embellishing stories of older members of the order to entertain themselves. It was a habit that he was not entirely free of himself. The story of the *Electi*'s displeasure with Feronantus and his exile was one of the more widely whispered tales.

Raphael had heard enough legends and tall tales in his travels to know that each contained a kernel of truth. In the case of stories about Feronantus, the reoccurring motif was that the Master of the Rock was a strategist of unparalleled depth.

Istvan was staring up at the sky again, babbling to one of his recurring ghosts, and this digression had become lengthy enough that the others seemed less inclined to wait him out. Yasper and Eleázar were bickering about who should get the last dregs of the *arkhi*, playing up their mock outrage to their captive audience, and no one paid much attention to the Hungarian's mutterings.

Except Feronantus, who was unmoved by the theatrics of the Spaniard and Dutchman.

Raphael leaned forward, his eyes on the bickering pair, but straining to hear what Istvan was saying.

"...can't go to the sea...can't see the sky...yes, it hurts... the head... don't let it look at me...I don't care about your pain...I didn't—no, it wasn't my fault...there is no—no, let me go...I didn't want...I didn't!... who cut him down? Who did it? Who cut *it* down?" Istvan shuddered suddenly, his legs bouncing against the ground. "The staff," he growled. "Where is the All-Father's staff? She lost it, didn't she?... When her favorite son...I don't know...no... no, no, no—" He shook his head. "Not my fault that they lost it. Not my—I don't want...so many horses...don't let it look—"

His voice was getting louder now, and his motions were more agitated. "The bitch lost it," he said. "It's not my fault. I never—fuck you! I will cut off your balls. The crows will eat your guts. Whoreson. Turd-eating cur. *Stop looking at me!*"

This last was delivered to the company as Istvan leaped to his feet—his eyes wild, his face straining and purpled with rage. His chest heaving, he gulped in great draughts of the night air. He stared around the circle, and whatever haze had obscured his vision gradually cleared. His mouth snapped shut, and he scuffed sand at the fire before he stalked off into the darkness.

Raphael cleared his throat. "That was my fault," he apologized. "I was the one who was staring."

"You do that a lot," Cnán offered, giving his polite lie some credence.

Yasper snorted with laughter. "Who wouldn't?" he asked. "That horse-lover is crazy."

"Perhaps he has cause," Raphael mused. His eyes strayed to Feronantus, who was staring at the fire as if nothing had happened.

You know who he was talking to, don't you? he silently asked the old knight.

DIFFERENT WORLDS

AFTERWARD THEY LAY together in each other's arms. Gansukh's hands, dry and rough as the leather they handled, gently abraded her smooth skin as they brushed over it. That porcelain pale surface had yielded gently in his grasp, and the warm pulse beneath traveled from her heart to his fingertips, the rhythms of her body ebbing and flowing, rising and falling. She touched her head to his tanned chest, and her breath fell upon him like spring wind, warm with the promise of life. Outside the *ger* the watch fires still burned, and they made the walls of the *ger* glow. Her hair was sleek as a midnight stream. Under the thick fur blanket her hand clasped his, and he felt how tender it was, how untouched by work or war.

She was of a different world, a soft world, and here she was in his harsh land. It was shaping her as surely as wind and rain carved the rock. There was the faintest ochre tinge to her shoulders where the sun had begun to tan her as it did him. There was a callus on her finger, just between the knuckles, where the bowstring was held. This hand once had never touched a weapon, this heart once believed violence unthinkable. Now his world had marred her.

And her world had affected him too. She brought him alien customs and manners, philosophy, polite civilization. The ways of the Mongols were ancient, customs passed down through seasons beyond count: births in the spring; nomadic grazing throughout the summer months; harvesting during the fall; surviving through the cold winters. It was an endless hardship, but it was what made a man a Mongol. These men now, who swaddled themselves in silk, sat on jeweled thrones, and never lifted a hand to tend livestock, what were they?

"What do you think will become of the empire?" he asked Lian.

She raised herself up on her arms, hair sliding down perfect shoulders. "You'd ask about history at a time like this?"

"I wasn't asking about history. I was asking about the future."

She favored him with a smile as she stretched out a hand for her robe, discarded so frantically some time ago. "History *is* the future. Its cycles repeat themselves like the seasons."

"You are always teaching me," Gansukh grumbled, running his hand down her exposed back. He took delight in how she shivered at his touch. "So what does history have to say?"

Lian elegantly slid her arm into the sleeve of her robe. "Every empire decays, in time. They become old and corrupt, and fall apart, or they become soft and complacent, and are conquered by the young and ambitious."

"Will the Mongol Empire suffer the same fate?" he asked.

She paused, the sleeve of her robe pulled halfway up her arm, and gave him a raised eyebrow. It was a look she had given him many times during his studies, an expression that said, *This question is not mine to answer.*

"I think..." he sighed, and lay back to stare at the ceiling of his *ger.* "It has already begun. The *Khagan* carries a great sadness within him, and the drink only deepens it. These—" He shook his head. It wasn't the fights between the foreigners that bothered him. It was...

everything they represented. They were not fights for survival or for the glory of the empire. They existed for purely base, selfish reasons: the fighters were there to entertain the *Khagan*; the *Khagan* was there to vicariously feel the joy of battle.

"What if he cannot rid himself of his sickness?" he asked, more of himself than of her. "It festers, like an arrow wound that is not properly dressed. The skin may grow back, but the head of the arrow is still inside the body. Eventually, the rot will kill him, and when he dies, the empire will fall as well." He pointed at the thick pole rising in the center of his tent. "Take that down, and the whole *ger* collapses," he said.

"And yet you do not abandon him," she said as she slid her other arm into her robe. "You still see something worth saving in him."

"I do," he said. "I must, because—" He stopped, unwilling to give voice to what lay in his heart. He listened to the whisper of silk as Lian tied her robe. *Was she getting ready to leave?*

"What if he does heal himself? What happens when the empire spreads across the world, from sea to sea?" He broke the near silence with his questions. Not because he thought she might know the answers, but because he didn't want the unspoken question to become true. "What will we become when there are no more lands to conquer? Will we become *civilized*, provincial administrators of our new lands? Instead of feeling the wind and rain on our faces, we will throw on more layers of silk and fur and hide inside our new fortresses. Instead of counting horses, we will tabulate numbers on our abaci. We will not chase the seasons across the steppes. We will stay in one place all year, and be neither Mongols nor Chinese. We will be..." *What?* he wondered. *What will we become?*

"But what of the people you rule?" Lian said as she knelt beside him, her hair hanging down across her robe and jacket. "They will learn Mongol customs, they will bear half-Mongol children. As they change you, you change them. As I have changed you. As you have changed me."

Gansukh toyed with the yellow fringe on the lower edge of her jacket, contemplating asking her to take all her clothes off again.

"How old were you when you first killed a man?" she asked.

Gansukh frowned, annoyed at the intrusion of violence into his thoughts. "Ten," he said.

"So young! How did it happen?"

"We were herding goats to pasture. My father, my uncle, and myself. Five men of the Spring Hawk Clan came down from the hills, thinking they could take our goats. They rode noisily, trying to scare us with their numbers."

"Five against three. They thought they had an advantage."

Gansukh nodded. "They were poor shots, though. I was frightened, but my father and uncle did not flee. They calmly took up their bows, and my father admonished me to do the same. My uncle and father each killed one as I was trying to ready my bow. And then we each took one of the remaining three." Gansukh let go of Lian's jacket and touched the hollow of his throat. "Right here. That is where my arrow landed."

Lian's eyes went to Gansukh's throat, and she swallowed heavily.

"Even then," Gansukh said, "I was an excellent shot."

"Was it easy?" she asked.

"If I hadn't fired my bow, they might have killed me. As it was, we lost two goats to their arrows." He shrugged. "The Spring Hawk Clan never challenged us again."

"What did it feel—" She hesitated, and he watched her quietly as she struggled to ask her question. Her shoulders hunched forward and her body shivered slightly.

"He was some distance away," Gansukh said softly. "He fell off his horse and we left him. I never saw his face." He reached for her hand. "The first man I killed with a blade was in Volga Bulgaria. To stare into a man's eyes as he dies is a much different experience. Some enjoy the feeling." He squeezed her fingers. "I did not."

"I'm afraid to sleep," Lian whispered. "I'm afraid that *his* ghost will be there, haunting my dreams."

"You took a man's life to save mine. Would you rather my ghost haunted your dreams?"

She shook her head, and in the weak light, he saw the gleam of a tear tracking down her cheek.

"Then you did the right thing," he said. He tugged gently at her jacket.

She slid down onto the bedding next to him, burying her face against his chest, and he let his arms fall around her. He held her tight and listened to the ragged sound of her breathing.

How long will this last? he wondered. *How long will any of it last?*

These questions remained unspoken and unanswered, long after Lian had fallen asleep, and he found their roles reversing. However, when he slipped from the bedding, she did not stir.

Gansukh remembered this too. The exhaustion that comes in the aftermath of the first kill. *You cannot sleep for all the thoughts racing around your head*, he thought, *but your body demands it anyway.*

* * *

He was dreaming about escaping from his cage again, though this time he did not try to steal a horse and ride out onto the steppe. This time, when he managed to get out of his cage, Haakon stole toward the center of the camp. The *Khagan* slept in the enormous tent on wheels. It was easy to find, and once he sawed his way through the heavy fabric, it would be equally simple to slay the man inside.

It was all very easy in his dream, but Haakon knew the reality would not be as simple. The Khan of Khans was always under the protection of his elite guard, who would not be blind to his efforts to cut a hole in the tent. He would have to fight at least one man, and the noise of combat would draw others, until he fell beneath a sea of Mongol warriors.

It was a fantasy. Nothing more. A way to pass the time, and while he wished his mind would dwell on more practical matters, he did not fret at the presence of such desires in his head. They meant he had not given up, that he still sought to stay alive.

Haakon stirred, sloughing the weight of sleep. His cheeks and left jaw ached, and his throat ached when he swallowed. The physical reminders of his fight the previous night. All in all, his bruises were slight in comparison to his opponent's. Eating might be a little more painful, but then, the Mongols hadn't been feeding him much more than a bowl of watery slop. Very little chewing was required.

He rolled onto his side, opened his eyes, and froze.

A Mongol crouched outside his cage, staring at him with evident curiosity.

Haakon stared back. The man's jacket and leggings were utilitarian and plain, well-worn and well-traveled, and his face, while not as dark as some of the riders who had traveled with the first caravan, was clearly weathered by the sun and wind. He wore no markings, unlike the white-furred men with cruel mouths and hard eyes who made Haakon think of hungry wolves when they stared at him. This one was different. No less feral. Unlike many of the silk-robed Mongols who had wandered by his cage to gawk, there was clear intelligence in this man's gaze.

Seeing that he was awake, the Mongol made a noise in his throat and indicated that Haakon should sit up. Haakon considered ignoring the man's gesture, but after a moment he pushed himself up to a seated position and coolly stared at the Mongol. He kept his face expressionless: if he smiled, he might appear a fool; if he grimaced, it might be taken as a threat.

The man seemed familiar, and Haakon suspected he had been at the fight the previous night. He tried to recall details from the sea of faces that had surrounded the ring of stones, but other than the *Khagan* and a few of the others who had also stood on the raised platform, he could not remember any of the faces in great detail.

The Mongol tapped his chest. "Ghan-sook," he said.

Haakon nodded. Easy enough to understand. "Hawekoon," he replied, drawing out the syllables much like he had for the general weeks ago.

From somewhere inside his jacket Gansukh produced a strip of dried meat. He tossed it close to the cage and watched as Haakon crawled over to the bars to retrieve the meat. He tore off a piece with his teeth and chewed it slowly, letting the taste linger in his mouth. It was fresher than the strips the guards had been giving him, and Haakon suspected it was from the warrior's own supply. He raised the remainder to his lips and tipped his head in thanks.

Gansukh grunted and stood up, his knees popping. He began to pantomime, and Haakon quickly interpreted the gestures to mean, *You fought another man; other man lost.*

Haakon nodded again. "Yes," he said in Mongol tongue. "I fight."

Gansukh smiled. "You fight," he replied, and then he said something else, which was beyond Haakon's limited vocabulary. Reading Haakon's shrug, Gansukh took to pantomime again, though this series of gestures was harder to follow. He pointed at Haakon, mimed holding a sword, made mock slashes in the air, and then he pointed to himself and pretended to be...

Haakon shook his head. "I don't understand," he said in his native tongue. He tried to think of how to say the same thing in Mongolian. He could say "no," but that wasn't what he wanted to tell the warrior.

Gansukh tried the pantomime again, refining his gestures. *You fight* was easy to read. *I...watch.* Haakon nodded, following that much. The last part was trickier.

Haakon smiled as he deciphered Gansukh's signs. *He wants to see* how *I fight*, he realized.

Haakon took his time getting up, stretching his stiff limbs as best he could in the cramped space of his cage. He bristled somewhat at the idea that he was expected to perform for this man, but another part of his mind considered the benefit of this man's interest. At the very least, he might be able to bargain for more dried meat.

Haakon put his hands together as if he were holding a sword and settled into a simple stance. He had to duck his head forward and hunch his shoulders due to the cage, but Gansukh seemed to understand what he was doing.

The warrior mimed drawing a sword of his own and he held it out before him, the imaginary tip pointed at Haakon's chest.

Haakon responded, twisting his hands up to beside his head. Imagining his own sword point, he thrust his hands forward quickly, and Gansukh clapped his right hand to his left shoulder, crying out in mock pain.

Haakon laughed. The young warrior played the fool well, and his judgment as to where Haakon's point would have struck was sound. Gansukh left off his playacting and brought his hands together over his head with a sharp clap. He swung them down, a quick overhead stroke of his imaginary sword, and Haakon reacted instinctively.

In his mind's eye, he saw where the blade would fall, and he brought up his hands to parry as he slid a half step to his right. He barked his knuckles on the rough ceiling of his cage, and he growled lightly in his throat. He knew the appropriate response—he could hear Taran's voice, telling him to strike quickly and true, making the long diagonal cut from the shoulder to the groin—but there wasn't enough room to perform that motion.

Haakon lowered his arms and shrugged. "Can't fight in cage," he said.

"A horse can't run when it is hobbled," Gansukh replied with a nod. He looked down at his hands as if he were examining his imaginary sword, and then with another curt nod, he departed, leaving Haakon to wonder what the young warrior had hoped to learn from their mock battle.

* * *

The shaman's tent squatted on the verge of the caravan, leaning, like an old tree, away from the rest of the tents. The shaman's horse, a bony gray gelding, quietly cropped a ridge of dry grass nearby, and an unruly pile of colorful blankets lay near the loose flap of the tent.

As Master Chucai approached the tent, the old gelding raised its head, regarded him for a moment, and then resumed its unhurried grazing. Chucai eyed the pile of blankets, and having gotten a whiff of the smell coming from them he decided to keep his distance. He cleared his throat noisily as he peered past the pile into the dim interior of the tent.

There was a rattle of wood and metal, and part of the pile moved. A bony foot extruded, and soon after—from another side—a hand followed. As the pile quivered and shifted, Chucai caught sight of a cracked set of antlers, festooned with bits of dull metal and shards of bone. The antlers rose up like the ghost of an ancient spirit, and a cracked and weathered face emerged from the blankets. There was a bulbous knob of a nose and a ragged hole that Chucai suspected was a mouth; only one of a set of eyelids managed to flicker open.

Chucai bowed, holding his beard against his belly so that it didn't drag on the ground. "O servant of the wind and sky, I seek your guidance," he began. "There is a matter that puzzles me greatly as of late."

The shaman continued to shift around in his expansive layers of clothing as if he were trying to find a more comfortable position. Or perhaps he was simply trying to find something he had lost among the voluminous folds of his robes. Either way, his expression did not change, and the gaze of his single eye remained fixed on Master Chucai.

"The great Spirit Banner of the *Khagan*," Chucai continued. "Ögedei received it from his father, and I wish to know how his father—Genghis Khan—acquired it."

"Temujin."

It took Chucai a moment to realize that the shaman had said something coherent. *Temujin*. The name by which Genghis Khan had been known before he had become the great leader who had united the clans. "Yes," he acknowledged. "Temujin."

"Temujin went into the mountains," the shaman croaked. "Genghis Khan returned."

"With the banner?" Chucai asked, trying to interpret what the shaman was telling him.

"The womb of the spirits," the shaman said. "The belly of Eternal Heaven."

"Is that where the banner came from? Is there a spirit in it?"

The shaman wheezed and cackled, a nasty barking sound that was strange enough to spook the gelding, which raised its head and snorted noisily at the laughing pile of blankets. "There are spirits everywhere, bearded master," the shaman explained when the stream of laughter dried up. "If you shatter a rock, do you shatter the spirit too, or does it live in every shard? When you cut down a stalk of grain, does the spirit pass into every seed?"

"I do not know," Chucai said.

"If you cut off the head, does the body die?"

"Yes," Chucai admitted. He smoothed down his beard. "I had hoped to learn more about the Spirit Banner, wise one. I have not come to engage in riddles."

The shaman opened his other eye and stared fixedly at Chucai. "I am talking about the banner," he croaked. "You are not listening." A bony finger jabbed forth from the robes. "Why does the body die?" the shaman asked again. "Why? Is it because the spirit has abandoned it?"

"I suspect it has more to do with the head being separated from the body," Chucai replied, reluctant to play the shaman's game.

"But you could sew the head and body back together," the shaman said.

"It's—" Chucai shook his head and sighed. "I confess the mystery of death is beyond my knowledge."

"It is not death you should concern yourself with," the shaman snorted. "Life, bearded master. That is what you should be worrying about. *Life.*"

"Is the banner alive? Is that what you are telling me in this maddening fashion?"

"The banner is a piece of wood," the shaman snapped, his voice suddenly harsh and dry. "It is the spirit that is alive."

raphael's book

NÁN STARTED AWAKE as Feronantus prodded her gently with his boot. She lurched upright, feeling the sky wheel around her, and she slapped her hands against the ground in an attempt to right herself. Blinking heavily, she tried to recall the last few moments of the previous night, yet there was nothing in her head but a hideous yowling sound. She tried to lick her lips, and found her tongue too dry to provide any moisture.

The sky was shifting away from black, bands of purple and blue sliding into one another, each one lighter than the last, until they became a roseate glow over her left shoulder. A few bright stars still twinkled in defiance of the coming dawn—laughter light from the heavens.

She raised her arms, no longer assailed by the vertigo of being suddenly awoken, and shook the sleep from her frame. She had not drunk as much as some of the others, but her mouth still felt like it was coated with sand. She peered at the misshapen lumps of the other members of the company as Feronantus moved among them, prodding and poking with his boot as he went. There was a great deal of groaning and complaining that rose in the old knight's wake.

"Up, you lazy dogs," Feronantus barked. "You lie about like indolent princes, waiting for me to wipe your asses and prechew your food for you."

"Ach," Yasper swore, cradling his head in his hands. "That sounds revolting."

"Which?" Raphael asked.

"The latter," Yasper shuddered. He put a hand over one eye, tilted his head to the side, and opened and closed his mouth several times. "I should not have slept on my side," he groaned.

"I'm glad you did," Eleázar said. "Every time you rolled over, you started to make a horrible choking noise."

"I did not," the alchemist said.

"You did," Vera noted. "I had a wolfhound once that made a noise like that when he was choking on a rabbit bone."

Yasper popped his lips a few times. "What happened to him?" he asked when his efforts appeared to have little effect on his internal condition.

Vera stretched until something moved into its proper place in her back. "He ate one rabbit too many."

Cnán, who had been counting bodies, came up one short, and shifted her attention to the horses. "Where's Istvan?" she asked, discerning a similar shortness in the number of horses.

"Scouting," Feronantus replied. He rocked Rædwulf with his foot. The Englishman hadn't reacted to more subtle attempts to wake him.

"In his condition?" Vera asked.

Nimbly avoiding an angry swipe of Rædwulf's hand, Feronantus let the big archer's body slump back against the ground. "His *condition* roused him before dawn. At which time, he and I had a discussion about Graymane and our route." He glowered at the Shield-Maiden. "Unlike the rest of you, Istvan can handle his drink, and woke this morning with a clear head and a willing spirit. Which is why I gave him the *easiest* of the tasks that we will undertake today."

The last elicited a groan from Yasper.

"What news of Graymane?" Raphael asked quietly, and Cnán recalled the circumstances under which they had found Istvan: ahead of them, bewildered, and lost in a haze of freebutton madness.

"He did not tarry at Saray-Jük. Whoever he is, he no longer concerns himself with trying to stop us. I doubt he understands our true mission, but we did not flee back to the West after our assault on his camp. He must suspect our goal lies in the East. He hopes to beat us there."

Eleázar shook his head as he folded his blanket. "And raise the entire Mongol Empire against us," he said.

"We're doomed," Yasper sighed.

"This changes nothing," Feronantus reminded him. He swept his gaze across the whole company. "He does not know whom we mean to strike, or when, or where. He knows nothing of import, and the sheer...*impossibility* of what he suspects means it will take some time before he can convince anyone to listen to him. Even then, he must mobilize a response, and still *find us*. By then, it will be too late."

"Aye," Percival nodded. "We must be swift and true."

"We will still meet Benjamin at the rock, and we may still travel with him along the trade route, but speed matters. More so than ever." Feronantus nodded toward the cluster of hobbled horses. "This will be our last full camp. From here on, we must become like them. We must eat, sleep, and piss from the saddle. Kiss the ground, my brothers and sisters, for you will not rest upon its breast for some time."

Rædwulf, who had propped himself up on one elbow, lay back down, his arms splayed out.

Feronantus looked down at the archer for a moment, and something akin to a smile tugged at the corner of his stern mouth. "Yasper," he called. "We are in need of your potions."

The alchemist, who had been routing around in his saddlebags, paused, his expression suddenly wary. "How so?" he asked.

"Rædwulf—" Feronantus prodded the archer gently with his foot—"will be bringing down several more deer this morning. The meat will need to be cured."

"That—that'll take a week," Yasper complained. "Even if I had the supplies."

"You have until first light tomorrow," Feronantus countered. He shoved Rædwulf again. "Get your bow and knife. I suspect the Dutchman will find a way, but he'll need as much of the day and night as your swiftest arrow can provide."

Rædwulf grunted and rolled to his feet, his lackadaisical attitude vanishing like a wisp of smoke.

"Percival, Eleázar," Feronantus continued, his voice the flat and hard tone of command. "Go with Rædwulf. He will need strong backs. Vera and Raphael: find their water source. Cnán—" he paused, and this time the smile did actually quirk his lips—"help the alchemist find his elusive salt."

* * *

They rode in comfortable silence: Vera, as if she could read the multitude of thoughts whirling through his brain, led their effort to find the stream Rædwulf and Yasper had seen the other day; Raphael let his horse follow hers, while his mind churned. More than once his hand strayed to his saddlebag, where he kept his private journal.

The book was a treasure he had picked up some time ago when he had passed through Burgundy. He and several other Shield-Brethren had provided protection for a group of Cistercians returning to their abbey at Clairvaux, and while one of the brothers recovered from an arrow wound received on the journey, he had explored the abbey. The monks had been pleased to discover a like-minded soul in one of the martial orders, and the abbot had personally given him a tour of the abbey's substantial library.

He was drawn to the Cistercians' collection of illustrated manuscripts like a magpie to a piece of shiny brass, and he spent numerous afternoons with the scribes, endlessly asking questions like a curious child and watching—with rapt attention—as they painstakingly copied text from aged scrolls that were in danger of crumbling from the slightest touch. The chief scribe, so amused by Raphael's guileless enthusiasm, had a book made for the inquisitive knight—a sheaf of blank pages bound between two unadorned boards. The book lacked the extravagance (and weight) of the tomes commissioned by Burgundian nobility, but it was also of a size that fit easily into a saddlebag.

Bring it back to us, the chief scribe had told him. *When it is filled with your words.*

It was a strange request, and for many months, Raphael had been reluctant to besmirch the virgin parchment of his book. Such hubris to think that *his* words would be worthy enough to be placed on the same shelf as the *evangelion,* the *horae,* and the psalters he had seen in the library at Clairvaux! When he needed to meditate, to empty his mind before battle, he would look at the blank pages and lose himself in the striations in the parchment. Over time, each page took on its own character, the lines and whorls suggesting images that were hidden in the parchment; and one day, he had taken a piece of charcoal to a page in an effort to manifest the ghostly image.

Other images followed; eventually, he added annotations. His awkward scrawl looped around the heads of his portraits like textual halos. Cryptic references piled atop one another, creating striated layers of history that charted both the passage of the seasons and his route across Christendom. The early text was Latin, but gradually he started to default to whatever language was most relevant to the event he was trying to capture. Doing so, he discovered, helped keep the tongue fresh in his head. The few notations he had scribbled down about Benjamin were in Hebrew, for example, while his record of the visit to the tomb of St. Ilya were a combination of the Ruthenian script and Greek, the closest approximation of the Slavic alphabet that he knew.

Eventually, the urge to look through its pages became too great, and he tugged the book out of his saddlebag. He wasn't sure what he hoped to find in the pages of his journal, though much like the *horae*—the Book of Hours—that Burgundian nobles had commissioned for their wives, perhaps what he sought was not illumination but comfort. His recollection of the past, the faces he drew so that he would not forget them, the names and deeds of those who died: these were subjective records, his attempt to mark the passage of time.

Raphael was unsettled by the events of the previous night, both Percival's admission of despair and Istvan's erratic interjections. He was not overly superstitious—among his brethren, he had a reputation for healthy skepticism—but he could not shake a sense of foreboding. *Too many visions*, he reflected as he turned the pages. *Our path is occluded by this confusion.*

"You remind me of the *hesychasmos*."

Raphael looked up from his examination of his journal. "Who?" he asked.

"The priests of *Pechersk Lavra*," Vera said. "They would stand for hours in the cathedral, meditating." She raised a hand and rubbed several fingers together. "Worrying their *chotki*—their prayer ropes."

Suddenly self-conscious, Raphael closed the journal and absently slipped it back into his saddlebag. "Saying their prayers," he nodded. *Seeking comfort in their rituals*, he thought. *Is that what my book has become?*

"They called it the *Scala*, a ladder they were trying to climb." She shrugged. "A mental exercise, I suppose, and not unlike some of our own drills, but I never did understand what purpose a ladder served. You cannot climb up to Heaven."

"No, of course not," Raphael said thoughtfully, recalling the aerie of Francis of Assisi at the top of La Verna. *The closest you can get to God and still have your feet upon the ground.*

He shifted in his saddle, setting aside the memory of the nearly blind friar and his scarred hands. "Do the *skjalddis* offer tribute to the Virgin?" he asked.

"Mary?" Vera asked, a cautious note in her voice. "Or are you referring to the older traditions?"

"I have seen so many ways of worshipping God that I don't care to judge any," Raphael offered, a wry smile tugging at his lips. "The Shield-Brethren heritage goes back a long way; most of those in Petraathen have forgotten our origins, and those in Týrshammar have been under the sway of the Northmen for many years. The old ways linger, though: the glory offered by battle, the sanctuary of the sword, the visions offered to those who are worthy..."

"The *Christian* worship of Mary does not include visionary practices," Vera pointed out. She spoke bluntly, as always, but Raphael had learned to read some of her subtle mannerisms. Lately, he had begun to detect an austere wit in her words.

"Does she not offer guidance then?"

"Little has been offered, of late." Vera nudged her horse closer to his, as if to make their conversation more confidential, even though they were surrounded by miles of open terrain. "Your brother, Percival, for all his Christian trappings, appears to still believe in these older traditions..."

"Yes," Raphael said. "As does Istvan, I fear."

And Feronantus too? He wondered silently.

Vera snorted. "Istvan is addled by his mushrooms. His mind is too broken."

"Did you hear what he said last night?"

"Madness and nonsense," she said, her eyes flashing. "That is all I heard."

"He spoke of the All-Father. And of a staff. And—"

"Odin carried a spear. Not a staff."

"Odin?"

"The All-Father." Seeing Raphael's expression, Vera laughed. "You are a child of Christendom, my friend, regardless of how enlightened you strive to appear. We may appear Christian—like yourselves—but the *skjalddis* remember our roots too. Our grandmothers and their mothers before them were Varangian, and we remember the stories of the cold sea, of the war between the giants and the *Aesir*, and the tales of *Yggdrasil*."

"Egg—?"

"*Yggdrasil*," Vera repeated. "The World Tree."

Raphael shivered. "What happened to it?"

"Nothing. It stands at the center of the world. The fields of *Fólkvangr* are supported by its branches, and *Hel* lies beneath its roots."

"He said it was cut down."

"Who? Istvan? He is mad, Raphael. You cannot believe anything he says. If *Yggdrasil* were to be cut down, *Ragnarök* would be upon us." Vera shook her head. "The Mongols are a scourge upon the world, but they are not the end of it. They are just men. They are not..." She trailed off, unwilling to speak of a greater terror. She raised an arm to indicate the open steppes. "This place inspires fear in its endlessness. You cannot let its emptiness rule your mind, Raphael. We all seek guidance, but we cannot invent it where it does not truly exist."

"What about Percival and his vision?" Raphael asked. "Do you think he is mad as well, or has he been granted guidance?"

Vera lowered her arm and pointed. "Look," she said. "I see a shadow. A gully. I suspect we'll find our water source there." She snapped her reins, and her horse snorted as it began to trot toward the shadow snaking across the plain.

Raphael gathered his reins, but did not immediately follow. She hadn't answered his question, and he suspected she would pretend to have forgotten he had asked it. She had welcomed his attention, even going so far as to allow him to think that he knew her, but he wasn't that naive. Like all of them, she wore a great deal of emotional armor.

But it wasn't her reticence that worried him, nor whether she believed that Percival had been granted spiritual guidance. It was the *possibility* of such guidance that continued to confound him. If Eptor's madness had been the Virgin's Grace, or Francis's insistence that God had left a mark on his flesh was true, then Percival's vision could be true. As could Istvan's.

Ragnarök, he thought. *Yggdrasil*.

He thought of Damietta, and the zeal with which Pelagius, the legate, had seized upon the idea of having Eptor's madness interpreted as prophecy. What were the Crusades but zealous men striving to realize some vision they thought they had been given? Pelagius had invented a myth to convince the army to march on Cairo; the crusaders had been slaughtered because of his lie.

Feronantus had been listening to Istvan, and Raphael wondered again what the old knight had heard in the other's mad mutterings. Feronantus had been at Týrshammar a long time. What stories had he heard from the children of the Varangians?

And had he come to believe those stories?

CANTATE DOMINO CANTICUM NOVUM 21

THE CUSTOM, AS old as the Church herself, was that the names. would be announced by the most senior cardinal. He would draw the names from the chalice, one by one, and read each aloud to the assembled host of cardinals. He would then hand the slip to his assistant, the second-oldest cardinal, who would repeat the name. Finally, using a needle, the slip would be strung on a red thread that had been prepared by younger priests and left in the room the night before.

Bundled together on the red threads, the first three had been inscribed with *Bonaventura*. This came as no surprise, although based on his unexpected standoff with Senator Orsini the day before, the collective assumption was that Castiglione would be getting most of the remaining votes.

When Cardinal Torres read the name on the fourth strip—*Father Rodrigo Bendrito*—Fieschi noted the reaction of several of the cardinals. Gloating quietly, they glanced around at the others as if to say, "Ha! Take that!" There was, briefly, an air of repressed amusement in the room.

But when the fifth strip also contained Father Rodrigo's name, the cardinals looked startled, glancing almost guiltily at each other.

Fieschi raised his hand casually to cover the smile he couldn't quite suppress. Their expressions were only going to grow more pronounced over the next few minutes.

Fieschi had been watching the faces of the others during the election process and had kept a dutiful count. He already knew that every remaining slip of paper in that chalice had Bendrito's name on it. The crazy wayward stranger, the common priest lost in his own world of madness, was about to be elected as the next Bishop of Rome. Fieschi settled back in gilded anticipation.

The sixth strip: *Bendrito.* The scores were now even. Alarm was exchanged between certain parties; astonishment from others. Colonna and Capocci, the eternal clowns, traded looks that bordered on perverse delight. *They do not understand what they have done. It is all childishly unreal to them,* Fieschi thought with contempt. *All that matters is their petty satisfaction in watching Bonaventura lose.*

"Father Rodrigo Bendrito," Cardinal Torres read aloud. His aged face showed no expression as he handed the seventh strip to Cardinal Colonna, who repeated the name and added it to the others. Every cardinal in the room sat up in his seat, or shifted about, some with consternation, others relief. Since there were ten cardinals voting, Bonaventura needed seven votes to win; Father Rodrigo, by having claimed four votes, now made that impossible.

"That's that, then," Annibaldi ventured. "Another deadlock. Send up the black smoke." He started to stand.

"No," Fieschi said sharply. "We cannot say there is a deadlock until *all* the votes have been read."

Every head in the room turned to look at him, all equally surprised at such a statement from Bonaventura's most vocal supporter.

"We must do this honorably," Fieschi said with dripping condescension. "All the votes must be counted, even though we know there will be no success in it."

"It will be a deadlock," said Torres in a tone of concession, clearly disliking ever having to agree with Fieschi. "Arithmetic gives us that."

"Count the votes," Fieschi said. "We must have a record, amongst ourselves, of where we stand."

The eighth strip of paper: *Father Rodrigo Bendrito*. Again the return to darting glances.

"We should annul the votes," said de Segni. "If we stop now—"

"And what is your precedent for breaking with this long-standing ritual?" Fieschi asked. "This is our tradition. We must remain firm of purpose and trust that God's will be done."

The ninth strip of paper: *Father Rodrigo Bendrito*.

"This is a terrible jest," Bonaventura said nervously. "Six of you are making a mockery of this process!"

Cardinal Torres reached in for the last slip of paper, looked at it, and with a dumbfounded expression, turned to Cardinal Colonna for aid.

"Not six," Colonna said, taking the slip from Torres. "Seven. This name is also Father Rodrigo Bendrito." To Fieschi, Colonna seemed perversely delighted. "Fathers, we have our new Pontiff."

Immediate chaos overtook the chamber. Nine cardinals leaped from their seats, a rainbow of different hues of amazement, from outrage (Bonaventura) to awe (da Capua) to delight (Capocci)...

"You did this!" Bonaventura shouted over the hubbub, crossing threateningly toward Fieschi, who alone remained sitting.

"Did I?" Fieschi said archly. "I have only one vote. There are seven votes for the priest."

"If you had not changed your vote!" Bonaventura nearly screamed.

"If *any* of us had not," Fieschi agreed.

"A common priest is not worthy to be *Pope*!" dei Conti snorted derisively.

"Ah, now," Fieschi warned with calm condescension. "The first Pope was a fisherman."

In response to the panicked commotion within, a guard outside the chapel had cautiously unbolted the door and opened it wide enough to look in with one eye. Seeing the commotion, he ventured to open it a little more.

"Your Eminences?" he said, completely unheard beneath the squawking and arguing.

But Fieschi saw the guard enter and, rising at last, strode comfortably past his upset fellows. He smiled paternally at the young man. "You may burn the wet straw," he said. "We want white smoke—a new Bishop of Rome has been chosen."

The guard's face relaxed into a smile. "At last," he said. "Praise God."

He closed the door behind him without bolting it. Fieschi turned back to face the hubbub of his nine fellow cardinals. Several voices were already demanding that they throw out the vote and try again.

"Brothers," Fieschi said calmly, raising his voice. He looked more feline than hawkish now. "Brothers, please calm yourselves. It is too late to throw out the votes. The world has been informed we have a new Pope. We must prepare to announce him."

Nine pairs of eyes stared dumbfounded at him.

"What right had you to tell anyone?" demanded Rinaldo Conti de Segni.

"Was there not a two-thirds majority cast?" Fieschi responded. "Is that not a deciding vote? We have been secreted away for far too long—this announcement frees us! Why are you not overjoyed at being liberated from our captivity?"

"But the result..." said Annibaldi. He was seconded and thirded and fourthed by others in the room.

"The result stands," Fieschi said. "There are no grounds for repealing it."

"He's not a bishop," Gil Torres rebutted. "There has never been a man made Pope before he was a bishop."

"I don't think there is a law about that," Fieschi mused. "But perhaps there should be. Let's ask the new Pope about it." He put his hand on the door as if he would open it.

"Wait, wait, *wait!*" shouted a number of voices from the circular chamber, as others demanded, "Let's talk this through!"

Fieschi turned his back to the door, his eyes flashing cold gray light. Everyone took a step away from him and fell silent. "What is there to discuss?" he said sharply. "We have voted in a leader of the Church. If we feel he is not up to the task, then we must assist him to it. Is that not our duty as cardinals of the Holy Church? I certainly intend to do so. I hope you will all join me, but that is your choice." He smiled coldly, enjoying the moment of drama immensely.

The other nine regarded each other dismally, then stared down at their feet, shoulders slumping, subdued.

"Well then," said Fieschi after a triumphal moment, and threw up his hands to God. "*Habemus Papam!*"

* * *

And then Father Rodrigo was back in the crypt of St. Peter, in this time and this place, this world—this universe. The vision had ravaged his mind, torn out his senses, retuned his perception of the world beyond insanity...but it was over. It had been a test, and he had survived.

The message he had been given, in that feverish dream in the farmhouse near Mohi—the images and mystic understandings he had scribbled feverishly onto a slip of paper, now lost along with his satchel—he had thought, all these long miserable months, that this prophetic vision contained a message he was meant to bring to the leader of all Christendom.

Now he saw the fallacy of that. *How arrogant of me*, Rodrigo thought, *to suppose I could prophesy the future of the world.* There were only a few people who could understand anything as vast as what he had scribbled on the piece of paper. One of them, he sensed, was the kind Englishman, but he was dead.

But understanding the vision meant very little. In the wide world's larger scope, that vision counted for almost nothing. It was a password, or a hazing ritual, that was all: a means by which he was challenged to enter into a realm of mystical insight. The higher powers of the cosmos had asked his unconscious mind to demonstrate that it knew the secret code, and that secret code was no mere phrase of words, but a shattering prophetic vision, to live through with his entire being.

His vision was not the *fruits* of a mystical initiation; it was merely the *invitation* to be initiated.

Rodrigo was still trembling. He brought the cool metal of the communion cup to his temple and rolled it gently, side to side, across his forehead. He found the smoothness, and the rolling gesture itself, calming. The metal absorbed the fevered heat he was emitting, yet remained cool. *Of course it did*, he thought, *of course it does*. Now at last, he was purified. He was rational. He was sane. He could look back on his strange, fevered behavior since Mohi and see it for what it was, and know that he had come through it. He was challenged, and he had survived.

Having proven he could survive a loss of sanity, at last sanity was restored to him.

First, I must find Ferenc, he thought. *The poor boy must be bewildered here without me—he doesn't have the language, and no experience surviving in a city. And I will need him in what lies ahead. For there is to be no rest for the weary.*

He had a responsibility now, a calling; he understood that, just as he understood that until today, he could not have guessed why he was really summoned to Rome. To give a message to the Pope? Ha! What good would that do? One mortal sharing words with another mortal; a transfer of information, nothing more. The spirit of the Christ was far more dynamic than mere words and information.

He looked around the tomb, stood up, tested his balance. He was fine. He felt light on his feet, in fact; his wound was entirely healed, he could not even remember which hip had been wounded. Somebody had changed his clothes since the previous day, and what he wore now was clean and softer than anything he could remember. He had even been accoutred with sandals, a rosary, and a new satchel. *Sanity is such a blessing, when your setting is serene*, he thought. No wonder he had taken leave of his senses outside Mohi; how else would he have survived?

"Very well, then," he said to the tomb, quietly. His hand was still clenched around the cool metal, the ever-cool metal, of the communion cup. He tucked that hand into his satchel and smiled benignly around the little tomb. "Thank you, Father," he said to the coffin of St. Peter. "You are far wiser than the rest of us, and upon this rock, let the new Church, when the time shall come, be built again."

He turned his back on the tomb, crossed the candlelit room, and strode up the steps with a slow, comfortable assurance he had not known possible.

At the top of the stairs he met a fresh-faced young priest whom he thought he recognized, but he could not figure out why.

"You were down there quite a while, Father," said the priest. "I was getting worried. I almost came down after you to see if you had hurt yourself."

"On the contrary, my son," said Rodrigo with smiling beneficence, "I have never been so well."

* * *

The cardinals sat around a highly polished wooden table, eating fruit and arguing. They grudgingly acknowledged that the vote was final, now that it had been announced, and that they had, in fact, elected a raving madman to be the next Bishop of Rome. What they could not agree upon was what to do about it.

There were three schools of thought.

First was Bonaventura and the de Segni cousins—Rinaldo and Stefano. They were bound and determined that the vote be somehow invalidated, and had sent junior clergy off to ferret out moldering codices of canon law in the bowels and attics of the church, seeking some justification to excuse them doing just that. They did most of the shouting, because—as far as Fieschi could make out—they wanted to make sure nobody else had a chance to even think straight until they had shaped events to their own liking.

If nothing else, they would probably turn to Orsini for help and ask him to arrange for the Pontiff-elect to be assassinated. This group, in short, was in a dither.

Then there was the group led by Castiglione, who were shocked but not panicked by what had happened. They believed that the vote should hold on legal principles, but that the madman should then be gently induced to decline the honor. This would send all the cardinals back into seclusion for another vote, but now within the sanctity of the Vatican compound, and not as victims of Orsini's oppression.

And then there was the unlikely triumvirate of Colonna, Capocci, and Fieschi. For different reasons, these men felt that the vote should hold, and Rodrigo should be enthroned. It was uncommon (but not impossible) to raise as Pope a man who was not a bishop; this was an easy technicality to fix: he could be made bishop, and then anointed Pontiff.

"I am curious. Why do you support the outcome of the election?" Fieschi asked the other two. Obviously the two clowns could not be trusted, but perhaps they would let slip some useful observation that could sway some of the other prelates.

Colonna shrugged. "I'm an old man, and I'm tired of being here," he said. "If this fellow is accepted, then I can finally go home and change my clothes and start acting like a cardinal again."

"So sloth is a primary motivator," Fieschi said, attempting dry humor but sounding instead as accusatory as he felt.

"Absolutely," said Colonna. He clapped his right hand down on his friend's knee. "Capocci, my dear fellow, tell the nice villain why you are taking such a perverse position on this topic."

"My position is the most honorable one in this room!" protested Capocci, waving his bandaged hand dismissively at everyone else. "We've made our bed and now we must lie in it, simple as that. Those of us responsible for leading the masses of Christendom, we have fallen to such a state that we would allow such a man to be elected, and having done so, we have to live with the circumstances. We have only ourselves to blame."

"That's a much better response than mine," said Colonna. He turned to Fieschi. "I want to change my answer to make it more like his."

Fieschi rolled his eyes. When he returned his attention to the other two cardinals, he found them staring at him with accusing malice. "And may we dare ask why the great and honorable Fieschi has betrayed his preferred candidate?" asked Colonna.

"You may ask," Fieschi said. "I am not bound to answer you."

The other two looked at each other. "Well, that proves it, then," said Capocci.

"Indeed," said Colonna, and the two turned to face him together. "You're definitely up to something nefarious," he informed Fieschi pleasantly. "Which means we're going to have to stop you."

"And hold you accountable," Capocci added ominously.

Fieschi turned his head away from them, refusing to be baited. Capocci could prove nothing. And Rodrigo would be his man, his puppet, he had no fear of that at all—but it was annoying that he would have to brush off these two gadflies along the way. *I will make sure the new Pope excommunicates them*, he decided. *That will get rid of them nicely.*

* * *

Rodrigo had tried to excuse himself and break away from the young priest, but the young man was strangely reluctant to be dismissed. He begged Rodrigo's pardon and followed him through the great church, toward the door, politely asking Rodrigo where he was planning to go, suggesting that perhaps he would be more comfortable resting in the deacon's office.

"Have you been assigned to keep an eye on me?" Rodrigo asked with a knowing smile. They had stopped at the grand western entrance to the basilica. Rodrigo was eager to be gone from these staid halls of ancient power. The days when such magnificence signified sanctified holiness had long since passed; he understood what must come next, and nobody else in the Vatican compound did.

The young priest blushed. "Yes, Father," he said, glancing down.

"There is no shame in your task," Rodrigo said. "When I first arrived in Rome, I was a raving madman. I was mistakenly placed in seclusion with the cardinals. When we were all brought here, the cardinals—very good men—were concerned that I might harm myself if left to my own devices. I understand. Previously, there was just cause for such concern. But my son," he said, with a reassuring smile, "I am now a changed man."

The younger priest frowned in polite confusion. "Father... ?" he murmured.

"I cannot explain what happened in Saint Peter's tomb, but it was a gift, a blessing—a blessed event," Rodrigo said, and rested his hand paternally on the youth's shoulder. "My madness was taken from me—and so were my physical wounds! I am well again, and in no need of chaperoning."

The young man looked at him, troubled, and blinked several times. "The Holy Sepulchre is known to have miraculous healing properties," he said at last. "And I am very glad to hear of their effect on you. However, Father, I must stand by my oath, and that is to keep you in my sight at all times until I turn that responsibility over to one of my fellows."

Rodrigo sighed patiently. "So be it. I commend you for your dedication to your office. Will you, in that case, accompany me on a constitutional? I am a native of this city, and it has been a very long time since I have freely walked its streets. I have a yearning for that, and I hope your duty does not prevent me from it."

The younger priest considered this. "Father, perhaps we can make an arrangement that is to your liking, but allows me to fulfill my obligation." He glanced down again, unwilling to gaze upon Rodrigo as he continued. "As it happens, I...have other duties to which I will be called. I would have to turn your care over to another anyhow. Let me see if I may do that now."

Rodrigo smiled benignly. "You are thinking that a new chaperone, meeting me as I am now, clearly rational and well recovered, would not feel the burden of sticking to me like a burr, as you perhaps do because you saw me before I was healed."

The young man reddened. "Really, Father, I simply have other duties. I am scheduled to receive confessions until dinner."

"Very well," said Rodrigo, gesturing back into the church. "Lead me to my next keeper. Rome is not going anywhere."

The junior priest looked relieved. "Very well, Father. Just this way, if you please." He turned and began to cross through the nave of the church, trusting Rodrigo to follow.

Which Rodrigo did. The communion cup within his satchel bumped against his hip as he walked.

the frog and the stone

22

THE PALE-HAIRED WARRIOR, Haakon, knew some of the Mongol tongue. His accent was very bad, but he could make himself understood, and Gansukh suspected his comprehension was much better than his pronunciation. *No wonder he watches us so closely*, Gansukh mused as he wandered through the sprawling camp. *He's listening and learning.*

A tiny smile flickered across his face. He would keep this tiny nugget of information to himself. Using the pale-haired youth to rile Munokhoi was a dangerous proposition, but an entertaining one. Given the pace at which the journey to Burqan-qaldun was progressing, he would need distractions. He couldn't keep shadowing Munokhoi; sooner or later, the *Torguud* captain would catch sight of him and take umbrage at the attention.

He didn't need to start a fight with Munokhoi. He just needed to be sure the other man's attention was directed somewhere other than at himself or Lian.

Gansukh wandered toward the eastern edge of the caravan where the Imperial Guards had set up a makeshift archery range. He walked over to the line scratched in the bare ground where the archers stood.

Behind him he heard the guards' conversation fragment, and he waited patiently. Finally, one of the them heaved himself to his feet and approached.

"Brother Gansukh."

Gansukh turned his head and regarded the one singled by the others. "Are you from the mountain clans?" he asked, noticing the colored threads braided into the man's hair.

The other man nodded.

"The days are long out here on the plain, aren't they, brother?"

"Tarbagatai," the man supplied. He wiped a hand across his face. "No longer than the nights, I suppose," he said with a shrug.

Gansukh offered a bark of laughter. "That is true." He waved a hand at the targets. "It has been a long time since I hunted in the mountains. I found the light to be different there. Night came swiftly, and if you were tracking prey, you had to be quick about making your kill. Otherwise, the sun would vanish and so would your target. Out here, though, the day seems to last forever."

Tarbagatai squinted at the targets, his tongue working at the inside of his lower lip. He seemed to be wondering if Gansukh was making sport of him, and Gansukh made no effort to guide the younger man's thinking. After his encounter with Namkhai and the Imperial Guard the other night, he had realized how few friends he had among the Khan's elite guard. Lian's schooling and his mission had kept him aloof from the men of the *arban*, a dangerous situation for a front-line warrior such as himself. If the caravan came under attack again, he needed some confidence that his fellow Mongols wouldn't see him as an adversary.

"Care to test your skill?" he asked, nodding at the nearby rack of bows.

Tarbagatai laughed. "I have heard the stories about you," he said. "In the *Khagan*'s garden. How you felled a deer with one arrow."

Gansukh shrugged as he wandered over to the rack. He let his hands roam across the bows—stroking the hardwood curves, fingering the sinew of the strings—and he finally selected a likely candidate. Smoothly, he strung the bow, and then offered it to Tarbagatai. "Maybe I was lucky that day," he said.

Tarbagatai snorted, and dismissed the offered weapon with a wave of his hand. His gaze darted toward his lazy companions. "I'll use my own," he said, and he called for one of them to fetch his bow.

Gansukh wandered back to the line, and standing shoulder to shoulder with Tarbagatai—who was slightly taller—he looked out at the scattered targets, counting them, noting their distance. "In the mountains," he said, "if you have a good position, you can see everything."

Tarbagatai nodded. "Anyone can shoot one arrow and hit one target."

Gansukh smiled at the mountain man's tone. Respectful, and yet slightly challenging at the same time. Tarbagatai had known who he was when he had approached, and he was certain the story of the deer in the *Khagan*'s garden wasn't the only story that had been passed around. The cup at the *Khagan*'s feast. The wrestling match with Namkhai. His ongoing feud with Munokhoi. All of these stories contributed to his reputation among the Imperial Guard, but every member of the Guard had been hand-picked for his own prowess and reputation. Stories meant little; actions counted for more.

The consensus about his match with Namkhai was that it had been a draw, and only because the Khan had allowed them to withdraw from the field. Opinion was split on who would have truly won, but regardless, no one could recall anyone ever besting Namkhai before. And Namkhai, of course, hadn't spoken one way or the other.

There was some allure to challenging Chagatai's envoy, then. There were few other opportunities for members of the Imperial Guard to distinguish themselves.

"We could pretend these targets are Chinese raiders," he offered. "A race to see who can kill more of them?"

The other guards wandered over in the wake of the man who brought Tarbagatai his own bow, eager interest plain on their faces. The pair in the back began to speak in hushed tones, making wagers.

Tarbagatai glared at the pair for a second, and then shook his head slightly, as if he were pushing their wager from his mind. The mountain man looked over the targets once more. "Ten," he said. "A full *arban*. Shall we have ten arrows each?"

"I would hope you would not miss that many," Gansukh said with a laugh. "How about six? That should be enough to warrant a clear winner."

Tarbagatai agreed, and with a word, sent one of the men to fetch two quivers of arrows. Each archer selected six, and Tarbagatai stuck his in the ground before him—a neat line, waiting to be snatched up.

Gansukh slowly pushed each of his arrows into the dry ground, making sure they were all firmly planted with their fletching pointed straight up. He opted for a tight cluster of shafts, a grouping that his hand fell upon naturally without requiring a look.

Tarbagatai would have to chase his arrows. Each shaft was a little farther away, and eventually, he would have to take a tiny step to his left in order to reach the last few arrows. Such movement wouldn't take much time, but in this contest, that tiny delay might make the difference.

"Ready?" Gansukh asked, laying his first arrow across his bow.

He heard the creak of a bowstring being drawn back, and Tarbagatai grunted.

"One of you," Gansukh called to the onlookers as he raised his own bow, "give us a word and we shall start." He peered along the straight shaft of his arrow at the first target. His right arm quivered for a moment before his muscles relaxed into a well-remembered position, and his breathing slowed. His belly tensed, and his vision shifted. The target—pale thatching stuffed into the ragged end of a log—sprang into greater focus, while everything else softened and dropped away.

"Hai!"

Gansukh loosed his first arrow before the man had finished shouting. He had heard the sudden influx of breath from behind him, and had known the cry was coming. His arrow flew true, burying itself deep in the thatch of the first target, though he did not hear the sound of its impact. Tarbagatai released his first arrow in concert with a horrific battle cry, as if his shout would give the arrow more loft in its flight. The sound was startling, more so for being projected right into Gansukh's ear, and he hesitated for a split second, caught off guard by the racket. Ruefully, he snatched up his second arrow, nocked it, drew back the bowstring, and let it fly.

His second arrow struck a target that already contained one of Tarbagatai's arrows. His shaft was closer to the center, but the mistake was already made. As he reached for his third arrow, he silently commended Tarbagatai on his clever ruse.

There was no time for further recriminations. The mountain man was quick, and Gansukh lost himself in the rhythm of archery: nock, pull, release. As soon as an arrow was clear of his bow, he would focus on the next target. He tried not to wonder if he was shooting at the same target as Tarbagatai; to worry would be to hesitate, and to hesitate would be to lose.

As he released his last arrow, he heard an echoing twang from over his shoulder, and he released the breath he was not aware he had been holding.

The archers and their audience stared out at the field of targets, watching as the two arrows buried themselves in the thick thatch of the farthest target. The rustling impact of the arrows in the dried stalks was like the fluttering noise of a bird's wings—two beats so close together that they could be easily mistaken for one sound.

"Every dog is dead," Tarbagatai announced, clapping Gansukh on the shoulder. "You shot well."

"Indeed," Gansukh replied. "As did you." He looked around and saw no arrows in the ground, and then let his gaze roam across the targets once more. This time he checked every target more closely. "We seem to have shot all our arrows, Brother," he pointed out.

"Yes, and we did not mark them ahead of time," Tarbagatai laughed. "Do you remember which ones were yours?"

Gansukh pointed at the nearby target that sported two arrows. "That one was already dead when my arrow hit it," he said.

Tarbagatai grinned. "But what of the last?"

Gansukh shaded his eyes with his hand and made a show of peering at the farthest target. "It is very far away," he said, "and I have developed a thirst. Perhaps we can check later."

Merriment danced in Tarbagatai's eyes as his grin stretched even wider. He raised his bow and let out a loud whoop of joy. "Yes," he chortled. "Let us have a drink in celebration."

As the other men noisily agreed with the resolution of the match and eagerly dispersed to gather skins of *arkhi*, Tarbagatai put his hands on Gansukh's shoulders. "I would follow you into battle, brother Gansukh," he said, and the intensity of his gaze matched the fervor of his words.

Gansukh returned the embrace, and found himself considering a strange idea. Could he lead men like Tarbagatai? To have the Imperial Guard at his command? The idea presented itself with no preamble, and he was surprised to find himself considering it.

And then he remembered the siege of Kozelsk, and the idea was like a black stain in his mind. He wanted to make it go away, but it only spread.

The *arkhi*, when he shared a skin with Tarbagatai a few minutes later, was incredibly sour in his mouth, and he fought the urge to spit it out.

* * *

She shouldn't have stayed, but she had, and when Gansukh stirred shortly after dawn, she had lain still and kept her breathing as even as possible, hoping he would think she was asleep. With her eyes lightly closed, Lian listened to Gansukh as he rolled out of the tangled mass of furs and blankets that were their shared bed. He stretched, grunting and mumbling to himself, and noisily fumbled his way into his clothing.

Trying to be quiet, and failing miserably. She fought the urge to smile.

Once he was gone, Lian continued to feign sleep, slowly counting to one hundred in her head before she moved.

She had been sleeping in his tent since the night of the Chinese raid, though they had not been intimate that first night. He had given her the bed and had slept next to the flaps of the tent, letting her know that no one would enter the tent without his knowledge. His protective gesture had been touching; and no less so when, a few hours later, she had prodded him with her foot and found him completely unresponsive. He had become her protector, but he did so without making her feel like property.

She had power over him, whether he realized it or not, and as she rose and dressed, she wondered what she was going to do with that power. A few weeks ago, the answer would have been clear, but she found her resolve wavering. *Don't be a silly girl*, she thought angrily as she pushed back the flaps of the tent and stepped outside.

She wandered toward the heart of the caravan, taking note of the increase in activity around the cluster of *ger* where the caravan masters were quartered. The *Khagan* and his entourage might move today.

A clump of women came toward her, and Lian recognized Second Wife and her attendants, and she scuttled around the nearest tent, trying to avoid being seen. If spotted, Jachin would insist on hearing any gossip, especially anything about the Chinese raid.

She just couldn't bear to talk about it. Not with *that* woman.

The women's voices followed her, and her heart started to tremble in her chest. They couldn't be following her, could they? She was being irrational, but that didn't stop her from quickening her pace and changing her course several times. And when she spotted the flag raised over Master Chucai's tent, she quickly made a decision and altered her course for his *ger*.

Jachin would never follow her in there.

She slapped the open flap of Chucai's tent and waited impatiently, glancing over her shoulder. There was no response, and so she slapped it again, more firmly this time, and jumped back as one of Chucai's servants suddenly appeared in the *ger*'s open mouth.

"Oh," she started. "I...I am here to see Master Chucai," she finished.

The servant stared at her, one eyebrow partially raised, and made no move to stand aside. His rigid posture made it clear that a shift in power had occurred. Rumors of her relationship with Gansukh were already circulating, and Chucai's servants were taking advantage of the gossip to remind her that there was a difference between being the slave of a powerful man like Master Chucai and being the kept woman of a horse rider.

Lian sucked in a large breath, using the motion to draw herself up to her full height and to throw out her chest. "At his command," she amended, with more than a little of regal haughtiness in her voice.

She should have come to see Chucai earlier, but there was no sense in castigating herself about that now.

The servant nodded without blinking, and stepped aside. She swept past him, flicking her hair with mock distain as she did so. Playing her old role, while part of her was certain the man would see right through it. He could see she was filled with nothing but doubt.

"Ah, Lian."

Chucai's traveling home was a replica of his small office at Karakorum. He was seated behind a wooden desk, working by candlelight. His travel trunks sat on one side of the *ger*, neatly arranged in a row; on the opposite wall, his long fur coat hung on a collapsible wooden rack.

"Sit down," he said, waving a hand toward the stool next to the trunks. If he was surprised to see her, he gave no sign.

Lian sat, placing her hands, right over left, on her lap. She waited while he finished reading the scroll. He read, untroubled and unhurried by her presence, and she did not fidget. Fidgeting was for nervous girls, for scared women who were not in control of their lives. Squirming was what bored slaves did, and she was neither.

"It is a curious situation, is it not?" he asked as he began to roll the scroll up.

"Yes, my Master," she replied immediately, her eyes downcast. Mainly so he would not spy any of the confusion and frantic wonderment she was experiencing.

"On one hand, I think you may have overcommitted yourself to your assigned task; on the other, I admire the *security* it has provided you."

She knew he had seen the terse exchange at the entrance of his *ger*, and though he wouldn't admit to having instructed his servant to act that way, Lian knew Master Chucai well enough to read the underlying message in both his words and his servant's attitude. "Yes, my Master," she breathed, carefully stressing the last two words without seeming to grovel.

"And of course there is the matter of why you might feel the need for such protection." Chucai looked at her then, holding her with his piercing gaze. Not accusatorily, but with an air of knowing, as if it were indeed true that he knew everything that went on in this camp, just as the same impression was true within the walls of Karakorum.

Lian blinked. "Munokhoi," she said, giving name to the true dread that had kept her awake the previous night.

It should have been the dead commander, Luo, but when she closed her eyes, it wasn't his face, with his staring eyes and accusing mouth and the black tears that dripped from the gash in his neck, that haunted her dreams. It was the cruel visage of the *Torguud* captain.

"Before the Chinese bodies were even cold, he was here in my tent, standing right over there, railing at me about you being a Chinese spy."

"What?" Lian spluttered, too surprised to form more words than the one.

Chucai squared up the ends of the scroll with a practiced twist of the cylindrical shape. "Indeed. It is an interesting accusation. And when I thought to ask you myself, you were—"

"I swear to you I am not—I would never—I am not a spy!" Lian tried to quell her rapid breathing, to lessen the feeling she had of being squeezed by a giant hand.

Chucai stared at her, letting the silence stretch between them to an almost unbearable length. "Yes," he said eventually, releasing her from the penetrating intensity of his gaze. "I do believe that you are not."

Lian gulped a breath and nodded gratefully. "Thank you," she managed. Being subject to the gossipy attention of Second Wife and her attendants might not have been such a bad fate after all.

"However, I also believe the *Torguud* captain's accusation that you were trying to escape, though he has, in all likelihood, completely forgotten this little detail by now. A fortunate omission in his record, don't you think?"

Lian made no reply.

"Even though I *believe* you did not lead the attackers to us, what *I* think is of little consequence." Chucai offered her a tiny smile, completely absent of any affection. "At least, in this matter."

Lian regarded him warily, a serpent of fear slowly twining itself around her lower spine. If she had come to his tent immediately after the raid, would his attitude toward her have been better? And yet, he sat here speaking to her as if she had been expected, as if he had, indeed, summoned her to hear this very...obtuse...conversation.

"Your opinion matters in all things, Master," she said, lowering her gaze to her hands. Her fingers were knotted in her lap, and with some effort, she extricated them from one another.

Chucai chuckled. "Yes," he said. "Yes, it does. In some areas, my opinion is all that is required. What I think is best is what is done. And what is done by my command causes ripples. Like a stone dropped into a pond. The frog, thinking it is safe from predators, may suddenly find its protective lily pad disturbed. Removed from beneath it, even."

"Am I the frog?" she asked.

"Are you?" Chucai raised his hand and mimed dropping a heavy stone. He leaned forward as if he were examining the results of his action.

"Munokhoi fears change," Chucai said after staring at the results of his imaginary stone. "He does not like being outside the city walls. Too provincial. Too many wild animals, untamed creatures like...ponies." Chucai laughed. "Yes, our brave *Torguud* champion is afraid of a *young pony*."

The serpent twisted even higher up Lian's spine. *The young pony,* she thought, and in thinking of him, was afraid for his safety. And hers, as well.

"What is to become of me?" she heard herself asking.

Chucai raised an eyebrow as he sat back in his chair, running his fingers through his long beard. "What should become of you?" he asked in a somewhat bored tone.

And she knew, in that instant, that Chucai was done with her. The failed escape attempt, the relationship with Gansukh, the threat of Munokhoi: these were all matters he no longer wished to concern himself with, and he had, in fact, realized a simple solution to all three. When she walked out of Chucai's *ger*, it would be for the last time.

She should have been more thrilled. Chucai had, in effect, freed her, but where could she go? They were days from Karakorum, and if she tried to ride off again, Munokhoi would relish the opportunity to hunt her down. And Gansukh. Would he follow her? Would he protect her against Munokhoi?

She put her hand over her mouth to stop a half sob, half giggle from escaping. After all these years, what she had yearned for was being offered her, and all she could think of was how to reject this freedom. How could she restore her usefulness to Chucai?

At least until the Khagan's *caravan returned to Karakorum.*

"The Chinese," she started, grasping at a fleeting memory from the night of the attack. "While I was being held captive by the Chinese, I heard one of their commanders talking about..."

The *Khagan*'s advisor remained slumped in his chair, but his fingers were no longer idly stroking his beard. "Go on," Chucai said carefully.

"He spoke of a sprout, and...and a banner—"

Chucai leaped out of his chair, startling her into silence. He leaned on his desk, looming over her. "What did he say?" Chucai demanded, his voice sharp.

Lian swallowed nervously, her hands fluttering in her lap. The change in Chucai's demeanor was not what she had expected, and she squirmed under his intense gaze. Her mind raced, trying to recall the conversation between Luo and the other Chinese man. "They...they said they wanted a sprout—that was why they attacked the *Khagan*'s caravan, but...but they were not able to find it. And so they tried to steal a banner instead." She sat up, realizing which banner Luo and the other man had been referring to. "The *Khagan*'s Spirit Banner," she breathed.

"Hsssssst," Chucai uttered, slamming himself back into his seat.

Lian fell silent. She kept her gaze on her lap, mentally calming her fingers and her breathing. Now was not the time to speak. Whatever she had heard from the Chinese meant something to Master Chucai; it was best to let him tell her, versus her trying to puzzle it out.

For now, at least.

"A sprout," Chucai said eventually.

Lian let her gaze flick up, but Chucai was staring into the space over her head and did not notice. "Do you know what he was talking about? Have you seen such a twig?" he asked.

Lian shrugged. "A twig, Master? I have seen many twigs." She felt unduly coy in saying it, but sensed a change in Chucai's mood. If there was a way she could benefit from this change, she had to try to take advantage of it. "Perhaps you could enlighten me a little more."

Chucai snorted and shook his head. "You would know it if you had seen it," he snapped. "I'm not talking about the sort of branch of flowers that Jachin has her handmaidens bring her. This would be..." He waggled his fingers at her, glowering.

Chucai doesn't know either, she realized. She dropped her gaze so that he couldn't read her expression. "I have not, Master," she said. "Though I would be more happy to keep an eye out for it, while I..." She left her sentence unfinished, hoping he would fill it in for her.

"While you what?" Chucai asked, his demeanor returning to its previous stony state.

The panic returned, squeezing her body. She was like the frog, swimming frantically in an enormous pond, with no shelter in sight. No lily pads. Just open water.

"While I...do nothing, Master," she ended lamely. Her dreams of freedom were nothing more than childish whimsy.

"Exactly," he replied with finality.

The frog, waiting for the stone to drop.

a fateful choice 23

TEGUSGAL WAS NOT the most physically imposing of men, but there was a quality in his gaze that Dietrich found both refreshing and worthy of a modicum of respect. They sat across from each other in a tent in the Mongol compound, separated by a narrow table on which a small pitcher of *airag* and two cups sat, both untouched.

To one side stood the priest, Father Pius, a nervous look on his face as he waited to translate for whomever would speak next. His eyes darted between the two dangerous men, looking rather like a mouse caught between two cats.

"Will he take the deal?" Dietrich asked when the silence overtook his patience. The priest turned and spoke rapidly to Tegusgal in the Mongol tongue. As he did, Dietrich loosened the pouch from his belt, laying it on the table with a jingling sound that no man, no matter his creed or homeland, could fail to recognize. The *Fratres Militiae Christi Livoniae* had lost many things, but its wealth was still in some part preserved, and Dietrich had brought enough coin with him to finesse certain situations.

Tegusgal reached for the leather pouch, loosening the string and digging out a single coin. He held it aloft between callused fingertips, and his eyes were dark and hooded. He flipped the coin and caught it, then said something in his own language.

The priest nodded in his nervous way, then translated. "He wishes to know why."

Dietrich frowned, suddenly in muddy waters where the stones on which to put one's feet could not be seen. A clumsy answer could upset everything the coin was about to purchase. Still, the coins were already on the table. It was too late to turn back.

"Because there are times," Dietrich said, "when a higher purpose must be put before all other things. When honor must be defended, even if doing so seems mad and foolish."

That was the truth of it. There were other benefits to this arrangement—matters which Tegusgal could ascertain for himself easily enough—but the settling of accounts was of paramount import to Dietrich. His return to Rome would not be coated in shame. His masters would not be able to accuse him of failing in his assignment or speak derisively of his efforts at protecting the honor of his battered order.

"This is such a time," Dietrich finished, and let it lie there in the space between them, with the coins.

The priest translated the words into the Mongol tongue, and Tegusgal's only response was a soft grunt. The Mongol's attention was on the sack of coins, his fingers dipping in and drawing out coins at random. Finally, the man's dark eyes flickered toward him once more. Tegusgal's lips curled into a cruel smile and he said a single phrase, short and direct.

The priest translated. "He finds your deal agreeable."

* * *

Zug hustled beside Kim through the maze of tents that formed the fighters' camp, an air of energy and urgency informing their pace. They rushed past fires where meat roasted on spits, dodged around clumps of men bent over impromptu games of knucklebones, and diverted from their path to avoid a crowd forming around two men who were settling a disagreement over a camp girl by bare-knuckled brawling. They were running out of time.

They had not been able to speak with Madhukar. He had been impossible to find since word had come from the guards that he was to fight next in the arena. Worse still, they had been waiting for confirmation from the street rats that the Rose Knight, Andreas, would be the Western fighter. Zug had thought it too risky to warn Madhukar of the plan far in advance, and now they only had a few minutes before Tegusgal's men arrived and escorted the wrestler to his bout. By the time they reached the tent, Zug and Kim were both winded.

Gasping for breath, Kim flipped back the flap on the wrestler's tent and stared in shock. Madhukar was calmly seated on a mat, a girl massaging each of his massive arms while a third tried to dig her delicate hands into the hard muscles of his shoulders and neck. He was wearing a narrow loincloth that was only a token nod toward modesty. He was not even remotely ready to fight in the arena.

"What has happened?" Kim asked, and Zug could hear the strain in his voice. Zug felt at a loss as well, and he struggled to keep his panic in check.

Madhukar glanced up, his face twisting into a dour mask of displeasure as he did. He gave a gesture with his right arm, speaking bluntly in his halting grasp of the Mongol tongue. "Tegusgal changed his mind," he grunted. "Said other man would fight instead."

A cold fist wrapped itself around Zug's gut and tightened into a viselike grip. Did the Khan's man know something of what they were planning? *No*, he pushed that fear aside, *if he knew, Madhukar would be locked in a cage now, not having his limbs massaged by lithe slave girls.* Tegusgal might toy with them, but he would not take any chances. If he knew, he would have come for Kim and himself already.

"Why?" Zug asked; at the same time Kim asked, "Who?"

Madhukar answered both of them with a shrug that only confirmed what they already feared. Why would Tegusgal have explained anything to the big wrestler? He barely treated the fighters in the Circus as anything above well-bred dogs, even at his most generous.

As there was nothing else to be learned from the taciturn wrestler, Kim and Zug turned away from Madhukar's tent. They wandered, somewhat aimlessly, toward the middle of the camp, somewhat stunned and unsure what to do about the chance for freedom that might, even as they stood there, be slipping away like grains of sand through their open fingers. Zug felt a fury boiling inside him. It was a reaction to the futility of their circumstances, he knew, a response that was distracting to a warrior, but it was not unexpected. He wanted to scream, to grab any of the slaves and other oppressed fighters wandering blithely past and shake them. Grab them by their hair and force them to face the visceral truth of their circumstances. He inhaled slowly and deeply, drawing air in through his nose and letting it back out even more slowly through his pursed lips. Embracing such a fury would be a fatal mistake, and all chances of their plan ever succeeding would vanish.

"The boy," Zug said, looking at Kim. "We could still get word back to the Rose Knights."

Kim's face was drained of color, the ashen pallor of death. "He's already come and gone," the Flower Knight said, as though hope were a delicate vase suddenly dropped and shattered on the ground, the reality only now sinking in.

"Then everything rests on him," Zug said, looking toward the arena. "One man. Fighting alone."

Kim jerked his head back, a smile fighting its way onto his lips. "We tried to make it otherwise, didn't we? But that is the way it always is, in the end."

* * *

There was cheering in the streets when he came. Hünern was a town inundated with violent men and aggressive souls whose lust for battle had brought them from lands far and wide. Where the fighters passed, common men got out of their path, women hid themselves, and children stepped aside.

Not so with the *Ordo Militum Vindicis Intactae.* The people raised their faces to look up at the banner of the Rose Knights as it passed. Every story they had heard was instantly solidified as an unassailable truth in their minds. Every hope they had ever harbored in secret was suddenly given new life. Even those who had not been there when Andreas had come to First Field and demanded to be allowed to fight for all of Christendom would remember that day as if they had stood next to the knight when he had issued his challenge. The crowds looked upon the Shield-Brethren, and loved them.

The memory of the crowds was a balm on Andreas's mind as he walked down the long tunnel of the arena. His mind was agitated, more so than usual, spinning around on all the aspects of the plan that were out of his control. When he had dismounted from his horse and had been about to enter the arena, a small figure had launched himself out of the crowd and thrown himself into Andreas's arms. Hans had held him tight and whispered a message into his ear. *You will be facing a friend. He will guard your back as you do what must be done.*

Despite his courage, there was fear written plainly across the boy's face. Only a fool would presume that whomever went into the arena with such intentions would walk out again, whether the Khan lived or died.

The plan—like all good plans—was simple, and Andreas's fingers flexed about the shaft of his spear. When he and his ally stood opposite one another, they would have the opportunity to strike at the Khan directly. Andreas was well practiced at hurling shafts, and that practice had not stopped since the arena fights began. He had a good arm for throwing, even battered as he was. With a man to guard his back, the only other thing he would need was a wind that was kind.

"Be careful," Hans had said as the crowd separated them. Andreas had not had time to answer, and he could only nod grimly before the boy's tear-streaked face vanished into the press of bodies.

The light at the far end of the tunnel summoned him. His heart quickened as his thoughts became less hurried, less confused. The plan was simple. His action would be clear. Now was the time when the Shield-Brethren would live up to the legends spoken of them. They had accounted heroically for themselves in the lists, and Andreas had endured blow after blow at First Field, holding onto their place long enough to buy their allies the time they needed to gather what friends they could. Now, at last the efforts were coming to fruition. Their days of hiding were coming to an end, and today would be the spark that ignited all of Hünern.

He had only to throw his spear, and throw it well. The rest would be in the hands of the Virgin.

He reached the final archway and paused for a final quick prayer, and then he stepped into the arena proper, where he was immediately assaulted by the deafening roar of an aroused crowd. Distantly, he marveled at the physical weight of the sound that fell upon him, glad of the thickness of his helm, and he tried to push all of that confusion aside as he looked around the killing ground for his opponent.

Andreas drew in a sharp breath at what he saw. Across the sand stood a tall, broad-shouldered knight, wearing full maille armor and a steel helm that gleamed in the sunlight. Steel plates of the sort many knights had begun to add to their maille adorned his shoulders, and his steel-sheathed hands rested upon the hilt of an unsheathed, broad-bladed greatsword, its point resting in the dirt. A white surcoat draped across his chest, reaching down to above his knees.

Stitched on the unblemished fabric was the red cross and sword of the *Fratres Militiae Christi Livoniae.*

Andreas blinked several times, glancing around the arena with some vain hope that he was mistaken in what he saw. Or what he didn't see. There was no one else. He was alone before the Livonian.

The man raised his sword in a formal, seamless salute. Andreas's heart was now pounding in his ears as he faced his unexpected foe. Memories of the alehouse, of staring down at the Livonian *Heermeister* from the saddle of a stolen horse flashed through his mind. Had their allies in the Mongol camp been compromised? Had Hans? Was this a deliberate gambit on the part of the Khan, or merely the revenge of a Grand Master humiliated in the street? Uncertainty started to give way to something else, something less noble.

With a calming breath and a tightening of his grip on his weapon, Andreas forced the fear away as he returned his opponent's salute. This was not the first time in his life that Andreas had endured an ambush, nor the first time that he had been taken unawares. When thrust into an unfamiliar situation against expectation, it was the way of the untrained novice to falter in the face of reactive terror. Andreas was a knight initiate of the *Ordo Militum Vindicis Intactae*—branded, blooded, and proven. This was a *complication*, and not a failure of the plan.

The roaring chant of the crowd faded to a distant din as Andreas focused his attention on the task at hand. Had they stood in the open field, the greater length of Andreas's spear would have been more than enough to keep his foe at bay. Here in the arena, the space was smaller, limited. He would not have the room necessary to keep the Livonian at bay forever, and the thick maille that swathed the man from head to toe would be an obstacle even in the face of strong thrusts. It made no sense to wait, then. Time was not his ally today.

He exploded forward, charging across the sand, and as he closed the distance he unleashed a series of rapid thrusts at the Livonian's body: head, feet, chest, head again, feet. Each strike was more rapid than the previous one. Forced to back away or check each attack with the strong of his blade, the Livonian gave ground. With each strike, Andreas shortened his grip upon the spear, bringing him ever closer to physical reach of his target. The Livonian continued to retreat, checking each thrust, his attention on the flickering point of Andreas's spear.

Closer, closer. Then his chance came.

Andreas aimed a thrust at the Livonian's groin. The Livonian's blade snapped into a ward to drive it off, but now Andreas was close enough to grapple. The butt end of his spear shot across the Livonian's arms, entrapping them together as Andreas hammered him hard in the neck. *Hips beneath the other man,* his tireless reminder to his students rang in his head as he leveraged his foe and sent the Livonian sprawling.

In the two heartbeats it took Andreas to steady himself enough to pursue, his opponent had already regained his feet and his sword. They stood facing one another again, and as he took the other man's measure, Andreas felt a chill run through him.

He doesn't even look winded.

* * *

Kristaps watched as the Shield-Brethren hesitated a mere fraction of a second at the sight of him standing ready. Behind his helm, Volquin's Dragon smiled. *You're afraid, little knight. Afraid, and stupid to let me know it.*

Once more, he raised his sword in salute. Amid the storm of shrieking faces that surrounded them, Kristaps was a focal point of channeled calm. The Shield-Brethren of Petraathen were the stuff of legends told from one end of Europe to the other. Kristaps knew all the stories, had believed them himself once upon a time, and he knew the lie they all imparted. No man, no matter how skilled, was ever anything more than bone, blood, and flesh, kept breathing only because another man hadn't yet cut him open.

God willing, he would cut this one open. And all of his brothers as well. That was the debt owed. That was the promise he had made and that he intended to keep, as long as he could wield a weapon. As long as he too could breathe.

Kristaps kept his sword up, watching the other man, how he moved, and taking note of what it might tell him of the way that he thought. From the stories Dietrich had told him the night before, Andreas was a bold fool, according to his *Heermeister*, an audacious soul who might be assumed to leap before he looked. Kristaps doubted this was true. The Shield-Brethren were exceptionally trained, to a fault. Their actions might appear like those of a careless fool, but they always knew the risks. They always planned ahead.

Andreas's first assault had been a clear indicator, and in another time and place, Kristaps might have congratulated Andreas on the feint that had resulted in him being thrown. But it had been a mistake. *He should have followed through and killed me*, Kristaps thought as the spear tip came at him once more, lancing through the air. *Because now I know the measure.*

Kristaps stepped into the latest thrust, his blade sweeping the point aside. Abruptly Andreas made a rowing motion with his weapon and too late Kristaps saw what he was doing as the butt smashed into his chest. He gave a sharp breath and drew back. He brought his sword up and then down, aborting a second rotation of the spear.

A fighter learns how to endure a blow without giving ground, without wincing and crumpling around the pain. It is a basic survival skill, one mastered quickly and readily. In an open field, the advantage would have belonged to the Shield-Brethren, the limitless range of his potential movement allowing him to constantly keep

Kristaps at bay. The arena hemmed both of them in, however, and a fighter who fled from every blow would eventually be pushed up against a wall.

He who was trapped first died.

They had separated again, following his disruption of Andreas's attempts to beat him with the knobbed end of his spear. Andreas came at him once more, thrusting in rapid succession at his midsection, his head, and his foot. *Smart plays,* Kristaps thought as he kept his distance, *but there was only so much he could do with that attack.*

Kristaps swept his sword upward from a low guard and intercepted the next thrust. He locked the shaft with his weapon and then stepped in to tuck it behind his arm. Andreas knew what he was doing and stepped in too, throwing his head forward. Their helmets slammed together, and Kristaps tried to take the brunt of Andreas's furious head butt on the ridge of his helmet.

His ears ringing, Kristaps shoved Andreas away. A smile spread across his face as he reset his guard and circled his opponent.

This was going to be more of a challenge than he thought.

* * *

Andreas had faced members of the Livonian order before, but this one was different. He was strong and skilled, and that was to be expected, but there was more to him than simple martial prowess. There was a disturbing familiarity in his movements, even in the way he forced separation and covered his retreat. *He's been trained by one of ours.*

Andreas couldn't rely on wearing his implacable foe down. The blows he had landed so far had been fierce, but they were the sort of trauma that would leave bruises and cause stiffness tomorrow. They weren't going to change the fight *today.* Andreas could feel the Khan's box behind him, its occupant at the heart of all his endeavors here. This Livonian was not a friend, that much was certain, and the only way he could accomplish the plan—and it was his alone, at this point—was through victory.

He'd bested his own brothers before; he could do the same here. *End this,* was his final thought on the matter. *There is no more time.*

Andreas launched himself forward with a powerful thrust aimed at the Livonian's neck. His opponent stepped off line and to his left, his left hand darting from the pommel of his sword to midway up the blade, dashing in faster than Andreas could retreat. The spear was ultimately a weapon made to keep opponents at range, but when the enemy bypassed the point and stepped inside, then that advantage was utterly lost and the weapon could rapidly become a liability. As the Livonian stepped forward, the tip of his blade hooked Andreas's hand against the shaft, and had it not been for the maille that protected his limbs, the back of his hand would have been cut straight to the bone.

He tried to withdraw, but the Livonian had already slipped behind him, and the pommel and grip of the greatsword were looped around his neck. He dropped his weight, but found the Livonian had beaten him to that trick first. The sky and the ground reversed their positions as he flew backward, landing painfully on the ground.

The Livonian was coming for him. The spear had landed within arm's reach, and Andreas snatched it up, waving it around from where he lay on his back. The motions were forceful and wild, but they had the desired effect of forcing his opponent to back up enough to let him regain his feet.

The Livonian stared at him, his posture bespeaking absolute confidence. Abruptly, the man spread his arms wide, leaving his chest open to attack. *He's goading me,* Andreas realized, *and I have no choice.*

With a cry, he launched himself forward, the spear lancing toward his enemy's chest.

* * *

The Shield-Brethren was starting to panic. With a smile, Kristaps gave ground as his opponent lashed out with his spear, trying to buy enough time to regain his footing. *Get up*, Kristaps thought, as he retreated from the slashing spear tip. The Shield-Brethren had been expecting a different opponent; Kristaps doubted he would have brought the same weapon to the arena had he known whom he was fighting. Ordinarily, fighting against a spear was a severe disadvantage, but the First Sword of Fellin had been at Schaulen and other fields of battle, and he knew the walls of the arena reduced his opponent's advantage. There were far fewer ways to fight a man with a spear, and once desperation started to creep in, the options became even more limited. His opponent was starting to panic; his fear was plain in his motions as he struggled to regain his feet. A desperate man forgot his advantages quickly, and was more prone to carelessness at the slightest hint of an opportunity for a quick victory.

They stood apart now, panting. Kristaps watched the other man assess him. His own blood was up and his mind alert and sharp. The Shield-Brethren could not touch him.

With deliberate slowness, he spread his arms wide, leaving his body undefended. *Come*, his posture said, *let me make it easy for you.*

The Shield-Brethren took the bait. It was his only chance, and both men knew it. He was quick, but speed could not counter strategy when his enemy was ready for it. It was a well-delivered strike, and would have skewered Kristaps like a pig had it landed.

Kristaps stepped forward, bringing his sword to the center just in time to catch the spear tip upon the base of his blade, pushing it aside. The thrust was broken, but the Shield-Brethren's momentum was not. Kristaps levered his greatsword forward the mere foot of distance necessary to plant its point squarely in his enemy's chest. It was not enough to penetrate the maille and padded gambeson, but Kristaps watched with satisfaction as the man jerked violently at the blow and fought the urge to crumple. A rib might have cracked, muscles torn by the sudden contraction.

He raised his blade for another blow, preparing to bring the sword down in a bone-breaking strike that would shear through maille and shatter limbs, but the Shield-Brethren's hand shot beneath his elbow, keeping his sword arm at bay. A desperate effort that would only prevent what came next for a few more seconds. The Shield-Brethren's arm was extended now, and it was Kristaps who was inside the range of his weapons. His left hand slid from the pommel of the greatsword as he twisted his hips, hooked the shaft of the spear, and drove it behind the Shield-Brethren's legs.

This is the first of many blows owed you and yours. Kristaps smiled, and snapped his hips back, levering the Shield-Brethren with tremendous force and hurling him to the ground. He managed to roll, struggling to regain his feet as Kristaps watched, now holding his greatsword in his right hand and his enemy's spear in his left. *You are unarmed. You are wounded. You have already lost.*

He hefted the shaft and threw it back toward his foe. Goading him now. *You are no threat to me.*

* * *

The trap had been sprung, and Andreas had landed badly. When he struggled to his feet his breath was coming in difficult rasps, his head throbbing with pain. The stillness of his enemy was unnerving, absolute in its predatory, watchful confidence. Andreas had begun the fight in uncertainty, his resolve shaken. Now, feeling the agonizing fire in his chest, the only possible end to this confrontation was making itself clear. *I am going to die.*

The spear sailed toward him, and he caught it reflexively. The motion of snapping his arm out to seize the shaft sent ripples of white-hot pain through his chest, shoulders, and back. He was losing the battle rush, and when the sword tip had struck him, something had broken. His legs were sluggish, and his maille and gambeson made it feel like he was carrying two or three full-grown men on his shoulders. The Livonian stood before him, his sword at the ready, watching with the contemptuous contemplation of a cat enjoying a game with a mouse before it has a meal. The sun was relentless in its attention, and what felt like rivers of sweat were coursing down his back and legs.

Behind the Livonian, the colorful flags atop the Khan's box fluttered, calling to him.

All at once the fear was gone, and Andreas gasped at the sudden clarity that lay before him. The goal of this battle, whether the advantage had been his or not, had never been about survival. It would have been nice had the Virgin allowed him and his absent ally to walk away laughing with a grand tale to tell his brothers back in Petraathen when this was all done and past, but that had always been an indolent dream. *Even Hans had known.*

His hands tightened on the spear, and he set his teeth against the pain. Andreas had heard stories from older brothers, speaking of the times when they had believed death upon them, how their senses became sharper. When fear fled, everything became serene and perfect. One last gift from the Virgin before she came to collect her brave warriors.

It was all he needed. One last gift. *One last throw.*

He sprang toward the Livonian, his spear flickering before him in a last flurry of thrusts. The Livonian defended himself, almost lazily, as if he could not quite believe that his opponent thought this assault would bear fruit. His enemy sidestepped the first thrust toward his midsection, swatted the spear tip aside as it came again at his helmet, and then—becoming bored with the same sequence being forced upon him once again—rushed in with a killing blow. It was exactly what Andreas had expected. He let the spear whirl around in his hands as the Livonian came at him, and smashed the butt of the weapon into the flat of the greatsword's blade, sending it veering off its course and to the side. *Control the motion, control the body.*

The butt of the spear was now between the Livonian's weapon and his body. Andreas slammed his weight into his enemy's flank, and used the shaft of the spear to hook his foe's neck. He dropped his hips, twisted all his weight against the pain, and sent the Livonian through the air, his body crashing into the ground. *Get out of my way.*

The crowds were roaring in his ears, expecting a finishing move. But Andreas ignored his opponent, continuing his mad dash across the sand. His legs cried out in pain; he ignored them. His chest was afire with the agony of each breath, but he would only need his lungs for a few moments longer.

The Khan's box hung before him, a massive work of wood painted with red and gold and decorated with the stolen fineries of a thousand looted kingdoms. A pair of gleaming curtains shielded its occupants from the rays of the summer sun, stirring now in the wind. Andreas held one arm before him to steady his aim. *You should have known better,* he thought. *Out of the reach of a sword, but not my spear. A gift, Onghwe Khan. I give you my life, so that I might take yours...*

Limbs burning, chest screaming, Andreas set his weight and threw his weapon, as hard and as far as he had ever done. As he watched it sail through the air, white-hot agony seared through his body—from his shoulder to his hip—and all feeling went out of his legs and his right arm. The world spun and he was no longer looking up at the Khan's box. A shadow passed overhead, and all he could see was the red and wet sand of the arena. He tried to lift his head, tried to find the Khan's box. Had his spear found its mark? *Virgin, into thy hands I place my—*

INTO HYPERBOREA

"WHERE ARE WE?" Yasper squinted up at the sky, as if assessing the location of the sun might be of some assistance in an otherwise futile effort at divining their location. In all directions, the steppe went on forever, a flatness marred only by the scraggly knobs of wormwood.

The landscape was—though Cnán didn't want to belabor the point—not much different from what it had been for the previous phase of the moon. "We're getting close," she said, catching Raphael's eye and hiding a smile.

"Close to what?" the Dutch alchemist wanted to know. He idly scratched his jaw, an unconscious tic most of the men had adopted since they had shaved their beards as part of Feronantus's initiative to blend in more readily.

Other than Raphael and Istvan, the men were very Western in appearance, and given their need to move quickly and effortlessly across the broad steppe they needed to be less conspicuous. With much grumbling, they had shaved their heads and beards, and with the assistance of a salve concocted by the alchemist and daily exposure to the sun, their skin tones had been darkened as well.

"We're close to that bush over there," Cnán said, pointing.

"Ah," Yasper said, throwing up his hands. "Now I know exactly where we are." He dropped his arms until he could look down one arm at the bush (which looked like every other bush for miles in any direction) and along the other at the route they had been following. "Yes," he said, wrinkling his nose and peering down his arm, "it is a good thing I have the latest inventions from Arabia to guide us." He wiggled one of his thumbs. "We are, and this measurement is exceptionally accurate—"

"To within one thumb width, at least," Rædwulf interjected.

"Better mine than yours," Yasper chortled. "As I was saying, yes, we are exactly *halfway*." He raised his arms again and looked at the company, rather pleased with himself.

Istvan chewed on the end of his mustache and glowered. Both Percival and Feronantus dozed in their saddles, oblivious to the alchemist's wit. Eleázar was a half mile ahead, riding point, and of the remaining quartet—Vera, Raphael, Rædwulf, and Cnán—only Cnán regularly engaged Yasper. She liked the quirky Dutchman's company; he had a lively insouciance and an inquisitive eagerness that made the long days and nights of their journey palatable. When she had made this journey west before, she had ridden along for many, many months, and she could recall very little of the journey.

Cnán stole a glance at Feronantus and Percival. They were alike in many ways, even though many years separated them. Feronantus was, in fact, old enough to have fathered every member of the company and, in some cases, of such an age that he could be someone's grandfather. Percival was younger than the other Shield-Brethren, but it was his bearing and his *vision* that lent the impression of gravid wisdom, the sort that usually comes with having survived many hard winters. In fact, she was starting to think that he was not much older than she, and this realization had caused her some distress a few days back.

"I am quite serious, though," Yasper continued, dragging her from her thoughts. "Where are we?"

"It's not far now," she replied, enjoying the consternation her words wrought on the alchemist's face.

"Weren't we supposed to meet that trader, Benjamin?"

"We are."

"When? We didn't meet up with him after the river. You found a note that we were supposed to go somewhere else. A rock, wasn't it? Some sort of landmark that would be obvious. How many days' journey was that supposed to have been?"

"Six," she said. "But we were chasing Alchiq, remember?"

"I thought we were looking for Istvan."

Cnán shrugged as if to say those two things were one and the same. "We went north when we should have been going south."

Yasper groaned. "I knew we should have stayed closer to the trade routes."

"We'll be there soon," Cnán assured him.

"You still haven't told me where *there* is."

"Soon." She nodded toward the horizon. "Can't you see it?"

Yasper whirled in his saddle, leaning forward like a hunting dog catching a scent. He even quivered a bit in excitement. "Where?" he said, a tiny quaver in his voice.

Rædwulf pointed, and Cnán marveled at his eyesight. She *knew* the rock lay in that direction; she had felt the gentle tug in her belly earlier in her day that said she was going in the right direction, but she hadn't spotted the lone finger of stone jutting up from the steppe yet. She had been looking for it, and even though the air was crystalline in its clarity, she couldn't see it yet. But, apparently, Rædwulf could.

"A day's ride," the tall Englishman said.

Raphael glanced up from the tiny journal he was constantly scribbling in. "Only then will we be halfway," he pointed out.

Yasper stood in his saddle, straining to see the tiny dot on the horizon that Rædwulf could see. "Next time,"—he sank back down—"can we pick a target closer to home?"

Cnán caught Raphael looking at her, an oddly gentle look in his eyes, and she gave him a wistful smile before ducking her head and kneeing her horse lightly to get it to trot a little faster. *Home*, she thought. *Where is that for a lost little leaf like me?*

* * *

"Oh, my friends, I did not recognize you!" Benjamin leaped down from his horse and approached the Shield-Brethren's horses. The trader offered them a wide smile and a wider embrace, hugging each one of them in turn, except for Istvan, who deigned to get down from his horse. "The steppe has changed you," he observed. "Well, most of you."

"Only on the outside," Raphael quipped, disengaging himself from the trader's hug.

"It is a very clever disguise." Benjamin fingered Raphael's plain cloak, and the gleam in his eye said he had felt the ridged texture of the maille beneath the simple homespun cloth. "From a distance, you look like Kipchaks or Cumans, not altogether unusual in this region, and this one"—he indicated Cnán—"always adds a bit of Eastern flair to your company. Up close, I would still think Cumans, what with your garb and your saddles. Most would not think twice about who you were." He tapped his forehead. "But I have traded this route too long to not notice the little things."

"We did not expect to confound you, Benjamin," Feronantus explained. "We only hoped to become invisible to the dull-eyed so that our passage would not be remembered or hindered."

"It is a good strategy," the trader nodded. "When you did not arrive at the caravanserai as immediately as we had planned, I suspected your mission had waylaid you. When the survivors of your encounter with the *jaghun* started to limp through, I knew you would not dare to meet me there. Fortunately, knowing your companion," he glanced at Cnán, "I suspected you might be able to find this place."

He slapped Raphael on the shoulder. "Oh, but I have been enjoying the wild tales that have preceded you. I have heard a number of stories about Western devils rising out of darkness, spitting fire, and walking across water."

Raphael laughed. "I suspect the last may be overly embellished."

"It was not my place to dissuade these people of the errors in their stories. I am but a humble trader," Benjamin said. "I would not dream of interfering with the fabrication of local legends."

"What of Graymane?" Feronantus asked. "The one called Alchiq."

"An elusive ghost, that one." Benjamin's face lost some of its levity. "As I came east, I made inquiries and heard very little. The few who spoke of him tended to whisper their rumors, as if they were worried he might hear them. Though I cannot imagine how, as everyone agreed that he was hurrying east, leaving a trail of dead horses in his wake. He asked many questions too as he rode—too many, in my opinion. He heard few satisfactory answers, which have led others to wonder about the cause of his ferocious curiosity."

"How many days ahead of us?" Feronantus asked.

"Enough."

"Aye," Feronantus sighed. He raised his eyes toward the impressive spire of the rock. "We will rest and resupply tonight; tomorrow, we will acquire fresh horses and ride on. Friend Benjamin, I would ask a boon of you. We had hoped to utilize your expertise on our journey, sheltering ourselves in the midst of your caravan, but I fear your need to stop and trade will only hinder our pace. Events, I am afraid to admit, have left us bereft of not only one of our numbers but also of time. We must get to the *Khagan* before Alchiq can reach and warn him. If we cannot beat him there, we must hope that his warning is delayed or otherwise ignored. Otherwise..."

"Yes," Benjamin mused, resting a finger on his lips. "I see your predicament. My caravan can offer you more invisibility than you already possess, but it will, alas, move at a rate that will not be to your liking. If I were to abandon my cargo to one of my caravan masters, he would, most likely, rob me blind and leave my camels in Samarkand." He shook his head. "Hardly a suitable end to a trade caravan that has gone back and forth along the Silk Road for nearly three generations."

Feronantus said nothing, and Cnán leaned forward to scratch her horse along its mane. She—and the rest of the company—had become accustomed to their leader's long silences. It was rarely due to an extended bout of thinking on Feronantus's part, but more for the sake of others in the conversation. Feronantus had already considered, rejected, and postulated several possible solutions, and in his mind he had already settled on the most suitable answer. He was simply waiting for the rest of them to come to the same conclusion.

Cnán found her own readiness to follow Feronantus's conclusions without convoluted mental peregrinations of her own both comforting and unsettling. She was allowing herself to become complacent with the company, letting them do her thinking for her.

"No decision need be made immediately," Benjamin said. "Come. Let us eat and rest. We have much to discuss before the morning." He beckoned to the company as he strode toward his camp.

Cnán grinned. Benjamin was a very adroit trader. He had neatly avoided Feronantus's trap.

* * *

Raphael had never seen a land as flat and inhospitable as the steppe. Scoured clean by the wind, the landscape east of the river where they had fought Alchiq's *jaghun* had been brutal in its emptiness, as if this were a land abandoned by God. There were animals and plants that thrived on the endless plain, enough that a desperate party could sustain itself, but such a life was spent being cold, miserable, and constantly hungry.

According to Cnán, it was only going to get worse until they reached the Mongolian Plateau on the other side of several mountain ranges.

Raphael doubted the rest of the company were familiar with Herodotus and Pliny, ancient historians who had tried to make sense of the myriad of travelers' tales that described the distant edges of the known world. Alexander had used Herodotus's *Histories* as his map of the East, and the Macedonian conqueror redrew all of the known maps by the time of his death. Pliny, hundreds of years later, tried to make further sense of the tangled histories of the peoples encompassed by Alexander's reach, but he never traveled to all of the places that he wrote about.

It struck Raphael as both strange and marvelous that he, a bastard born in the Levant and raised in Al-Andalus, was seeing more of the world than either Herodotus or Pliny. Both had written of a land called Hyperborea, where the north wind lived in a vast cave. They repeated stories of one-eyed giants and gryphons, forever at war with one another, though it was difficult to see what was worth fighting about on these barren steppes.

As the company settled itself following a simple feast (one that was mouth-wateringly delicious in comparison with their diet of salted meat and dried berries over the last few weeks), Raphael took it upon himself to investigate the rock. *Perhaps*, he reasoned, *I might find some gryphon feathers.*

The rock was a mystery, a prominent landmark in a land that had none. It was shaped like a sundial's gnomon, oriented east to west with the higher end in the east. It cast a significant shadow, and were they staying a day or two more, Raphael would have wanted to scale it. He was intrigued by the allure of the view from its pointed peak. How far could he see from the prow of this rocky ship? Who else had been up there, and had they left any markings for later travelers to decipher?

Boreas may have smoothed the sharp edges of the rock, but there were still narrow channels cut in the limestone as if from water (leading Raphael to speculate that the weather had been vastly different in this region once) as well as pockets and divots filled with twigs and down from generations of nesting birds. Much like an oasis in the desert, the rock offered shelter and solace, providing a place where men and animals could pretend the surrounding land was not intolerably harsh.

Benjamin's camp was situated on the southern side, and Raphael hiked around the thicker end of the rock, mainly to see the other side. It was the same as the other, though at this time of year, the shadows were longer. He clambered across the rough scree and laid his hands on the rock directly, marveling at how cool the stone was to the touch. Letting his right hand rest on the rock, he walked east, idly wondering if he could circumnavigate the rock before nightfall. He chided himself on such frivolous thinking. As the day cooled, there might be beasts that would come out of hiding to hunt, and he was out of earshot of the camp.

He paused, his hand dropping to the hilt of his sword as he caught sight of movement ahead of him. He relaxed as he recognized Cnán's shape, but his curiosity was immediately piqued as he wondered what she was doing. Her posture suggested she was looking for something.

His foot dislodged a rock, which clattered noisily as it rolled, and the Binder whirled in his direction. So as to not spook her further, he raised an arm and called out a greeting. He slid down from the rocky sill and strode toward her, making no pretense at having been spying on her. "Ho, Cnán. I see you have been curious about the spire as well."

Her face was guarded, and she was clearly wrestling with deciding how to reply, if at all.

Raphael beamed, opting to appear as nonthreatening as possible. "Do you know who Herodotus was? He was a Greek scholar, and he wrote this wonderful book called *The Histories*. He attempted to collate the stories of the known world into a comprehensive narrative—it is very impressive." He knew he was babbling, but he wanted her to be at ease. "He wrote of a people known as the *Arimaspoi*. They had one eye in the center of their foreheads. Very warlike."

"I am not familiar with them," Cnán said slowly, peering at Raphael with thinly veiled unease.

"Their mortal enemies were gryphons. Do you know what a gryphon is?"

Cnán shook her head.

"It is an enormous bird that has the body of a lion and the head and wings of an eagle. Many cultures regarded it as a sacred creature, a symbol of the divine power of their gods. To adapt the gryphon as your symbol was to harness the magic of the gods, and I imagine the Arimaspoi hunted them, for their feathers among other things."

"I have seen no feathers," Cnán said, shifting from one leg to the other.

"Nor have I," said Raphael sadly. "Can I ask what it is you are looking for?"

His question caught Cnán off guard, and she blinked owlishly. She sighed heavily when he said nothing more, waiting for her to offer some explanation. Beckoning him to follow her, she started walking east.

Raphael followed, wisely keeping his mouth shut.

After a few minutes of walking, Cnán spotted something that was indiscernible to Raphael. She led him up to a crack in the rock face that stretched far above their heads, and Raphael was surprised to realize the crack was both wider and deeper than he had first thought. One slab of the rock overlapped the other, hiding the true depth of the crevice from casual examination. Cnán squeezed through the narrow gap, and Raphael stopped, eyeing the tight space with some trepidation. He might fit, but he wasn't so sure he wanted to find out. Especially if he managed to force himself through and then couldn't get back.

"I'll be right back," Cnán said, and before he could argue otherwise—*and what would be the point of telling her to stop, really?*—she slid farther into the crack and turned a corner he hadn't realized was there. He stood beside the crack, somewhat at a loss as to what he should be doing while he waited, and just as he was starting to think he *could* squeeze through the gap, Cnán returned.

She slipped back out of the crack and showed him a strip of braided horsehair. It had been tied in an intricate series of double and triple knots, and he knew there was some purpose to the order of them, but he couldn't discern it. "You found something from your kin-sisters," he said.

"Aye," Cnán said. "A weather report." She tucked the horsehair braid into her a pocket of her jacket.

"Is that all?" Raphael asked.

"No," she said tersely, but after staring at him for a moment, chewing her lower lip, she relented. "Some of us are firmly rooted in the soil of our birth. Others, like myself, travel endlessly. The ones who put down roots know everything there is to know about where they live. The wanderers know less about their destination, but they know how to get from one place to another. Spots like this one are where we leave messages for each other. Some of them"—she patted her pocket—"are as simple as notes about the weather, about local warlords and who is fighting whom in the region, or about the location of caches of food and money. Others are..."

Raphael looked at the crack once more, suddenly desirous to try to squeeze past the lip of stone. *Maybe without my armor...*

"Come," Cnán said, grabbing his arm, not altogether gently. "Let us return to the camp." She tugged him. "Even if you could squeeze through," she said softly, "you would not be able to read any of the messages." She pulled the horsehair braid from her pocket and waggled it in front of his face. "'There is no snow in the gap,'" she quoted. "Can you decipher these knots?'"

Raphael shook his head.

"Let it remain a mystery then," she said. "Like your gryphons."

* * *

After dinner, by the light of a roaring fire, Benjamin laid down a large piece of cowhide and unrolled his map of the trade routes. The company clustered around the worn palimpsest, trying to make sense of the marks and letters that had been written and rewritten over many years.

"This is the Yaik," Benjamin explained, tracing a thin line that ran along one edge of the map. "This is Saray-Jük, not far from where we had planned to meet, but wisely, you bypassed that caravanserai and came here"—his finger traced to a small triangle—"instead."

"The middle of nowhere," Yasper quipped.

Benjamin smiled, and dropped his finger to the closest line on the map. "We are north of the Silk Roads, and as you can see, they tend to run much farther south. There are two, primarily. One runs north along the Tien Shan Mountains, through Urumqui and Turfan, and the other runs much farther south, beyond the Taklamakan Desert. Both take you to the heart of China, which is not where you want to go." His finger had been moving across the map as he spoke, highlighting each of the places as he mentioned them, and when he finished, he moved his finger up into a large blank spot where, seemingly at random, he spotted and tapped the map. "Karakorum, the imperial palace of Ögedei Khan, *Khagan* of the Mongol Empire, is here."

The members of the company examined the map for a few minutes, silently considering the information that Benjamin had given them.

Percival cleared his throat and leaned forward, his finger gliding across the map to a point that almost seemed to summon his finger, an *X* that was the result of two mountain ranges coming together. "What of this place?" he asked.

Benjamin glanced at Feronantus and Cnán briefly before he answered. "It is a pass called the Zuungar Gap," he said.

"What do you know of this gap?" Feronantus asked.

"It's a high pass," Benjamin said. "A long and narrow course through the mountains. If there is, indeed, not much snow, it will be an easy route." He traced a finger along the map. "You stay on the western side of the Tien Shan until here, cut over through the gap, and you will find yourself on the edge of a place known as the Gurbantünggüt. As deserts go, it is not as bad as some, and travel across it will be fairly easy until you reach the Altai Mountains, which are not as imposing as the Tien Shan—the Celestial Mountains—but they have other dangers." He paused to draw breath, and he glanced at Cnán, a flicker of a smile touching his lips. "Once you have crossed *those* mountains, you will be on the Mongolian Plateau. From there, it is only a week or so hard ride to Karakorum."

"Is that all?" Yasper asked.

"It is a dangerous route," Benjamin continued, "and one I would not attempt if I was not *certain* about the weather."

Feronantus looked carefully at Raphael, Percival, and then Cnán, and then spoke for all of them. "I think we are," he said.

Percival beamed, and Raphael wanted to run away from the firelight, out in the darkness around the rock, where he could berate God and no one would hear his blasphemy.

TENEBRAS IN lucem

FERENC WAS INTRIGUED by this cardinal Oddone de Monferrato. His eyes seemed to be in a permanent state of gaping. Helmuth had explained to him how much this man had been through, what he had seen and survived, especially far away from here in the little island nation of England. But to Ferenc, he looked like a deer startled by everything happening to him and around him.

They were a motley little group, returning to the city: Léna, the cardinal, and the soldier named Helmuth; Ocyrhoe and Ferenc, in clothes much too big for them—like children dragged along on a family outing. Helmuth was there as the eyes of the Emperor, to keep Monferrato in line and in view. Léna had requested permission to go with the party, and her reasons had not been made clear to the others, but Ocyrhoe suspected she wanted to ascertain for herself what had happened to the other Binders in Rome.

Ocyrhoe looked so happy to have her company that Ferenc was actually a little jealous. His primary sense of purpose since arriving in the city was to be of use to her; now he had to share that purpose with somebody else. He noticed Ocyrhoe going out of her way to pay attention to him, to let him know that she was still glad of his company, but that struck him as condescending. He had drained his face of expression as they began their journey back toward the city walls; he stopped signing to her or even speaking to Helmuth.

He decided he did not respect Helmuth. The Holy Roman soldier had an arrogance that Ferenc did not think was justified. Not that arrogance was ever justified, but he could abide it in people who were clearly in some way superior. Helmuth was ugly and large, and seemed preoccupied with appearing as subservient as possible to Emperor Frederick. This, perversely, seemed to be the root source of his arrogance, which made no sense to Ferenc.

Léna—to Ferenc's mind—was similarly suspect. She was standoffish, and Ocyrhoe seemed so desperate to make a good impression on her, to demonstrate that she was not foolish or inadequate. He did not like to see his friend embarrass herself this way. Even before they had departed, he had tried to warn her about Léna.

She is going to Rome to replace you, Ferenc had signed to her. *You will be useless in Rome if Léna is also there.*

She had given him an impatient look and waved him off. But then, about an hour later, as they approached the gates of the city, Ocyrhoe slowed down to let Helmuth and Monferrato pass her, joining Ferenc as he brought up the rear.

Hello, she signed on his arm, smiling.

Hello, he signed back, fingers lax.

Soon we will save Father Rodrigo, she signed again, heavily tapping his forearm, as if to focus his attention.

He made a doubtful face.

This cardinal will vote and break the tie, and then they will all be released, and Father Rodrigo will be with you, she signed.

He shrugged in grudging acknowledgment.

And then what will you do? Tell me please, she signed, with an intense look.

Ferenc withheld his answering fingers. He had never stopped to think about this, not once since Mohi. Everything had been an unwelcome quest for him, from the moment of his mother's death at the hand of the Mongols. First with Father Rodrigo to get to Rome; then with Ocyrhoe to free Father Rodrigo. The priest had never wanted anything but to get close to the Pope; surely, after all this time sequestered with the high-up Church authorities, that would be easy for him now, whoever the Pope was.

So what would Father Rodrigo do next? That would determine Ferenc's course. Months ago he had stopped thinking about wanting anything for himself. Everyone and everything he knew and loved had died or been destroyed. He had no reason to go back, and nothing to go toward. The more he thought about this, the more it felt as if the hard dirt road beneath his feet was giving way like quicksand.

He felt tapping on his forearm and realized Ocyrhoe was trying to communicate with him. *Are you all right all right all right?* she kept asking.

All I know is useless, he signed back.

Ocyrhoe nodded solemnly, and he was sure she understood exactly what he meant. They ran forward to catch up with the others, but at that moment, the others stopped.

"We approach the gates," Léna announced from the front, turning to face them. "From here we need our tracker and our native to get us to the Septizodium."

Our turn to be in charge, Ocyrhoe signed with a small smile, and then grabbed his sleeve and pulled him forward.

* * *

Rodrigo had had no difficulty convincing his new chaperone, Brother Lucio, that there had been some mistake—he was merely supposed to be treated well and made comfortable, but not actually guarded. And so, when he explained that he dearly missed his native city and wanted the liberty to explore his old haunts, especially around the basilica, he was allowed to go, with only a young page boy, Timoteo, shadowing him.

Rodrigo remembered the city so clearly, although he was not used to approaching it from this side of the Tiber. From where he stood, a broad bridge, hundreds of strides long, led to the northwest corner of the city proper. This was the only part of the city that relied on water rather than walls to protect it.

He crossed the bridge and strode along the broad avenues. There was a vague memory of passing through here while he was feverish and wounded—how disturbingly loud and confusing everything seemed then...just a few days ago, was it? He knew where he was now, and he did not mind the bustle. He followed one road that led him almost due southeast, as Timoteo silently followed at his heels, lugging a water skin and saying nothing.

Rodrigo recognized certain buildings—merchants' shops, this intersection, that ruined shrine...a pleasing familiarity washed over him with the soft autumn warmth of the sun.

After walking the distance of several bowshots—he was still thinking in terms of battle!—Rodrigo paused in the crowded avenue and turned to the boy. "Do you see that wall?" he asked, pointing to an entire city block hidden behind an unbroken stone barricade. Distinctive rooftops rose up beyond the wall, interspersed with thick treetops, carefully trimmed. Timoteo nodded. "Do you know who lives there?" Rodrigo asked. The boy shook his head.

"That," said Rodrigo, as if sharing the secret to a magic trick, "*that* is the home of the Orsini family. When I was a child, they were like powerful kings...in my imagination. But now I have actually met Orsini, in the flesh, and he is just a regular man like me." Rodrigo smiled. "Perhaps even more regular. And should we move another thousand paces, along this street, on the left, we will come to an even larger and more magnificent palace. That is the home of the

Colonna family. When I was your age, they too were great as kings in my estimation, and I feared them. But now I have met Cardinal Colonna, and he too is just a mortal man. In fact, he is friendlier than most men."

Timoteo stared at Rodrigo without speaking, probably baffled as to a proper response.

"And when I was a child, everyone in Rome knew that those two families absolutely despised each other."

"They still do, Father," said the boy. "Everyone knows that."

"Well then, my wise one, I will tell you something both enlightening and entertaining," Rodrigo said, smiling beneficently. "Yesterday, I saw Cardinal Colonna and Senator Orsini in the same room, forced by circumstance to be civil. It was like watching actors in a play. I felt as if I was in the audience of a very subtle, special comedy. I thought, all those stories I heard when I was a child—and here are these two characters, acting them out, for our amusement!"

The boy smiled sheepishly. "What did they do?" he asked.

"Cardinal Colonna kept making jests at Orsini's expense," said Rodrigo. "It was not very Christian of him, but he *was* rather witty. And Orsini kept growling at him like this." Here Rodrigo attempted to imitate the throaty rumble of a bear. The page boy grinned. "They were in front of lots of people they thought were important, and so they could do no more than that."

Timoteo frowned. "You mean the cardinals? Those are people who are important, aren't they, Father?"

Rodrigo gave the boy a knowing smile. "My son, in the eyes of Heaven, we are all as little children. No one of us is more important than another. In fact, the more important we think we are, the less we stand out in the eyes of the Lord. Remember that, if you yourself someday become a man of God." He looked around the avenue. "We have a ways to go yet before we reach our destination."

"What is our destination, Father?"

"I fondly remember the area around the Colosseum," Rodrigo said. "I recall there is always a nice bustle of people. I would like to be surrounded by a bustle of people. That way, if I have something important I need to say, I have only to say it once."

He gestured for the boy to walk along beside him. Timoteo happily followed. Rodrigo knew that the boy found him both gentle and amusing, and likely regarded him as no more eccentric than the other priests.

Rodrigo wandered on, humming old melodies, following pleasant memories, turning, turning, taking this lane, then that, looking up between the leaning, towering buildings. An hour later he saw that the young boy was no longer with him—had somehow lagged behind and was now out of sight and earshot.

Rodrigo smiled some more. All would be well; nothing was amiss. The boy would find him again, if God willed it to be so. Father Rodrigo Bendrito was blessed in such things, for Providence was with him.

Providence, and what he carried concealed in his robes.

* * *

"What do you mean he isn't here?" Colonna demanded of the sheepish young priest. "You were assigned to keep an eye on him. He was half dead. Where could he have gone?"

The young man lowered his eyes, looking as if he wouldn't mind a nice straightforward crucifixion instead of a grilling from the entire College of Cardinals. "He went into the crypt, and I allowed him time alone down there. He seemed greatly recovered when he came out, and I turned him over to the care of Brother Lucio, as I was scheduled to take confessions in the chapel. I cannot account for Brother Lucio's care of him, nor do I know where Brother Lucio himself is now."

Fieschi turned his attention away from this useless young cleric and seared the half dozen guards around them with his eyes. "Find Brother Lucio," he ordered. "Bring him here at once."

The ten cardinals stood in the antechamber to the bishop's conference hall. Despite the relief of being free from months of deprivation and now surrounded by arguably the most sumptuous decorations in all of Christendom, the ten cardinals were so beside themselves they took no notice of their surroundings at all. Sunlight streamed in at an angle from one set of open doors. It was magnificent, almost literally golden, and it cast their shadows artfully across a marble floor. Not even da Capua, the most artistic one among them, noticed the beauty.

"This is a calamity," Fieschi said angrily to the others. "The leader of the Church has gone missing." He tried to remain calm, but a worm of doubt was gnawing in his belly. He glanced at Colonna and Capocci, wondering if they were responsible for this mishap.

"Perhaps we need to get another leader, then," de Segni said in a sharp, bitter tone. "One who is voted into power because people want him in the position."

"You are both overreacting," said Annibaldi blandly. "The man is surely somewhere in the immediate area, and as soon as he is retrieved, we will explain the unusual circumstances. He is, after all, a man of God. He will surely do the right thing."

Fieschi chewed his lower lip, glaring at Capocci. He was trying to account for the movements of the two clowns since all the cardinals had left the voting chamber. Had they spoken to anyone since? Had either of them wandered off for a little while?

* * *

Rodrigo moved slowly through the crowded city, toward the main gateway to the Colosseum. It was perhaps a mile away, but his stroll took longer than it usually takes to walk such a distance—in part because of the crowds, but also because Father Rodrigo was in no particular hurry. He ambled more than strode, and with a small smile or even a sigh of nostalgia he imagined pointing out to young Ferenc places of historical or personal significance. He pretended for now that Ferenc was still with him. He wanted to thank Ferenc for bringing him home, and he wanted the boy to feel welcome in this city, welcome enough to call it *home* as well. He wondered where Ferenc was. He would have to find him, and make sure he was safe.

Somehow, the boys always strayed...

But there was something else he had to do first.

* * *

"But he was absolutely unremarkable," Brother Lucio insisted, from his knees. He had been impelled to this level by the collective glowering of cardinals—glowering so intense it seemed to add to his earthly weight. "I had been told I'd be put in charge of a demented invalid, but the man who was handed off to me was as healthy and rational as any man in this room." He dared to look up at them, cringing. "I am always obedient, but this was an imposition on my day, which was already a very full one. It is the beginning of the entry of the grape harvest into the compound, and it is my responsibility to oversee it. So when a perfectly lucid priest assured me that he did not want to be a source of trouble, I did not see the need to doubt him."

"Where did he go?" Fieschi said coldly.

Brother Lucio shook his head. "He said he wanted to go into the city, because he was a native and had not been here for a long time. I managed to spare Timoteo, one of the lay boys who help us with organizing the harvest influx. The two of them left over the Ponte Sant'Angelo."

"When?"

"About an hour ago, perhaps two." Lucio looked extremely ill at ease, which Fieschi felt was entirely deserved.

"And nobody knows where they went?" Fieschi demanded. "They are at large in Rome?"

"They could not have gone far," Lucio began in an apologetic voice, but was cut off by Fieschi's hand slapping him hard across the face.

"You negligent fool!" he snarled. "You've misplaced the Pope!"

Despite themselves, Colonna and Capocci snickered at the sound of this. Fieschi whirled around, his scarlet cloak swirling like wine in a cup, and glared at them. They immediately repressed their grins, but this only made them look like naughty schoolboys. Muttering, Fieschi turned away from them and looked at the other cardinals.

"Perhaps he is headed for the Septizodium," he suggested. "We should send guards there at once."

"Yes," said Capocci in a meaningful voice, rubbing his bandaged hand gingerly. "I'll wager he is looking for his friend Cardinal Somercotes."

"Perhaps he is seeking his childhood haunts," Castiglione suggested. "Are there any records of his background? Do we know where he was ordained or who he studied under?"

As much as Fieschi did not want to admit it, this was a sound idea. He looked around the room irritably for someone else to order around. There were now a dozen priests and two bishops standing with them, all equally unable to do anything about the situation.

"You," Fieschi said, randomly pointing to one of the older priests. "Discover where this Father Rodrigo studied, and where he served before he went to Hungary. There must be some particular church he has affiliations with in the city, and he may be headed in that direction."

The man bowed hurriedly and left. The other priests looked torn between relief at not being given the assignment, and forlornness at being stuck with the glowering cardinals until further notice.

* * *

The boy, Timoteo, ran up beside Rodrigo, panting and wide-eyed.

"I thought I'd lost you!" the boy cried.

"I am here, no harm. I have been walking and thinking."

"They will be looking for us. We have been gone too long!"

"Then let them find us."

They passed by the dumping ground that a thousand years earlier had been the Forum, the center of Roman government and religion. There were many markets in the city of Rome, but one of the largest was in the open space between the Forum and the Colosseum. The cemented combination of debris and ruined buildings had raised the height of the ancient Forum so that it seemed to peer and hover awkwardly over the western edge of this market.

He remembered climbing those rubbish-strewn ruins as a child, and he even remembered a section—if it was still intact—where part of a wall of the Temple of Vesta had fallen, without breaking, onto its side, creating a flat area not unlike a dais. The accidental acoustics of half-fallen columns around it had made it an effective place to shout from, if, as a child, one wanted to get the attention of several hundred market-goers and market-sellers at once. He had done that when he was younger than the lad who followed him—Timoteo. He even remembered how to get there.

Rodrigo approached the awkward, angular bulge on the earth that was the ruins of the Forum. The boy stumbled up after him.

"This way, my son," Rodrigo said with a smile. "I am going to show you a secret way into the marketplace, and then you are going to witness something that people will talk about for generations to come."

He led the boy up a wobbly crest of boulders and broken walls that formed an uneven series of steps and stairs. They moved sideways across what had once been the upper portico of some great administrative building. The stone was warm and reflected the bright afternoon sunlight. It felt wonderful, so wonderful, to feel the sun shine upon him in his native city. Rodrigo watched the familiar pathways of years gone by unfold before him, unchanged but by the smallest degree. When they reached the edge of the portico, he gestured to the boy to look.

Below them by some dozen feet spread the western edge of the enormous market. It was mostly a fruit and vegetable market, but to the north there were several horse traders, and farther east the mercers' stalls began.

Timoteo took in an awe-filled breath at this unusual perspective. "It's beautiful," he said. Then, pointing to a small crowd gathered together and facing a single point, he asked, "What is that?"

Rodrigo looked and huffed dismissively. "Nothing has changed since my early days here. That, my son, is a false prophet, preaching some heresy to gullible innocents whose souls he may well damn for all eternity. Such men as he are popular in gathering spots like this. Look, there is another one," he said, and pointed to the south where a smaller band of women with market baskets stared slack-jawed at a man in a bright blue robe who stood on a cart, gesticulating madly. "And there too." A bowshot to the east of him there was another man, this one dressed in sackcloth, shouting abusively into a growing crowd made up mostly of young men.

"Where do they come from?" Timoteo asked, genuinely alarmed at seeing souls led astray. "Why does anybody listen to them?"

"That," said Rodrigo, "is an excellent question. Let us attempt to find the answer to it. Will you come with me?" He gestured forward. The portico ended but abutted the fallen temple wall that Rodrigo had anticipated. He had to take one unnerving jump across a gap the breadth of an arm; the gap was deep, and he could see the jagged stubs of ruined columns below. For the boy's sake, he acted as if it did not bother him.

The boy, perhaps for Rodrigo's sake, acted likewise, and jumped right after him.

Now they stood in clear view of hundreds of people. Rodrigo glanced down at the boy. "*Et in semitis quas ignoraverunt ambulare eos faciam. Ponam tenebras coram eis in lucem, et prava in recta,*" he said, and seeing the boy's confusion, he offered him a genial smile. "It is my time," he explained, "I have something to show them." He reached into his satchel and pulled out the communion cup he had brought with him from the tomb of Saint Peter.

Timoteo's eyes grew very wide.

* * *

A guard entered the antechamber where the cardinals were clustered in their confusion, a squirming figure thrown over his shoulder. He dumped his cargo in the middle of the marble floor, and gesturing at it, he offered a terse explanation. "This one ran up to me like he was being pursued by the Devil," he said. Out of the corner of his eye, Fieschi saw da Capua hastily make the sign of the cross to ward off any truth to the man's statement. "Name's Timoteo, he says. He's seen something. Maybe what you're looking—"

"Of course," Fieschi said, waving the guard away from the boy sprawled on the floor. The boy was still half hysterical, and with little prompting from Fieschi, his story spilled out in frighteningly rapid rush of words. The cardinals listened to his story, and their expressions changed from incredulity to disbelief to—for more than a few—horror. Especially when he reached the part about...

Fieschi nearly pounced on him. "Magical priest?" he said, furiously gesturing the others to back away. "This man. Was his name Bendrito? Father Rodrigo Bendrito?"

"Yes, Your Eminence," Timoteo said, trembling even more now that he was being stared at by so many angry, well-dressed men. "I was assigned to go with him into the city."

Annibaldi glanced up and signaled to one of the several extraneous guards by the door. "Release Lucio," he said, "but bring him back here." Then his eyes, like all the others in the room, went back to the boy.

"He took me to the marketplace at the Forum," the boy said. "He was kind, he seemed normal, until we got there, and then...and then..."

"And then *what?*" demanded Fieschi. "What happened? Where is he? Why did you leave him there? He could be anywhere now!"

"Oh, no, Your Eminence," Timoteo said, gaining courage. "He'll be very easy to find. You'd have a hard time *not* finding him, I think."

"What does that mean, boy?" Fieschi demanded, as all the cardinals exchanged confused looks.

"He began preaching," said the boy, and stood up, taking a deep breath as if to reassure himself his lungs could still do that. "Like all those crazy preachers in the marketplace. He began prophesying and talking about the Mongol invaders bringing an end to the world, and how to defeat them."

There was the slightest collective sigh as all the cardinals exchanged knowing glances. "So he is still demented," said Fieschi. "Despite reports to the contrary."

"He did not seem demented, Your Eminence," Timoteo said. "He got a lot of attention right away. Well, not he himself so much, but..." his eyes widened. "Your Eminences, I know you won't believe this, but he was carrying...he said it was...it did look—"

"What?" Fieschi demanded.

The boy seemed on the verge of tears, but his face was caught between despair and such a wild delight that Fieschi could not help but feel a sense of dread creeping over him.

"It glowed," the boy said. "When he held it up. It was so bright, and it blinded me. I put up my hand to shield my eyes, but he turned it and it only glowed more brightly. He smiled at me, and...and he said it was—"

"Damnation, boy!" Fieschi could not contain his impatience. "What was he tossing around out there?"

"The Cup," the boy said, staring around at the group. "The Cup of Christ."

"*What?*" demanded most of the voices of the room, followed immediately by Colonna and Capocci breaking into quiet guffaws.

"I saw it," the boy insisted.

Fieschi watched his face closely. At heart, Timoteo seemed a practical young fellow, and the reactions of the cardinals had made him swallow hard. Perhaps he was wishing he'd never said a word, but Fieschi suspected the boy would defend his story vigorously, now that he had told it. He would elaborate now, adding more details to the story. It was quite wonderful, actually, he reflected, to see how God shaped the world with such subtlety.

The priest was mad, clearly, and this boy's testimony was only going to further the cardinals' impression of the priest's insanity. The new Pope would need strict guidance, they would all see that, and it would be so much easier for him to insert himself...

"I was standing right next to him," Timoteo said. "It materialized from nowhere, and then suddenly he was holding it in his hands, and the sunlight hit it, and rays spread out from it in all directions—" here Timoteo excitedly and awkwardly tried to demonstrate emanating rays. "It was almost as if the light was reaching out to touch people, people in the crowd, and you could see it, you could see when they were touched, their faces changed, they lit up, they suddenly could not take their eyes away from him. It was the most miraculous thing I have ever seen in my life!"

The boy had gone quite far enough. Such a story could be dangerous, after all, if it got around. "That's blasphemy," said Fieschi sharply. "There is nothing miraculous about it, it was just a trick of the light. Why did you leave him there unattended when you were ordered not to?"

"But he wasn't unattended, Your Eminence," the boy said. "Hundreds and hundreds of people were hanging on his every word—"

"The child exaggerates," Fieschi said with contempt, and turned away from him. He gestured to one of the bishops. "Send guards to the Forum to find Father Rodrigo before he disappears again. Tell them to look for the crazy preacher."

"There are a lot of crazy preachers in that marketplace," Capocci pointed out with a smile.

"He...you will find him, surely," Timoteo said hurriedly, trying to be helpful. "He is the one that hundreds of people are flocking to. He could have jumped off the ledge where we were standing and been caught and carried away by them, they were so packed together, jostling to come closer, to see this miracle—and more were moving toward him every moment. I was sure we would be separated by the crowd, for there were people climbing up the ruins to get near to him. I thought it was my duty to come back here and inform Your Eminences of what was happening. Of...what I saw." He blinked at Fieschi, wide-eyed innocence. "Have I done wrong?"

For a moment, Fieschi was too flabbergasted to speak.

"It seems our new Pope already has both a calling, and a following," Colonna announced philosophically. "We really must give him more credit."

* * *

Ferenc, Ocyrhoe, and the rest of the party from the Emperor's camp entered the city without incident from the Porta Labicana, and took the left of the broad roads. This led a mile west to the Colosseum, where a turn to the left would lead south to the Septizodium.

The day was hot and dry, and the streets too noisy for comfortable conversation. Ocyrhoe led the way with Ferenc beside her, the adults abreast behind them. Occasionally Ocyrhoe would glance over her shoulder to make sure they were still close on her heels. Each time, she saw them making assorted faces of displeasure. She took it as a personal insult that they did not like her city.

When at last they reached the ruined Colosseum—and she exacted some satisfaction from the amazed expression on surly Helmuth's face—she was surprised to notice that all the foot traffic was suddenly heading only in one direction: westward. People were moving into the market area between the Colosseum and the Forum, but nobody seemed to be leaving.

Ocyrhoe knew her city well, knew how to read its pulses as if it were a living organism. Beside her, Ferenc was equally distracted, picking up on other clues from his own training: something strange was afoot.

The two of them stopped at the same moment. Ocyrhoe did not even bother to sign. She simply glanced ahead toward the marketplace, just out of view around the bend of the Colosseum, and then looked back at Ferenc, raising her eyebrows. He raised his too, and nodded.

From the market, echoing from the walls, boomed a great voice, and around that voice, the murmurs of entranced listeners... like the lowing of contented cows in a field.

"Father Rodrigo," Ferenc said.

Ocyrhoe nodded.

Without explaining, they turned together toward the market, ignoring the protests from their companions, who held back for a moment, then ran to keep up.

HE NEVER FALTERED

RUTGER LEAPED TO his feet as the spear sailed through the air. The collective voices of the audience turned from raucous cheers to screams of panic. The Shield-Brethren in attendance at the arena wore maille and carried weapons under their cloaks and plain robes in preparation for the culmination of Andreas's plan. But everything had gone horrifically wrong the moment one of Dietrich's men had walked into the arena instead of one of the Khan's fighters. The Shield-Brethren had all been waiting for the fight to end, hoping that their brother would be triumphant, but fearing they would be forced to watch him fall. Forced to watch one of theirs die, unable to do anything to prevent it. And their plan would have come to naught, undone by the Livonian Grandmaster's desire for revenge. Everything undone.

But Andreas—bold, stupid, heroic Andreas—had refused to give up. He had tried to save them anyway.

Rutger's eyes followed the path of the shaft as it vanished between the curtains of the Khan's box. He stared at the billowing curtains, trying to ascertain if it had hit its target. His lips moved in a silent prayer. *Give me some sign.*

A Mongol swathed in silks and drenched in blood staggered into view, the spear through his midsection. He was thin, dressed like a functionary.

Andreas had missed his target. The gambit had failed.

Everything was undone.

The death of the Khan would have made for much more confusion, which they had planned to use to their advantage. As it was, their enemy was simply aroused and angry, actively seeking the presence of enemies within the crowd. They had to flee the arena before anyone realized they were there. Before anyone thought to look more closely at their bulky clothing. They could not afford to be caught in a riot.

* * *

Hans wanted to scream, but his throat had seized. Wedged as he was between two watchers in the common stands, the cacophony of the crowd would have drowned him out anyway, yet he struggled to make his voice work. As if the sound of his voice might somehow change the gruesome scene before him. He struggled to make a noise as the Livonian's hand brought the heavy sword down on the Rose Knight's shoulder. The blade did not bounce off the maille, but sheared through the mesh, cutting deeply into the body underneath. *I told him there would be a friend.*

The deafening roar of the crowd overwhelmed him, hurting his ears and making the wood floor tremble and shake. *The world is falling apart,* he thought, *and we will all fall through the cracks.*

Andreas fell, a violent spray of blood all around him—in the air, in the sand. Hans wanted to look away, but his eyes—like his mouth—refused to obey. He could no more look away than he could stop what was happening with his tiny voice. *Get up!* he silently begged, though he knew Andreas would not. He had seen blood like this when the Mongols had sacked Legnica, and he knew the wound was fatal. He knew there was nothing God could do to save the Rose Knight. Nothing anyone could do.

They knew, he realized, staring at the red cross on the other man's chest. Somehow, the Livonians had known of Andreas and Kim's plan. And if they had known...

The others. I have to warn the others. Now it was his legs that wouldn't move. He had to do something—anything—but he was frozen in place, held captive by the horrible spectacle.

He did not want to watch, but he couldn't tear himself away as the Livonian raised his sword again.

* * *

The crowd was shrieking now, no longer cheering the wild battle down below. The Livonian had struck Andreas at the shoulder, and the greatsword had sliced through his maille, splitting Andreas from shoulder to hip. The sand was a filthy pit of red mud, and Andreas—*somehow, by the Virgin!*—was still alive.

Rutger forced his way to the rail, trying to ignore what was happening as he looked elsewhere. The gates were open below, and Mongol guards were streaming into the arena. In the stands, panic was already tearing through the crowds as some of the onlookers tried to flee the riot they knew was coming while others surged toward the rail. He spotted several of the Shield-Brethren, confusion and frustration writ over their features. Nearby, Styg was openly weeping, his mouth screwed up into an expression of inescapable horror. As he watched, something died inside the young man and his mouth snapped shut. He surged forward, shoving his way toward the rail.

"No!" Rutger intercepted him, hauling him back from the wooden barrier. The pain in his hands made him gasp, but he held on, holding the young man back.

Styg fought him, great sobbing gasps quaking his body. "We can't let him do this!" Styg shouted at him, and Rutger stole a glance over his shoulder at the killing floor below. "That's our *brother!*"

The Livonian was still cutting, his sword rising and falling like a butcher's cleaver, even though the body beneath his blade was clearly dead.

"Aye," Rutger snarled, hauling the young man around so that he would no longer look upon the bloody spectacle of the field. "And if you go down there, you will join him. Others will follow you, and it will all be for *naught*. We are done here. Get to the horses!"

He barked at the other Shield-Brethren within earshot. "Go, now. Get back to the chapter house."

He wasn't sure if they heard him, but they could read his command in the anguish of his face, in the bared ferocity of his teeth, in the wild fury of his gaze. They *understood* him, and obeyed, fleeing the retribution that was to come.

To the chapter house, he thought. They would regroup, grieve briefly, and then they would ready themselves. His mind raced, leaping across a dozen different courses of action as his men melted into the teeming chaos of the fleeing crowds. He gave Styg one last shove, ensuring that the young man was moving in the right direction, and then he spared one last glance back at the arena and the Khan's box.

A Mongol dignitary, wrapped in bloody silk, the spear jutting out of his body, sprawled against the railing of the Khan's pavilion. The curtains had been pulled close around the box, and the roof of the pavilion was swarming with the Khan's archers.

Andreas, he thought as he let himself fall back in the crowd. *It should have been me.*

* * *

Roosting crows cawed irritably from the rafters of the barn. Hünern had become a ghostly ruin. The Mongols had withdrawn into their camp, barring their gates and shielding their Khan. The streets were empty but for a few stragglers, too drunk or senseless to seek shelter. Even the birds had gone into hiding.

Dietrich knew the silence wouldn't last. The Mongol retreat was a strategic withdrawal so that they could order their ranks. Once they got over the initial shock of the assault, they were going to ride out in full force. While their main focus was going to be on the Shield-Brethren, there was little doubt in his mind that every living soul between them and the *Ordo Militum Vindicis Intactae* was going to be counted as an enemy.

If they survived, there was still the issue of Kristaps's actions to be dealt with. War had been declared between the two orders.

"Have you taken leave of your *senses?*" Dietrich snarled at Kristaps when he found the man. "I didn't tell you to kill him while his back was turned."

Kristaps stood before a water trough in the barn that was serving as a basin, washing Andreas's blood from his sword. From tip to hilt, the weapon had been coated with the blood of the Shield-Brethren, and no one had dared try to take the blade from Volquin's Dragon.

"I've likely saved our order, *Heermeister,*" Kristaps replied with an unnerving calm. The knight looked at Dietrich, and the *Heermeister* was struck by the utter lack of feeling in the man's unflinching gaze.

"By starting a war?" Dietrich snapped. He was in no mood for double-talk, and Kristaps's implacable stare was unnerving.

"By making our intent clear to those who *truly* hold the power here," Kristaps replied bluntly. "When the knight made his dash to throw his spear, how would it have looked if I'd let him live? Especially given that you bribed my way into the fight.

They would have seen two Western orders putting aside their differences to defy the Khan. What vengeance comes next would as likely fall on our heads as theirs. To save us, I had to defend the Khan's honor."

Silence hung between them, filled by the chatter of crows in the rafters. In the distance, a bell started to toll. Dusk was upon the city, and the dolorous tone of the bell made Dietrich shiver involuntarily. Night was coming, and only God knew if any of them would see another sunrise.

He had ordered his men to start striking their camp. They had to be ready to ride at a moment's notice. The compound had served as suitable shelter for his order, but it would not protect them at all when the Mongolian wrath was unleashed. Even if Kristaps was correct in his assessment, it would only buy them a little time. The Mongols would turn their attention to the other orders once they finished destroying the Shield-Brethren. He couldn't overlook what had happened at Mohi. The Mongols did not discriminate.

There was something else, though. A thought nagged at Dietrich, and he stared at the First Sword of Fellin, trying to elucidate his concern. "You made your point when you killed him," he said, now holding his knight's gaze. *I will not be cowed. I am your Heermeister.* "You did not need to mutilate his body."

Kristaps said nothing, though whether his silence was due to genuine regret, which Dietrich doubted, or because there was no proper way to excuse his behavior, was not apparent.

The big knight had already doffed his maille, and he slowly slid the sleeves of his gambeson up to his elbows. He raised his forearms to Dietrich, revealing circular scars on both arms. Old burns, seared deep into the meat of his forearms. In the fading light of the day, they looked like heraldic devices, though smeared and stretched across the skin.

Kristaps's blue eyes flashed. "They mutilated me first."

* * *

But for the evening birds and the distant tolling of a bell in Hünern, the Shield-Brethren toiled in silence. Armor was being donned, swords sharpened, and those horses that were not yet readied were being saddled. Rutger felt the pain in his joints acutely, a grinding heat in the knuckles of his fingers. It had robbed him of his place in the order years ago, and the succeeding years had slowly buried his disappointment until he had come to accept the lesser role of quartermaster. But there was a need to hold a sword again.

Eventually, the Shield-Brethren gathered around a pyre erected from the remaining firewood. Rutger counted thirty somber faces. Full knight initiates, squires, and the *untested* like Styg and Eilif who had more than proven their worth in the past few weeks. Andreas had been right, Rutger realized as he looked at the assembled men. *They were boys no more.* He was surrounded by his brothers—the only family he had ever known—and their hearts and minds were as focused to the task ahead as their bodies were ready. There were no other men among whom he would rather stand when it came time to die.

The Mongols had taken what was left of Andreas's corpse and nailed it to the walls of the arena. While he would have preferred to give Andreas a proper burial, dying in an effort to retrieve the body was an utterly foolish way to honor their fallen brother. What few personal items that remained would be enough, a symbolic gesture that would hearten the men and honor the spirit of their departed companion.

A torch was offered to him, and he managed to wrap his stiffening fingers around the piece of wood. Thirty pairs of eyes turned toward him, and he knew it was time.

Time to tell them why. Time to tell them the reason they all took the oath.

"We are all dying," he said bluntly. Feronantus would have done a better job. His old friend was a much more gifted orator, but as the most senior brother present, the duty was his now.

What happened to all of them was his responsibility. He tightened his grip on the torch, afraid that his clumsy fingers would betray him and let go of the flaming brand before he was done speaking.

"High-born and low, peasant or king," he continued, "our lives come to the same end. The Virgin claims our souls, and the earth and sky claim our flesh and blood. She whose honor we have sworn to defend measures our deeds in life, and those who are found worthy are taken to her hall where we spend eternity beneath the tree that is the root of all. Those of us who remain honor the memory of our worthy dead by hanging their pommels in the Great Hall of Petraathen."

Rutger paused, a lump at the back of his throat, a wetness swelling behind his eyes. "Brother Andreas was worthy," he said, his voice breaking. "Honest in word and deed; unflinching in his courage; first to act when the call came. When we floundered in our duty, he remembered. When we wished to hesitate, he struck. Andreas was everything that a knight of the Shield-Brethren must remember to be. When we forget who we are, when fear seizes us or when doubt assails our hearts, we need only think of our brother Andreas to find our strength again."

Styg raised a longsword encased in a worn leather scabbard. Upon its pommel was a design similar in composition to the sigil of the order, but unique. Every brother owned a blade, given to him when he proved himself, that bore his own symbol. When he died, it was the sworn duty of his brothers to return the weapon to Petraathen. The blade would be reused, given to a new initiate, but the pommel would be struck free and permanently housed in the Great Hall. Andreas's sword would have been lost with his body, but for the fact that he had not carried it with him into his final match.

The blade had stayed here at the chapter house, and so they possessed it still.

Rutger carefully transferred the torch to his left hand. With his right, he drew Andreas's sword from its scabbard. His hands felt like they were on fire, each knuckle a burning coal beneath the skin. "This blade is the finest steel our smith could forge, and when we go into battle, this sword is our virtue and our strength. But our brother did not take *this* sword into battle. Instead he took his faith and his love." He raised the blade. "It is our tradition to break and reforge a blade once its wielder has fallen, but I submit to you that this sword should never be broken. It should hang, whole, in the Great Hall for all eternity as a reminder of our brother's faith. It never faltered. *He* never faltered..." His voice wavered, threatening to lay bare his grief, and he tightened his grip around the hilt, the pain in his joints hardening his resolve. "We are the Knights of the Virgin Defender. We are the Shield of Saint Mary."

He said the older name next, the Greek words hard in his mouth, and he saw confusion on the faces of some of the younger men. *It is time they knew.* "We have stood fast for many lifetimes," he explained. "We live to see our brothers die in battle. We too will die violent deaths. But our vows remain. Our strength remains." He raised the sword high and let his pain fill his voice. "Andreas," he cried. "*Alalazu!*"

His brothers answered with the same. The still air was filled with the sound of swords being drawn and voices raised in salute. *Alalazu! Alalazu!* The battle cry of the Shield-Brethren shook the branches of the trees and rattled the old stones of the ruined church, and before the echo of the first salute had died away, a second followed. And then a third.

In the wake of their salute, they heard the sound of horses. The rhythmic rumble of hooves against the hard ground. The jingling sound of steel against steel.

"Mongols," Styg spat.

"No," Rutger countered. *Too heavy.* "Mongols don't ride chargers."

The sun had nearly set, a redness bleeding in the western sky, and the horsemen riding into the camp appeared to be swimming out of a sea of blood, the last light of the day glinting off helmets and shields and maille. White surcoats marked with red crosses and black ones marked in white hung on the riders as they filed into the clearing, their combined numbers several times that of Rutger and the Shield-Brethren about him.

Rutger lowered Andreas's sword and stared at the host of Templars and Hospitallers. As he waited for some sign as to their presence, the lead Templar slid from his horse. His short hair and closely cropped beard were steel gray, and his face was a stone-etched mask. "I am Leuthere de Montfort, commander of the Templars at Hünern," he said in a rough-edged voice turned hoarse from many years in the field. "Who commands here?"

Rutger stepped forward from among the circle of Shield-Brethren. "I am Rutger, knight initiate of the *Ordo Militum Vindicis Intactae.* My brothers look to me for guidance." Having said the words, he felt their weight settle upon his shoulders. *I will lead them, Andreas,* he vowed. "Do you come for blood?" he asked plainly. The Livonians had made themselves enemies of the Shield-Brethren today, openly and with all the hatred that could be mustered. He was somewhat surprised that the other orders would feel the need to mete out justice.

One of the Hospitallers dismounted and strode forward to stand beside the Templar. "I am Emmeran, commander of the Knights of Saint John," he said. Like Leuthere, he was armored for battle. His face was kinder, however, though at the moment it was etched with a solemn expression. "The Livonian atrocity committed upon your brother was ill done. You should know that their *Heermeister,*

Dietrich von Grüningen, had come to both our orders previously, speaking ill of you and your brothers."

Leuthere nodded in agreement with the Hospitaller. "I apologize for the bluntness of my question," he said, his gaze still unreadable. "Your man, when he threw his spear at the Khan today...was he acting alone?"

A desperate hope seized Rutger as his mind warred with itself over whether or not to tell the truth. He was surrounded by a host of knights that was several times larger than his small company of Shield-Brethren. He exhaled slowly, and in his mind's eye, all he saw was Andreas, smiling at him. *Wouldn't you rather choose the manner of your death?*

Rutger opened his eyes and looked at the unlit pyre for their fallen brother. *I hope you rest in the arms of the Virgin*, he thought. With a grunt, he threw the torch atop the bundle of wood, and it clattered across the pyre, scattering wisps of flame. As the oil-soaked wood ignited with a huff, he turned back to the Templar and Hospitaller. "The plan was of his making," he said, "but it was done with our knowledge and support. Our brother did not act alone."

Emmeran and Leuthere exchanged a look, and then the Templar's mouth cracked into a smile. It looked almost bizarre on that stony face. "Surely he did not think he could take on the entire Mongol host by himself?"

Rutger shook his head, trying not to let the small hope burning in his chest erupt into something larger. "No," he said, his eyes flickering back and forth between the two men. "Such an action requires more men."

The Hospitaller's eyes glittered in the leaping firelight. "That is our thought as well," he said. "Which is why we have come to join you."

THE LONG AND WINDING ROAD

"NOW I UNDERSTAND why the Silk Road runs along the edge of a desert," Yasper groused, slapping his arms against his body in a futile effort to keep his body warm. He wore a fur hat, pulled down as far as his eyebrows, and he had let his beard grow out again. Wild and uncombed, it resembled a weaver's nest, and his voice issued from somewhere inside the bramble of wiry hair. "What I wouldn't do for a handful of hot sand. Doesn't that sound like paradise?" he said wistfully. "Just one handful of hot sand."

Raphael nodded, though the motion was hard to distinguish with all the frantic shivering he was doing. Even with woolen strips wrapping his arms and legs and an extra layer of foul-smelling furs the company had traded for a week prior, the cold air still managed to worm its way down his back. He was doubly glad he had stopped wearing his maille several days ago. The chain seemed to absorb the chill in the air, and more than once he had found his hands sticking to the metal links.

Of all the company, Feronantus seemed the least affected by the weather. He wore extra layers, like everyone else, but Raphael had yet to see the old veteran shiver. If anything, he seemed to find the frigid air bracing.

Raphael had only ever been to Týrshammar during the long summer months, when the nights were short and the sky never fully darkened. Over the last few days, he started to get a sense of what the winters in the northern stronghold must be like.

Of their own journey, there was one more pass to ascend before they reached the long valley where Boreas blew constantly. Raphael couldn't even imagine attempting this route if there was *more* snow. As it was, they had reached the snow line the day before, and by Cnán's reckoning, it was another three days before they would be able to pass through the gap and start their descent to the Gurbantünggüt Desert.

Like Yasper, Raphael had been having dreams—when he was able to fall asleep—about deserts. Along with dreams of the sun and fire, vast pinwheels of raging flame spinning across the sky.

As the horses slowly picked their way up the narrow mountain path, Raphael tried not to let his thoughts dwell on the significance of the pinwheels. It was unsettling to think they might be the same spoked wheels that Percival saw in his visions; if they were, did that mean he was gradually being won over by the persistent *truth* of Percival's vision? That the images the knight saw were, indeed, a message that issued from divine lip and hand.

Raphael had seen too much of what men did in the grip of visions. From the atrocities perpetrated in the Levant and in Egypt, to the mad works of that unholy inquisitor Konrad in his zealous pursuit of heretics in Thuringia, to the mystical zeal that was the source of constant torment and conflict within Percival.

It was not fair of him to judge Percival so, but over the last few months Raphael had begun to lay the blame of Roger's death on the Frankish knight. If Percival had not insisted on visiting the caves beneath Kiev in pursuit of the illicit artifact he had imagined he knew to be there, then Roger might not have been killed.

He was spending too much time reliving the past. It was an unfortunate aspect of his fascination with keeping a record of their journey. At first, his tiny marks in the journal had been a means of passing the time during the endless days of riding; later, when he started to look back upon earlier entries and find them lacking in detail, he began to write more earnestly, thinking of Herodotus and Thucydides and their histories of the ancient Greek world. During the long nights on the steppe, when he could not sleep and lay staring up at the endless spray of stars across the heavens, he began to think of the *Confessiones* written by Augustine of Hippo when the Christian theologian was of a similar age. In many ways, the *Confessiones* was a preamble to Augustine's truly revelatory work, *De Civitate Dei*, as if the theologian had to exorcise his own past before he could address the more complex philosophical inquiries of the later work.

Vera said he thought too much, and while she did not intend her words to be mean-spirited, there was more than a hint of truth to them. Raphael would not deny that he thought a great deal about an endless panoply of ideas; it was his boundless curiosity about God's creation, about his role within it, and how he was supposed to understand his purpose. Many never gave much thought to their ultimate purpose on the earth, and he knew that it was by God's grace that he was able to even conceive of *having a purpose*, but that self-knowledge only inflamed his desire.

Yasper and his alchemical recipes had not helped either. The scrawny Dutchman had his own codex, though the alchemist's was not nearly as well constructed as Raphael's, being an olio of parchment, cloth, hide, and a few scraps of what looked suspiciously like tattooed skin. Yasper kept the loose collection in an oilskin satchel, and he referenced it, annotated it, and fussed with it on a daily basis. Raphael's curiosity had led him to inquire about the alchemist's notes, and he had been intrigued by some of the Arabic passages Yasper had in his collection. Written by a Persian named Jabir ibn Hayyan, the material was not—as he had anticipated—a babble of mystical nonsense disguised as a treatise on philosophical medicine, but a well-reasoned discourse on the immutable nature of the soul. Jabir sought answers to the same questions as Augustine; it was only his rhetoric and his practical methods that were different.

What is my purpose? How may I best serve God?

* * *

"It is a beautiful view, isn't it?" Eleázar spread his arms to encompass the vista of snow-capped mountains. "Almost worth the trip for this alone, yes?"

Yasper shook his head, and nudged his shivering horse back onto the path.

"You must not take umbrage with Yasper," Rædwulf explained to Cnán. The pair of them were riding behind Yasper and Eleázar. "He was born in a place that has nothing but dikes and low hills that barely come up to here." He held his hand out, level with his horse's shoulder. "The first time he saw the Alps, he fell off his horse. He claimed he was struck dumb in awe and terror at the majesty of God's work. The other riders he was with thought otherwise and, on many subsequent occasions, performed entertaining pantomimes of what came to be known as the Low-Lander's Abasement before God."

"Does it happen often when he is talking to you?" Cnán asked, squinting up at Rædwulf. The tall Englishman smiled wolfishly. Glancing around, Cnán saw smiles on the faces of a few of the others who had paused at the scenic overlook.

There had been few opportunities for jovial camaraderie since they had left Benjamin at the rock. The trader had argued strenuously about joining the company, even after his detailed account of why such a decision was financially disastrous for him. Cnán had not understood the merchant's interest in the hard ride that the Shield-Brethren had before them, but as she listened to the trader's cogent argument, she grew to see that Benjamin thought he was in the company's debt.

A debt that, ultimately, Feronantus refused.

The route through the Zuungar Gap was not well traveled, Benjamin argued, and the villages and clans that dotted the route were not as open to strangers as many who lived more closely to the Silk Road. The company would need a guide and an interpreter if they were going to reach the far side of the gap.

It was Benjamin's informed guess that Alchiq would be keeping to the trade routes, where he could readily acquire fresh horses. Benjamin's proposed route along the Tien Shan and through the gap would be rigorous and more dangerous, but it would be quicker.

Rigorous, dangerous, and quicker: those had been the magic words that had betrayed Benjamin. Feronantus had nodded with a gravid finality that the others knew well when Benjamin stressed them. *Three reasons why you cannot come with us*, Feronantus had said. *You place too little value on your life.*

What of you and yours? Benjamin had retorted.

Each of our lives have no meaning, except that which we give them by our deeds, Feronantus had replied, and Cnán knew he was quoting some old dictum of the Shield-Brethren.

In the weeks since, Cnán had noticed how the weight of that saying—the burden of their journey—was starting to show on the old veteran from Týrshammar. He may have traveled to the far edges of Christendom, but the steppe was much broader than he could have imagined, and occasionally Cnán could read a crumbling despair in Feronantus's eyes when he stared at the distant horizon. What had, in the beginning, seemed like a simple plan—*ride east, passing over the Land of the Skulls and into the heartland of the Mongol Empire, and kill the Great Khan*—was becoming such an extended odyssey that he was beginning to doubt they would reach their goal in time to save the West.

"That one over there is Khan Tengri," Cnán said as the rest of the company reached the overlook, pointing to the white peak, blazing in the afternoon sun. "We are close to the Zuungar Gap." The mountain floated above a layer of blue and gray clouds, a slab of flying marble like the mystical and unreachable home of foreboding gods. "When the sun sets," Cnán finished, "the snow turns red."

Istvan hawked and spat, and Cnán wasn't sure if the Hungarian's reaction was one of disbelief or if he was engaged in some manner of warding ritual. More and more, she had begun to see the Hungarian as a deeply superstitious man, one who was both haunted and hunted by some spirits only he could perceive. He hadn't been completely taken by the influence of the freebutton mushrooms for many weeks, but she suspected he still had a secret cache of them on his person and that he would, from time to time, chew one.

"*Tengri*," Yasper mused. "Isn't that the name of the Mongol god?" The light from the distant mountain peak seemed to be reflecting from his face. "Does he live up there?"

Cnán shook her head. "No, the Mongols aren't like that. They believe in spirits. Everything has a spirit—the rocks, the trees, all the animals—and these spirits are all part of the world that flowed from Tengri."

"That is not dissimilar to the Christian view of the soul," Raphael pointed out.

"Ah, but the Christian soul is unique and distinct," Yasper countered. "Your soul inhabits your body, and when your body perishes, *your soul* goes to Heaven. It is still your soul. I suspect—and correct me if I am wrong, Cnán—when something dies, the Mongols believe its spirit flows back to Tengri where it is reabsorbed into the great expanse that is their god."

Cnán shrugged, indicating that this conversation was already well beyond her.

"You are separate from God, good Raphael," Yasper continued. "I suspect the Mongols and their world are not. In fact, I am sure we will find a shrine near the top of the gap that is dedicated to the rocks and the trees that manage to thrive at this height, so close to the realm of the Sky God." Yasper seemed genuinely thrilled by the idea.

"I'm sure the Church will be delighted to send missionaries to endlessly debate this distinction," Feronantus observed dryly.

"We could let these two debate it now," Rædwulf said. "We have many days left in our journey."

Feronantus smiled at the longbowman's enthusiasm. "I am a fighting man," he said. "Not a theologian or a philosopher. All of this talk is well beyond my simple understanding, and I fear such discourse will be meaningless to me."

"I think your understanding is far from *simple*," Raphael noted dryly.

"Perhaps," Feronantus said. "But it is *my* understanding." The old veteran tapped his horse with his reins, nudging it back to the sloping path. The others, sensing the time was over for scenic viewing and rhetorical discourse, followed until only Cnán and Raphael remained.

"There," she said, pointing. "Do you see it?"

Raphael nodded. There were winds blowing at the top of the mountain, and a gauzy curtain of white mist fluttered at the tip as if it were caught upon that high spire. Below, the slope of the mountain was changing color—gold to crimson.

"I have heard stories about the Shield-Brethren, though I have little faith they contain but the merest morsel of truth to them. They are like many fanciful tales one hears along the trade routes," Cnán said as the others moved out of earshot. "You pretend to fight for the Christian God, but you swear your oaths to someone else, don't you?"

"Does it matter?" Raphael countered. "If the oath I am swearing is to protect people like you and other innocents?"

"Do you all swear the same oath?" she asked.

"We do," Raphael said.

"But it means something different to some of you, doesn't it?" she pressed.

"Aye," he said softly. "I fear that it might."

Ahead of them, Khan Tengri became drenched with blood.

* * *

The wind howled so vociferously and with such zeal that, for the rest of the day after they breached the gap and began their rapid descent down the other side, Raphael's ears were blocked. His head was filled with the shrieking echo of Boreas, the angry north wind that had attempted to drive them back with the sheer volume of its outrage.

But they had doggedly kept moving, hauling their horses by the reins when the beasts balked at going any farther. He had taken part in the crusade in Egypt, and the disastrous march on Cairo had tested him vigorously; others in the company had been in similar campaigns, and they knew their wills were stronger than any temporary pain. They knew the only way to complete any journey was to focus on the ground in front of them. Place one foot, and then the next. Do not look at the unmoving horizon or the immobile sun. One step at a time. The Shield-Brethren can always take *one more step*.

The gap was a narrow slit, as if God—or *Tengri*—had cut a notch in the shoulder of the mountain, and the wind shrieked with near physical violence as they dragged their terrified horses through the rocky defile. On the eastern side of the gap, the land dropped away rapidly. By nightfall, which came so quickly that Raphael wondered if God had snuffed out the sun as soon as it had passed beyond the notch of the gap, they were already below the snow line.

The route descended into an endless forest filled with tall and narrow trees, unlike any evergreen that Raphael had seen before. The needles were like the trees in the West, long and pointed, but the trees held their branches close to their trunks. In the West, the evergreens spread their branches wide, as if they were offering shelter to any weary traveler; the trees on the eastern slopes of the Tien Shan struck him as being wary of strangers.

He felt as if he was constantly being watched as the company made their way down into the long valley. This land knew they were invaders and regarded them with a great deal of suspicion.

He slept poorly that night.

Shortly before midday, the evergreens began to thin out, invaded by squat, broad-crowned leafy trees. Rædwulf recognized them as walnut trees, and he and Yasper dismounted from their horses to fill several bags with the hard-shelled nuts. Istvan enjoyed cracking the nuts with his bare hands.

Raphael suspected the walnuts signified the presence of water, and an hour later, the company discovered a crystalline tarn nestled in the basin of the valley. A rocky moraine at the southern end formed a natural dam, and the water was bluer than the pale, cloud-dappled sky.

And much colder.

Feronantus called a halt and announced they would overnight on the bank of the lake. They had been traveling hard for several weeks, and the strain of the journey was clearly etched on everyone's face. The sun was warm on the rocks, there was little wind (especially in comparison to the howling gale of the gap), and there was food and water in ready supply. It was a good camp.

Yasper broached the lake first. With some effort, he pried his stiff clothing off. Venting a shrill battle cry, he dashed for the water.

His voice became more agitated as his pale legs entered the lake, and his words turned blasphemous. But he kept going, and eventually his head disappeared beneath the surface. He reemerged almost immediately—shuddering, his lips blue and teeth chattering—but his mood was irrepressibly jubilant. "It's warmer than it looks," he shouted to the rest of the company, all of whom wore doubtful expressions. He splashed water at Istvan, who danced back from the spray as if it were hot coals.

"You first," Vera said to Raphael in response to his raised eyebrow. Her expression brooked no argument.

IN THE SHADOW OF BURGAN-GALDUN 28

AS THE TERRAIN became rockier, the caravan folded itself into a narrow formation and wound its way along a more circuitous route. To Gansukh, perched on the flat, sun-warmed crown of a rocky promontory, the elongated caravan looked like a serpent, fat and swollen with a recent meal. Sluggishly, it slithered around uprisings of crumbling rock. Beyond, a day's ride back, lay the grasslands. They had found the edge of that endless sea and left it behind.

Now was the time for an ambush. There were numerous tactical advantages in this terrain: how the narrow track forced the caravan to spread itself out, making it more difficult for the patrols to guard it well; the rocks offered so many more hiding places from which to launch an assault; these same rocks provided cover for a retreat. Why had the Chinese attacked them in the lowlands? They had had inferior numbers, and the caravan had been stationary with a defensive perimeter established.

Gansukh shaded his eyes and peered at the tiny shapes darting around the bulky midsection of the serpentine caravan. The *Torguud* and their endless patrols, eternally vigilant and restless since the attack. Like an anthill after it had been probed with a stick.

His horse nickered softly. His mount had spotted another horse, one that it knew, and Gansukh caught himself hoping the approaching rider was Lian. He knew it couldn't be, and as he glanced over his shoulder, he squashed the momentary thrill of the idea.

The horse was black, and the rider wore black. His long beard trailed behind him.

"Master Chucai." Gansukh scrambled to his knees, thought about standing, and then realized, in an awkward reversal, that he would be taller than the other man. Instead, he remained on his knees. A ridge of stone pressed against his left knee, and he wobbled slightly as he offered a perfunctory bow.

Chucai nodded in return as he dismounted from his horse. He effortlessly scaled the spur of rock and stood with his feet spread apart. "They can see us quite easily," he said, taking in the view.

Gansukh brushed a dusting of fine grit from his leggings as he got to his feet. "You are an imposing figure," he pointed out, "and you don't blend in well. I would hope that they see us."

Chucai regarded him with a sidelong glance. "And you? Prior to my arrival, would they not have mistaken you for a Chinese raider?"

"Even if they had, they are too far away." Gansukh thought of the archery contest with Tarbagatai a few days ago. "There are good archers in the *Torguud*, but they would have to ride much closer before they could hope to hit me. They are shooting up; I would be shooting down. My range is better. By then, I would hope they could tell the difference between one of their own and a Chinese archer."

Chucai nodded. "There is a great deal of optimism in your thinking."

"More strategic than optimistic," Gansukh corrected.

"Of course," Chucai acknowledged. "This location also offers us some privacy."

"Yes, it does," said Gansukh, wondering why that was important and fearing the reason at the same time.

"I too engage in what might be considered *strategic* thinking, albeit it with less optimism. In my position, I am called upon to make important decisions regarding the *Khagan*'s safety and well-being. Normally, I make those decisions without any need for discourse with those who will carry out my decisions. I order; you, and others like you, obey. That is how the empire continues to function."

"Of course, Master Chucai." Gansukh inclined his head.

"But these are not normal times, are they?"

Despite his confusion at Chucai's appearance and a bit of annoyance at the interruption of his reconnaissance, Gansukh allowed a wry smile to cross his lips. The Khan of Khans was going to the sacred homelands of the Mongol people, where he would hunt a mystical animal at the behest of his shamans, all so that he might reassert his control of the empire. Meanwhile, his general, Subutai, was preparing to expand the empire past the distant lands conquered by his father, the greatest leader the Mongol people had ever known. No, these were not normal times.

"In these times, is it possible that members of the empire might be thinking more of themselves?" Chucai asked. "It is possible that they might place their own desires and wants above the desires and wants of the *Khagan*—and, by extension, the empire?"

Gansukh cleared his throat, weighing whether Chucai actually sought a response to this question or if this was one of those instances in which it might be best to simply wait for a clear directive to which he could respond. His eyes darted toward Chucai, noting that the *Khagan*'s advisor was staring at him intently, one eyebrow partially raised.

"It...it is possible," Gansukh said. And then, with more bravery, "But, for some individuals, they always think thusly."

"Does the empire then overlook their lack of duty—shall we say—because they are useful to the empire? What happens when they are no longer useful?"

Gansukh shrugged, more casual than he felt. "They are discarded," he said, opting to not shirk from the point he felt Chucai was trying to make.

"Discarded," Chucai mused, stroking his beard. He seemed, to Gansukh, to be playacting, giving the moment more gravity than necessary, as if to frighten Gansukh. *But why?* Gansukh thought. *Does he want me to confess to something? Have I not done all that he has asked in regards to the* Khagan? His heart skipped a beat. *Lian!*

"Do you know why the Chinese attacked the *Khagan*'s caravan?" Chucai asked suddenly.

"The Chi—Chinese?" Gansukh stuttered.

"Yes, the Chinese raiders. Do you think they were trying to assassinate the *Khagan* or was there another goal? Thievery, perhaps?"

Gansukh swallowed heavily. He tried not to let his relief show. Chucai wasn't asking about his relationship with Lian. "I don't know, Master Chucai," Gansukh said, his chest relaxing. "I spent most of the attack as a prisoner."

"Yes, so I have heard. And during this imprisonment—most embarrassing, if I may say so—you didn't hear them talk of their plans?"

Gansukh felt his face flush. "They spoke Chinese, Master Chucai."

"Oh yes, of course. And Lian hasn't... ?"

"Taught me Chinese?" Gansukh shook his head. "You may certainly ask her, Master Chucai, but I believe she will tell you she was having enough trouble teaching me the proper way of speaking Mongolian."

Chucai laughed. "Well spoken," he said. "What of their tactics, then? What of the *Torguud* response?"

Gansukh sensed that Chucai had changed his mind about his line of questioning. He wasn't sure what he had said—or not said—but Chucai appeared to be mollified on some topic. Or perhaps he is simply setting it aside for now, he thought, admonishing himself to listen carefully to Chucai's questions. "I am not a member of the *Torguud*," Gansukh said carefully. "It would be presumptuous of me to speculate on their martial response."

"Oh, very tactful," Chucai said. "Lian's instruction, I suspect."

Bristling, Gansukh held his tongue and bowed his head slightly in return.

"The reason I ask," Chucai continued, "is that there may be a *strategic* advantage gained by soliciting your opinion in a certain matter rather than simply giving you an order," Chucai continued.

"I can only hope to be of service, Master Chucai," Gansukh offered.

Chucai raised an eyebrow in response to Gansukh's obsequious response. "I am going to ask Munokhoi to relinquish his position as captain of the *Khagan*'s private guard," he said.

Gansukh's heart thudded loudly in his chest, and his cheeks and forehead were suddenly hot in the sun. His knees trembled, and the landscape wavered slightly as he tried to calm his racing thoughts. He had no idea what sort of expression was on his face, though he was certain Chucai could tell the statement had caught him off guard. *Was this what he was referring to when he talked about men failing to follow the* Khagan? he wondered. Had Chucai's question had nothing to do with him after all?

In a moment of rare talkativeness, Chucai explained himself. "Munokhoi is unfit to lead the men out on the steppes"—he indicated the land spread out below them with a sweep of his arm—"or here in the mountains. Did he send you here to watch over the caravan? No. That was *your* decision. You saw the need to look over the terrain before the *Khagan* crossed it. Munokhoi thinks like a man who has spent his life behind walls."

Gansukh scratched behind his right ear. "You need someone who has fought beyond the *Khagan*'s walls," he said slowly, belaboring Chucai's point.

Gansukh waited a moment for Chucai to continue, but he wasn't terribly surprised when the *Khagan*'s advisor said nothing. This was a not uncommon gambit on Chucai's part: to start a conversation, and then let it peter into silence. He had infinite patience: as a hunter, he could probably outwait even the most cautious deer; as a veteran of the *Khagan*'s courts, there was no one more skilled than he at making silence excruciating. The more he learned from Lian, the more Gansukh had understood the merits of Chucai's techniques. People were more likely to believe something they felt like they had a hand in creating. Order a man, and he will dutifully comply; let him possess an idea as his own, will he not leap to implement it with great enthusiasm?

Gansukh couldn't help but think of Ögedei's decision to leave Karakorum for Burqan-qaldun. Had he not, in some small way, manipulated the *Khagan* into believing the idea was his?

"Master Chucai..." he began.

"Hmmm?" Chucai seemed to have forgotten he was there.

"This is an unusual circumstance that I find myself in," Gansukh said. "As you say, typically you would simply inform me of your decision, and I would carry it out. Yet, you come to me now and appear to want my input on a certain matter."

Chucai nodded absently, his attention still on the landscape below.

"Yet, I doubt that you haven't thought through every consequence of every possible decision already. Do you expect *me* to have better insight on this matter than you? Or am I supposed to change your mind?"

"Change my mind?" Chucai raised an eyebrow. "What choice do you think I have made?"

Gansukh regarded the *Khagan*'s advisor warily, a response to Chucai's question hanging in his throat. *Why else would he have come all the way up here to tell me this? Does he want me to ask for the position?* Gansukh rejected that idea almost as soon as it came into his head, but it wouldn't go away. *Me, a* Torguud *captain.* There would be certain benefits, of course. And while there were many in the *Khagan*'s service who wouldn't trust him, much like he had earned Tarbagatai's admiration, he could win them over. All he had to do was demonstrate the depth of his allegiance to the *Khagan*—and wasn't this entire hunting expedition the result of his efforts to show his devotion to the *Khagan?* The men would drift toward him. He had led men before; he could do it again.

But what of Munokhoi? Awkwardly, Gansukh felt a pang of empathy for the man. Cruel and self-serving as he was, he had served the *Khagan* well for many years, otherwise he never would have been promoted to his current position. It was unnerving to see how easily he could be pushed aside, and for someone who was such an outsider. *What would stop Chucai from doing the same to me?* Gansukh wondered.

And Lian? What would her reaction be? Would she see it as Gansukh choosing the *Khagan* over her? *It is what I would be doing,* he admitted to himself. Would she attempt to escape again, and would he be forced to go after her? Would he be ordered to put her to death for disobedience?

Gansukh took a deep breath to calm his addled nerves. His mind was twisting itself into knots, trying to examine all the possible outcomes. He felt like he was playing that Chinese game that Lian had told him about—black and white pebbles on a wooden board; rules she explained in less than two minutes; followed by an hour-long conversation about strategy that had numbed his mind. Chucai was clearly a master at *weiqi*, and Gansukh felt as if he were playing his first game, already on the defensive.

Don't think of it like a game you don't understand, he realized. Think of it in terms of something you are good at. What are the options for a warrior who feels he is cornered and on the defensive? Think more strategically. What is the best defense?

Shifting roles. Becoming the attacker. Fighting back.

"What *is* your goal, Master Chucai?" Gansukh asked.

For a moment Chucai's expression remained blank, and Gansukh flushed, his guts tightening with dread that he had spoken too bluntly. But then Chucai's eyebrows crept up, and the corners of a bemused smile peeked through his beard. Though he didn't understand Chucai's reaction, it was better than the one he had anticipated.

"That is a very direct and astute question, Gansukh," Chucai said. "Mistress Lian has told me—on numerous occasions, in fact—that you are prone to speaking your mind. Even with all of her efforts to obscure that tendency beneath layers of courtly civility."

Gansukh felt his face redden even more, but he didn't break the other man's gaze. *Do not lessen your assault.*

"Sun and rain and good seed will not produce a crop from fallow ground." Chucai's smile broadened. "I know you are a warrior and a hunter, but surely you understand that basic tenet of farming, yes?"

"Yes, Master Chucai." Gansukh kept his annoyance out of his voice.

"Does a farmer give up if his land is bad, or does he find new land?"

"He finds new land."

"And while he is searching for new land, what of his family, of his horses and cows?"

"He must still provide for them."

"So, it follows that fertile ground must be found—quickly—and the farmer must continue to plant his seeds, cultivate his tender plants, and reap his harvest as he always does, with as little disruption as possible."

"With all due respect, Master Chucai, there is no way to remove Munokhoi from his position without some disruption."

"Of course not," Chucai snorted impatiently.

"Replacing him with me would be...*very* disruptive," Gansukh pointed out. Even if he *were* a good choice to replace Munokhoi, such a decision would only further enrage the already hotheaded *Torguud* captain.

Chucai lifted a finger and touched it to his lips. "Would it? Don't you think the empire would benefit more from advancing you than it would lose by *discarding* Munokhoi?"

Gansukh didn't like the way Chucai was twisting his words; and behind his calm facade, there lurked another series of barbed questions, waiting to entrap Gansukh. And then, within the span of a heartbeat, Gansukh realized a way out of this predicament. "There is another who would be more suitable," he offered. "Brother Namkhai."

Chucai shrugged slightly, his finger remaining against his lips. Realizing Chucai had already considered Namkhai, Gansukh rushed to explain his thinking. "I'm not suggesting Namkhai because I am trying to shirk my duties to you or the *Khagan*, Master Chucai. It is not that I feel I am unworthy of the position—I am worthy of it—it is just that..."

Chucai's expression suggested he was listening intently to Gansukh's words, but that they weren't quite enough to convince him.

Gansukh thought rapidly, trying to verbalize key reasons that would support his claim. "Namkhai is a steppes rider too, plus he has been with the men longer. He knows them as well as they know him. I do not know many of the men."

Chucai gave him a tiny nod. *Keep talking.*

"I have seen Namkhai stand up to Munokhoi when Munokhoi has been caught up in rage, irrational and unable to command. The men respond to Namkhai's leadership. They will respect him more quickly."

"Respect is an important quality to have in a leader," Chucai offered as encouragement for Gansukh to keep talking.

"And Munokhoi does not resent Namkhai like he resents me. The perceived insult would be less grave and the reaction less severe."

"Would it be?" Chucai considered Gansukh's words. "There is some wisdom behind your suggestion, Gansukh. Even as hastily offered as it is." He smiled fleetingly, and then his expression deadened. "But you speak of Munokhoi's reaction being *less* severe..."

"Yes," Gansukh agreed.

"There will still be a reaction," Chucai said. "His resentment of you will not be lessened. It will simply be *unburdened*, no longer shackled by the strictures of his rank."

Gansukh sucked in a quick breath. Munokhoi would be free to come after Lian. Ever since the gladiator match between the two Westerners, Munokhoi's furtive glances made Gansukh think of a wary predator—biding his time.

Chucai had to be aware that this would be a likely outcome of stripping Munokhoi of his rank. He found his hands clenching into fists as his temper flared, a reaction that Lian would have chided him for. He could almost hear her voice: *this is the reaction he expects you to have.* Though he was tempted to accuse of Chucai of playing a deadly game, Gansukh calmed his breathing and stared at his hands until he could force them to relax.

"Namkhai is a good choice, Gansukh," Chucai said, ignoring Gansukh's mental distress. "A better choice, in many ways."

Gansukh felt a strange mixture of elation and disappointment at Chucai's words. The emotional rush was confounding. On the battlefield, such confusion—this temerity and second-guessing about one's decisions—was deadly. He needed to keep focused.

"However, that is all he will ever be," Chucai explained. "He does not have the same broad-mindedness that Chagatai Khan saw in you when he selected you as his emissary. Namkhai has not been to the far edges of the empire; he has not been exposed to different martial cultures." Chucai fixed Gansukh with his fierce gaze. "He has not watched his brothers die in the streets of foreign cities. He has not truly faced death, and as such, cannot tell his men how to be strong at such a time."

Gansukh dropped his gaze, the crazy welter of emotions racing around his brain falling silent in the face of Chucai's praise. "You honor me too much, Master Chucai," he muttered.

Chucai was silent for a moment. "Perhaps," he offered. "Still, recent revelations have made it clear that if the empire is to maintain its strength, it needs less blind devotion and more..."

"More what, Master Chucai?"

"Are you asking as a *Torguud* captain or a free warrior of the steppes—one who thinks more of his needs than the needs of the empire?"

Gansukh hesitated, sensing a trap. "My apologies, Master Chucai. I was merely asking as a concerned warrior of the empire, who only seeks to assist the *Khagan* in any way that the *Khagan* wishes."

Chucai laughed. "You are much less a fool than anyone takes you for, Gansukh."

Gansukh chuckled. "Please do not tell anyone otherwise."

"Oh, I won't." Chucai sighed as he played with the trailing end of his beard for a moment. "It would have been much easier to address your problem with the weight of the *Torguud* guard behind you."

Gansukh tensed as Chucai's hand tightened on his shoulder. "*That* problem is my own, Master Chucai. It is best I dealt with it directly."

"Yes, Gansukh," Chucai said. "That would be for the best. Much less *disruptive* that way. Much less."

Gansukh did not watch Chucai mount his horse and ride away. He stared down at the snaking caravan, his eyes following the tiny dots of the *Torguud* riders as they patrolled.

He wondered which one was Munokhoi.

He could wait until the caravan was in range, and then he could solve his *problem* with a single arrow. It would be so much easier.

Gansukh sighed and shook his head. While an arrow was efficient, it would have consequences that could be as equally disastrous. No, he had to find another way. A less disruptive way.

Patience, he told himself as he walked back to his horse. *A true hunter knows to wait until his prey shows itself.*

* * *

When the caravan reached the Kherlen River, it was greeted by a contingent of twenty horsemen. Each rider carried a pole with a sky-blue banner that snapped and whipped in the wind as the party galloped toward the caravan. The *Torguud* parted for the riders, and they swept through like a sudden squall of rain. As they reached the dense cluster of mounted guard near the *Khagan*'s *ger*, they reined as one and dismounted in near-unison, each landing swiftly on the ground and dropping to bent knee. Sky-blue arrowheads woven into their robes marked them. *Darkhat*. Guardians of the lands sacred to Genghis Khan—his birthplace, his tomb, and region beyond. Burqan-qaldun.

Some of the *Torguud* shuffled nervously, attempting to keep their horses at ease. The *Darkhat* remained still, waiting for Ögedei to emerge from his *ger*. The tableau remained frozen for what seemed to be an inordinately long time, and then the flaps of Ögedei's *ger* were thrown back, and the Khan of Khans emerged.

Ögedei leaned against the railing of the narrow platform, and stared thickly at the *Darkhat* host as if he could not account for their sudden appearance in his camp. Just as he seemed about to lose interest in their presence, one of the *Darkhat* shot to his feet and raised both arms in salute to the *Khagan*.

"Hail, Ögedei *Khagan*," he said. "I, Ghaltai, welcome you to the lands of your father."

"Hail, Ghaltai, faithful and eternal servant of my father's legacy," Ögedei replied. He waved an arm to encompass the other *Darkhat*. "Hail, faithful servants."

Ghaltai was not a tall man, but he was stocky, with thick weather-beaten skin. His eyes were thin, almond-shaped slits in his face. "What brings you to these lands, O *Khagan*, with so mighty a retinue?" he asked.

"A pilgrimage," Ögedei replied. "We will need your guides to take us through the mountain passes."

"That we can gladly provide," said Ghaltai with a bow.

"Oh, yes," Ögedei said as if the idea had just occurred to him. "My father's grave. I wish to see it." His gaze roamed over the assembled *Torguud* until he spotted Munokhoi. "The caravan will continue without me," he instructed. "I will catch up with it by nightfall."

"My Khan—" Munokhoi began.

"You have your orders, Captain."

Ögedei shuddered slightly, surprised by the voice at his elbow.

Chucai stood a respectful distance behind the *Khagan*, but with his height, he still seemed to tower over the slumped figure of the *Khagan*. "Your task is to ensure the safety of the caravan," he explained. "Namkhai and a few others will accompany the *Khagan*. As will I." He inclined his head toward Ögedei. "With your leave, of course, *Khagan*. I too would like to pay my respects to your father, my late friend."

"Of course," said Ögedei thickly, a grimace twisting his mouth into an ugly sneer.

***

The windswept plain between the Kherlen and Bruchi Rivers was filled with wild grasses. Closer to the rivers, ash and cedar trees grew, leaning toward the flowing water. A rounded boulder, taller than a man seated on a horse, lay in the center of the plain. It was such an anomaly in the landscape that Chucai's gaze was drawn to the distant crag of Burqan-qaldun, and he wondered how far the massive rock had traveled to end up in this field.

The stone was the only marker of Genghis Khan's interment. There were no pavilions of gold and silver, no field of banners, no sculptures or monuments. Just the rock, in an untouched plain of wild grass, at the confluence of the Kherlen and Bruchi Rivers. As Genghis had wished.

Chucai, Ghaltai, and the rest of the honor guard remained at a respectful distance as Ögedei dismounted and approached the boulder. The *Khagan* sank to his knees, head bowed in prayer.

Before he had become Genghis Khan, Ögedei's father was a simple man named Temujin. When he was nine, he was promised to Borte—daughter of Dei-sechen, of the *Onggirat* tribe—and he eventually married her six years later. Their marriage was interrupted by *Merkit* raiders who had never forgiven a theft by Temujin's father. He had stolen Hoelun, a woman intended for their clan leader, and the *Merkits* saw the theft of Borte as due compensation for their loss. They also intended to kill Temujin, but after three days of searching for him among the woods and bogs surrounding Burqan-qaldun, they gave up. Temujin, as the stories went, stood in this valley and swore in the presence of Burqan-qaldun, the great mountain that had kept him safe, that he would rescue Borte.

Not only did he rescue his wife, but with the assistance of friendly clans he defeated the *Merkits*, beginning what was to become the unification of all the Mongol peoples under his rule.

The empire started here, Chucai reflected. *One man. One promise.* He shivered slightly, dismissing the chill as nothing more than an icy gust of wind finding its way inside the collar of his jacket. He recalled the vision thrust upon him in the wake of the Chinese attack on the caravan: the endless herd of wild horses, their manes flowing like clouds—the never-ending empire. *Born out of Temujin's love for Borte.*

"Your tribe has dwelled in these lands for some time, have they not?" Chucai asked Ghaltai, pushing aside these idle, and yet troubling, thoughts.

"For many generations," the *Darkhat* rider replied.

"After Temujin became Genghis Khan, he came back to Burqan-qaldun," Chucai said. "What did he find here?"

Ghaltai made a show of looking around the wide plain, and then shrugged. "Open sky."

Chucai gave him the look that normally withered visiting dignitaries who presumed to be important enough to warrant disturbing the Khan. Ghaltai, nonplussed, met his gaze.

"Tell me about the banner," Chucai said. And when Ghaltai pretended to not understand, Chucai leaned toward the *Darkhat* and lowered his voice. "It was old when Genghis raised it as the standard for the empire, and it is older now. It should be a dead piece of wood, but why does it thrust forth new growth?"

Ghaltai's weather-beaten face paled. "I—I do not know of what you speak," he said.

"You know something," Chucai hissed, unwilling to let the *Darkhat*'s reticence get in the way of learning something about the history of the banner. "Tell me."

"There is a legend," Ghaltai began after a moment of reflection. "Before *Borte Chino* mated with *Qo'ai Maral,* when *Tengri* walked this land—"

Chucai snorted derisively before he could stop himself, and seeing Ghaltai's expression, he offered an apologetic nod.

"The people who lived here taught the birds to fly in formation and the bees to gather in swarms. When the Wolf and the Doe mated, these wise men gave this knowledge as a wedding gift. *Teach your children*, they said, *so that they may grow to become the strongest clans under the Eternal Blue Heaven.*"

"But the clans did not unite until Genghis brought them together," Chucai pointed out. Ghaltai's story sounded like yet another fable that had become *truth*, another fanciful explanation for Genghis's rise to power. He had heard so many of these stories over the years; in fact, he and Genghis had laughed together about a number of them. They were the idle stories that belonged to the uneducated—the superstitious who would flock to a passionate visionary and follow him anyway.

"The clans were waiting," Ghaltai said with an unsettling fervor. "They were waiting for someone to claim the legacy of *Borte Chino* and *Qo'ai Maral*. My father's father led the *Darkhat* when Genghis returned to Burqan-qaldun. He told his father, who, in turn, told me when I was old enough to take his place, that Genghis was visited by *Tengri* in a vision. *Tengri* told him where to find the sacred grove, the place where Wolf and Doe first laid together. Beyond the mountain. Genghis went there alone, and—"

"And when he returned, he had the banner," Chucai said, filling in the last detail of Ghaltai's story. "But you don't know where or how he found it."

Ghaltai nodded. "We guard the way to the grove, but we do not venture onto the path."

Squinting, Chucai raised his face toward the mountain. "Ögedei Khan has had a vision as well," he said. "He has come to hunt a bear in the sacred grove." When Ghaltai did not respond, he lowered his gaze and looked over at the *Darkhat* rider.

Ghaltai sat rigidly in his saddle, and he would not meet Chucai's gaze. "It is a place of powerful spirits," was all that he would say.

IN THE AFTERMATH

FTER THE DEATH of the Rose Knight, Hans remembered very little. He had managed to avoid the tumultuous press of bodies throwing themselves out of the arena, mainly by virtue of his size, but the streets had been so chaotic, filled with so many Mongol warriors with bared weapons, that he had gone to ground. Like a frightened rabbit. He knew a half dozen routes back to his uncle's brewery and the safe haven of the tree, and most of those paths could only be traversed by a boy his size or smaller, but he hadn't felt safe.

Nowhere was safe.

And so he hid. Beneath the southern stands of the arena, he found a corner of the foundation where the Mongol engineers, in their haste to assemble the edifice, hadn't quite closed. The hole was narrow and dark, and he managed to rip his shirt and scrape his shoulder, but he got in. Crawling around in the dark until he felt stone and wood behind him on two sides, he curled up in a ball. Only then did he let himself cry, and he bawled until he had no tears left.

He must have fallen into an exhausted stupor—not quite sleep, but not quite consciousness either. When he came to his senses, wiping the crust of dirt and dried tears from his stiff eyelashes, he heard nothing. No pounding feet. No screams. No shouting, nor clashes of steel. Stiffly, he pried himself out of his corner sanctuary and gingerly crawled back toward the dim light of his entry hole. Distantly, he heard the raucous screams of angry crows, the sort of cries the black birds made when they were trying to intimidate each other. When they were trying to drive other birds away from a prize of putrescent carrion.

Hans cringed at the thought of what lay outside, scooting back on his hands and rear until he was pressed into his safe corner again. It wasn't Hünern outside anymore, it was Legnica—the day after the Mongolian engineers had breached the city gates and the mounted warriors had streamed into the city.

He wasn't old enough to fight with the rest of the men in the defense of the city, but he was old enough to understand what the women were planning should the walls fall. He was old enough to know that he should hide, someplace where no one could find him. Not even his own family. Their children would not become slaves, the mothers of Legnica vowed, and when the Mongols came, the women took their children to the wall.

He was not the only boy to survive the hammer and hilt, blade and knife, that took every boy and girl child of Legnica, the frantic solution laid upon each child by their parents to keep them safe from the ravenous pillaging of the Mongol Horde. They were all marked for having been cowards—a darkness each could easily read in the eyes of the others; bound by this shadow, they swore oaths to one another beneath the cracked branches of the old tree in Hünern. Never get caught. Never betray one another. Never give succor to the enemy. *Think of the living.*

He had survived the fall of Legnica. Days after the Mongols had finished plundering the city, he had crept out of his hole, shivering and weak from hunger. The city stank of death, and the stone walls of those few buildings still standing were smeared and stained

with blood. There were corpses everywhere, bloated and stinking with maggots and flies. The sky had been dark with crows and
vultures.

He forced himself away from the stone wall and crawled toward
the hole in the arena's foundation. *It can't be as bad.* Hünern was
silent, daring him to find out.

The arena was empty, but some sense—that same animal cunning that had kept him sane and safe while hiding in Legnica—
warned him to stay hidden. He crept slowly along the edge of the
stands, eyes and ears alert.

Wood creaked overhead, and he froze, pressing himself against
the wood. Barely daring to breathe, he listened intently for the
sound to be repeated, and after a few moments, he heard the weak
groan of the timber as it was forced to support a heavy weight once
more. Voices followed, guttural snatches of conversation, and Hans
listened intently, trying to discern what the pair of Mongols was
discussing.

They hadn't seen him: that much was clear. The men were both
bored and on edge—*guard duty*, Hans guessed, *watching the arena*. But
why was the unanswered question. Satisfied that he wasn't in danger
of being spotted, Hans crept toward the back of the arena, a dangerous curiosity tugging at him.

Each of the arena's numerous exits was typically sealed by a
heavy wooden gate, but they were all an afterthought, and their
timbers were the leftover scraps from the initial construction. There
were gaps in the gates, and most of them didn't quite marry with the
well-worn path. There was a gap large enough to squeeze through
beneath the gate nearest Hans's hiding place, and he—gingerly,
carefully—eased through the hole.

Once through the gate, he lay flat on the ground, trusting that
the dirty dinginess of his clothing and hair would make him blend
in with the rough and knotted wood of the gate. Raising his head

not much more than the width of two fingers from the ground, he let his gaze roam around the open field outside the arena for any movement.

There were a few huddled shapes. *Corpses*, he assumed, judging by the interest being shown by numerous crows. A few sported the familiar fletching of Mongol arrows, and after examining the position of these bodies in comparison with the others, Hans was able to discern a history of what had played out in the field.

Most of the dead had probably died in the riot, cut down by Mongol swords or trampled in the madness that had followed Andreas's valiant attempt on the Khan's life. The remainder—the ones sporting arrows—were closer to the wall, grouped in a cluster, almost as if they died trying to reach a specific spot on the arena wall.

Curiosity dared him to look, and he crawled belly down along the gate until he reached the wall. The gate was inset slightly, and with a final, nervous glance around, he pushed himself up to his hands and knees. Leaning forward, he peered around the corner, directing his attention up.

At first he couldn't quite understand what he was seeing. A leg. An arm. The ragged edge of a maille shirt. And then a horrible realization hit him: a body had been nailed to the wall. It was in pieces, the limbs hacked from the torso, and little effort had been applied in putting the pieces back in their proper position. Hans leaned out farther, trying to spot some identifying mark, and he finally spied the head.

"No," he sobbed, sinking back against the wall, and as soon as the word had slipped free of his lips, he wanted to take it back. He wanted to grab the sound with his hands and shove it back into his mouth, as if by swallowing the word, he could reverse time and erase the image burned into his brain.

Andreas.

Overhead, the timbers creaked as the guards reacted to his tiny cry. They began jabbering at one another, and before they could investigate, Hans was on his feet. He sprinted away from the arena, his feet flying across the dusty ground. Behind him, the guards shouted, and he heard the whistling hiss of an arrow as it flew past him. Dodging the dead, he kept his head down and his eyes forward. His whole body—lungs aching, heart pounding—was solely focused on reaching the welcoming embrace of the nearest alley and the shadows that would hide him from the arcing arrows of the Mongol guards atop the arena walls.

He didn't look back. He had seen enough.

THE GIFT OF THE SPIRITS

*I*N OTHER CIRCUMSTANCES, Chucai might have marveled at the scenery of the valley at the foot of Burqan-qaldun. He might have stood quietly in a reflective *qi* pose, and let his breathing become one with the gentle sighing sound of the northern wind. If he didn't have the responsibility of managing the entirety of the *Khagan*'s vast empire, he might have lain down on the ample grasses and watched the white clouds chase one another across the vault of Blue Heaven. It was a hard man who was not moved by the beautiful simplicity of the site where Genghis Khan lay entombed, and the austerity of the Great Khan's grave only furthered the myth that Genghis truly understood his place within the endless expanse of the known world.

However, Genghis *was* dead, his empire was nearly double the size it had been during his life, and his third son—while perhaps the most capable of his children—was a drunk. Chucai did not have the luxury of admiring the unspoiled beauty of this sacred place. The empire, if it was to survive, needed leadership. It needed a strong *Khagan*.

Chucai ran his hand through his long beard and let his gaze bore into Ögedei's back. The *Khagan* had been kneeling at his father's gravesite for an interminable time now. At first, the *Khagan* had been speaking in a low voice, offering a solemn prayer to his father's spirit

377

and the spirits of this valley; now, the *Khagan* was still—so still, in fact, that Chucai wondered if Ögedei had fallen asleep.

Gansukh's impetuous actions had touched a long-slumbering part of Ögedei's spirit, and for all the administrative headache the trip to Burqan-qaldun had caused, Chucai had been pleased at the initial elevation of the *Khagan*'s attention to all matters concerning the empire. But the delays and the constant presence of the court—even as diminished as it was on this journey—had mired the *Khagan* again. The siren lure of the drink was too strong, and Ögedei loved it too much.

Was the hunt for the bear going to be enough to drive that thirst from Ögedei, once and for all?

Voices from the direction of the *Torguud* escort roused Chucai from his ruminations. Piqued by the movement among the bodyguards' horses, he turned his attention from the kneeling *Khagan*.

Namkhai and the other *Torguud* had surrounded an interloper. The horseman was not *Darkhat*, though he was clearly Mongolian, and his attire was both well cared for and weather-beaten. His sun-darkened face was familiar to Chucai, though he could not quite place the man, and his unrestrained hair had been bleached of all its color by years of sunlight.

"Who is this man?" he demanded as he rode over to the cluster of *Torguud* riders.

"He claims to be an old friend of the *Khagan*'s," Namkhai rumbled.

"Here? Now?" Chucai scoffed. "The nearest outpost is how many days away?"

"Two, Master Chucai," the interloper called out. He raised his arm—slowly, so as to not startle the already tense *Torguud*—and pointed. "In that direction. It used to be an old *Merkit* village before Temujin and the clans took it over. Do you remember it, Master? Or was that before you came to the Great Khan's household?"

"The *Merkit* are no more," Chucai said. "We are all Mongols now."

The gray-haired man smiled. "Some of us remember, though, because we were there."

"Who are you, old man?" Namkhai demanded.

"His name is Alchiq." Ögedei rode up beside Chucai, and though his face and beard were wet with tears, there was a smile on his face. "He was my father's man. On one of my first hunts, he helped me carry the meat from my kill back to camp." His smile became a broad grin. "I thought you were dead."

"Not dead, my Khan," Alchiq replied, sparing a withering glance at Chucai as he placed a closed fist over his heart and bowed his head. "Just far away, in the West."

Ögedei appeared to not notice the glance as he waved his hands at the *Torguud* surrounding the gray-haired man. "He is an old companion," he commanded. "Do not treat him as an enemy."

But he was, Chucai recalled, *when you first became enamored of the spoils of the empire. He was one of those who stood at your side—exhorting you to drink, to enjoy the privileges of being the Khan of Khans.*

The dissolution had begun with the desire to build Karakorum. Shortly after vanquishing the Jin Dynasty—one of the last conquests left unfinished by his father—Ögedei had decided to build himself an imperial palace, much like those his armies had demolished throughout the Chinese provinces. Chucai could recall the arguments about the foundation of such a fixed camp, and one of the few regrets he had concerning his governance of Genghis's legacy had been telling Ögedei that Genghis never would have built such a place.

I am not my father, Ögedei had shouted at him, and there had been such finality in those few words, such outrage and such pain, that Chucai knew he had indelibly damaged his relationship with the son of the Great Khan.

And now this man, this gaunt and weather-hardened *Mongol*, had returned, and in his gaze, Chucai saw an obdurate devotion that had refused to wither. When Alchiq had been exiled from the nascent palace of Karakorum, his only duty—his *final* duty to his *Khagan*—had been to go someplace far away, to wander past the edge of the empire and die. Like the decency a dog has when it realizes it is too old to hunt.

While Chucai ruminated on Alchiq's arrival, Ögedei pushed his way past his sluggish and reluctant *Torguud*, and warmly clasped Alchiq's hands in his own. "You have returned at the right time," the *Khagan* said, pulling the older man half out of his saddle in an effort to hug him. "You are an omen of good luck, sent by Blue Heaven to bless my hunt."

"No, my Khan—" Alchiq began. His mouth closed to a narrow line and his nostrils flared as he smelled the wine on the *Khagan*'s breath.

"Yes!" Ögedei blustered on, ignoring Alchiq's change of expression. "The hunt!" He turned in his saddle, seeking to make eye contact with Namkhai. "I am done here. I have paid my respects to my father, and the spirits of this place have responded. They have sent me an old friend. They approve of my quest. They approve of *me*."

"Of course, my Khan," Namkhai replied smoothly. He turned in his saddle and, with a quick series of hand gestures, informed the bodyguard of the *Khagan*'s desire to ride back to the caravan. The riders fanned out into a teardrop formation.

Namkhai is the right choice, Chucai thought, watching the other riders respond to the wrestling champion's commands. *I will inform Ögedei tonight that Namkhai is his new* Torguud *captain*.

"You will dine with me," Ögedei said to Alchiq. "I will hear of everything that has happened to you in the last few years."

"There is one thing—" Alchiq started.

"It can wait," Ögedei said, and with a wild cry, he snapped his reins. His horse leaped to a gallop, and the *Torguud* followed, smoothly parting around Alchiq, Chucai, and the few *Darkhat* who had accompanied the *Khagan* to Genghis's grave.

Ghaltai, the *Darkhat* leader, hesitated for a moment, and then he and his men followed the *Khagan* and his bodyguard, leaving Chucai and Alchiq behind.

Chucai stroked his beard and stared at Ögedei's old companion, daring Alchiq to lock eyes with him again. The surprise had worn off, and his own mental guard was back up. Exiling Alchiq and the few others who had been a bad influence on the *Khagan* had been the right decision. They had all been drunks, and he had hoped the shame of the exile would have been enough to give them the requisite excuse to drink themselves to death, but such a supposition had clearly failed in Alchiq's case.

"He's still drinking," Alchiq frowned.

"Yes, he is," Chucai said. *We both failed.* He brushed that thought aside as readily—and with the same indifference—as if he were brushing dust from his sleeve. *The past is dead; there is only the future of the empire to consider.* "Do you recall the penalty for breaking your exile?"

"I do."

"Then why have you returned?"

"The *Khagan* is in danger. I—I had to warn him."

"You could have sent a messenger."

"Would you have believed a messenger?"

Chucai offered Alchiq a withering smile as his answer.

"That is why I came," Alchiq said, a fervent finality in his voice. "My *duty* was clear."

And so are your eyes, Chucai noted, and the irony of Alchiq finding salvation in exile was not lost on him.

* * *

The *Darkhat* had met the *Khagan* with a great deal of noisy ceremony when the caravan reached the Kherlen River, two *arban* of identically clad warriors on splendid horses thundering across the water. Only one of the *Darkhat* spoke, offering greetings to the *Khagan*; the rest had sat like imposing statues on their horses, staring into the distance as if they could see the enormity of the empire's history laid out in the caravan's wake.

They were meant to be imposing, and Gansukh had noticed the effect their stoic intensity had on a number of the younger *Torguud*. When the *Darkhat* had arrived, they had galloped toward the *Khagan*'s *ger* without pause, as if they expected the *Torguud* to get out of their way. The *Khagan*'s Imperial Guard had moved aside for the oncoming riders, and—just like that—the *Khagan*'s men had already ceded the mental advantage to the newcomers. Without even realizing it, they had accepted a presumed subordination.

After the *Khagan* departed for the grave of Genghis Khan with a retinue of his own men and half of the *Darkhat* riders, Gansukh had had an opportunity to watch the remaining *Darkhat* as they preceded the caravan to its final destination.

The caravan was being taken to a valley on the southern slope of Burqan-qaldun. It was not—as he had inaccurately assumed—the location of the Sacred Grove that the shaman had spoken of back in Karakorum, but a long meadow that would provide sufficient open ground for the many *ger* as well as pasture for the horses and running water. The grove itself was closer to the mountain, through a vale of rock and—according to the vague nonanswer offered by one of the *Darkhat* when Gansukh had inquired—beyond a waterfall and a field of singing rushes.

All very mysterious, intentionally off-putting so as to maintain an air of secrecy and mysticism. Gansukh was a humble steppe warrior—sure to be mentally constricted by long-extant clan superstitions that would keep him docile and respectful. So that he wouldn't question what his eyes were telling him; so that he wouldn't allow his curiosity to ask too many questions.

The *Darkhat* armor was worn—not from use, but from age. Their horses, while sure-footed and well-groomed, were no longer young stallions. Gansukh was fairly certain his pony could outlast any of the larger *Darkhat* horses in a long-distance race. While all of the *Darkhat* carried bows, nearly a quarter of them had quivers that were only half full. And the men themselves? None of them were his age, and, in a less formal setting, he probably would have referred to more than half of them as *grandfather*.

He ruminated on these details during the remainder of the day, and as the caravan slowly trundled down a gentle slope toward the sunlit meadows of their camp, Gansukh was struck by an odd discrepancy. No one was waiting for them.

It was not a significant social failure. The *Khagan* had not yet rejoined them, and such pomp was typically reserved for his eyes, but Gansukh found himself wondering why there had not been more riders waiting for them in the valley. Typically, when receiving visitors, an *ordu* chief would send out his best warriors as escort, and he would greet them himself when they arrived at their destination.

There are no more Darkhat, he realized. The two *arban* that had met the *Khagan* at the river were all the *Darkhat* fighting men. The clan was dying out.

He tried to dismiss this conclusion as the caravan came to a halt and began the lengthy process of settling into camp. Once he had removed his saddle and gear from his horse and performed the remedial tasks of brushing and feeding it, he joined the other men who were clearing the field for the *ger*. The busy work would keep his hands and mind occupied, so that he would not dwell overlong on the conclusion he had reached.

It wasn't just the *Darkhat* clan he kept thinking about; it was the empire as a whole.

the man who would be pope

ERENC'S EYES NEARLY popped out of his head, making him look like a younger Monferrato. "Father Rodrigo!" he gasped, grabbing Ocyrhoe's arm and pointing excitedly.

Too far away to tell, she signed on his arm, reluctant to believe the evidence of her ears.

Ferenc and Ocyrhoe paused at the edge of a crowd of at least a thousand people, no longer milling and murmuring, but transfixed, all eyes trained on a small man dressed like a priest, standing halfway up a huge mound of rubble, head bowed as if in prayer. Ocyrhoe could not see his face clearly, but he held out something that flashed and gleamed—something brilliant, golden, almost hypnotic in the steady sunlight. The cattlelike lowing sounds had subsided into a profound quiet. Ocyrhoe was used to the city and its busy, noisy throngs, but she was not used to so large a group falling mute all at once, unified in utter silence.

The three adults—Léna, Cardinal Monferrato, and the soldier, Helmuth—came up behind. The cardinal was breathing heavily through his mouth.

After a long break, the priest on the mound lifted his head and resumed his harangue. His voice rang out clearly over the onlookers and echoed from the far walls.

Ocyrhoe had seen many prophesiers in many marketplaces, but never before had she seen one of them attract this kind of attention. And his words! She shook her head, still unwilling to believe what she was hearing. He was preaching violence.

Ferenc shook his head and exclaimed out loud, "It *is* Father Rodrigo!" Around them, outliers glared in disapproval and lifted hushing fingers. Oblivious, Ferenc spoke to Helmuth, the one man who could understand his native tongue. "That is the man we have come to Rome to save!"

Helmuth frowned. "We did not come to Rome to save anyone," he said. "We came to bring Cardinal Monferrato to vote for the Pope."

Ignoring him, Ferenc turned back to Ocyrhoe. *Tell me what Father Rodrigo's saying*, he signed.

Ask Helmuth, she begged off. *Too many words.* She couldn't tell Ferenc what the priest was saying.

The cardinal was staring open-mouthed at the man on the rubble pile. "Who is that?" he demanded. "How is it this boy knows him?"

Ocyrhoe wondered how best to explain. After a deep breath, she began. "It is Father Rodrigo Bendrito, a Roman priest who once lived near Ferenc's home. Ferenc and Father Rodrigo traveled together to Rome, and then Father Rodrigo was put into seclusion with the cardinals in the Septizodium. As he is not in the Septizodium, that could mean the others are no longer imprisoned there, either."

Monferrato closed his eyes a moment, as if hoping to open them to a different, saner reality. "He is preaching a Crusade. He is telling these people to rise up and defend Christendom against the Mongols."

"I hear what he's saying as well as you," Ocyrhoe said. The man's face pinked. He puffed and looked outraged that she had dared to address him so abruptly. Out of the corner of her eye, Ocyrhoe saw Léna frown. "He was very ill when they arrived here, both physically and mentally," Ocyrhoe said quickly, trying to find some explanation that the cardinal would find suitable.

Monferrato blinked owlishly at her, and she shrugged, not sure what else to tell him. She had no idea why the priest was exhorting the crowd to launch a Crusade against the Mongols. It seemed so unlike the kindly—albeit somewhat dazed—man she had met in the Septizodium.

Beside them, Helmuth was translating Rodrigo's rant to Ferenc, who looked as if he were watching eels do circus tricks. Ocyrhoe felt somewhat mollified; Ferenc couldn't believe what Father Rodrigo was saying either. He replied to Helmuth in a tone that Ocyrhoe took to be a defense of the priest, and used the word *Mohi* several times.

Léna started upon hearing the name. She snapped her fingers in front of Ferenc's face to get his attention and repeated, "Mohi?"

When Ferenc nodded, she turned her attention to Helmuth. "What was he saying?" she demanded.

The Emperor's guard shuffled nervously, his face pale. "He talks of the battle at Mohi, as if he and the priest were there." He said something to Ferenc in Magyar, and Ferenc nodded tersely in reply. "They didn't just witness it," Helmuth continued. "They were on the battlefield."

"You poor boy," Léna said softly. She touched his arm, her fingers dancing lightly across his skin, and Ocyrhoe was surprised when Ferenc pulled away from Léna's touch.

Léna hesitated for a moment, and then she turned to the others. "The priest and this young man were present at one of the most atrocious battles Christendom has ever witnessed. It was a battle no one should have had to witness—least of all a man of God—and what the priest saw must have driven him mad." She indicated Ferenc.

"With what sanity he had left, he must have asked this boy to bring him back to Rome, perhaps to seek redemption—or whatever peace might be left for him. But now it would appear that his madness has consumed him, and he is infecting the rest of the city."

She listened intently to Father Rodrigo's sermon, as if hearing him differently now. She had the same expression on her face that Ocyrhoe had seen previously—her attention both intent and distant.

Privately, Ocyrhoe thought Father Rodrigo looked much healthier than she had ever seen him. And he spoke with a great deal of verve. His words were clear and direct. He spoke without hesitation or confusion, as if the message he was delivering to his rapt audience was one that he knew quite well.

It was a strange message, one she did not understand fully. He spoke of trees—cedars—being cut down and the darkening of stars. He spoke both of the need for faith and the end of the Church, and when she glanced over her shoulder at Léna, she noted that the Binder woman was mouthing words almost in concert with Father Rodrigo.

A disturbance rippled through the crowd and further discussion as to the sanity of Father Rodrigo was cut short by the arrival of other figures on the makeshift pulpit. From around the side of the mound of rubble came a young boy and half a dozen men dressed in white uniforms, each with an image of crossed keys emblazoned on his chest. Three of the men carried pikes, and were already pointing their tips down toward the crowd. The other three men rushed Father Rodrigo and brandished swords close to his face. He gave them a curious glance, then returned his attention to the crowd, calling upon them again to take up arms, to drive the darkness back to the East, whence it had come.

The guards looked disgusted and reluctantly sheathed their swords. One of them circled from behind and grabbed Father Rodrigo around the neck, while the other two lifted his legs and tied his ankles. They then tossed him like a pig carcass, pulled back his arms, and used a length of rope to bind his wrists behind him. The cup he had been holding fell clanging to the stones. The guards, still manhandling the unresisting priest, did not notice. Ocyrhoe did, and when she glanced at Ferenc, he nodded, indicating he had seen the cup fall too.

Behind her, she heard Léna draw in a sharp breath.

The crowd, released from the spell of the priest's prophetic ranting, turned ugly. Swiftly, a chain of possession from the vendors' carts materialized, and the angry citizens began to pelt the soldiers with vegetables.

The soldiers ignored the fusillade of vegetables. One even reached out and intercepted a flying cabbage, giving the crowd a brief bow and a crooked grin. Within a few heartbeats, they had efficiently draped Father Rodrigo over the largest man's shoulder and departed in the direction from which they had come.

The crowd growled and surged to the left, as if it would move, in one unit, around the ruins and follow the soldiers and the trussed-up priest. But as quickly as it moved forward, it fell back again like a wave on a beach meeting a sea wall. A phalanx of uniformed, helmeted men equipped with yet more pikes erupted into view. The crowd's shouts of protest twisted into cries of alarm, then pain, and the mass swayed sideways and back to get away from the prodding, jabbing weapons.

Without another word, the five travelers grabbed each others' hands and shoulders and fled down a small street that led south, away from the market. After a score of paces, they stopped and stood in a circle, staring at each other, husking out frightened breaths.

"What just happened?" Cardinal Monferrato demanded.

"Guards...from the Vatican," Ocyrhoe said. "They wore different uniforms from the men who serve the Bear—Senator Orsini. They will likely take this priest to Saint Peter's or the Castel Sant'Angelo. We should go there, not to the Septizodium."

"Why? Isn't the Septizodium where the cardinals are being held?" Helmuth shook his head. "The Emperor does not care about this priest friend of yours, and neither do I. He wants us to go to the Septizodium."

"Those soldiers take their orders from the College of Cardinals," Ocyrhoe argued. "How could the cardinals be commanding them if they were still imprisoned in the Septizodium? How would they even know—"

"Child," Léna said sternly, and Ocyrhoe silenced herself at once. "What was the message you were given to deliver, by the English cardinal?"

Ocyrhoe already understood the point of this lesson. "It was to bring the Emperor's men back to the Septizodium," she said in a resigned tone.

"You are under oath," Léna said simply. "Does a Binder interpret the message that has been given to her or does she simply deliver it?"

Ocyrhoe lowered her eyes. "She delivers it," she said. "But I think it is a waste of time to go there."

"What you think matters less than what you are sworn to do," Léna said, not unkindly. "It is a characteristic that many rely on with the Binders." A note of bitterness crept into her voice, which caused Ocyrhoe to raise her head, but Léna, seeming to anticipate Ocyrhoe's gaze, was already looking away. "Let us continue with what we came here to do," she said softly.

Ferenc had been watching them all with increasing impatience, and at this lull in the conversation he grabbed Ocyrhoe's arm and urgently pointed back in the direction Father Rodrigo had been taken. It took no translator for her to understand what he wanted. She gave Helmuth a plaintive look, and the German soldier brusquely translated to Ferenc what had just passed between the two Binders.

Ferenc squirmed and flung up his arms in frustration, then grabbed her forearm. She wanted to pull away—he could not possibly understand—but he did not. *Lie to them about where we are going*, he signed.

At that, she snatched her arm from his fingers as if she'd been burned. "No!" she said angrily, and shook her head. "Never. Never!"

* * *

"You obviously have no control over anything that is happening," said Senator Orsini furiously. "How are you of the slightest value to me? I should demand payment for all the choice viands you have supped upon at this table. I might as well have thrown them to my dogs. At least I know *their* loyalty is solid."

Cardinal Fieschi seethed and twitched with frustration. "Total control is impossible, and not even useful. There has been a hiccup in our plan, but don't you see it has allowed things to unfold in a way that can be even more fruitful?"

"No," said Orsini. "I don't see that at all, nor do I care for your inference that I am too stupid to understand your clever plan. In fact, I am so unmoved by your cleverness—"

"Orsini, what is it we want?" Fieschi demanded. "We want a Pope we can control, do we not? One who will repel the advances of the Emperor."

"We would have had that in Bonaventura. And it is your fault Bonaventura is not now the Pope."

"If anything, it is to my credit he is not," Fieschi shot back. "But even if I'd voted for him this last round, he would not have won. Do you understand that? It would have been another deadlock. Unless Frederick were to release one of the cardinals he holds hostage, and allow that man to come back to Rome, it would always be a deadlock. Even after removing one of Castiglione's supporters from the equation entirely, there was no way to avoid deadlock."

"Deadlock is better than chaos," Orsini huffed. "Currently we have chaos. I should never have trusted you to steer anything. I will remember that when we really do have a Pope in power. The Bishop of Rome and the Senator of Rome will have plenty to talk about, but you have lost your place at that table."

Fieschi could feel the heat rise in his face so intensely he wondered if even his eyeballs had turned red. *You imbecile*, he wanted to shout at Orsini. *Are you really so blind you do not see how much more is at stake? Rome means nothing compared to the world that the Church commands. You are nothing but a convenient tool, and you are rapidly becoming inconvenient.*

Instead, he forced a tight smile and said, with tempered condescension, "If you will listen to me for but a moment, you will realize that I have actually helped to *set* that table. We have the Pope in a room a half mile from here. The citizens of Rome have already heard him speak and they were mesmerized by his rhetoric. We will be able to steer him in any direction we desire, and the masses will eagerly follow. He offers us power that would be unimaginable if Bonaventura had been elected." He sat back in his seat and crossed his arms, looking up at the Bear smugly.

Orsini made a dismissive face. "What do we care what the masses do?" he snorted. "They have no power."

Fieschi altered his tight smile into a sympathetic one. "Come with me to the Vatican compound and you may change your mind. It took me two hours to get here because the mob was so thick. There is something hypnotic about that priest. Come with me and see for yourself, and then dismiss the masses—if you dare."

Orsini shook his head stubbornly. "If he has that kind of power and he's a madman, then he is extremely dangerous and must be killed immediately."

"But he is pliable," Fieschi insisted calmly. "I saw Somercotes win him over easily. If we stage the next few days carefully, I am confident that I can make him my creature. And then all that power is ours to use as we want."

"And if you fail?" Orsini said. "I do not share your confidence in your abilities."

"If I fail, then get rid of him, and we're back to where we were before," Fieschi said. "A deadlocked College of Cardinals and no Pope."

Orsini thought about this for a few moments. Fieschi watched him, and was careful not to make a sound or indulge in even the slightest movement lest he trigger Orsini into some truculent response.

Finally Orsini asked, grimly, "What are the other cardinals doing about all this?"

Fieschi made a dismissive gesture. "Some of them are poring over old codices of canonical law trying to establish if we may..." He lifted his hands. "Annul the election? Force a resignation? I doubt they will find any definitive answer or procedure, but the longer we stay here, the more time they have to create an argument against keeping him."

"Are you the only cardinal who wants to see him remain the Pope?"

Fieschi shrugged. "The only one who counts," he said firmly. "I have two unlikely colleagues, but they are mostly interested in entertaining themselves. They're not taking any action, they are just sitting back to watch what unfolds."

"Is one of them Colonna?" Orsini asked in a disgusted voice.

Fieschi sat upright and said sharply, "Do not refuse this course simply because you don't want to agree with Colonna. That is childish. The entire Colonna-Orsini feud is childish. Do you even remember what your ancestors first argued about?"

Orsini made a dismissive gesture. "If you genuinely believe that you can bring this man under your sway, so that he will be my tool,

then I will consider—but only *consider*—ensuring that all civic authority in the city is dedicated to carrying out his enthronement."

"That is the only sane way to persevere in this," Fieschi said,
feeling a wave of relief that he was careful not to show. Let Orsini
think Father Rodrigo was to be Orsini's tool.

He knew better.

* * *

A dried, charred smell wafted toward the five as they approached the
alley that ran behind the Septizodium. "We turn left here," Ocyrhoe
announced. "There is a hidden entrance that only Ferenc can find."
Ferenc glanced at her and smiled with sheepish pride, knowing what
she was telling them. "Then there is a series of dark passages. We will
need at least a candle. Do you still have the candle from this morning?"
she asked Monferrato. "The one you used to irritate the Emperor?"

Every time she spoke to him, he seemed startled and slightly
annoyed. She wondered how many girls other than servants ever
spoke to him, cardinal as he was. "That was part of the excommunication ritual," he said. "I gave it to my colleague."

"Well, we'll need to get a candle from somewhere else, then, or
a lantern," she said. "But first we'll show you the doorway. It's just...
Oh!"

They had turned the corner as she spoke. The charred smell hit
their faces, wafting on languid curls of smoke that emanated from a
large, ragged opening in the rock face, a few dozen paces away.

This was the secret entrance to the Septizodium, but it stood
wide open—in fact, the hinged rock that served as the actual door
had been lifted away, as if by the hand of God, and lay in the street.
Amazed, she turned to Ferenc, who was already staring at her.

"That's the entrance. Something has happened," she said, as
calmly as she could.

"I think there has been a fire," the cardinal said in a concerned voice. Ocyrhoe rolled her eyes. She was not prone to sarcasm, but this man was just too easy a target.

"Let's take a closer look," Léna calmly intervened.

"Yes, absolutely," Helmuth said, so quickly that Ocyrhoe suspected he was embarrassed he was not the first to suggest it.

They walked toward the entrance. Ocyrhoe glanced up at the surrounding rooftops but saw no guards—no one at all. The alley was deserted. As they approached the entrance, preparing to enter with Ocyrhoe in the lead, an echoing, percussive sound issued from the darkness. And then, softer, the sounds of footfall, coming closer to them.

A low, blocky form emerged from obscurity: a small, hunched man, a shovel slung back over his shoulder, wearing the ill-fitting livery of a low-ranking servant. His face was wrinkled, furtive, sad. He stepped through the doorway and paused with disinterest, lowering his jaw slightly when he saw them all gathered. "No entry allowed," he said, sounding bored. "There are guards back there, they'll just chase you out." He took another step to move past them.

"Can you tell us what happened?" the cardinal asked.

The old man shrugged. "Fire. Someone died."

"Who died?" Ocyrhoe demanded.

Again the old man shrugged. "Cardinal."

"Which one?" Monferrato demanded shrilly.

"Foreigner. English, I think."

Ocyrhoe gasped before she could catch herself. Ferenc tapped her arm. She ignored him and turned to Léna. "The man who sent the message is dead." She tried to push aside the strange upwelling of emotion—she'd only met Somercotes once, yet she found herself disoriented by the news. "How do I fulfill my obligation now?" she asked, almost childlike. "I was to bring the Emperor's men to Cardinal Somercotes, but he...no longer lives."

Léna gave her an understanding look. She reached for Ocyrhoe's right hand, lifted it, gently pressed the hand into a fist, and rested the fist against Ocyrhoe's breastbone. "You are like the fox, unbound here and unencumbered," she prompted.

Ocyrhoe began to echo the phrase before Léna had even finished. Then she heaved a huge sigh, both saddened and relieved that her mission was over. She saw Ferenc watching the two Binders with a wary, envious look.

During their exchange, Helmuth had continued to question the worker, who met the soldier's demands with a series of shrugs and other signs of stolid disregard—and only a few mumbled words. After releasing the old man with a disgusted kick at his backside, Helmuth informed the rest of the group, "The other cardinals were escorted to the Vatican compound yesterday."

"I knew that," Ocyrhoe said matter-of-factly. Helmuth glared at her. Ocyrhoe had never encountered so many fragile men in her life. They must feel very insecure indeed if a girl talking back caused such unrest.

"Let us go there," said the cardinal.

Helmuth grimaced. "The way will be congested," he said.

"It would have been much less congested earlier," Ocyrhoe said, unable to still her tongue.

"Silence, brat," Helmuth said.

Léna smiled, silencing both of them with a look. "A path will present itself," she said calmly. "I am sure of it."

THE BOY AND THE TREE

32

HE REFLECTION IN the horse trough was a hollow-eyed phantom. Ripples in the water added lines, distorting his mouth into a quivering frown that split his face in half. Dietrich slapped the water, disturbing the image even further, and turned away from the wrecked face staring up at him. He dried his face with a rag that was probably dirtier than he was. As much as he tried to push the matter out of his mind, he could not avoid the truth. It kept creeping up on him—staring back from the water in the horse trough, leering from behind the eyes of his men. Doubt. Fear. Panic.

He had lost his way, and he was leading the *Fratres Militiae Christi Livoniae* to ruin. Had *Heermeister* Volquin suffered this same realization shortly before the battle at Schaulen? Dietrich recalled the fury in Kristaps's eyes when the knight had revealed the ugly scars of his failed Shield-Brethren initiation. That same fervor had driven Volquin, and he had been blind to the trap at the river. The *Heermeister's* obsession had nearly destroyed the order; the Teutonic Knights had taken pity on the survivors of Schaulen, welcoming the lost Livonians into their ranks. Many of the Sword Brothers wore the black cross rather than the red, and were content to leave the past buried along the muddy banks of the Schaulen River.

But some had strained under the Teutonic yoke. These men—veterans of the Northern campaigns, survivors of Schaulen—secretly spoke of taking the red cross again, of taking their own lands, of regaining their old glory. They chose him to lead them, and all they had needed was a sign that their purpose was just and right.

And they had been given that sign by the Pope himself. The Sword Brothers found an unexpected patron in Rome, and once Dietrich had sworn himself—and the order—to serve not just the Church, but the men who secretly ruled the Church, they could wear the red cross again.

But the memory of Schaulen proved difficult to shake.

Dietrich sat on the bench beside the trough and stared at the tumbledown wall of the barn that was the extent of their holdings in Hünern. Was this all that *he*, Dietrich von Grüningen, the fourth master of the order, had accomplished? Would history even remember him?

He shuddered, shaking himself free from the grip of this tenacious melancholy. Such weak-mindedness! This would not be the legacy of his command. He would right himself; he would find honor and glory for his men. The rest—the ones who still wore the black cross—would come back. He knew they would.

The Fratres Militiac Christi Livoniae *will survive*, he vowed. Whatever storm threatened, he could not shrink from his duty: his order must survive. No matter the cost, no matter the danger, he must not shirk his responsibility.

Having dispersed the phantom of failure, Dietrich whistled for his squire and began the slow, deliberate ritual of donning his armor. As his squire ensured that maille was fitted properly over gambeson, that surcoat hung properly, and that sword rested at the proper angle on his hips, Dietrich von Grüningen, fourth master of the *Fratres Militiae Christi Livoniae* considered his meager options.

He had been given one order by his master in Rome, and after securing the safety of his men, that was his only other responsibility. *Destroy the Shield-Brethren.*

His squire offered him his helmet, and Dietrich shook his head. He would not need it. Not where he was going. His dressing complete, Dietrich strode out into the main compound, hand resting on the hilt of his sword.

Burchard and Sigeberht were waiting for him. Constant companions, their devotion was absolute. *With a hundred like them, we would be strong,* he reflected as he looked at their stoic faces.

"Is my horse prepared?" he asked.

"As you asked, *Heermeister,*" Burchard murmured. "Where do we ride?"

"The Mongol compound," Dietrich answered. "I must speak with Tegusgal."

* * *

The tree had never had any leaves, as far as Hans could recall; to an outsider, the tree was a scraggly ash, grown from a wind-tossed achene that had sprouted in the unkempt wilderness of a neglected alley. It would never get enough sun. It would never get enough water. But it refused to die, and Hans and the other boys—the Rats of Hünern—adopted it as their own. It was their standard, and beneath its twisted arms, they felt safe. Protected. Sheltered from the cruelty of a world gone mad.

Axis mundi, Andreas had said of the tree when he had last visited the tiny shelter. *It is the pillar of your world,* he had explained. He had reached up and touched the highest branch of the stunted tree. *Though it has some growing to do before it can hold up Heaven, don't you think?*

Andreas was dead. But the tree still lived. *He* still lived. Hans wrapped his arms around the tree and pressed his cheek against the rough bark. Only then would he let himself cry.

But he had no tears. He was as dry as the tree.

"Hans."

He jerked upright at the sound of his name, and instead of flee-ing he only hugged the tree more tightly. When his name was spoken a second time—the tone of voice filled with compassion and tender-ness—he dared to look around for the speaker.

His uncle, Ernust, peered under the dirty tarp that hung over the narrow entrance to the tree's tiny enclave. Ernust's face was streaked with dirt and soot and a stain of something darker—*blood?* Hans's brain offered an idea—and then refused to speculate further—about the source of the smear.

"Boy," Ernust said. "Are you hurt? You came running in here so fast, it was if the Devil were..." He dismissed the rest of his observa-tion. "Are you hurt?" he repeated.

Hans shook his head.

"Yesterday..." his uncle began. The portly man sighed, at a loss for how to finish his thought, and ran his hand across the rounded dome of his head. His eyes flicked over Hans—head to toe and back—and the boy read all the unspoken words in his uncle's restless gaze. "It is time to go, Hans," he said. "There is nothing left for us here, and the Mongols won't wait for the mob to find its strength. They're going to ride out—soon—and kill all the knights. Not just the Rose Knights—though they will be first—but every man who can possibly lift a sword. It will be just like—"

"A Livonian killed him." Hans barely recognized his own voice—flat, echoing with exhaustion. He wanted to lie down beside the tree and cover himself with one of the dusty blankets used by the Rats. He wanted to lie down and let the bleak despair of his words flow throughout his body. Let it fill him until he drowned. "Not one of the Mongols. He was killed by *one of us.*"

"No, boy," Ernust said sadly. "They're not like us. None of them are. They fight for their own causes, for their lords and at the whims of their lords. Never for us. We are nothing to them. We board their animals. We feed them. We give them shelter. We *care* for them, and they do not think of us. They think only of themselves."

"Andreas didn't," Hans countered.

Ernust shook his head. "The others are preparing to leave. There will be no one left to drink our brews—no one who will give us coin for it, anyway. We have to go with them. Back to Löwenberg." He let loose a hollow laugh. "Not that we'll be safe there for—"

"I'm staying," Hans said, tightening his arms around the tree. His fervor surprised him, as did his certainty.

His uncle's face lost its doughy softness, and he fixed Hans with an intent stare that was supposed to be intimidating. "He's dead, Hans. I know he offered to take you with him, but he can't. And the rest won't keep his word. If they even survive. *We* have to survive, and that has little to do with waiting for a hero to rescue you."

Hans flinched at his uncle's words, but his initial reaction passed quickly, and he stared silently at his uncle. Ernust sighed and ran a hand across his head again, looking down after at the smear of dirt and blood on his palm. Neither said anything, and the narrow sanctuary filled up quickly with a portentous silence.

His uncle was a prudent and savvy man, the sort who could see past the tragedy of the Mongol invasion and realize the opportunities present in the ragged tent city of Hünern. During his short stay with Ernust after his mother's death, Hans had heard stories about why his uncle had left the family enclave in Legnica for the untrammeled landscape around the new settlement of Löwenberg. The forest needed to be cleared, fields planted, and houses built: all thirst-making work. The same was true for Hünern, albeit work of a bloodier sort. And what his uncle said was true: the brewers—as well as the carpenters, millers, smiths, leatherworkers, cooks, whores, and all the rest—served at the whim and mercy of the knights. When the knights were gone, the rabble dispersed as well.

Think of the living, boy.

Why wait? This was his uncle's sensible suggestion. There was no shame in leaving. They weren't combatants. They were merchants, brewers of ale and spirits. The market in Hünern was drying up. Why wait to be the last to leave?

Andreas's face came to Hans. Not the gap-mouthed rictus nailed to arena wall, but the calm visage that the Rose Knight had worn as he had walked onto the sand. The knight had not been afraid. He knew his duty, and he approached it with honor. In the end, when he had turned his back on the Livonian to throw his spear, he had not hesitated. He had not fled. He had not turned away from his true purpose.

"No," Hans said quietly. "I can't leave. They need me."

Ernust closed his eyes. Overhead, the sun slipped out from behind a cloud, and the tree's shadow reached across the sanctuary, the branches seeming to grab for his uncle's feet.

"You're daft, boy," Ernust said, squinting at Hans. "Who needs you? The knights? They already know they are in danger."

"The others—the ones the Khan keeps in cages—I can help them." *I need to help them.*

"What can you possibly do?" Ernust asked.

He had had a lot of time to think about what Kim and the Rose Knights were up to. The messages passed back and forth had been purposefully cryptic, but it had been clear to him that their plan was to defeat the Mongols. He wasn't sure how killing the Khan would have accomplished that goal. As important as Onghwe was, he was only one man; the rest of the Mongols wouldn't simply run in terror if their Khan died.

"The knights are going to fight back," he explained. "They don't have any other choice. They won't run. It is not in their nature to run."

Ernust raised his shoulders and sucked at his teeth. "That is why they'll die," he said with some frustration. "That is why everyone will die. That is why we have to go."

"But they're not alone," Hans said. "They have allies." He smiled. "Friends who can strike at the Mongols from behind."

"No," Ernust shook his head, understanding what Hans was suggesting. "You can't do that, boy."

"I have to," Hans insisted. "Otherwise—" his voice broke, and he shook his head angrily. "I can tell them where the cages are. I can tell them how to free their friends."

* * *

The city was eerily quiet. The aftermath of the riot following Kristaps's fight with the Shield-Brethren had imbued the entire settlement with the gravid sense of an impending storm. A stillness hung over every street, ramshackle house, and building like a smothering blanket. Even the priests and monks remained hidden as he and his men had stopped by the church to retrieve the terrified Father Pius.

It would not do to find himself unable to communicate with the Khan's commander when the need was most great.

They did not reach the Mongol compound. Dietrich heard the horses coming before he saw them, felt his own steed stir at the vibrations that were sent through the earth when many hooves pounded it in unison.

The Mongol host flowed through the streets like water around rocks, blending together in a mass of maille and lamellar-armored bodies, the fletching of innumerable arrows protruding from quivers in a plethora of varying colors. Dietrich also saw spears and curved swords, as well as many, many faces glaring at the four of them with naked hatred.

Dietrich raised his arms away from his weapons as they approached and quietly instructed Burchard and Sigeberht to do the same. Pius trembled beside him, and he hissed at the priest, telling him to remain still. "Translate what I say," he instructed.

Tegusgal rode at the front of the host, a tall banner rising from the back of his saddle. His lamellar armor was painted red, and around his neck was a thick necklace of gold links, the only marking that distinguished him from the mob of mounted warriors.

"I am not your enemy!" Dietrich called across the open space between them, and he waited nervously, his right palm itching to touch his sword hilt, as Pius stuttered a translation.

Tegusgal stared flatly at Pius, giving no indication he had understood the priest's words. Pius started muttering under his breath, a Latin prayer, and just as Dietrich was about to command him to be silent, the Mongol commander responded.

"He says that with so few men, you could hardly hope to be," Pius translated. The priest swallowed heavily as Tegusgal continued. "He asks if you have come here to beg for your life with more gold."

Dietrich refused to be riled by the comment, even though he felt a somnambulant sense of pride struggle to awaken in the back of his mind. "Tell him I have something of infinitely greater value," Dietrich said. "I know he rides to battle with the knights. But does he know which are the ones he seeks?"

Tegusgal laughed when he heard the priest's words, and his men guffawed and howled with laughter in the wake of his response.

"He doesn't care," Pius said. "He says you are all going to die."

Dietrich smiled. "God willing," he said with a nod in Pius's direction. "But not today."

Pius hesitated.

"Tell him," Dietrich thundered.

Shivering, Pius stuttered a translation of Dietrich's words, crossing himself as he spoke the words.

Tegusgal rose up his stirrups, his face darkening, and several of the warriors in the first rank behind him reached for their bows.

Dietrich lowered his hands, resting them on his saddle. He waited, impossibly patient, a tiny smile on the edge of his lips.

Burchard's horse nickered nervously, and the big Livonian made a tiny noise with his lips to calm the animal.

Finally, after an eternity of staring at each other, Tegusgal barked a short question.

"He wants to know why," Pius translated.

"Because I know his Khan is angry at him. The Shield-Brethren knight nearly slew his master. He failed to protect his liege, and he's out here today with"—Dietrich ran his eyes over the host of Mongols, trying to get a quick count, and giving up after a few moments—"with more men than he needs to curry some favor." He waited while Pius translated, and before the Mongol commander could reply, he continued. "He needs to slay the Shield-Brethren *first*, otherwise his Khan will know that he doesn't know *who* is the real threat. Tell him that I can show him where the Shield-Brethren are. I can tell him how they hide themselves. I can tell him about their sentries, about their fighting techniques, about how they're waiting to ambush him."

Father Pius's voice droned in the morning air, filling the space between them with words that Dietrich could not understand but hoped were the ones that he had spoken. Everything rested upon this opportunity. *I must not waste it.*

Abruptly, Tegusgal snapped his fingers, cutting Pius off. His spoke savagely in response, angrily gesturing for Pius to translate.

"He wants to know why he should trust you. You are betraying your own people."

"They aren't my people," Dietrich said. He leaned forward. "Were the actions of *my man* in the arena not clear enough?"

Tegusgal regarded him coldly as Pius translated. The Mongol commander grunted as the priest finished, and glancing over his shoulder, he said something to the men behind him.

"What did he say?" Dietrich demanded.

"I—I don't know," Pius responded.

Tegusgal spoke again, and with a gulping hiccup, Pius translated, his voice quivering. "What do you want?"

"Safe passage for my men," Dietrich said without hesitation. "Kill all the knights you want, but me and my men are leaving this shithole."

"Hai!" Tegusgal barked when Pius finished translating, and before any of the Westerners could react, four Mongols raised their bows and loosed arrows. Dietrich flinched, but the arrows were not intended for him.

Sigeberht fell back, toppling off his mount without a word, and Dietrich caught sight of an arrow jutting from his left eye socket. Another was buried in the maille around the base of his throat.

Burchard groaned and leaned forward, remaining—for the moment—in his saddle. He fumbled with a pair of Mongol arrows—both had struck him high in the chest—and tried to speak, but all that came out of his mouth was a spatter of dark blood. His hand slipped, leaving a red smear across his horse's mane, and then he too fell to the ground.

Tegusgal spoke, and Pius translated, his voice a quavering whisper. "He'll kill all the knights he pleases. It is not for you to tell him otherwise."

Dietrich ground his teeth and stared at the Mongol commander. His hand drifted toward the hilt of his longsword, and a number of Mongol bows creaked as their owners drew them back.

Tegusgal held them off with a raised hand. He spoke again, his voice brusque and commanding.

"He will consider your proposal," Pius whimpered, "while you show him the camp of the Shield-Brethren. Should he be victorious there, he may grant you—"

"What?" Dietrich demanded as Pius faltered to a stop.

"He may grant you a head start," the priest wailed.

GRAYMANE'S RIDE 33

THE STRIKING DIFFERENCE between a normal night's rest and the camp being constructed in the valley beneath Burqan-qaldun was the frenzy of the preparations. Jachin had watched the proceedings for a little while but had grown quickly bored by the monotony and had returned to the warmth of her nonmoving *ger*. Lian remained outside, happy to have an excuse to remain free of Second Wife—for a little while at least.

Since her conversation a few days prior with Chucai, the freedom she had been enjoying in moving around the camp had become tainted with uncertainty—an effect she was certain Chucai had considered in the course of his chat with her. She had served with Master Chucai long enough to be fully aware of his predilection for manipulating people—she had even taught him one or two tricks—but that didn't make being the recipient of his machinations any easier. More so when he spoke truly, without the sort of slippery guile that he normally employed when trying to get people to do what he wanted. She suspected Chucai's true intimation in their conversation about the frog and the stone was not that the stone would swamp the frog—it was an amphibian, after all, and could survive being dunked in water—but that the sudden weight of the stone would strip away the frog's hiding place. She would be exposed—bait meant to entice a predator. In this case: Munokhoi.

She recalled the incident with the drunk guards in the alley. She had been able to put them off with the warning that she was protected by someone powerful in the *Khagan*'s court, but that protection was only valid if the men threatening her concerned themselves about repercussions for their actions and if that protective shield was actually true. If she lost Chucai's protection, then what would stop Munokhoi from assaulting her? In fact, given the animosity between the *Torguud* captain and Gansukh, she feared Munokhoi would relish assaulting her as it would provoke a reaction from Gansukh. Such a reaction would be the only excuse he'd need to get into a deadly fight with the *Khagan*'s young pony.

Lost in thought, she wasn't aware of the approach of another person until a hand reached around her waist from the left. She jumped at the sudden touch and found herself reacting in a way that Gansukh had taught her—right thumb on the back of the stranger's hand, grabbing the edge of the fingers with hers and twisting up and out as she spun sharply to her left. As she spun around, raising her arm, she recognized the man who had snuck up on her.

"Ah!" Gansukh's mouth was twisted, caught between trying to smile and holding back a grimace. He brought his right hand up to her neck in a mock counter—a real warning that she was hurting him. "I should have never taught you that wrist lock," he said, massaging his wrist after she let go.

"No, having taught it to me, you should have known better to sneak up on me *like that.*" She punctuated these last two words with a finger to Gansukh's chest.

Gansukh laughed, pretending to be physically shaken by the force of her strident poking. "Ah, what's a little rough contact between—" He paused, reading something in her expression. "What is it?" he asked, his tone losing its levity.

"Nothing," she said.

He caught her hand as she tried to withdraw it, and pulled her toward him. She minced forward, letting herself be dragged close. "I don't believe you." He touched her hair lightly, his hand hesitating—wanting to stroke her head, but not wanting to be so affectionate in public. "I haven't seen you for several days."

"I know. Second Wife has been in need of company, and Chucai asked me to report on her moods."

Gansukh smiled. "And he needed you for that? I could tell him her moods. *Anyone* could tell him her moods."

Lian fought the urge to smile. "Also, as long as I am with Jachin, I am..." She wrestled momentarily with telling Gansukh what had been on her mind right before he had grabbed her. She fought the urge to lean into his touch—to let him hold her. "It's...Munokhoi," she said.

"Ah, I see." Gansukh nodded, a thoughtful expression tightening his face. "Has he threatened you?"

Lian shook her head. "I haven't see him, but I know he hasn't forgotten what happened during the Chinese raid."

"He is to be relieved of his command," Gansukh said. He moved to Lian as he spoke, his voice dropping to a conspiratorial whisper. "I don't know when it is going to happen, but I suspect it will be soon. And when he is stripped of his rank, he will no longer be protected by the rules of the *Torguud*."

This was all the confirmation she needed for her suspicions. Without the rules of the *Torguud* mandating his behavior and protecting him from reprisals, he would be even more liable to seek revenge for the injuries done to his reputation. "Are you... ?"

Gansukh shook his head, a hard smile pulling back his lips. "Do you take me for a scared boy from the steppes?" he asked, mock outrage in his voice. There was a gleam in his eyes, an excitement that was equally frightening and thrilling to see.

"Staying with Second Wife is a good idea. It puts you out of harm's way," Gansukh continued, trying to soothe Lian's fears. Trying to pretend that he hadn't revealed the hunter's delight in his heart.

She felt a momentary pang of guilt as relief washed over her. She didn't need to be the bait that drew Munokhoi out. She didn't have to put herself in danger.

Gansukh was already planning on hunting Munokhoi. He knew what had to be done, and he had no reticence about doing it.

A commotion beyond the nearest rank of *ger* gave Lian an excuse to break away from the confusing elation and horror brought on by this train of thought, and they separated to a more discrete distance as they hurried through the *ger*.

A large crowd gathered near the *Khagan's ger*: courtiers, merchants, *Torguud*—both on horseback and on foot—and other riders, bearing the sky-blue banners of the *Darkhat*. As she and Gansukh approached the verge of the crowd, a ripple ran through the host as they parted to allow someone to approach the steps of the wheeled *ger*.

Ögedei ascended to the platform and turned to address the crowd. He planted his feet firmly on the wooden platform, standing more firmly than he had earlier, and when he spoke his voice was strong and clear. As if his words came straight from an equally clear and resolute mind. "I have offered my prayers to the spirit of my father and to the spirits of our ancestors, *Borte Chino* and *Qo'ai Maral*. They have accepted my prayers and blessed my sacred mission." The *Khagan* paused as the audience cheered his pronouncement, and Lian noticed he did not lean on the railing for support while he waited. "We have come to this sacred land to hunt a great beast, a martial spirit of our ancestors. Our success in this hunt will ensure the prosperity and longevity of the empire." Another cheer interrupted him, and he swayed slightly as if buffeted by the fervor of those gathered.

"Clan *Darkhat* has shown us this pleasant valley," Ögedei continued, "and this will be our camp for the duration of our stay. By the pleasure of the Blue Wolf, let us not stay long!"

The audience erupted into noise once more, and Ögedei's final words were lost in the cacophony of voices. The *Khagan* threw up his arms, exulting in the adoration of his subjects, and then he turned and disappeared into his *ger*.

"There will be a feast tonight," Gansukh whispered, his mouth close to her ear. "That is when the hunt begins."

Which hunt? Lian thought, a shiver running along her arms.

*   *   *

Unlike the intricate and complicated preparations necessary to organize the caravan, setting up camp and preparing for a feast were activities that the host of servants, attendants, tradesmen, and guards knew by heart. Oddly enough, these few hours were some of the only unstructured time Master Chucai had. Typically, he would withdraw to his *ger* and spend a few hours in delightful solitude, but tonight, as the camp buzzed with preparations for an immense feast to celebrate the *Khagan*'s hunt in the morning, he sought out two men: Alchiq, the old drunk, and Ghaltai, the leader of the *Darkhat*.

He found Alchiq near the wagons carrying the prisoners from the West. The gray-haired veteran was assisting with the sparse meals for the caged fighters, and when he noticed Chucai watching, he handed off his bucket of slop and rice to the caravan master.

"Good evening, Master Chucai," he said, offering a short bow. "May I be of assistance?"

"How is it that a one-time companion of the *Khagan*—a man who commanded at least a *jaghun* in his time—is now serving slop to foreign prisoners?" Chucai asked with some curiosity. The idea of Munokhoi serving in this stead floated across his mind, and he quickly dismissed such a possibility as unlikely.

"After you exiled me, I drank a great deal," Alchiq said. "I rode and I drank; I didn't care where I went, just as long as I could refill my skin of *arkhi*." He gestured at the row of cages behind him. "Serving men like this was all I was suited for."

"And yet, earlier today, you wanted to serve your *Khagan* again."

"I've never stopped wanting to serve," Alchiq corrected him. "But I was a drunk. I stood by the *Khagan* and gave him an excuse to drink. We had conquered the world. What did it matter what we did next?"

Chucai said nothing; the man clearly had a speech he had been waiting a long time to deliver. Better to let him get it out.

"But it did matter, didn't it?" Alchiq said. "That was why you banished me and the others. Why you kept reminding the *Khagan* of what his father had accomplished." Alchiq shook his head. "We all hated you; we thought you were the poison that would destroy the empire." He spat in the dirt.

"Why did you come back?" Chucai asked.

"I was with Batu Khan as he conquered lands in the *Khagan*'s name," Alchiq said. I was there when he stormed Kiev, and I rode with his men when they tried to take the white citadel at the top of the hill." Alchiq lifted his long hair off his neck and showed Chucai the ravaged line of scar tissue that ran down his neck and disappeared into his robe. The flesh was bubbled and ragged as if the skin had been liquefied and then allowed to cool.

"We tried for two weeks to take the citadel," Alchiq continued, "and would have continued to throw ourselves against its walls until every last one of us were dead if Batu had had his way. It was General Subutai who pulled him away from the siege. There were only a handful of warriors in the keep, the general argued, and there were other lands to conquer. Beating down those walls was not worth the effort, not when there were richer prizes to be won more easily. Batu relented, but he left some of us behind. To wait for the day when those gates opened and we could finish them off."

Alchiq stared at the cage that held the red-haired giant. "I waited a long time," he continued, his voice more thoughtful. "I commanded more than a *jaghun*, Master Chucai, but, over time, more and more of them wandered off, chasing after Batu's army. My men and I ranged far from Kiev, policing these lands as subject to the *Khagan*'s rule, exacting tribute as we saw fit. But we always came back to Kiev. We always came back to see if those gates had opened. But they never did. Not for us."

"Why come back here?" Chucai asked again. "Shouldn't you have reported your failure to Batu?"

Alchiq smiled at him, a fierce feral grin. "I didn't fail. They came out eventually, and I was waiting for them. My *jaghun* caught them near the Ijil Mörön, the big river also known as *San-su*."

Chucai sucked on a tooth and shrugged, indicating the geographical subtlety of Alchiq's story was lost on him.

"The Ijil Mörön lies *east* of Kiev," Alchiq explained. "And while my men slew all of the *women* who came from the white citadel in Kiev, the others decimated my men not a week later."

"Wait—" Chucai's attention snapped to the older man's words. "Women? Others?"

Alchiq nodded. "The warriors in the white citadel were all women—they were called *skjalddis* by the people who survived Batu Khan's conquest. They left their citadel to travel east, escorting a group of men whom I have fought twice now and barely survived both times. Each time I met this band, they were farther east, closer to the center of the empire."

Chucai laughed, unable to help himself. "You think they are coming here? To threaten the *Khagan*?" he asked.

"I do not know what their goal is, but I fear it is to strike at the heart of the empire."

"How many were there? Fifty?"

"Less than a dozen."

"Against three hundred of the Imperial Guard? Against the *minghan* who can be summoned from Karakorum?" Chucai scoffed. "I think you overestimate their chances."

"Maybe," Alchiq said. "But how long has it been since the empire has fought a worthy foe? Has anyone since Genghis Khan been in a battle he could not win? Does the *Khagan* know what it takes to defeat an enemy that will not submit?"

Alchiq had been watching the white-haired prisoner while he spoke, and Chucai's gaze was drawn to the young prisoner. The youth was slouched against the bars of his cage, his head turned partially away from them—his gaze fixed and unfocused on the slope of a nearby *ger*. One of his hands flopped out of the cage. He gave all the impression of being dazed and indifferent to anything going around him, and Chucai was struck by the stark difference between this lassitude and the way the youth had stared at everything when he had first seen him outside Karakorum.

Alchiq gave a curt nod, and angling his body away from the cage, signaled Chucai with a finger to his lip and then to his ear. *The boy is listening.*

"It took me many years to realize you were right, Master Chucai," Alchiq said. "I *was* the poison that would have destroyed the empire. But not anymore. I'm the one who is going to help you save it."

Chucai stared at the white-haired boy with a mixture of wonderment and curiosity. *A spy?* Was Alchiq suggesting that the boy was an *advance scout*—of all things—for a party of warriors from the West?

The idea was ludicrous and incredibly daring or...it was a paranoid fantasy concocted by the *arkhi*-damaged brain of a bitter old soldier.

Either way, Chucai realized, *this man is an annoying complication*. It was far better for him to stay here, watching the prisoners, than to be whispering these sorts of ideas in the *Khagan*'s ear. He had enough trouble with Ögedei as it was. He didn't need the additional headache of the *Khagan* being spooked by outlandish theories from old drunks.

* * *

Haakon was still mulling over the conversation he had overheard between the black-bearded man and the quiet gray-haired Mongol when a pair of guards approached his cage. One of the two whacked on the bars with a spear shaft, getting his attention, and he slowly scooted back to the center of the cage. The other man busied himself with the lock on the door, and Haakon filed away his thoughts for later reflection.

Provided there was a chance to reflect later.

The Mongols had fed the prisoners earlier, a tradition the caged fighters all understood: a decent meal meant they were going to fight soon.

Once his cage was unlocked, Haakon crab-walked out. He stood upright, stretching for a few moments, and then allowed himself to be prodded in the direction of the feast—an orange glow over the peaks of the line of *ger*. Voices, flush with wine and *airag*, buzzed like angry bees lurking in the folds of the *ger*. He shook his arms out as he walked, trying to loosen his muscles and work out some of the knots he couldn't quite rid himself of in the confines of the cage.

He tried not to think about the word he had heard the old warrior use. *Skjalddis*. Shield-Maidens.

The fires were bigger than before, enormous bonfires that scared away the darkening gloom of the evening, and the crowd was thicker, and more terrifying—the fires distorted the shadows on every face. The fighting ring was marked with a combination of rock and timber this time, and as he stepped over a freshly hewn trunk of an oak tree, he estimated that it was smaller too. The *Khagan*'s wheeled *ger* did not abut the fighting space as it had previously; a narrow platform had been hastily erected along the curve of the ring closest to the fires.

On the opposite side of the ring, guards had shepherded his opponent into position, and Haakon eyed the smaller man carefully. A Kitayan, not unlike his Mongolian captors, but darker of skin and leaner. He wasn't much older than Haakon, and his face was dotted with scruff from a beard that steadfastly refused to grow in fully.

A weapon clattered on the ground next to Haakon. He felt the weapon's impact more than he heard it, as the crowd erupted into a shouting mass as soon as the sword landed. Across the ring, the Kitayan darted for his own weapon, scooping it up and charging across the open circle. Haakon wasted a precious second looking around for his wooden sword.

The Kitayan presented a flurry of quick jabs, and Haakon—out of position from having been slow to get his weapon—could barely keep ahead of them. But he still ascertained quite a bit about his opponent's style during the first series of rapid strikes: the Kitayan had a shorter reach, he wasn't as strong as Haakon, and he thought he was quicker.

Haakon beat the next strike aside with much more strength than was necessary, forcing the Kitayan to redirect his own blade. As soon as he felt the other's sword clear his blade, he flicked his wrist, snapping the wooden point toward his opponent's face.

The Kitayan reacted badly, throwing his sword up in a frantic block. The wooden swords clacked together noisily, and for a second, the Kitayan held the block, trying to muscle Haakon's blade. All he accomplished was holding his—and Haakon's—blade steady for a moment.

Long enough for Haakon to reach out with his left hand and grab the tip of the Kitayan's sword. Wrapping his fingers around the wooden point, he twisted his wrist sharply.

It was a training response—*grab what is close to you*—and attempting this move with sharp steel was decidedly dangerous. It was important to remember that wood was different from steel—a distinction that had caught Haakon off guard during his gladiatorial bout for the *Khagan*.

Haakon twisted and pulled, yanking the other man's weapon out of his hands as the audience cheered and stomped their feet with approval. He tossed the Kitayan's weapon aside, not caring where it landed, as he reversed his own weapon so as to bash his opponent in the face with the pommel. The Kitayan stumbled backward, his chin tucked into his neck as he tried to get away from Haakon's wooden hilt.

He didn't bring his hands up to block his face. Instead he fumbled with his shirt, and the motion was incongruous enough that Haakon sensed something was not quite right. *He wasn't that clumsy.*

Firelight gleamed off polished metal as the Kitayan reversed direction, lunging toward Haakon. Something narrow and sharp was clenched in his fist, and Haakon dropped his right hand quickly, trying to block the Kitayan's lightning attack. The wooden sword bounced off the Kitayan's arm, spoiling his aim, and Haakon felt a finger of ice run up his chest.

The Kitayan danced away, his right arm tucked against his side, his fist held tight against his waist. Hiding whatever was clenched in his hand.

Haakon glanced down at his chest and saw the ragged tear in his shirt. The icy line on his chest was burning now, and when he pressed a hand against the cut, it came away red.

The Kitayan had a knife. A very sharp knife.

THE NOOSE TIGHTENS

CROUCHED BEHIND THE wreckage of a weathered barrel, Hans watched the meeting between the Mongols and the Livonian *Heermeister*. He had been attempting to approach the Mongol camp stealthily, but too many of the obscured and secret routes used by the Rats had been demolished in the riotous hours following the Rose Knight's death. He had been forced to skulk along the more well-traveled routes, and as a result, he had stumbled upon the standoff. His well-honed sense of self-preservation—the Rat sense that kept all the boys alive—warned him that he shouldn't tarry, but as surely as the sun had risen, he couldn't tear himself away. Especially after he heard the Livonian *Heermeister* offer to betray the Rose Knights.

He pressed his head against the barrel, and his fingers dug into the soft wood. He clenched his lips shut, trying to suppress the wordless cry quaking in his throat. Was there even time to warn them?

He flinched at the sound of the Mongol commander's shout, and he recovered from this fright in time to see both of the *Heermeister*'s bodyguards topple from their saddles, pierced by Mongol arrows. He stared, transfixed as firmly as the *Heermeister* and the priest, as the Mongol group surged forward, surrounding the two remaining horsemen. There was some confusion for a moment as Mongol warriors seized the reins of the four Western horses and got them turned around, and then the entire war party galloped down the street.

Leaving the two dead Livonians.

One of them was still alive. The Livonian bodyguard lay on his side, facing Hans, and the man's eyes rolled loosely in their sockets. His mouth kept opening and closing, like he was having trouble breathing, and blood dribbled out. His hand clawed at the ground, one of the fingers bent awkwardly—the lowest knuckle had been crushed by the hoof of a Mongol horse.

Hans didn't know what he could do to ease the man's suffering, but he couldn't bear to watch him die. He edged out from behind his shelter, drawn toward the dying man by a primal sympathetic urge to provide what succor he could.

A hand grasped his shoulder and pulled him back. A tiny yip leaped out of his throat, and he lashed out with hands and feet in a frantic attempt to extricate himself from his captor's grip. The man holding him grunted once as Hans's elbow connected, and then Hans was wrapped in a tight embrace. "Hold still," a voice hissed in his ear. Hans continued to struggle as he was bodily carried into an alley.

Fearing what would happen when he was out of sight of the dying Livonian—as well as any other passersby—he redoubled his efforts to escape from his captor's strong arms. The man holding him let go, spinning him around, and as Hans caught sight of the man's face, he took aim and swung his fist as hard as he could.

A hand caught the blow, turned it aside. The face behind it was weathered and aged, with a look not unlike wind-scarred wood or stone, worn down by time. Its gray eyes were alight with both amusement and a fierce intensity that Hans dimly recognized.

"Ach, you are quick," the old man said. When he saw Hans hesitate, he lifted his chin so that the young boy could look upon his face more fully. "Do you recognize me, boy?"

Hans, his fist still clenched, nodded. "At the chapter house of the Rose Knights."

"That's right. After you met Andreas, he sent for me. Do you remember my name? I am Rutger. The Rose Knights are—"

Rutger gasped as Hans, recognition coming to him like a bolt of lighting, impulsively rushed to embrace the older man. A bemused expression on his face, Rutger lowered his arms around the boy and held him close. "We've come to keep Andreas's promise," he said. He pressed his cheek against Hans's head. "Our fallen brother will not be forgotten."

* * *

The air inside the *ger* was stifling. Zug lay as still as possible, for every motion was a struggle against the torpid air. His body complained endlessly about the beating administered by the guard, and while none of his bones were broken, his frame was covered with bruises and dried blood. To be spared grievous injury suggested the Mongols were not yet done punishing him.

All he could do was lie still and wait. Wait for the end to come.

Yet, his mood was not as dark as the bruises. He had endured worse discomfort. He had lived with pain before. This suffering would not last.

The fly that had dragged him out of his stupor buzzed in his ear again, and he tried to remember how to make the sack of flesh work, how to move his bones. *Zzzzzzzuuuuuu—*

It wasn't a fly. It was a man's voice.

Orange and white sparks—like crazed fireflies—danced across his eyelids as he dragged them open. There was some light—the day had not yet passed—but it was a weak glow through the gaps in the hide walls of the *ger*. Most of the shadows were gray shapes flitting at the edge of his vision. He stared at the iron bars of his cage for some time, waiting for the pain behind his eyes to pass.

This was the same cage he had been in after his fight in the arena. They had beaten him then too, but the worst part of that punishment had been the quivering shakes as the demons in his blood cried out for alcohol. Those demons were gone, pissed out some time ago, and all that remained was the old hollowness. The ragged ghost who had haunted his mind since he had left home. *Dead man*, it whispered in the bleak emptiness. *Dead...*

With a groan that he felt all the way down to his toes, he forced his shoulder to move, and he rolled onto his back. He let his head flop over until his cheek rested against the sticky sand scattered across the floor of the cage.

He was not alone in the cage. Huddled against the bars was another sack of flesh. Black hair, matted with blood. Face swollen and purple with bruises. Did he look that bad?

The other figure peered at him with one eye, the other hidden beneath a mass of puffy purple flesh. "Zzzzuuuuggg..." The voice issuing from the man's throat was a ragged whisper that slowly crawled across the sandy floor of the cage.

"Kiiii—" Was that his voice? He didn't recognize it, but the noise brought a smile to the other man's face. A bloodstained smile.

"Still here," Kim whispered. He coughed, or maybe he laughed. It was hard to tell. "They should have killed us."

Zug swallowed, his throat raw and parched. "They made a mistake," he managed.

In his head, the old ghost laughed.

* * *

May God have mercy on me for my lies, Dietrich prayed as he rode in the midst of the Mongol raiding party. All he had wanted was to save his men from the same ignoble defeat that had slain so many at Schaulen, and all he had accomplished so far was the ugly deaths of his bodyguards—two of the most loyal and trusty knights in his command. It was as if God were punishing him already for his hubris. How dare he think his order more worthy of salvation than any other knights of Christendom. Did they not worship the same God? Yet, he had offered to sacrifice *them* in order to save his own. Was such an act worthy of a Christian soldier?

These are the decisions a Grandmaster must make, he reminded himself, recalling his last visit to Rome and his audience with the Pope. Gregory IX had offered his ring for Dietrich to kiss, and the *Heermeister* had gotten down on one knee and kissed the old man's hand. *Sacrifices must be made,* the Pope had said, offering Dietrich his other hand, and Dietrich had kissed the smaller gold ring as well. The one with the broken sigil. He had sworn fealty not only to the Church and the Pope, but to something older than both.

Beside Dietrich, Father Pius clung to his horse like a wet rag. The priest had not stopped whimpering since the Mongols had swept both of them into their column, and the way the priest was quivering in his saddle, Dietrich was surprised the coward hadn't pissed himself.

"They will release us," Pius squeaked, his voice thin and shrill. Dietrich wasn't sure if the priest was asking him what was—in his mind—an entirely rhetorical and pointless question, or if the priest thought that endless repetition would make the words true. Twice now the priest had tried to engage the Mongols in some sort of discourse, but the warriors closest to them had only laughed at the priest's timorous words. The second time, one of the warriors had whacked Pius about the head and shoulders with his bow, finding even more amusement in the noises the priest made with each blow. Eventually Pius realized the only way to make the man stop his abuse was to stop shrieking.

"They will kill us, as soon as they remember we're not useful to them," Dietrich growled. He didn't say it to frighten the priest even more, but to focus the man's attention. "More specifically, they will kill you as soon as they no longer need my words translated. Your survival depends on mine. Do you understand?"

The priest stared at Dietrich, eyes frozen with fear. Pius's horse snorted and danced a few jerky steps as the priest lost control of his bladder.

The Shield-Brethren were housed in an old monastery north of the ruins of Koischwitz, and while Dietrich surmised it was possible to approach the chapter house through the woods between the destroyed hamlet and the old ruins, that approach would be noisy and difficult for a host of riders. By fielding a sizable war party, the Mongols had sacrificed stealth and speed for numbers. Dietrich did not know how many Shield-Brethren were at the chapter house—this was one of the many details they had kept hidden by virtue of their distance from Hünern—but he suspected Tegusgal had more than double the numbers of warriors. In which case, a direct approach made sense. Dietrich had made no suggestions as Tegusgal had led the party across the narrow bridge spanning the sluggish river that lay to the west of Hünern.

The bridge had been a narrow span occasioned by local herdsmen and the isolated merchant prior to the Mongols' arrival, and as the influx began around the arena, some effort had been applied to shoring up the old pillars and replacing the more rotten planks. Once improved, the bridge became more used, which led to more wear and tear on the timbers, necessitating yet another pass at repairing it. The second time, Mongol engineers got involved; nearly overnight, the bridge doubled in width, and a small shack was erected on the Hünern side.

Onghwe Khan knew the value in controlling the roads. While the man had a reputation for being dissolute, he was also cannily aware of the fundamental ebb and flow of humanity. Dietrich suspected his rumored boredom was nothing more than an affectation, though he never wanted to find out one way or another.

Surrounded by mounted Mongol warriors, Dietrich and Pius galloped across the wide bridge, and the group swung north, putting the river on their right. Dietrich—with some annoyance—marveled at the speed and fluidity with which the host moved, each mount keeping pace with the others with neither thought nor order required. They slowed as they got out into the countryside, allowing themselves to be seen by any who still moved out in the open. Tegusgal was intentionally projecting power by way of visible force, Dietrich realized, to garner fear. It was not enough to destroy his enemies; it needed to be seen and left undisputed.

Dietrich's charger, larger than the tallest of the Mongol horses by several hands, chewed on its bit at being trapped in the center of a mass that moved slower than it liked, but Dietrich held it steady. For the time being, he was a prisoner. There was nowhere to go, and no reason to push the Mongols to ride faster.

His and Pius's usefulness would come to an end soon enough.

The Mongols began to shift around him, and Dietrich found his horse being nudged toward the front of the formation. The Mongol party slipped past him like beads of water sliding off a broad leaf, and in short order, he was in front of the host. He felt like a game beast hunted for the sport of some bored nobleman in his own lands, and some of his apprehension about what was to come next drained away, leaving only the burning shame and humiliation of his position.

He was riding to his death. His plan had been flawed from the outset, the feeble machinations of a tiny mind that could only react in fear. What did he really know of the Shield-Brethren's location? Of their defenses and their armament? He was going to ride right into the camp of the *Ordo Militum Vindicis Intactae*. God would decide what happened next. He had no other option. The longer he tarried, the more obvious it would be to the Mongols that he had no idea how to deliver on what he had offered them.

When that happened, Tegusgal's archers would fill him with arrows. The image of Burchard and Sigeberht dead in the street flashed unbidden across his thoughts, and an involuntary shudder shook his frame. He was almost as bad as Pius.

He bent his thoughts toward the Shield-Brethren instead of dwelling on the dead. They were using an abandoned monastery, and he tried to imagine how they would apportion themselves throughout the ruins. They would need some open ground where they could pasture and exercise their horses. Would they set up an archery range? They would have to forage for food, and they had enough mouths to feed that they would have to use some of the horses as pack animals. Horses would balk at continually moving through dense undergrowth. There would be paths in the forest, tracks made by the constant coming and going of the hunting teams. Dietrich started to pay closer attention to the gaps between the trees as the woods grew thicker around him and his Mongolian entourage.

He tried not to think about the bow that each man carried, about how quickly he had seen them nock and shoot an arrow. The small of his back itched. Even in armor, he felt naked.

His eye was drawn to a gap between a trio of mature oak trees. On one of the trees, he spotted a series of too-regular markings. At a distance, it would have been easy to miss the cuts, dismissing them as happenstance, but up close, he could see they were made by a knife blade. They were at the right height too for a man riding on a horse. The branches of the tree on the left side of the gap didn't reach across the opening as they should either. There was one, curling low in the front, but behind it, there was a suspicious dearth.

Dietrich nudged his horse toward the gap, ducking beneath the leafy screen of the foremost branch. Once past, it was easy to see where someone had taken a blade to other branches, cutting them back from the path. Still leaning forward, he cast his eyes across the track, noticing the confusion of marks left by numerous horses coming and going.

Should he follow this path? It was a narrow track, wide enough for one horse only. If it led right to the Shield-Brethren chapter house, he didn't want to be in the lead. That would only make his betrayal more evident. The Shield-Brethren would see him first—a knight of the West—and then the Mongols would come pouring out of the woods. They would all know he had led the enemy to them.

Not that any of them are going to survive.

He glanced over his shoulder. The Mongol party had come to a halt behind him, gathering around the tiny gap in the trees. Beneath his armor, goose bumps danced on the flesh of his chest. Expressionless faces, staring at him; eyes alight with murderous glee. Pius was near the back of the mob, his cheeks wet with tears. The priest's lips moved, but Dietrich could not hear his words, though he could imagine the prayer the priest was saying. *Libera nos a malo...*

Tegusgal barked a command at him, waving a hand at the trees. Several men on either side of the Mongol leader raised their bows. Arrows were nocked.

Dietrich raised a hand, indicating that he understood Tegusgal's command. He didn't need Pius to translate, and he briefly wondered if by acknowledging Tegusgal, he had just signaled the end of the priest's usefulness. Without waiting to see, he tapped his horse lightly in the ribs and turned his attention to the narrow path into the woods.

* * *

Rutger brought him to a squalid camp behind the fire-blackened remnants of a wall. There had been four walls once, encompassing a house that had probably belonged to Hünern's burgher. Tents had been strewn up along the surviving wall, creating a makeshift shelter that had once been home to a crew of brutish Franks, vicious men who had shown little compunction about killing those who they saw as intruders. Hans and the Rats had learned to stay well away from the Black Wall—as they had called the camp.

It was empty now, and Hans could only guess as to the demise of the Franks. Had they all been slain in the riots or had their bluster run away and they along with it?

Before Hans had a chance to ask Rutger about the previous inhabitants of the camp, other Rose Knights began to join them. They were dressed much like their quartermaster—in filthy rags and plain habits. Occasionally, though, Hans could catch sight of what lay beneath their clothes. A silvery glint of maille, the dull sheen of boiled leather, the dark knobs of hammered studs. *Armor.* As the men solemnly huddled around Rutger and Hans, the boy felt something akin to what he felt when he slept among the roots of the spindly tree the Rats claimed as their own. He was in the presence of something older than he could imagine, something that had the strength to endure all adversity.

Rutger put a firm hand on Hans's shoulder. "The boy knows much about the layout of the Mongol camp." The older man squeezed Hans's shoulder. "Tell them."

He began with some hesitation, still awed by the stern focus of the knights around him, but as he spoke he slipped into the patter he used with all of the boys who had come and gone into the Mongol camp on his behalf. He knew every detail of what lay behind the walls of the Mongol compound. He had spoken so often over the past few months that the minutiae of the camp were etched in his mind like carvings upon ancient stones. The Shield-Brethren listened intently, and when he finally ran out of breath, they asked a few questions, prompting him to recite certain details once again. How many guards were at the front gate? Where was the back gate? How many archers in the towers along the front? Where were the barracks? How quickly did the Mongols react to an alarm? What about the prisoners who the Khan used as fighters in the arena? Where were they held?

When he finished, he listened quietly as Rutger walked through their plan, adjusting it as necessary in light of Hans's information. He and the Rats had planned excursions in the past, but they had been the raids of boys—unkempt plans for thievery and mischief. The Shield-Brethren spoke of more brutal matters, of the efficient ways to kill men, of the ways to break an enemy's will to fight. Certain elements of the plan might have struck Hans as dishonest or unbecoming actions of a knight had he been more of an innocent, but given what he had seen nailed to the wall of the arena, he found the simplicity of their plan to his liking. It was both cunning and jarringly direct.

Could it work? He felt something like hope spark in his chest, but it was a tiny flame, and a cruel wind could snuff it out quickly.

"Styg, what of our riders?" Rutger asked.

"They'll be ready," Styg answered. He had come with Andreas on that day when the Shield-Brethren had stolen the Livonian horses. He was tall, dark-haired, and—though young—he exuded a confidence that Hans wished he could emulate as readily. "Halvard and Yvor have collected enough from the Mongol watchers to clothe themselves." He glanced shyly at Hans, as if he wanted to speak with the boy but felt awkwardly confined by the current situation.

"Very well," Rutger said. "I will go to the cart. The rest of you go to your men and wait for the signal."

"What of the prisoners?" Styg asked.

Hans had told them they were scattered about the compound. Tegusgal did not want them housed too close to one another. Such proximity could easily foment rebellion.

Rutger shook his head. "Our priority is the gate."

"The boy knows where they are housed. His idea has merit."

"It is too risky."

Styg laughed, and Hans was surprised to see Rutger recoil from the younger man's reaction. "What difference will two men make?" Styg asked. "If we are that desperate to hold the gate, then we have already lost. Let Eilif and I go. If we can free the prisoners, then the Mongols will be fighting on two fronts. There are—how many? Two dozen?" He glanced at Hans, who nodded. "Was this not the reason Andreas wanted to make contact with them? They have the same enemy. Given the chance, I know they will fight at our sides." Styg gestured at Hans. "He knows as well. These men are our allies. We can *trust* them." He thrust his chin toward the sprawl, away from the Mongol camp. "What if the others do not come?"

"By the Virgin," Rutger swore, "you are going to haunt me forever, aren't you?"

Hans did not follow Rutger's speech, and as he glanced at the other Rose Knights, he saw that many of them did not understand their master's question either. Rutger passed his hand across his face, covering his eyes for a brief moment. His fingers were bent and crooked, and they shook. "Very well," he sighed, lowering his hand.

"But not the boy," he amended, cutting off Styg's enthusiastic reply. "The boy stays on *this* side of the wall, with someone to watch over him."

Styg nodded, curbing his tongue.

"Go," Rutger said. "Before I change my mind. Wait for us to draw their attention."

* * *

Before he saw the chapter house, Dietrich expected to smell it: the burning fragrance of green wood, the crisp tang of smoldering meat, the hearty aroma of baking bread. But as his horse trotted along the narrow path, he smelled none of that. There was only the scent of wet ash in the air, the morning dew still damp on partially burned logs that had lost their heat during the night.

Concerned, he snapped his reins against his horse's neck. There was only one reason why he would be smelling cold fires, and as he broke through the edge of the clearing, he quickly saw that his fear was well-founded.

The chapter house was deserted.

The central building of the old monastery was a pile of rubble scattered across the northern verge of the clearing as if the chapel had been knocked over a half century ago by the idle hand of God, and an arc of roofless outbuildings abutted the ragged front porch of the chapel. A small graveyard bounded with a low stone wall lay to the east, and the forest encroached from the west, taking over what had once been the monastery's pasture; Dietrich spied a number of stout trunks arranged along the leading edge of the birch and oak trees. Archery stands, he noted, his eyes picking up other signs that the ruins had recently been inhabited. A thin strand of white smoke curled up slowly from one of the circular fire pits on his left. Picket stakes, minus the rope between them, had been driven into the ground next to the graveyard. Other bits of wood sticking out of the ground indicated where the tents had been, and a long scrap of dirty cloth still clung to the jagged stones of a large gap in one of the walls of the chapel.

The Shield-Brethren had been here recently, and they had not been gone long. The midafternoon sun shone down on a camp that had been hastily and recently abandoned, put into disarray by the chaos of a rapid departure.

Through the breach in the forest, the Mongols poured into the camp. Dietrich's charger snorted and pawed the ground as the Mongols flowed around them as if they were a stone in the midst of the torrential flood that had just broken through a dam. Dietrich tried to calm his horse as Tegusgal passed nearby, barking orders at his men. Mongols slid off their horses and disappeared into the old stone ruins.

Tegusgal pointed at Dietrich, snapping more orders, and Dietrich didn't need Pius to translate. The Mongol's displeasure was readily evident on his face.

"Wait," Dietrich shouted, holding up his hands. Out of the corner of his eyes, he saw several Mongols raising their bows. He was out of time. "The Shield-Brethren were here," he said, "but they haven't run away. They aren't cowards." When an arrow didn't immediately pierce him, he paused long enough to take a breath and look around for the priest. He had to make them understand. If even for only a few minutes more. Long enough for him to...

Pius was still alive, huddling on his horse like a wet rag draped across a saddle. Dietrich waved his hand at the shivering priest. "Tell him," he snapped. "Tell him what I just said. Our lives depend on it."

Pius began to translate, but his voice was so soft that Dietrich could barely hear him, and he shouted at the priest to speak more loudly. Pius flinched, nearly fell off his horse, and started again.

"Your mighty force outnumbers them," Dietrich continued when Pius's translation elicited no arrows. "They would be fools to simply wait for you here. How defensible is that chapel?" He pointed at the broken building behind Tegusgal. "How long could they keep your men from breaching its walls? The history of their order goes back many, many years, and it has never been their way to lie down and die when confronted by hardship. They are at their most dangerous when you think you have them cornered."

Dietrich glared at Pius as the priest faltered in his translation. Under Dietrich's insistent gaze, the priest shuddered and then continued translating.

While the priest spoke, Dietrich let his reins go slack in his hands, and he tightened his right leg against his charger's barrel. The horse flicked its ears and shook its head as it started to perambulate.

Tegusgal frowned, turning in the saddle as the men he'd sent to search the old building reemerged. The look on their faces was all Dietrich needed to see. They tried to make a report, but Tegusgal cut them off with an angry wave.

"He's going to kill us," Pius hissed, and Dietrich waved him quiet.

As his horse ambled in a wide arc, Dietrich used the animal's motion to indicate the ring of trees surrounding the ruined monastery. "Where would you hide if you had fewer men?" he asked.

Tegusgal's eyes flickered toward the tree line as Pius translated the question. In that instant, when the Mongol commander's attention—as well as the attention of most of his archers—wasn't on him, Dietrich snatched up his reins and drummed his heels against his horse's barrel. He was pointing in almost the right direction—the narrow breach in the woods that was the path they had followed to the Shield-Brethren camp.

If he could make it that far, he might have a chance.

THE NIGHT OF
THE FISH CUTTER

35

NIGHT CAME QUICKLY in the mountains, and as the sky bled to black, the warmth of the day vanished. A half dozen bonfires were built, crackling piles of orange and yellow flame, and their light and heat summoned everyone to the center of the camp. A wooden platform was raised for the *Khagan* so that he could watch the festivities and all of his subjects could watch him eat and drink. Beside the platform, a gladiator ring had been erected, and already there were clusters of moneylenders haggling over bets.

The festival would last a good part of the night.

Master Chucai prowled along the periphery of the long fire pits where the *Khagan*'s numerous cooks worked furiously. They didn't have the luxury of the permanent kitchens of the palace at Karakorum, but they were managing to craft an endless variety of baked and stewed and sweetly charred victuals. Occasionally, Chucai would stop a servant, loaded down with a steaming tray of food, and sample something off the top of the plate as he reiterated his desire to speak with the leader of the *Darkhat*.

The servant would nod, scurry off to deliver his tray of hot food, and upon his return, he would tell Chucai the same thing as all the others before him: the *Khagan* was in a most jovial mood and was enjoying Ghaltai's company; the *Darkhat* commander felt it was unseemly to excuse himself at this time.

Chucai chafed at being denied, and what irritated him even further was the fact that he could not simply interrupt the *Khagan*'s meal and demand to speak—privately—with the *Darkhat* commander. Ögedei was annoyed with him, and it was likely the *Khagan* would simply berate him for interrupting the dinner party with what Ögedei—in his addled state—would think was nothing more than Chucai's constant meddling in the affairs of the empire.

All of which would make Chucai's job more difficult.

His conversation with Alchiq buzzed around the corners of his mind too. The idea that the *Khagan* might be in danger. If the Chinese raiders had been trying to kill the *Khagan*, that night would have gone very differently. The Chinese—outnumbered several times over by the *Khagan*'s *Torguud* escort—had managed to get far enough into the camp to steal the banner. How safe was the *Khagan*?

And the constant confusing complication of the banner. Where had it come from? Why was it important to the Chinese?

Chucai noticed a pair of men returning from the feast, and realized one of the two was more heavily attired than the other. As they approached the ruddy glow of the cooking pits, he noted the blued shadows of the second man's cloak. *Ghaltai.*

"They are bringing out the fighters," the *Darkhat* commander said as he came up to Chucai. "I told the *Khagan* I needed to take a piss."

Chucai nodded sagely at the other man's duplicity. "I appreciate you coming to see me," he said. "I have a matter which I would discuss privately with you."

Ghaltai grunted. "I *do* need to piss," he said gruffly, making as if he were going to walk past Chucai.

"Do," Chucai said, laying a hand on the *Darkhat*'s arm. "I wouldn't want you to be uncomfortable while on your horse."

Ghaltai looked at Chucai's hand. "I am an honored guest of the *Khagan*," he said softly.

"He's been drinking," Chucai said. "Plus the fights will have started. He won't notice you are gone."

"Where am I going?"

"I want you to take me somewhere."

Ghaltai shook off Chucai's hand. "You presume much, Master Chucai. I am not one of your servants."

"No, you serve the *Khagan*. And the empire." Chucai nodded toward the noise and light of the feast. What had Alchiq said? *I've never stopped wanting to serve.* "Surely you've noticed the empire isn't what it used to be," Chucai said to the *Darkhat* leader.

Ghaltai looked in the opposite direction, his face suffused with shadows. "He may be the only one who doesn't see it," he murmured.

"I want to know where Temujin went," Chucai said. "I want you to take me to that place."

"There is nothing there," Ghaltai hissed, whirling on Chucai. "Nothing but spiderwebs and dust." His eyes were wide, filled with firelight.

"Then what harm is there in showing me?" Chucai asked. When Ghaltai didn't answer, he shrugged. "What harm is there in helping the *Khagan* see what he has lost?"

Ghaltai spat into a nearby cooking pit, his spittle sizzling as it was vaporized by the heat. "No," he laughed hollowly. "What harm ever came from knowledge?"

* * *

Shortly after the *Khagan* had announced the feast celebrating the hunt, Gansukh had started to hear snatches of the news as it passed among the *Torguud*: Munokhoi was no longer commanding the Imperial Guard. There was no official announcement—he knew there wouldn't be—but like a shadow flitting across the sun, something *changed* at the camp.

As the day waned and the feast got underway, Gansukh sensed a presence near him, like a predator slowly stalking its prey. Unlike a nervous deer, he did not stand still and stare about him, wondering from which direction his death would come; he kept moving, wandering and weaving through the maze of tents. He doubled back on his trail—sliding underneath wagons and ducking through the open framework of the half-erected *ger*. A merchant hollered at him to assist with carrying rugs, and he happily agreed to the task, using the long tube as a shield as he went back and forth along the same route for a half hour.

On the third trip, he caught sight of Munokhoi. The ex-*Torguud* captain paced him on the other side of the row of *ger* on his right. When he dropped off his armload of rugs and returned to the merchant's wagon, Munokhoi was no longer there. But Gansukh had seen enough of his stormy expression to know he wouldn't be far away.

When the crowd started to gather for the fights at the feast, he worried momentarily about the press of bodies. It would be easy to slip up next to a man in the confusion and slip a knife in his back, and so he made sure he stayed on the western side of the gladiator ring where the light from the bonfires was brightest. As the audience grew more excited about the fights, he sidled toward a cluster of *Torguud* who were clustered around a pair of busy moneylenders.

"Ho, Gansukh! I hear the blond one is fighting." The mountain clan archer, Tarbagatai waved him over to the cluster of guards. "Did you bet on him last time?"

"I did," Gansukh replied. "And when we return to Karakorum, I believe someone owes me twenty-five cows."

"Twenty-five?" Tarbagatai scoffed. "Who was such an idiot to bet that many?" The *Torguud* standing next to the young archer elbowed him roughly, and Tarbagatai paled as he realized what he had said.

"Yes, well, that idiot was me," Gansukh mused, glancing about. "But thankfully someone took my bet. I suppose that makes me clever, doesn't it? And the other one the idiot—"

"You boast rather mightily for a man who not only didn't kill any of the Chinese raiders but also managed to be captured by them."

Gansukh looked for Munokhoi and found him standing much *too* close on the left. The ex-*Torguud* captain's eyes were bright, and his head glistened with sweat.

"Captured?" he laughed at Munokhoi. "I was *infiltrating* their ranks. My plan was working fine until you rode by, slaughtering anyone who wasn't on a horse—including fellow Mongol citizens. What was your final tally? More or less Chinese?"

The crowd shrank as people surreptitiously found excuses to be elsewhere, giving the two rivals ample room for anything that might happen. *Not here,* Gansukh thought. *Not now.* There hadn't been enough provocation—or enough drinking—to warrant drawing his knife.

"Twenty-five cows are nothing," Munokhoi sneered, ignoring Gansukh's question.

"I am glad you think so because it was more than I had last time," Gansukh said. "Though, I am happy to have them now. I am going to send them to my father; he'll be very pleased. That many head will provide nicely for my family all winter," Gansukh said. "Though if I had double that number, I could marry that girl from the *Sakhait* clan whom my father always wanted me to."

"And your Chinese whore?" Munokhoi spat.

Gansukh stroked his chin. "She has expensive tastes, doesn't she? Maybe I will need more than fifty cows," he said, a touch of alarm in his voice.

Tarbagatai and several of the *Torguud* guffawed. One of the moneylenders waved his hands at Gansukh. "Are you placing a wager or not?" he cried.

"Fifty cows," Munokhoi snapped.

Gansukh spread his hands. "I only have the twenty-five," he apologized.

Munokhoi's teeth flashed in the firelight as he grinned. "Pray your man doesn't lose."

* * *

This was how differences were settled at court—by wagers and proxies. It was not the way of the steppe, and as he watched the pale Northerner square off against the lean Kitayan, Gansukh reflected on what he had learned about being *civilized* since he had come to the *Khagan*'s court. Had he become a better man based on what he had learned?

He hadn't slipped up behind Munokhoi and slit the other man's throat. *Yet.* Though he wasn't entirely sure Munokhoi wasn't still planning on doing the same to him. Would he be remembered as the *better* man if he didn't stoop to such a debased level of violence? He wouldn't care; he'd be dead. Was there any consolation to be found there?

He'd rather be the one who survived. No amount of courtly learning was going to smooth out that rough edge. He would do what it took to survive. Kozelsk had taught him that. It seemed like a much better lesson to live by than anything he had learned from Lian.

The crowd surrounding the fighting ring gave a collective gasp, and Gansukh blinked away his idle thoughts, focusing on the pair of fighters. What had he missed?

The Kitayan had a knife.

"Hai!" Namkhai shouted from his position next to the *Khagan*'s platform, and there was a rippling surge through the crowd as newly anointed captain of the *Torguud* pressed forward, presenting their spears.

The two fighters paused, though neither lowered their guard nor looked away from each other.

"My Khan," Namkhai called out, seeking direction. "The Kitayan man has a knife."

The crowd held their breath, and the only sound was the crackling rumble of the bonfires and the low creaking noise of the platform as the *Khagan* levered himself up from his low seat. "That's a tiny blade," he slurred, peering at the fighters. "Is it good for much more than gutting carp?"

Someone laughed in the audience, and Gansukh knew without looking that it was Munokhoi. Had he given the Kitayan man the knife? The idea was troubling.

"Gansukh," Ögedei was standing near the edge of the platform, searching the faces arrayed below him. "Didn't you win a bet on the pale-haired one last time?"

Gansukh raised his arm so the *Khagan* could find him in the crowd. "I did, my Khan."

"What did you say about him? Something about *tactics* making up for a lack of strength?"

"I may have, my Khan."

Ögedei grunted, and swung his head around to peer at the fighters again. "Namkhai," he called out.

"Yes, my Khan," the new *Torguud* captain exclaimed.

"I seem to recall you giving me a very poor answer when I asked you about this fighter," Ögedei said.

"I said..." Namkhai hesitated. Gansukh caught the big wrestler glancing in his direction. "I said I would be wary of the scrawny ones."

The *Khagan* waggled his finger at Namkhai. "That is what you said when I gave you a second chance," he corrected. He glared down at Namkhai for a moment, swaying slightly, and then his gaze traveled slowly across the multitude of faces. "A second chance," he roared suddenly. His face was scarlet, the veins in his neck standing out against his skin. He swiveled his head ponderously on his quivering neck, staring ferociously at the audience as if he dared anyone to challenge his statement.

"Namkhai, does this man pose a threat to me?" His voice was ragged and strained, his throat still constricted.

"My Khan?"

"Does this dog of a Kitayan have the *slightest chance* of getting within an arm's length of me with that knife?" The *Khagan* found his voice again, unleashing his question in a thunderous shout.

"No, my Khan!" Namkhai replied, trying to match the *Khagan* in volume.

"Are you certain? Do I have to ask you a *second* time?"

"No, my Khan!"

Ögedei staggered back to his seat and collapsed on it, gesturing for a servant to bring his wine cup. "Then let him keep his fish gutter," he said. "Let us see a little blood tonight."

* * *

First the spears had been lowered at them, and then the Great Khan had started shouting. Haakon and the Kitayan had remained still throughout the tirade, unsure of what was going to happen. Haakon tried to follow what was being said, but most of his mind was filled with trying to settle on the best defense and offense against the Kitayan's knife.

When they weren't immediately threatened with the spears, Haakon suspected the Kitayan was going to be allowed to keep his knife. He had to be ready. He had already been cut once, and was certainly going to be cut again. He had to figure out how to beat the Kitayan before he lost too much blood.

Haakon's wooden sword was longer, but that advantage didn't match up to the deadly edge of the knife. He could hit the man a dozen times with the sword, and he wouldn't stop fighting. But one slice of the Kitayan's knife to his neck or thigh and he'd bleed out.

The Great Khan's platform was over his left shoulder, and Haakon couldn't watch what was going on there and keep a ready defense against the Kitayan at the same time. Holding his sword tightly, he stopped trying to watch for some sign from the Great Khan. The Kitayan was the real threat. He should be giving his opponent his full attention.

The Kitayan was distracted; the hand with the knife in it was down at his side, held close to his stomach. It wasn't the best position, but it was ready enough, and Haakon watched the Kitayan's legs and hands. Waiting for some sign. *Should he wait that long?*

He heard a man shout a response, and he distantly realized that was probably the captain of the *Khagan*'s guard, responding like a good warrior. Haakon exhaled slowly as the *Khagan* asked his question again. *Here it comes,* he thought; *don't wait for him to make the first move.* The captain replied again, still shouting his acknowledgment of the *Khagan*'s command, and as soon as the *Khagan* spoke once more he could feel the audience's attention shift. *Don't wait,* the spirit of his old *oplo* whispered in his head.

Haakon struck. He lunged forward, taking an enormous step as he stretched his arms out. The Kitayan was caught off guard by how quickly and dramatically Haakon closed the measure, and he yelped in pain as the wooden sword smacked him on the head with a mighty crack.

The Kitayan slashed upward with the knife, and Haakon twisted his sword to his left, trying to smack the Kitayan's wrists with the wooden blade. *Get him to drop the knife.* The Kitayan staggered, dropping his center of gravity, and the sword skipped off his upper arm. Haakon felt his arms going too far to the left, and the Kitayan's hands were on the outside, the knife blade coming up and around Haakon's hands. Haakon skipped back, swinging the sword around in a clumsy backhand at the Kitayan's closest knee. He made contact, but the Kitayan didn't flinch or stumble. A weak blow. Not enough to distract him.

The Kitayan snapped his arm out, flicking the knife at Haakon's face. He jerked his head back, and he felt the tip of the knife slice his cheek.

He was in the wrong position. His hands were low, and his opponent's weapon was inside his guard. This wasn't a sword fight anymore; it was close quarters combat. If he had a steel sword, he wouldn't be able to use it effectively.

But the weapon in his hands was nothing more than a piece of wood, and wood didn't have an *edge* to worry about.

Haakon snapped his wrists up, and his sword smacked the Kitayan on the underside of his knife arm, near the elbow. He maintained the contact between flesh and wood and stepped into the other man, putting his weight behind the shove. The Kitayan lurched back, and Haakon caught the knife hand just behind the wrist with his left hand. Pulling down with that hand, he used the wooden sword as a lever and forced the Kitayan off balance.

The Kitayan tried to cut him with the knife, but Haakon's grip restricted the range of available motion. Haakon smashed the sword against the Kitayan's elbow—once, twice—and the man grunted in pain. Haakon twisted and pushed, and the Kitayan bent over in an effort to keep his arm from being dislocated. Haakon continued to drive his opponent before him, and when he dropped to his knees, the Kitayan went first, his face smashing painfully into the rocky soil.

Haakon twisted the arm until the Kitayan screamed, and then he pushed off the fallen man, stripping the knife free of the Kitayan's now slack fingers as he stood.

The audience howled with delight, and the ground rumbled from many feet, stomping in unison. Haakon shivered, knowing what they wanted to see, and slowly, the knife held loosely in his left hand, he turned toward the raised platform. In his mind, he saw Onghwe Khan's pavilion in the Circus arena. He had just won his match and was still holding Zug's knife.

The *Khagan*'s platform was much closer.

His fingers toyed with the knife, moving it around in his hand. Moving it into a better position to throw.

A giant figure burst through the crowd next to the platform, shoving his way into the circle. He wasn't as tall as Krasniy, the red-haired giant who was also a prisoner, but his shoulders were as wide. He jabbed a finger at Haakon, exhorting him to drop the knife.

Could he do it? Would the knife fly true?

Haakon pretended to not understand the muscular Mongol's words. He recognized the man's voice as the one he had heard earlier, responding to the *Khagan*'s questions. He shrugged, holding up his wooden sword as if the stick was the item being discussed. In his left hand, his fingers stopped fussing with the knife, settling on a good grip.

The Mongol kept coming—not hurriedly and not cautiously, but in long confident strides across the fighting ring. His path put him between Haakon and the platform.

Haakon backed up, maintaining a visible pantomime of confusion, though he let go of neither weapon. Each step took him farther from the *Khagan*, increasing the distance the knife was going to have to travel if he threw it.

Was he strong enough to make the sacrifice?

The Mongols would kill him. He might be able to keep the captain at bay for a little while with the wooden sword, but the crowd would turn into a frenzied mob. They would overwhelm him. Would they tear him to pieces immediately or would they torture him first? What if he missed the *Khagan* or didn't deliver a mortal wound with the thrown knife. Would his punishment be any less severe?

The Kitayan sat up, blood dotting his nose and lips. His right arm hung awkwardly at his side, and his eyes widened as he caught sight of Haakon.

As the Kitayan was struggled to get to his feet, the tall Mongol reached down and easily picked up the Kitayan. The Kitayan shrieked as the Mongol hurled the smaller man.

Haakon was completely unprepared. No one had thrown a human body at him before, and he froze. He caught a quick glimpse of the whites of the Kitayan's eyes and the man's open mouth, and then one of the Kitayan's elbows glanced off his cheek as they collapsed in a heap. The air was forced from his lungs as he was caught between the Kitayan and the ground. He struggled to push the stunned man off him.

A shape threw a shadow across him, and he looked up to see the ridged line of the captain's knuckles zooming in at him, and then more shadows came, blotting out all the light.

* * *

"Can you believe that?" Tarbagatai shouted in Gansukh's ear.

"I can," Gansukh laughed, slapping the young archer on the shoulder. "I have had personal experience with Namkhai's strength."

The crowd was frenzied with excitement, and the tumult of their jubilation was so pronounced that speaking loudly enough for someone other than your immediate neighbor to hear was impossible. Gansukh couldn't hear the conversation Munokhoi was having with the moneylender, but the ex-*Torguud* captain's body language was easy to read.

Munokhoi shook his head sharply, his hands clenched into fists. The moneylender shrugged, unperturbed by Munokhoi's ire, and when the ex-*Torguud* captain stepped even closer, threatening the smaller man with his angry presence, the moneylender waved at the nearby cluster of *Torguud*. Munokhoi backed off with a sneer as the *Torguud* drifted toward the cornered moneylender.

Gansukh wandered over, wearing as innocent an expression as he could muster. "Fifty cows," he said loudly. "My family will really appreciate those cows, Munokhoi."

"I owe you nothing, country boy," Munokhoi snarled.

"Well, someone owes me some cows," Gansukh said, ignoring Munokhoi and directing his attention toward the moneylender. "If Munokhoi isn't going to pay what he owes, maybe I should be asking *you* for them instead."

"Me?" The moneylender was incredulous.

"I clearly heard him make the wager, didn't you?"

The moneylender waved his hands, clearly not wanting to be a part of the conversation.

"I wonder how the Kitayan came by that knife?" Gansukh made a show of puzzling over this question. "Isn't it odd that Munokhoi was so eager to match my wager? Almost as if he—"

Growling like a cornered wolf, Munokhoi stormed up to Gansukh, grabbing Gansukh's jacket with both hands. He put his face close to Gansukh's. "You are not as clever as you think," he raged.

"I do not doubt that," Gansukh replied. He stood very still, his hands loosely at his sides. As long as Munokhoi had both hands on his jacket, Gansukh wasn't too worried about what the other man might try. "Still," he continued, "the issue isn't who is more *clever*, but which of us has a better grasp on sums."

Munokhoi bared his teeth, his eyes focusing on the tip of Gansukh's nose. "I will kill you, country boy," he whispered.

Gansukh merely smiled, holding Munokhoi's gaze.

Munokhoi's hands tightened, and Gansukh heard the grinding strain of Munokhoi's jaw as he clenched his teeth. With a mighty effort, Munokhoi composed himself and let go of Gansukh with a tiny shove. "A lucky bet," he growled.

"The Blue Wolf favors me," Gansukh acknowledged with a small nod.

Munokhoi pursed his lips, holding his words in check. He glared at the surrounding crowd, and Gansukh could see him assessing the general mood of those who were paying more attention to this disagreement than the aftermath of the fracas in the fighting ring. Munokhoi's jaw worked for a few seconds, and then he spat—decisively—on Gansukh's boot. "You'll get your cows," he said, though the tone of his voice suggested otherwise. He stalked away, elbowing his way through the press of bodies that were sluggish to open a path for him.

"I'm sure I will," Gansukh called after him, a mocking lilt in his voice. Just enough to gall Munokhoi one last time. *Push him a little farther. He's already so close to the edge.*

* * *

Ghaltai led Chucai along the twisting course of an empty riverbed. The ground was rough, and Chucai gamely stumbled after the sure-footed *Darkhat*. The moon offered enough illumination to see the other man but not enough to reveal all the loose stones and jagged pieces of rock that filled the old waterway. They had left the horses an hour ago, and Ghaltai had refused to light a torch—partly, Chucai was certain, as petty revenge for Chucai having dragged him away from the feast.

But mostly because the *Darkhat* was afraid. Was he a superstitious old fool who had lived in his self-important exile too long, or was there something to his apprehension about the spirits of the mountain? Chucai had ample time to consider both possibilities, and as much as he wished it were otherwise, the simple reason they were climbing the mountain in the dark was because he couldn't dismiss the possibility that the latter concern of the *Darkhat* was actually true.

The route steepened, forcing Chucai to pay more attention to where he put his feet. Ghaltai scrambled up the incline, and Chucai resorted to clawing at the loose rock with his hands for the last few steps before he reached a narrow plateau.

He paused and looked back, making note of their route, and realized it was pointless to try to discern the track in the dark. The riverbed followed a complicated course through the exposed strata of the mountainside; it wasn't a route he could trace back down with his eyes. He would simply need to stay in the riverbed, and trust that it would take him to lower ground. *The spirits provide a way*, he thought, *but you have to trust them.*

They were on rocky ground, a flat expanse that jutted out from the base of a rocky pinnacle that towered high overhead. The ground sloped downward as he walked away from the ledge, and Chucai realized it was an old pool. Striations and runnels in the rock face revealed where the water had once cascaded down from the peak, pooling on this flat spot before leaping over the edge again and gouging a serpentine path down to the valley far below.

Ghaltai led him toward a darker spot on the rock face, and when he walked right up to the wall and vanished, Chucai realized the darkness was a rough opening the rock. He followed the *Darkhat*, reaching out and touching the wall on either side of the narrow passage. The rock was smooth, worn by time and tools, and he let his fingers trace along the cool rock as he blindly followed Ghaltai into the mountain.

The tunnel turned to his left and dipped down. He heard a distant sound, a steady dripping noise—water falling into water—and the air remained fresh and pure. As the sound became louder, the darkness became less absolute. At first, he merely thought his eyes had become accustomed to the gloom, but as he started to notice tiny glimmers in the walls around him, he realized he was seeing evidence of some sort of illumination. The tunnel turned again, and now nearly able to see both hands touching either wall, he went around the curve and found himself in a large cavern.

The ceiling was more than twice as tall as he was and covered with a layer of luminescent lichen. There were several dark holes in the ceiling, and judging from the purity of the air in the cavern, Chucai surmised they were actually open to the sky. As he wandered into the cavern, he caught sight of the pale moon peeking down through one of the lowermost holes.

The cavern was longer than it was wide, narrowing in the back to a series of three passages, and the chamber was empty but for a series of five platforms, large discs of stone raised a few *aid* off the dark and dusty floor. The discs were clearly man-made, with narrow lips and sunken centers. Two of them held water, and the sound he had heard was the steady *drip-drip* coming from somewhere in the ceiling into the larger of the two pools.

The stone in the water-filled pools was lighter than the surrounding stone, and Chucai bent to inspect the floor. Part of the thick layer of sediment strewn throughout the cavern had the gritty texture and color of ash.

There had been a fire.

The ash marked the walls, where the stone wasn't covered by the creeping lichens. On the right-hand wall, there was a texturing that didn't seem random. Chucai used his sleeve to wipe away some of the grime, and when he reached the lichen, he used a stone to scour the wall clean. Eventually, he uncovered a large drawing, carved into the rock.

It was a picture of a tree, gnarled like an old man, with thick roots that reached all the way to the floor and a tangled mass of leaves of branches that went up farther than he could readily reach.

SUMMUS PONTIFEX
ECCLESIAE UNIVERSALIS

ODRIGO WAS BEGINNING to wonder if he had been forgotten. He did not mind the solitude, but his stomach—so recently filled at the Septizodium—was reluctant to return to the previously lean weeks leading up to his arrival in Rome. It grumbled again, and this time—as if God had heard the noisy sound of his belly—the door to his chamber opened, and two men slipped into the room; each held a platter, one with fruits and cheeses, the other with cold sliced meat. He recognized them from the Septizodium, though they were now wearing much more regal clothing than they had previously. With kind smiles, they set the plates on the small table beside where he sat, and both of them gestured invitingly toward the food. Capocci—the shorter one—had white bandages on his hands.

"Do you remember us?" the taller of the two men asked as Rodrigo began to eat.

Rodrigo frowned in concentration, his hand—holding a grape—frozen near his mouth. "You are Giovanni Colonna," he said. "You were the first—no, the second—man I met in the Septizodium." He put the grape down on the plate. "And you are Capocci," he said to the other man. "You examined my teeth, before..."

Rodrigo felt an immense weight in his stomach, as if the few morsels of food he had just swallowed were now turning to stone in his belly. "Your hands are burned," he sighed. "You did not come out of the fire with us. You went back in and tried to rescue Cardinal Somercotes."

"Yes," said Capocci. "I did." He seemed embarrassed by Rodrigo's observation, and the sight of his bandage-covered hands only appeared to make his shame greater.

"In light of the devilry caused by that accident," Colonna said, drawing everyone's attention away from Capocci's wrapped hands, "we have elected to intrude upon your private vigil. There is an urgent matter we need to discuss."

Rodrigo nodded toward each of them. "Of course, Your Eminences."

"Do you know who the current Pope is?" Colonna asked.

"Gregory...oh, no," Rodrigo corrected himself. "Cardinal Somercotes told me that Gregory has died." How strange: that news, when first he'd heard it, had been devastating, for back then he had not really understood the nature of his great mission in Rome. Now that he knew the real purpose of his coming here, seeing the Pope was almost irrelevant. "And we were brought here—to the Vatican—to elect a new Pope. Has that happened?"

"Yes," said Capocci. "But do you know who he is?"

Rodrigo grimaced. "No."

"Well, we're here to tell you, and it will probably be a surprise."

Rodrigo was fairly confident he was beyond being surprised by anything, at this point. But he wished to be polite, so he gave them a curiously expectant expression.

"Your Holiness..." Colonna began.

"Your *what*?" Rodrigo asked, knitting his brows.

"Your Holiness—*you* have been elected Pope."

This was a remarkable statement, yet Rodrigo felt calm hearing it. Something about it resonated, almost as if he had been expecting such an announcement. It fit into the evolving tapestry of his day: of course he did not need to take a message to the Pope, if he himself *was* the Pope. In fact, his being the Pontiff was convenient, as it meant he would not have to convince some other man of the importance of his mission.

"All right," he said, after a moment. "All to the good."

Capocci and Colonna looked at each other, surprised.

"This is not a jest, Your Holiness," Capocci said. "You may have reason to think of us as occasional pranksters—and you would be entirely within your rights to do so—but in this matter we come to you in absolute earnest. There was a vote. You were elected Bishop of Rome."

"I see. That means somebody must first invest me as a bishop," Rodrigo said. "Is that what you are here to do?"

The two cardinals looked at each other. "I suppose we could do that," Colonna said.

"We would need more witnesses," Capocci pointed out.

Colonna shook his head. "It is all very unexpected and very unusual," he said. "There may be precedence. We don't know yet. The College of Cardinals is divided on this matter."

"And will be for some time," Capocci interjected.

"I was chosen," Rodrigo mused, "though I was not even a candidate."

"Yes," Colonna said.

Rodrigo smiled. "I find that very reassuring. Clearly this is the will of God."

Again both men seemed taken aback by Rodrigo's calm acceptance, but they recovered quickly. "That is an excellent perspective, Your Holiness," Colonna said.

Capocci nodded in agreement, a satisfied grin on his face. "As your friends," he said, "which both of us are, unreservedly, we wanted to remind you that the Papacy is a sacred office. But it is a political appointment as well. If there are no complications, and you are, in fact, anointed as the head of the Church, there will be many people working diligently to influence you—even manipulate you. Everyone will tell you that they have only your best interests at heart, or the best interests of the Church."

"We want you to know," said Colonna earnestly, "that they are all full of crap. Your Holiness."

Rodrigo revealed surprise, then polite amusement. "I see," he said. "So I should not listen to them? I should listen only to the two of you, is that right?"

"No, no," they both replied quickly, and Capocci went on: "We have promised ourselves not to try to guide. If you ever want to ask either of us for advice, we are here, but we will never impose our will on you, overtly or covertly. We merely beg you to hold others at a similar distance."

Rodrigo considered this. "Is there anyone in particular whose influence I should suspect?" he asked.

A pause. "Is Your Holiness asking for our advice?" Colonna said carefully.

"Yes," Rodrigo said plainly.

"I seek only to offer guidance," Colonna said.

"Of course," Rodrigo said.

Capocci looked down at his hands, as if to extricate himself from this conversation.

"You must be very wary of Cardinal Sinibaldo Fieschi," Colonna said.

* * *

After sunset, Orsini's carriage finally managed to cross the bridge. Orsini had had second thoughts, which then twisted into third, fourth, and fifth thoughts; the two men had argued the entire way, and the less-than-cordial debate continued even as they were led through the receiving chamber.

Orsini was still questioning Fieschi's plan as they strode into the shadowy central hall, lined on both sides by heavy oaken doors leading to adjoining rooms, as well as entrances to other corridors.

In one of those rooms, Fieschi knew, Father Rodrigo was being held.

"The man has lost his senses," Orsini said. "Most societies bar syphilitics or other diseased heirs from taking the reins of power—so too should the Church. It is a disservice to Christendom to let a simpleton be Bishop of Rome."

"You mean it's a disservice to you, because you cannot control him," Fieschi retorted. "But I can. You must trust me."

"Well, that's easy to do, as you've proven to be such a man of your word so far," Orsini muttered. "You will go down in the balladeers' books as consistent, reliable Fieschi."

"I will go down in the chronicles of the ages as effective, efficient Fieschi," the cardinal corrected. "Or rather, I will not go down in the chronicles at all. I am so effective as to be invisible. Where is the priest? Po—Father Rodrigo?" he demanded of a waiting servant, a willowy ostiarius who hovered near the interior door.

The slender man bowed. "He is in the room the cardinals put aside for him when he was carried...when he returned from the Colosseum. He is holding an audience with two of the cardinals."

"Take me there," Fieschi ordered.

"Both of us," Orsini amended.

Fieschi looked askance at him. "This is my realm, *Senator* Orsini, not yours. Civil authority has no place here. I thank you for the use of your carriage, but you may return it to your palace now."

Orsini's face darkened to sunset purple. "Do not ever talk to me that way."

Fieschi smiled coldly. "Do you see how upset you have just become? So very easily? You have just displayed the very reason I will not have you come with me to see him. I require absolute and total calm to get and keep his attention. Anger and suspicion? He will sense them with the fine-tuned perception of a madman. Stay away from him until I tell you that he's fit for you. And that you are fit for him."

"If you were capable of swordplay I'd throw a gauntlet at your feet this moment," Orsini said between clenched teeth. "But you, oh, elevated prelate, you would never condescend to something as barbaric as fencing. You just strangle and burn your victims."

If he said it to cause trouble for Fieschi in front of the help, he was not successful. Fieschi's face stayed absolutely calm; in fact, he glanced at the ostiarius with an expression of conspiratorial condescension as if to say, *Such a shame these laymen are so misguided.* The ostiarius—knowing well who his true master was—then shot Orsini a subtly disapproving look.

"Come, then," Fieschi said to the Vatican doorkeeper, who gestured toward a small door nearby. As they began to cross the hall, Orsini followed, deliberately close to the cardinal. "Senator, you are not invited," Fieschi said without looking back at him.

"Inform the cardinal I will enter," Orsini directed the ostiarius.

The slender porter seemed to shrink a little at this contretemps. "My sincere apologies, Senator Orsini, but the cardinal is correct that ecclesiastical law holds here. His word outweighs yours. If he does not wish you in the chamber, you may not enter."

"It's for your own good, friend Bear," Fieschi said, still not looking at him.

"Very well then," Orsini said, the words almost strangling him. "I shall wait just outside."

They were nearly at the door, which opened suddenly. Colonna and Capocci exited, closing the oak door quietly behind them. Not noticing the newcomers in the dim light, the two men paused to confer.

"That did not go at all as I expected," Capocci said heartily. "But I must say I am not displeased."

"Agreed," Colonna said. "He'll change the course of history, but I think he'll do it quietly."

Fieschi released a groan of annoyance. Capocci started and stared at him, then at Orsini, several paces off.

"The two of you have already gotten your claws into him?" Fieschi demanded, in the tone of a chastising parent.

Colonna and Capocci recovered quickly. "Claws?" said Colonna, the venerable uncle. "Are you suggesting that we have just come from unduly influencing the man who is to be our next Pope?"

"*Tried*," Capocci corrected. "That we have *tried* to unduly influence the man."

"Yes, of course," Colonna corrected himself. "*Tried*. How could we possibly corrupt a man as pure and uncorruptable as that one?"

"I don't think such a thing is possible," Capocci agreed.

"Enough!" Orsini snapped. "You two make a mockery of your offices."

Capocci regarded the Senator with an unruffled expression. "I have suffered recently for my office, Senator Orsini," he said quietly, all traces of humor gone from his voice. "While I do not tempt God as readily as you—"

"Why are you not with the other cardinals?" Fieschi interrupted coldly.

"They are over in the Castel Sant'Angelo," Colonna answered. "Poring over codices and scrolls that various clerks and acolytes have found for them. They are not convinced we should go forward installing Father Rodrigo as Saint Peter's heir. Of course they are mistaken, for he has been duly elected, and we were all witness to it."

"This is all most irregular," Orsini said uncomfortably, his voice hollow in the long, dark hall.

Colonna gave him a murderous look. "Not half as irregular as what we were subjected to in the Septizodium," he said. "Senator, you are out of place here, and I strongly recommend you escape back to your side of the Tiber."

"He's leaving now," Fieschi said firmly, as Orsini prepared to add his own imprecations. "Aren't you, Senator?"

"I have come to pay my respects to the new Pope," Orsini said brusquely, but he turned this way and that, indecisive, uncomfortable—very like an embarrassed youth.

Colonna sneered. "You have no respects to pay," he growled, his tone withering, his voice like a lion's. The doors seemed to hum and flex along the hall. He advanced toward Orsini, hands balled into fists. "You, Senator, are a man without respect. You have no power here. Leave immediately or I shall ask several of our larger priests to haul you out bodily, like the sack of manure you are, and dump you into the river."

Orsini glared at Colonna, but did not move.

The tall cardinal inclined his head a fraction. "Good evening, Senator," he said, his brusque tone making it clear the conversation was over.

Orsini blinked, and with a snarl creasing his lips, he spun on his heel and stalked out of the hall.

Fieschi watched the Senator go, briefly admiring Colonna's brash dismissal of him. "If you two are finished attempting to coerce the priest—" he started.

"His Holiness," Capocci corrected.

Fieschi waved a hand to indicate how little he cared about such niceties. "May I have a word with him?" he asked. "Or are you going to threaten me like you did the Senator?"

Colonna glanced at Capocci. "Did I threaten the Senator?" he asked.

Capocci shrugged. "That felt more like a warning than a threat."

"That is what I thought too," Colonna said.

Fieschi was unmoved by their banter. "A word," he said, "or two. With the Pope."

"By all means," Colonna said with a welcoming wave, as if he had not just made Fieschi repeat himself. "Have at him. We've left some food, and we can send in wine if you are going to have more than two words with him."

"I can have someone else bring wine," Fieschi said, refusing to be ruffled by Colonna, "should that be necessary."

"Very well," Colonna said with a nod. "Come, Rainiero," he said to Capocci. "Let us leave this dreary place and take a stroll in the evening air."

"Yes," Capocci agreed. "We should take advantage of our newly restored liberty."

The two cardinals took their leave, and Fieschi did not stay in the hall to watch them depart. They had wasted enough of his time already. He ran a hand down the front of his robe, using the motion to calm his annoyance, and then he opened the door and stepped into the room.

The priest was sitting quietly at a small table, nibbling at several plates of food the two cardinals had left behind. He looked up as Fieschi entered the room. His gaze was unfocused, and he stared at Fieschi for a long moment as if he did not recognize the cardinal.

No, Fieschi realized, *he looks at me as if he does not* wish *to recognize me.*

"Good evening," Fieschi said, his voice caring and sympathetic. "It has been a rather exciting day. You must be quite overwhelmed by all that is happening around you.

Father Rodrigo shrugged. "I was overwhelmed by some guards when I was speaking to my people," he said. "Other than that, I find most things here are manageable. And I find it quite agreeable to be Pope."

Fieschi paused, caught off guard by the priest's candor. "Are you aware that some of my fellow cardinals are opposed to your becoming Pope?" he asked cautiously.

"I do feel compassion for their concern, but their strife is of their own making, is it not?" Father Rodrigo said evenly. "They elected me, did they not?"

"They are trying very hard to *un* elect you," Fieschi said. "It would behoove you to have a champion in this matter."

"Why?" Father Rodrigo asked, showing little concern. "Do I not already have a champion?"

"Oh, dear God, please don't listen to Colonna or Capocci," Fieschi said. "Surely you have seen for yourself what mischief they can get up to."

"I have also seen for myself what mischief *you* get up to, Cardinal," Father Rodrigo said, his voice finally taking on a bit of bite. "Anyway, I was not referring to them. I was referring to our Lord. Does He not extend His grace to me upon my election?"

Fieschi gaped. "You are still quite mad, aren't you?"

Father Rodrigo thought for a moment before answering, "If I say no, you'll say that is proof of my delusions, and what does that gain you? But if I say yes—acknowledging my own madness—does that not imply that you *knowingly* elected a madman to be your supreme Pontiff? I fear neither answer is very useful to you, my son."

Fieschi swallowed several times, trying to clear a sudden obstruction in his throat. *Where had this rhetorical skill come from?* Previously, the man had appeared to be little more than an addled parish priest. "I have come to you this evening to offer my assistance," he said, forcing aside his rage. "I had the honor of being a valued servant and confidant of your predecessor, Gregory IX. I humbly offer my services likewise to you."

"Thank you," Father Rodrigo said. "If I am ever in need of a jurist or an orator, I will keep you in mind. Otherwise, I cannot imagine you and I will have much to discuss." He returned his attention to the plates.

Fieschi bristled. *How dare he be so dismissive?* "This is—"

Father Rodrigo raised a single finger, and Fieschi was struck dumb by the subtle command of the motion as well as an utter disregard for the differences between their respective stations. "Until the College of Cardinals reconvenes to unelect me, I believe the correct way to address me is 'Your Holiness.'"

Fieschi felt the blood drain from his face. "Your—, Your—" he spluttered, unable to use the honorific.

"Yes?" Father Rodrigo said after a pause. "Would you like to take confession, my son? I don't know if, as Pope, I am supposed to hear confession. Perhaps you could ask one of your fellow cardinals. Do you suppose Cardinal Somercotes is busy?"

Fieschi stiffened, his previous awkwardness vanishing. "What are you up to?" he snapped. *This is all a joke arranged by those two fools,* he thought. "Whose tool are you?" he sneered.

"The Lord's," Father Rodrigo replied calmly. "Whose tool, my son, are you?"

THE HORSE AND THE CART

IETRICH HAD TO run. If he paused to consider his flight from the abandoned Shield-Brethren chapter house, Tegusgal's Mongol archers would end his life. Was that not justification enough for his actions? To flee meant to live. His brothers-in-arms had not fled at Schaulen, and they had died. Was that not the ultimate lesson the *Fratres Militiae Christi Livoniae* should have taken from that morning at the river crossing? Outnumbered, overwhelmed, and caught in the open: the enemy had surprised them. Retreating so as to find better ground, to face the Samogitian rabble another day, was an *expedient* solution. A practical one.

But his predecessor, Volquin, had stood his ground. Lithuanian light cavalry, much more nimble in the swampy lowlands around the river, had shattered the main body of the order's cavalry, and as the Livonian *Heermeister* had tried to rally his men into an effective wedge against the approaching infantry, he had been struck by an errant spear. Before he could regain his footing in the muck, the pagan foot soldiers clashed with his men. Volquin was struck again and again, beaten by sword and club until his armor split. Until the river turned red with his blood and the blood of his faithful.

Dietrich von Grüningen was not Volquin. Nor did he aspire to be. He simply wanted to live.

His horse wanted to dally as it approached the verge of the forest, and Dietrich beat his heels against its barrel, drumming his desire mercilessly into the reluctant animal beneath him. An arrow whistled past his right ear, burying itself into the knobby trunk of an oak instead of the back of his head. He mentally cursed his hubris for not wearing a helm, and his shoulders tightened instinctively as if they could collapse in on themselves and make his body a smaller target. He ducked lower across his horse's neck as the first branches of the forest whipped by, and he heard the desultory *thunk thunk* of arrows striking the trees around him.

He missed the first curve of the path, his horse plunging into the undergrowth. He cursed as the unruly branches of the oak trees clawed at him. Holding the reins tight in one hand, he struggled with the clasp of his cloak before a branch snagged it. Such an ignoble death: to be pulled off his horse by a tree branch. His horse, grunting and snorting, blundered through a tangle of ferns and spindly shrubs—leaves and branches alike slashing and whipping at the animal's flanks.

A heavy bough loomed, and Dietrich threw himself flat against his horse's back. His cloak went tight against his throat, and he clenched his neck muscles. Digging his fingers between the tight fabric and his neck, he felt it tear, and the pressure against his neck vanished. Gasping, he sat up and looked back. His abandoned cloak hung from the thick branch, a ghostly shadow of the man he once was.

His horse stumbled across the path, and he jerked its head to keep it from blundering into the undergrowth again. His horse was bigger than the Mongol steeds, and while keeping to the forest made him a harder target, he couldn't move as fast.

Was he only delaying the inevitable? Once he broke free of the woods, there was nothing but open land between him and Hünern. Could he outrun the Mongols? And then what? Run back to the Livonian compound like a wounded animal and cower in the shadows of the wrecked barn? He couldn't imagine his men—especially Kristaps!—cowering with him.

As he weighed his choices, his mount reached the narrow gap he and the Mongol party had recently used to enter the forest. His horse leaped through the slot between the trees, leaving the forest behind, and he blinked heavily in the sudden light. The sun had passed its zenith and was starting its long tumble toward the horizon. It hung in the western sky, God's dazzling eye, and he felt himself being pulled toward it. There were a few hours of daylight left. The ruins of Legnica lay to the west. Could he find somewhere else to hide until nightfall?

He turned in his saddle, blinking away the radiance of yellow and white spots that suffused his vision. The forest shook behind him, the trees seeming to caper and dance in his wake. A rank of many-armed monsters, gesticulating wildly so as to frighten him away. He swiped at the tears clouding his sight, and noticed the arrow caught in the links of his chausson.

* * *

The practice of war often relied upon both patience and deception, and the exercise of the latter invariably relied upon a concerted use of the former. Every year the encroachment of winter froze his hands a little more—the numbness in his fingers, the tingling in his joints, the constant ache in his wrists. The only real practice Rutger got anymore was in exercising his *patience*.

For many years he had trained in the yard with the younger men, and occasionally he had been called to be their *oplo*. But more often than not, he was simply one of the experienced swordsmen whom the trainer called upon when he needed to make an example of a student's failure to properly follow the lesson. For Rutger, since the teeth of winter had started gnawing away at his joints, holding his sword *poorly* was something he had gotten very good at.

His mind, however, compensated for his lack of martial dexterity, and he studied assiduously the records maintained by Týrshammar's lord, learning the more subtle arts of combat—the devious ways in which a commander can forestall engaging an enemy, the violent methods of reducing the number of combatants one must face before ever having to draw one's sword, and the artful practice of patience. Of waiting for your enemy to blink first.

Fog had rolled into the valley overnight, a damp layer that had clung to the wreckage of the city. His joints ached fiercely, and he had wanted nothing more than to sit by a roaring fire, cradling hot stones wrapped in an old scrap of leather, but the phantasmal fog had made it easier for the Shield-Brethren to slip into the chaotic squalor of Hünern. The sun had slowly burned off the fog without stirring up any wind, and the day had collapsed into a slow, torpid afternoon. After the death of Andreas and the following riots, the city seemed content to lie still, licking its wounds.

The Mongol compound was surrounded by walls built of bricks made from sun-baked mud—the choice of a foreigner clearly, though the weather had been unexpectedly mild over the last few months. A palisade of logs would have been a better *permanent* solution, but perhaps the use of mud was simply a reminder to all that the Mongols never intended to stay long. The Mongols had cleared a wide pomerium, though had not bothered to dig much of a ditch along the base of the walls. There was one gate—two panels of oak planks covered with hides and iron studs—and it stood between a pair of narrow towers, both made from a combination of brick and lumber. Each tower housed two Mongol guards, and they had spotted Rutger and his wagon almost as soon as he emerged from behind the Black Wall.

He was coming from one of the main routes through the area of Hünern that Hans had called the Lion Quarter, and his route was one taken every day by merchants as they brought their meager wares through the ragged city to the open markets near First Field and the arena. A man and a cart were not unexpected along the edge of the pomerium closest to the ruins of Hünern, and as he had anticipated, his presence did not unduly alarm the watching Mongol guards.

The wagon trundled and bumped along beneath Rutger, its wheels thudding over the uneven ground as he kept the horse moving at a slow, ponderous pace. It hadn't taken much to disguise himself as a poor laborer, filthy haired and rag-clad, and truth be told it was even less difficult to feign physical weakness when every bump of the wagon made his joints complain. He kept watch on the towers, however, taking stock of the presence of the guards and their attentiveness.

Or lack thereof, which only increased the chance that his plan might actually work.

The odds were against the Shield-Brethren. The Mongols had too many men, and they were all sequestered within a highly defensible compound. A frontal assault would be so damaging to his numbers that they would fail before they even breached the wall. The only possible solution was to trick the Mongols, and given their paranoia—panic and dread in equal parts—such a trick would require as much luck as it would deception.

If it all came down to luck—regardless of how much favor the Virgin gave them—they were already dead, and Rutger tried to keep those thoughts far from his mind.

He expected at least ten guards at the gate—the Mongols ate, slept, shit, and patrolled in groups of ten. Four in the towers meant at least six more inside the gate. Would there be more? He didn't know, and Hans's only insight was that there were usually two *arban*—the Mongol word for the tenman squad—scattered near the gates during normal circumstances. There was also more foot and cart traffic then, and Rutger would have put more men on the gate himself, but would he keep that same level of security if the gate were closed?

It depended on several factors: the number of able-bodied men at his disposal, the expectation of an attack (and the size of the attacking force), the amount of time the garrison would have to respond to any alarm. Also, in his experience, more men on the wall didn't increase the chance of spotting sneaky attackers. Too many men, and they would get lazy in their watchfulness, assuming the man next to them would be as watchful or more. Fewer men meant more responsibility, for no man wanted to be the one who missed seeing the enemy approach.

The four sentries were armed with spears, curved swords, and bows. Of the three, only the last caused him any concern, and even though he knew there were twice as many Shield-Brethren archers scattered within the ruins on his left, the range was great enough to stir his blood as he crept along the verge of the pomerium. It was a tricky path to follow: too close and the guards might become suspicious; too far away and they might be suspicious as well. If he had nothing to hide, then why would he be riding as far away from the camp as possible and still be taking this route? When the time came, would he be close enough?

He didn't dare look over his shoulder, though the urge to do so was nigh unbearable. The signal would be plain enough, and it didn't matter if he saw it. The Mongols were the ones who had to spot the plume of smoke.

* * *

It was hard to do nothing. After that fateful day when he had first met Kim in the church, and all during the following weeks when he had sent numerous boys through the gates of the Mongol compound for the sake of passing messages between the Flower Knight and the Shield-Brethren, Hans had been at the center of a secret web of intrigue against the Mongol invaders. He had no illusions about actively *fighting* the Mongols, but what he had been doing felt just as important. Earlier, when the Shield-Brethren quartermaster, Rutger, had been asking him questions about the layout of the Mongolian compound, he had strained to remember every little detail that the boys had relayed to him. The Shield-Brethren had listened intently, committing it all to memory.

Now, Hans could only watch as the two Shield-Brethren scouts, Styg and Eilif, prepared to scale the wall of the Mongolian compound. The fourth member of their group—a long-faced young man named Maks—crouched next to Hans behind the jumble of brick and burned logs that hid them from sight.

He wanted to be going with them. After all this time of watching others do the dangerous work, Hans chafed at staying behind. He had argued strenuously with the three Shield-Brethren when they had first approached the wall, but Eilif had cut his arguments short with a single statement. *If what you have told us is true, we don't need you; if it isn't, we're all dead.*

It was a brutal assessment of his value to the Shield-Brethren, coldly delivered, and Hans had been stunned by it.

In the past, there would have been guards patrolling the entire length of the walls. The top of the wall was wide enough for one man to walk along, and sentries patrolled the entire circuit of the wall via a series of easily anchored ladders. Before Styg and Eilif had approached the wall, they had waited and watched for what had seemed like an interminable amount of time, and had seen no sign of a patrol.

Styg thought it was highly likely that the ladders had been taken down on the far side of the wall. The Mongols had decided the height of the walls was security enough, and the presence of men on the walls would only attract archers.

In which case getting up this side of the wall was the easy part. Once at the top, Styg and Eilif could take a quick peek. Hopefully they wouldn't be peering into a nest of suspicious and angry

Mongols, waiting for foolish knights to do exactly what they were doing.

Using a wooden mallet and tent stakes, Styg cautiously ascended the mud-brick wall, leaving behind a trail of hand-and footholds for Eilif to follow. Hans sucked in his breath and held it as Styg reached the top of the wall and—very gingerly—eased his head up until he could peek over the top of the wall. Styg risked a quick glance, and then raised his head slowly to take a longer look at the Mongol camp. Hans half expected the Shield-Brethren's head to snap back, a Mongol arrow in his eye, but nothing happened. After a slow and methodical examination of the compound, Styg retreated down the stakes to join Eilif at the base of the wall. He looked toward Hans and Maks's hiding place and flashed them a quick smile.

The route was clear. All they needed was a distraction.

"That's it," Maks breathed. "They're ready." Letting out a huge *whoosh* of pent-up air, he clapped Hans on the shoulder. "Let's go, my friend. There's nothing more we can do here."

Hans hesitated, staring at the series of stakes pounded into the wall. Maks's hand tightened on Hans's shoulder, as if he sensed the direction of Hans's thoughts. He held Hans back like one would hold a hound back from a downed bird.

Hans stared at the stakes. In his mind, he was already scaling them...

* * *

Dietrich felt no pain from the arrow, and the fletching bounced in response to the motion of his horse and not in time with it, suggesting that the head of the arrow had failed to fully penetrate the maille of his chausson. He grasped the shaft, and without applying much pressure at all, worked the arrow free. Mongol arrows were shorter than those used by Christian archers, and the tips were less uniform in construction. This one was a ragged shard of white bone lashed to the wooden shaft, and the very tip of it was stained with blood.

A more religious man would have attributed his safety to the hand of God, slowing the arrow's flight so that it barely creased his flesh, but Dietrich recognized that his luck was more due to the animal between his legs than divine intervention. He threw the arrow away, and squeezed his legs more tightly around his horse's barrel.

His thoughts went to Father Pius for a moment, and he wondered as to the priest's fate. There was no point, however, in dwelling on what had happened to the priest. *He's with God now.*

What had he said to Tegusgal earlier that afternoon? God willing, *he* wouldn't die today. So far, God appeared to be listening, but He was certainly taking others to His breast. *How long do I have?* Dietrich wondered.

His horse crossed fallow farmland at a gallop. Hopefully the open terrain and his charger's stride were increasing the lead he had on the Mongols. He glanced back once, but his horse was running so hard that it was difficult to judge distances with the constant juddering motion of the horse. *Far enough for now,* he thought. As his horse leaped over a narrow streamlet and reached the rougher ground along the river, Dietrich made up his mind and turned his mount south. Back toward Hünern.

ONE OF OUR KHANS IS MISSING

IT WAS HARD to sit and wait. Riding across the endless steppe had been trying for many reasons, and each of the company had dealt with the exhaustion and hardship of the journey in his or her own way, but there was no good way to pass the time while sitting still in enemy territory and *waiting*.

The Shield-Brethren were camped a half day's ride from Karakorum, the capital of the Mongol empire. The city sat on a wide plain, not far from a river left shallow and sluggish after a dry fall, its course a deep cut across the flat plain. At night they could see the glow in the south of the many torches, lanterns, and fires from the city, and during the day they walked the horses in the narrow depression where they made their camp, cleaned their gear, and kept watch for any movement on the plain.

They spoke little. They had been in each other's company for many months now and were all comfortable enough with each other that none felt the need for making idle chatter, which left them alone with their respective thoughts. Some, like Yasper and Istvan, found a great deal of entertainment there; others—and Raphael knew he was guilty of this as much if not more than the rest—dwelled on the past.

The last entry he had written in his journal had been the night at the rock when Feronantus had turned down Benjamin's offer to guide them to Karakorum. Feronantus had used an old maxim inflicted upon all the trainees during their first year at Petraathen as his rationale, but Raphael suspected Feronantus had said it for the company's benefit as well.

Each of our lives have no meaning, except that which we give them by our deeds, and by how our comrades remember us.

He had written it down that night, when he had been unable to sleep. Since then, every time he had opened his journal, those words quelled any desire he had to continue the record of his journey.

He did not want to be one upon whom it fell to record the deeds of his fallen comrades.

He had been holding a piece of charcoal for some time, his fingers now black with dust, when his endless reverie was disturbed by a tiny motion on the plain. He propped himself up on his elbows, shading his eyes. Two horses, one rider. Riding north. He waited until he was sure, and then he slid down the bank to tell the others that Cnán was coming back from Karakorum.

Whatever he had meant to write could wait, he decided.

* * *

Yasper was ecstatic when he realized the second horse was laden with supplies. In fact, he was so overjoyed that the others stood back and let him single-handedly unburden the horse of its saddlebags, caskets, satchels, and boxes. He arranged everything on the ground beside the horse and proceeded to open every bag and container and take stock of the supplies that Cnán had procured. "By Aristotle's hairy knuckles," he swooned as he opened a lacquer box and discovered tiny sugar-glazed cakes. "They're still warm."

"What's the bad news?" Feronantus asked.

Cnán offered him a rolled scroll, and went to sit on the rough-hewn bench that Eleázar and Rædwulf had constructed the other morning in an effort to stave off boredom. Stiffly, she began to unwind the dirty wraps wound around her lower legs. "He's not there," she said.

"Who?" Percival asked.

"Where?" Rædwulf asked at the same time.

Feronantus started to unroll the scroll, and waved Raphael over to help him. Together they unwound the long piece of cloth and revealed the map Cnán had acquired. It was beautifully done in watercolor, with the intricate markings that Raphael knew were Chinese. Delicately drawn white and pink blossoms scaled up one side of the map, and nestled in a bramble at the top were three long-beaked birds with red streaks on their wings.

"Ögedei is not in Karakorum," Cnán explained as she pulled off her boots and wiggled her toes. "He left over a week ago, heading north into the mountains."

Raphael peered at the map, trying to figure out locations from the few geographical details that were present. He thought he found the Orkhun River, the one that lay a few hundred paces to the west of their current location, and along its bank was Karakorum. He tapped the map, and Feronantus nodded, concurring with his guess. He ran his finger toward the end he held, the top of the map, trying to make sense of the lines and markings.

"Is that where his winter palace is?" Feronantus asked.

Cnán shook her head. "He's not going to his winter palace. Not yet. He's off on a pilgrimage." She finished flexing her toes and looked over at Feronantus with a tiny smile. "The *good* news is that he didn't take *all* of his Imperial Guard with him."

"Oooh," Yasper sighed, holding out the lacquer box. "You have got to try these." He went back to licking his fingers.

* * *

After delivering a short version of her scouting trip to Karakorum, Cnán announced she was going to take a nap. She had slept little in the last few days, and not at all since dawn the day before, and it had taken all of her willpower to keep her eyes open long enough to find the Shield-Brethren camp. She knew the cornucopia of salted meats, dried and ripe fruit, and sugared confections would keep the rest of the company occupied for a few hours while she slept.

Plus there were two small casks of ale. With any other group, she suspected her news would be desultory to the company's morale (in which case the ale would bolster sunken spirits); however, she suspected the Brethren would find her report uplifting and welcome the ale as a surprising bounty.

The sun had fled the sky by the time she woke, and she was drawn to the light of the crackling fire that Eleázar had built in the stone-ringed pit. One of the casks had been opened, and judging from the merriment she heard in a few voices, its contents had been drunk.

"Ho, the Great Provider awakens," Eleázar chortled as she approached the group gathered around the fire. He passed her a bowl of dried figs and a piece of salted deer meat. She accepted both, her stomach grumbling with eagerness for sustenance.

Yasper and Raphael were arguing over the ingredients used in the sugar cakes she had brought. She smiled to herself as she listened to their speculations, which grew more and more fanciful. She had not had sweets like this since she was a child, and it had been a childish indulgence on her part when she had run across the baker in Karakorum's extensive market. The glaze contained spices she had tasted nowhere else but in China, and they reminded her of a tiny period of her life when she had been innocent and happy.

It made her happy now to hear people she would consider friends arguing so vociferously—and with such joy—over the flavors hidden within tiny seedpods, roots, and flowers. This argument suggested the world was not altogether a bleak place, that there were ways in which even those most bereft of home could find family.

"It is cassia, I tell you," Raphael was arguing. "I have had it before, in the Levant. It has a taste that is neither bitter nor sweet, and somewhat dry. The spiciness comes from this pink strand, a piece of a root is my guess, sliced very thinly."

Istvan cackled with laughter, drawing everyone's attention. The Hungarian stared into the fire, not seeing anything but the shivering dance of the flames. "Sliced very thinly," he whispered.

"Is he—?" Cnán leaned over toward Vera, keeping her voice quiet enough that only the Shield-Maiden could hear her.

Vera shook her head. "I have not seen him under the influence of the freebuttons for months. This is a different madness," she whispered. She said a word in a language Cnán did not understand, though she nodded anyway. She could surmise what Vera meant. Blood-fever. Istvan's predilection for the mushrooms had infected his blood, and he would never be truly free of the visions unleashed by the freebuttons.

Feronantus cleared his throat. He poured a tiny measure from the open cask into his cup, and then passed the cask to Percival, on his left. "We have eaten and drunk and argued"— he raised his cup toward Yasper and Raphael—"of the provisions you have brought us, Cnán. Now it is time for us to hear of the other matters you have procured from your visit to the heart of our enemy's empire."

Cnán swallowed her last piece of salted meat, felt it get stuck in her throat, and realized that Percival had filled his cup and was holding it out to her. She accepted it, blushing only slightly, and washed the meat down into her belly.

"In the late fall, the *Khagan* usually moves to his southern camp," she started after she handed Percival's cup back. "This year he not only left early, but he went north instead of south."

"As you mentioned earlier," Feronantus reminded her. "He went on a pilgrimage."

"Yes," Cnán nodded. "Every year, there is a large festival near the harvest season where the *Khagan*'s brother, Tolui, is honored. Within a month after this festival, Karakorum empties out for the winter. This year, however, there is still a thriving market and a number of traders who are in no hurry to return to their routes. They have not sold all their goods."

"Is it a bad year for commerce?" Raphael asked.

"No, they expect the *Khagan* and his retinue to return."

Yasper groaned. "We're early. Now we're going to have to sit here in this hole until he comes back."

"Not necessarily," Cnán pointed out. "There are two *minghan* quartered in Karakorum. The *Khagan* is surrounded—night and day—by one thousand warriors. If you were going to assassinate him, you would not be able to accomplish it while he was in the palace."

Yasper's face fell even farther. "I guess we should have thought of that before we left Legnica," he said as he scanned the faces of the others, looking for some sign that he had not stumbled into a moonlit pagan ritual.

"How many men did he take with him on his pilgrimage?" Feronantus asked.

"Three *jaghun*," Cnán said.

"And where was he going?"

"A place called Burqan-qaldun. A sacred site in the mountains to the north of here. He goes to commune with his ancestors," Cnán shrugged. "Or to receive guidance from the spirits the Mongols worship. Or even to appease the mood of his people by proving himself a great warrior by slaying a cave bear. Or all three of these things. I heard them all as reasons."

"But the location was consistent?"

Cnán nodded. "Yes. Burqan-qaldun."

"Very well," Feronantus said. "Do you know where it is?" he asked Raphael.

"I think so," Raphael said. "If the map is accurate."

Cnán let loose a huff of surprise. *What map is ever accurate?* she wondered. "It will be fine," she heard herself saying.

"Then our course is clear," Feronantus said. "We chase after the *Khagan*. He is vulnerable away from the security of his palace. We shall find an opportunity at this Burqan-qaldun. That is where we end his life."

a day of rest

39

HE *Darkhat* leader had mastered the art of catching a nap while riding his horse, and his steed dutifully followed Chucai's horse as they picked their way along the narrow track that wound down to the valley. The moon tripped along the rim of the horizon, ready to flee at the first glimmering of dawn. The bonfires of the feast no longer filled the valley with red-orange light; they, like the rest of the *Khagan*'s caravan, were slumbering. The nocturnal birds—owls and tiny swifts—had fallen silent too, no longer chasing prey and filling the night with their cries. This last hour before dawn was always the emptiest, the time when the world appeared to be holding its breath.

Chucai was no stranger to this hour; he had always found the silence enormously satisfying. This was the time when he normally did his *qi* exercises, and the persistent ache in his lower back from all the time spent in the saddle over the last few weeks was a reminder of how long it had been since he had properly exercised. *Today*, he promised himself. There was much to think about, and the mental clarity of the exercises always helped.

The carving of the tree in the cave had done little to illuminate the mystery surrounding the Spirit Banner, though Chucai's suspicions were now confirmed. He had to learn more about the history of the banner.

Ghaltai stirred as a quarter of *Torguud* riders approached. The men recognized both the *Darkhat* and Chucai, and they let the pair pass without issue. Ghaltai yawned and rolled his shoulders as their horses picked up their pace, sensing the end of the journey. When the two men reached the edge of the camp, Ghaltai reined his horse to a stop. "I will go join my men," he said.

Chucai nodded. Chucai had had a number of questions for the *Darkhat* commander after they had emerged from the subterranean temple, but Ghaltai had refused to provide any answers. *I have shown you,* was all that he had offered. *I will not speak of what we have seen. It is not for me to offer any explanation.*

On one hand, Chucai suspected Ghaltai's words were motivated by petty revenge for Chucai having pulled him away from the feast, but Chucai suspected Ghaltai's reticence also stemmed from a long-standing superstitious apprehension.

Not that he could blame the *Darkhat* chieftain. The banner unnerved him too.

He was tired. Everything seemed too obtuse for him to figure out. A good rest would reinvigorate his brain; he would see things much more clearly after a few hours of sleep.

His servants were all still sleeping, and he didn't bother waking them. He could manage his own preparations. He would just sneak into his *ger*, lie down for a few hours, and—

There was someone in his *ger*, lying on the floor beneath a pair of fur skins. A brazier sat nearby, its coals cold and gray. Chucai kicked the supine figure—none too gently—startling him awake. The man sat up.

"Master Chucai," Gansukh said sleepily. "I have been waiting—" The young man yawned mightily, his words getting lost in the open depths of his mouth.

"Whatever it is," Chucai snapped, "it could have waited until midday, at least."

Gansukh adjusted the skins around his shoulders. "I doubt that," he said. "I would not count patience among Munokhoi's qualities."

"What does Munokhoi have to do with you *sleeping* in my *ger*?"

"I couldn't very well go back to mine, could I?"

"Why?" Chucai sat down in his chair. "What are you talking about?"

"You missed the fights last night, didn't you?" A sleepy smile crawled across Gansukh's face. "Well, let me tell you a story then..."

* * *

It seemed like only moments after he had gotten rid of Gansukh and lain down, intending to get a few hours of sleep, that Chucai started awake. Where there had been darkness in his tent, there was now light.

Seated in the center of his *ger* was the *Khagan*'s shaman. Beside the old man, the brazier—which had previously been filled with cold ash—glowed with an orange light. The bits of metal attached to the shaman's clothing gleamed as if they were tiny chips of fire clinging to the oily cloth.

"What do you want, old man?" Chucai growled. Part of him thought this was nothing more than a dream, and he resented the phantasmal intrusion.

The shaman chose this moment to fall into a paroxysm of coughing that made every shard of bone and bit of metal attached to his headdress and robe jangle frantically. With a final wheezing cough, he got something unstuck. He worked it around in his mouth for a moment and then spat in the brazier. A finger of flame reached up and grabbed whatever noisome thing that had come from the shaman's throat. "Nothing is more visible than what is hidden directly in front of you," the old man intoned.

Chucai slumped back on his bedding, turning his face toward the ceiling of his *ger*. "I am tired, old man," he said. "I do not have time for your games."

"The empire does not sleep," the shaman said.

Chucai shook his head. *Hadn't he said something similar to Ögedei once? Years ago, when the* Khagan *had first started drinking heavily.*

"Does a tree ever stop growing?" the shaman asked.

Chucai sat up in a rush. "You told me about the spirit that never dies," he heard himself saying as he recalled his previous conversation with the old shaman. "Is that what the tree is? Is that what the banner is? A living spirit?"

"All life comes from *Tengri,*" the shaman whispered. "All life returns. Nothing is lost."

"What is the banner?" Chucai demanded.

"The banner is a piece of wood," the shaman said.

He said that before, Chucai remembered, fighting a swell of frustration. "And what of pieces that might be cut from it?" he asked.

The shaman smiled, and an involuntary shiver raced up Chucai's spine. The light from the brazier highlighted the lines on the shaman's face, a pattern that resembled the twisted branches of the tree carved on the wall of the temple.

"Not *what*," the shaman said, shaking his head. "Ask yourself *why.*" He clapped his hands, and a cloud of smoke erupted from the brazier.

The smoke filled the *ger* and Chucai tried to wave it away, succumbing to a coughing fit nearly as physically wracking as the one he had seen the shaman suffer. His eyes watered, and he squeezed them shut, wiping at the tears.

When he opened his eyes, the shaman was gone. As was the smoke and the fire in the brazier. The coals were cold and gray, much like they had been when he had first found Gansukh in his *ger*.

There was no sign the shaman had been anything other than a dream.

***

Ögedei hurt all over. He wanted to lie still beneath the pile of furs on his sleeping platform until the pain went away, but the aches in his body were there even when he was immobile. He groaned, shuffling around beneath the pile of furs, and he felt someone grab his foot. He tried to pull away, but their grip was strong. Dimly, he heard the muffled sound of a woman's voice, and he gradually realized it belonged to Jachin. She was telling someone that the *Khagan* was not to be disturbed, a sentiment which he heartily endorsed.

She remained, though, and her hands began working on his foot. She massaged each toe individually, her hands slick with scented oils, and once each toe had been worked on, she moved on to his ankle, and then his calf, and then his thigh, and then...

Her ministrations helped, albeit briefly. For all her efforts, the headache remained, and its pounding rhythm sent aching waves cascading through his body—down his spine, echoing through his chest, into his pelvis, and down his legs to his feet and toes, which started to throb again.

He dug his way out of his bedding, and squinted at both the light and the sight of Jachin hovering nearby. She had a cup in her hand. "Water," she said.

He groaned and started to burrow under the furs again, but she stopped him. "Drink it," she said. She did not have the same forceful personality as Toregene, but the concern in her voice was enough to arrest his burrowing. Lifting his head slightly, he accepted the cup and sipped from it. The water was cold, freshly drawn from the nearby river, and his body shivered as he found himself gulping the water. She poured him another cup, and this one he drank more slowly.

"I have sent someone to get your cook, who will make you soup," she said, and when he started to protest, she shook her head and pressed her hand against his chest. "It will ease your discomfort," she said. "Lie still. Rest."

It was all that he wanted to do, anyway. He felt a distant urge to piss, brought about by drinking the water, but he couldn't imagine getting up right now to do so. He would have to venture outside his *ger*—into the sunlight—and he feared he would burst into flames.

It was best to stay here, lying very still, as Jachin commanded. The aches would pass. They always did. This was the spirits' revenge for his drinking. In the past, he simply kept the pain at bay with another cup of wine, but as he sprawled on his bed, covered by a heavy layers of furs, he knew such succor would not be forthcoming. He could smell the fermented stink of his own sweat, a stench that made his stomach rebel.

He was a drunk. He knew his father would not have approved. For the most part, such awareness didn't disturb him. Those thoughts only came to the forefront of his thinking at times like this, when he was in the aftermath of a bout of heavy drinking, and he knew—like all thoughts of inadequacy and fear—that they would pass. He was the Khan of Khans, ruler of the largest empire the world had ever seen. He was the master of thousands and thousands of fighting men. He was not a slave. He could stop drinking if he wanted to.

In fact, he was going to do just that. *As soon as I return to Karakorum*, he promised, squeezing his eyes shut. Rainbows danced across the inside of his eyelids as the headache flared again—*thum thum*—and then relented, releasing its hold as if it had accepted his promise.

He heard voices, the muffled sound of more than one person talking, and his nose encountered a delicious aroma—fish, garlic, ginger, and the sharp tang of a Chinese pepper. He opened his eyes, blinking heavily in the pale light.

The flaps of the *ger* had been pulled back, enough to allow a single figure to enter and still keep most of the sunlight out. *Soup*, he thought, somewhat surprised he could even consider eating. He sat up as the man carrying the tray approached his bed. The flaps of the *ger* were lowered, and as his eyes adjusted to the happy dimness again, he recognized the weathered face and the long gray hair of the man who brought his food.

Alchiq.

"Where is my cook?" Ögedei grumbled.

"He was only too happy to allow me the honor of bringing you your food, my Khan," Alchiq said, a touch of a smile twisting his lips.

Ögedei grumbled some more, but kept the words to himself.

"Master Chucai said I should attend to your needs," Alchiq said.

"Why?"

Alchiq shrugged. "He did not say, though when has he ever explained his commands?"

"Ha," Ögedei said, scooting toward the edge of his sleeping platform. His stomach growled, vociferously eager for food, though, and he wondered if it was strong enough for such fare. "He is like an old fruit tree: as he gets older, he gets stiffer and his fruit becomes more sour." He picked up the wide spoon that was resting beside the bowl and gingerly slurped up a mouthful of the broth.

It burned all the way down to his stomach, and his scalp started prickling immediately. "Ah," he complained. "It is worse than I thought. This isn't food. Why is my cook trying to poison me?"

"He's trying to make you sweat," Alchiq said, favoring Ögedei with his unwavering gaze.

Ögedei stared at his old guard for a moment and then, trying his best to ignore the pain still lacing his throat, he scooped up several of the floating pieces of fish with the spoon. "You used to drink with me," he said around a mouthful of fish. "In fact, I remember you being able to drink *more* than me."

"I do too, my Khan," Alchiq replied.

"But not anymore."

Alchiq shook his head slowly.

Ögedei sighed. "Now I understand why Chucai was eager to let you close to me again." His stomach quailed as he filled his spoon with more broth. "I will need some distraction if I am to get this all down," he said. "Tell me of the West. My sons and their cousins are conquering it in my name, but I know so little about it." He laughed. "Did you ever imagine that our empire would be so vast that there would parts of it that I have never seen?"

"I did not, my Khan."

"My father did." A huge sigh welled up from his belly, and he shuddered as it worked its way out of his body. His cheeks felt wet, and he swiped a hand across his face. "This soup," he laughed raggedly, "it is very spicy."

"It is, my Khan." Alchiq had the grace to look away.

smoke signals

A TRIO OF BILLOWING columns of gray smoke marred the otherwise clear sky. The late afternoon sun winked through the twisting plumes, and Dietrich shook his head in disbelief as his horse galloped around a copse of oak trees that hugged a bend in the river.

The bridge was on fire.

No wind stirred the scene, and the pluming smoke billowed and roiled at its own whim. The plain near the bridge had been flattened by the passage of so many horses and men that it was nothing more than a flat field between the high banks of the river and the verge of a narrow band of trees that demarked fallow fields to the west. There was no shelter on this plain—it was exposed ground that Dietrich had hoped to cover swiftly before his Mongol pursuers could get within arrow range. His goal had been the bridge, but that hope died in his breast as soon as he realized where the smoke was coming from.

The road to Hünern was blocked.

Desperate, Dietrich urged his horse toward the river, pulling up short of the steep incline of the bank. Had he the presence of mind when they'd earlier crossed, he might have paid more attention to the depth and speed of the water. To misjudge either would be the death of him, especially dressed as he was in armor, and he did not have time to discard it. With the Mongols at his back, he dared not even try. He could force his horse into the water, but the animal would probably drown trying to carry him and swim. It was too great a risk, and it would take too long to discard his maille.

He heard the Mongols coming, their voices echoing with equal parts glee and anger. Dietrich suspected they would not kill him quickly.

His horse snorted and tossed its head. It sensed his panic and wanted to get away from the smoke. Dietrich glanced at the bridge one last time, his brain struggling to put together a viable plan, and his brow furrowed as his frenzied mind finally focused on a fundamental peculiarity of the scene.

The smoke was pouring from a quartet of squat barrels. There was no real fire, just lots and lots of smoke. Dietrich tugged on the reins and urged his horse toward the bridge. The animal balked, and in a flash Dietrich understood the nature of the obstruction.

The smoke would keep the horses away, but the bridge was intact. He couldn't ride across, but he could walk. In fact, if he could move one or two of the barrels, he might be able to lead his horse across.

* * *

After a quick glance to make sure they weren't looking at him, Rutger ignored the guards as they became agitated. They were looking behind him, and if he looked, he suspected that he would see the rising plumes of smoke from the bridge. The fires had been lit. Everything was going to happen in short order now. He allowed a tiny grin to crease his lips as he kept his head down. He was within bowshot of the walls. The plan could still come undone.

He heard the sound of the horses approaching, and the pair flashed past him. They were Mongol ponies, with a pair of stocky

Mongols clinging to the saddles. He offered a silent prayer to the Virgin as the pair approached the gates. *Let them pass.* One of the guards shouted down to the men at the gate as the others jabbered and gesticulated at the approaching pair.

Sentries from the bridge, bringing news.

Wood rattled behind the walls, and with a groan the heavy gate creaked open. The two sentries galloped toward the gate as Rutger gathered up the reins of his stolid dray horse. His knuckles burned, but he clenched the straps tight in his fists.

As the two horsemen reached the gate, they suddenly pulled back hard on their reins. Their horses jerked and bucked at the sudden bite in their mouths, and everything became chaotic at the gate. The two horsemen slid off their mounts, and sliding steel from their sleeves, they slit the throats of their steeds.

Rutger snapped his reins and shouted at his draft horse, spooking it. Behind him, beneath the heavy tarp covering the bed of his wagon, he heard the pair of hidden Shield-Brethren stirring. Slapping the reins again and again, he drove his startled horse toward the open gate.

The first Mongol sentry died with a surprised look still on his face as one of the two new arrivals—Shield-Brethren, wearing the clothing and armor of Mongol warriors—drew his sword and hacked the man's head from his shoulder in a single, fluid strike. The second sentry had lifted his spear into a ready position, but the weapon was useless against the second knight's thrown hatchet. The hand ax struck him in the face, knocking his conical helmet askew and splitting his skull.

In the sentry towers, the four Mongol archers were hurriedly readying their bows, and Rutger spared only a quick glance at them as his horse and cart closed in on the confusion at the gate. Two of the guards jerked back and disappeared from view as arrows launched from hidden Shield-Brethren positions near the Black Wall struck them, and the remaining pair ducked out of sight behind the mud wall.

And then Rutger was at the gate. His horse tried to avoid the two dead horses, but it was hampered by the heavy cart and its cargo. The horse stumbled, and the cart lurched as its wheels struck the unmoving mass of a dead horse. The horse screamed and reared, flailing with its front hooves, and the Mongol sentry, standing in front of the panicked horse, jabbed it with his spear.

The sentry realized almost immediately that he was focusing on the wrong target, and he tried to pull his spear back, but the point was lodged in the chest of the horse. When a Shield-Brethren sword caught him under the chin and slit his throat, he died with a disappointed frown on his face.

The two Shield-Brethren in the cart threw off the oiled tarp cover that had been covering them and leaped from the wagon, swords drawn. They joined the pair disguised as Mongol riders, and the remaining Mongol guards found themselves outnumbered.

Rutger reached behind him and snatched up the longsword lying in the bed of the cart. It was Andreas's blade, and the worn impressions of the younger man's hand in the leather grip only made him grip the weapon more firmly. With two large swings he cut the tethers and straps holding horse and cart together. The dray horse, bleeding copiously from the spear wound in its chest, staggered a few steps away from the gate and collapsed.

"*Alalazu!*" Rutger shouted, raising his sword and signaling to the men who were hidden in the rubble of Hünern. They came, pouring out of the alleys and shattered doorways, a ragged host of armored knights, swords and axes and spears held ready.

He scrambled down from the wagon, crossed the threshold of the open gate, and raised his eyes to the guard towers. The surviving sentries were hiding from his archers, and as he looked up, another flight of arrows skipped and bounced off the wall and wooden braces of the sentry towers. Of the two surviving guards, only one was still unhurt. Shooting back at the Shield-Brethren archers meant standing long enough to become a target, and since the fracas at the gate had begun, retreating to the ground meant closing with the invading Shield-Brethren. They had panicked, and the sole survivor hadn't realized he could shoot down at the men *inside* the gate yet.

He cast about for how to climb up to the tower and spotted the narrow stairs on the right side of the gate. As his four men clashed with the remaining Mongol gate sentries, he ran for the steps, taking them two at a time. The Mongol guard saw him coming, and stood up, reaching for his spear.

Rutger paused, a half dozen steps from the top, and stared up at the snarling Mongol. The man coughed suddenly, the anger draining from his face, and the spear slipped out of his hands. He coughed a second time, blood flecking his lips, and he stepped forward, his foot coming down on empty space. He fell off the wall, and Rutger counted three arrows jutting from his back as he plummeted to the ground.

Rutger continued up the stairs, pulling a strip of red cloth from within his dirty shirt. He waved it over his head as he crested the tower, and when the fluttering banner was not immediately pierced with arrows, he stood tall and proud, waving the banner wildly. *"Alalazu!"* he shouted.

The second wave came, sprinting across the pomerium. His archers, coming forward to provide support for the knight initiates who were already inside the walls. They scrambled over the wagon and the dead horses, pouring into the Mongol camp.

They had taken the gate. Now they had to hold it.

* * *

As soon as they heard Rutger's battle cry, Styg and Eilif rose from their supine positions next to the wall and darted up the embedded stakes. Styg pulled himself up to the narrow top of the wall, lay flat, and then swung his legs up and over, letting his momentum carry the rest of his body along. He bent his knees to absorb the shock of landing on the hard ground. As Eilif thumped to the ground beside him, he eased his sword out of the scabbard strapped to his back.

The attack on the gate would draw most of the Mongols' attention, leaving them free to find and free the Khan's captive fighters. Rutger's plan called for the warriors of Christendom to break the Mongols' spirit, and there were two prongs to their assault. The first attack was a bold initiative against the front gate of the Mongol compound, a noisy assault intended to slay as many Mongols as possible before the knights were overwhelmed by the Mongols' superior numbers. The second strike was more precise: free the prisoners and point them at the Khan's private tent. Of all the fighting men present, the captives had the most incentive to risk what would probably be a suicide mission.

It was the sort of mission Andreas would have loved, and Styg hoped they could execute it well enough to honor Andreas's sacrifice. *Virgin steady my hand*, he prayed, *that I might do even half as well as he.*

Eilif freed his blade as well, and with a nod they crept into the maze of tents, paddocks, and cages that made up the Mongol encampment. This area had been uncultivated land before the Mongols arrived—open meadows and fields of wild grasses—and the native grasses had been trampled so thoroughly that only tenacious clumps of parched weeds still grew around the bases of some of the tents.

Here and there, men would pop out of these tents—Hans had referred to them as *ger*. With helmets askew and weapons bared, the Mongols would race for the sounds of violence at a mad, disorganized dash. Styg and Eilif moved slowly and stealthily, freezing whenever panicked warriors dashed for the gate, hoping to remain unobserved. The Virgin was watching over them, shielding them from the eyes of the alarmed Mongols, but such favor would not last indefinitely.

According to Hans, the *ger* most likely holding the prisoners was rectangular with orange walls, and it was located within the second rank of tents along the southern wall. They had tried to pick a spot to climb the walls as close as possible, but they still had to hunt through the maze to find the one *ger*.

It was a race. Could they find the prisoners before being discovered?

Eilif hissed, and Styg caught sight of movement behind the half-opened flaps of the *ger* beside him. A tall Mongol with a long mustache ducked out of the tent and stopped in his tracks, staring at Styg for a long, unblinking moment, and then his face broke into an ugly smile.

Styg darted forward, and the Mongol ducked back, disappearing into the darkness of the tent as he dodged Styg's thrust. When he returned he had a blade of his own. And a friend.

The first Mongol lunged at him, and Styg responded by side-stepping the man's attack, bashing the blade even farther to the side, and then snapping his own sword straight at the Mongol's face. He buried a good three inches in the man's forehead, and when he jerked his hands back and down, teeth and bits of skull ripped free along with his blade.

The second Mongol had to step around his dead friend, and he used that wide step to drive a powerful two-handed backswing. Styg's hands and blade were low—he couldn't get them up quickly enough to block the Mongol's attack—and he swept a leg back as he raised his sword nearly parallel with the Mongol's stroke. The curved sword slammed against the quillons of his longsword, and Styg kept moving, pushing off against the Mongol's blade. His hands rotated, right over left, and his blade whirled around into a diagonal slice that connected with the back of the Mongol's neck.

As the Mongol collapsed, blood spurting from a cut that nearly separated head from trunk, Styg blinked and remembered to breathe. His heart pounded in his chest like a thunderous drum. The attack had happened so quickly. If he had stood and thought about what he should have done, either of his Mongol attackers would have succeeded in cutting him instead. He had simply reacted, letting his training guide his arms and sword. *You must stop thinking about holding your sword*, Andreas had told them during one of their first training sessions. *It is an extension of you*, here *and* here. Touching his head and his chest. *We will do these exercises until you understand this. I want to forget all of your names and see only* swordsmen *on this field*.

Styg shook off the thoughts, sensing the melancholic trap that a fighter could easily fall into after combat. He had used his sword to take a life. That act changed a man—there was no doubt of that in his mind—but to stop and dwell on that transformation would be as foolish as *thinking* while fighting. If he survived, he could dwell on his first blooding all he liked.

He looked about for some sign of Eilif, and saw none. *The orange tent*, he reminded himself, and he jogged to his right, getting away from the two corpses before someone stumbled upon the scene. If Eilif was still undetected, Styg mused, it might fall to him to lead the Mongols away from the tent to give his friend enough time to free the prisoners.

That is, if he hadn't been spotted.

Continue with the mission, he chided himself. He came around the curve of another tent, and was surprised to find a thick post standing in the middle of an open space. A man, his hands bound by leather straps that, in turn, were lashed to an iron ring set in the top of the post, half leaned, half sat on the ground. His hair was long and unkempt, and he wore no shirt. Styg could make out the puckered edges of a still suppurating wound on the man's back.

A coarse shout sounded behind Styg, and he glanced back toward the tent with the two dead men. The bodies had been found, and already a Mongol was running toward him, sword drawn.

Styg darted toward the block of wood and, as he came abreast of it, he swung his sword. The blade severed the leather straps, and he pivoted around the block, swinging his sword in a wide arc in his wake. The Mongol drew up short, avoiding Styg's wild swing, and once the blade had passed, he leaped forward with a howl. Styg caught the Mongol's cut on the strong of his blade and let the momentum of his enemy's attack drive his pommel upward and into his enemy's face with skull-cracking force.

The freed prisoner stared uncomprehendingly at the senseless Mongol lying on the ground next to him. Styg kicked the Mongol's curved sword toward the man, hoping the sight of the weapon would bestir the man. The man reached for the weapon finally, fingers wrapped around the hilt with a practiced familiarity.

We all know what to do with a sword, Styg thought as he moved on, seeking the orange tent.

He caught sight of a piece of orange felt, and relief washed over him that he hadn't been running in the wrong direction. Drab and worn down with mold and rain, the tent's coloration was not unlike that of a rotting gourd, left too long in the field.

His elation was momentary, cut short by more shouts behind him. He glanced over his shoulder and spotted three more Mongols rapidly approaching. They all carried spears.

His hand tightened on his hilt, memories of watching Andreas fight the Livonian in the Circus filling his head.

Spears against swords. Not a good match.

* * *

The smoke burned Dietrich's eyes and throat as he slid off his horse and dashed toward the bridge. He didn't have time to figure out who had put these barrels on the bridge or why. The Mongols were coming, and if he could clear a path, he might still escape.

His boots clattered on the wooden boards of the bridge as he approached the first barrel. Up close, he could hear the hissing frustration of the fires inside the nearest barrel as it tried to devour the green and wet wood that was the source of the smoke. The barrel was surrounded by a primitive fire circle, and he kicked the broken rock aside. Clenching his eyes shut against the billowing smoke, he wished he still had his cloak to cover his nose and mouth. Trying to breathe as little as possible, he bent and shoved with his shoulder. The barrel slid across the bridge, rocking slightly, and he staggered against it, inhaling a lungful of smoke.

Coughing, his eyes watering, he hunched over. His eyes were filled with tears, and his throat ached, but he couldn't stop to hack up all the smoke he had inhaled. He had to shove the barrel off the bridge. He had to keep moving. The Mongols were coming. He had to get his leg to move.

Wiping tears from his eyes, he stared stupidly at his recalcitrant leg. He had removed the arrow earlier. The one that hadn't penetrated his armor. Why was it back? Forgetting about the smoking barrel for a moment, Dietrich reached down and touched the long shaft of the arrow protruding from his right thigh.

It was longer than the other one, he dimly realized, and the fletching was different.

Through the haze of smoke, he saw horsemen approaching. More arrows began to land around him, skipping off the planks of the bridge, burying themselves into the wood of the barrel next to him. Shorter arrows, fired from Mongol bows.

"No," he coughed. *This isn't fair. This isn't the way it was supposed to end.*

He wasn't going to die like Volquin. That wasn't his destiny. He grabbed his stiff leg and hauled it with him as he staggered around the barrel. He was going to survive. He was going to escape.

An arrow punched him in the shoulder, spinning him around, and he tried to arrest his fall, but his right leg crumpled under him. A brilliant spike of pain shot through his hip and made him cry out. His head rebounded off the bridge and his vision darkened. *No. I will not die today. God is protecting me.*

Sprawled on the bridge, Dietrich found he could breathe more easily as there was less smoke. He could see more readily as well. The edge of the bridge wasn't too far away. Could he crawl that far? He dragged himself through the talus scattered across the bridge, one agonizing inch at a time. Arrows continued to fall around him, and he dimly heard shouts and the clanging sound of steel on steel. The Mongols had been engaged by another host, and if his world had not been reduced to nothing more than this painful crawl, he might have wondered who had sprung this trap on the Mongol host.

It was only as he tipped over the edge of the bridge and fell into the river that he caught sight of the arrow in his leg again. The white fletching. Chicken feathers.

A Templar arrow.

And then the water closed over him, and he knew nothing else.

ThE MousE's TRAIL

ONFERRATO'S SEDAN CHAIR had gotten them into the compound, though Monferrato had been dismayed to learn that he missed the vote and apoplectic to realize that a simple priest had been elected. Ocyrhoe thought the cardinal's eyes were going to pop out of his head when he learned that the College of Cardinals had not immediately invalidated the election.

"How is this possible?" Monferrato had spluttered to the ostiarius who was leading them through the dark halls of the Castel Sant'Angelo.

"You had best speak to Cardinal Fieschi," the tall ostiarius said, his pace quickening as if he could escape further interrogation.

"Where is he?" Monferrato demanded.

The ostiarius slowed, confusion showing on his face. "He is with the other cardinals," he said. "But I thought—"

"We do," Léna said smoothly. She indicated Ocyrhoe and Ferenc. "However, these are longtime companions of the Pope. He will want to see them immediately. After which, you may escort Cardinal Monferrato to see Cardinal Fieschi." Unlike the cardinal, her voice was calm and soothing, and it had an immediate effect on the ostiarius, who nodded eagerly and started walking again.

Monferrato started spluttering again, his eyes bulging even more, and Léna forestalled any further discussion by putting a finger to her lip and shaking her head.

Ocyrhoe grabbed Ferenc's hand and hurried after the ostiarius. She didn't need to be part of their argument; she only wanted to see Father Rodrigo.

Their guide took them to a hall with multiple doors, and he chose a small one on the left—it seemed terribly unassuming to Ocyrhoe to be the door that led to the Pope. But she said nothing as the ostiarius opened the door and indicated they were to enter. Still holding Ferenc's hand, she stepped through the door into the narrow chamber beyond.

Ocyrhoe was struck by the difference in Father Rodrigo, meeting him this time. First, of course, he was physically much healthier—which made him look younger. But more than that, he radiated beatitude—an emotional stability that she could not associate with the man she'd first met.

She enjoyed watching the affectionate blandishments Ferenc and Bendrito showered on each other. She could not follow the language they spoke, but she could read their faces and body language, and sense the emotional pitching and tossing that Ferenc was going through as he listened to Father Rodrigo speak.

Finally, after perhaps a quarter hour, Father Rodrigo turned to her and began to speak in the language of Rome. "Sister, Ferenc tells me you have been good to him and he is fond of you," the new Pope began.

"That is mutual, Father. Your Holiness," she corrected herself without hurry.

"He tells me that you are a native of the city and that you can help us to escape."

"They are holding you captive here, then?"

"Ferenc tells me you saw me speaking in the marketplace. Did it look like I left there by my own free will?" He gestured around the room. "I have just been made *Summus Pontifex Ecclesiae Universalis,* yet, I reside in a small, windowless room with no pot to defecate in, eating cold food. Do you think I am here by my own choice?"

Ocyrhoe squirmed a bit under the intensity of Father Rodrigo's gaze, hoping that he wasn't suggesting what she feared he was. Based on Ferenc's gleeful expression, though, she suspected that *escape* was exactly what Father Rodrigo had in mind.

* * *

By the time the new Pontiff had finished his private audience with the strange hunter-boy from the north, a temporary suspension of the endless canonical discussions among the cardinals had been called; everyone agreed to turn in for the night, and to resume conversations, arguments, investitures, or whatever else the future might hold, starting the next morning.

Ocyrhoe and Léna were put together in a room on the first floor; at the new Pope's insistence, Ferenc slept in his room. Helmuth and Cardinal Monferrato were also put together in another guest quarter, closer to the rest of the cardinals.

Father Rodrigo's room, not surprisingly, had a guard placed in front of it. That did not worry Ocyrhoe. In the dark hours of the morning, with a small kitchen knife and a kneading blade she had purloined from the castle kitchen, she let herself out of the room. Léna had not stirred as she had slipped out of bed and made her way to the door. Ocyrhoe did not feel that what she was about to do was at all contrary to her identity as a Binder, but still, she sensed Léna would discourage her from following her instincts.

Her plan was simple enough—the sort of misdirection that came naturally to her as a child of the streets. Like a mouse, she laid out a trail for the guard to follow. She planted a number of obvious clues— a piece of torn fabric, some bits of wax from a candle, a wedge of plaster, and powder from that plaster—down the hall, around another corner, and aimed directly at the door of Cardinal Fieschi's room.

When she finished her false trail, she crept back to the corner near Father Rodrigo's room. The guard was leaning against the wall, his lack of vigilance suggesting he had no idea who he was guarding. She tossed a pebble in his direction, making sure it bounced and rattled against the base of the wall. As soon as the guard roused himself, she scampered noisily away from the corner. There was a dark niche not far from the next corner, deep enough for her to hide in, and she pressed herself into the slot shortly before the guard stumbled around the corner.

She was counting on the guard's boredom, that he would be more interested in following a trail of evidence that would result in the capture of a sneaky thief than the endless monotony of guard duty.

The guard paused as he came around the corner, looking around cautiously. Ocyrhoe held her breath, waiting for him to spot the piece of torn cloth. He did, and bowing over like a hound, he began to creep along the hall, his eyes clearly scanning for more clues. He passed by her hiding place without even looking in her direction. In another few heartbeats, he reached the corner and disappeared from view.

Ocyrhoe darted out of her hiding place and silently—like a mouse—ran back to Father Rodrigo's chamber. She quietly picked the lock on the door with the kitchen knife, pushed up the simple latch with the dough blade, then slipped into Father Rodrigo's small room and shut the door behind her. Ferenc and Rodrigo were already awake and dressed. A candle stub burned by the bed, throwing their shadows up against the high stone and plaster of the ceiling.

Father Rodrigo smiled benevolently. Did nothing disturb the man now? Perhaps a Pope was beyond fear.

Ferenc looked nervous and happy to see her.

Already she was loosening her satchel to pull out the map she had drawn. The moon was low but the compound in general never really slept; once she got them safely outside, away from people who would recognize their faces, they could walk off openly without causing suspicion. All the same, the map showed the most indirect, untraceable, forgotten pathways leading out of the city. Beyond the city walls, she could no longer help them.

She smiled in the candlelight and reached out for Ferenc's hand. *Good-bye, my friend*, she signed, and then threw her arms around him in an embrace.

Ferenc went first, the idea being that the sight of the young Magyar might not raise as much alarm immediately as the sight of Father Rodrigo wandering around the halls. Father Rodrigo paused at the door to the room. "Will you stay here?" he asked, his eyes bright in the candlelight.

"Here?" Ocyrhoe whispered.

Father Rodrigo nodded. "An empty room is an easy mystery to solve, but a room that contains something other than what is expected will be confusing." A small laugh slipped out of him. "Is that not what we find in our hearts?" he asked, though Ocyrhoe thought he wasn't speaking to her. "We fear we are empty vessels, but we aren't, are we?"

"No, Father," she whispered. An oddly familiar and yet foreign shiver ran through her body, not unlike the sensation she had felt when she had first laid eyes on the priest in the marketplace"God bless you, child," Father Rodrigo said, resting his hand on her forehead. His flesh was warm and dry. And then he was gone.

Ocyrhoe waited in the empty room, feeling a little bit empty herself. What a bizarre and unexpected few days this had been! What unimaginable outcomes had developed from it!

She looked around the room in the flickering light of the candle stub. I'll sleep here then, she decided. *Tomorrow morning, when they come for him, they will find me instead. They will be furious, but Léna will not allow them to hurt me.*

She was confident of that.

She blew the candle out, pulled back the cover of the bed, and snuck under it. It was much nicer than the bedding she and Léna had been given. This would actually be quite nice, she decided, sleeping in a Pope's bed, and allowed herself to smile. From the Emperor's camp to the Pope's bedroom in a single day! Sleep began to tug at her mind, and she welcomed it.

Until she heard voices outside the room. Male voices, and one of them a little bit familiar—Cardinal Fieschi. She looked around. There was no place in here to hide, and no way to escape before he entered.

An empty room is an easy mystery. Something unexpected is altogether more confusing.

She flung aside the covers, scrambled out of the bed, pulled the covers back in place, and knelt beside the bed in a position of prayer.

The door opened.

Fieschi entered, carrying a torch, already incensed. "A thief? In the palace? Are you a fool?" Handing the torch off to the guard behind him, he flicked the latch. "It's not even—"

He had spotted her, and the change that came over him was frightening in its ferocity. He lunged at her, teeth bared, hands like claws, murder in his eyes.

THE ARCHERY COMPETITION

G ANSUKH FELT WELL rested, all things considered. He had not expected to sleep that night, and it was only by a stroke of luck that he had stumbled upon the fact that Chucai had left the camp. Chucai's *ger* had seemed like a perfect place to hide from Munokhoi.

The ex-*Torguud* captain had nearly assaulted Gansukh at the fights, barely managing to contain his volcanic temper. Gansukh was certain Munokhoi was waiting for him somewhere in the camp, and if the positions were reversed, he would have certainly lain in wait near his *ger*. He had been of half a mind to sleep in Munokhoi's *ger*, figuring that the ex-*Torguud* captain's rage would keep him alert and fixed in place outside of Gansukh's *ger*, but in the end that had felt too risky of a proposition.

What he needed was another opportunity like that of the night before to publicly mock the ex-*Torguud* captain without being seen as challenging him. It wasn't a very clever plan, but it would get the job done as long as there were witnesses—people who would attest that Munokhoi attacked first, without provocation—then any response on his part, including a fatal one, would be seen as self-defense. No one would be fooled, but propriety would be maintained.

He had learned that much from court—the maintenance of propriety. The phrase even sounded like something from one of Lian's endless scrolls. The *understanding*—the unspoken rule of acceptable behavior—was that it didn't matter who knew what you had done, as long as you gave the court an excuse to pretend otherwise. And if you took care of a persistent thorn, you were given latitude.

Of course, this was all predicated on Munokhoi playing along—at least with the part where he was supposed to lose his temper publicly—but this plan didn't leave as bad a taste in his mouth as the option of assassinating Munokhoi.

He was running out of time, however. The *Khagan* was supposed to leave for his hunt today.

"Ho, Gansukh!" It was Tarbagatai, eager as ever. The mountain archer jogged up to Gansukh, his round face nearly bursting with some irrepressible news. His face fell slightly when he realized Gansukh's hand was on the hilt of his knife. "Did you not sleep well, friend?" Tarbagatai asked. "You seem jumpy."

Gansukh relaxed. "I slept quite well, in fact. It's just..."

"Oh," Tarbagatai said, nodding. "It's—yes, the fights... I...I think I understand." His brow furled, betraying the fact that he probably did not have as much clarity as he claimed.

Gansukh realized the mountain clan archer wasn't that much younger than himself—only a few years. *What a difference those years made*, he thought. *I would be just like him if I hadn't gone to Kozelsk, if Chagatai Khan hadn't picked me as his envoy.*

"I'm sorry," Tarbagatai said, dropping his gaze. "I have said something to offend you."

"No, no," Gansukh assured him, brushing aside his melancholic thoughts. "Forgive me. I am...distracted this morning. It is the excitement of this..." he struggled to focus his attention, "of the *Khagan*'s hunt."

"Yes," Tarbagatai agreed. "But not today."

"What?"

"You haven't heard? The *Khagan*"—Tarbagatai mimed drinking from a cup—"We will go tomorrow." He brightened. "I have never participated in a hunt with the *Khagan* before."

Gansukh reflected on the hunting technique typically used by the *Khagan*. "I fear it will..." He paused, all too aware of the other man's enthusiasm. "It will be fantastic," he amended, clapping Tarbagatai on the arm. Privately he was relieved to have another day in the camp. Another chance to draw Munokhoi out...

Tarbagatai smiled, losing the consternation that had been clinging to his face. "We could...practice," he said, trying to appear nonchalant. "To be sure that we are ready for tomorrow."

"Practice?" Gansukh asked.

Tarbagatai gestured at the bow slung over Gansukh's shoulder. "Our archery. You have your bow with you. You wouldn't have to borrow one this time."

Gansukh touched the horn-and-sinew shape of his father's bow. "Oh, yes, I suppose," he feigned a look of sudden realization, "but I am supposed to pick flowers with some of Second Wife's attendants this morning. They wanted someone along to ensure no wild animal disturbed them."

"Of course," Tarbagatai said, clearly crestfallen. "Very well, then, Gansukh. Perhaps some other time."

Gansukh kept a straight face until the mountain archer had turned his back and started to walk away, and then he relented, releasing the laugh that was clamoring to get out of his mouth. "I am joking," Gansukh said in response to the hurt look on Tarbagatai's face. "I would enjoy a rematch. I think that is an excellent idea."

Tarbagatai guffawed. "When I saw you with your bow, I hoped you would," he said, grinning and ducking his head like a tongue-tied boy talking to his first courtesan.

"Yes, we do think alike, don't we?" Gansukh said. "A free afternoon. Good weather. It is a perfect opportunity to match our skills once more." He offered Tarbagatai a guileless smile, and he let it stretch wider in response to the other man's grin. He felt a twinge of shame for lying to Tarbagatai, but he couldn't admit to the mountain archer the real reason he was carrying his bow and sword with him around camp.

One more day.

He hoped it would be enough.

* * *

Jachin was uncharacteristically quiet when she returned from the *Khagan's ger.* Lian shooed the other attendants out of Second Wife's sumptuous *ger* and attended to the distracted woman herself. She helped Jachin out of her silk gown and into her favorite robe. It was plain and unadorned—not the proper costume for the *Khagan's* second wife—but she knew it was warm and soft. Its simplicity also allowed Jachin to put aside her role as wife of the *Khagan,* and Lian suspected Jachin wanted some respite from the burden of her office.

Let us just be girls, she thought as she quietly combed out the snarls in Jachin's long hair.

"Do you love him?" Jachin asked suddenly. She had said nothing since Lian had sequestered the two of them in the *ger,* quietly accepting Lian's ministrations. Lost in thought.

"Who, my Lady?" Lian asked quietly. Her hands had hesitated for only a fraction of a second with the comb.

"The *Khagan* calls him *young pony.* That one. What is his name?"

"Gansukh, my Lady."

Jachin turned her body and looked at Lian. "Do you love him?" she repeated.

"I am but a humble attendant to the *Khagan*'s court," Lain demurred, dropping her head into a more submissive pose. "I would not assume to love a proud Mongol warrior."

Jachin grabbed her chin and raised her head. She peered intently at Lian's eyes, and Lian was surprised at Jachin's expression. She had thought Second Wife would have been angry or annoyed at her refusal to answer, but what she saw in Jachin's own gaze was a frank honesty, a plain desire for companionship, for *understanding*.

"Yes, my Lady," Lian said quietly, gently removing herself from Second Wife's grip. "I do."

Jachin dropped her hands to her lap, fussed with them for a moment as if she didn't quite know what to do with them. "Does he love you in return?"

"I...I think so," Lian replied.

Jachin nodded. She gestured for Lian to give her the comb. "Turn around," she said. "I want to brush your hair." Jachin's face was composed, her lips firm. Lian complied, and she sat quietly as Second Wife took out the ornamental sticks in her hair and began to brush it. "Tell me about him," Jachin said.

Lian did—haltingly at first, but the words came more easily after a while. Jachin even laughed lightly when she told the story about the dancer in the market and the bells.

"Ögedei loved me," Jachin said quietly when Lian finished. "Once." She gave a tiny laugh, choking back some other emotion.

"I know, my Lady," Lian said. She glanced down and noticed two dots of moisture darkening her robe. She carefully wiped her cheek so no more tears would fall.

* * *

On the other side of the river, a long meadow sloped down to a sparse wood of alder and cedar. The *Torguud* had set up a series of targets—small shields lashed to spears that were rammed into the ground—ranging across the field to the edge of the wood, and as Gansukh peered at the tree line, he noted more targets within the shelter of the trees. Each of the targets had a slash of red paint across it, signifying the heart of the imaginary enemy.

A handful of *Torguud* were already practicing, and Gansukh and Tarbagatai milled about somewhat aimlessly while they waited. Gansukh kept scanning the forest below them as well as the line of scattered *ger* on the other side of the river, keeping an eye out for Munokhoi.

"That is a very nice bow," Tarbagatai said, breaking their silence.

Gansukh unslung the weapon in question and offered it to Tarbagatai, who ran his hands along the smooth shape of the bow. "Is this goat horn?" the younger man asked after his examination.

Gansukh nodded. "My grandfather killed it so that my father could have its horns. This is the first bow he ever made, and when I..." he paused, recalling the story he had told Lian about his first kill. "When I came of age, it became mine."

"I made this one," Tarbagatai said, offering Gansukh his bow. "It took much longer than it should have."

Gansukh admired the shape of Tarbagatai's bow. It was darker than his, made from some wood other than birch, though the *siyah* were light, like the tips of antelope ears. The string was looser than he preferred, and he wondered if Tarbagatai had switched his string yet. The air, while warm in the sun, was generally colder than it had been in Karakorum. He would need to use a tighter string. *Or maybe he just likes a little more play.* Gansukh toyed with the tension in the bowstring a little longer, and then handed the weapon back to its owner. "The product of your own hard work. It is an excellent bow. I hope that it serves you well."

"Is there going to be shooting or talking here today?" The new speaker was a stocky man, wide in the neck and gregarious in his expressions. He and a half dozen other *Torguud* had wandered up while Gansukh and Tarbagatai had been admiring each other's bows. The newcomer planted his feet wide and put his hands on his hips as he voiced his jovial query. He looked like nothing more than a smaller version of Namkhai, and Gansukh realized the similarity was not accidental. Namkhai had a cousin in the *Torguud*. *What is his name?*

Tarbagatai came to his rescue. "There will be more talking than shooting now that you are here, Sübegei."

"Is that so?" Sübegei laughed. "Someone has to bore your enemies so they will stand still long enough for you to hit them." He gestured toward the archery targets. "Come on, you two. We heard there was going to be a contest."

"Still have some money from last night, eh?" Gansukh asked.

"I understand you have forty-nine more cows than you know what to do with," Sübegei said. "Maybe we can help you part with some of them."

"What makes you think I know what to do with the *first* one?" Gansukh said, and the group laughed uproariously. He grinned at Tarbagatai and motioned the younger man toward the crooked line of dark rocks that marked the edge of archery field. "How shall we do this?" he asked.

Sübegei overheard him and offered his own interpretation of the rules. "Seven arrows," he said. "Tarbagatai gets dark fletching; Gansukh will have the light-colored fletching." He gestured at the archers who had just finished shooting, and they started to dig through their quivers to assemble the requisite arrows. There were some friendly disagreements about what constituted *light* and *dark* among the arrows.

Sübegei rolled his eyes and shrugged at Gansukh's inquiring glance. "You'll be judged for speed and accuracy," he continued, ignoring the altogether too-complicated process of arrow selection.

"The archer who finishes first will be awarded one additional point, and then we'll examine the targets. Does that sound fair?"

Gansukh gave Tarbagatai back his bow and received his own in turn. "That sounds fair," he said as he slipped the string loose and bent his bow to restring it properly. Tarbagatai agreed too, and both men stepped up to the edge of the range and collected their arrows. Gansukh took the other arrows out of his quiver, placing them on the ground, and arranged his seven carefully so they were ready to be pulled. He noticed Tarbagatai lagging behind him, the younger man carefully copying every motion—the mountain archer wasn't going to make the same mistake he had last time when he had failed to set up his arrows for rapid shooting.

Gansukh nocked the first arrow and looked down the range, checking the location of each of the targets. There were ten targets in all, but no more than two were at any given distance, and they started fairly close—not much more than ten strides away. He would start with the closest pair—that would allow him to gauge the distance more readily—and he suspected Tarbagatai would employ the same tactic. But Gansukh also suspected Tarbagatai would be seduced by possibility of the extra point for firing all his arrows first, and in his mind, Gansukh had already conceded that point. He knew Tarbagatai was faster, so he had to be more accurate.

"Quiet," Sübegei called behind him, and when the assembled soldiers didn't stop their chatter quickly enough, he raised his voice. "Shut up, you louts!"

Gansukh turned his head to the left and glanced at Tarbagatai; the mountain archer favored him with a tiny grin. "Are you ready?" Tarbagatai asked, and Gansukh nodded. As the crowd finally settled down, Gansukh returned his attention down range. The morning sun made the red paint gleam, and a slight breeze wafted up the rise. The conditions were perfect.

"Archers!" Sübegei cried. "Ready!" Gansukh raised his bow, pulling the string back to his ear. His shoulders were tight, and he tried to relax. He tried to focus on the first target, but something seemed amiss. A bead of sweat slid down the left side of his face, almost going into his eye, and he blinked heavily.

"Fire!" Sübegei shouted, and Tarbagatai let out a tiny grunt as he released his arrow.

Gansukh took one step back.

He heard a whisper of sound, the fluttering noise of an arrow as it passes. He sensed more than saw a black blur flying past him, moving from his left to his right. Without thinking, he stepped forward and turned, causing Tarbagatai to flinch, fumbling his second arrow. Gansukh ignored him, looking across the river for his target.

Looking for the source of the arrow that would have hit him if he hadn't taken that backward step.

Behind him the crowd was making noise—not all of it pleasant—and Tarbagatai had stepped back from the edge of the range, his eyes wide. Gansukh studiously ignored all of the distractions, his eyes scanning for some sign of Munokhoi.

He was out there. Gansukh hadn't imagined the arrow.

"Gansukh, hold," Sübegei tried to get his attention. "Put your bow down."

Growling in his throat, Gansukh lowered his arms and let out the tension in his bowstring. His eyes kept scanning the row of *ger*, looking for any sign of movement. Finally, he relented, letting out a pent-up rush of air. "I am sorry, Tarbagatai," he said, looking toward the mountain archer. "That was very unsporting of me. I was..." he cast about for some suitable explanation, "momentarily dazzled by the sun. Disoriented." He let out a short bark of laughter. "I was so frightened by your first arrow that I thought I was in the midst of a terrifying battle."

Tarbagatai raised an eyebrow, but the tension remained in his face and shoulders. "You are a bad liar, Gansukh."

"Bah," Gansukh said, dismissing Tarbagatai's claim. "It is a good thing to be bad at, don't you think?"

Tarbagatai managed a weak grin.

Gansukh glanced at the row of *ger* again. "Shall we try again?" he asked, even though part of him wanted to charge across the river and search for the elusive Munokhoi. "I promise to be less frightened of your magnificent shooting."

Someone in the crowd groaned noisily, and a voice piped up: "Make him give you his bow if he does it again!"

Gansukh nodded in agreement. "Fair enough. You may have my bow if I am nothing less than virtuous in my shooting."

Tarbagatai tried to remain aloof, but his gaze lingered overlong on Gansukh's bow. "I suppose we can try again," he said.

Gansukh gestured at the crowd. "My opponent will need two more arrows," he called.

"Only one," Tarbagatai corrected. He pointed. "I'll keep that first one." Tarbagatai's first shot was dead center in the nearest target's red heart.

"Fair enough," Gansukh said, squinting at the target.

An arrow was provided, and Sübegei counted them off again. Gansukh shot slowly, striving for accuracy, and Tarbagatai took care with his shots as well, knowing that Gansukh would not be rushing. Still, in very little time, the quivers of both archers were empty.

"Extra point for Tarbagatai," Sübegei called. The crowd shouted, pleased with the performance of both men. "Let us go check the arrows," Sübegei said, and the crowd moved forward, sweeping both Tarbagatai and Gansukh up with it.

Gansukh let the group pass around him, and once the bulk of the men were past, he turned to his right and walked in a straight line, his eyes scanning the ground for the straight shaft of dark arrow.

He didn't have to walk far. Munokhoi's arrow was buried in the scrub grass, and only a short span of the shaft and the fletching were visible. Gansukh looked back, tracing the path of the arrow, and gauged from between which two *ger* Munokhoi had most likely shot the arrow. He stepped purposefully on the shaft, breaking it beneath his boot, and then went to join the others.

* * *

The flaps of Gansukh's *ger* sagged open like the slack mouth of a dead man, and Gansukh knew what he would find inside. He paused, out of direct line with the opening, and looked around once more, checking for any out of the ordinary movement.

He had seen no sign of Munokhoi since the incident with the arrow at the archery range, but he knew that meant little. The ex-*Torguud* captain was watching him, stalking him throughout the camp. Waiting for an opportunity to strike with impunity.

The fact that Munokhoi hadn't openly assaulted him meant the ex-captain was still aware of the consequences of assassinating another Mongol, especially one whose death the *Khagan* would notice. In some ways, that made him more dangerous.

Satisfied that there was no one watching him, Gansukh approached his *ger* and cautiously peeked inside. As he suspected, all of his gear was in disarray. Munokhoi had been here and had taken out his frustrations on Gansukh's belongings. Gansukh wrinkled his nose as he smelled the acrid stench of urine. Munokhoi had done more than shred his shirts and slash all of his water skins; he had pissed all over everything.

Gansukh sighed, and calmly laced up the flaps on his *ger*. He had come to Karakorum with nothing more than what fit in a pair of saddlebags on his horse; he could survive being reduced to that again. In some ways, Munokhoi's wanton destruction was a blessing—a reminder of who he really was. Most of the clothing he had acquired at Karakorum wasn't all that functional out on the open steppe, and Gansukh felt oddly free of the weight of those belongings.

I am a Mongol clansman. I belong outside—the steppes beneath my feet, Eternal Blue Sky above my head. I want nothing else.

He had his knife, his sword, his bow, and his horse. On the first night of the trip, he had sewn a tiny pocket on the inside of his favorite jacket—a home for the lacquer box and the sprig. At the time he hadn't given the urge to do so much thought, but now he was glad he had.

He did not understand the importance of the tiny twig, but it had meant something to the shaman and Ögedei. The sprig, in some ways, was the reason the *Khagan* was taking this trip. Ögedei had told him to hang on to it until the *Khagan* found himself worthy of it once more. *Worthy of what?* It didn't matter; it was Gansukh's job to keep it safe.

***

The afternoon shadows were getting long as Gansukh wandered past the fighters' cages. There were only six men left now, and they all had suffered minor injuries during the last round of bouts for the *Khagan*'s entertainment. The red-haired giant had lost a chunk out of his left forearm when his opponent had desperately tried to chew his way out of the giant's crushing bear hug. The one who braided his beard had almost lost an eye.

Gansukh drifted past Haakon's cage, watching the young man as he calmly and slowly performed a series of exercises that worked the muscles in his upper body. He had stripped off his ragged shirt, and the cut across his chest was red and swollen, but it looked like it wasn't infected. The bruise on his cheek had turned a sullen purple color.

Haakon noticed Gansukh and brought his hands together in the traditional greeting. Gansukh responded in kind, somewhat amused by the youth's efforts to learn the local customs. "Hai, Haakon," he said. "Your wound heals well?"

"Yes, friend Gansukh," Haakon replied. "I am a valuable cow." His accent had gotten better.

Gansukh couldn't help but grin. "That you are."

"Knife for me next time?"

Gansukh shook his head. "I'm sorry. I don't—" He realized Haakon wasn't speaking to him, and when he followed the Northerner's gaze, he found a gray-haired Mongol standing a few paces behind him. In a flash, Gansukh read his history: the slight bow to his legs, the deep lines around his eyes, and the seasoned darkness of his aged skin. This man had been a horse rider his entire life.

"I suspected he knew our tongue," the gray-haired man said as he came abreast Gansukh.

Bewildered, Gansukh tried to understand what had just transpired between the prisoner and the gray-haired rider. "Who are you?" he asked.

"My name is Alchiq," the rider said. "I was this one's age when Genghis Khan brought the clans together. I have served the empire ever since." He turned his attention to Gansukh. "You were at Kozelsk," he said, "with Batu Khan."

"I may have been," Gansukh said.

Alchiq offered him a smile that didn't go all the way to his eyes. "You were. You opened the gates so that the Khan's army could take their revenge for their fallen brothers."

Gansukh flinched. "You must be mistaken," he said. "I was just a scout. I never..."

Haakon was staring intently at him, studying Gansukh's face. Gansukh swallowed heavily and pushed away the memories of Kozelsk that were threatening to surface and changed the subject. "You gave the knife to the Kitayan."

Alchiq nodded. "I did." He too was watching Gansukh closely, watching for some reaction in Gansukh's eyes to his admission.

"Why?"

"To see how well this one could fight. To see what he would do if he was given an opportunity."

"An opportunity for what?"

"The *Torguud* captain—Namkhai—is a very large man," Alchiq said. He held up his fist, showing it to Haakon. "He has a big hand, yes?"

Haakon raised a hand and touched his bruised cheek. "Big hand," he echoed.

Alchiq walked up to the cage, his hand still clenched in a fist. "I know you, *Skjaldbræður*." He opened his hand and slapped the bars of the cage, grinning at Haakon's reaction.

Alchiq gestured for Gansukh to follow him, and when Gansukh opened his mouth to ask a question, Alchiq shook his head. The gray-haired man waited until they had passed the last cage before he spoke. "The boy listens too intently," he said by way of explanation. "He *spies* on us from his cage."

"That word you said. *Skold—*"

"*Skjaldbræður*," Alchiq corrected.

"What does it mean?"

"How long did Kozelsk hold Batu Khan at bay?" Alchiq asked, seeming to not hear Gansukh's question. "Seven weeks?"

"Something like that," Gansukh replied, somewhat flustered by the change in topic. "I don't recall exactly."

"And how many experienced fighters did that city have? Once the gates were open, how many hardened warriors did we find?" He poked Gansukh in the chest. "How many did *you* kill?"

Gansukh rolled his tongue around his mouth. "A handful," he lied.

Alchiq pursed his lips. "A *handful*? Batu let his army raze the city so that the West would know his anger at being denied, but the damage was done. There was a tiny garrison in that city, and the rest were old men, women, and children. They held off the entire might of the *Khagan*'s army for nearly two moons. Batu sent word back to Karakorum that he needed more men, that the West was so bountiful that his army could not carry all the wealth they were plundering. But that wasn't the truth, was it? The armies of the empire had gotten soft. They had become accustomed to their enemies running in fear when they saw the banners of the Mongol Empire. Subutai recognized the danger, but Batu did not. The other Khans did not." Alchiq jerked his head in the direction of Haakon's cage. "There are others like him. Other *Skjaldbrædur*. They will not yield to us. They will never stop fighting us."

"You've fought them," Gansukh said, realizing Alchiq had answered his previous question in a roundabout way.

Alchiq nodded. "Ten of them took on an entire *jaghun*. They lost one man. I killed him. I snuck up on him and broke him when he was collecting water." He let out a short laugh that was void of any humor. "And then I ran."

"There is no shame in that," Gansukh said.

"I was not seeking your approval, boy." Alchiq poked Gansukh in the chest again.

Gansukh caught Alchiq's finger and pushed his hand away. "I wasn't offering any," he snapped.

Alchiq brayed with laughter, and he slapped Gansukh with good humor on the arm. "Try not to confuse your enemies with your friends, *young pony*," he said. "I spent many years being angry at the wrong people, and now those years are gone. What do I have to show for it?"

Gansukh recalled the disarray in his *ger*, and his irritation subsided. "My apologies, *venerable goat*," he said, his tone only slightly mocking.

"The *Khagan* begins his hunt in the morning," Alchiq said. "You and I will be joining him. We must be wary of being hunted ourselves."

"Of course," Gansukh nodded. "It would be an honor to join you." Internally, his guts tightened. *Hunted.* If he hadn't dealt with Munokhoi by then, he would be leaving Lian unprotected. He had to warn her.

It was only some time later that he realized Alchiq had been talking about something else entirely.

* * *

I will kill them both—pony and goat.

Munokhoi sat cross-legged in his *ger*, calmly chewing on a slice of salted meat. His mind was restless, buzzing with plans and ideas. In a metal brazier, a tiny flame danced, the only illumination in his *ger*. Shadows danced all around, a capering festival of spooky figures that moved in accordance with the shivering delight Munokhoi felt inside.

He had shadowed Gansukh all day, and other than the single arrow fired during the archery contest had not revealed his presence. He had shoved his fist in his mouth to stop from giggling aloud when Gansukh had finally gone back to his wrecked *ger*. Oh, how satisfying it had been to drink dry all of Gansukh's skins and then slice them with his knife. And then, a half hour later, the supreme pleasure at *passing* that same liquid there. *I have stolen nothing,* he had thought as he pissed all over the sleeping furs and the ruined clothing.

Listening to the gray-haired fool and Gansukh talk by the prisoners' cages, it had been difficult to contain his rage when he learned that the old man Alchiq had given the Kitayan the knife! After the first fight, Munokhoi thought Gansukh might stoop to some dangerous subterfuge in an effort to embarrass him, and he had watched for some sign that such a plan was in the making, but he hadn't suspected that Gansukh might have an accomplice. The old man had a foxlike cunning, and giving a blade to a prisoner was a very dangerous ploy. Their plan could have gone awry quite easily, but they had gotten lucky instead.

Their luck would end tomorrow. They were both going on the hunt with the *Khagan*. There would be time enough to take care of everything while in the woods, and then his honor would be restored. The *Khagan* would see how bad a decision it had been to promote that loud-mouthed wrestler. The *Khagan* would take him back.

Tomorrow, Munokhoi thought, gleefully. *I will kill them both tomorrow.*

IN THE ENEMY'S CAMP

AT THE ROSE Knight chapter house, Tegusgal could not help but laugh when the sniveling Livonian worm bolted. *Where did he think he was going? Did he actually think his horse was fast enough to outrun his Mongol hunters?* Tegusgal shook his head as the Livonian *Heermeister* fled the chapter house grounds, and he gave some thought to letting the man go so as to sweeten the eventual hunt. He eyed his men, as some of them started launching arrows after the fleeing knight, and he sighed. They were restless, tense, and the sport would improve their morale. He whistled, giving them the freedom to chase after the foolish *Heermeister*.

Yipping like excited hounds, his men drove their horses into the woods.

Tegusgal fingered the hilt of his dagger, eyeing the quaking priest who remained. "Please, please," the man begged as Tegusgal kneed his horse. "Spare my life, and God will reward you."

"I do not believe in your god," Tegusgal reminded him as he drew abreast.

The priest whimpered, and his horse snorted and shook itself as the man's bladder let go. Tegusgal wrinkled his nose at the man's shameful terror, and with a casual swipe of his knife, he silenced the priest.

Eyes bulging, the priest tried to stop the blood from coursing out of the wound in his neck, covering his frock and staining the wooden cross he wore. Tegusgal shoved him, and arms flailing, he fell off his horse.

Tegusgal wiped his knife off on the blanket beneath the priest's saddle, and then slapped the riderless horse on the rump. It galloped off, assuredly delighted to be rid of its stinking, whimpering rider. He sheathed his knife and spurred his horse after his men, leaving the dying priest and the empty chapter house behind.

His mare thundered through the forest in pursuit of his men and their quarry. The stupid fool of a knight didn't understand that by running, he was summoning the greatest hunters in the world to give chase. Every Mongol warrior knew how to chase prey on horse-back, how to outlast it, and how to bring it down once it had worn itself out. The *Heermeister* was about to discover how pointless it was to try to outrun the Mongol hunt.

He burst out of the forest, on the heels of his hunters, who had fanned out in a broad arc across the fields. The *Heermeister*'s horse was large and strong, and on open ground, it could run faster than Mongol ponies. But Tegusgal knew it didn't have the same stamina. Eventually it would falter, and his men would close the distance. Even now, some of his faster riders were coming into bow range.

The chase wasn't going to last much longer. In fact, they would be on the *Heermeister* before he reached the bridge.

Tegusgal frowned. There was smoke, a black plume rising into the late afternoon sky. He slapped his horse with his reins, urging it to run faster, and as he crested the last rise before the bridge to Hünern, he saw the source of the smoke.

There were barrels on the bridge, spewing columns of thick smoke. The *Heermeister* was off his horse, doing something with one of the barrels. He looked like he was trying to tug it into position.

Tegusgal's men hadn't slowed down. They saw the barrels too, and the struggling figure of the foolish knight. Some of his hunters were already standing in their saddles, firing arrows at the knight, trying to stop him from finishing his task.

Tegusgal shook his head. That wasn't right. The knight hadn't put the barrels there. He hadn't the time. He was trying to move them aside so that he could get his horse across the bridge. He was still trying to flee. *Who put the barrels there?* Tegusgal wondered. *And why?*

He got his answer when the ground started to shake with the thunder of heavy hooves. From the wood on his right, a host emerged, sunlight gleaming off naked steel and polished helms. The riders—sitting astride tall chargers, Western battle steeds—wore white and black; their shields were covered with red and white crosses. His rallying call was lost beneath the many-throated battle cry of the attacking Western knights.

The ambush was sprung, and Tegusgal's hunters were unprepared for the massed charge of the Templars and Hospitallers. The host slammed into the flank of his men, scattering riders. Tegusgal's men were disorganized, caught between the knights' charge and the river. His numbers and the fabled mobility of the Mongol horse rider meant nothing in the face of this crushing assault. Tegusgal yanked his horse's head away from the pitched battle. "Fall back to the river," he shouted as he beat his heels against his horse's barrel. No one heard him in the pandemonium of battle. Steel clashed on steel. Men shrieked. Horses screamed. Arrows hummed through the air.

His men were all going to die. This was a rout. He had to escape. He had to warn Onghwe Khan. His worst fear was being realized: the knights of Hünern were fighting back.

* * *

The ululating war cry of the Shield-Brethren rippled through the air like the charge before a lightning strike as the knights of the *Ordo Militum Vindicis Intactae* clashed with Mongol attackers bent on retaking the gate of their compound. In the front rank of the Shield-Brethren host, Rutger's sword stroke crashed through a Mongol's guard, and the blade cut the Mongol from neck to mid-chest. The man gurgled, clutching at Rutger's sword as the quartermaster pulled it free, and then he crumpled to the bloodstained ground. Rutger checked the man on his right, making sure he wasn't in danger of being overrun by his opponent, and then he pivoted to his left, swinging his sword at an overeager Mongol who raised his curved sword over his head. He caught the Mongol in the back—under the armpits, where the armor was weak—and his sword bit deep into the man's body.

Rutger was exultant. Gathered around him were his brothers, their energy a tangible force weaving them all together into a single fearsome multiarmed monster. They breathed as one; they thrust, parried, and retaliated as one fighter. Each man protected the man next to him, and none felt any pain or exhaustion or fear.

They stood in the narrow throat of the gate, surrounded by the bloody corpses of their enemies. A gleaming ring of swords defended the entryway, rising and falling and dancing left and right, completely synchronous in their movement. Overhead, Shield-Brethren archers in the guard towers harried the stragglers of the Mongol force, making men stumble and flinch as the men next to them would suddenly slip and fall and not get back up.

Eventually the Mongols retreated, falling back to their tents to lick their wounds, count their dead, and consider their next assault. Rutger lowered his arm, the intense pain in his hands finally making itself heard in his brain. He nearly dropped his sword—Andreas's sword—but he fought the pain and kept his grip tight. *I have faced worse*, he counseled himself. *I still stand.* He glanced up and down the line, and saw that it remained intact. None of the Shield-Brethren had fallen, but in so quick a look there was no time to tell how much of the blood that covered every man was that of the enemy. Some wounds, he knew, would not be felt until the battle lust eased.

"Check your weapons and your armor," he croaked. "Thank the Virgin for your fortune." He glanced toward the Mongol tents. "And get ready for them to come again."

They only had to hold the gate until the others arrived, and then they could truly take the battle to the Khan.

* * *

As the spear-wielding Mongols approached, Styg pivoted on his left foot, putting one of the Mongol tents at his back. He was outnumbered—fighting against three men who wielded weapons that could keep his sword at bay—but he would not die without taking as many of them with him as possible. He may not be a full knight initiate of the *Ordo Militum Vindicis Intactae*, but he fought for the Virgin nonetheless. His death would be costly for his foes.

During the training sessions at the chapter house, Styg had seen Andreas take on multiple initiates numerous times. Both Feronantus and Taran had drilled in all the young fighters the same fundamental battlefield maxim. *More men meant more opportunities for confusion.* A single fighter had a distinct advantage: everyone else was an enemy. He didn't have to worry about where his allies stood or what they were planning.

The middle one attacked first. He was the tallest of the trio, and his reach was longest. Styg sent a silent prayer to the Virgin and lunged toward his attacker. He swept his longsword from right to left, smashing the spear aside with the flat of his blade, which fouled the approach of the Mongol on the left. Styg flicked his sword back, extending his arm as far as he could—much farther than he would if he were facing another swordsman—and his blade sliced across the face of the Mongol on the right, splitting the man's cheeks and severing the tip of his nose.

The spear he'd knocked aside came back at him as its wielder attempted to recover, a reverse of the arc on which he had sent it. The predictable motion of a fighter's reflex. Styg had been expecting such a response, and as the weapon swung toward him, he let go of his sword with his left hand and tried to grab the shaft of the spear. The Mongol reacted quickly, yanking his spear back and out of Styg's reach.

Suddenly Styg was painfully aware that the Mongol whose face he had wrecked was still standing.

The Mongol screamed, his face a horrific mask of blood, as he yanked a dagger free of his sash and lunged at Styg. The blade sliced through Styg's surcoat, dragging across the maille underneath, and before the Mongol could slash him again, Styg grabbed the Mongol's armor and pulled the man to him. He smashed his head down, helmet striking the Mongol's already ruined face with a satisfying crunch, and then shoved the man away. *Stay down*, was his fleeting thought.

There was little time for much more thought than that. He was out of position, and as he tried to bring his sword up, one of the other two Mongols slammed into him. His grip slackened on his sword as he and the Mongol stumbled back against one of the nearby tents. He wasted no time lamenting the loss of his sword, twisting in the Mongol's grip in an effort to grapple with the other man. The Mongol growled, showing his teeth, and he shook Styg like a child's doll. He hauled Styg off the resilient tent and threw him to the ground. Styg tried to roll, but he couldn't get his hands in front of him in time, and he sprawled awkwardly on the ground.

He spotted his sword and tried to scramble toward it, and got a boot kick in the belly for his efforts. Maille was good protection against sharp weapons, but it did little to diminish the impact of such bludgeoning force; Styg curled up as he felt his stomach try to hurl itself out of his throat.

He had to get up. He couldn't beat them off from the ground. If he could reach his sword...

It lay out of reach. Tantalizingly out of reach.

The Mongol kicked him again, and he felt something crack along his left side. He flopped on his back, staring up at his attackers. One of them raised his spear, preparing to jab Styg in the face.

The spear-thruster coughed suddenly, spitting out a stream of red blood, and he stared down at the bloodied blade that had sprouted from his chest. He jerked and collapsed to his knees as the curved sword was savagely pulled out, and his friend fumbled for his own sword. He got his blade half out of its scabbard when the bloody sword sliced his throat open. He stumbled and fell, landing on his stomach, head turned toward Styg—staring, his mouth gaping like a dying fish, blood spurting from the mortal gash in his throat.

The sword-wielder who had saved Styg was the fighter he had freed from the post. He was shorter than Styg by half a head, but compactly built, thick muscles crisscrossed with pale, white scars. His face was a study in brutality, like a weathered chunk of wood carved with a dull chisel.

After making sure that the skewed Mongol was expiring, the scarred man shoved the dying man over, and offered Styg his hand. Styg grasped the man's rough hand and was hauled upright. "Thank you," Styg said. He made a fist and put it over his heart. The fighter stared at him for a second, searching his face with his dark, emotionless eyes, and then he made a noise in his chest and made a similar motion.

Little more needed to be said.

Styg's legs shook slightly as he picked up his longsword, the proximity of his death starting to sink in. When he stood up, a wave of dizziness washed over him, and he tried to breathe slowly through his nose and mouth. Deep, calming breaths.

The scarred warrior was striding toward the orange tent.

Styg shook himself like a dog, trying to shed the last remnants of the death fear that had nearly gripped him, and then he hurried after the other man.

* * *

Tegusgal forced his mount into the river, ignoring the sporadic arrows that splashed nearby in the water. The current rode up on his legs as his horse struggled to keep its footing in the deepening water. Nearing the center of the river, his horse would be forced to swim, and he peered through the acrid haze from the burning barrels, trying to find a flat stretch on the opposite bank where he could drive his mount ashore.

His men were scattered. Trapped against the river and hammered by a ferocious host, his men had fallen back on their traditional tactic of splitting and flowing around the force assaulting them, but there had been nowhere to go. Splitting meant fracturing into smaller groups, and those groups had little chance against the mounted knights. They were being chased up and down the riverbank, cut down like wild dogs as they fled. Tegusgal was one of them—a dog running for his life. He struggled to stay in his saddle as the current sloshed angrily around his horse, trying to scoop him free of his mount.

If he let the current take him, his armor would drag him down. The river was too deep and the bank too far. His horse lost its footing and began to swim, and the current pulled him under the bridge, the rushing roar of water blotting out every other sound. A body rushed past him, slamming into one of the wooden piles. The man was still alive, his mouth gaping in a rictus of terror as he tried to hang on to the bridge, but the river threw water over him and he slipped under the surface.

Tegusgal and his horse shot out from under the bridge, buoyed along by the increased churn of the river. His horse struggled, its head straining toward the opposite shore. It needed no encouragement from him. He held on to the reins, and a heartbeat later, he felt the animal's movement stutter beneath him as its hooves found the bottom again. With a mighty surge the horse rushed the bank and emerged from the river.

He could not think of a more beautiful sound than the noise of hooves against stones. His horse grunted and strained as it clattered up the bank. Water streamed out of his armor, his clothes, and his saddlebags, and he wished it would run out faster. As soon as the horse reached level ground, he pulled back on the reins and forced it to stop. He didn't want to look, but he had to see what was left of his men. Humiliation and outrage at what he saw ignited a fire in his gut. The knights were massing near the bridge, having completed their destruction of his men. They were moving the barrels already, pairs of men rolling them off the bridge. In a few minutes, the host would ride across the bridge, returning to Hünern.

Tegusgal had little doubt where they intended to go, and he dug his heels into his horse, urging it toward Hünern. He wouldn't be able to get to his master soon enough to warn him of the coming assault, but he would be able to help Onghwe escape.

Escape. He spat, trying to clear his mouth of the bitterness of the word. If he survived, he would summon the wrath of the entire empire. He would make these knights pay with their lives.

The company, divided

THEY FOLLOWED THE *Khagan*'s caravan. The track of hundreds of men and horses, along with an endless number of carts, was easy to follow. After two weeks of constant riding, they left the steppes behind and followed the tracks into a forest around the base of a tall mountain. The following day, the forward riders found sign of an extensive camp, and the company sequestered themselves in the forest while Cnán slipped into the camp to find news of the *Khagan*'s plan.

Rædwulf and Yasper were on watch, and they were surprised to see her so quickly. As she rode past their hiding place, they continued to eye the forest suspiciously. "Were you followed?" Rædwulf asked.

"No," Cnán said breathlessly. "There is something else I have to tell Feronantus."

"What?" Yasper asked.

"I found Haakon," she said.

"Haakon?" Yasper was incredulous.

She nodded. "He's a prisoner in the *Khagan*'s camp."

The others, when they heard the news, immediately began to discuss plans for rescuing the boy. Feronantus cut that discussion short with a chop of his hand. "The *Khagan*," he said. "What of his plans?"

"He is going to hunt a bear," Cnán said. "In a valley north of here. They had an enormous feast last night, which means they are planning on heading out soon. Probably in the morning."

"Then we leave immediately, and find the bear first," Feronantus said. "That will be our opportunity—our only opportunity."

The company fell silent, and though Cnán could tell that Feronantus wanted them to be moving, to be getting on their horses and riding north to find the bear and lay a trap for the *Khagan*, she had been with the Shield-Brethren long enough to sense why Feronantus was waiting. The company would ride faster once they were all thinking of the same goal.

Right now, there was another matter still on their minds ...

"What about Haakon?" Raphael asked.

Feronantus stared at him, his gaze hard and unflinching, as if he were disappointed that it was Raphael who had finally voiced the question.

And yet, at the same time, Cnán knew Raphael was the only one who would have voiced the question on everyone's mind. It wasn't insolence that led Raphael to question Feronantus's orders, it was a different quality entirely.

"Our mission is to kill the *Khagan*," Feronantus said softly. "How does risking ourselves and exposing our presence aid our mission?"

"What happens after?" Cnán asked, surprised that it was her voice that broke the somber silence.

"After?" Feronantus asked her in return.

"Aye," Raphael said. "After we kill the *Khagan*."

Yasper groaned. "Do we really have to talk about this now?"

"We should never *talk* about it," Vera said, her face hard. "It only creates fear. We all know what happens."

Yasper stroked his beard. "Well, if you're going to put it that way, *now* is the right time to talk about it." He peered at Feronantus. "What does happen after we kill the *Khagan?*"

"Does it matter?" Feronantus asked.

"Look, you Shield-Brethren are an exceptional lot. Stoic. Iron-willed. Ready to die every time you draw your swords. Suicide missions like this are the sort of thing that brings everlasting glory to your name. But me?" Yasper tapped his chest. "I wouldn't mind seeing the cities of the West again. Paris, I hear, is spectacular in the spring."

Istvan snorted and spat. "Buda," he said. "Paris is a shithole in comparison."

Yasper pointed at Istvan. "This is the sort of impassioned discourse that makes this company so charming. Paris or Buda? Don't you want to be able to see both and decide for yourself?"

"I have seen both," Feronantus said quietly. His face was impassive, carved from stone.

"As have I," Eleázar said. "And I would not mind seeing them again."

Something in Eleázar's tone touched Feronantus, and his eyes flickered toward the Spaniard. "We have to find the bear first," he said. "It is our only opportunity to lay a trap for the *Khagan.*"

"None of us are disagreeing with you on that point, Feronantus," Raphael pointed out. "We joined with you on this desperate mission because we believed it was the right choice. We trusted you to lead us, to see us to victory. But we are not young initiates—wet behind the ears—who know little about soldiering. Our goal—as much as Yasper thinks otherwise—is not to die gloriously, but to live. A successful mission means going home again. *All of us.*"

"They're going to kill Haakon," Cnán said. "You know they will. After the *Khagan* dies, they're going to kill every Westerner they can find." When Feronantus did not speak, she grew angry. "You're leaving him to die!" she shouted at him.

Feronantus whirled on her, his eyes blazing, and with a thick hand, he grabbed the front of her jacket and pulled her close to his face. "I have sent many—*many*—men under my command to their deaths. I have watched a good number of them die. Do not presume to lecture me on the morality of my actions, little Binder. I, alone, carry the weight of my decisions, and you have *no idea* how heavy that burden is." He squeezed his hand, gathering the fabric of her shirt in his fist. "Yes," he growled, "I am leaving the boy to die, because I must in order to save thousands of other lives. Lives of men, women, and children who I will never meet. These people will never know my name; they will never even know what I have done for them. What others have sacrificed for them. But in order to save them, *I* must let the boy die."

He shoved her away and turned toward the remainder of the company. "If the success of our mission depended upon it, I would let all of you die," he snarled. "You knew this risk when you agreed to follow me east. You have had months to face this truth and pre-pare yourselves. We have traveled thousands of miles together. We are deep in the heart of the empire of our enemies. We are hope-lessly outnumbered. Yes, it is highly likely that we are all going to die." He closed his eyes for a moment. "We all took the oath," he said, his voice gentler. "We all gave ourselves to the Virgin, knowing that few—*very few*—who so swear are allowed the luxury of dying in their beds. And those of you"—he opened his eyes and looked directly at Yasper—"who have not sworn the same vow are braver by far."

Yasper looked away, his mouth twisting. Cnán was glad Feronantus did not look at her. She wasn't sure she could withstand the force of his gaze. She didn't want to acknowledge what he had just said.

"I would be honored to die beside any one of you," Feronantus said. "I have seen Paris, Buda, London, the Levant. I have spent decades in the North, watching generation after generation of boys leave Týrshammar to take their oaths and become men at Petraathen. Few of them ever return. And now I have seen the other half of the world. It has been a good life, and if I were to die in the course of our mission, it would be a good death. But"—and he looked at each of them in turn—"dying in the next few days is not my plan."

Raphael made a noise in his throat. "So, you do have a plan," he said. He cocked his head to the side. "Or is it a *vision?*"

Feronantus gave Raphael a hard stare, and out of the corner of her eye, Cnán saw Percival glaring at Raphael too.

"Get on your horses," Feronantus said, the tone of his voice signaling an end to the discussion. "We have one last hard ride ahead of us."

"No," Cnán said quietly.

Feronantus walked to his horse as if he hadn't heard her, put his foot in the stirrup, and rose into his saddle. Gathering his reins, he raised his craggy head and gazed at her. She met his stare, and didn't blink. She didn't look away.

"I'm not going," she said. "You don't need me. I'm not a fighter. I will only be in the way when you prepare your ambush."

She expected more of an argument, and she even steeled herself for a cold dismissal from Feronantus, which made his reaction all the more confusing. "May the Virgin protect you, little leaf," Feronantus said with unexpected tenderness. His face changed, losing some of its ferocity, and she was startled to read a deep longing in his gaze. "We have been enriched by your company, and you are always welcome at any fire or hearth that we call home. I speak for myself—and I hope I speak for the others as well—when I say that what is mine is yours, Cnán."

Cnán opened her mouth to speak, and found her throat wouldn't work. She nodded dumbly, fighting back the tears that were threatening to run down her cheeks. She raised her hand awkwardly. After all they had been through together, to be bereft of each other's company so suddenly was more painful than she had imagined it would be. Judging by the expression on more than a few of the faces of the company, she was not alone in her despair.

"I do ask one favor," Feronantus said.

Cnán nodded. "Yes," she managed.

"Do nothing to rescue the boy until after the *Khagan* has departed for his hunt."

She laughed, the sound hiccupping out of her body. She wiped at her face. "Of course," she said.

Feronantus smiled at her, and she wanted to run to him and leap into his arms. "Good luck," he said. "We'll see you again." He said it simply, but there was a stark finality to his words, as if there was no question in his mind.

"You will," she said, trying to match his resolve.

He snapped his reins against his horse and left the glade without looking back. The others lingered, each one offering her a farewell, and she managed to hold her tears in check until they were all gone.

the exodus

ERENC WAS CONFIDENT that, given time, he could find his own route to the city walls. But Father Rodrigo had sagely suggested they trust Ocyrhoe's map instead. She knew the bolt holes, the unmarked alleys, the routes taken by the city watch. The map's route was easy to follow, more so because the city streets were mostly deserted, and sooner than he expected, they were outside the city walls.

So much easier when the city guard wasn't chasing them.

Father Rodrigo walked as if he had been hitched to a wagon; each step seemed incredibly laborious, and only after his foot came down did the rest of his body follow.

Ferenc was exhausted as well. The excitement of his reunion with Father Rodrigo and their subsequent escape had worn off. They had little in the way of supplies—one blanket he had grabbed from the room before they had left, a water skin, and his flint, all shoved into a ragged satchel the priest was carrying. In the morning, they would have to find sustenance. In the morning...

Ferenc wondered again why the priest had been so intent on escaping. There was food, a roof over his head, and—if he understood correctly what had transpired—the entirety of the Vatican was at Father Rodrigo's disposal. Why then the urgent need to slip out of the city? Had they just spent months traveling *to* the city?

He did not entirely understand Father Rodrigo's thinking, and since the priest had been in the Septizodium, he had found the man's attitude and awareness disturbing. It was as if a different man had come out from the one that had gone in. This one—the haggard priest staggering along the moonlit track ahead of him—was almost like a stranger to him.

"We should rest, Father Rodrigo," he said gently, "though we must not light a fire. We do not want to attract anyone's attention. But if we bundle ourselves together in the blanket, we may keep warm through the night."

Father Rodrigo's response had been a wordless grunt, a reminder of the way they had communicated in the first months after Mohi, when the priest had been terribly sick. But, unlike then, he came willingly when Ferenc led him to the shelter of a tall tree, and he fell asleep almost immediately upon lying down on the ground. Ferenc arranged the blanket as best he could to cover both of them, and he stared up at the night sky, listening to the priest's breathing.

The weight is gone, Ferenc thought as his eyelids grew heavy. *Whatever he carried from Mohi to Rome is no longer with him.* There was something else—a lighter burden, but one no less valuable than the message he had carried previously.

With that thought Ferenc fell into a fitful sleep of his own. He dreamed about cavernous tunnels whose openings were covered by red curtains, and of the women who kept disappearing into these tunnels—women who wore long coats of maille. They wore no helms, and their long, unbound hair flowed down their backs, like the manes of horses.

In the morning, there was dew clinging to everything, and even with a flint Ferenc doubted he could have started a fire. They were, as he feared, cold, hungry, and damp. It would be easier to find an outlying village and offer his labor in exchange for breakfast.

"Why did we run away from Rome, Father?" he asked as he stretched, letting his gaze wander about the countryside.

"We did not run away, my son," said Father Rodrigo simply, as if this were all the answer that Ferenc could possibly need. "We have a task to perform. One that we could not have accomplished inside the city walls."

"What task is that, Father?"

Father Rodrigo offered him a puzzled expression. "To release the power of the Grail, of course." He patted the tattered satchel he had brought with them.

Ferenc stuck a finger in his ear and worked it back and forth, as if he could dislodge the words he had just heard. *The Grail?* He remembered a cup Father Rodrigo had been holding on the ledge above the crowd. It had fallen from his hand when the soldiers had grabbed him. Was that the Grail? But how had that cup found its way back to Rodrigo?

"What...what does it do?" Ferenc asked. He recalled the crowd's reaction to the cup: astonishment and awe. But he hadn't seen what had been so remarkable about the cup. It had looked like an old drinking mug, tarnished with age.

"That is not the right question, my son. Instead, consider what it is that the Grail wants *us* to do," Father Rodrigo replied with a small smile. "We are but vessels through which it operates. I must show it to the people of Italy, of Germany and France. I must show it to everyone, and the Grail will tell them what it wants from us."

That was not a promising, or elucidating, answer, and Ferenc eyed Father Rodrigo's satchel with suspicion. He had packed it himself. He didn't recall putting a cup in there, nor any opportunity when the priest might have done so. "What did it want yesterday in the marketplace?"

"It wanted me to rouse up the people of Christendom and urge them to shake off the danger of the Mongols. It wanted me to prevent the arrival of a prophecy—to prevent the world from coming to an end."

Ferenc's stomach tightened into a knot. His voice leaped up almost an octave as he demanded, "Mongols? The ones from Mohi? Father, you were there. You know what they did, what they can do. We cannot fight them. Even with everyone from the market yesterday. We will be killed!"

"Calm yourself, my son," Father Rodrigo said. "I am not talking about a marketplace of people descending on an army. I mean we must gather *all* of Christendom, every man, woman, and child, and all together, as a united front, we will confront them and drive their evil from our land."

"Everyone?" Ferenc repeated, saying the word with exaggerated care. "*Everyone?*"

"Everyone."

Ferenc considered this. "How?" he asked, unable to comprehend such a mass of people.

"God will provide," Father Rodrigo said, a serene calm descending upon his face. The priest stared into the distance, a wry smile on his face.

Ferenc sighed, faced with the entirely reasonable conclusion: however calm and rational Father Rodrigo seemed, he had taken leave of all of his senses. The fever may have finally left him, but it had burned away too much of the priest.

"Excuse me, Father, I need to relieve myself," Ferenc said. He picked up the blanket and carefully draped it around Father Rodrigo's shoulders. The priest patted Ferenc's hand and continued to smile at nothing in particular. Unwilling to look upon the priest's face any more, Ferenc turned his attention to the nondescript countryside of grass and occasional copses of trees. Then he purposefully began to walk to the east, looking for something in particular.

A hundred paces off, he found it: a view out over a shallow valley, filled with the tent city of Emperor Frederick. Ferenc had suspected they were near it, and his intention the previous night had been to skirt the camp. Now, he decided, the best thing to do was march right into it.

The English Cardinal Somercotes had sent them to the Emperor. Father Rodrigo had liked Somercotes. By association, then, Frederick was probably not a villain, peculiar as he was. Another thing to consider: Ocyrhoe had told him that Frederick cursed a lot. That meant Frederick was not pious. And *that* meant he was less likely to be seduced by Father Rodrigo's story. Even if the Grail really did have special powers—which Ferenc doubted—it was probably safer in the hands of an Emperor than those of a raving churchman. It saddened him to think this, for Father Rodrigo was still by far the most beloved living human to him...but he could not ignore the obvious.

With a sigh, he turned back to fetch the priest.

* * *

"You're a woman, can't you make her speak?" Orsini demanded irritably. Léna turned her calm, subtle gaze from the Senator to the girl.

Ocyrhoe imagined a hand pressed over a mouth, and tried to project this image to Léna. She had had so little training before her other sisters had vanished that she doubted she knew how to communicate properly in this fashion.

"She is not going to say more," Léna said confidently. She had not even made eye contact with Ocyrhoe. "I believe she is under an oath to somebody and part of that oath requires secrecy. If that is the case, she will *never* speak. She will die sooner than speak."

Ocyrhoe tried to keep alarm off her face. She was *not* under an oath, and she was *not* willing to die to help Father Rodrigo and Ferenc escape. Had Léna gotten her message, and was she now bluffing on her behalf? If so, it was a clever ploy; if not, then Ocyrhoe feared she was in more danger than she had originally thought.

"Your Eminences," Léna offered. "I understand your distress over the discovery of this girl in His Holiness's chambers." She glared at Fieschi as she said this, and Ocyrhoe wondered how much she had seen of the manner in which Fieschi had dragged her out of the room.

At first she had thought the cardinal had meant to harm her, but he had simply been trying to snare her—much like the manner in which a cat pounces on a mouse. Fieschi had been angry, ready to strike her, but the sudden appearance of Léna had given him pause.

"Leave her with me," Léna said. "I will find a way to give you the information you require in a manner that does not break her oath."

Fieschi grimaced. "I don't care what sort of ethical justification you want to give it, just as long as we get what we need." Ocyrhoe noticed that his distaste did not extend to his eyes. He was watching them carefully. Too carefully.

"Fine. Leave. Now."

Orsini was the more startled of the two by her command, and as he huffed with indignity, she fixed him with a withering stare. Wanting to make himself larger before feeling diminished by letting a woman order him around, but when he noticed Fieschi's lack of outrage he deflated—slowly—as he departed.

"Speak," Léna said sharply as soon as they were alone.

Ocyrhoe shrugged. "The priest asked me to help him escape, and Ferenc wanted to go with him. I drew a map for them to get out of the city, and I distracted the guard at the door so they could get out. But once they were out, I was stuck inside, and Fieschi found me."

Léna made an aggrieved noise. "Why did he want to escape? Why did you help him? Where was he going? How could you possibly consider this appropriate behavior for a Binder?"

Ocyrhoe held her hands up in weak protest. "I was not behaving as a Binder; I was behaving as a friend."

"Once you become a Binder, you are *always* a Binder. Especially when your *friend* is the Pope. Your actions will bring *chaos* upon the city, little one. You have interfered with matters that you had no right—"

Desperate for justification, Ocyrhoe interrupted, "What if he had employed me as a Binder?"

Léna blinked, surprised. "To do what, exactly?"

"I...I was to carry the message of his departure to the cardinals. As indeed I did, the moment Fieschi opened the door. I did not even have to tell him verbally; my presence was enough."

"Such flippancy is dangerous, girl," she warned, punctuating her words with the same glare she had used on Orsini.

"I truly have no information beyond what I've told you," Ocyrhoe said, less ruffled by the look than Orsini had been. "I don't know why he left or where he was headed. He said he was a prisoner, and that he shouldn't be. He asked for my help. Ferenc is my friend, and I wanted to help him. And Ferenc wanted whatever Father Rodrigo wanted. So..."

"So you decided to take matters into your own hands, regardless of how much pain and suffering that might cause others. Is that it?" Léna stared at her. "If he is truly mad, then you have set him loose in the world. Do you understand the folly you've committed?" Her voice was softer, though no less stern.

Ocyrhoe looked down, her cheeks flushing. "Yes," she said in a small voice. "I'm so very sorry. But there is nothing I can do to help you find him."

"I know, child." Léna placed her hands on the sides of Ocyrhoe's head and kissed her lightly on the crown of her skull. "But that doesn't mean you don't know where he has gone."

Ocyrhoe looked up at Léna. "I don't understand," she said.

Léna brushed Ocyrhoe's hair back from her face. "Which gate did you send them to?"

"Flamina. I thought the sooner he got out of the city, the better."

"Give them that much," Léna said.

"What will they do to him if they catch him?" Ocyrhoe asked.

"What do you think they will do?" Léna asked. "He is Pope. Why should he fear the people who serve him?"

Ocyrhoe shook her head. "I think Fieschi wants to kill him."

"Would you dare say as much to the Senator?" Léna asked. "While the cardinal was standing next to him, in the same room?"

Ocyrhoe froze. All of a sudden she couldn't breathe, much less shake her head. *The Bear had taken my sisters*, she thought frantically. How could Léna have forgotten that?

"You must consider your actions carefully," Léna said softly, and the woman's words released Ocyrhoe from the terror that had gripped her. "You must know the repercussions of what you do before you act. Regardless of your concerns about the cardinal, is the priest not safer here than out in the wilderness where any brigand or ruffian could harm him? He only has Ferenc to watch over him. That may have been enough before, but now Father Rodrigo wants to preach to the people. Is that not dangerous for him in his state?" She stared at Ocyrhoe for a moment, waiting for her to nod in agreement. "When I call in the cardinal and the Senator, you will tell them which gate. Yes?"

"And then what?" Ocyrhoe asked, panic twisting in her belly. This time she got the words out. "Orsini silenced our sisters. I see how he looks at me. He wants to do the same again."

Her outburst gave Léna pause. "I will make sure he doesn't hurt you."

"How can you do that?" Ocyrhoe demanded, trying to stall the inevitable. "He took all of them, even when we realized they were disappearing. He still got everyone except me. They were my family and they could not protect me. How can you assure me otherwise?"

An odd look came across Léna's face. "Trust me, little one," she said. Her expression melted into a soft smile. "I will have a talk with the Senator soon. That's all it will take. Just a little chat."

TO ETERNAL GLORY

GEDEI KHAN TOOK his morning meal late and alone in his *ger*. After Alchiq's visit he had spent the remainder of the day in repose, mostly napping off the effects of the copious amounts of wine he had drunk, but some introspection had flitted across his mind during the long afternoon. It was the sort of post-drinking-binge thinking he avoided as much as possible, as it was full of all manner of recriminations and self-loathing, but this time he let it run its course. When it was gone, he had fallen into a deep, dreamless slumber and had woken this morning feeling quite rested.

Still, he did not rush into the hunt. Now that his brain was free of the fog of the wine, the importance of this hunt was that much more evident. He wouldn't go so far as to admit that the health of the empire rested upon the death of the Great Bear, but the symbolism of the hunt was significant. He was not superstitious—the empire had left all that behind when the clans came together and formed *one* people—but he understood the value in giving his subjects an event they could claim as a watershed moment in their lives. A token of the empire's strength and everlasting value. It was best to delay such rewards, to further emblazon their reception with as much gravity as possible.

The *Darkhat* scouts knew where the Great Bear roamed—less than a day's ride to the north. Master Chucai had suggested he take a *jaghun* with him, but Ögedei had scoffed at such an idea. *What beast would not flee in terror before a hundred men?* Half as many might still be too many—surely his trackers alone could find the bear's den—but to take less would be to incite Chucai, and he was not in the mood to suffer that man's persistent disappointment. It was *his* hunt, after all.

I will take four arban, he decided. Two would be his strongest guards, including the new *Torguud* captain. The other group of men would mostly be trackers, including both Chagatai's envoy and Alchiq. One cook, Master Chucai, and the shaman would make up the remainder of his hunting party.

He would have preferred to leave Master Chucai behind. His advisor was beginning to annoy him again and, much like the previous time when their relationship had become antagonistic, Ögedei knew Chucai's mood would only improve when the *Khagan*'s drinking lessened. Of course, knowing this only made him want to drink *more*, and it would be so easy to lay the blame for his drunkenness at Master Chucai's feet. But it wouldn't change anything. Chucai would still be an arrogant son of a whore, and Ögedei would still thirst for wine.

The previous night he had dreamed that the Great Bear had eaten Chucai. He had been greatly refreshed when he had woken. Why couldn't he have that dream every night?

The guard, Alagh, ducked into the *ger* and bowed to the *Khagan*. "My Khan."

"What is it?" Ögedei asked with a sigh. He could guess. *I think of him and he appears.*

"Master Chucai asked that I tell you the hunting party is ready. The day of your great hunt has finally come."

"He couldn't come tell me himself?"

"My Khan?" Alagh was flustered and mildly frightened by the question.

Ögedei grunted and waved, dismissing the guard, who quickly fled from the *ger*. Ögedei picked at the leavings on his plate, dawdling a few moments longer. *I should reassign that one*, he thought, staring at the entrance of his *ger*. Alagh was one of the pair who had guarded him the night of the Chinese raid, and of the two he was the more skittish. Like a young colt, recently born. Both overly curious and easily frightened. Once, he would have enjoyed having men like that around him. They tended to be eager to please. He recalled his new *Torguud* captain's dispatch of the blondhaired fighter—quick and efficient. The difference was that Namkhai expected *more* of him as *Khagan*—he could read the desire quite readily in the wrestler's face.

Ögedei looked at his hands. *I will kill the Great Bear*, he thought. *I will be worthy of my father's legacy once more.*

His hands shook only a little bit.

* * *

Jachin could not decide on which scarf to wear. She had woken well before dawn to get ready for the momentous day. The *Khagan* would be leaving the camp, and Second Wife could not be happier. Soon their endless exile from Karakorum would be over. She had been giddily happy as she had ordered her servants to prepare her finest outfit.

Of course, such delight had given way to irritation: her servants hadn't packed the right clothes. Some of her coats were too wrinkled. Her handmaidens had forgotten that she preferred to have her hair back over her *left* ear, not her right. None of her scents had the right floral note—they had all gone rancid overnight.

And finally, it was time to choose a scarf, and Lian could not suffer Jachin's frenetic nervousness any longer. As Second Wife

shrieked at her servants, threatening to tear all of her clothes off—
Do you want me to stand naked before the Khagan?—Lian slipped out of
Jachin's *ger*.

The morning sun had warmed the valley enough to drive off
the limpid fog, though many of the banners still gleamed wetly. The
ground was damp, and she could feel the chill of the approaching
winter through the thin soles of her shoes. The weather had been
pleasant the last few days, but the nights got very cold. She skipped
lightly as she walked through the camp.

Outside the *Khagan's* wheeled *ger* the hunting party was gathering. The *Torguud*, in their finest armor, were fussing with their
saddles. The *Darkhat* guides stood in a clump, stoic as ever. A tiny
man, covered with tassels and bells and bits of metal and bone, was
hand-feeding the smallest pony she had ever seen. She spied Master
Chucai moving through the ranks of the *Torguud*, and he caught
sight of her but gave no indication of pleasure or displeasure at her
presence. And, over by the fire pits, she spotted Gansukh and a gray-
haired man.

Sparing one more glance in Chucai's direction, she hurried over
to the pair. "You...you are going on the hunt?" she asked.

"It was not my—" Gansukh said. He glanced at his companion briefly and then took her by the arm and led her a few
paces away. He stood so that his body was shielding her from the
company being assembled. "It was not my idea," he apologized,
"though I should have known it was going to happen. What the
Khagan wants..."

She was more flustered about this than she had expected to be,
and she flushed as she realized how badly this news was affecting her.
"Did you... ?"

He shook his head. "Stay with Second Wife," he said crypti-
cally. "I will finish that matter when I return."

"What matter?" she asked.

His forehead creased. "Munokhoi," he whispered. He stepped closer to her. "Don't go anywhere alone, if you can help it," he said. "Stay with Second Wife."

She shook her head, not wanting to hear his words. Not wanting to acknowledge what he was telling her. She was embarrassed by the fear and despair that were burning in her stomach. Like a hot coal that slowly blackened all that touched it. Slowly she realized her fear had little to do with Munokhoi and more to do with the fact that Gansukh was leaving.

She knew that the men going with the *Khagan* were not going to be in any danger—their presence was mostly ceremonial, once the bear had been located—but it was the realization of *loss* that was eating at her. *What the* Khagan *wants...*

Once the hunt was over, Gansukh would go away. Afterward, Gansukh's presence at court would either be irrelevant or an irritant; either way, the *Khagan* would send him back to Chagatai.

"Don't go to my *ger*," he said. "There's nothing left."

Her body quivered. *Nothing left.* It was all coming to an end.

He read her fear in her face, and some of it leaped to his eyes as well. He stroked her cheek lightly, and she turned her head away, unable to bear his touch. "Lian," he started, and then he fumbled with his jacket. He took her hands, pressing a rectangular shape between them. "I'll be back," he said, squeezing her hands tight around the thin box.

Someone shouted from behind Gansukh, and he turned his head. One of the *Torguud* stood on the platform of the *Khagan*'s *ger*, and he beat the base of his spear against the wooden platform to further command the assembly's attention.

Lian transferred the object to her left hand and grabbed Gansukh's jacket with her right. "Wha—?" he started, but she cut him off by pressing her lips to his mouth. She broke the contact before he could properly respond to the kiss, and somewhat reluctantly, she released her hold on him.

"Good hunting," she whispered.

"Lian—"

She shook her head, cutting him off.

Many voices shouted behind him as the splendidly attired form of Ögedei Khan emerged from the *ger*. Dressed in a plum-colored fur-lined jacket and matching trousers, the *Khagan* carried a cup of tea in one hand and a curved bow in the other. He stood there, surveying the crowd, seemingly indifferent as the audience erupted into wild pandemonium.

Gansukh hesitated, confusion still written across his face, but as the *Khagan* began his speech, he tore himself away from Lian. She closed her eyes as he turned away, and her tiny sob was lost in the tumult of the burgeoning crowd.

"Many years ago," Ögedei began once the cheering subsided, and his voice was soft enough that the crowd became instantly silent so as to hear his words, "my father came to Burqan-qaldun. He slew the Great Bear, and its spirit helped him bring the clans together."

Lian opened her eyes, drawn in by the *Khagan*'s voice. He stood, regal and proud, on his raised platform, and with quiet dignity, he took a long sip from his teacup. "This," he said as he raised the cup, "is Chinese tea. I would not be drinking it were it not for my father." He hurled the cup down, and it shattered on the cold and hard wood of the platform. He thrust his other arm in the air, holding the curved bow high. "This is a Mongol bow," he shouted. "This is how my father hunted. This is how my father made his empire. This is how I will claim what is mine."

Ögedei looked down on the audience, and his gaze settled on Jachin. And how could it not, with as many skirts and scarves as she wore? He gave her a beatific smile, and Lian's heart jumped. For a brief instant, the *Khagan* ignored everyone else and focused on Second Wife, and Lian knew the effect the *Khagan*'s attention would have on Jachin—it would sustain her the entire time the *Khagan* was gone on his hunt. Longer, even. Somewhat selfishly, Lian knew that Jachin would be so much easier to deal with during that time. She would be lost in her own imaginary world, rapt with bliss.

"Such a dumb cow. So easily beguiled." Munokhoi's voice was quiet and controlled, and all the more frightening for it.

Lian's heart hammered in her chest, and she found herself unable to breathe. She had not heard the ex-*Torguud* captain's approach, and she was too frightened to do anything but press her left hand against her waist, hiding the tiny box with her hand and body as best she could.

"She will not protect you," Munokhoi continued, coming closer to her. She could feel his presence now, a burning heat directly behind her. His breath stirred her hair.

Her hand dropped to her side, and she let out a tiny cry as his hand smashed on top of her right hand, pinning her fingers against the hilt of the knife she kept hidden in her skirts. "Do you think to stab me with your lover's knife?" He pulled her hand back, twisting it behind her back. Out of sight of the crowd. "Here?" he whispered, his mouth close to her ear. "With all these people watching?"

She struggled briefly, but it only made him hold her more tightly, and the proximity of his body—and the oily stench of his breath—made her shudder and stop.

"I can kill you any time I want," Munokhoi whispered. "Your protector is leaving, and Second Wife will be too busy pining for the man who doesn't truly care for her to notice how frightened you have become." He inhaled deeply, smelling her hair. "I like the way you smell when you are scared. I can only imagine what you are going to smell like when you know you are going to die."

Lian tried to calm her breathing, tried to remember the lessons Gansukh had taught her, but her mind was like a cloud of wild butterflies. All she wanted to do was run, but Munokhoi's grip on her arm was too tight.

"I am going to kill your lover," Munokhoi sighed, "and then I am going to kill you. Maybe I will bring back his head so that he can watch you die." He chuckled, and she couldn't stop the shiver of revulsion that ran through her body.

She felt his leg against hers, and she finally remembered what Gansukh had taught her. Gathering her courage—a tiny spark of defiance that bloomed as soon as she reached for it—she stomped down with her heel, trying to catch Munokhoi's foot. Simultaneously, she grabbed for his groping hand. If she could get a hold on his thumb...

His hand vanished as she was pushed from behind. Stumbling forward, she caught herself before she fell down, and still moving away from where she had been standing, she looked over her shoulder.

Munokhoi was gone.

The *Khagan* had finished his speech, and his horse—a magnificent white stallion—was being led through the crowd to the edge of the *ger*'s platform. The crowd continued to cheer, swords, spears, and bows rising and falling as they chanted the *Khagan*'s name.

Lian scuttled toward the crowd, trying to look every direction at once—hoping to find Gansukh, dreading that she might catch a glimpse of Munokhoi.

* * *

Gansukh tried to find Lian. When the *Khagan* had appeared, the crowd had become chaotic. More people had suddenly surrounded the *Khagan*'s ger, every one hoping to bask in *his* glory as he set out on this momentous hunt. He and Alchiq had joined the other hunters, waiting for the *Khagan* to finish his speech. Gansukh had started to fret with his horse's tack. The last part of his conversation with

Lian had been interrupted; he had wanted to tell her about the contents of the box. But he couldn't find her in the crowd, even from the height afforded him by sitting astride his horse.

The *Khagan* had descended the stairs from his *ger* and was fussing with his horse's bridle. The rest of his entourage had already mounted, and their horses were becoming restless. It was clear to most of the riders that there was nothing wrong with the *Khagan*'s tack, but no one dared say anything. They all waited, patiently; so did the crowd, but Gansukh could read an undercurrent of boredom creeping into some of the faces around him.

Where is she? He felt fairly certain that Munokhoi would come after him first, a certainty that had only increased in the days since the Chinese attack. The ex-*Torguud* captain liked to cause others pain, especially those who could not fight back as effectively, and so he knew Munokhoi would wait to deal with Lian. But now, scanning the crowd, he wasn't so sure. And he was leaving the camp for at least a day. What would Munokhoi do while he was gone?

The *Khagan* swung himself up in his saddle, finally satisfied that the straps of his reins were not frayed or twisted. Ögedei adjusted his position in his saddle, and raising one arm over his head, he tried to stir the audience's fervor again. But a little too much time had passed and some of the initial excitement of the *Khagan*'s hunt had waned; now the crowd's enthusiasm felt a little forced.

Ögedei brought his hand down sharply and snapped his reins. His white stallion leaped forward with a snort, scattering courtiers who hadn't been paying close enough attention. Namkhai gave a shout to his *Torguud*, and the honor guard followed the *Khagan* in a thunder of hooves. Master Chucai and the trackers followed, the shaman on his tiny pony bringing up the rear.

"Hai!" Alchiq shouted, slapping his reins against his horse's neck. The gray-haired hunter galloped after the hunting party, leaving Gansukh as the last.

His horse snorted, eager to join the rest, and Gansukh searched for sight of Lian one last time.

Ögedei had given him the sprig to keep safe, and the decision to leave it with Lian had been a sudden one. He had sensed she was worried that he wasn't coming back, and on one hand, he wasn't terribly worried about the *Khagan*'s hunt. The escort would more than protect the *Khagan* from a rampant bear should things go awry. On the other, there was Munokhoi.

Munokhoi will come after me first. He tried to believe it, but his heart quailed. What if he was wrong? Not only was he was leaving her to die, he had entrusted her with the sprig. Had he just given it to his enemy?

Someone whistled shrilly, and Gansukh caught sight of Lian finally. Her face was drawn—frightened, concerned, steadfast—and her left hand was clenched tightly around the lacquer box that held the sprig. She pointed in the direction of the galloping horses. The fear vanished from her face as she slowly traced her thumb across her throat.

Gansukh was suddenly cold in the warm late-morning sun. He locked eyes with Lian and nodded, understanding what she was telling him. He slapped his reins, encouraging his horse to join the others.

The hunt had begun. It would be finished out there, in the woods.

UNCAGED

HANS CROUCHED BEHIND the Black Wall, sheltered by the straining afternoon shadows. He could clearly hear every detail of the battle at the gate; in the chaos of battle, Hans knew, it was all a whirling wind—a thick cloud of noise and violence that deadened the senses and mind with its intensity. It was bad enough hearing it; he didn't need to see it too. He had had enough of watching men kill one another during the siege of Legnica.

Maks, on the other hand, could not tear his gaze away. He stood, shifting nervously from foot to foot, at the edge of the wall, peering down the alley at the gate of the Mongol compound. His hand kept tensing on the grip of his sword, a nervous reaction each time a new scream echoed on the air, as if he might tell from whose throat it sprang.

"They'll win," Hans said, and immediately felt foolish for speaking the words. It didn't matter if the Shield-Brethren won or lost; he knew what Maks wanted was to be part of the battle. It was the same feeling he'd felt every time that he'd sent one of the other boys to carry a message in his stead.

Abruptly Maks looked back at him, and by the sudden calmness in his stance, Hans realized the young man was weighing a decision. "They need me," Maks said. "And you should not be here in any case. Go back to your uncle, boy. I must fight with my brothers." He pushed away from the wall, turning toward the alley, and then paused. He reached behind him, slid his dagger out of its sheath, and offered it to Hans. "In case you run into any trouble on the way back," he said, and then he left, sprinting down the alley to join his companions.

Hans stared at the dagger in his hand. Long and narrow, it possessed a triangular cross section and a single edge tapering to a deadly point. More screams ripped through the air, accompanied by a renewed frenzy of metal clashing on metal, and Hans shivered, immobilized by the deadly weapon in his grip.

He should listen to Maks's command. He should go back to his uncle and flee Hünern. But that would mean going with Ernust to Löwenberg. *They promised to take me with them*, he thought, his hand tightening on the handle of the dagger. If he went to Löwenberg, would the Shield-Brethren come and find him? Would they send someone for him? He shook his head. If he left with his uncle, he would never know who won. He would never know if he had been helpful. He stood paralyzed, the sounds of the combat echoing in his ears; the dagger was a heavy weight in his hands.

I will never know...

His mouth tightened into a hard line, and he turned away from the alley, heading back along the wall in the direction he had gone several hours earlier with Styg, Eilif, and Maks.

Styg had pounded stakes into the wall of the Mongol compound. Hans had no illusion that he was going to fight the Mongols, but he knew the layout of the compound better than anyone else. Could he trust Styg to remember all of the details of the map he had sketched in the dirt?

Once he was out of sight of the gate, he broke into a run. He could still be useful.

The Shield-Brethren needed him more than his uncle did.

* * *

Styg and the scarred man found Eilif inside the large tent, crouched next to the first of two large iron cages. The Shield-Brethren scout was wrestling with an iron lock, cursing the mechanism's failure to yield to his efforts. He glanced up as the pair approached, and Styg was taken aback by his brother's frantic expression.

They could hear the sounds of the pitched battle at the gate—the mingled cries of the victorious and the shrieks of the dying. How many of those wailing voices were the cries of their friends dying? Styg understood Eilif's consternation; he had been struggling for some time with the lock, growing more and more frustrated with his continued failure.

"There must be a key," he said, trying to calm Eilif. "We will find it." As he came closer to the cages, Styg recognized the one Haakon had faced in the arena—Zugaikotsu No Yama. The other one had to be Kim, the Flower Knight, the man Andreas had faced at First Field. Both had been brutally beaten, their faces swollen and their bodies crisscrossed with ugly scars and welts. Styg smelled sweat, piss, and blood, and knew these men had been in these cages since Andreas had died.

Kim started talking to the scarred fighter, his words slurred and thick. The scarred fighter responded, pointing to the two Shield-Brethren. Kim nodded, and pointed at the heavy locks on both cages, as if none of them had noticed them yet.

"Everything else about this place is made from sticks and bones," Eilif groused, "but not these damn locks. They're solid, and I can't figure out how to jam them open." He ran his hand through his hair, a helpless expression painted on his face. "We need a key, but I have no idea which one of the Mongol guards—"

The scarred warrior put his hands on Eilif's shoulders and carefully pushed him aside. He stood before the lock on Zug's cage, staring contemptuously at it as though there was nothing more loathsome in the entire world, and Styg could almost feel him feeding all of his hate, all of his rage, into this lump of rain-rusted iron. Zug had been talking to the warrior, but he broke off suddenly as the fighter raised his stolen Mongol sword and brought it down with all of his might on the loop of metal at the top of the lock.

Styg could see no change in the metal as the fighter smashed his sword down on the lock a second time. Within the cages, Zug and Kim were now considerably more animated than they had been, as if freedom were only one mighty stroke away. Styg caught sight of the fiery delight in their eyes, and he shivered. *Yes*, he thought, *I want you to be unleashed too.*

"Lakshaman," Eilif said quietly, nodding at the scarred man. "He fought the Livonian. Do you remember?" Styg, eyeing the furious intent in the scarred man's face, remembered. Lakshaman had fought against a better-armed and better-armored opponent and won. This man, with his scars and his knives, had taken that warrior with every advantage, and fed him his own preordained victory on the tip of his own rondel.

Suddenly Styg had little doubt the lock would yield.

There was a deafening *clang*, and sparks flew, dancing across the dirt floor. Zug's cage trembled. Lakshaman raised his weapon, and Styg noted how pitted and scarred the edge of the blade was, jagged like broken teeth. Styg was arrested, rooted to the spot as the whole world seemed to fade into the nothing but for Lakshaman and his jagged blade. Styg's heart pounded in his chest as Lakshaman brought the sword down one more time, screaming in inchoate fury. Everything rested on the strength and fury of one man, battered and scarred by brutal masters, against a simple iron lock.

Lakshaman's sword snapped, and Styg and Eilif ducked as a large piece of the blade bounced off the iron bars of Zug's cage with a resounding clang.

The sword was not the only thing that had broken. The lock lay on the ground, snapped in half.

Lakshaman, breathing heavily, tossed aside the useless hilt of the Mongol sword. Zug tentatively touched the bars of his cage and slowly pushed the door open, as if he couldn't quite believe what he was seeing. The door moved, and a ferocious grin spread across his face. He was free.

Kim cleared his throat, and when he had their attention, he pointed at the lock on his cage. The look on his face was easy to interpret.

One more.

When Lakshaman raised his sweat-slicked face and looked at Styg, he shrugged and went to get another Mongol sword. He knew where a few were lying, no longer needed by their owners.

* * *

There was someone climbing the spikes Styg had driven into the wall.

Hans had found his way back to the spot where the Shield-Brethren had entered the Mongol compound readily enough—he knew every route through the broken alleys of Hünern, but instead of darting to the wall and scaling the spike ladder, he had ducked behind the same broken wall he and Maks had hidden behind previously. He had seen no one during his dash—not surprising, given the mood in the city—and so the sight of another person was startling.

More so that it was a Mongol warrior.

In fact, it was none other than Tegusgal, the captain of the Khan's guard.

The Mongol's armor was battered and stained—both with soot and blood—and his helmet was missing. From what Rutger had said when they were all gathered behind the Black Wall, Tegusgal and his Mongols should have been caught in an ambush on the other side of the river. The Templars and Hospitallers had been in charge of making sure none of the Mongolian cavalry made it back to the compound. Hans felt his stomach tighten at the thought that the other knights had failed.

But Tegusgal was alone, sneaking into his own camp—which suggested that the ambush had been successful. Tegusgal was returning to his master like a whipped dog.

Hans gripped Maks's dagger. His heart was beating fast. And before he talked himself out of the idea, he darted from his hiding place.

Tegusgal was climbing slowly. He had been wounded in the left arm, and the injury was making the ascent difficult. Hans knew he could climb faster. Even while holding Maks's dagger in one hand.

He ran to the wall and scrambled up the ladder of spikes. Tegusgal, having reached the top, braced himself on the wall. He looked down, hearing Hans on the spikes below him, and he stared, incredulous at the sight of the boy coming after him.

Hans didn't slow down. As soon as he got close enough, he launched himself off the spikes, Maks's dagger in his hand. The tip pierced the back of Tegusgal's calf, the force of Hans's blow driving the metal point in far enough that the tip grated on the bone in Tegusgal's leg.

Tegusgal howled, his foot slipping off the stake. Hans hung in the air, both hands around the hilt of the dagger. Blood ran down the back of Tegusgal's leg as the Mongol tried to shake him off.

a change of plans

KJALDBRÆÐUR

The word burned in Haakon's head for the rest of the day after the gray-haired one had caught him off guard. He hadn't imagined that a Mongol would know of the Shield-Brethren, much less of his affiliation with the order. Had the gray-haired warrior been at Onghwe's arena? He couldn't recall. The first weeks were a dull blur in his head. Other than his chance encounter with the Great General, Subutai, he could not remember the faces of any of the Mongols.

Where had he learned about the Shield-Brethren?

After a while an answer came to him, and it made his blood run cold. The gray-haired one had laughed when he had spoken the word, the savage glee of a man who thought he was stronger. A man who had survived battle and who was now fearless.

They're dead, Haakon realized. *Feronantus and his band. The Mongols found them. They're all dead.*

This news distressed him, and for several hours he struggled to understand why. As he lay in his cage, his head resting against the bars so he could see the sky, he gradually laid to rest a vain hope he had nursed ever since he had woken up in the cage. The Shield-Brethren were dead. No one was going to rescue him.

He was going to die in this foreign land. No one would sing of his deeds after he was gone. He was a nameless gladiator, and he lived at the pleasure of the *Khagan*, who was little more than a petulant child, constantly drunk on power and wine.

"Hssssst!"

Haakon shook off his maudlin fear and rolled onto his side. He peered out of his cage, looking for the whisperer.

Krasniy, in the next cage, waggled his fingers to get Haakon's attention. Haakon nodded, indicating that he had seen the red-haired giant's gesture. Krasniy held up a small object, nearly invisible in the dark, and Haakon nodded again. Krasniy pointed at the sky and then drew an arc with his finger, from east to west—sunrise to sunset. Haakon understood.

Tomorrow night, Krasniy was going to use the arrowhead he had been hiding since the Chinese raid. The *Khagan* was leaving on his hunt in the morning; by nightfall, no one in the camp would be paying much attention to the prisoners in their cages. It would be the best chance they had to escape.

Haakon lay back down on the floor of his cage, and after a few moments of trying to find a comfortable position on the unyielding floor, he fell asleep.

A plan always quieted the mind.

* * *

After the *Khagan*'s hunting party had left, Lian had gone to Gansukh's *ger*, even though he had warned her to avoid it. She only had to unlace the flaps partway to understand Gansukh's command. The destruction and the smell within mortified her, more so because even though it was Gansukh's *ger*, it was the only place within the caravan—within the entirety of the *Khagan*'s empire—that she might have been able to feel a feeble sense of security and freedom.

Munokhoi had taken that from her.

Lian had stumbled through the camp—her heart numb, her mind a confused cascade of thoughts. Munokhoi said he was going to kill her when he returned from killing Gansukh. If the ex-*Torguud* captain did return, that would mean Gansukh was dead. Would Master Chucai protect her? That was unlikely. She was a pawn in his endless court games—a piece whose use was, unfortunately, coming to an end.

Even if she found someone else to protect her, wouldn't she still be nothing more than a slave? Her life would never be her own.

Lian paused between two *ger* and fumbled in the pocket of her jacket, where she had slipped the tiny box that Gansukh had given her. It was an unadorned lacquer box, the sort that appeared seamless. She had had one like it when she was a child, and she knew the trick to getting them open. The lid was stiff and moved slowly, but she managed to open the tiny container.

Inside was a small twig crowned by three green leaves. It looked healthy and vibrant and not at all like a dried sprig cut from a tree. She touched the leaves gently, and found them soft and pliant. She raised the box to her face and sniffed. The scent was crisp and fresh, not quite mint and not quite lavender. Looking at the twig lessened her panic and confusion, and easing the lid back onto the box was more difficult than she expected.

This is what Chucai wanted, she thought. This is what the Chinese came for.

"*Lian!*"

Her hand closed reflexively around the box, and as she turned, she tucked it away in her jacket again. "Jachin," Lian said as she spotted the approaching woman, trailed by a trio of her handmaidens.

"We have nothing to do until the *Khagan* returns," Jachin said as she swept up to Lian. "I, for one, am going to take a bath." She rolled her eyes at her handmaidens. "If these simpletons can ever manage to shore up my *ger* well enough that the water doesn't keep running out of the tub."

"Perhaps it might be best to not fill the bath completely," Lian suggested, attempting to quickly fix Second Wife's problem.

"I might as well not even bother in that case." Jachin shook her head. "Next you'll be suggesting that I have the servants rub my skin with wet clothes in lieu of actually submerging my body."

"Oh, my Lady, no." Lian moved her hand—the one that had just shoved the box and sprig into her coat—up to her mouth as if horrified by the idea. "That would be akin to suggesting that you strip naked and jump in the river.

"Jachin snorted. "Just like the men?"

"Well, not *just* like them."

One of the handmaidens giggled and Jachin laughed outright before frowning playfully at Lian. "I do not think the *Khagan* would approve," she said. "No, I want to please him when he returns from his hunt. Even though he will be elated, he will be tired from the long day of riding. I want to be ready for him. I want him to take me to his bed on the night of his victory. I want to be—" She broke off, and surprisingly, blushed. She toyed with her hair, staring off over Lian's shoulder.

"Of course." Lian fought the urge to fidget, to try to flee from Jachin before Second Wife got it into her head to insist that Lian keep her company while she bathed.

"Toregene would tell me to leave the *Khagan* alone on his victory night. He would come to me if he *wanted* my company," Jachin said, nodding to herself. "But that is what she wants. Of course, left alone, the *Khagan* would choose her. Not because he likes her, but because she is First Wife." She wrinkled her nose. "It is all so easy for her. She doesn't have to worry about being forgotten, about being left alone, night after night."

Lian thought of the ruin of Gansukh's tent, of sleeping alone amid that wreckage, and nodded.

"Toregene is lazy," Jachin said, a smirk curling her lips. "She is. She thinks everything will come to her because of her station. That her son will become *Khagan* after Ögedei is gone, but she doesn't understand him."

"Not like you," Lian said politely, sensing some sort of comment was expected of her at this point. "You are always thinking of what is best for the *Khagan*."

"A true wife always does," Jachin purred, eyeing Lian. "As I am sure you think about Gansukh."

Lian's breath caught in her throat. "Gansukh?" she asked.

Jachin smiled at Lian. "Oh, you don't need to be so coy with me. I know you are thinking about him. It is so plain on your face."

"I—" Lian tugged at the hem of her jacket, finding something to do with her hands. "My Lady, I would not presume to think that such a proud warrior as Gansukh would want me."

Jachin laughed. "He's already had you, Lian."

Lian blushed. "That is not what I meant, my Lady. I am a slave. I am owned by Master Chucai, and—"

Jachin waved away Lian's words as if they were nothing more than minor annoyances. "The *Khagan* may do anything he pleases, Lian. He could simply tell Chucai that you are no longer his." She laughed, clapping her hands delightedly. "Oh, wouldn't that make him so angry!"

"Who, my Lady?"

"Master Chucai. He thinks he is in charge of the *Khagan*, and not the other way around." She leaned forward, her voice dropping to a conspiratorial whisper. "The *Khagan* detests him. He told me himself. Just the other night."

"My Lady..." Lian began, unsure what she should say. Her heart was unexpectedly racing in her chest. Freedom from Chucai. Could it be so simple? It would be easy enough to convince Second Wife of her desire to be with Gansukh, that such a union could only be accomplished by releasing her from bondage. Jachin, inveterate romantic that she was, would be delighted to be instrumental in the consummation of her relationship with Gansukh (beyond the mere physical one they already enjoyed). Also, there was the perverse joy that would come with seeing Chucai put in his place by the *Khagan*.

"My Lady is most kind to think of my happiness," Lian murmured. *Would that be enough?* she wondered.

"It is done," Jachin said. "I will tell the *Khagan* tomorrow. He will be ready to agree to anything after I have..." She trailed off, and her handmaidens giggled behind her. Jachin smiled broadly, entirely too pleased with herself.

"I...I am in your debt," Lian said.

Jachin clapped her hands delightedly. "I am going to take my bath now," she announced. "I must prepare myself for a *very important* audience with the *Khagan*." She smiled at Lian. "You should prepare yourself as well," she said with a wink. "For when the hunters return. And later, you and I can share stories about our men."

"Of course, my Lady," Lian dipped her head and remained in the submissive pose. It was an old trick that worked well with some of the ladies at court. Pleased with the gratitude proffered by slaves they would wander off, not realizing that it was they who had been dismissed by the servants and not the other way around. It worked in this situation too, as Jachin, humming happily to herself, wandered off toward her *ger*, her handmaidens trailing behind.

Lian watched the four ladies depart, her mind racing once more. A debt to Jachin would never be paid in full; Second Wife would constantly remind Lian of what she had done. Regardless of her freedom from Chucai—of her relationship with Gansukh—she would not be *free* of Jachin. In which case, wasn't she still a slave?

Her hand drifted to the tiny bulge in her coat.

What if she left the empire instead?

* * *

Cnán waited and waited. She grew tired of waiting, slept, and woke, wondering if the *Khagan* was ever going to leave his camp. She hid her horse not far from the Mongol camp, and donning a dirty robe and a rose-colored scarf that she had pilfered the last time she had crept into camp, she wandered into enemy territory once again. She stayed among the maze of *ger* and wagons that belonged to the merchants and staff that served the *Khagan*. There was a mix of ethnicities among this rabble, and when someone did pay attention to her, she seemed no more or less exotic than those around her.

There was a bustling urgency in the camp, and she knew the *Khagan* was finally leaving. As more and more of the camp drifted toward the center where the *Khagan*'s *ger* was located, she wandered toward the cages where the prisoners were held.

Haakon was still there.

She didn't reveal herself. Not yet. It would give the boy unreasonable hope if she made contact with him. She didn't know when she was going to try to free him, nor exactly how she was going to get him away from camp. She needed a little time to think yet, and nightfall would come soon enough.

That was when she would free the young Northerner.

She found an unattended pot hung over a fire pit, and she scooped out its contents into a wooden bowl. She pilfered a half loaf of bread that lay forgotten near a pair of wooden benches, and squatted down behind a half-assembled wagon to stuff the food into her belly.

She still had to wait, but at least she wouldn't be hungry.

* * *

The *Khagan*'s camp was in the most isolated location in all of the empire, and there was no friendly Chinese village for hundreds of miles. Lian knew that fleeing now was a fool's choice, but the isolation worked in her favor. There were fewer guards with the *Khagan* here than there were at Karakorum, and most of the trackers were away with the *Khagan* at this time. When the *Khagan* returned, there would be a celebration that would last several days. If she was lucky, no one would really notice she was gone until it was too late to track her.

Except Gansukh.

Would he come after her?

Part of her hoped he would, but she shoved those feelings aside. She had to escape. She had to do it now.

She knew Jachin was taking a bath, which meant the *ger* used by her handmaidens would probably be empty. After slinking in and stealing a few articles of clothing and a bag to carry them in, she wandered toward the makeshift pasture on the northern side of the caravan, intending to investigate the possibility of stealing a horse—a dangerous proposition, especially given the punishment for horse thievery among Mongols—but as she caught sight of Gansukh's lonely *ger* one last time, an idea occurred to her.

She didn't bother unlacing the flaps this time; she simply used her knife to cut through the ties. Inside the smell assaulted her, but she breathed through her mouth, ignoring the worst of the acrid reek. Munokhoi had broken everything that could be broken and taken his sword to the rest. She rummaged through the wreckage until she found Gansukh's store of extra supplies: needle, thread, candle, cloth, sharpening stone, flint.

Working quickly, she arranged everything that would burn readily along one wall of the *ger*, piling the furs and the straw from Gansukh's sleeping mat on top. Her hands shook slightly as she used the flint, and it took her three tries to coax a steady flame from the slightly damp straw.

The flames were tiny and threatened to go out as she watched. She blew on them a few times until they grew steadier. As she stepped back to the flaps of the *ger*, she watched the flames. They weren't going to go out, but it would take a little while before the pile really caught. Long enough for her to be nowhere near the *ger* when it started to burn.

As she turned to leave, she heard voices outside the *ger*, and she carefully peeked out. Two *Torguud* were wandering nearby, arguing about the evening meal. They noticed nothing amiss about Gansukh's *ger*, though more likely they hadn't even looked. They were very intent in their conversation.

Waiting, Lian glanced back nervously over her shoulder. The flames were a little taller than before. She didn't have as much time as she thought.

As soon as the men were out of earshot, she ducked out of the *ger*, laid the flaps carefully over one another, and strode off quickly for the horse pasture.

On her way there, she passed the row of cages that housed the prisoners from the West. She stumbled to a halt when she realized one of the cages was empty. The blondhaired Westerner was housed in the adjacent cage, and he was staring at her eagerly, almost as if she had caught him doing something illicit.

Her breath caught in her throat. *The prisoners were trying to escape.*

* * *

Krasniy sawed savagely at the thick rope that looped around the door of his cage while Haakon kept watch. After the excitement of the *Khagan*'s departure, the camp became very quiet, and after a heated discussion, they decided this was the best opportunity they were going to have for escape.

Krasniy went to work on the rope, and when the arrowhead didn't cut through the thick rope quickly, Haakon's apprehension started to mount.

If they were discovered...

It was best to not worry about such possibilities. They were committed to their course of action now, and as fraught as the spontaneous plan was, they were actively attempting to escape. They were fighting for their freedom, and as the first rope parted and Krasniy began work on the second, Haakon's fear was replaced with a growing elation.

Freedom.

The last rope parted, and with a hoarse shout, Krasniy shoved the door of his cage open. Moving stiffly, he lumbered over to Haakon's cage and shoved the arrowhead through the bars to him. As Haakon picked up the tiny saw and went to work on his ropes, Krasniy indicated he was going to look for weapons. Haakon nodded absently, his attention focused on keeping the slippery arrowhead moving back and forth along the same axis of the hempen rope.

He had just finished sawing through the first rope when the dark-haired woman appeared not far from his cage. He hadn't heard her coming, and he could only stand there stupidly, the arrowhead hidden in his fist, staring at her. Beside him, Krasniy's empty cage with its open door was all the evidence anyone needed to understand what was going on.

Haakon stared at the woman, quickly trying to figure out what he could do—if anything—to keep her from raising an alarm. And when voices did go up in the camp beyond the first row of *ger*, he flinched. They had been discovered already! He wanted to bang his head against the cage door in frustration.

Much to his surprise, the dark-haired woman quickly strode toward his cage, pulling a knife out of her robes. He stood back from the bars and watched—both mystified and elated—as she hacked at the rope holding his cage closed. Her knife cut through the rope very quickly in comparison to the laborious effort it had been taking with the arrowhead. "Escape?" the woman said in the Mongol tongue as she pulled open the door of his cage. She motioned to him, pointing off to his left. "Now," she said.

Behind her, he spotted Krasniy returning, a bloody sword in his hand. The woman sensed his attention shifting to behind her and she turned around, quickly backing a few steps away from the cage, trying to keep both him and Krasniy in her field of view.

"We have to go," the woman said. "Now. There is very little time."

Krasniy looked at Haakon, who could only shrug. He had no idea where the woman had come from, but the fact that she had helped him with the ropes on his cage suggested the three of them had the same plan in mind.

"Okay," Haakon said, ducking out of his cage. He stood upright, feeling his spine rattle and crack, and he filled his lungs with air. It felt good to stretch, even though time was of the essence. Off to his right, he noticed a lazy finger of smoke drifting into the air, and the sound of excited voices drifted toward them from that direction.

A diversion? he wondered. His gaze was drawn to movement and he saw a tiny woman, her head swathed in a red scarf, watching them from the row of *ger*. She stood awkwardly, staring at the cages, and there was something about her bearing that struck Haakon as familiar.

She looked in his direction as she reached up and removed the scarf from her head. Haakon stared, shocked to recognize her. "Cnán... ?"

* * *

The Chinese woman complicated the situation, especially when the other prisoners started to make noises about being freed as well. Cnán gestured at Haakon to follow her, and started walking briskly toward the tree line to the west of the camp. The young Northerner would either follow her or not, and she couldn't really do anything about the others—the giant man covered in red hair or the Chinese woman who had helped Haakon escape. In her mind, she could already hear Feronantus admonishing her for the number of strays she had picked up, and she felt her face flushing with embarrassment as she strode out of the camp.

She hadn't thought through Haakon's escape. She hadn't really considered the complications that would arise with trying to free just one of the prisoners. She glanced over her shoulder—happy to see that Haakon was following her, not as happy to see the other two coming as well. At least they'd moved away from the cages before other prisoners made too much noise.

They had to move quickly.

She picked up her pace when she reached the tree line, and behind her she heard Haakon hiss at her, trying to get her attention. She didn't slow down, not wanting to stop until they were some distance into the woods.

The red-haired one, she heard, was not very good at moving quietly through the woods.

"Cnán!" Haakon grabbed her shoulder and pulled her to a stop.

"We can't stay here," she said. "We have to keep moving."

"In a moment," he said. He was slightly out of breath, his cheeks flushed with excitement. His beard had come in more fully and he seemed taller. Perhaps that was only her memory of him—thinking of him as a mere boy, even though he hadn't been.

"I wasn't expecting your friends," Cnán said.

Haakon looked over his shoulder. "That one is Krasniy," he said, nodding at the red-haired man who was clumsily making his way through the forest. "I do not know the other one." He smiled. "I never expected to see you again."

She flushed at his attention, and gently removed herself from his grasp. "I couldn't..." she started.

"You aren't here alone," Haakon said. "One of the Mongols talked about the Shield-Brethren. Like he knew them."

Cnán started. "Alchiq?"

"Aye," Haakon nodded. "I think that is his name. Older man. Gray hair."

"That is the one," Cnán said. She suppressed a shiver. If Alchiq was with the *Khagan*, the Shield-Brethren might be walking into a trap.

"Excuse me," the Chinese woman said in the Mongol tongue, having caught up. "We cannot stay here. We have to move farther into the woods."

Cnán glared at her. "Who are you?" she demanded.

"I am Lian. Like your friends, I wish to escape the *Khagan*'s reach."

"You can't come with us," Cnán said. "I don't know you."

"Nor I you," the woman responded. She glanced at Haakon. "But I know him."

Cnán noted that Haakon appeared to be following their conversation. "But I don't know you," he said to the woman.

"I like your new friends, Haakon," Krasniy boomed as he joined them. "Very pretty." He laughed at Cnán's expression.

Cnán shook her head. "Come on," she said. "We need to be far away by nightfall."

"Where are we going?" Haakon asked.

"Anywhere but here," Cnán muttered.

Haakon didn't budge as she started to walk away, and she stopped too, looking back at him. "We have to go," she reiterated.

"Where are they?" Haakon asked.

"Who?"

"The Shield-Brethren. They're in danger, aren't they?"

Cnán shook her head. "They're always in danger," she replied.

"They're trying to kill the *Khagan*." Haakon didn't phrase it as a question.

Krasniy guffawed at Haakon's pronouncement, but his laughter subsided when he glanced at Cnán's face.

"Yes," she said.

"I want to help them," Haakon insisted. "If Alchiq is with the *Khagan*, then it may be a trap." He turned to Lian and spoke in the Mongol tongue. "How many warriors with the *Khagan*?"

She shrugged. "Four, maybe five *arban*."

"Fifty men," Haakon said to Cnán. "How many Shield-Brethren?"

She shrugged, not wanting to tell Haakon the true number. "A dozen or more," she lied.

"Who leads them? Is it Feronantus?"

Cnán felt herself growing impatient. "This isn't important. We have to flee."

"It is important," Haakon insisted. "Because we're going to help them."

"You are out of your mind," Cnán snapped. "We are deep within the Mongol Empire. We have very little in the way of supplies. We are—you are—clearly a stranger in this land. We only have one horse. We can't afford to go riding into...into—" She struggled to find the right words.

"Battle?" Haakon supplied. He smiled at her and glanced at Krasniy. "Where else would we go?"

Cnán let loose a tiny cry of frustration. *Completely stubborn*, she thought. *Just like Feronantus.*

"They are my friends," Haakon said. "They are my family."

She glared at him. Was that not the same reason she had defied Feronantus to stay behind and rescue Haakon? Had she not—over the long journey from the West—come to think of the Shield-Brethren as family? She couldn't find fault in Haakon using the same reasoning in his argument.

"Fine," she snapped. She pointed at Lian. "What about her?"

Krasniy laid a large hand on the Chinese woman's shoulder. "She can be with me," he said, a broad grin on his face.

Lian tossed her hair back from her shoulder and smiled up at the giant man. Cnán was unsure whether Lian had been able to follow their argument, but she could tell from the anger in the woman's eyes that Lian understood the meaning of Krasniy's hand on her shoulder.

"Come on," she said with a hint of resignation. She turned and started to weave her way through the woods.

This whole rescue was turning out to be much different from what she had planned.

AN IMPERIAL BREAKFAST

FREDERICK SQUINTED AT the pair who had interrupted his breakfast. "You seem to have traded down," he said to wide-eyed Ferenc. "We gave you a cardinal and you have brought us back a mere priest. And where is the rest of your posse?"

"Your Majesty, he doesn't understand you," the priest said in a grandfatherly voice.

Frederick sighed. "I know. You were not present for the farce yesterday, a tedium exacerbated by the fact that even as I was being excommunicated—again—the cardinals were electing a new Pope. I have heard there was white smoke sighted. Are you here to inform me of the identity of the new Pope?"

"I am, Your Majesty," the priest said.

Frederick waited for the priest to continue. "And that man is..."

"I am he," the priest said. "The new Pope."

Frederick started to smirk, but upon noticing the unblinking sternness of the priest's expression, he delicately raised a hand to hide his amusement. "Of course you are," he said. "Obviously." He spread his hands in a welcoming gesture. "Splendid. Well, here you are, already coming to give me grief," he said, a mocking tone creeping into his voice.

The priest gave him a puzzled look. "You do me a disservice, Your Majesty, in thinking my intentions are malign."

"Ah, a benign Papal visit then. And so early in your reign. To what do we owe this honor?" Frederick asked. He signaled a servant waiting by the tent flap, and made a gesture demanding wine. He leaned back in his carved wooden chair. "I do wish you spoke Italian or German," he said in Ferenc's direction. "It would be nice to get a second opinion as to whether I should believe this story or not."

"Ferenc is a good boy," the priest said as if protecting him. "He would not tell you anything unless I gave him permission. So you may as well just talk to me directly."

"Very well then," Frederick replied. "This comedy continues. I have no other choice but to play my role in this, do I?" When the priest did not answer, Frederick continued. "Have you selected a name for yourself, or is there a Christian name your mother gave you that still suffices?"

"Rodrigo," the priest said with a tiny bow of his head. "Rodrigo Bendrito."

"Well met, Rodrigo Bendrito. Or would you prefer *Your Holiness?*"

The priest demurred responding, offering a much more pious and humble nod of his head instead.

"I shall split the difference then," Frederick offered. "Tell me, Father, what brings you here."

"We are paying our respects."

Frederick laughed. "You don't know my history with the Church, do you? It is amusing, admittedly, to have the Pope here, in *my* tent, offering respect when he is so newly anointed, but you must understand that I am more than a little reticent to believe such a statement." He waved a hand at Ferenc. "Your companion can tell you. He was witness to my most recent excommunication."

Father Rodrigo's face lost some of its serenity. "The Church has lost its way," he said quietly. "I do not cling to what it was. I have seen..." He shook himself as if he were shrugging off a heavy blanket. "I do not believe in your prior transgressions," he said.

Frederick blinked. "Are you *un*-excommunicating me?" he asked. He glanced at Ferenc, who seemed both oblivious to their conversation and pleased that they were talking. "You're no help," Frederick noted.

He sat forward in his chair, returning his attention to Father Rodrigo. "This is a most curious turn of events," he said. "And suddenly, I find myself being drawn into your delirium. If you are indeed Pope, what a marvelous thing it would be to discover a *friend* in Rome. So, yes, tell me. Is there any reason other than a mutual exchange of respect that brings you into my camp?"

The priest reached for his satchel as if to reassure himself of its contents. "I have been called to service by God. I must raise an army against the infidels. I seek to call a crusade."

"In person?" Frederick asked incredulously. "Usually one sends bishops and priests out to do that sort of ugly legwork."

"I believe my appearance is the only way to move people to action: show them I am doing, myself, what I think they should be doing. I moved a great many people in Rome yesterday, and I intend to move others as I travel."

"I see, I see," Frederick said, nodding. He crossed his arms, then slumped back farther in the chair and crossed his legs. He stared intensely at Father Rodrigo, his mind a welter of thoughts. Was this man as barmy as he seemed, or was he truly the new Pope? There was an intensity to the priest's gaze, and he spoke his words with an equal fervor. But he had also met zealots like this before, and even though they believed—so very ardently—that they spoke God's truth, so many of them had found only an ugly death. "And may I ask, since the boy cannot understand me, what has happened to the cardinal I released yesterday?" he asked, mainly to give himself another few moments to think. *Had Léna a hand in this?*

"Oh, yes, that sounds familiar." Father Rodrigo said. He turned to Ferenc, and they had a brief exchange in Magyar. Then Father Rodrigo turned back to Frederick. "Cardinal Oddone de Monferrato, would it be?"

"The very same," said Frederick. "He was to be the tiebreaker in the Papal vote."

"They voted before he arrived," Father Rodrigo explained. "Apparently it was quite a surprise when I won."

"I'm sure it was," Frederick laughed. The page boy reentered with a flagon of wine and three cups. The Emperor pointed to a camp table deeper inside the tent, and the boy crossed to it and began to pour the wine. "And how did you come to be a candidate?"

"I have no idea," Father Rodrigo said. "When Ferenc and I arrived in Rome, I was mistaken for a cardinal and tossed into the Septizodium. I was sick and weak, and I cannot account for anything that happened there."

"But apparently somebody decided to put you forth as a candidate."

"I don't know who, or why," Father Rodrigo said. Frederick studied his face. Barmy or not, the priest radiated calm sincerity.

"I realize the vote is in confidence, but have you a sense of who your allies were?"

"Oh, yes. The kindest man of all was killed in the fire—"

"What?" Frederick demanded.

"There was a fire in the Septizodium, an unexpected blaze that released us from our prison. Sadly it also released Robert of Somercotes from this mortal coil entirely."

Frederick uncrossed his arms and legs and sat up very straight. "What the *fuck* has been happening in that godforsaken city?" he demanded.

The priest remained calm. "I believe the fire may have been set deliberately as a way to force the issue of the election, perhaps, or for more nefarious reasons. Once rescued, we were all moved to a horse stable, and from there to Saint Peter's, where the cardinals elected me to be the next Bishop of Rome. But they wanted to keep me locked up. They would not let me speak to my flock, and so I had to run away."

Frederick stared at him, wide-eyed. "This is the most god-damned improbable story I believe I have heard in my life," he declared. "And that is saying a *lot*, my friend."

Father Rodrigo nodded amicably. "Yes, it does have the sense of a dream, doesn't it? I have wondered myself, but having recently been infected with dreams, I know now that I am awake. So very wide awake. And my health has been restored, allowing me to carry out my mission."

Frederick pursed his lips together, struggling to find a rational explanation for the priest's presence and story. It beggared comprehension, but...he couldn't ignore what Léna had told him prior to her departure from his camp. *Opportunities will present themselves. Take care that you recognize them.*

He signaled to the boy for his wine cup. "I will ask you about your mission in a moment," he said, "but first let us return to my first question: tell me about your supporters. Besides the English cardinal, who befriended you?"

Father Rodrigo smiled as if nostalgic. "Most of the cardinals were very pleasant to me. Two fellows named Colonna and Capocci especially took me under their wings, so to speak—"

"Indeed?" *So we have the same friends*, Frederick thought. *Or at least, your friends are not my enemies.*

"Yes, and there is Cardinal Fieschi. He is most attentive," Father Rodrigo concluded carefully.

That made no sense at all. Fieschi and Colonna would never be on the same side of any issue. Frederick frowned, and dismissed the boy offering wine.

"Fieschi? Sinibaldo Fieschi? You are sure of that?" Frederick said. "If both Fieschi and Colonna are your allies, I'm pretty damn sure that one of them is not actually your ally, but wants you to *think* he is."

"Which do you think is not my ally?" Father Rodrigo asked, a curious cunning in his eyes.

What am I supposed to read in his face? Frederick found himself wondering. The priest continued to surprise him with these alternating moods. He appeared harmless, a simple priest struck daft by some beatific vision he thought he had had; but at other moments, there were these flashes of a deep intelligence and passion.

"The fire in the Septizodium," he said carefully. "You said it was unexpected. Unexpected for you, perhaps, but not for everyone."

"*Ignis succensus est in furore meo,*" Father Rodrigo said.

Frederick couldn't help himself and rolled his eyes. "God, you priests and your Scripture. Yes, I get it. The fire was born out of someone's anger, but whose?" He stared at the priest. "Somercotes died in the Septizodium," he mused. "Who benefited from that *accident*? Orsini, for one. Somercotes was English, hardly an advocate for a Roman Pope. Did he have men set that fire to cover up some other nefarious deed? Or did he have a man inside?"

"*Et ardebit usque ad inferni novissima,*" Father Rodrigo said quietly.

The fire that burns in the lowest pit of Hell, Frederick thought, still considering whether to believe what the priest was suggesting. He held his hand out. "I'll take the wine now, boy." The page immediately held out the chalice. Frederick drank it off in one gulp and handed back the cup. "Have some wine," he said, gesturing to the other two cups. He looked directly at Ferenc and repeated the gesture.

As the two visitors rose and crossed to the table, Frederick carefully considered what the priest was suggesting. The fire in the Septizodium had been set on purpose, mostly likely to hide the suspicious death of Cardinal Somercotes. Did he know who committed the heinous crime? he wondered, and of what use was that knowledge—to the priest, to him?

He had his doubts about the man's claim to being the Pontiff-elect, but he also knew to keep an open mind for such a possibility. The machinations of kings and caliphs and popes affected all of Christendom, and a vast portion of his duties as Holy Roman Emperor were to understand these games better than anyone else. He had learned, long ago, to keep an eye out for the chaotic oddity that might change the rules. In the case of Father Rodrigo—madman or Pope—what was he supposed to do? The priest wanted to engage in this foolhardy business of all-out war? He doubted the man could actually accomplish the goal he sought, but what he thought meant little. What mattered more was the Church's reaction, and Frederick strongly suspected the Church—if any of what the man said was true—would want to lock him up somewhere, against his will, to keep him from discrediting the Church with his public declarations.

When they finished their wine, Ferenc and Father Rodrigo returned to their stools. Frederick noticed that the boy had left his cup beside the decanter, while the priest still held on to his. His fingers tapped against its rim, and he was unaware of the noise he was making.

"Two more questions for you," Frederick asked. "First, this foreign boy that's with you—"

"Ferenc," Father Rodrigo said affectionately; Ferenc turned nervously toward him. Father Rodrigo made a soothing gesture and murmured something in Ferenc's language. "He was with me at Mohi, and he accomp—"

"Jesus Christ, you were at *Mohi*? Having seen that, you still want to call a crusade?" Frederick asked, eyes widening. "That settles it, you're definitely mad."

"I believe I was, Your Majesty, but I have been healed by God's grace," Father Rodrigo replied evenly.

"So you came from Mohi with this feral creature," Frederick prompted. "You were thrown into the Septizodium—"

"Yes, and he tried to rescue me with the assistance of a waif of a girl, Osie...Osie-someone."

"Ocyrhoe," Ferenc said promptly.

"Yes," Frederick said. "I've met her. Archetypal urchin, not what I go for. I sent Ocyrhoe and Ferenc to the Septizodium in the company of three normal adults—a cardinal, a soldier, and a woman. Where are they?" Seeing the priest's expression, he mentally expressed his displeasure—mainly to keep from profaning God *that much* in front of the priest—and pointed at Ferenc. "Ask him," he snapped.

The priest and the boy had a brief exchange, as Frederick kept moving the pieces around in his mind. The man had to be deranged, however pacific his exterior behavior.

Father Rodrigo turned his attention back to the Emperor. "When they arrived at Saint Peter's, Ferenc and Ocyrhoe were allowed to have a private audience with me. Ferenc has not seen the others since then. Ocyrhoe stayed behind after she helped us to escape."

"Your story grows more fucking bizarre with each utterance," Frederick said. "I'll have to thank Fieschi for the entertainment next time I see him."

"You're not going to send me back to him, are you?" asked Father Rodrigo, worry darkening his face for the first time.

Frederick looked at him and thought about all the possible ways there were to answer that. "Of course not, Your Holiness," he said at last. He turned and signaled to the boy standing by the entrance of his tent. "Before we discuss what is to happen to you, let's eat, shall we?" He mimed eating to Ferenc, who perked up and nodded. "It is much easier to make important decisions with a full belly," he said.

Father Rodrigo nodded absently, his empty hands resting lightly on his satchel.

UNEXPECTED ALLIES

N THE OTHER side of the open field, the Mongols massed. They outnumbered the Shield-Brethren at the gate by no small number, but they appeared to be in no hurry to assault the gate again. Behind the roiling mob of infantry, horsemen rode, parading back and forth. *Rallying the men*, Rutger thought.

"That's a lot of Mongols," Knútr observed. The blocky Shield-Brethren had lost his helmet during the initial fracas, and the right side of his head was sticky with blood. He grinned, and Rutger noticed one of his pupils was larger than the other. "They seem a bit...nervous."

Knútr was correct in his assessment. The Mongol vanguard jeered and shouted at the Shield-Brethren, trying to goad the knights. Rutger didn't understand any of the insults being shouted, but he was familiar with training-yard bullying. They *were* afraid, and all the bluster in the world couldn't hide the fact that their superior numbers were not decisive enough an advantage for them to press the attack.

Rutger knew they would come eventually. The men on horse-back were shouting at the infantry, whipping them into a frenzy. Calling them cowards, unworthy dogs that were an embarrassment to their Khan. How could they face their families, their fathers, if they ran from this meager band of nameless knights? Rutger knew what was being said. He had used the same words himself. *Bolster their courage. Call upon their sense of duty. Inflame their rage.*

The Mongols would come again. They had no choice in the end.

The cart had been hauled to one side of the gate, and the dead horses (along with a number of Mongol corpses) to the other, forming a definite channel around the gate. The Mongols would have to funnel into it in order to attack the Shield-Brethren; it was an ancient tactic that had been used successfully over and over again. Reduce the killing field so as to strip away the enemy's advantage of numbers.

Rutger dimly remembered a siege in the Holy Land—he couldn't even recall the name of the castle now—that had lasted six weeks. The Muslims breached the wall twice, but each time the defenders had managed to beat the invaders back, inflicting such grievous casualties that the Muslim morale quailed. It took the Muslim Sultan so long to reestablish control of his army that the Christian engineers had been able to reseal the breaches. Eventually reinforcements from Jerusalem had arrived, and the Sultan had fled.

Reinforcements. Nodding, Rutger looked over his shoulder, scanning the open ground outside the walls for signs of movement. *Where were they?*

With a ragged howl, the Mongols came again. Spears and arrows flew in advance of the angry mob, and Rutger heard a coughing gurgle off to his left as one of the hurled spears found a target. "Stand and hold," he shouted, his voice ragged and hoarse. He forced his fingers to tighten around the hilt of his sword as he readied himself for the charge. It was only the boon of battle fervor that made the pain in his hands tolerable.

From the guard towers above him, his archers began to loose arrows into the front rank. He could only spare a few men for archery duty, and the six men he had chosen were known for their speed and accuracy. He couldn't match the Mongols for numbers, but he could make each arrow count. As the Mongols charged, each arrow dropped its target, befouling the charging men who came after. In this way the Mongol line, instead of being a heavy wave that crashed over them, became a ragged and chaotic crowd, with men jostling one another as they tried to close the holes in their ranks.

The Shield-Brethren line stood firm, a waiting wall of sharp steel.

Rutger was consciously aware of the first man, a Mongol with yellow beads strung in his hair. He thrust his spear at Rutger, and Rutger sidestepped the attack, moving inside and driving his sword into the man's open mouth. The Mongol with the yellow beads died, and that was the last man Rutger remembered as the bulk of the Mongol charge slammed into the Shield-Brethren line. His world became a chaotic blur—filled with spear points and curved swords, men shouting and screaming, and the distant awareness of his own arm, rising and falling.

He saw Knútr fall, run through by two spears, an arrow jutting from his right shoulder. Another brother went down, the front of his helmet cleaved by a Mongol sword. Rutger could not tell which of his men it was, and he felt a momentary spasm of regret as the press of bodies surged over the fallen knight. The Mongols kept coming, slowly forcing the Shield-Brethren back.

Rutger's maille saved him from a sword stroke to his left side that nonetheless sent ripples of pain through his body. He clamped his arm down, trapping the blade against his body, and wrenched it out of his attacker's hand. He buried a hand's worth of blade into the man's befuddled face.

That was when he heard the shouts, not from in front of him, but from behind. "Clear the way!"

Rutger grasped the shoulder of the man next to him and shoved him violently against the inside wall of the gate. The desperate move saved both of them as a thunder of horses stormed past. He caught sight of a moving banner of white and silver, the riders all dressed in gleaming white surcoats. The host of horsemen struck the Mongols like a battering ram, splintering them into a disorganized mob. Those who weren't trampled outright fled before the onslaught of the freshly arrived knights.

As the tide of battle turned, one of the knights fought his way back to the gate. His sword was drenched with blood, and it matched the image stitched proudly across his bloodstained surcoat. The crimson sword. Above it was an equally red cross.

The sigil of the *Fratres Militiae Christi Livoniae*. The Sword Brothers.

The knight cleared his sword of blood, sheathed it, and pushed his helm up. Rutger stared in anger at the face revealed—the face of the man who brutally butchered one of their own in the Khan's arena.

These were not the reinforcements he had expected.

*　*　*

When *Heermeister* Dietrich did not return from his fool's errand, Kristaps had taken charge of the Livonian host in Hünern. He sent a quartet of men to investigate the *Heermeister*'s absence on the off chance that Dietrich had only been delayed, and the rest he set to dismantling their camp. Regardless of the success or failure of the *Heermeister*'s audience with the dissolute Khan, it was time to leave Hünern. The riots following his fight in the arena had upset the delicate balance in the tent city.

It was all an illusion anyway. The Mongols were wolves, and they looked upon the West as an unguarded flock of wooly sheep. Kristaps had seen the handiwork of the Mongol Empire in Kiev; he knew of its rapacious appetite. The West ran around in circles, bleating in foolish ignorance. They had been seduced by the Khan's facile lure of martial combat, thinking that a single victory in the arena would save them.

He had shown them otherwise, hadn't he? The death of one of the Shield-Brethren had brought their tenuous truce to a bloody end. And now they saw the true nature of the wolves from the East. Now they knew they had no choice but to fight.

Yet, Dietrich wanted to run away. The coward.

As his men loaded their horses, taking way too long to accomplish such a simple thing as striking camp, his scouts returned. They found Dietrich's bodyguards, dead in the streets, and of the *Heermeister* there was no sign.

It wasn't hard to figure out what had happened.

Regardless of his disappointment in Dietrich's leadership, the *Heermeister*'s disappearance provided a useful incentive to the remaining Livonians. It was better if Dietrich was dead and not captured, as the murder of the *Heermeister* was an insult that could not be ignored. Kristaps was the First Sword of Fellin, a legend within the Livonian Order. He had survived the battle of Schaulen, and he had slain one of the famed Shield-Brethren in single combat. When he addressed the Livonians in a voice that quaked with rage, they listened.

Kristaps was tired of running, tired of hiding in the marshes and the forests. He wore the white, not the black, and the sword on his surcoat was red. Why was the sword in his hand not that same color? Why was it always sheathed when there were so many enemies of God close at hand? Why were the Sword Brothers not *fighting* for the glory of God?

The men had raised their voices in response to his questions. They too wanted glory. They wanted to scatter their enemies. They wanted to save the West. It was not difficult to whip them into a frenzy. The Sword Brothers would not sit idly by as their *Heermeister* was tortured and killed by unclean heathens. They would not *flee*; they would fight.

Kristaps's plan was neither complicated nor subtle. They knew the location of the enemy camp. They would ride into the heart of it and claim reprisal for the crimes inflicted both upon their order and upon Christendom. They would show the West that the Shield-Brethren were not the only order capable of demolishing the enemies of God.

The ride through the city had been exhilarating, and when they found the gate of the Mongol compound wide open, Kristaps had not hesitated to give the order to charge. Galloping through the gate and scattering the Mongol host clustered there had been nearly as cathartic as cleaving the Shield-Brethren knight's corpse in the arena. The motion of his sword about him as Kristaps rode was a rhythmic expulsion of his frustration. He laid about him with powerful strokes, cleaving helms and severing arms, venting all of his anger. His horse, goaded into a frenzy by his fury, ferociously trampled the wounded and dying. This was his true purpose, that for which God had given him his strength. That the Shield-Brethren had failed long ago to harness it was a sign of their foolishness, of their weakness.

He broke them, these strange-faced killers from a far-off land, who fancied themselves conquerors and subjugators. He shattered them, rode them down, and trampled them into a bloody paste in the dirt where they fell. It was only when the Mongols were fleeing the field that he pulled himself free of the blood fury and took stock of the circumstances he and his Livonian brothers had altered.

The gate had been open when his host had arrived, and the Mongols had been engaged with a small force guarding it. Men wearing Western armor.

He pulled his horse away from the fighting and returned to the gate. Pushing up his visor, he examined the puny force that had been holding the gate. They wore the Red Rose.

One of the Shield-Brethren detached himself from the group and Kristaps marked his face. Kristaps recognized him from the stands at the arena. He had been the one holding the young one back. The other Shield-Brethren stared at him with faces clotted with anger and suspicion, like dogs staring at a master from whom they received only kicks and curses.

He chuckled as he shook his blade, freeing it of cloying blood. He was going to enjoy what came next.

* * *

Rutger became acutely aware that he was holding Andreas's sword, and part of his mind clamored for him to raise it against the man who had killed Andreas. He held his ground, though, knowing such an assault was exactly what the mounted Livonian wanted.

Andreas's killer sat astride his horse with the demeanor of a king—untouchable and in absolute control of his surroundings—a tiny smile on his face. His blue eyes were so cold their gaze seemed to knife right through Rutger's maille, more readily than any Mongol sword. He wore maille with solid steel upon his shoulders, his surcoat soaked with Mongol blood. He carried a shield upon his left arm; his single-handed sword, having been cleared of blood, was back in its scabbard, and strapped to his saddle was the great two-handed sword he had used to kill Andreas. He sat utterly still, like a cat watching his terrified prey.

He won't give me the satisfaction, Rutger realized. The Livonian's rage was clear in his bright blue eyes, but there was also an unmistakable intelligence. Whatever hatred he bore for the Shield-Brethren, he kept it in tight control. *Now is not the right time*. Rutger lowered his sword and carefully walked toward the waiting knight.

When they were close enough that shouting was not needed, the blue-eyed knight spoke. "Your men owe me their lives," he said in an offhand way.

"We owe you nothing," Rutger spat.

The Livonian looked around the blood-spattered field. "My men broke their advance. They would have overwhelmed you otherwise."

"We did not call for your support," Rutger said.

"We came, nonetheless," the Livonian smiled.

"This does not assuage you of the blood debt between us," Rutger said.

The blue-eyed knight laughed. His posture was relaxed, unperturbed, as if this were a casual training-yard discussion taking place rather than words exchanged hastily in the midst of a battlefield. "Of course not, old man. I would be disappointed otherwise." He gestured, drawing Rutger's attention to his scattered riders. "You will not claim it today, *Virgin-defender*. There is much still not done here."

"Where is your master?" Rutger demanded.

The knight leaned forward. "I would ask the same of you. Where has Feronantus gone? Why do I not see that old war hound here today?"

In a flash, Rutger finally recognized the Livonian knight. It had been many years since he had seen the other man, and he had been so much younger. "You," he gasped. "I know you."

The Livonian laughed again. "Do you remember me now?" He pulled his helm down, hiding his face from Rutger's accusatory gaze. He drew his sword, causing Rutger to take a step back in alarm.

"I kill only Mongols today, old man. My men will follow my lead. Pray to God that your fellow Brethren follow yours."

"Kristaps," Rutger spat. "This isn't finished."

"No," Kristaps replied. "It is far from over." He spurred his horse away from Rutger, returning to the assembling host of his bloodied men.

Rutger shuddered, his hands aching fiercely. He shouted over his shoulder, summoning the surviving Shield-Brethren. As much as he yearned for it to be otherwise, he knew Kristaps was right.

Old feuds would have to wait. There was other killing to be done first.

THE SECOND VOTE

AFTER OCYRHOE TOLD the Senator and the cardinal about sending Ferenc and Father Rodrigo to the Porta Flamina—and the subsequent flurry of activity as Orsini had ordered his guards to scout the roads and countryside around Porta Flamina—she and Léna were left alone again in the small room that had once been Father Rodrigo's room. The Castel Sant'Angelo was being thoroughly searched as well, she knew, on the off chance that everything said so far was a lie.

"I understand why they want me," Ocyrhoe said after listening awhile to the distant sound of guards stomping around in the hallways. "I abetted fugitives. But you had nothing to do with it. You should be allowed to go back to Frederick."

"I'm not going anywhere until I learn what has happened to the Binders of Rome," Léna said. "That requires me to spend some time with Senator Orsini."

"You aren't safe with him," Ocyrhoe pointed out with a note of alarm.

Léna smiled at her. "Our sisters have gone missing. The Senator knows what has happened to them. How could I not try to learn the truth?"

Ocyrhoe shuddered. "I do not want to be alone with him."

"You're a child; you're not even fully trained," Léna said. "That you survived the Senator's efforts to this point is almost miraculous. Fear is natural, Ocyrhoe; it is guilt which you must not succumb to."

"I could have done more," Ocyrhoe mumbled, embarrassed that Léna had so clearly seen the source of her fear.

"In any crisis, survivors will always berate themselves that they could have done more," Léna said, almost to herself. She blinked and then her sharp focus returned to Ocyrhoe. "I should get you out of Rome," she said, almost as if to herself.

"Where would I go?" Ocyrhoe demanded, alarmed. "The farthest I've ever gone outside the city walls was the Emperor's camp two days ago! I'd rather stay here with you and face Orsini."

"Do not take offense at this, child, but you would only be a hindrance to me," Léna said. "If you want to be of assistance to me, put yourself as far away from here as possible," she said with a firm but reassuring tone.

"Why?" Ocyrhoe asked.

"As long as you stay here, you can be used against me," Léna said. "In much the same way that I can be used to *bind* you. Do you not see how Orsini has kept you here? You fear you cannot leave because of your missing sisters, but what have you done to rescue them? Can you do anything? How does this inaction serve them, or you, or me?"

"But I'm their prisoner here, I can't just leave," Ocyrhoe said. "And I have nowhere to go outside the city, I have no experience in the wilderness, I don't know how to get food, I'll have nowhere to sleep..." A terrifying vulnerability brought her to the brink of panic and made it hard for her to think straight enough even to form words. "What do I do? How can I survive, let alone as a Binder? Is there someone you can send me to? Is there someplace I should go to? Will Frederick take me back with him to some other city where they still have Binders who can teach me? What about—"

"Calm yourself!" Léna said, raising her voice.

Ocyrhoe pressed her lips shut and looked up at her with frightened eyes.

"Thank you." The elder Binder crossed the room with the energy of a captive tiger running out of patience with its captors. "I cannot answer any of those questions. You may certainly go back to Frederick's camp, since it is easy to find, but I would not suggest you stay there long."

"Can't you come back with me?" Ocyrhoe nearly begged. "Isn't he expecting you? Aren't you bound to serve him?"

"Not constantly," Léna retorted. "I am not *his* Binder, I am a Binder who works *with* him. I have, in fact, worked with the Church too. The previous Pope, Gregory IX, found me useful from time to time. If I do not return to Frederick's camp by the time they return to Germany, he will simply leave without me. He knows I will wend my way back toward his court as opportunity arises."

"Well then..." Ocyrhoe was trying very hard not to sound like a frightened child, but that was difficult as she felt, at that moment, exactly like a frightened child. "Could you not go back to the camp with me, just long enough to ask him to take me with him, and then you could come back here to face off with the Bear?"

Léna looked at her. Just looked. Said nothing. Did not send her any mental images or feelings. Ocyrhoe met the gaze, hoping at first that something promising would come of it. Nothing did. Ocyrhoe was left with her own fear and longing, and she understood what Léna was telling her: "It is up to me alone to find my place in the world now," she said, very much hating this truth.

Léna's expression softened. "You have been learning how to do that for a while now, and you have done very well."

"I have had my city to protect me. Outside those walls I will be as exposed as a black fly on a white wall."

Léna gave her a sympathetic smile. "Have greater faith in your ability."

"It is a moot point anyhow, since I have no means of leaving," Ocyrhoe pointed out. Suddenly, captivity seemed comforting.

"You will find, in your life as a Binder," Léna assured her, "that what you need will be offered to you, in unexpected ways and times. I do not know how you will come to leave the city, but I am confident you will. And soon."

* * *

Orsini had gone back to his palace in disgust. He had made it very clear what he thought of Fieschi's comportment during the recent events. It had taken every atom of restraint Fieschi had to remain composed throughout the diatribe.

The entire Vatican compound was in hysterics over the absence of the unanointed Pope. Liberated from the Bear's oppressive blustering, Fieschi now found himself saddled with the equally irritating presence of his fellow cardinals. They had collected together in the round chapel where the vote had first been cast. After agreeing upon this as a meeting place, they seemed unable to agree on anything else at all.

"I'm relieved for the fellow Bendrito," Annibaldi said.

"I would do the same thing in his position," Capocci said in agreement. "We gave him a dreadful job, and he did not want it. He has abandoned the throne of Saint Peter."

Fieschi regarded Capocci warily, trying to ascertain the bearded cardinal's mind-set. *His allegiances can be as tangled as his beard*, he thought.

"Perhaps, the word you mean to use is *abdicated*," Colonna provided.

Capocci shrugged, idly chewing on a strand of his beard, as if he couldn't be bothered with the minutia of language.

"Regardless," Bonaventura added, sensing an opportunity, "we should thank him for having made such a difficult decision so quickly and with such firmness of purpose."

"We are without a Pope once again?" de Segni asked, sounding weary.

"Must we go through another round of voting?" Gil Torres nearly wailed.

"I am here," Monferrato offered, eyes wide as always. "I was sent to break the tie."

"We cannot vote for another Pope while we currently have a living one," Fieschi argued, with less vehemence than he was feeling. While he had doubts about his ability to control Father Rodrigo—even if they could find the fellow—Fieschi was also doubtful he could control the outcome of a new vote. At best, Father Rodrigo was still his best chance of keeping the Church on the right path. The confusion of the election, the fire in the Septizodium, what he had done for God in those subterranean halls: all of these things were feeding a growing insecurity, a bleakness born of all these doubts. A bleakness he could not afford to let control him.

"We don't know that he is living," Colonna said. "There is no way to prove that."

"We also don't know that he is dead," Fieschi retorted. "Nor is there any way to prove *that*."

Capocci's eyes shifted back and forth a moment, and Fieschi found himself dreading what crazy idea was about to sprout from that man's head. "Yes there is!" Capocci suddenly shouted. The various muttered arguments and conversations in the room hushed, and his ten fellows turned to him.

"Listen to me," he said. "We can engineer a solution. That there is a new Pope is known by all of Rome—we have burned the straw, they have seen the white smoke, and news travels fast. Every baron in Christendom has some spy or messenger in the city, waiting to hear the news so that they may return home. We cannot pretend we do not have a Pope. However, nobody has any idea what he looks like. Nobody outside the Vatican compound even knows his *name*. Now, couple that with the following observation: if we disregard Father Rodrigo's existence, and take another vote right now, we'll have a stalemate, even with our eminent new brother joining us"—and here he gestured toward Monferrato—"we would have a stalemate now, and a week from now, and probably a month from now. And during that day or week or month, the whole world thinks we have a Pope, and wants to hear from him. So we must give them a Pope—*immediately*." He looked around the room with anticipation, as if he were seeking somebody who could guess what his next words would be and shout them out like an eager student. Nobody did. Not even Colonna. "Therefore," he prompted, "we present them with a Pope, so that we do not look like a group of incompetent idiots, we anoint this Pope as if he were the one we voted in, we enthrone him—and then, right away, we kill him."

With a flourishing gesture, he leaned back on his heels and smiled at them all.

"*What?*" Bonaventura demanded, horrified, into the stunned silence that followed.

Capocci stared at them as if he could not imagine why they were all so shocked. Then his face lit up. "Ah!" he said, still buoyant. "My mind was working faster than my mouth. What I mean is: we pretend that somebody in this room has been elected Pope. We go through all the motions of crowning that man, with the understanding—shared by all of us, but not to be told to another living soul, not even our most faithful servants—that within a fortnight, the pseudo-Pope disappears forever, and we claim that he has died."

The shocked silence remained, but now the cardinals were all exchanging glances rather than staring slack-jawed at Capocci. Even Fieschi held his tongue, waiting to see how his peers would react. The idea was ludicrous, but in its insanity was a very narrow path out of the current disaster.

"We'd need to have a body," Colonna said at length, an implicit acknowledgment that he was willing to entertain the plan.

"There are bodies enough in Roman morgues," Capocci said.

"What happens to the man who volunteers to do this thing?" da Capua asked. He too seemed cautiously interested now.

"I think that's up to him," Capocci said. "It is an enormous service he will be performing, saving the appearance of our integrity. We have no actual integrity—I think we have demonstrated that quite thoroughly by now—but the *appearance* of it will be deeply comforting to our flocks. It is almost a kind of martyrdom. If I were such a man, I would ask for a bucket of gold and a nice quiet hermitage in which to spend my days in happy anonymity."

"Nobody in this room would consider such an absurdity," de Segni snorted. "Every man here is brimful of ambition or he would not have become a cardinal."

"That's true enough," said Gil Torres. "But as the senior-most cardinal alive, I can tell you that ambition wanes as surely as it waxes. I would not put myself forward for the sacrifice, but I can imagine it might be attractive—to the right man."

"What about the priest?" Torres asked. "The one who is already Pope?"

"Ah," Capocci said, "this is the clever bit. If we do this quickly enough and we all swear that it be true, then Father Rodrigo's claim simply becomes the spurious ravings of a country fool. He's just a pretender to the position, and if he's insane enough to insist that a conspiracy has been perpetrated..."

Fieschi had to admit there was a certain elegance to the solution. Perhaps it wasn't a matter of controlling the next Pope, but simply leaving the position vacant. He had been able to accomplish quite a bit during the *sede vacante*—including turning the bullheaded Senator to his side. The cardinals would scatter soon after a successful vote, leaving Rome to him. During the time it took to recall all the cardinals—including the ones that Frederick had managed to intercept—he would have ample time to fully dominate Rome.

And after Rome, what next? Sicily?

Fieschi smiled. The doubts would fall away, readily enough.

"Would my fellow cardinals be willing to consider this?" Capocci asked. "Shall we at least entertain it for discussion?"

"How about a show of hands?" Colonna suggested.

"Wait a moment," Castiglione said. "Seven of us voted for Father Rodrigo. We caused this strange catastrophe, and so it should fall to one of the seven to make this sacrifice." The dei Conti cousins and Bonaventura—the only three who did not vote for Father Rodrigo—all visibly relaxed, while the half dozen others eyed each other nervously. "But of all those seven," Castiglione continued, "the one who bears the greatest shame for writing down Father Rodrigo's name is me. I wrote his name because I did not want to be elected. The stress of these past few months, and most of all these past few days, forced me to look honestly at my own *ambition*, to use Cardinal de Segni's term. The rest who voted for Father Rodrigo did so for reasons of their own, but I am sure they were sound ones. I, however, voted for him to shirk my own duty, and so the burden of guilt for all of this falls upon my shoulders more than on any other's. I volunteer to be the Pope who dies."

There were gasps of amazement from around the room. "This is a feint!" Bonaventura shouted above the din. "You will take power and threaten us all with blackmail if we try to remove you!"

"Of course I won't," said Castiglione. "If I had that kind of ambition, Cardinal Bonaventura, I would not have voted for Father Rodrigo, and then we would not be in this ridiculous position. Furthermore, if I volunteer to do this and then seize the office for real, I am sure Orsini will dispatch me very quickly."

The Senator could certainly be called upon to do what was necessary, Fieschi thought, and a tiny smile tugged at his lips. "Well," he said dryly. "That sounds very convincing. How about the rest of you?"

The narrow path lay open before him. *Yes, let them choose this man,* he thought, *that will work out just fine.*

mongol-a-mongol

SHORTLY AFTER THE hunting party left the confines of the valley, it ascended a narrow ridge, and Ögedei reined in his horse to admire the view. The valley was a long indentation that ran east to west, as if *Tengri* himself had reached down and dug a trough through the verdant forests that blanketed the lower slopes of Burqan-qaldun. The air was clear and crisp, and Ögedei could see the tiny shapes of his subjects moving among the colorful mushroom shapes of the *ger*.

I will build a palace, he decided, caught up in the crystalline clarity of the moment. *I will have all the materials brought here. No trees will be cut down. No rocks moved. It will stay pristine—just the way it is today.* He stared at his *ger* and fixed its position in his mind. The palace would be built in the exact same spot.

"My Khan?" Namkhai's broad face was impassive, but there was the barest hint of a question in his voice.

"I am admiring the view, Namkhai," Ögedei said. "Is it not a magnificent day?"

"It is, my Khan."

"A man could accomplish anything he desired on a day like today, could he not?"

"He could, my Khan." Namkhai's stony mien cracked slightly, allowing a brief smile to escape.

"And there would be no reason to rush, would there? A man's destiny will wait for him, yes?"

"It never arrives before he does, my Khan."

Ögedei laughed. "A wrestler *and* a philosopher. You are filled with surprises, Namkhai. Once I have slain the bear, will you compose a song in my honor?"

"I regret not, my Khan."

He is fearless, Ögedei thought. *He does not shirk from telling me the truth, even though it might displease me.* He glanced over his shoulder, taking in the rest of the hunting party, and his gaze lingered on Alchiq and Gansukh. *Would that I had a* tumen *of men like him, there would be no stopping the Mongol Empire.* He casually laid his hand on the shaft of the Spirit Banner, the tall pole stuck into a leather boot attached to his saddle. In his mind, he saw a sea of horses spanning from horizon to horizon, their manes flowing like waves. His hand tightened on the banner as the horsehair tassels whispered gently in the slight breeze.

* * *

By midafternoon, the hunting party had ascended into the forest that lay heavily about the shoulders of the mountain. Sunlight trickled in solid streams through the branches of the trees, and swarms of golden motes danced in the radiance. The hunting master and his dogs ranged in front of the main party, keeping company with the trio of *Darkhat* scouts. Chucai and Namkhai flanked Ögedei, and the remainder of the *Torguud* followed them in a clump. The other scouts were arranged in wide arcs on either side. There had been no sign of the bear yet, but Ögedei wasn't terribly concerned.

His mount's steady gait echoed throughout his body, knocking loose memories that had lain covered for many years. He had forgotten the pleasure of the hunt—his senses awake and marveling at the proliferation of details that his mind, taut like a bowstring, was readily processing. He was ready, quivering like one of the hunting master's hounds, waiting for some sign of his quarry.

"It has been too long," Ögedei remarked to Chucai. "I should hunt like this more often. Too much time has passed, and this," he poked his stout belly, "has grown too large."

"You are still a better hunter than most," said Chucai, perfectly composed upon his black steed. "I, for one, have not hunted since before your father elevated me to my position at court."

"Father!" Ögedei laughed jovially. "No one could match my father. I remember a time when he provided for the entire army. A buck, each and every night. He hunted alone and always brought one back."

"Bashkiria, my Khan," Chucai said. "Yes, I recall that campaign. There was more food than we could possibly eat. I gorged myself on venison on more than one occasion."

"Life was simpler then, wasn't it?" Ögedei said. "When we got hungry, we would hunt; when we were tired, we slept; when we wanted something..." He sighed and his hand idly patted his belly again.

"The empire has grown mighty, my Khan," Chucai said silkily. "It has done so under your guidance, and many are thankful every day. The spirits are pleased with your efforts."

Ögedei stretched in the saddle, working out the tension that had settled in the middle of his back from the ride. "The spirits stir slowly in this disused body," he said.

Chucai hesitated, and then swallowed his words with a quiet "mmm." He turned his attention to the forest around them, taking particular note of the lichens that mottled the bark of many trees.

Ögedei considered insisting that Master Chucai reveal what was on his mind, but the *Khagan* could guess what words had been repressed. He knew he was rotund and out of shape, just as he knew where he had hidden a pair of wineskins in his saddlebags. Chucai would speak in the obsequious language of the court for only so long before his tongue would get the better of him, and in this case, he would be speaking the truth. All he had to do was stretch out his right hand, dig around in the saddlebag on that side of his horse, and he could lay his hand on that disappointment. He hadn't been able to abandon his thirst entirely. His strength of will had improved immeasurably, but it was still nothing more than a newborn babe. Easily smothered.

There was too much silence in the air for the *Khagan*'s comfort, and he turned to Namkhai and said, by way of changing the subject, "Have you ever brought down a beast as mighty as this?"

Namkhai shook his head. "The great bear is going to be a mighty challenge, my Khan," he said. "Arrows alone might not be enough to penetrate its hide."

"The dogs will weary it." Ögedei waved a hand in the direction of the snapping pack who yearned to be freed of their yokes. "When they are done, when they have blooded it, then it will be my turn."

"It may take down one of our hunters before then," said Namkhai. "A wounded beast is dangerous. Perhaps we could set a trap for it with spears. Harass it until we can drive it into impaling itself."

Ögedei shook his head. "Where is the honor in that?"

Namkhai looked at him with heavily lidded eyes and only shrugged.

"Harass it, bleed it even, if that allows us to trap it, but *I* must kill it. That is what the spirits want. I must deliver the killing blow so that I can take in its spirit. How else will the spirit of the Great Bear know who it must fill?

Namkhai shook his head. "You have a great challenge before you, O Great *Khagan*," he said. "May the Blue Wolf favor you."

Ögedei felt his blood surge in his ears, a sudden pounding as his heart beat more heavily in his chest. *Just like Chucai*, he thought wildly, *he doubts that I can do it*. His hands tightened on his reins, and he felt his neck muscles tense in preparation of the shout that was beginning to swell from his belly. With a great deal of difficulty, he swallowed his ire. *He has no faith*, he realized, and instead of letting his anger out, he shoved it back down, deep into his belly. *I will show him. I will show them all.*

In his mind, he could see himself wrestling with the bear, armed only with a curved sword. Towering on its hind legs, foam flecking its enormous jaws, it raged and snarled at him. He stabbed it, over and over, ignoring its ineffective swipes at his armor with its giant paws. It tried to pin him, tried to bite his throat with its sharp teeth, but he plunged his sword deep within that open mouth, ramming the blade back and up and into the bear's brain.

Let them doubt me, Ögedei thought. *I can—I will—do this.*

On the last stroke, his hand had been steady. He did not waver. He did not hesitate.

* * *

Gansukh rode on the right rear flank of the hunting party, his eyes scanning the forest. A beast as old and venerated as the *Darkhat* spoke of would have terrorized this area for so long that it would make little effort to hide itself. He watched the groupings of smaller saplings for signs that some of them had been rudely forced aside. He read the patterns on the bark, looking for the white scars left by claws being sharpened. Would it hide its kills? Gansukh doubted so, and he kept an eye out for the carrion birds that would circle around the rotting carcasses of the bear's prey, picking at the dead until there was nothing left.

He also kept watch for Munokhoi. The ex-*Torguud* captain was not part of the hunting party. He had carefully examined every face of the forty-plus men the *Khagan* had brought with him. Nor had he expected that Munokhoi would have joined the group. Too many of the men would have noticed the ostracized ex-captain's presence and said something. No, Munokhoi was in the woods, though he did not know how close.

As the hunting party made its way through the woods, Gansukh drifted farther and farther away from the main host. If Munokhoi was trailing them, waiting for an opportunity, then it would be best if he was out of sight of the *Khagan*'s host. Offering himself as bait.

Sometimes the easiest way to catch a predator was to pretend to be prey.

As the morning wore on, he found his vigilance flagging. There were too many shadows under the trees. Hunting in the woods was much more tiring than hunting on the steppes.

His horse shifted its gait, dancing around the moss-covered hump of an old log, and Gansukh squirmed in his saddle. He was no stranger to riding long distances with a full bladder, but that didn't make the experience any less uncomfortable. He had pissed from saddleback often enough, but it was easiest when he could look ahead and see that his horse wouldn't need to change its gait. Here, in the forest, the ground was uneven and the occasional branch tried to grab his horse. Performing the necessary contortions *and* managing his horse was a little more complicated. Stopping to relieve himself would be simpler.

He pulled his horse to a halt, dismounted, and looped his reins around a low branch of a nearby sapling. He opened one of his saddlebags and retrieved a handful of dried berries. His horse snorted as he offered the treat, its breath warm on his palm. "I'll be right back," he said with an affectionate pat between its ears.

He walked a few paces away, adjusting the bow slung over his shoulder. He undid his sash to make water over the gnarled roots of an immense oak. The tree leaned crookedly, an aged malingerer that refused to point in the same direction as its surrounding brethren. Gansukh let out a sigh of satisfaction as the pressure of his bladder lessened.

He was, not unlike other wild animals in the forest, marking his territory. If the hunting party was anywhere near the bear's cave—and the lack of bear sign suggested they weren't very close—he would have been more circumspect in his pissing. It wasn't so much that such behavior was rude—one animal to another; it was that four-legged predators had a much better sense of smell than the two-legged kind. Urine carried a very distinct odor, and leaving such a stain would only alert them of his presence.

A grim smile touched his lips as he finished. Munokhoi had pissed all over his gear. Such a feral response, one wolf marking the territory of another.

He started to retie his sash, and then paused, his senses suddenly alert. He didn't turn his head, but he tried to read as much of his peripheral surroundings as he could. He listened intently to the sounds of the forest: the rustling of the leaves as they were stroked by the gentle caress of the wind, the creaking and croaking of insects, the crunching sound of his horse's jaws as it chewed on long grass that it had pulled up, and the *distant* chatter of birds.

Close by, it was too quiet. An uneasy silence.

His horse raised its head, ears flicking. Its nostrils widened as it smelled the breeze.

Gansukh left his sash half tied and, slowly, put his hands on his bow.

His horse wasn't frightened by the scent, which meant whatever was out there in the woods wasn't the bear—or a wolf or some other predator.

He heard the arrow, a rustling that whispered through the trees. It hit its target with a meaty *thwap*, and his horse let out a dreadful scream. It reared, a long black-fletched arrow protruding from its neck. Blood spattered from the wound, and the beast stumbled as it found its range of movement limited by the reins tied to the sapling. It snorted, its eyes wide with fear and pain, and then it stumbled again, falling heavily against the nearby tree.

Gansukh had instinctively dropped to a crouch as soon as he had heard the arrow, his back pressed against the thick trunk of the leaning oak. He unslung his bow and quickly reset the string, a series of motions his hands performed automatically, unconsciously.

His horse collapsed, its body shuddering with pained breaths. Each one was shorter and more violent than the last. The grass around its head glistened with blood. It couldn't lie its head down; the reins were still caught in the tree. The fletching on the arrow in its neck matched the arrow he had broken the day before.

Gansukh's eyes were drawn to the quiver of arrows nestled among his saddlebags. He had no idea where Munokhoi was. The other man would be moving to a better position, but he had no idea how long that would take. He couldn't stay where he was for long.

If he could just reach his arrows...even one would be enough.

He shifted his weight, readying himself, and his foot slipped. He glanced down, remembering why the roots of the tree would be wet, and noticed a fist-size rock close to his left boot. He pitched it downslope, hoping it would make a great deal of noise as it rolled through the brush. As soon as he hurled the rock, he made a mad dash for his fallen steed. He didn't have time to release his quiver from the straps holding it in place; all he could do was grab a handful of arrows.

He kept running, his eyes scanning for a suitable hiding place. An arrow sang past his head, and he changed his direction, forcing Munokhoi to adjust his aim. Gansukh spotted the ragged shape of a giant stump, nearly waist-high, and he dashed toward it, skidding across the ground as he tried to slow his headlong rush. An arrow smacked heavily into the moss-covered wood above his head as he scrambled to cover.

The upper part of the stump had become hollow over time, and there were numerous gaps in the bark. Shifting back and forth between several of the larger holes, he spied on the upward slope.

Such scouting was torturous, but he kept at it, hoping to catch some flicker of movement that would indicate Munokhoi's position.

A shaft of light was eclipsed, and Gansukh fumbled with one of his precious arrows. Holding its fletching with his right hand, he tried to lay the arrow across his bow but it didn't seem to catch, and he tore his gaze away from his secret spy hole to see what was wrong.

The arrow in his hand was too short, missing its head and a portion of the shaft. It had snapped off during his dash to safety. Cursing, he threw it aside and grabbed another one, visually checking this one before laying it across his bow.

He peered through the bark hole again, moving his head from side to side to increase his field of view. Had he missed his chance? He ground his teeth in frustration and leaped to his feet, drawing his string back and loosing an arrow. He immediately fell back to his crouched position, peering through the gaps.

He didn't expect to hit Munokhoi, but his arrow drew a response. He heard a hollow *thock* as one of Munokhoi's arrows sunk into the old bark. He prepped another arrow and stood up again. He tried not to focus on anything in particular, waiting a fraction of a second for something to move, some target to suggest itself. He sensed motion without actually seeing it, and loosed his second arrow.

At this range, without having time to aim properly, it was next to impossible to hit his target. He could only hope to draw Munokhoi closer. He counted his remaining arrows—three—and decided he didn't have enough to play this game with Munokhoi.

A booming noise echoed through the forest, and something heavy crashed into the stump, knocking great holes in the wood. Bark pelted Gansukh, and like a startled deer, he sprinted away from his hiding place. He dashed through a clump of spiny bushes, branches clawing at his bow and clothing, and slid to a stop behind an aged spruce. His heart pounded in his chest, and the echo of the thunder still rang in his ears.

Smoke came through the trees, a gray haze that drifted slowly downslope. The upper portion of his previous hiding place looked as if it had been clawed by a giant bear; ragged strips of bark poked up from the crown of the stump like crooked fingers.

There was no bear. Gansukh had heard nothing prior to the sudden boom, nor had there been any subsequent sound of a large animal crashing through the underbrush. It could not have been a lightning strike either. The sky was clear of clouds, and no fire had been started. It had to have been Munokhoi, but what sort of sorcery was it?

Gansukh remembered the night of the Chinese raid. When he had been chasing Lian, he had heard similar booming noises. Afterward, some of the *Torguud* had spoken of a Chinese weapon, a portable cannon that used fire to hurl shards of metal and pottery with incredible force.

Looking at the wreckage of the stump, Gansukh imagined what such a weapon would do to him. His armor would offer no protection. But the handheld cannon had to be cumbersome to wield, otherwise Munokhoi would have used it when he had first attacked. He wouldn't have waited until Gansukh had been hiding. In fact, Gansukh theorized, he had only used it because he hadn't been able to get a clear shot with his bow. *I would have done the same*, he thought, risking another glance. *If your target is obscured, make him move or make his hiding place no longer safe.*

Munokhoi had both bow and fire thrower, and Gansukh had only three arrows. He was at a disadvantage, but he thought he knew what Munokhoi was thinking.

An arrow struck the trunk of the tree above Gansukh's head, and he didn't flinch. He glanced at it, noting its angle and orientation in the tree, and rose to his feet, mentally reversing its flight path as he drew his bow back and loosed an arrow. It disappeared into a thicket to the right of the last tendrils of drifting smoke, and as he ducked back behind the tree, he noted movement in the brush.

He had to coax Munokhoi close enough that the ex- *Torguud* captain would try to use the Chinese weapon again. Gansukh suspected it would take Munokhoi some time to ready the weapon—his attention would be devoted to that task. That would be Gansukh's opportunity to get a clear shot. He had to have time to aim his arrows. He had to see his target without being seen.

Gansukh poked his head out once more, and another arrow hissed past. He darted in the other direction, upslope but still away from Munokhoi. He paused behind every large tree—varying the time spent in cover so that Munokhoi couldn't anticipate when he would emerge again. He kept looking for a suitable hiding place, and finally spotted a fallen tree that had lodged between two other trees. The trio of trees made for excellent cover—he could stand upright and still be hidden from view—and the long trunk of the fallen tree provided him the means to crawl away from cover without being seen.

He made it to the other side of the barrier without being hit by an arrow, and he caught his breath before he carefully poked his head out for a quick peek. He saw no sign of Munokhoi, and he shifted to the center of his cover. Grabbing onto the thick bark of the fallen tree, he hoisted himself up to risk another look. An arrow skipped off the bark, not far from his head. It vanished into the forest behind him as he dropped back down.

Munokhoi was still coming. Gansukh didn't have a lot of time with which to accomplish his ruse. He dropped to his belly and began worming his way along the ground. When he had gone several body lengths, he got to his knees and slowly rose to a half crouch, peering over the dead tree. He had chosen a spot where a leafy fern had spouted from the trunk, and he was confident he wouldn't be seen.

His ruse had worked. He could see Munokhoi clearly, kneeling behind a large bush. His bow lay on the ground beside him, and he was busy stuffing something into an iron tube held cradled in one arm.

Gansukh nocked one of his two remaining arrows and, holding the bow sideways so that he wouldn't reveal himself prematurely, he drew back the string. Rising slowly to a standing position—his thighs quivering at the glacial pace of his motion—he aimed carefully. Munokhoi sensed his presence right before he let go of the bowstring, and Gansukh had a brief glimpse of the ex-*Torguud* captain's wild eyes before he ducked back down behind the log.

Gansukh scrambled farther to his left, not worrying too much about being quiet, and finding another fern to obscure him, he risked another glance over the log.

Munokhoi was gone, but he had left a leather satchel on the ground. Gansukh wasted a few seconds peering at where Munokhoi had been crouching, trying to ascertain any other sign that his arrow had struck its target, and movement in the nearby bush warned him in time. Munokhoi's arrow shredded the leaves of the fern as he ducked. That one would have hit him if he hadn't moved.

He saw a gap between the tree trunk and the ground and realized he had gone as far as he readily could. The gap grew wider on his left, and Munokhoi would be able to track his movement.

The Chinese weapon thundered again, and Gansukh flinched even though he was protected by the dead tree. Wood splintered and cracked nearby, and he looked upslope to see a spindly tree start to topple. Munokhoi's cannon blast had destroyed the tree's trunk, and the tree was falling right toward him. Its looming branches were like a hundred eager hands, reaching for him.

Gansukh scrambled out of the tree's path, and the trunk missed him—striking the heavy log and rebounding. It slid downhill, its branches clawing and tearing at his clothes. He tripped and struggled to free himself of the tree's clutches. After being dragged a few paces, he managed to roll free of the branches, still clutching his bow.

But he had lost his last arrow.

His heart racing, he ran, weaving through the trees to spoil Munokhoi's aim. Arrows whistled through the branches around him as he fled, and some of them smacked into trees, sounding like a flat hand swatting a horse's rump. *Run faster, young pony, run faster.*

As the arrows faltered, he began to pay closer attention to his surroundings: Where was the brush thickest? Could he find a hollow log to hide inside? Were the shadows beneath a copse of evergreens dark enough?

None of these places mattered though if he didn't have an arrow. All he needed was one clear shot, but there had to be some bait for Munokhoi. How to best the hunter at his game? Where could he hide that Munokhoi wouldn't think to look for him?

The forest had gotten thicker, the trees bristling with densely packed branches. He stopped beside a wide alder with a generous shroud of thick branches. *The owl falls upon its prey from above,* he thought, mentally charting a path up through the branches of the tree. *The hare doesn't see the owl until it is too late.*

He draped his bow around his neck so that it lay close to his chest. Branches poked at his face as he began to climb, and his heart leaped into his throat when one branch snapped as he put his weight on it. He looked down once, and his head started to swim as he saw how far off the ground he was, but he tamped his fear down and kept going. He paused once more, balancing on one foot, to hack at a relatively straight branch with his knife. Finally, he found a pair of thick branches that would work as a perch, and he steadied himself against the rough trunk.

He held his arm out, measuring the length of the branch he had cut. Satisfied that it was both long and straight enough, he trimmed it down and then carefully set about stripping off the bark. There were a few tiny buds, and he cut them back, smoothing out the shaft with delicate strokes of his knife. Once all the knobs and burrs were gone, he whittled one end to as fine a point as possible, and then he cut a deep notch in the other end. The last step was to peel back the soft wood on either side of the notch so that he could create make-shift fletching from leaves stuffed under the flaps.

It wouldn't fly very far and, judging by the gentle curve he hadn't been able to work out in the shaft, it would pull to the right. But it was an arrow nonetheless.

Settling in to wait, he laid his rough arrow across his bow and kept his right fingers loosely curled around the leafy end. He kept his breathing shallow and measured, ignoring as best he could the cramps and aches that came from holding one position too long. The branch on which he was standing was narrower than his feet, and he couldn't shift his footing too much without danger of slipping. He watched the landscape below, constantly scanning for some sign of his prey. *I am a patient owl.*

The hare came.

Down below, Munokhoi stole through the forest. He didn't step on a single branch, and he eased through the brush more readily and silently than the wind. His bow was held ready, and Gansukh couldn't tell if he was still carrying the Chinese fire thrower. Munokhoi's head swung back and forth, his eyes taking in every brush and branch, but he never looked up.

Gansukh drew his bow back slowly, cringing at the slightest creak of the wood. Munokhoi was going to pass on his right, and the best shot would be when the ex-*Torguud* captain was abreast of him, presenting his own right side to Gansukh. He could take the shot now, but the range was farther than he trusted his ready-made arrow. He had to wait. He held his breath and aimed, feeling the bow become an extension of his body.

As Munokhoi passed Gansukh's tree, he paused, his head swiveling back and forth. His brow furrowed slightly as if he sensed something out of place in the wood.

Gansukh released his pent-up breath, his fingers opening. His bow sang, and there was a flutter of leaves.

Munokhoi took a step back, and looked down at the shaft of fresh wood protruding from his chest. Shock registered on his face for a moment before he toppled to the ground, disappearing from Gansukh's view

Gansukh let out a whoop of elation as he half clambered, half fell down the tree. The hunt wasn't over yet, though. He had to be sure Munokhoi was dead. He doubted his arrow had been fatal. He had to get close and slit his throat. Leave nothing to chance.

Munokhoi lay on his back, blood spattered across his jacket and the branches of a nearby bush. He stared up at the panoply of the forest, and his face was contorted in a grimace. Gansukh's arrow was embedded in the right side of his chest, sticking nearly straight up.

Gansukh approached cautiously. While Munokhoi seemed dead, his right hand lay concealed beneath his leg. Such positioning could be a coincidence. It could also be a trap.

Trying to keep as much distance as possible, Gansukh stooped over Munokhoi's body to reach for the arrow. If Munokhoi was only feigning death, he would react when the arrow was pulled out. Gansukh clutched his knife tightly as he leaned over his fallen foe.

Munokhoi let out a blood-curdling scream as Gansukh yanked the arrow out. The ex-*Torguud* captain sat upright, his hand—holding a dagger—shooting out from behind his leg. Even though he had expected such a surprise, Gansukh seized up in terror, as though he were facing not a mortal man but an evil spirit. Munokhoi's dagger tangled in Gansukh's half-tied sash, and he slapped his left hand down, trying to grab Munokhoi's wrist. He made contact, stopping the thrust, and as he started a tug-of-war his feet were swept out from under him as Munokhoi twisted on the ground.

He landed on his back with a *thud*, his knife slipping out of his grip, and Munokhoi rolled atop him, pinning his right arm to the ground with a knee. Blood dripped from the wound in Munokhoi's chest, dotting Gansukh's jacket. Munokhoi spat in Gansukh's face, his breath heavy with the stink of *airag*. "You are weak," he growled. Gansukh still had a hold on Munokhoi's wrist, and he held Munokhoi off, barely. The dagger inched closer to his throat.

Gansukh bucked his hips, trying to throw Munokhoi off balance, and when that failed, he tried to kick his leg up high enough to hit Munokhoi in the back of the head, but the ex-captain was leaning too far forward, bearing down with all of his weight. Gansukh bucked again, but this time he tried to extricate his right hand from beneath Munokhoi's knee. He managed to pull his arm free, without his own knife, but an empty hand was good enough. He dug his fingers into Munokhoi's jacket, searching for the bloody arrow wound with his thumb.

Munokhoi howled as Gansukh ground his thumb into the open wound. Gansukh bucked again, and Munokhoi's weight lessened on his chest. Gansukh heaved, rolling onto his side, finally throwing Munokhoi off.

He scrambled for his knife, found it, and then lunged after Munokhoi. As Gansukh charged, Munokhoi braced his hands against the ground and lashed out with a foot, but Gansukh twisted his body enough so that the foot struck him on the shoulder instead of the face. He grabbed at the leg, shoving it to one side so that he could more readily stab at the other man's stomach with his knife.

Munokhoi brought his other leg up, attempting to trap Gansukh between his thighs. He batted Gansukh's outstretched hand aside, and as the pair collapsed into a heap of tangled limbs, he began to squeeze with his legs.

Gansukh struggled to free himself. Munokhoi's legs were constricting his range of motion—one of his arms was pinned at his side—and he was going to have trouble defending himself from Munokhoi's blade. Gansukh lashed out blindly with his knife, feeling the blade cut fabric and flesh. Munokhoi grunted, and his legs loosened. As Gansukh scrambled out of Munokhoi's grip, he kept slashing with his blade. Munokhoi began kicking, and Gansukh retreated before one of the other man's boots connected with his face. There was blood on his knife and on his hand.

Munokhoi rolled away too, using the motion to propel himself into a crouch and from there to an upright position. He favored his left leg, and there was a bright wash of blood running down the side of his pants. Munokhoi's gaze was charged with feral rage, his mouth contorted into a savage grimace. He stood ready to fight, oblivious to the wounds he had received.

Gansukh had seen this blindness to injury before. Men who refused to lie down and die, no matter how many arrows stuck out of their bodies or how many times they had been stabbed or cut. He had even heard of a man who continued to fight with a severed arm until his heart had pumped nearly all of the blood out of his body.

He wasn't surprised that Munokhoi would be filled with this invincible bloodlust. In fact, he was prepared to call upon it himself. After everything, Munokhoi was not going to walk out of the forest. Gansukh was going to be the survivor of this fight. "You are nothing," he hissed. "I will leave your corpse for the scavengers."

Munokhoi's response was a snarl of raw hatred and a lightning-fast lunge. Gansukh darted to the side, staying away from Munokhoi's knife and keeping to the other man's wounded side, but Munokhoi grabbed his left arm and tried to pull him close. He slashed at Munokhoi's neck with his knife, and Munokhoi tumbled forward, shoving his shoulder. He stepped back, stumbling slightly, and Munokhoi slipped behind him, making ready to slit his throat like a sheep.

Gansukh contorted his body, trapping Munokhoi's arm with his own. They were locked together now, each straining to overpower the other. Whoever lost control first would lose his life. Their faces reddened with anger and effort as they twisted in a macabre dance, trying to break each other's hold. Trying to drive their knives deep into flesh. They were evenly matched, unable to gain the advantage while keeping the other's knife at bay. Munokhoi slipped his arm over Gansukh's wrist, attempting an arm lock, and Gansukh wriggled free and nearly managed to throw Munokhoi in return.

Munokhoi recovered and stabbed at Gansukh's side, but there wasn't enough speed or force to his blow, and Gansukh was able to stop the blow by grabbing Munokhoi's wrist and pushing his hand away. Growling with frustration, Munokhoi hurled himself forward, thrusting with his chest. He snapped at Gansukh's cheek with his teeth. Gansukh pulled his head back, and Munokhoi lurched farther up his chest, still straining to bite. He latched onto Gansukh's ear, grinding his jaws together. He shook his head back and forth, like a dog worrying a piece of raw meat.

Gansukh felt blood flowing down his neck. He wanted to jerk his head away, but he knew if he did it would only increase Munokhoi's blood rage. But letting Munokhoi gnaw on his flesh wasn't helping either. He twisted his body, trying to slip his shoulder against Munokhoi's chest, and he felt Munokhoi's grip loosen on his right wrist.

The hand holding the knife.

Gansukh jerked his hand up, wrenching his wrist free of Munokhoi's grasp, and he drove his blade swift and deep into Munokhoi's neck.

Munokhoi shivered and jerked his head back. His jaw had locked, and he tore a piece of Gansukh's earlobe free. Gansukh retaliated by yanking his blade forward and then pulling it back, tearing a deep slash across Munokhoi's throat. Munokhoi started to choke, and when he spat the piece of Gansukh's ear out, blood spattered from his mouth.

Gansukh tried to shove him away, but Munokhoi, eyes bright with spite, clung to him like a leech as he staggered and fell. Munokhoi coughed up a gout of blood when Gansukh landed on top of him, and he weakly tried to fend off Gansukh's blade. Gansukh stabbed Munokhoi again and again—in the chest, in the neck. Blood flowed freely from the copious wounds, and Munokhoi's motions became more and more feeble. His skin paled, his mouth went slack, and finally his eyes lost their mad gleam. Only when he no longer showed any reaction to being stabbed did Gansukh finally stop. Leaving his knife embedded in Munokhoi's chest, Gansukh slid off the dead body and crawled a short distance away. Bent over, he threw up again and again until the bloodlust was purged from his being.

At last the bloody work was done.

* * *

Late in the afternoon, the hunting party rested by a stream that gurgled happily along a rock-strewn course. The horses drank their fill and quietly nosed around, cropping the tender grasses that grew along the bank. Ögedei had been only too happy to get out of his saddle, and he moved a little stiffly as he walked back and forth along the river's track.

Namkhai took the opportunity of this rest to check on his men, and he walked among them, making small talk and inquiring of what they had seen (or hadn't, in the case of bear sign). Of all the host, only the old rider—Alchiq—didn't dismount. He stayed in his saddle, quietly chewing on a piece of salted meat.

"Where's Gansukh?" Namkhai asked.

Alchiq nodded past Namkhai's shoulder, his expression unchanging, his mouth moving slowly around the jerky.

Namkhai turned and spotted Gansukh emerging from the forest. Ögedei's young pony raised a hand in greeting when he saw

Namkhai looking at him, and he angled his horse toward the two men. "Hai, Namkhai," he said.

"Hai, Gansukh," Namkhai said. "You fell behind." He looked around and spotted the short shaman and his equally tiny pony. "Even the old wizard got here before you."

"I saw a squirrel," Gansukh offered as an explanation.

Namkhai stared at the young rider, considering what he saw. Gansukh sat stiffly in his saddle, and his clothing was rumpled and ill fitting. The left side of his face was turned away, a posture that seemed forced and awkward—as if he were hiding something from Namkhai's view. Though he seemed both dazed and exhausted, his face was at ease, with a tiny satisfied smile. There was a blotch on his neck, a dark stain that hadn't been completely wiped away.

"It was a very big squirrel," he said in response to Namkhai's quizzical eyebrow.

Namkhai nodded thoughtfully as he let his gaze roam over Gansukh's mount. It was a darker color than he remembered, and both the saddle and the cloak bound to the cantle were much finer and less travel-stained than he would expect of a horse rider like Gansukh. "I do not like squirrels," he said finally.

Alchiq chuckled, and then spat a chewed bit of meat on the ground. "Who does?" he said innocently. "Nasty rodents. That one will not be missed."

Namkhai laughed. "No," he said. "Not in the slightest." He bowed his head to Gansukh once more. "That is a beautiful horse," he said. "I suspect such an animal would cost…fifty cows or so. A suitable payment for outstanding debts, don't you think?"

Gansukh patted the horse's neck. "Suitable enough," he said. "I am satisfied."

"As am I," Namkhai said.

ET FACTUM EST ITA 53

ND THUS IT was done.

When the votes were tallied, the cardinals were in agreement. Castiglione would be their new Pope, and the very result Fieschi had been fighting against the last few days had, ironically, become the solution to his troubles. Castiglione would not be Pope long enough to unduly influence the Church.

It was not an optimal solution, but it was one that would allow him time to lay a more solid foundation for the next election. When they could dispense with the nonsense of worrying about whether the Holy Roman Emperor could influence the election in any way.

There was still the minor annoyance of what to do about Father Rodrigo should he resurface, but, as Capocci had pointed out, in several days it would no longer matter. All of the cardinals looked eager to put the grievous error of their first vote behind them. Da Capua, in fact, had such a permanent crease in his forehead that Fieschi suspected that he would, within the year, retire to a monastery and live out his days, staring at the walls and plucking his lyre.

De Segni and Capocci took responsibility for informing the few priests, bishops, and lay servants necessary to ensure cooperation in the *Papal mummery*, as Capocci called it.

Fieschi went outside, squinting in the midday glare, and began to cross the broad central meadow of the Vatican compound toward the Castel Sant'Angelo. The board was decent there, compared to the miserly rations served from the makeshift kitchens outside Saint Peter's.

He was nearly to the castle when he heard footsteps behind him. He turned quickly, to see a young messenger approaching at a run. "Cardinal Fieschi!" the young man cried as he arrived. "I was told you are Cardinal Fieschi?"

"I am," he said, with a frown of caution.

"I have a message for you from His Majesty, Emperor Frederick," the young man said, bowing while gasping for breath. "I am to wait for your response before returning."

He handed Fieschi a small piece of parchment that had been folded into thirds and sealed with the imperial eagle. Intrigued, Fieschi broke the seal, unfolded the parchment, and read.

The note was short and to the point, written in Frederick's own scrawl. *Do come for a visit soon, dear Sinibaldo. There is a delicate matter that I wish to discuss.*

The missing priest, he thought, interpreting Frederick's message. *He didn't get very far.* He should have suspected that a madman wandering around the countryside would have been found by the Emperor's men. He glanced up at the dome of the basilica. *Did it matter that the Emperor had the missing priest?* he wondered, and then he smiled as an idea occurred to him. If the priest was mad, and he could convince the Emperor that this madness was part of a larger conspiracy, then perhaps he could redirect Frederick's attention elsewhere.

* * *

The heavy wooden door was thrown open so forcefully it bounced from its hinges and almost ricocheted back at Cardinal Fieschi.

"I know where he is," he gloated.

"Who?" Léna asked as if she didn't know who the cardinal was talking about.

"Your young friend will be with him," Fieschi said, ignoring Léna's question. He pointed at Ocyrhoe. "You will be coming with me," he said.

"I will?" Ocyrhoe squeaked.

"Why are you taking the child?" Léna protested stridently. In her head, Ocyrhoe heard an echo of Léna's earlier words. *You see? What you need will be offered.* Though she could not see how being remanded to the angry cardinal was going to help her escape from Rome.

"Frederick has sent me a message, asking for a meeting. He has the mad priest and I suspect he wants to ransom him back to me. I am not so foolish as to go alone," Fieschi sneered. "Nor am I going to be caught in a political trap. The girl will help me convince Father Rodrigo that Frederick is not his friend."

"And if she doesn't?" Léna asked.

Fieschi gave Léna a feral grin. "I will still have you, here, under my guard. If Frederick wishes to negotiate the return of the priest, I will have something he will want to negotiate for."

"And the girl wouldn't be more useful to you here as your hostage?" Léna asked.

"In the last few days," Fieschi snapped, "this child has caused me more headaches than Robert of Somercotes—"

"Dead so unexpectedly," Léna sighed sadly.

Fieschi paled slightly, at a loss for words all of a sudden. "We depart at once," he growled, with an impatient gesture. "They are saddling a pony for you."

Ocyrhoe gasped. "I don't know how to ride."

"All you have to do is sit," Léna said reassuringly. And then to Fieschi, "What if the Holy Roman Emperor's intent is not as malicious as you make it out to be?"

"Do not insult me," Fieschi snapped. "I have known Frederick a long time. I know how he thinks. He won't pass up an opportunity to force concessions from the Church. What do you think his blockade of Rome was for? I don't trust him."

"He will be saddened to hear that," Léna pointed out. "He considers you one of the most rational men in Rome."

Fieschi slashed his hand through the air, silencing her. "Be that as it may, you will stay here," he said.

"Well, I'm happy to stay," Léna observed, and for a second, Ocyrhoe thought Fieschi was going to change his mind, but when Léna smiled innocently at the cardinal, he stormed out of the room.

"Off you go," Léna said, shooing Ocyrhoe toward the door.

"Wait," Ocyrhoe argued. "I don't understand any of this. I thought you said you weren't tied to Frederick. How can he be trying to get you back if you don't belong to him?"

Léna put a finger to her lips. "The cardinal seems to have overlooked that point," she said with a wink. "Let's not tell him, shall we?"

* * *

It was a dry, dusty day, even as the shadows began to stretch eastward. Ocyrhoe liked the rocking motion once she had gotten used to it, and to her surprise, her mount sped up, slowed, and shifted at the precise moment she was wondering how to make it move in those ways. As if the pony were itself a Binder, or at least communicated as Binders do. *Animals do not have a spoken language*, she thought. *They must have other ways in which to communicate.*

From the height of the pony, the Holy Roman Emperor's camp looked very different to Ocyrhoe's eyes; she could see the boundaries much better now than before, when it was all just a big jumbled maze and she was breathless with anticipation at fulfilling her first Binder assignment.

From Robert of Somercotes.

She wondered again at what had passed between Léna and the cardinal when Cardinal Somercotes's name had been brought up. The cardinal had died in the fire, and it was her understanding that it had been a tragic accident, but there had been a mocking note in Léna's voice. She marveled at how the older Binder had given such a simple declaration such weight. And Fieschi's reaction! What was he hiding?

If they weren't about to arrive in the Emperor's camp, Ocyrhoe would be more concerned about being in Cardinal Fieschi's presence. She had seen his face when he had lunged at her early this morning. He was just as dangerous as the Bear, maybe more so.

Where the camp met the road, guards stopped the group, asking the riders to dismount and for the cardinal to descend from his carriage. Helmuth had returned with them, so they were admitted immediately into the campsite. The mundane details of daily life teemed around them in the tent city—chickens crooning in cages, women scrubbing laundry in tubs, bakers shaping loaves beside portable ovens, metalworkers and leatherworkers intent upon their crafts. The size of the camp itself did not impress Ocyrhoe—it was smaller than even one neighborhood of Rome. But the fact of its mobility, of its inhabitants and creators having traveled hundreds of miles together to erect this temporary town, it was a marvel she could not quite get her mind around. Cities were permanent things, yet...

She recognized the Emperor's pavilion. Strange to think it had been but one overnight since she had left here; how much had happened in so short a time! A week ago she had known nothing of Father Rodrigo, Ferenc, cardinals, or emperors.

All the sides and tent flaps were rolled up to the eaves of the tent, so they could see the Emperor, and he could see them, a good twenty paces before they arrived. Frederick was sitting in the camp's one oak chair, low-slung camp stools scattered before it, as if he were expecting a party. A guard stood at the entrance and others were stationed around the perimeters; a page boy stood behind Frederick's chair. Otherwise he was alone. When they were half a dozen strides distant, Frederick opened his arms wide as if in greeting. He smiled.

"Damn him," Fieschi muttered. But his voice, for once, lacked rancor.

"Welcome to my home away from home," Frederick called out. "Won't you join me for a cup of wine?"

They entered into the shade of the pavilion. Helmuth, in the lead, saluted, said, "Sire!" then bowed briskly and stepped away to the right. Ocyrhoe wanly imitated his bow.

"Hello, my young friend," Frederick said to her, amusement in his eyes. Ocyrhoe managed to squeak out, "Sire" and scurried to the left, away from Helmuth.

She watched Fieschi and Frederick as they looked each other in the eye without speaking. Neither wore the challenging or angry expressions she had expected—their faces were both neutral, almost pleasant. Neither one would break the stare.

"I outrank you, Sinibaldo," Frederick said eventually. "I expect you to at least bow your head."

"I will prostrate myself with gratitude," Fieschi promised, "as soon as you return him to me."

Frederick gave him a small, mocking smile. "Who? The priest?" He put a finger to his lips. "No, I am mistaken. The *Pope*. Yes, is that who you are speaking of?"

Fieschi closed his eyes a moment, took a careful breath, and said through gritted teeth, "He is not—"

"Oh, and what was it that he had with him?" He waved away Ocyrhoe's brightening expression with a wave of his hand. "No, not the boy. The other thing. The cup. Yes, that's what it was. The Cup of Christ."

"What?" Fieschi exploded.

"The Holy Grail," Frederick said patiently. "You got my note, clearly, and your rapid arrival confirms my suspicion." He glanced at Ocyrhoe for a brief second, and she was surprised by both the merriment and caution in his eyes. "I am glad I kept my language circumspect—"

"What suspicion?" Fieschi asked, his face even darker with rage than before.

"You wouldn't come trotting out of the safety of Rome for a mere priest, especially one as addled as that poor man is. Even if he was your newly elected Pope. No, dear Sinibaldo, I think you've come for something much more important."

"I have no idea what you are talking about," Fieschi raged. "The Holy Grail doesn't exist."

Ocyrhoe heard a ragged breathlessness in the cardinal's voice as if he were struggling to hide a different emotion entirely. *Panic.*

"Oh, I beg to differ, my dear friend," Frederick countered heartily. "A *dozen* or so members of my entourage, after setting eyes on the cup, wished to traipse after the priest on his idiotic crusade; my guards had to physically restrain them. I thank *God* I have some atheistic sentinels who were immune to the goddamned allure of the thing."

Fieschi was still changing color, paling now. "What do you mean, follow after him? Where is he?"

Frederick shrugged. "No idea. I released him into the wild, a few hours back. I thought it was only sporting to give him a head start if Cardinal Fieschi was on his trail."

"*Goddamn your—*" Fieschi started. The sentinels around the pavilion instantly stepped inside; soldiers passing by on the avenue beside them stopped and turned toward them, as if the entire camp were prepared to assault Fieschi should he shout again. He took a very large breath and let it out forcefully, holding his hands up in a ceding gesture.

Frederick regarded him calmly. "I have already been excommunicated this week—in a much more official manner—so I will look upon your outburst as nothing more than—"

"Where is the priest?" Fieschi demanded, his voice quiet but firm. "Why did you let him go?"

"Well, he was very intent on his mission," Frederick said, in an approving tone. "And his mission did nothing to challenge my authority. His resolve was very admirable. I admire that in a religious authority, especially in one who thinks he is the Pope. Very useful. And appropriate. So I chose to assist him. He and his undomesticated little hunter friend. Gave them clean clothes, and a good meal, and plenty of supplies for the road ahead." Then as an afterthought, "Oh yes, and a couple of horses. Some of my fastest, as they are both excellent riders." He grinned at the expression on Fieschi's face. "You are bursting with the impulse to call me a shithead. It's all over your face, Sinibaldo. Unfortunately, there are witnesses who would be stricken to hear such language coming from the mouth of a cardinal, especially after that previous outburst."

"Frederick!" Fieschi snapped in a constricted voice. "What are you talking about? What have you done?"

"Did I not just fucking *itemize* it for you?" Frederick said with mock exasperation. "Would you like me to write it out for you? I can do it in crude pictures if that will make it easier for you to grasp."

Ocyrhoe ducked her head and pursed her lips together as hard as she could bear. Hearing Fieschi spoken to this way was a reviving antidote to the events of the past days.

Fieschi huffed with frustration, turned away, and began to stalk around the tent like a caged animal. The sentinels followed him with their eyes, adjusting their positions to discourage him from leaving. Ocyrhoe watched his face change mood over and again, as a dozen different strategies and tactics were dismissed. Finally, he returned to his position in front of the Emperor.

"I am here as a representative of the Holy Roman Church to seek your assistance in the retrieval of Church property."

"Go ahead," Frederick said agreeably, gesturing toward the avenue outside. "I'm not stopping you. Though if you are referring to the Grail—and I find it curious how quickly you've gone from complete denial of its existence to calling it *Church property*—I should point out that I'm not entirely sure it *is* Church property. At least, not the physical manifestation of it. Oh, I'd be happy to have a long and interesting discussion with you about the metaphysics of the Cup of Christ, given what I've seen with my own eyes, but—"

"I am speaking of the man," Fieschi ground out.

"The Pope is Church property?" Frederick asked.

"And all artifacts that he might carry," Fieschi amended hastily.

"Oh yes, of course, my mistake," Frederick snorted, waving his hand toward the door of his tent. "Be my guest, though I am out of fresh horses. Perhaps you could untether one of the nags from the carriage that carried your august personage here and ride it, though I suspect that would be a most uncomfortable ride."

Fieschi again resorted to a groaning sigh to release his frustration. He paced about the tent, his mouth working around words that never came out, and then he stopped and whirled toward them again.

"You, *Binder*," he said, directing his ire at Ocyrhoe. "You are the cause of all this. You have meddled beyond your reach. I will—"

"Has she?" Frederick interrupted.

Fieschi whirled on the Emperor. "Stay out of this," he snapped, shaking a finger at Frederick.

"I'd like to, but if you're going to go blaming all of this nonsense on a small girl—who, I would like to remind you, is not a true Binder, inasmuch as I understand any of their strange rituals and observances—I think that reflects poorly on your own judgment. Which, frankly, is already suspect. I would hate to see that reflected in, say, the next Papal election."

Fieschi slowly curled his finger back into his hand. "She helped the priest escape."

"From a prison you put him in in the first place." Frederick shook his head. "Sinibaldo, this is beneath you. It gives me great joy to watch you sputter and foam like an old toothless woman, but after a while, the joy passes and watching you"—he raised his shoulders and sighed—"it fills me with an unremitting sadness."

Fieschi curled his hand into a fist, and then realizing what he was doing, he lowered his hand. Regaining his composure, he attempted to affix a smile on his face. "This jest has been ill-timed, Frederick. I am under enormous pressure to facilitate the resolution of this *sede vacante*. Perhaps, you might rise above your own childish predilections once in a while."

"I might," Frederick offered.

Fieschi nodded curtly. "We are going to return to Rome. This meeting has been a farce. Given your blasphemous words concerning one of the Church's greatest symbols and your carefree attitude concerning the disposition of Rome's missing priest—"

"Pontiff," Frederick corrected.

"*Priest*," Fieschi snarled. "It is a tragedy that the Holy Roman Emperor, in a time of great religious strife, could not be bothered to respond appropriately to a call for assistance from a beleaguered and otherwise devoted Church."

"Very nicely spoken," Frederick said, clapping lightly when Fieschi finished. "I almost feel *bad* for indulging in my—what did you call them?—my childish predilections." He winked at Ocyrhoe. "Almost."

"Perhaps you will respond more appropriately the next time the Church seeks your assistance," Fieschi said slowly, his face darkening again.

"Perhaps," Frederick said. He waved his hand. "Thank you for stopping by, Cardinal Fieschi. You may go now. Oh, and when you say *we*, I assume that is limited to yourself and your immediate attendants, yes?"

Fieschi's eyes darted toward Ocyrhoe.

"While I may not be leaping to your aid, Cardinal Fieschi, I cannot—in good conscience—let this girl return to Rome with you. Not after you tried to blame all of your current troubles on her. Letting you keep her would be akin to throwing her to the lions, don't you think?"

Fieschi's lip started to curl, and Ocyrhoe was worried that he might press his argument with the Emperor, but he came to a decision. "Keep her," he snapped. "If she ever enters Rome again..." He left the threat unfinished, stalking out of the tent before any more could be said.

Ocyrhoe watched him go, both stunned and awed by what had just transpired. It had been delightful to watch the Emperor castigate the cardinal, and in the end it had turned out as Léna had wished. She was safe, and out of Rome.

"Well," the Emperor said in the silence that filled the tent in the wake of Fieschi's departure. "That was an interesting conversation." He looked at Ocyrhoe. "And here you are," he noted.

Ocyrhoe had presence of mind to bow before the Emperor. "Here I am," she said quietly, her mind still awhirl.

Frederick leaned forward, peering at Ocyrhoe. "Why did the cardinal bring you along?" he asked. "Is it because he thought you might be useful to him?"

"They...they are my friends," she said.

"And because they are your friends, Fieschi thought you might influence them, yes? Perhaps turn them against me?"

"I don't know what the cardinal was thinking," Ocyrhoe admitted.

"I'm not sure *he* did either," Frederick murmured. "It is true that I gave your friend and the priest horses," he continued. "The cardinal will send riders out to find them, and given the priest's condition, I doubt they will be lost very long, and that concerns me because, unlike the cardinal who prefers strut about and squawk denial like an outraged peacock, I am concerned that the priest is carrying something he shouldn't. Something dangerous."

the fight for hünern

R IM TOOK A deep breath as he stepped out of his cage. He'd dreamed of the possibility of freedom, or at least dying in the act of attempting to secure his freedom, and now, he could not quite believe this might come true. The rage he had expected to be coursing through him was strangely absent. As he stood free of the cage, he felt only an all-encompassing certainty of purpose.

It was time to repay what had been done to him, to all of them. He met Lakshaman's gaze and saw the same unmistakable sense of clarity in the other man's eyes. He turned to Zug, expecting to see the same expression, but his gaze was arrested by the appearance of several Mongol guards at the entrance to the *ger*.

The guards, summoned by Lakshaman's noisy attempts to break the locks, were not entirely caught off guard by the escaped prisoners, but they were startled by the pair of Rose Knights. They paused a second too long, uncertain who to attack first.

Zug closed with the foremost of the three, intercepting a wild slash of the man's curved sword by stepping under the cut. Zug seized the Mongol by the wrist, and levered a powerful palm strike to the guard's elbow joint. The Mongol screamed as his elbow shattered. Zug, seizing the curved sword as the man released his hold on it, delivered a spine-snapping kick to the man's hip that sent him careening into his companion to the left. The third Mongol's attack was met with steel, and Zug used the momentum of the bind to wind his sword around and into the side of his enemy's terrified face.

The uninjured Mongol extricated himself from his screaming friend in time to receive a death blow to the head from the sword of one of the Rose Knights, and Lakshaman pushed past the Rose Knight to shove the remaining Mongol down. He placed a foot on his chest to hold him in place, and then broke his neck with a savage heel kick to the side of his head.

Zug walked out of the tent with a supple insouciance that Kim found both intoxicating and infuriating. The Rose Knights trailed behind him, babbling in their tongue. Zug ignored them, walking with a purpose that seemed to agitate the young knights further with each step. Kim jogged after them, Lakshaman trailing behind him. Finally Zug stopped, looked at the young men, and then quietly shook his head. "Khan," he said, enunciating the word clearly so that the Rose Knights would understand.

One of the knights nodded, and pointed off toward a line of flags that indicated the location of Onghwe's massive tent. Zug nodded in a different direction, and the knights started jabbering at him again.

Zug looked at Kim. "Make them understand," he said.

"Why me?" Kim retorted. "I agree with them. The Khan's tent is *that* way."

"I know where it is," Zug growled. "But my *naginata* is stored over there." He pointed. "I want my skull-maker."

* * *

Tegusgal's leg was slick with blood, and some of it dripped off the heel of his boot, spattering Hans's hair. Hans hooked one hand around Tegusgal's boot, and flailed with his feet, trying to get purchase on the stakes in the wall. Tegusgal shouted, jerking his leg, and as Hans felt the dagger slip, he swung himself to the right, throwing his hand out to grab at Tegusgal's other foot.

He hung there for a moment, suspended between both of Tegusgal's legs. The dagger tumbled past his face, falling out of Tegusgal's leg, and he watched it bounce off the dusty ground. His hands were sweaty, slowly slipping off Tegusgal's boots, and the blood from the dagger wound was making his grip even more tenuous. He wiggled his legs, trying to reach the spikes in the wall, and Tegusgal made a different sound—a scream of panic rather than rage—as he let go of the wall.

They both landed hard on the packed dirt at the base of the wall, and the breath was knocked out of Hans. His hip hurt from where Tegusgal had landed on him, and he tried to extricate himself from beneath the Mongol captain. His right shoulder ached, and when he tried to use his arm, his wrist complained.

Tegusgal groaned, responding sluggishly. He sensed Hans moving beneath him, and he tried to stop the young boy from escaping, but his grip was weak.

Hans spotted Maks's dagger and twisted his body in order to reach it. His fingers could almost touch the bloody blade when Tegusgal grabbed his leg with much more conviction this time and held him tight.

"You—" Tegusgal snarled, but his words were cut off when Hans kicked him in the face. He fought back, managing to get a grip on Hans's pant leg and, from there, gain control of the boy's flailing leg. He grinned, blood running from his nose.

Hans grinned back. All of this struggling had allowed him to grab Maks's dagger. He sat up and thrust the dagger with all his strength at Tegusgal's face.

The Mongol tried to cover his head with his arms, twisting out of the way, and Hans missed Tegusgal's head. The dagger slid into the gap at the top of Tegusgal's armor, hitting the soft flesh beneath. Tegusgal shrieked and let go of Hans's legs. This time, Hans scooted back on his rump as quickly as he could, putting some distance between him and the wounded Mongol captain.

Shivering with pain, Tegusgal yanked the dagger out of his neck, and a squirt of blood spattered across the dirt. Gritting his teeth, the Mongol captain started to push himself upright. "I am going to kill you slowly," he coughed. On his knees, he fumbled for his sword, his fingers slipping off the hilt. He tried again, getting it half drawn, when a rock bounced off his chest.

He stared at it stupidly, wondering where it had come from. Hans glanced over his shoulder and saw a flash of movement in the rubble behind him. *The Rats*, he realized giddily.

Tegusgal shook off his confusion and finished drawing his sword. A second rock struck him in the face, and he shouted in pain, his attention finally going to the wreckage behind Hans. More missiles followed, most of them not much bigger than a bird's egg, but many of them were thrown with precision, battering Tegusgal.

Hans's Rats—the cadre of boys who had carried messages time and again into the Mongol compound—were shouting now as they threw rocks at the Mongol captain. Jeering and taunting. Fighting back.

Tegusgal raised his sword, trying to protect his face with the blade, and several stones rang off the blade. He was still trying to get to his feet, though Hans could sense that his intent was now to flee.

Hans scrambled for the dagger.

A particularly well-thrown rock caught Tegusgal in the center of the forehead, and the Mongol captain swayed, momentarily stunned.

The fusillade of rocks subsided as the Rats paused to check their handiwork. Tegusgal shook his head, spattering blood, and then he grinned at the urchins watching him from the wreckage. His face was dark with cuts and bruises, and his teeth were stained red. He wasn't beaten. Not yet.

Hans found himself thinking about Andreas, and he didn't hesitate. He jumped at the Mongol commander, stabbing with the dagger.

Tegusgal's mouth changed shape, and his eyes got big.

* * *

Styg and Eilif had not been able to follow the conversation between the three escaped prisoners, but after a moment of firm hand gestures, the stern-looking one simply shrugged and started walking. Away from the fluttering flags they could see over the tops of the tents.

"He's not going toward the Khan's tent," Styg said.

"Does it matter?" Eilif asked, clapping him on the arm.

The camp was in an uproar, not because the prisoners had been freed but because Rutger and the other Shield-Brethren had commenced their assault on the gate. As Styg hesitated, listening to the sound of battle, he heard horses as well. The reinforcements had arrived.

"Come on," Eilif said. "We're going to lose them."

Styg jogged after Eilif and the escaped prisoners. He didn't know where they were going, but he trusted they were going to end up at the Khan's tent.

Don't stop, Rutger had instructed all of the Shield-Brethren shortly before Styg and Eilif had split off on their special mission. *Kill every Mongol you meet. That is the only order you must remember. Kill them all.*

It really didn't matter how he got there, did it?

A group of panicked slave girls came running around the corner of a tent, and Styg darted to his right to avoid them. For a moment, he lost sight of the others, and when he was trying to spot them again, he caught of a quartet of Mongols trying to control a towering figure with dark skin and thick black hair.

The man was the largest human Styg had ever seen in his life, and the Mongols were trying to tie him to a post, but the man's massive arms were like tree trunks, and he was not cooperating readily. One of the Mongols was trying to lash his hands together while the others jabbed him with their spears. Each time he resisted, the spears would prick him, though none so deeply as to do more than make him hesitate.

Styg glanced around for the others one last time, and then changed course.

The first Mongol never saw Styg coming. Styg's blade cut his spine, and he collapsed immediately. The second turned in time to catch Styg's pommel on the side of the head. One of the remaining Mongols swung his spear sideways, and Styg blocked the shaft easily with his sword, but the man yanked the spear back as soon as there was contact and darted the spear point back again, on the inside of Styg's guard!

Styg slapped his left hand around his blade and yanked his sword toward him as he twisted his body away. He felt the spear point catch on his maille as it trailed across his side. Off balance, his sword half caught between his body and the spear, Styg realized there was no easy way to extricate himself from this situation without giving the man an opening. He simply let go of his sword and grabbed the Mongol's spear with both hands.

The Mongol warrior stared at him, dumbfounded at Styg's foolishness, and then he remembered what he and his companions had been doing before Styg's interruption. His eyes widened as he struggled to yank his spear out of Styg's grip, and after a second he let go of the spear and tried to pull his sword out of its scabbard, but he was too late.

The Mongol was suddenly—and very violently—smashed to the ground by the body of the fourth Mongol.

In the frenzied moment, everyone had forgotten the muscular giant. He had yanked on the ropes the fourth Mongol clung to, and before the hapless soul could disentangle himself, the giant had swung him like a club into the other still standing Mongol.

With a wordless yell, the giant advanced on the two sprawling men, and Styg got out of the way as he grabbed up a fallen spear and drove it through the chest of one man, through the leg of the other, and finally lodged the point deep in the ground. The Mongols struggled, pinned by the spear, and with a bellow of rage that Styg could swear shook the ground, the behemoth kicked each of the downed men in the head. The second one's neck snapped at a horrific angle with a cracking nose that made Styg wince in sympathetic agony.

The immense man turned toward them, and Styg stared, open mouthed, up at the towering man. The giant stared at the Styg, chest heaving, eyes shining with murderous fire. He touched his hands to his chest, said one word—*Madhukar*—and held out his hands, still bound with rope.

"I think you and I share the same enemy," he said. He grinned as he cut the man's bonds with his bloody sword.

the caue of the great bear

GEDEI COULD NOT remember the last time he had been awake before anyone else. In Karakorum, the servants knew to let him sleep as late as he desired, though invariably Chucai would send a frightened messenger with some poorly veiled excuse of a crisis that demanded his attention. Some days, the desire for drink woke him; he had either drunk too little or too much the night before, and the spirits that lived in the wine would tug him away from sleep. His mouth would be dry, and they would whisper incessantly in his ear about how easy it would be to rinse out the dust with a mouthful of wine. During the long journey to Burqan-qaldun, he would wake to the sound of the camp preparing for another day: wood being chopped, meals being prepared, *ger* being disassembled, pack animals being loaded again.

It had been many years since he had slept away from the constant commotion of civilization, and many years before that since he had slept outside with only a sleeping roll between him and the ground. It was not surprising, in that case, that he had slept poorly. It had been the constant mention of his father that had put him in a foul mood as he had lain down to sleep the previous night. He had stared up at the stars for a long time, lost in thought, as more and more of the men around him surrendered to their dreams.

All spoke of Genghis Khan as if they knew him, as if they were anything more than lap dogs and lackeys to him, but none of them knew the Great Khan as well as he did. And he would never confess to them that the man had been an enigma to him.

He never understood why Genghis had chosen him over his brothers to lead the empire. Jochi had been stronger and Chagatai was smarter; even Tolui—dear sweet Tolui—had been better suited to lead than he. And yet, Genghis had ignored all of the evidence and chosen him—the middle son who no one believed was capable.

Late the night before, he had recalled a dream from months earlier, during the late summer at Karakorum. He had dreamed of abandoning the empire—just he and Toregene. They shared one horse and rode west until they reached the endless sea where the sun doused itself every night. There, on the beach, they had built a shelter out of driftwood and palm fronds. He had learned to fish from the shore, and she haunted the rock ledges where the noisy birds nested, harvesting eggs. It had been a simple life, unlike any he had ever known, and it had been satisfying. When they had gotten hungry, he fished; when they had been tired, they slept. The sun fell down from the sky, boiled the sea, and went out; the next day, it was there in the sky again. Nothing ever changed. The dream hadn't been a vision; it was nothing more than the idle spark of a desire that he fueled enough to become a tiny flame, lurking in his heart.

The previous night, sleeping on the ground, beneath a sky filled with bright stars, was a small taste of what that life would be like. Now, with the sky obscured by the predawn fog, the ground wet with dew, he discovered that the burning desire for a simple life had been extinguished. That dream was nothing more than cold ash in his mind, a fantasy that belonged to someone else.

Ögedei rolled his dry tongue around the inside of his mouth, and his attention drifted to the nearby bundle of his gear. Nestled deep inside one of the bags were two flasks of wine. He'd only need one to quench the worst of his thirst. He could save the other one for after he slew the Great Bear.

He rolled over, turning his back on the bag and its secret contents. His knees and back complained as he got to his feet, and he used this soreness as an excuse to walk away from his sleeping roll. A little exercise would get his blood flowing. They had camped near a stream; he could get a drink from there just as easily, and the clear, cold mountain water would wash away the cobwebs of the night.

Under a nearby tree sat a pair of *Torguud*, and one slapped the other as Ögedei limped past, trying to rouse the sleeping guard. He should have stopped and berated them for failing to both stay awake, but he found himself sympathizing: the hard ground was no substitute for a warm *ger*.

As he made his way to the river, his head was filled with thoughts of Karakorum—the comforts of home, the ease and luxury that he had earned after many years of crisscrossing the steppe in pursuit of his father's dream. Why did he need to kill this bear, anyway? What did he really have to prove? Genghis had given him the empire, and it had expanded under his rule. It was so large that it took all of Genghis's sons and their sons to rule it. Wasn't that enough?

Ögedei knelt at the edge of the stream and cupped his hand in the rushing water, wincing at the frigid temperature. He scooped water into his mouth, and gasped as the cold water made his teeth ache. He scooped several more handfuls into his mouth, feeling cold rivulets of water stream down his throat. Bracing himself, he splashed water on his face and rubbed his skin vigorously.

It didn't help his mood.

He heard someone approach, and he turned in acknowledgment. It was Alchiq. The gray-haired hunter knelt by the stream, his knees popping, and dipped a small bowl into the water. He stood, sipped from it slowly, and then he offered it to Ögedei.

Ögedei dismissed the offer. Why hadn't he thought to bring a bowl to the river? How dare Alchiq embarrass him like this? Why hadn't he stopped him from getting his hands wet? He glanced down, noticing how much water had splashed on his shirt from his own actions, and his annoyance increased. He was *Khagan*, and here he was slurping water from a river like a mongrel dog, sleeping out in the open like some herder's sheep. This was all beneath him.

"You're thinking about going back," Alchiq said.

Ögedei glowered at him.

"They'll go, if you order it, but do you think they will forget what you did? What you *didn't* do?" Alchiq shrugged, taking another sip from his bowl. "You'll have to kill all of them. Including the big one, and the young one, the one who knows how to *hunt*."

Ögedei held out his hand for the bowl, and after Alchiq handed it over, he drank from it, peering over its rim at the gray-haired hunter. "Would you kill them all for me?"

Alchiq lifted his shoulders and calmly let his gaze swing across the camp, almost as if he were marking how he would accomplish that task. "I am yours to command, my Khan."

"Would you kill the Great Bear for me too?"

Alchiq brought his gaze back to Ögedei. "You won't ask me to," he said.

"But would you?"

"Would you help me kill all of these men?"

"What? That is a ludicrous question."

"Is it?" Alchiq asked. He knelt by the river again, refilling his bowl, allowing Ögedei the luxury of not answering the question. He stood and took another drink from his bowl. "A man earns those things that he carries with him his entire life. Both his victories and his secrets. What he doesn't earn haunts him, always." He clapped Ögedei on the arm, a surprisingly familiar motion, and gave the *Khagan* a rare smile. "Kill the bear, my Khan," he said. "Accept your destiny."

Ögedei did not know what to say, and after Alchiq left him, he stood for a long time at the edge of the stream, staring at the water.

* * *

Gansukh tugged at the hem of the shirt, wishing—once again—that Munokhoi had been slightly taller. Though, if he had been, events in the woods might have gone differently. He sighed and wriggled his shoulders one final time before relenting to the constant confinement of the ex-*Torguud* captain's extra shirt.

He could have returned to the hunting party the previous day covered in blood, but when he calmed down after killing Munokhoi, he had realized that the less said about the fight in the woods, the better. Namkhai had noticed when he had caught up with the *Khagan*'s party, as had Alchiq and Chucai, but the different clothes and horse had gone unnoticed by the others.

He had caught Ögedei staring at his ravaged ear after the evening meal, but the *Khagan* had said nothing. Even though the cold water from the stream had given him a headache, he had dunked his head into the stream three times, scrubbing his hair, his face, and both ears between each immersion. He was surprised—and a little pleased—that he had slept at all, given how much his ear had been throbbing in the night.

This morning, though, most of the stinging was gone, reduced to a dull ache that would, he suspected, persist for several weeks while the wounds healed. He would be marked for the rest of his life, carrying the visible scar of the fight in the woods.

At least he was alive. Missing part of an ear was an acceptable sacrifice.

After the men had taken care of their horses the day before, the *Darkhat* had drawn the *Khagan* a map in the dirt. The valley forked, and the northern fork became a narrow rocky vale. Somewhere up there, hidden in the boulder-strewn hillside at the end of the valley, was the bear's cave. The southern fork was rocky as well, though it was filled with a dense forest of evergreen trees. The bear hunted in those woods, but it always returned to its cave in the northern fork. In some ways, it didn't matter in which fork the bear was, because once they entered the valley, there was no way out except past them.

When they reached the valley, the *Torguud* became the rear-guard, and the hunters spread out to the side and in front of the *Khagan* as the hunting party rode toward the northern fork. The sky was clear of clouds, and the morning mist had already burned off the floor of the valley. Thin wisps of fog still clung to some of the rocky knobs on the surrounding hillsides.

Gansukh was surprised by the variety of trees. He recognized ash, alder, oak, and cedar, but there were several other evergreens that he did not know. The trees hugged the edges of the valley, growing thicker the farther they ventured into the valley. The trees were tall too, as if they had never known fire or ax. Gansukh heard numerous birds singing and calling to each other, and he saw signs of small animals—squirrels, rabbits, and other rodents and scavengers.

The bear never had to go far to find food, and for a little while, Gansukh wondered if the *Darkhat* had been wrong and the bear had been dead for many years. The proliferation of life in the valley was, instead, a testament to the lack of predators.

The sun moved overhead as they reached the rocky spur that signified the split between the two ends of the valley. The hunting party paused briefly—some dismounting to piss, others chewing a quick snack of dried meat—and then continued to the left, moving past the outcropping of rock that split the valley into two forks.

The forest thinned out, and the trees gave way to fields of rocks and the scraggly bushes of the steppe. They started to come across piles of bear scat; after the first one, everyone sat up a little straighter in their saddles, and bows were strung and readied. As the hunting party approached the end of the valley, the hillsides forced them to ride closer together, and there was some confusion among the riders as to who would lead.

Ögedei finally pushed his horse to the front, silencing Namkhai and the chief hunter's arguments with a curt shake of his head. The *Khagan* readied his spear, and the hunting party crept forward.

One of the *Darkhat* pointed out the dark hole of the bear's cave, and the hunting party came to a halt. A hushed conference was held, debating the best way to approach the bear's cave, and Gansukh sat a little ways off. His opinion wasn't needed, and he would only be in the way of the *Khagan*'s triumphant kill. It was his job to watch now, to be a party to Ögedei's triumph.

Alchiq's horse ambled up to his. The gray-haired hunter was peering intently up at the dark cave. He grunted, catching Gansukh's attention, and then pointed.

Gansukh looked, shading his eyes from the sun to see what Alchiq was pointing at. There was a clear trail up the slope, the route the bear took time and again, and it looked like there was a flat shelf in front of the cave where something caught his eye.

Gansukh looked at Alchiq, who shrugged as he slid off his horse. Carrying his bow ready, the gray-haired hunter darted forward, leaping from cover to cover as he approached the cave. Swearing under his breath, Gansukh glanced over at the clustered hunting party, wondering if anyone had noticed Alchiq. No one had, and with a final curse, he climbed down from his horse and followed the gray-haired hunter.

They were too far below the cave to see properly, but Gansukh had seen what had caught Alchiq's attention: a wooden spar, jutting up at an angle that didn't seem natural.

As he ran after Alchiq he heard Namkhai shout behind him. He ignored the *Torguud* captain's cry, and dogged Alchiq's heels as the gray-haired hunter raced toward the cave. They scrambled up the slope together, no longer caring to move silently. The hunting party was making enough noise now to alert anything that might be waiting for them up at the cave.

Breathing heavily, Gansukh reached the flat shelf at the cave a half step behind Alchiq, and he came to a sudden stop as he saw what was waiting for them.

The body of a Great Bear was crucified upon huge crossed logs driven into the ground in front of the cave. Its front legs splayed out, arrows driven into its paws. Its head was held in place by a length of rope. The beast's tongue protruded from its mouth in an obscene and unnatural twist.

Alchiq slowly walked up to the dead beast. His head was almost level with the bear's shoulders; directly in front of him was a long shaft jutting from the bear's chest. Gansukh stared at the object, uncomprehendingly.

It looked like an arrow, but it was the longest arrow he had ever seen.

Alchiq turned around, his eyes restlessly scanning the hillside around them, searching for something that, judging from the savage grin on his face, he had been expecting.

"They're here," he said.

a binder's choice

IN THE WAKE of the cardinal's departure from the Emperor's tent, Frederick waved his hands, and his guards withdrew. In a few moments, only he and Ocyrhoe remained, and he gestured for her to join him at the narrow table where several plates of food were arrayed. She hesitated, awkwardly aware of the ragged condition of her clothing and the matted tangles of her hair. The Emperor's clothing was made of silk, and she could only imagine what it was like to wear such opulent clothing. She felt like the city rat she was, transported into an unknown wilderness, a forest so dense with trees and brush she could barely see the sky. So unlike Rome. So unlike anything she had ever known.

The Emperor sat on one of the stools beside the table and began to eat: salted pork, grapes, slivers of sliced fruit, hunks of dark bread. Her mouth watered as she drifted toward the table. "Sit," Frederick said. "Eat." He poured water from a jug into a plain cup. Into another cup he poured a measure of wine. "Earlier today I had a meal similar to this one with your friends," he said, ignoring her reluctance to join him. He indicated the cups on the table with a piece of meat. "We drank from some of my finer tableware, which would normally be completely unremarkable but for an odd bit of roguish sleight of hand." He stared at her intently as if she should know what he was talking about.

She shook her head.

"The priest truly does think he is in possession of the Holy Grail," Frederick said without further preamble. "What do you think of such nonsense?"

"I know very little of such things, Your Majesty," Ocyrhoe said, her hand darting out for a grape.

Frederick grunted and stared off into space for a few moments. "He is a curious fellow, your priest. One moment, he seems quite harmless; the next, sadly broken from his experience at Mohi; and the next..." He shook his head slightly. "I have met my share of zealots, little Binder, and most of them cannot hide their insanity. They are like moths that have been blinded by a candle. Father Rodrigo, on the other hand, concerns me. If he were a moth, he would be blind, burned, and still insistent on leaping into the flame again." He picked up his cup and sipped from it. "And he doesn't want to go alone."

Ocyrhoe didn't know what to say. The Emperor's assessment of Father Rodrigo made her stomach knot. She reached for the cup of water and drank from it slowly.

"We were having a perfectly pleasant conversation this morning," Frederick continued, "albeit one that was marred by the occasional outlandish remark concerning apocalyptic prophecies and divine inspiration, and then the priest produced a cup from his satchel and announced it was the Holy Grail." Frederick smiled. "I laughed at him, I must admit, which was probably not the most circumspect reaction, but I was taken aback by his claim. He was, after all, trying to convince me that one of my own cups was the holy chalice." He tapped a fingernail against the rim of his cup. "Just like this one. I offered him wine, and when my back was turned, he slipped the cup into his satchel so that he could produce it again."

He shook his head. "I knew it was my own cup. I had had a boy bring three into the tent. I had one, there was a second sitting on this table, and the third—well, the third was in Father Rodrigo's hand and he was telling me that it was the Holy Grail and, with it, he was going to call a crusade against the infidels and nonbelievers. And by God, I believed him."

Ocyrhoe nodded slowly. "I saw him preaching to a crowd at the marketplace," she said. "They weren't shouting at him or throwing vegetables. They were listening, and he had a cup there too. I could feel the mood of the crowd change when he showed it to them. They became more..." She searched for the right word.

"Entranced?" Frederick provided.

"Yes, entranced. They would have followed him if the Vatican's guards hadn't intervened." She wrinkled her nose. "But, I saw the cup fall," she said. "He dropped it, and I don't remember where it rolled. I don't know that anyone retrieved it." She looked at Frederick's cup. "And it was gold. Not silver."

"Yes," said Frederick absently. "And the one he produced this morning was silver at first, but it appeared to change color..."

Taking advantage of Frederick's inattention, Ocyrhoe snatched a piece of the meat from the trencher and shoved it into her mouth. She was not used to pork—the unpleasant smell of it hung over the whole camp—and her mouth cringed from the heavy salting, but she chewed it nonetheless. She groped for her cup, gulping water to help wash down the dry meat. None of this stopped her from reaching for another piece.

Frederick watched her eat, the corner of his mouth turning up in mild amusement. "We used to be friends," he said, "Cardinal Fieschi and I. I used to have a much less...antagonistic relationship with Rome. I went on a crusade for the Church, in fact. It was the only crusade since our initial conquest of Jerusalem that could be considered a victory for the Church, and I did it with very little bloodshed. Does the Pope reward me for such a victory? No. He excommunicates me. *Twice*." He shook his head. "And now this disaster in Rome: the *sede vacante*, this strange Pope who may not be Pope, the disappearance of the Binders in Rome—oh, yes, I know about your missing kin-sisters—and, finally, the question of the Cup of Christ. What am I to make of this...oddity that Father Rodrigo placed on my table? That entranced members of my camp?"

He drummed his fingers on the table, idly chewing on his lip as he thought. Ocyrhoe kept eating, emboldened now by the Emperor's mental distance.

"I fear Fieschi will be Pope someday, and at which time I will lose the friendship of a cardinal and gain the enmity of a Pope," Frederick said with a sigh. "Though I admit to some culpability in straining that friendship. I do admire Cardinal Fieschi's self-control in not forcing himself upon the Church at this time, though I guess I can't blame him. This election was a fucking disaster from the beginning."

Ocyrhoe choked on her piece of meat, and it was only after gulping the rest of her water that she was able to breath easily again. "What do you know about my sisters?" she finally managed.

Frederick nodded. "I'm sure Senator Orsini was simply following orders, blindly being led by a hand that he thinks will continue to feed him, but he is, in the end, very provincial in his thinking. Which would be more ironic—given his status in Rome, that once great center of civilization—were it not for the larger game afoot." He leaned forward, resting his elbows on the table. "What did Léna tell you when she sent you back to me?"

"She...she didn't," Ocyrhoe stuttered. "The cardinal ordered me to come along."

"He did, did he?" Frederick smiled. "And she said nothing to you before you left?"

Ocyrhoe tried to remember anything that Léna might have imparted to her that would be worthy of the Emperor's notice, and she couldn't recall anything specific. "She said I needed to leave the city, and when I said that I couldn't because of the guards, she told me to be patient. Something would happen that would aid me."

"And it did, in the person of the cardinal. Not what you expected, was it?"

"Very little has been since...since my sisters vanished, Your Majesty."

"Yes, well, I expect it will get stranger still yet," Frederick said wryly. "Do you believe that the cup Father Rodrigo carries is actually the Grail?"

He seemed very focused on that question, and Ocyrhoe wished she knew what she was supposed to say. "I do not know, Your Majesty."

"I suspect Fieschi was going to try to *bind* you to retrieving it for him," Frederick said. "Though I am not quite certain why he thought that might be possible."

"I don't understand. Bind me how?"

"To a message. In the same way that you were bound by Cardinal Somercotes to bring me news of the cardinals' captivity."

Ocyrhoe did not understand what he meant, and she was uncertain if she could confess that or simply play along. She wished this situation were a dream from which she might will herself awake. Her very sinews felt as if they were about to leap out of her body and run back to Rome, leaving her a pile of enervated bones on the rug-covered ground of the pavilion.

Frederick, sensing her tension, laughed and slapped his leg. The joyous expression was strange on his unhandsome face, but she believed his jocularity was freely expressed. "Let us not talk of being forced into a course of action," he said dryly. "Let us consider a choice freely made. Hmmm?" When she nodded, he continued. "Let us presume for a moment that you knew where Father Rodrigo and Ferenc had gone and that you were allowed to join them. Knowing what you know about the priest and his mission—which, I grant, is very little—would you be inclined to join him or stop him?

"How...how would I stop him?" she asked.

"You saw him in the marketplace. Do you think the guards would have been able to remove him from the crowd if he *hadn't* dropped the cup?"

"It frightens you," she said, sensing the truth of her words as they came out of her mouth.

Frederick sat back on his stool, his face becoming still and unreadable. "I am concerned, little one," he said somewhat brusquely. "Do not conflate such into more than it is."

"You want me to steal the Grail," she said, the Emperor's intentions as clear as if he had spoken them aloud.

"So does Cardinal Fieschi," he said. His expression was complicated to read now: at once trying to remain friendly and confiding, but a sternness had settled on his brow. "Which of us would you obey?" Ocyrhoe looked down, cowed but determined to maintain her position. "Why must I obey either of you?" she asked. "The Senator took my sisters and the cardinal did little to stop him. You profess to knowing of their disappearance too, and what have you done to aid them? And yet you ask me to thieve for you? For the Church?" She shook her head.

Frederick remained still, studying her, and she focused on her hands to avoid his scrutiny.

"If I were to tell you—to insist, as a matter of fact—that the cup that Father Rodrigo has taken is, indeed, nothing more than a cup from my table, would that not make his action thievery? If you were to believe the cardinal's clumsy rhetoric, whatever Father Rodrigo is carrying is Church property, property that has been stolen as well. You would be returning something that does not belong to the priest. Doing so would be the right thing to do, in fact, and I don't think it is such an onerous thing for me to ask of you."

Ocyrhoe immediately looked up and stared at him, with the frank rudeness that usually only small children can get away with.

"No? Then why don't you do it yourself?" she asked, and when he didn't answer immediately, she continued. "If *retrieving* this cup is such a simple duty, then why do both the Holy Roman Emperor and one of the most powerful cardinals in Rome want me to do it? Do you think I am too simple to notice the contradiction? Do you think because I am female, or common, or young, that I don't recognize hypocrisy and manipulation when I see it?" Amazed at her own brazenness, she quickly amended, "Your Majesty." But she kept his gaze.

Frederick was the one who looked away, blinking rapidly. "Christ Almighty," he said to himself. "No wonder she arranged *this*." He looked back at her, and grinned. "I apologize, young lady. Very well. I intended no offense, and I will prove it now by including you in my thoughts about these matters. Tell me, what do *you* think of this nonsense with the cup?"

Ocyrhoe's thin lips pressed together briefly to control a flaring of anger. "You are mocking me, Your Majesty," she stated.

He shook his head. "I'm not. Truly. I think the world of Léna"—he chuckled and shook his head—"and I would never mock one of her kin-sisters. Alas, I have been boorish enough to insult one, though, by implying she is simple, so please grant me the opportunity to make amends."

Ocyrhoe took a deep breath and let it out in a sigh, willing her fearful indignation to subside enough so she might think straight. He really wanted to know her opinion, and it was abundantly clear to her now that he wasn't going to stop asking until she replied. "In the marketplace, I saw the priest hold up a cup as if it were a relic. But I was not very close to him, and from what I did see, it seemed to be shiny but it was otherwise unremarkable." She tried to recall more details of the event in the marketplace: the way the crowd reacted to

Father Rodrigo, the play of light on the object in his hand, the odd hollowness of his voice, the crawling sensation she felt in the back of her head. "But it did affect those who looked on it. The crowd thrilled at the sight of it," she said slowly, swallowing a strange thickness at the back of her throat.

"But you found it unremarkable?" Frederick asked.

Ocyrhoe shook her head. "It had no power over me, if that is what you mean."

"Yes, that's what I meant," Frederick said. "While I was not as smitten by it as some in my camp, I must confess to being *lulled* by its presence. I *knew* it was a cup from my table, but such awareness did not make itself felt upon my mind until well after the priest had removed it from my sight. So, the question that continues to intrigue me is this: does the influence derive from the man or the cup?" He levered a finger at her. "What do you think of the man Rodrigo?" he asked.

She grimaced, caught off guard by his brusque question. She squirmed under his gaze, not wanting to give him an answer, but knowing she couldn't avoid doing so. "He is a good man," she said carefully. "I think he has suffered a terrible injury. Not physically, but in his mind. I do not think he is a mystic or a prophet or anything like that. Something has not healed right in his head."

Frederick nodded. "How does this *attraction* work? If it stems not from the cup nor from his person, then how can you account for his power over the people?"

Ocyrhoe shrugged. "How different is it from the influence any powerful ruler has over his subjects? Does it worry you because you feel it too? That you might be like the rest of us?" She was somewhat shocked by these words. She would not have spoken so bluntly to her own foster mother, and yet, here she was, speaking thusly to the Emperor of the Holy Roman Empire.

He gave her an avuncular laugh. "You have an unexpected feistiness I rather like." He sobered. "However, as much as I know you would find delight in me admitting that I am, like yourself, nothing more than a rat from the streets, albeit in finer clothing, put aside this ferocity. It's getting in the way of our discourse. Where does this power come from?"

She did not entirely trust his motives but, in the back of her mind—in much the same way she sensed the presence of Léna or her sisters—she knew her answers were providing a way. To what and how she had no idea, but she only knew her path was not yet set. "My only thoughts are...farfetched, Your Majesty," she said.

"To hell with orthodoxy. Tell me what you think."

Using her two hands to illustrate her point, Ocyrhoe said, "The man is nothing alone, and the cup is nothing alone, but when the man works with the cup"—here she brought her hands—palms up—together, interweaving her fingers—"it is as if there is a..." She searched for the right word, and found one, floating there in her head as if it were waiting for her to latch onto it. As if whispered from someone else's lips directly into her ear. "An *alchemical* change. They become more than the sum of their parts."

Frederick sat back in his chair, his expression both piqued and hooded. "An interesting word choice, my young friend. Not the sort of explanation I would expect from a poorly dressed street rat." His lips quirked around a smile. "Take no offense, please," he said, anticipating her reaction. "Given the overbearing reach of the Church within Rome's walls, it is surprising to find someone who knows of the concepts of *al-kimia*."

He pronounced the word differently than she had, and instinctively she knew he was referencing an older tradition, much like the cloth merchants in the market would assess the quality of each other's wares with cryptic references to the source of the materials. There was a light dancing in his eyes now, a flame of mirth that he was trying very hard to tamp down.

"It would seem remarkable how similarly our minds work, wouldn't it?" he asked. "But I guess I shouldn't be surprised." Clapping his hands together between his knees, he leaned forward. "Answer me this, then: why is not everyone affected by it? That is the part I cannot make sense of."

"I think it has to do with any given person's nature," Ocyrhoe said. She suddenly felt shy. Answering the catechism of his first few questions had been awkward, but not entirely uncomfortable; now, something had changed in his demeanor, and his questions had a new intensity. He actually wanted to know her opinion, and she found the onus of providing useful information intimidating. "Perhaps in these days of such upheaval, when there is no Pope, when there are terrifying stories of invaders from the east, there are some people who *wish* to have an apparent savior appear, and so given the chance to believe they have seen one, they *will* believe." She raised her shoulders. "Others do not."

"I agree with that, but I cannot imagine *anyone* alive right now not wishing for some kind of savior to appear," Frederick argued. "I wish it myself, and I'm the most dedicated atheist alive."

"It...it isn't about faith," Ocyrhoe offered. "Consider this: Ferenc is absolutely devoted to Father Rodrigo; he loves him dearly, and he would believe anything the priest told him. But was Ferenc entranced by the cup? Even when Father Rodrigo brandished it?"

Frederick shook his head.

"Maybe, to him, it is just a cup. Maybe, it hasn't occurred to him that such an object would be anything other than what it appears to be," Ocyrhoe offered.

Frederick grimaced thoughtfully, looking at her, nodding slowly. "That is it," he said conclusively. "Thank you. Such pure and clear understanding." He sighed, and looked away from her for a long moment, staring out into the avenue where the life of the tent city continued to stream past. "Such maddening cleverness," he said quietly, speaking not of Ocyrhoe but of someone else who was not present.

But who had been. *Recently*, Ocyrhoe suspected.

Eventually he turned back to look at her. "Given all this, then, would you take the cup away from the priest?"

Ocyrhoe frowned. "I already told you I will not steal it, not for the Church and not for the Crown. I don't see how this conversation changes that."

He held up a finger to his lip. "Soft, girl. Listen to me. I am not ordering you as a ruler. I am suggesting that you do this as a favor to the boy and to the priest himself. No good will come of that poor madman wandering through the wilderness, occasionally turning heads. He will inspire enough people that they may be moved to take action and raise arms against the Mongols. But—"

She raised her hand to protest, but he reached across the table and grabbed her by the wrist, pulling her toward him. His pale blue eyes flared almost green.

"*But*," he repeated in a low, intense voice, "and this is the most important *but* that you are going to hear in your young life, so listen to me. *But* he will not raise enough of a force to be effective against the invaders. If the Grail were truly some kind of holy relic, and the entire population of Europe really was moved to rise up against the Mongols, that would be one thing. But the fucking thing does not have that power. It is an illusion. The number who will be moved will be just large enough to convince themselves they are strong, *but* they'll be wrong, and they'll be slaughtered, and their families will be bereft. That is what will happen if Rodrigo keeps hold of that goddamned cup. The man and the cup must be sundered. It is the kindest thing that you can do for him. And for scores or maybe hundreds of families whose paths he is about to cross. Take the cup away from him."

He stared into her eyes, and she saw sweat forming on his brow. He was barely controlling his breath. She realized, with shamed amazement, that he was speaking not as a conniver or controller, but as a ruler concerned about the well-being of those he ruled. A ruler who feared he, himself, was not strong enough to perform this task.

"Yes," she said, suddenly frightened. "I will."

AN AUDIENCE
WITH THE KHAN

A MONGOL, KNOCKED INTO a cook fire during the initial surge of horsemen, had lived long enough to run—shirt and hair on fire—into the rows of tents. Rutger assumed he had died from the burns, but before he had expired, the flames had leaped from him to several tents. The fire was spreading, and a haze of ash and embers was starting to fill the air. A storm of glittering snow.

The battle had moved away from him, and he took advantage of the respite to catch his breath. His lungs ached from battlefield exertion, and he gulped air as best he could. There was no time to rest, even for a moment. Even with the Livonians bolstering their numbers, they were still outnumbered. As long as they could keep the Mongols off balance and disorganized, they stood a chance. They had to keep fighting.

Off to his left, Rutger caught sight of Kristaps, who had lost his horse and now fought on foot. He fought with a relentless energy, his Great Sword of War rising and falling with methodical precision. Rutger felt a pang of envy at the other man's strength, but he pushed that thought away. He was under no illusion about his age or his health.

The front line was not a place for him any longer.

Ahead of him, four knights—three Shield-Brethren and a Livonian—staggered out of the smoke. Arrows followed them, and one of the Shield-Brethren fell. A howling group of Mongols came next, swords and spears eager for blood. Trailing behind the war party was an enormously fat Mongol with a blood-spattered cudgel.

"Behind you!" Rutger shouted, waving his sword and starting to run toward the three men, but his lungs seized. He stumbled, gasping for breath. *Not now*, he pleaded, *let me finish*. His throat convulsing, his body shaking as it tried to draw in enough air, he could only watch as two groups smashed into one another.

Rutger was still catching his breath when a number of Shield-Brethren rushed past him to join the frenzied melee. He recognized one—the initiate, Maks—and he wondered why the young man was here and not protecting the boy, Hans.

The Mongols were shouting a name—*Ashiq Temür*—and Rutger saw the fat Mongol shouting in response, issuing orders to the men around him. Rutger pounded his hand against his chest as he limped toward the battle.

The panic holding his chest eased, and his lungs inflated in a rush. His vision both darkening and lightening, Rutger felt his strength return, and he moved more quickly to aid his brothers. He slew two Mongols as the battle surged around him, welcoming him back to the fray, before he had a chance to take stock of that state of the melee.

He was in the midst of a straining mass of bodies, sword ringing against sword, spear thrusting into maille and cloth, men on the ground grappling with daggers and bare hands. He caught sight of the fat Mongol, Ashiq Temür, and he struggled to move in that direction.

His attention was suddenly interrupted by a screaming Mongol who came at him from the side. Forced to react, Rutger pivoted backward, twisting his midsection just out of range as he rotated his sword to a high guard and snapped his hips back, bringing his sword edge down in a cut at the Mongol's head. The Mongol intercepted the stroke, and wheeled his curved sword around Rutger's blade.

As was the case in any fight, the ones who lived were the ones who had some skill, and as the battle wore on, Rutger found that the men he faced were showing more and more of it. The Mongol's response to his parry was fast, and he had to snap his hilt up in order to keep the line closed. The Mongol's blade slid down his with a hiss of metal grating across metal, and Rutger ducked as he sidestepped. He was now beneath his enemy's blade and inside. With a quick pull, he freed his blade from the bind and slashed it across the Mongol's torso, gutting the man. He stepped through, turning, and reversing his hands, finished his opponent off with a cut to the back of the neck.

He spotted Maks again, and he watched as the young warrior closed in on Ashiq Temür. The fat warrior caught the first stroke of the initiate's sword on his cudgel as he tried to get closer to the young man. Maks kept his distance, lashing out with his sword as he darted out of the way of the fat Mongol's club. His sword sliced across Ashiq Temür's arm, leaving a red line that immediately started to run with blood. *Keep your distance*, Rutger thought, a grim smile on his lips.

But Maks had nowhere to go. He had been spun around in the fight and now his back was to a tent. Instead of waiting for Ashiq Temür's attack, Maks moved first. But the fat Mongol was quicker than his bulk suggested. He got within Maks's measure and swept his bulky arm down, pinning Maks's sword against his body. Maks struggled a second too long, trying to pull his sword free, and he brought his hand up in a valiant—but hopeless—effort to shield his face from the Mongol's cudgel.

Rutger saw Maks's body jerk and spasm as his skull was shattered by Ashiq Temür's club, and when the fat Mongol stepped back, the young initiate—his face a bloody, unrecognizable pulp—fell as if bonelessly to the ground.

Rutger's chest threatened to seize again, and his blood pounded in his ears. *Another boy gone*, he thought. He heard his voice echoing in his head, screaming the Shield-Brethren battle cry.

* * *

The guards outside of Ongwhe's tent saw them coming and hesitated, frightened by the bloody figures running toward them. Zug had his *naginata*, and at his side were Kim, Lakshaman, and one of the Rose Knights. The guards had been stuck at the Khan's tent, unable to participate in the battle, forced to watch what little bit of the melee they could see. They were eager to fight—too eager, perhaps—and when the fight finally came to them, they reacted poorly.

A guard thrust his spear too soon at Zug, and he sidestepped it easily. With a tiny flick of his hands he smashed the shaft aside with the heavy *naginata* and swiped the blade across the narrow gap between the top of the Mongol's armor and the base of his throat. It was a tiny space, but with years of practice he had gotten very good at cutting it—straight across, side to side.

Nearby, a guard dropped to the ground, gurgling and clawing at the knife that sprouted from his throat. Two more guards charged him and he dropped down to one knee, pulling his weapon tight to his body. He kept the blade of the *naginata* pointed up, forcing the guards to go to either side of him or risk impaling themselves on his blade. The guards ran right into Kim and Lakshaman, who fell upon them in a frenzy of steel.

More guards poured out of the Khan's tent, and Zug lost himself in the battle that followed. The skull-maker sang its song, and he felt a tiny spark of joy in his chest.

Finally, he was doing the right thing.

When the last guard fell, weeping as he tried to staunch the earnest flow of blood from a severed arm, Zug strode toward the Khan's tent and thrust aside the heavy flaps.

The interior was surprisingly sparse for as large as it was. There were only a few tables and divans scattered on a sea of colorful rugs. On the far side, Onghwe Khan lounged on a long platform draped with silks and furs. A nearby table was covered with trays of food, and the Khan languidly held a silver goblet in one hand, seemingly unconcerned about the sudden appearance of armed men in his private tent. His body was draped with layers of colored silks, and though the lavish fabrics hid his frame, the enormous weight of his body could not be fully disguised.

He was completely unarmed and unprepared for the quartet's entrance, yet he did not look remotely frightened. Unlike the whore hiding behind him, her eyes wide with abject terror.

There were still more guards as well. Zug's eyes darted about the grand room, counting five armed men. They were approaching the front of the tent cautiously, their expressions running the gamut from fury to outright panic.

But the Khan was nonplussed. Zug returned his gaze to Onghwe's round face, seeking some sign that the Khan remotely understood what was about to happen to him. *How can he be so unaware of the danger?* he thought. *Is the Khan in the grip of some sort of pleasure drug? Is he insensate from wine?* The Khan's mouth opened slightly, his tongue darting out to run across his ruddy lips, and Zug felt only revulsion and fury at the years he had lost to this man.

The guards were approaching, and there was no more time for idle speculation. Zug stepped farther inside the tent, allowing the others to crowd past him. Kim wasted no time, leaping to attack the first man. The Flower Knight's spear pierced the throat of his opponent with a well-aimed thrust; he folded the man in half with a powerful kick to the abdomen, and then proceeded to leap over the collapsing man to smash through the guard of a second Mongol, who screamed as Kim's blade cut through his arm and lodged in his chest.

On Zug's left, Lakshaman parried a spear thrust with his sword, cutting at the guard's hands as the weapon went past him. The stroke took too long, and he didn't get his sword around in time to block the thrust from a second man. He let out a low grunt as the spear point entered his right shoulder. As Zug watched, Lakshaman grabbed the shaft of the spear and wrenched the spear-wielding Mongol closer to him. He rammed his blade through the man, and as the Mongol died, he let go of his sword and pulled the spear out of his shoulder. A hard cast knocked the remaining guard off his feet, and only then did Lakshaman retrieve his sword.

The last guard hesitated, and Zug glanced at the young Rose Knight standing next to him. Zug tilted his head toward the Mongol, and the boy grinned as he darted forward to engage this last guard.

Zug turned his attention to the Khan, but Lakshaman was already moving. The scarred fighter bounded to the top of one table, jumped between two divans, and then took an immense leap toward the reclining Khan. His sword was raised high above his head, and he let out an animalistic scream as he brought his sword down in a mighty swing.

The whore screamed, her voice a thin echo of Lakshaman's cry, and there followed a muffled *thud* that caught everyone's attention as Lakshaman's sword buried itself deep within the mass of pillows and furs.

But not the body of Onghwe Khan.

Zug felt his sweat go cold on his brow. He had never seen a man move so fast.

Onghwe was standing now, a plain sword in his hand as if it had been summoned by some arcane magic. The girl was still screaming, her lungs not yet having run out of air. Lakshaman was frozen, the muscles of his arms and back standing out in plain relief. Onghwe's face was no longer soft and his eyes were bright and fierce. He swung his arm, and Lakshaman's head, expression of surprise and disbelief permanently frozen on the scarred man's face, separated from his body and bounced across the rugs, leaving bloody blotches as it rolled.

Onghwe smiled, and Zug found himself staring at the face of a tiger who had just cornered its prey. "Over these many years, I have enjoyed watching you suffer," Onghwe said, shaking Lakshaman's blood from his blade. "Time and again, I thought you would lie down and die, but you were like an incredibly stupid and faithful dog. You never gave up. No matter how badly I abused you or beat you or pushed to the brink of madness, you never quit. You two are, without a doubt, the most impressive specimens I have ever captured."

He smiled and beckoned Zug and Kim to approach. "Come to me, my most faithful dogs. Your new friend too. You have no idea how long I have been waiting for this moment."

GUIDING THE EMPIRE

THE FIRST ARROW pierced the man standing in front of Ögedei through the hollow of his throat. The arrow buried itself to its fletching, and to Ögedei it seemed as if the man had suddenly sprouted a white flower at the base of his neck. The hunter jerked, a spatter of blood erupting from his mouth, and his eyes rolled back in his head as he clawed frantically at the feathers and shaft sunk into his neck. The arrow, longer than any Ögedei had ever seen, protruded from the hunter's back.

The second arrow punched through the skull of the man standing behind him, the broadhead point of the arrow sticking out of the man's face below his left eye. This man was dead as he collapsed, his arms flopping forward as if attempting to embrace Ögedei as he fell.

Namkhai slammed into Ögedei, shoving him against his horse. Ögedei's face was smashed against the horse's flank, and his exclamation of surprise turned into a muffled sputter through a mouthful of horsehide. Ögedei heard the meaty *thunk* of another arrow hitting flesh, and Namkhai grunted, and then the *Torguud* captain hauled him down to the ground.

One of the long arrows had gone through Namkhai's left shoulder, and as soon as the *Khagan* was down on the ground, Namkhai reached over his shoulder and, gritting his teeth, snapped off the back half of the arrow.

The hunting party was in complete disarray. The *Darkhat* and the shaman were the only ones who had remained on their horses when they had reached the end of the valley. The rest of the party had dismounted while Alchiq and Gansukh had scrambled up the slope to investigate the entrance of the Great Bear's cave. From the ground, Ögedei could only see a confusion of legs—of both men and horses—as the hidden archer continued to rain death down upon them.

"Spread out," Namkhai shouted at the men. "Get to cover and find those archers!"

Archers? he thought dumbly, imagining a host of giants hurling these long arrows at the hunting party. He groveled on the ground, his legs shaking, and he would have stayed where he was, clutching the dry earth, if his horse hadn't screamed and reared.

A shorter arrow stuck out from the animal's neck, and as it staggered and swayed toward him, he was forced to move. The horse collapsed on its side, nearly pinning Namkhai to the ground. Ögedei froze for a moment, blinking in shock at the sight of the long arrow that suddenly sprouted from the ground beside his outstretched leg, and then Namkhai grabbed his sleeve unceremoniously and shoved him in the direction of a cluster of leafy bushes.

Ögedei scrambled as fast as he could on his hands and knees. He threw himself around the edge of the bushes, clawing at the dirt and dragging his legs quickly to reach shelter. There were two men already hiding behind the screen of bushes, and as Ögedei crawled behind them, one of them cried out and fell on his ass. A long-shafted arrow stuck out of his gut, and he whimpered pitifully as he tried to gather his courage to touch it.

A pair of *Darkhat* riders passed behind his position, guiding their horses with their legs as they fired their bows. Ögedei didn't dare peek out to see what they were shooting at; he was relieved they were fighting back. Someone was shouting his name, but he couldn't make out who it was with all the chaotic noise from the men and the horses.

"It hurts. I can't feel my legs." The wounded man tugged at his sleeve. "My Khan," he moaned. "Help me." There was a lot of blood, and as the wounded man struggled to sit up, Ögedei spotted more blood on the ground beneath him. The arrow had gone completely through the man's body.

The other man tried to shush the wounded one, and his entreaties were cut short. The leaves of the bushes shivered, and the man jerked to the side, toppling into Ögedei. He writhed and wailed, and Ögedei took one look and shoved him away in horror.

The arrow had passed through the man's face, from one side to the other. He couldn't open his mouth very far, and his cries quickly became a choking gurgle as his mouth and throat filled up with blood.

The bushes offered no shelter against the long arrows. Ögedei might as well be standing in the middle of an open field.

* * *

They crouched behind the crucified bear, able to see the devastation wreaked by the long arrows below and still scan for the location from which the mysterious archer was shooting. Trying to track the arrows, Gansukh watched as the assassin—with deadly accuracy—slew three men. The *Khagan* was nearly hit several times before he managed to scramble into shelter, and each time, Gansukh felt his heart leap into his mouth.

"There," Alchiq said, pointing to a clutch of boulders on the southern hillside.

Gansukh squinted at the rocks, trying to ascertain the distance. "That's too far—" he started. His argument was cut short as he saw movement behind the rocks. A man stood, his bowstring drawn back to his ear. He loosed his arrow and vanished again. Gansukh tried to make sense of what he had seen: the bow had been nearly as tall as the man.

The arrow arced across the valley, seeming to gain speed as it plummeted toward the ground. It flashed through the branches of the bushes sheltering the *Khagan* and two other men, and Gansukh winced as he saw the arrow spear one of the men in the gut.

"We have to get closer," Alchiq snapped. "Otherwise we are all dead." He darted out from behind the bear, scrambling across the rocky terrain with the agility of a mountain goat.

Gansukh followed, and the pair leap-frogged each other along the rounded scope of the hill. Cover was sparse, and Gansukh felt widely exposed each time he paused behind the trunk of an isolated tree. Most of them grew at an angle on the slope, and if he stood upright, his lower body was exposed; if he crouched, his head stuck out.

Finally, they reached a range that seemed possible for their smaller bows, and Alchiq let loose the first arrow as Gansukh scrambled past him to a flat-topped boulder that seemed like a good shooting position. Alchiq's arrow skipped off the top of the largest of the three rocks they thought concealed the archers.

Gansukh peeked over the top of his rock, and he saw two heads briefly pop up. One of the pair was on the far side of the trio of boulders. That one had the shorter bow, not much larger than his and Alchiq's, and he shifted his aim toward their positions. The first arrow overshot Gansukh's position, ricocheting off a rock behind him with a brittle snap.

Gansukh stood, pulling his bowstring back and loosing his arrow in a smooth motion. He returned to his crouch, his eyes level with the top of the rock. His arrow vanished into the dark cleft between two of the rocks. Ducking down, he slid a handful of arrows out his quiver and balanced them on a nearby rock. Close at hand, easy to grab; he could stand, shoot, crouch, and ready another arrow without taking his attention off his target. Glancing back at Alchiq, he exhaled heavily, blowing out his cheeks.

As soon as he saw Alchiq stand and shoot an arrow, he did the same. He hesitated a split second, watching the flight of both arrows, trying to discern some meaning to the spatter of shadows behind the rocks. As he heard Alchiq move behind him, he shot three more arrows in quick succession.

Alchiq slammed into the rock beside him, grunted from the impact. "They're fools," he hissed, leaning to his left and peering down at the valley floor. "Ride!" he screamed, startling Gansukh. "Get the *Khagan* away from here." Muttering under his breath, he scooted around on his ass until he could peer over the top of their cover. He ducked back down almost immediately, and Gansukh heard the wooden rattle of an arrow bouncing off the top of the rock. "The archer isn't trying to hit the *Khagan*," he said to Gansukh, jerking a thumb toward the valley. "He had his shot. Now he's just slowing them down."

As Gansukh examined the chaos below, he saw a *Darkhat* horse take an arrow in the chest and stumble, throwing its rider. He counted bodies, and got the same number of horses as men. "There's another group," he said, divining the same strategy that Alchiq was seeing. "On horseback most likely."

Alchiq nodded. "He's got a longer range than us, but it means nothing when your targets are all scrambling for cover. His first two arrows were his only real chance at assassinating the *Khagan*." He gestured down at the scattered bodies. "This is sowing confusion. It is a tactic they do well. It suggests they are outnumbered. They want us to not think about how many of them there are, and where they are located. They want us running in blind fear."

"Back up the valley," Gansukh said. "Right into an ambush."

Alchiq rolled over and peered out beyond the far edge of their cover. "Where are the *Torguud* guards?" he wondered. "How far back did we leave them?"

As if in response, a booming echo rolled down the valley. "Chinese powder," Alchiq spat angrily.

Gansukh had recognized the sound too. "Munokhoi had one," he said. "A hand cannon. He got it from the raiders who attacked our caravan shortly after we left Karakorum. He had it with him when..." He tried to remember where he had last seen it. There had been a satchel that the ex-*Torguud* captain had dropped...

"It's a signal," Alchiq said. "Get the *Khagan*!" he shouted again, trying to catch the attention of the men below. "Now their real ambush will be sprung," he snarled.

Gansukh understood his frustration. They were trapped on the hillside, unable to aid the *Khagan*. An idea occurred to him and he tapped Alchiq on the shoulder. "Up," he said. "If we can't go down, let's go up. Get above the archers."

Alchiq gave Gansukh a nasty smile. "Flush them out," he said, nodding.

* * *

An odd serenity came over Master Chucai as the archers on the hillside started killing the *Khagan*'s hunting party. His *qi* was not agitated by the sudden and violent death being visited upon the men around him; instead he felt a placid calmness descend upon him.

Until he was turned as an arrow creased his jaw and punched through the tangle of his beard. He gasped as the world came rushing back: a tumult of sound making his ears ring, the rich scent of flesh blood, the texture of leather and horn under his hands as he grabbed his saddle and hauled himself onto his horse.

Behind him, the shaman cowered on his pony, his hands over his ears. The tiny man babbled, a string of prayers and magical cantrips meant to protect him from flying demons. Chucai leaned over and shoved the shaman out of his saddle; he grabbed the reins and led the pony as he kicked his horse into motion.

A *Darkhat* rider passed him, going in the opposite direction. The man loosed an arrow past his head, drew another from his quiver, and aimed without bothering to notice that he had nearly put an arrow into Chucai's eye.

Chucai understood the man's focus, and he was glad that someone was fighting back. It would make getting the *Khagan* to safety easier.

He swung around a cluster of bushes and spotted the *Khagan* lying on the ground next to two dying men. Both were begging the *Khagan* for mercy, and Ögedei was trying to back away from them while still maintaining as small a profile as possible against the ground.

"Ögedei," Chucai shouted. He shook the pony's reins at the *Khagan*. "A steed, my Khan." Ögedei looked around wildly at the sound of Chucai's voice, and he slowly focused on the pair of horses. "You...you want me to ride *that?*" he sputtered.

Chucai shook the reins at the addled *Khagan*. "Decide quickly," he snapped. "Do you want to be the Khan who was too proud to ride a pony and who died miserably in the woods? Or... ?"

Another arrow punched through the brush and silenced the cries of the gut-shot man. The other one, the man with the arrow through his face, shrieked and clawed at Ögedei's boot, begging to be rescued.

Ögedei scrambled to his feet and snatched the offered reins from Chucai's hands. He clambered onto the pony, his legs nearly touching the ground, and hunching over the small animal's neck he smacked it fiercely on the ears. It bolted, darting toward the other end of the valley, and Chucai spurred his own steed after the galloping pony.

He had to guide the empire still. He had to make sure it was going the right direction.

THE BIG BOSS

As Rutger fought his way through the crowd toward Ashiq Temür, he eyed the man's cudgel warily. The simplest weapons were oftentimes the most effective, and Rutger knew all too well that a solid blow from the big Mongol's weapon would shatter bone and pulp his flesh. Maks's crushed face was the only reminder he needed of the weapon's power. As he broke through the mob, he saw that the cudgel was more than a shaped piece of hardwood. Beneath the blood spatter and gore clinging to it, he could see the glint of metal. *Heavy and slow*, he thought, *I must be quick.*

He swung his sword, and Ashiq Temür saw him coming and raised his club to block Rutger's attack. Their weapons clashed, and Rutger's blade bit into the wood of the cudgel. The Mongol commander grinned, showing a mouthful of crooked teeth, as he twisted his arm down. Rutger couldn't get his blade free in time, and his arms were yanked to his left. Ashiq Temür stepped closer, movement that wasn't very smart if he was planning on hitting Rutger with his cudgel, but Rutger knew the big man had other plans in mind. He wanted to grapple.

Rutger stepped in too. He let go of his sword with his left hand, made a fist, and drove forward with all his might. Unlike the

Mongol, his hand was covered with steel plates, and his armored fist struck Ashiq Temür square in the nose. The Mongol's head snapped back and a bright flower of blood burst across his face.

Rutger wasn't sure who screamed louder—he or the Mongol. Even with the protection of his gauntlets, something snapped inside his hand when he hit Ashiq Temür's face.

Rutger felt his sword come free of the cudgel, and he darted to Ashiq Temür's left. He slid behind the Mongol's back and raised his blade so that he could grip the steel with his damaged left hand. Even though his grip felt imperfect—one of his fingers was not cooperating as it should—he yanked the sword toward him, slamming the blade against his enemy's throat. He twisted his hips violently.

On a smaller man the technique would have slit the man's throat and most likely snapped his neck, but Rutger felt the blade rasp off metal and leather. Ashiq Temür was wearing neck protection, and all he had done was attach himself to the bigger man's back like an enraged monkey.

Ashiq Temür dropped his weight and rotated his hips, and Rutger tried to hang on as he was wrenched around like a rag doll. The big Mongol flexed his shoulders, broadening his back, and his left elbow snapped back, driving into the aged quartermaster's gut.

Rutger knew the elbow was coming. He released his grip on his blade, taking the Mongol's strike against his chest. It knocked him back, and as Ashiq Temür whirled around, Rutger turned the stagger into a roll and the roll into a retreat. The ground shook as the cudgel hammered into the spot where he had been standing a moment earlier.

His spine popping, Rutger came up in a crouch. His chest was tight—not from the Mongol's blow, but from his overworked lungs—and his left hand burned as if he had been squeezing hot coals. He stayed low, his sword resting on the ground in front of him as he struggled to catch his breath.

Ashiq Temür towered over Rutger as he raised his massive cudgel for another ground-shaking blow. His mouth yawned open, braying a wordless battle cry, and the skull-shattering club arced down, eclipsing the late afternoon sun.

No, the thought flashed through Rutger's head, *I will not die today.*

He was fighting with Andreas's longsword. He would not let the weapon be lost on the battlefield. He would not let Andreas who had fallen before, or Maks or any of the other Shield-Brethren who had fallen today, go unremembered. He would not falter.

Rutger surged to his right, sweeping Andreas's longsword up into the path of Ashiq Temür's descending swing. He felt the blade strike flesh, jarring his hands. Shards of pain blasted through his left wrist and up his arm. The cudgel hit the ground and bounced to his left. Ashiq Temür stared, shock and surprise crumbling the corners of his wide-open mouth. Rutger wasted no time, and snapped his sword up, the tip of his blade slicing just above the leather collar wrapped around Ashiq Temür's neck. The Mongol commander groaned, a jet of dark blood spurting from his throat, and when he raised his arms to try and stop the flow his eyes widened.

Rutger's first cut had severed both of his arms, just above the wrist.

Ashiq Temür collapsed, sprawling on ground slippery with his blood. He died, open eyes staring at his severed hands, still clutching the heavy club.

Rutger turned away from the dead man, shutting him out of his mind. Exulting in the death of an enemy was both a waste of precious time and beneath the dignity of the Shield-Brethren. Every combatant carried with him the power of life and death; every breath was a blessing from the Virgin, and to be the one who continued to draw breath after battle was a testament to skill and training.

He couldn't tell which side was winning; the battle was still balanced on a knife's edge. Shield-Brethren and Livonian fought side by side against Mongol warriors. As one clump of combatants splintered apart, another group clashed. All the men fought with the same determination, the same zeal, trying to break the morale of their nemeses. The side that lost its momentum first would lose the field.

"*Deus Vult!*" The cry carried over the din of battle like a horn resonating out of a mountainous canyon. The cry came from many throats, shouting in perfect unison, and while the echoes of the cry were still reverberating, the ground started to shake with the thunderous approach of a mounted host.

His arm aching, Rutger raised Andreas's sword over his head. "*Alalazu!*" he cried, though his voice was so ragged that he doubted anyone heard him.

More horses came, seemingly everywhere at once, bristling with spears and swords and flails. The Mongols wavered, trembling like a field of reeds in the path of an angry wind, and then, as their companions around them started dying, they broke and ran.

The Templars and the Hospitallers had come.

* * *

With a quick flick of his eyes, Zug checked on Kim's reaction to Onghwe's revelation. The Flower Knight was staring at the dissolute Khan with an odd expression on his face. *What was Kim thinking?* Zug wondered. As if he had heard Zug's question, Kim turned and looked at him. The Flower Knight shrugged slightly, tossed his sword aside, and picked up one of the guards' discarded spears.

The tent was silent but for the whimpering of the whore, huddled on the platform. Zug and Kim moved noiselessly across the rugs, slowly closing the distance to their nemesis. The young Rose Knight hung back, clearly intending to guard the entrance against any other guards who might try to rescue the Khan, and Zug quickly put the boy out of his mind.

Onghwe's smile remained undiminished, and his hooded tiger gaze flickered back and forth between the two men.

Kim struck first. Without any warning, the Flower Knight was no longer creeping stealthily forward but was flying through the air, the tip of his spear lancing out at the Khan.

Onghwe darted to the side, moving with the speed of a biting snake. He seized the whore by the hair, and with singular strength, hurled her in front of him. She tumbled across the bed, arms flailing.

Kim tried to abort his strike, his features rearranging themselves into an expression of horrified shock, but the Khan's aim was too true. Kim's spear gored the woman through the chest, the point protruding hideously out her back.

In a gruesome second, the Khan had neutralized Kim's attack and rendered him weaponless. The Flower Knight's sword lay several paces behind him. Kim dropped the spear and drew back as the Khan advanced on him, his sword flashing in quick arcs.

Zug released the *kiai*—the heavenly shout. His strike came up from the floor, not as strong as the overhead strike but still quick enough. Still strong enough to split the dissolute Khan from groin to neck. The Khan would have to choose between killing Kim and dying, or evading his strike and allowing the Flower Knight to escape.

The Khan had seen Zug fight in the arena enough times to know that attempting to block a *naginata* strike with a sword was tantamount to inviting death, and he opted for evasion, leaping toward Zug with astonishing speed.

Zug anticipated Onghwe's approach. Every sword fighter, when facing off against opponents with longer weapons, strove to get inside, to diminish the effectiveness of the long weapon. Equally, every pole-arm fighter learned techniques to keep the sword fighters at bay. Zug pulled his *naginata* back, slashing in the opposite direction as he closed the line.

Onghwe, having avoided the first attack by moving to Zug's right and toward him, kept coming. He reversed his blade, catching Zug's downward slice against the flat of his sword. A dangerous parry, but as Zug had not been able to gather full momentum, the stroke only pushed the Khan's blade against his body—the sword blade shielding the Khan from the *naginata*'s cutting edge.

Onghwe's feet pounded against the floor as he rushed Zug, striking him in the middle of the forehead with the pommel of his sword.

Zug's world exploded into a flurry of vibrant colors. He tried to get an arm up to block another punishing blow as he reeled back, and Onghwe smashed him on the right shoulder. He stumbled against a divan, and off balance and unable to see through a rain of tears he fell, trying to turn his stumble into a roll or flip or anything that would take him away from the Khan's sword.

He tumbled clumsily off the other side of the divan, landing awkwardly on his left shoulder. Ignoring the pain racing up and down his arm, Zug scrambled to his feet, dragging his *naginata* with him.

The Khan's sword struck the haft of his weapon just below his right hand and sheared through the thick wood. Onghwe let out a tiny grunt as the tip of his sword hit the carpet beside Zug. He froze for an instant, his eyes glittering as he examined Zug's position—on his knees, his arms over his head, the *naginata* blade a long ways off. His sword was much closer to Zug's undefended right side; he could hit Zug sooner than Zug could get the *naginata* blade around.

Zug loosened his grip, letting the haft of the *naginata* move loosely in his right hand, and he jerked his left hand toward his right, thrusting the butt of his weapon. Onghwe jerked his head back, and Zug only managed to land a glancing blow on the dissolute Khan's cheek.

Onghwe whipped his sword around, a wild one-handed swing that Zug had no choice but to throw himself forward in order to avoid. He felt the sword whip over his head, and before Onghwe could swing on him again, he scrambled away, swinging the *naginata* around to make the Khan cautious in his approach.

But Onghwe wasn't pressing the attack. During their exchange, Kim had procured another spear and now returned to the fray. The Flower Knight thrust at Khan, and Onghwe twisted himself around, momentarily putting his back to Zug. He parried, spinning his blade around Kim's weapon and pushing it wide. He darted forward, attempting to use the same pommel smash he had used on Zug.

Kim wasn't about to let Onghwe get that close. He wiggled his spear, slipping it under the Khan's elbow to raise Onghwe's arm. He kicked, smashing his heel against the side of Onghwe's knee. Onghwe roared with pain and retreated, cautiously testing his weight on his right leg.

"Marvelous," he chortled as he put some distance between the two fighters. His face was flushed, glowing with sweat, and a dark bruise was already forming on his right cheek. "I haven't felt this alive in years." He laughed, consumed in equal portion by feral madness and giddy euphoria.

FINAL DOUBTS

FERONANTUS'S PLAN WAS simple: kill the bear, stake it out in gross parody of its rampant state, and wait for the *Khagan* to arrive. Rædwulf and Istvan would lie in ambush on the southern hillside, close to the rocky spur that split the main valley. The rest of the company would hide in the southern canyon until the *Khagan*'s party had scattered, and then they would ride into battle.

The last half year of hard riding came down to this: a dead bear, an ambush, and one final charge.

None of them expected to survive.

They said good-bye to Yasper shortly after they broke camp, and then a half hour later, to Rædwulf and Istvan. With three horses in tow, Feronantus led the party into the southern forest and stopped when he reached an open glade. They tethered the horses in a line and gave them enough rope to forage among the tall grasses.

As Feronantus, Percival, and Eleázar checked and adjusted their gear—Eleázar grousing noisily about having to fight from horseback where his enormous sword would be useless—Vera took Raphael by the hand and led him into the trees. They had all lost weight during the hard trek across the steppe, and Vera's beauty had become even more stark and austere. Her hair was longer, and she had taken to braiding it in the Northern style. The sun and wind had darkened her skin; it was not as dark as Raphael's, but she was not the pale ghost of a woman he had met months ago. Only her eyes remained unchanged—hard and unyielding, the same color as her maille.

"Stop staring at me like that," she said gently. "We knew this day was coming. We take death into our hearts when we take our oaths."

"Yes," he argued, "but that doesn't mean we have to like it."

She cupped Raphael's face with her hand. "I have liked very little in this world, Raphael of Acre, and you have shown me more affection than I deserve. I am sorry—"

He placed his hand over her mouth and shook his head. "I have said good-bye to too many friends today. I am done. No more." She relented, and tightly pressing her hand to his, she kissed his fingers. He pulled her close, and dropping their hands, their lips met.

She broke contact first, as he knew she would, but she didn't let go of him. Her teeth worrying her lower lip, she rested her head against his shoulder. "By the time the Mongol horde reached Kiev, we knew they were going to besiege the city for as long as it took to break our spirits, and we swore—my sisters and I—that we would never submit. We would never, willingly, open our gates to the Mongols, and the Virgin heard our prayer. They breached Kiev's gates and ravaged the city completely, but the walls of our citadel held. We took in too many refugees, and if the Mongols had been patient, we would have starved to death. But Batu Khan was too eager to press farther west. He thought the destruction of the city would be enough to break our spirit. But we didn't falter. We were *skjalddis*. We would never surrender.

"And then I took my sisters out of the city. I took them away from the Virgin's protection, and the Mongols found us." Her hand closed to a fist on his chest. "I killed my sisters as readily as if I cut their throats myself."

Raphael shook his head. "You can't blame yourself. Every commander feels responsible for his troops. They would not be a good commander otherwise. But you can't carry that burden. It will crush you."

"It won't crush me, Raphael." She raised her head and looked him in the eye. "My sisters guide my arm. They give me strength. They will be with me when I kill the *Khagan*."

"Vera..." He faltered. Her gaze was too guarded, too hard. His words would not be strong enough to penetrate her armor.

She kissed him lightly. "I'm sorry, Raphael," she whispered, her breath light on his cheek. "I wish there was more room in my heart." Her lips brushed his cheek as she squeezed his arm, and then she was gone.

* * *

He would have preferred an opportunity to play with the ratios of the various powders that he had found in the satchel, but Feronantus had been disinclined to let him go off and conduct explosive experiments on innocent trees. Time was limited; the resolution of their quest was upon them. He had one chance to get the mixture right.

He would have thrown his hands up at such an impossible challenge six months ago, but as a companion to the Shield-Brethren who looked upon the *impossible* as a noble challenge, he had become inured to the insurmountable. Creating an explosive reagent from an untested oddment of powders, tinctures, and salts was exactly the sort of conundrum God would put before him.

Especially after he had complained—somewhat incessantly, he was now willing to admit—about that damned Livonian stealing his horse back in Kiev. He had stumbled upon a veritable treasure hoard of alchemical ingredients in the ruined city. He had collected an entire bag of smooth stones that were nearly all the same shape and size, not too small and not too large—nearly perfect, in fact, for a *balneum cineritium*. The large grains of sand would have retained their heat so evenly. The idea of a portable *balneum* had been so tempting.

The jugs of *aqua ardens* had been an unexpected blessing. The two bottles weren't as volatile as a recipe he had made several years ago, but, as evidenced in the tunnels, the fiery water burned readily enough. The other jug could have been distilled further—he was certain he could have done it—and having several vials of purified *aqua ardens* would alleviate his current dilemma.

"Attend to your mind," he whispered to himself. The *aqua ardens* was gone; the treasure trove he had collected during the early days of their journey was gone. Dwelling on the materials he had lost was to engage in wistful daydreaming like an ale-addled simpleton. He had to keep his mind focused. The company was depending on him.

They had stumbled upon the location of the bear's cave late in the day after they had said good-bye to Cnán, and Feronantus had kept them busy, exploring the two-pronged valley, until well after moonrise. They had argued for several hours around a meager fire about the best way to entrap the *Khagan*. In the end, the simplest stratagem won out: let the *Khagan*'s party enter the valley, but don't let it leave.

The last part fell squarely upon Yasper's shoulders, and shortly after sunrise, he had surveyed the rocky terrain on either side of the western entrance of the valley. An avalanche was clearly the best solution, but how to move all those rocks? After an hour of clambering about less surefootedly than a mountain goat, he thought it was possible to bring down a number of rocks.

However, he would need a few supplies.

Feronantus had been loath to let him go wandering off into the forest, especially when they expected the *Khagan*'s hunting party late in the day. All the more reason Yasper had to find his alchemical ingredients sooner than later. *Without these ingredients*, he had argued, *I can't bring the hillside down. You'll have to come up with a different plan.*

Early the following morning, Yasper, Istvan, and Raphael went scouting again with two goals in mind: finding Yasper's alchemical ingredients and discerning the location of the *Khagan*'s hunting party. Consensus among the companions was that the *Khagan* had simply waited a day before leaving, but they needed to be sure.

Shortly after midday they found the hunting party and Yasper found his alchemical supplies, albeit in an unexpected fashion.

They heard a booming noise, and Yasper thought it was too singular and too close to be thunder, especially given the lack of cloud cover in the sky. Keenly aware that they were not alone in the woods, they dismounted and carefully led their horses through the trees. After the second rumbling echo, Yasper was sure the source of the sound was an alchemical explosion.

They nearly interrupted the duel between the two Mongol hunters, and had the pair not been so intent on killing one another they would have surely spotted the trio of Westerners. Istvan had wanted to kill them both, but Raphael had held him back, and after one had dashed off and the other followed, Yasper had been able to creep into the clearing and retrieve the dropped satchel.

He had nearly wept with joy when he opened it and examined its contents.

By nightfall, his joy had withered to consternation. Some of the powders were foreign to him, and he had no time for practical research. He woke often during the night, shivering with a sensation nearing panic, and in the morning when the rest of the company departed for their hidden positions within the valley, he was left alone. Just Yasper and the mystery of the powders and God, who wasn't offering any insight.

The white crystals, sweet to the taste, were a salt of some kind. The metal shards had no function as part of the alchemical explosive.

It was only after catching his finger on a rough burr and drawing blood that he had realized their purpose. They were tiny projectiles, meant to be packed in with the powders. When the incendiary device ignited, the alchemical energies released would hurl the shards in every direction.

He shuddered, imagining the effect they would have on unarmored flesh, and then shuddered even more as he divined how the Chinese used these powders. Feeling befouled, like he had just accepted a deal with some infernal demon to allow these thoughts into his head, he laid the ingredients out in a line, seeing their arrangement in a different light.

The dark powder tasted bitter, not unlike the calcinate that a sand bath would draw out of a cow's urine, and the red crystals turned to blue flame when he had tossed a pinch into the campfire. He recognized the ash readily enough, though it came from a pleasantly fragrant wood.

As he was wrestling with the ratios, the *Khagan* and his hunting party passed below his hiding place.

Yasper pressed himself flat against the rocks, and with an oath, he kicked sand over his tiny fire, trying to put it out. He inched to the edge of the rock and peered down, desperately hoping no one noticed the thin line of smoke.

He counted heads, and was taken aback when he passed forty. He figured the one on the black horse, wearing the gaudy plumcolored outfit, was Ögedei, the Khan of Khans. Yasper stifled a grin. *Rædwulf will be so jealous*, he thought, *when he learns how close I was.* He was not a very skilled bowman, but he thought he could hit the *Khagan* with an arrow from his position.

As he watched, one of the honor guard—a tall muscular Mongol—gave orders to the men, splitting the group into two. More than half were to stay at the mouth of the valley. A rearguard, Yasper surmised, to ensure the bear did not accidentally escape. *Little chance of that*, he thought, recalling the display that Percival and Rædwulf had erected. Shooting the arrow into the bear's chest *after* it had been strung up had been a masterful idea on Feronantus's part. A taunting flourish on top of an already arrogant display of defiance. It was bound to enrage the *Khagan*.

"Oh, shit!" The words hissed out of Yasper's mouth before he could stop them. He had recognized one of the riders in the group that was continuing on with the *Khagan*.

Graymane.

There was nothing he could do but watch as the *Khagan* and his much smaller hunting party—including the gray-haired rider who had plagued them so incessantly during their journey—rode into valley. The twenty or so left behind milled about for a while, uncertain of the best way to prevent a charging bear from leaving the valley. After a half hour or so, they settled down. As Yasper kept his vigil, his heart continuing to pound in his chest, they fell into the same routine as bored soldiers anywhere. They ate and drank, sharing among themselves, and eventually someone produced a bag containing some manner of marked bones. While three of them remained mounted, keeping a bored watch, the others passed the time by betting on the bones.

Yasper still had to figure out how to make an alchemical incendiary. The guards had positioned themselves on his side of the vale, making it somewhat easier if he managed to figure out how to send a cascade of rocks down upon them. He had marked a few he thought would bring along other rocks when they tumbled down the hill, and his plan had been to dislodge them by packing a mixture into key cracks. However, in order to ignite them in the right order, he would need a long fuse, one that burned at the right speed and with the right amount of flame.

All the vines he had found during his searches had been too full of juices—there wasn't enough time to dry and temper them properly. He had found fuses in the satchel, but they were all short, not much longer than the distance from the tip of his longest finger to the base of his hand. Even if he tied them all together, they weren't going to be long enough.

He sighed and rubbed his scalp vigorously. He was running out of time. It wouldn't take that long for the hunting party to find the dead bear. He had to act soon. Otherwise, the *Khagan* could still escape.

What were the right ratios?

He heard a distant cry, like the scream of a hawk as it dives upon its prey, but he knew it wasn't a war cry of a predatory bird. It was a scream of pain.

Rædwulf was shooting his arrows. The trap had been sprung.

Muttering to himself (and to God), Yasper scooped up the various pouches of ingredients and combined them as equally as he could into two of the larger pouches. After packing in a layer of metal shards, he shoved a fuse into each and tied them as tightly as he dared. He struck his flint against the nearby rock face, scattering sparks. The first fuse hissed, and he blew on it briefly to make sure the sparks became fire. The fuse caught, flaring into a sizzling finger of blue and orange flame.

He stared at the flame. *"Alalazu,"* he muttered. He didn't know the history of the Shield-Brethren battle cry, but it seemed an appropriate blessing for his impromptu solution.

He stood up and hurled the bag, aiming for the center of the cluster of guards.

The alchemical incendiary exploded with a delightfully noisy boom, and the concussive sound echoed back and forth between the hills. It was an unmistakable signal, in case the others were wondering when the fun was going to begin. Yasper peered out of his hiding place, trying to see anything through the gray haze that floated over the valley floor. He saw shapes that were, most likely, mounted riders, the men trying to calm their terrified horses. Other shapes materialized—men crawling and staggering. As the haze thinned, Yasper got a better glimpse of the carnage wrought by his device. His gorge rose, and he clamped his hands over his mouth and sat down heavily on his rump, breathing rapidly through his nose.

Several Mongols had been *shredded* by the explosion. He had seen what bears could do to a human body, and the lacerations and dismemberment wreaked by beast paled in comparison to the bodily destruction scattered about the field below. The only means by which he could tally the dead was to count those still living; the dead were in too many pieces.

His gaze fell upon the other alchemical incendiary, and he kicked it away, horrified to be near such a hellish construct. It slid across the ground, and his horror mounted as he watched it tumble across the remnants of the tiny fire he had built earlier. It rolled to a stop, the prickly tongue of its fuse resting against the ground. Yasper held his breath, praying that the capricious imps who did the Devil's mischief would not be watching.

They were. The fuse sparked and sputtered, and a thin blue finger of flame began to dance at the end of the fuse, flinging sparks with reckless abandon.

Yasper scrambled forward, burning his hand as he put it down in the not-yet-cold coals of his fire, and he grabbed up the lit incendiary, throwing it down the hill.

He threw himself to the ground and put his hands over his ears in a futile effort to block out the horrific sound he knew was coming.

* * *

They burst out of the forest in a line, riding abreast, their maille glittering in the sun. Feronantus: the Shield-Brethren battle cry on his lips, leaning forward in his saddle as if he were a young man again. Percival: his armor gleaming brighter than the rest, sword in one hand, mace in the other, his horse responding to the lightest touch of his knees—the results of months of continuous training. Vera: sword and shield ready, her face hidden behind the blank mask of her helm; the woman he had kissed in the forest was gone, and all that remained was the indomitable spirit of the *skjalddis*.

And he, Raphael: veteran of the Fifth Crusade, survivor of the siege of Córdoba, oath breaker, man of God though cast out from the Church. A knight initiate of the *Ordo Militum Vindicis Intactae*, at first for expediency and then because the order was the only family that would accept him. He carried sword and shield, for now was not the time to hang back with spear and arrow.

Now was the time to look your enemy in the eye when you slew him.

They came at a hard gallop, their horses' hooves pounding at the dusty ground. The Shield-Brethren rode to war, expecting to face insurmountable odds—one hundred, two hundred of the finest fighting men the Mongol Empire could field. They rode, anticipating a bristling barricade of spears and lances, and found...

...an empty plain.

Raphael sat up in his saddle, scanning for some sign of the *Khagan*'s host. When he and Yasper and Istvan had stumbled across its passage in the forest, they had been somewhat mystified by the size the track suggested, and they had assumed it was the advance party, the scouts who were ranging ahead of the main host.

He didn't bring that many men with him, Raphael realized.

Nearly simultaneously, he spotted horses coming from either direction. The ones on the left wore matching colors and were riding hard; on the right, the horses were scattered far apart, and a few had no riders. *This is it?* he thought, and he recalled Roger's boastful comment at the *Kinyen* in the chapter house near Legnica. *Ten thousand of them means ten thousand opportunities for confusion.*

He missed Roger fiercely. *How I wish you were here for this moment, my friend,* he thought. *You would have laughed, and all our hearts would have been lightened by the sound of your voice.* He gripped his sword more tightly. *I am sorry, Roger,* he offered as a silent prayer to the Virgin and the host of the dead whom she had gathered to her bosom.

And for a moment, he recalled Andreas—the young man he had met once on a German road. *Had the Virgin claimed him too?*

He might know the answer to his question soon enough.

And then the Mongol riders were upon them, and the time for memory and prayer was done.

ON THE ROAD
TO ROME

CARDINAL FIESCHI STARED morosely at the scenery as his carriage trundled back to Rome. He had already sent ahead several riders to alert Orsini. By the time his carriage reached the Vatican, the countryside surrounding Rome would be crawling with horsemen wearing the Bear's colors. Given his recent spate of foul luck, the Bear's men would stumble upon an overzealous squad of the Emperor's men and the resulting fracas would be the start of all-out war between Rome, the Church, and the Holy Roman Empire.

Was that Frederick's goal? he wondered. For as little as Fieschi missed Gregory IX—the man had been a tyrant to his staff, and Fieschi had tolerated it longer than anyone else—he briefly wished the man were still alive. He had an incredibly deft mind when it came to understanding the myriad layers of the conflict for Christendom. Orsini's effort to hide the cardinals in the Septizodium might have won the election for the Church, but what did that matter if Rome was immediately overrun by a mangy bunch of Germans and Sicilians?

He had been Gregory's right-hand man. He had run the College of Cardinals. He had bent the Senator of Rome to his will. He had dirtied his hands for the Church. But what had any of that gained him?

Gregory had been grooming him; Fieschi had no doubt that the previous Pope had been preparing the way for Sinibaldo Fieschi to become his successor. Perhaps he might even have taken the name of Gregory X. But the Pope had unexpectedly fallen ill during one of the heat waves that perpetually suffocated Rome in late summer. The man had caught a chill—seemingly impossible in the heat—and had died nearly overnight, leaving the Church headless. Between the Mongol threat in the north and the Holy Roman Emperor coming up from the south, it had been nearly impossible to call the cardinals back to Rome in order to vote.

He had worked so very hard, trying to keep the Church alive. But no matter how hard he tried, matters kept slipping away from him. First, the country priest who had stumbled into the election and wound up being elected Pope. Then, the matter of the girl and the witch network in Rome—he had warned Orsini the trouble they could cause, and he had placed too much faith in the Bear's ability to contain the witches. They had missed one—one tiny girl!—and she had caused so much grief.

He pounded his fist against his wooden seat. He knew he was feeling sorry for himself, wallowing in the doubt that had nipped at him earlier in the day when the question of the second election had come up. He was letting these tiny reversals get the better of him. He was letting Frederick get under his skin—the Emperor's words continuing to echo in his ear, nursing the doubt in his heart. Like a tiny breath that keeps a weak fire alive.

He couldn't stop thinking about the Grail.

Had the spirit of God come back? And what were the chances that the Cup of Christ was the only artifact of God's Grace that had been awakened?

He suddenly recalled the prophecy the mad priest had been carrying. The scrap of parchment he had taken from Father Rodrigo's satchel was in his chambers, and he recoiled at the thought of someone finding it there. He was going to burn it as soon as he got back to Rome. How he wished he could burn those words out of his mind.

A new order rises; if it falls, woe to the Church! Battle will be joined, many times over, and faith will be broken.

* * *

Léna found Cardinal Castiglione walking in one of the tiny gardens near the basilica. He was in the company of two other cardinals: Colonna, the tall missionary who had survived more than one imprisonment; and Capocci, the builder whose shrewd mind was equally at home planning cathedrals as it was putting down insurrections. "Your Eminences," she said, bowing, as they caught sight of her. "Such a pleasant afternoon for a stroll."

"Indeed," Castiglione said, eyeing her with a modicum of caution. "You are the woman who accompanied Cardinal Monferrato from Frederick's camp, are you not?"

"I am, Your Eminence. I am Léna, a—"

"Binder?" Capocci said.

She inclined her head. "More often I am simply an ambassador."

"For whom?" Capocci pressed her.

"Does it matter?" she said sweetly.

Colonna chuckled at her verve, while her words only seemed to cause Castiglione more distress.

"Do you have a message for me?" the cardinal asked.

"No," Léna said after a moment's hesitation. "I bear no message for *you* today." She cocked her head to one side, studying the three men for a moment. "Do you have one you wish me to carry?" "Why would I?" Castiglione asked.

Léna shrugged. "I have recently seen Cardinal Fieschi. He was in quite a hurry to visit the Holy Roman Emperor." She noted their reaction, reading the entire power structure of the Church in their faces. Castiglione's reaction was the one she found the most interesting. *The sort of outrage brought about by a lack of control*, she thought. *When someone you think is under your command makes their own decisions, forgetting to inform you.* Which led to an interesting question: why did Castiglione think Fieschi reported to him?

"Have you seen the Pope?" she asked innocently, and her question was rewarded with a nervous glance between Colonna and Capocci and further distress from Castiglione.

Now I see the heart of it, she thought, suppressing a smile. *It all comes together now.*

There was still much to do, and many pieces to still move about, but she felt her heart start to thrill at the idea of seeing a gambit come to fruition.

"I see," she said in the wake of their awkward silence. She dropped to one knee. "My apologies, Your Holiness."

"Get up," Castiglione said gruffly. "Stop this public abasement."

But you didn't deny it, Léna thought as she stood.

"I am so sorry," she said. "I thought I had heard that the priest—Father Rodrigo—had been elected, but I must have been mistaken."

"You were," Capocci said quickly.

"It is a clever ruse," she added, "letting everyone think this simple man is Pope—long enough to distract the Holy Roman Emperor—and then announcing yourself as the true Pontiff. If Frederick seizes the priest and attempts to ransom him, it is a simple matter to embarrass the Holy Roman Emperor for inventing a Pope and then trying to ransom him back to the Church. He will lose a great deal of face with the leaders of other nations. Why bother excommunicating him—which we both know has had little effect on his efforts to dominate Christendom—when it is easier to publically shame him?"

"Why indeed?" Capocci noted.

"Well, Your Eminences, Your Holiness," she bowed to each of them, "I do not wish to trouble you. You appear to have much to discuss. I am simply on my way to see Senator Orsini. There is a little matter he and I need to clear up. A small matter of unjust imprisonment."

She almost laughed at how readily Castiglione took the bait.

"Unjust imprisonment?" he echoed. A fire sparked in his eye and he stood up a bit straighter. When he spoke to her again, there was a righteous indignation in his words. "Yes, in fact, I do wish you to carry a message for me."

Léna smiled. "Give me the message," she said, invoking the sacred trust of the Binders.

"I, Goffredo da Castiglione, send a message to—no, let us do this correctly." He glanced at the other two cardinals, who gave small nods of encouragement. "I"—he cast about for the proper words—"Pope Celestine IV of the Holy Roman Church, send a message to Matteo Rosso Orsini, Senator of Rome..."

Léna listened the new Pope's first proclamation, repeating his words back to him at the appropriate intervals. *Yes,* she thought, *this will suffice nicely.*

ARROW'S FLIGHT

ANSUKH AND ALCHIQ were spotted before they were able to get high enough on the hill to have a clear shot at the pair of archers behind the boulders. But they were high enough—and close enough—that the two Westerners had to deal with them before they could go back to killing Mongols in the valley. In that sense, they had done all they could to save the *Khagan*, but as the tall Westerner turned his fearsome bow on them, Gansukh realized his own life was now in mortal danger.

The long arrows of the Westerner were not deterred by brush or tree trunks less than a hand's breadth in width. One of the broadhead arrows punched completely through the twisted roots he had been lying behind, the tip scratching his shoulder, and he stared at the razor-sharp arrowhead for a moment. *So much power*, he thought with a shudder. He scrambled over the roots, diving for the security of a jumble of rock. His shoulders remained clenched during his frantic dash, and even after he was nestled securely behind the rocks, he couldn't relax. Would the rocks be protection enough?

The other archer, a gaunt man with black hair and bristling whiskers, had a bow like his and Alchiq's. Deadly enough, and Gansukh couldn't ignore him entirely, but the real target was the tall man.

Gansukh laid another arrow across his bow as he slowly peered around the edge of his shelter. Alchiq's bow sang behind him, and he risked a glance as Alchiq's arrow flew toward its target. He could see the edge of a man's cloak, fluttering behind the rocks. He stood, held his breath for a second—waiting—and then released his arrow. He snatched another arrow for his quiver, laid it across the notch, pulled the string, and released. The fluttering cloth was still there, and his second arrow pinned it to the ground.

He ducked down, duck-walked to his left as far as he could without exposing himself, readied another arrow, and rose to his feet again. He exhaled, staring at the wild eyes of the black-haired man for a second as he looked up from tugging at his pinned cloak, and then Gansukh released his arrow.

Even as the arrow flew from his bow, he knew it was going to miss. The man was leaning to his left, straining against his pinned cloak. Gansukh reached for another arrow, got it nocked, and was starting to pull the string back when the tall man stood up. Gansukh released early—much too early—and his arrow flipped out of his bow like a feather flying off a duck's back. The man convulsed his body, a strange motion that made sense to Gansukh as soon as he saw what it accomplished, and then Gansukh was throwing himself to the ground to avoid the tall man's long arrow.

Hands and chest pressed against the ground, breath stirring up dust, Gansukh stared up at the arrow quivering in the rock upslope of him. The head wasn't buried deep in the stone, but enough that the arrow stood out straight. It quivered, as if were an angry wasp trying to sting the rock to death.

"Again," Alchiq hissed at him from a spot above and to his left

"You first," Gansukh whispered back, still transfixed by the rock-piercing arrow.

* * *

The horses were scattering, and by his count, Rædwulf had killed six. Istvan had killed the horse of the one they thought was the *Khagan*, and he had almost put an arrow into that man's purple jacket. *Almost.*

Rædwulf knew that if he didn't manage to kill the *Khagan* in the first few seconds, he probably wouldn't get the opportunity. Their location was far enough from the bear's cave that hitting a moving target—one that was doing its best to evade his arrows—was going to be very difficult. As soon as the hunting party dissolved into a confused mass of horses and men, he gave up trying for the *Khagan*. He focused on the slow-moving ones. And the horses. If they had to walk or run, it meant they stayed in range longer. He would have more time to kill them.

Except for the pair of archers who had climbed up to the bear's cave. He had glimpsed white hair on one, and he knew, without a doubt, that it was Alchiq. He knew what they were going to do, and he told Istvan to keep an eye on them. *Let them think they are getting close,* he had said. *And then we'll deal with them.*

They had gone upslope though, which presented a bit of a problem, but it wasn't an insurmountable issue. He would have to break off shooting at the men and horses to deal with them.

He tracked one last target, a tall man with a flowing beard astride a beautiful black horse, and with a twinge of guilt, he put an arrow in the horse's flank. He grinned as both horse and rider went down, the man's leg pinned to the horse's flank by his arrow.

Istvan cursed, and Rædwulf glanced over his shoulder. The Hungarian was pulling at his cloak, which appeared to be caught on something. Istvan stopped suddenly, raising his head and looking upslope. Rædwulf threw himself toward the rocks as another arrow whistled down from above. Istvan grunted as the arrow sliced through the meat of his arm.

Rædwulf turned, his hands positioning an arrow on his bow with unconscious alacrity. He drew the string of his longbow back, sighted, and when the Mongol he was aiming at fumbled his arrow, he loosed his own shaft with a sigh.

He was impressed at the speed with which the Mongol dropped out of sight.

Setting another arrow across his bow, he stepped to his right and kicked at the arrow pinning Istvan's cloak to the ground. The arrow snapped off, and he stepped forward into a wide stance with his left foot. He was out from behind the rock, but he had a clear view of the hillside. If either of the two Mongols moved, he would put an arrow right through them.

He hoped it would be Alchiq.

The Mongols rose together, and for a second he hesitated, torn between targets. Letting a blasphemous curse slip, he loosed his arrow, aiming for the gray-haired bastard who had dogged them endlessly, and then he tried to move back to the protection of the rock.

He made it, but something slammed into his right hip, and he leaned back against the stone, teeth clenched against the ribbon of fire running up his side.

A Mongol arrow jutted out of his hip, and when he moved, it moved too. It had pierced the flat bone, and would be hard to get out.

"Istvan," he snarled, looking around for the Hungarian. The other man wasn't there, and Rædwulf wasted a few precious seconds wondering where he had gone. Had he fled? Had he been hit as well and tumbled down the hillside?

It doesn't matter, he told himself, returning his attention to the arrow in his hip. He had to get it out. It was going to interfere with his shooting. He gripped the shaft, and a fresh wave of pain slammed through his body. *Break it off*, he commanded his hands. *There isn't time to pull it out.*

With a savage chop of his hand, he snapped the shaft of the arrow off, and the resulting pain brought tears to his eyes. He threw his head back against the rock, gasping for breath, straining against the vibrant colors that threatened to block his vision. The pain ebbed, and he could move his hip now without debilitating agony.

He reached for his bow, which had slipped to the ground next to the rocks. Bending was difficult, but he managed to hook his fingers around the horn end of the bow and tug it toward him. Just as he was maneuvering himself back upright, he heard the crunching noise of a boot against loose rock.

Alchiq stood above him, not ten paces away. His bow was drawn and the tip of the arrow was pointed at Rædwulf's heart.

The tall Englishman didn't flinch as the gray-haired Mongol released his arrow. It flew straight and true, and he heard it hit its target. *So this is what it feels like*...and then all sense and meaning passed.

The Guan Do

HE BATTLE HAD left the field near the gate, and Rutger slowly made his way toward the distant peaks of the Khan's pavilion. His heart was alternating between racing and standing still, and he couldn't stop his hands from shaking. The index finger of his left hand refused to bend, and he tore a long strip of cloth off the shirt of a dead Mongol. He couldn't get his gauntlet off, not by himself, and it would probably have to be cut free of his hand. In the meantime, all he could do was immobilize the finger as much as possible to prevent the pain from being too unbearable. He wound the cloth tightly around his hand, clenching his teeth against bursts of pain that made his hand twitch.

A pair of chargers emerged from the smoke on his right, sweeping across the field. When the riders spotted Rutger, they changed their course, heading toward him. They wore the white and black, respectively, of the Templar and Hospitaller orders, and as they reined their animals to a stop, Rutger recognized the two Masters. "The enemy has been broken," Emmeran called out in way of greeting. No amount of dirt and blood could completely obscure the pleased expression on his florid face. He brought his horse close to Rutger and leaned over.

Rutger took the extended hand with his left, and Emmeran had the grace to offer a compassionate nod when he caught sight of the dirty cloth wrapped around Rutger's left hand. There was a long bloody smear down the left side of Leuthere's surcoat, and based on the tiny rip in the white cloth, Rutger surmised the granite-faced Templar had taken an arrow to the ribs.

"They're in a panic," Leuthere said, "nothing more than a rabble. There is no organization to them, and unhorsed..." He shrugged, as if the fight between an armored knight and a Mongol on foot was no contest worth mentioning.

"What of Onghwe, their Khan?" Rutger asked. "Is he dead?" He waved his bandaged hand in the direction he had been heading.

Emmeran's face lost some of its enthusiasm. "Those of the enemy who still have spirit left have fallen back to protect their master, but they will not withstand our assault for long," he said.

"But has anyone seen him?" Rutger pressed. "Has anyone confirmed that Onghwe is even in his pavilion? If he senses the battle goes against him, he will flee. Have we accounted for all of his commanders? If any of them still live, they could be providing a cover for the Khan's escape."

Emmeran and Leuthere exchanged a quick glance, and Rutger felt an icy hand clutch his chest. "Who?" he demanded.

Leuthere shook his head angrily and jerked his horse's head around. The Templar master galloped off, leaving Emmeran to answer Rutger's question.

"The commander of the party who went to your chapter house," Emmeran explained. "We did not find his body among those at the bridge. We suspect he made it across the river."

"Where is he?" Rutger shouted, even as he realized the Hospitaller did not know the answer. He couldn't believe what he was hearing. If the Khan escaped and managed to flee back to the main Mongolian army at Mohi, he would return with a host many times larger than the force he had commanded at Hünern. The people of Hünern could flee, but that would only exacerbate Onghwe's rage, and Rutger knew the Khan would pillage and burn everything until his bloodlust was satisfied.

Breaking the Mongol grip on Hünern was an impossible feat—one so very nearly in their grasp—but without the death of Onghwe, their efforts would amount to little more than waking a slumbering bear.

They might win the day, but Christendom would only be even more imperiled by their actions.

"My men are scouring the camp," Emmeran said. "There is no way out but through the main gate. Even if some of the Mongols manage to escape, we will have weeks to hunt them down." The Hospitaller shook his head, a grim smile on his lips. "But the Khan will not escape."

Rutger's chest tightened, and his throat worked heavily. "I wish I shared your faith, Master Emmeran," he wheezed. "But I have seen too many battles that were thought won—" An icy lance of pain ripped through his upper chest, and he staggered. He tried to draw a breath, but his lungs refused to work.

"Master Rutger..." Emmeran began.

Rutger stared at his left arm. His entire body felt cold, except for his arm, which burned with such heat that he thought it would burst into flame. His legs quivered and he fell to his knees. Streaks of white light flashed across his field of vision. He stared up at the Hospitaller, trying to make sense of the shadows moving across the man's face.

A white light bloomed behind Emmeran and his horse, and Rutger blinked, tears starting in the corners of his eyes. "No," he croaked with the last breath in his throat. *It can't be. Don't take me*, he pleaded. *I am not ready.*

The light erupted, an explosion of thousands of white petals flying outward like a snowstorm falling upward, soft, downy flakes rising up to Heaven. In the center of the light, Rutger saw entwined branches and—

The exhausted heart of Týrshammar's quartermaster finally stopped.

* * *

Onghwe broke the momentary respite in the duel by throwing his sword at Zug. With a shout, Kim dashed forward, but the Khan fled, dashing back toward his enormous platform of pillows and furs.

Zug twisted his body, evading the well-thrown blade, though the tip of the weapon raked across his right ear. Blood began to flow, and tiny pricks of pain nipped at his skull as if he were being stung by an extremely angry and persistent hornet.

Onghwe started throwing pillows as he reached his bed, and the Flower Knight adroitly knocked the first aside with his spear, let another bounce off his chest, and ducked under a third. He kept closing on the Khan throughout, and after the third missile, he thrust his spear at the Khan's legs. The Khan, who had been digging through the layers of furs and pillows, found what he was looking for. As he pulled his legs back, getting out of range of Kim's attack, he twisted his body, and levered up the long pole that had been hidden beneath the opulent layers.

It was a *guan do*, similar to Zug's *naginata*, but the blade was shorter, thicker, and had a notch and a spike along the back edge. Onghwe whipped the pole-arm around, and Kim, having some experience fighting against this weapon, knocked Onghwe's first strike aside and thrust his own spear point over the top of the Khan's haft. Onghwe snapped the haft around, rotating it over Kim's thrust, and shoved the spear aside. He flicked the *guan do* blade, and Kim leaned back, letting the curved edge of the pole-arm blade whisk past his face.

Onghwe pressed the attack, flicking the *guan do* in tight circles, forcing Kim back as the Flower Knight blocked and evaded the flashing blade. Kim gave ground readily, and Zug approached from the Khan's right, flicking his own weapon at the Khan. The Khan adjusted his technique, and the blade of his *guan do* became a darting, flashing bird that leaped from both Zug's and Kim's weapons without pause. Zug was content to be patient, keeping the pressure on the Khan, knowing the other man could not keep up this incredible display of dexterity for long. Eventually he would tire.

The Khan's blade rebounded from his *naginata*, slashing low toward Kim, who had started to drift closer to the Khan. The Flower Knight leaped into the air, avoiding the *guan do*'s blade, and at the apogee of his leap he thrust his spear forward in one hand, and the point pierced Onghwe's shoulder.

The Khan snarled, and Kim barely got the haft of his spear up in time to block Onghwe's counterattack. Kim landed off balance, and the Khan's attack sent him reeling. He drew back quickly, seeking distance from the angry Khan, and he would have been in trouble if Zug had not leaped forward with a whirling slash of his own.

The Khan flicked the *guan do* up, catching Zug's blade, and then slammed the blade of the *guan do* down, sliding it along Zug's haft, aiming for the Nipponese man's hands. Zug shifted his arms, twirling the *naginata* as he forced the *guan do* wide and retaliating with another stroke. Onghwe jerked his left hand up, catching the shaft of the *naginata* just inside the metal blade, and he responded with a similar slash of his own. Zug countered and closed the distance, letting his weapon fall back against his body. He snapped the shortened end up, smashing Onghwe on the side of the head.

Onghwe's head snapped to the side, and he stumbled. Zug stepped back, giving himself some measure, and flicked his *naginata* blade up in a vicious swing. Onghwe tried to parry it but only managed to deflect the *naginata* enough that it glanced off the upper portion of his left arm. Zug felt the blade bite into flesh, and when the Khan reeled away, he saw blood soaking the sleeve of his robe.

"Your dogs smell blood," he snarled, and he heard Kim make a howling noise, as if he were summoning a pack of wild hounds.

The cry was picked up by other voices, and all three men paused.

At the back of the tent, the Rose Knight was no longer alone. He had been joined by the other knight—the one who had helped with the cages—and a familiar giant of a man, who kept up his howl longer than the others. Braced in his hands was a long club, topped with a heavy ball of rough stone.

Madhukar grinned as his howl trailed off. "Save a little bit for me," he said, hefting his club.

Kim's shout was the only thing that saved Zug from the Khan's sudden attack. Snarling, Onghwe rallied, lunging forward with the *guan do*. Zug flinched, and the blade sliced across the front of his right shoulder.

An inch higher and the blade would have cut his throat.

The Khan tried to seize the advantage, but Kim was suddenly there, at Zug's side, aiming a high thrust at the Khan's face. Onghwe retreated, smashing the Flower Knight's spear aside, and Zug saw an opening.

He brought the *naginata* around low, and flicked it up, beneath the Khan's guard. The blade passed between the Khan's legs, and he rotated his wrists and pulled up as the Khan danced back, fleeing from his weapon. He felt the blade tug as it sliced through cloth and flesh.

Kim pressed forward, his spear point darting high and low at the Khan. Onghwe parried Kim's attacks more easily, but his stance was unsteady. A heavy sheen of sweat covered his face.

He knew he had been cut.

Zug prowled to the left, staying just out of measure but close enough that he could spring forward should an opportunity present itself. Kim continued his flurry of attacks, forcing the Khan to defend himself. Forcing him to keep moving, to keep putting weight on his injured leg.

The inside of the Khan's leg was covered with blood, and he was leaving a bloody trail behind him as he staggered across the rugs.

Onghwe smashed Kim's spear aside with a heavy swing of his *guan do*, and, with a heavy snarl twisting his features, he lunged at the Flower Knight, thrusting his pole arm straight at Kim's face. The *guan do* didn't have a pointed end, and the only way the strike could hurt Kim was if the Flower Knight dodged to the side but didn't block or retreat, allowing the Khan to slash sideways. Kim twitched his head to the side as he leaned forward, and the *guan do* passed within a hair's breadth of his head. He wrapped his left arm around the haft of the Khan's pole-arm and trapped the weapon against his shoulder.

It was a dangerous move, as the blade of the *guan do* was poised right behind his head. The Khan would only have to rotate the blade in order to get the edge against Kim's skull.

But he never got the chance.

As soon as Kim trapped the Khan's weapon, Zug leaped forward, bringing the *naginata* around in a powerful swing. The blade sheared through the Khan's right arm and continued into his chest, where it stopped against his ribs. With a sharp tug, Zug pulled it free, and the Khan gasped, blood spattering from his mouth. Zug whirled the *naginata* around his head and with a reverse stroke, separated Onghwe's head from his body.

* * *

"It is done," Zug said quietly.

The Khan's body lay twitching on the rug-covered floor of his pavilion. His head had rolled a few paces away, and it stared at the rug, its mouth hanging open.

Kim hefted the Khan's *guan do*, comparing it to the guard's spear he had been using. It had been a long time since he had used one of these Chinese pole-arms. It was a slashing and cutting weapon, not at all like the spear.

It felt good in his hand.

"I don't suppose they are going to let us walk out of here," he said.

Zug offered him a tiny smile, the first sign of humor that Kim had seen from him in a long time. "No," Zug said, "they are going to be somewhat angry with us."

"Should we meet them outside?" Kim asked. "Would you rather die under an open sky?"

"I would," Zug agreed. He bowed, sweeping a hand toward the entrance of the pavilion. "After you, my friend."

"It has been an honor to fight beside you, Zugaikotsu No Yama."

For a moment, Zug seemed to be on the verge of saying something else, and then he swallowed the words. "The honor has been mine, Kim Alcheon," he said.

Kim kept the spear, figuring he could throw it at the first Mongol who came at them. Weapons in both hands, he walked unhurriedly toward the pavilion's entrance, where Madhukar and the pair of Rose Knights were waiting for them.

"I missed the fun," Madhukar sighed.

"Oh, the fun is not over yet," Kim laughed, slapping the taller man lightly on the arm. "Come, let us go tell the Mongols what has befallen their Khan. I'm sure that will provide more opportunities for your club."

He was going to die a free man; they all were. It was a fitting end.

Kim shoved aside the heavy flaps of the tent and stepped outside, surveying the field outside the Khan's pavilion. The air was filled with smoke, and the stench of blood and death greeted him immediately. There was less activity than he had expected, but there were still enough Mongols surrounding the tent to present rather insurmountable odds.

"Ho, warriors of the Mongol Empire," he called out, making sure he got all of their attention. "Here I am."

"Here *we* are." Zug emerged from the pavilion to stand next to him. The others stood beside them. Zug held up the Khan's severed head. "And here's your Khan." He dropped it on the ground and kicked it toward the mob of Mongols. "His *dogs* got the better of him."

An angry surge raced through the Mongols, and spears, swords, and clubs were all brought to bear on the pair. Kim didn't even bother to count the number of deadly weapons pointed in their direction. He looked and laughed. Not at the Mongol's reaction to Zug's contemptuous gesture, but at what he saw rapidly approaching the rear of the Mongol mob.

The knights of the West.

CONGREGABO TE

HE DAY WAS nearly over before Ocyrhoe found them.

Ferenc and Father Rodrigo had stopped on the side of the road, apparently for a meal. Father Rodrigo's satchel was lying flat open, the cup—unusually brilliant in the late afternoon sun—sitting in the center as if it had just been unveiled. Father Rodrigo himself towered over Ferenc, speaking loudly and rapidly in Magyar. Ferenc's body language was that of a person either in shock or grieving, seemingly paralyzed by Father Rodrigo's fervor.

Ocyrhoe dismounted from the horse she had been given by the Emperor—whose stables were not as bereft of suitable mounts as he had intimated. Ferenc spotted her first. He made no move to rise and greet her, but only struggled to offer her a weak smile.

"Your Eminence," she called to Father Rodrigo, and her use of the honorific broke through whatever fog was clouding his brain. His mouth snapped shut, and he stood still, staring at her and blinking, as if he could not quite remember how he knew her. Ocyrhoe put her hand over her heart, squeezing her fingers into a fist to hide from him how much they were trembling. "I greet you as a friend. Do you still recall me as such?"

Father Rodrigo's mouth worked, as if he were tasting her words. She recalled the meeting with Robert of Somercotes, and how Father Rodrigo had seemed to be in a daze until he had seen Ferenc. Even then, he had only been intermittently engaged with the rest of them.

Ferenc spoke up, and she heard her name mentioned. Father Rodrigo swung his head toward Ferenc like a dog finding a scent, and the priest blinked heavily as he listened to Ferenc's words. "Yes," Father Rodrigo said, "I do remember you." He straightened, his face brightening, losing its slackness as he tightened his mouth into a smile. "Have you come to join us on our crusade?"

Ocyrhoe glanced at the cup sitting on the satchel. It had lost some of its luster, as if the sun—which had been previously shining on it—had slipped behind a cloud. It was, as Frederick had mentioned, a silver cup, and not one of gold. She shivered, feeling nothing but apprehension about the cup. "What...what crusade?" she inquired, using the question to cover her nervousness. To give him more time to remember her because she was still not sure he did.

The first day she had ever laid eyes on the priest had been at the market near the Porta Tiburtina, and he had stared at her as if he knew her. His gaze had been wild and feverish, and while he seemed to recognize nothing else, he had known her. Now, his eyes were unclouded by fever, but he kept peering at her as if he thought she were someone else. *So little has changed since that day*, she thought, *and yet so much too.*

"The cedars," the priest said, his voice slurring. "I must save the cedars."

Ocyrhoe glanced around, not seeing the sorts of trees he was talking about. "Father Rodrigo," she said softly. "This crusade is—"

"*What?*" Father Rodrigo answered with a harsh, mocking laugh—unlike any sound she'd heard him make before. "I am the *Summus Pontifex Ecclesiae Universalis*. I am bound to serve God, and

He has revealed His plan to me. *To me.* Not Fieschi. Not any of the others. I was the one who carried His message from Mohi. *I* was the one who suffered. *I* am the one who is strong enough to carry it farther, and that is what I intend to do."

"Why?" Ocyrhoe asked in a plaintive voice. She wandered closer to Ferenc, resting a hand on his shoulder. He stirred beneath her, a shudder running through his body. "You want Ferenc and I to join you on this crusade, but where are you taking us? What are we supposed to do?"

"You are supposed to serve God. We are going to drive out the infidels."

"How?"

He gestured at the cup, which brightened visibly as he paid attention to it. "The Grail will provide a way," he said thickly. His hand shook.

Ocyrhoe recalled Léna's words back in the room Father Rodrigo had stayed in at the Castel Sant'Angelo. *What you need will be offered to you, in unexpected ways and times.* Father Rodrigo had the same faith. But she and Frederick had talked about faith too, in relation to the Grail. In a flash, she understood why Frederick had talked her into chasing after Father Rodrigo. Her faith in something else might be strong enough to withstand the Grail.

Her faith in her sisters.

She walked past Ferenc and knelt on the ground beside Father Rodrigo's satchel. "Will it?" she asked, peering up at him. She reached out her hand to touch the cup.

"Don't touch it," Father Rodrigo shrieked. He lunged for her, meaning to shove her away from the cup, and she spun away from him. She tumbled across the satchel, knocking the cup over.

Father Rodrigo loomed over her, his face blotted with shadows. "You will not take what is mine! You will not!"

She raised her hands defensively, alarmed by the change that had come over him. The cup rolled away from her, and she saw that it was nothing more than a plain silver cup. Identical to the one Frederick had drunk from during the meal they had shared. She kicked it and it bounced across the dry ground.

"God owns me. Only an agent of the Devil would try to take what belongs to God," Father Rodrigo shouted as he scrambled for the cup.

Ferenc finally shook himself free of whatever torpor had held him in place, and he grabbed Father Rodrigo, keeping the priest from reaching the cup. "Father Rodrigo," he pleaded, trying to get the priest's attention.

Father Rodrigo whirled, his hand striking Ferenc across the face. "Stand not in the way of God, heretic," he screamed. *"Vade post me Satana!"*

the flight of the khan

HE SHAMAN'S SADDLE was too narrow for Ögedei, and he perched on it awkwardly, half sliding off the side of the pony as it ran as fast as its short legs could manage. It was a bony animal too, and it ran with a stiff-legged gait that made Ögedei's teeth clack together noisily.

Chucai's powerful stallion was already pulling away from him, and the *Khagan* wanted to shout after his advisor. *How dare Chucai leave him?* But his own nauseating fear provided the answer: Chucai wanted to live too.

He was running away. He could not pretend otherwise as he bounced atop a short-haired pony, shrieking at it to run faster. It didn't matter what sort of image he presented to his men. None of them were pointing and laughing. They were all either dead or engaged in the same headlong rush for safety.

A long arrow caught Chucai's horse in the side, and it plowed into the ground. Chucai remained in the saddle as it fell, and as Ögedei bounced past, he saw why. The long arrow had gone through Chucai's leg first, pinning him to the horse.

The last Ögedei saw of Chucai was the other man straining and tugging to get his *other* leg out from beneath the fallen horse. His beard was tangled too, streaked with blood, and Chucai was shouting something in Chinese, a language Ögedei had not heard him use for a long time.

Ögedei didn't stop. He kept riding. He told himself it was what Chucai would have insisted he do.

The empire was all that mattered.

* * *

As the short-legged pony bounded out of the trees, Ögedei saw two things simultaneously that filled him with equal parts elation and dread. Directly ahead of him, he spotted a number of his *Torguud*. They were galloping fast toward him, and he raised his arm to signal to them. *To me!* he willed. *Your* Khagan *requires your aid*. And then, a flicker of light drew his eyes left, and he squinted against the sun flashing off metal armor.

Armored men, on horseback.

There were only four of them, but they came so relentlessly, their chargers galloping with such strength and determination, that his elation vanished beneath a wave of tremulous panic. Their armor gleamed, their faces were covered with blank masks of shining steel, and the crests on their chests appeared to be fiery roses.

The quartet split—the two on the right angling toward his approaching *Torguud*, the others thundering toward him. He lashed the pony mercilessly, trying to make it run faster, but he could feel it laboring heavily beneath him already.

Behind him, stragglers of his hunting party emerged from the woods, and they rapidly overtook his lumbering pony, reaching him a few scant moments before the two armored riders did. Metal clashed, a horse screamed, and two of his men were down. The armored riders surged through his paltry host, wheeling their mounts about for another charge. A *Darkhat* fired an arrow at one of the two attackers, but it skipped off the man's helm without causing him any harm.

An armored rider came at him, and Ögedei fumbled for his sword, his fingers slipping off the hilt. The charger's hooves pounded against the ground, and he could hear its heavy breathing. He finally got his hand on his hilt, pulled the sword halfway, and realized he wasn't going to get it free in time.

He looked up, deciding he would rather see his death coming, and was suddenly buffeted as another horse and rider passed between him and the approaching rider. The armored man's horse wheeled, nearly throwing its rider, and Namkhai, suddenly between him and his death, battered at the armored man with the long pole of the Spirit Banner.

Namkhai swept the banner around again, and the armored man hesitated for a second. Ögedei could not fathom why the man faltered. Had he felt the power of the banner? Had he seen the endless sea of horses that lived within the banner? Did he realize how pointless his efforts were? The empire was endless. It would run from horizon to horizon, from mountain to sea. It could not be stopped.

"Ride!" Namkhai screamed at him, startling him out of the ecstatic fervor that had suddenly gripped him. Namkhai hit the rider one last time with the banner, knocking him out of his saddle, and then his *Torguud* protector was reaching for him. Ögedei let go of the pony's reins and swung his right leg out of the way as Namkhai brought his horse closer. He leaned over, grabbing a fistful of Namkhai's trousers, and with a grunt he pushed off from the pony's saddle. He floated through empty space for an instant, and he was certain he had mistimed his leap, and then the back of Namkhai's horse slammed against his thighs. He snaked his arm around Namkhai's waist as the horse, now carrying twice the weight, stumbled briefly before finding its balance again.

Screaming a wordless battle cry as if he dared any man or spirit to stand before him, Namkhai urged his horse to run harder. The ground flashed beneath them, and Ögedei buried his face against Namkhai's broad chest, hanging on for dear life.

the strong heart

RSINI STRODE TOWARD the waiting room. He was agitated by Cardinal Fieschi's messenger, and while he had immediately sent the captain of his guard off to mobilize his men, he couldn't shake the feeling that he was chasing a wild horse that would never be tamed. Fieschi had made promises, and at first it seemed that the cardinal might actually be able to produce the results he said he could, but in the last few days, Orsini was beginning to doubt that the cardinal had the situation under control. And if the cardinal wasn't running things, who was?

A priest waited at the door, and when Orsini nodded, he pulled the bolt back and opened the door for the Senator. Orsini took a deep breath and assumed his most imposing attitude—shoulders back, gut forward, forehead glowering—as he entered the room.

The woman stood across from the door, quietly dignified, arms folded across her chest. She gave him such a look of knowing expectation that he almost stumbled, even though the floor was smooth and even. The muscles in his legs twitched, an autonomic response to an instinctual nervousness.

"Senator," she said.

Orsini tried to regain his swagger. "Lady," he replied, not quite mocking and yet still respectful. He stopped just inside the door, a wider stance than felt quite natural. He mirrored her, mockingly, by crossing his arms across his chest.

"Thank you for agreeing to meet with me," she said. "I am Léna, recently of the court of the Holy Roman Emperor, though I am not *bound* to his court."

Orsini sneered, catching the inflection of her words. "You are one of *them*," he said. "A Binder."

"I am," Léna replied. "And I have come to ask of my sisters who live in Rome."

Orsini dismissed the sneer from his lips. "What of them?" he shrugged.

"You are the Senator of Rome," Léna reminded him. "You don't know your city well enough to know what has happened to my kin-sisters? Or is there a different excuse you would like to offer?"

"I don't have to offer you anything," Orsini snapped. "You are an agent of the Holy Roman Emperor, and given his recent attitude toward Rome and the surrounding cities, he has almost declared himself a true enemy of the people."

"*Almost*," Léna said, emphasizing only one of his words. "The resolution of that question may hinge on your answer."

Orsini chewed on his lower lip, gauging the woman before him. Was she bluffing? Would Frederick dare invade Rome simply to find out what had happened to a few witches, none of whom would truly be missed.

"The cardinals have elected a new Pope," she said, changing the subject when it was clear he wasn't going to answer her question.

"A new Pope," Orsini said. "Yes, I know. They finally chose one yesterday."

She shook her head. "No, earlier this morning. Castiglione is their chosen man."

Orsini glowered a little longer at the woman, and when she was unmoved by his best impression of his namesake, he relented. "Of course he is," Orsini sighed, wondering how this disaster could have happened. *What happened to the crazy priest that would have been so pliable?* he wondered, and then his stomach tightened with doubt. *Had this been Fieschi's game all along?*

"He has taken the name Celestine IV," Léna continued.

"Is that all you wanted to tell me?" Orsini asked, tiring of this woman. "That Castiglione has been elected Pope? What does this matter to me?"

"It matters a great deal," Léna said with a smile, and Orsini found himself disliking her smile. "My sisters," she repeated. "Where are they?"

"You don't belong here," he snarled at her. "You are a spy for the Holy Roman Emperor. You are an agitator and a witch. I am going to call for my guards. You can join your—" He caught himself, barely in time.

"Ah," Léna said. "They are still alive. Well, that is fortuitous news."

Orsini waved his hand at her, no longer interested in hearing what she had to say. *At the very least,* he thought as he turned away to call for the guard, *I can ransom her back to Frederick.*

"Senator Matteo Rosso Orsini," Léna commanded. He found himself stopping and turning back to face her, against his better judgment.

She put her closed hand over her heart. "Senator Orsini," she said. "I am bound to you with a message from Pope Celestine IV."

"What nonsense is this?" he demanded, striding toward her. Intending to shut her up—forcefully, if necessary.

"The Pope wishes to inform you that his first act as Pope is to express his displeasure at the treatment of the cardinals in the Septizodium by ordering that you be excommunicated from the Holy Roman Church."

She smiled as she finished. Orsini tried to speak, but found he could not even open his mouth. An oak plank smashing him on the head would not have left him more stupefied than this.

Léna, after a polite pause, announced, "Thus delivered of my message, I am like the wind, unbound here but bound elsewhere."

She paused again, but he could do nothing more than stare at her, stunned. *Excommunicated...*

"I would expect that the Pope might reconsider his order," she said pleasantly as she started to walk toward him, "if you were to demonstrate some contrition for your acts of heinous torture against the citizens of Rome. Since the cardinals are no longer imprisoned in the Septizodium, perhaps you might think of some other poor souls who have been wrongly imprisoned."

She stopped and looked up at him. "Now, do you remember what happened to my kin-sisters?" she asked.

He found himself nodding dumbly.

"Good," she said. "I look forward to hearing news of their release. I might even be inclined to beg clemency from His Holiness on your behalf."

* * *

God believes your heart is strong enough.

At first, there had only been tiny pinpricks of light, shards of sun that dazzled as they fell on the leaves. But when they reached the vale of endless tents, the light had grown stronger. When Rodrigo glanced through the open flaps of tents, thinking he would see nothing but shadows, all he saw were glowing faces. Cherubic angels peering out at him, their rotund moon faces swollen with honey-sticky joy. And when he met the Emperor, the man who spoke with the voice of a black bird, he could no longer bear to raise his eyes toward the sky. Even though there was a heavy canvas tent over his head, he could still see the fiery explosions of God's spinning eyes.

As he grabbed the cup, all the light went away. It was as if there was a vast hole in the bottom of the vessel, a sucking abyss that began to inhale deeply as he squeezed the metal stem in his hand. He could see the light streaming toward the cup. It flowed across the table like water running uphill; it dribbled out of Ferenc's eyes in fat, squirming tears; it fell from the sparkling wheels in the sky in sheets of fiery rain. The cup continued to inhale, seemingly unperturbed by the quantity of light it was consuming, until there was nothing left but shadows.

In the resonant darkness, the black bird kept shrieking, and Rodrigo heard answering calls, the echoes of all the crows and vultures from the battlefield. Each voice splintered into tinier voices, like the cries of lost children—the orphans of Mohi, of Legnica, of every city the Mongol horde had destroyed in its relentless quest to trample the world.

Make them stop! he pleaded with the darkness. *Give them peace. Embrace them.* But if God was in the darkness, he did not respond to Rodrigo's prayer. The priest teetered on the edge of the abyss, the one that had nearly consumed him once before, buffeted by the screams and cries of all the dead birds.

His feet slipped, but he did not plummet into the empty vastness. He hung, dangling over the abyss, one hand wrapped tightly around the stem of the cup, and it did not move. Grunting and straining, he reached up and put both hands on it.

He remembered everything perfectly: his catechisms from the seminary, the holy words of God writ in the Bible, the insights gleaned from Brother Albertus, the last benediction from the Archbishop before the armies of the West were devastated on the plain near Mohi, the words spoken to him by the fair-haired angel at the farm. *Signa hodie lumen vultus tui super me...*It was only through arduous reflection upon everything he could recall that he could understand God. That he could understand his place in God's design.

There was still a glimmer of light in the cup. Every muscle in his body groaned as he raised himself so that he could sip from the floating cup. He put his lips against the warm metal, and as his flesh made contact with the Grail, it tipped toward him. A golden streak of light flowed into his open mouth, and he drank it eagerly, accepting it into his body, into his soul.

When he exploded, he knew he was the exultation of light that he had seen in his vision. The endless wheels within wheels were his existence, shattered and strewn throughout the profusion of possibilities, destinies, histories, implications, and connections. He whirled, each particle of his being shivering with an ecstatic thrill. He saw everything and heard nothing.

As the wheels began to slow, as his being began to coalesce once more, he started to weep.

He could see cracks in the vessel, and even with all this light and warmth, the cracks could not be healed...

* * *

Father Rodrigo struggled in Ferenc's grip. "What are you doing, boy?" the priest screamed. His eyes were wild and his face was pale with blotches of red—the same sort of coloration that Ferenc had seen during more than one of the priest's feverish fits. "She wants to steal the Grail. She's a child of Satan."

He didn't believe what Father Rodrigo was saying—he *couldn't*— and he felt more strongly the fear he had been trying to push away. He had seen the priest become lost in his fever fogs before, but never like this. Never with such little warning.

Without taking his eyes off Father Rodrigo, Ferenc listened to the sounds of movement behind him: Ocyrhoe's ragged breathing; her hands and knees moving across the rough ground; the sound of cloth scraping against the same. Father Rodrigo thrust out an arm, pointing over Ferenc's shoulder, and he heard Ocyrhoe's horse spook with a deep snort.

"Stop her!" Father Rodrigo shrieked.

"Father," Ferenc said, gently taking the priest's outstretched hand with both of his and pulling it toward his heart. "Look away. Calm yourself. I beg you. She is not your enemy. She only wants to help. *I* want to help." He squeezed the priest's fingers.

Father Rodrigo shoved Ferenc sharply, and he staggered backward and barely caught himself from falling. "Open your eyes, boy! *Domine, oculos habet, et non videbut.*" His eyes were frighteningly bright and large, and he pulled his hand free of Ferenc's grip. Shivering with rage, he grabbed Ferenc's shoulders and spun the boy around. "I have seen her in my visions, and she is all that stands between me and our salvation. Look!"

Ocyrhoe dashed across the road, her legs at awkward angles as if each wanted to flee in a different direction. She clutched both the cup and the priest's satchel against her chest.

With a roar, Father Rodrigo released Ferenc and threw himself at the fleeing girl, his hands grasping and clawing. Ferenc saw her, in her confusion and terror, grab the satchel even tighter to herself rather than attempt to avoid his outstretched hands. Father Rodrigo grabbed Ocyrhoe by the hair, yanking her to a stop. She cried out, struggling in his grip, and Ferenc flinched as she wrenched herself free, leaving a fistful of hair in Father Rodrigo's grip.

Ferenc shook himself free of the fear that was paralyzing him and sprang after Father Rodrigo. The priest heard him coming this time, shook him off as he tried to wrap his arms around the mad priest. Father Rodrigo threw an elbow back, catching Ferenc on the bridge of the nose, and Ferenc tried to blink away the flood of tears that sprang into his eyes.

The priest lunged after Ocyrhoe again, grabbing at her neck and shoulders this time. As he found his grip, he squeezed and lifted her so that she was poised on her toes. Her face was very red, and her hands flew to her throat, trying to pry loose his grip.

"Father, stop," Ferenc hissed. He grabbed Father Rodrigo's arm and pulled, but it was like trying to pull a full-grown tree out of the ground. He slapped Father Rodrigo, but the priest ignored him. Ocyrhoe sputtered and choked. She had dropped both the satchel and the cup, and her tiny hands beat ineffectively at Father Rodrigo's arms.

Ferenc looked at Father Rodrigo's eyes and saw no sign of the priest he once knew.

He stood on his toes, and wrapped his right arm around the priest's head and face. "I have to do this," he whispered. "I'm sorry." With his left arm folding in against his own chest, he grabbed Father Rodrigo's right ear in his left hand.

The priest's body tightened against his, dumbly realizing something was amiss. His hands stopped tightening, but he did not release Ocyrhoe.

Having gotten the man's attention, Ferenc carefully pulled a little with his right arm as he pushed with his left, forcing Father Rodrigo's head deosil enough to be uncomfortable. A nervous cry slipped from the priest's mouth, almost as loud as Ocyrhoe's rasping gasps for air, and Ferenc found himself almost unable to maintain his grip. He had heard the sound before when Father Rodrigo had moments of lucidity during his bouts of fever madness.

Out of the corner of his eye, Ferenc saw Ocyrhoe's frightened face and her mouth, opening and closing like that of a fish pulled out of the water. He felt the muscles in his arms tremble, and he tightened his embrace. He had to be strong.

"Release her," he said, his arms firm. "She is an innocent girl. When you wake from this madness, you will know yourself again. You will never forgive yourself if you do not let her go." His heart hammered in his chest, and he silently prayed that the part of Father Rodrigo that he had just heard cry out could hear him.

When he had hunted in the woods outside of Buda, he had, on occasion, needed to mercifully end the life of a wounded animal.

Don't make me do this, he pleaded silently.

PURSUIT

APHAEL CAUGHT THE Mongol's sword on his shield, and as his horse thundered past, he pushed his shield down and swung his sword in a heavy chopping motion. It bit through leather and flesh, tugging as it caught on bone, and then his opponent was behind him. Another Mongol rider was galloping past on his right, and he angled his horse after the man. He passed behind the other's horse, and the Mongol twisted adroitly in his saddle, loosing an arrow at close range. He pulled his upper body down toward his gut, tightening in his saddle in an effort to hide behind his shield. The arrow smacked hard into his shield, breaching its surface and protruding a few inches out the other side. He rose out of his crouch, swinging his sword, and the Mongol spun away, blood rising in a plume.

He caught sight of Percival smashing a Mongol's shoulder to a bloody pulp with his mace and following through with a merciful stroke across the enemy's throat. He looked for Vera and Eleázar—didn't see either of them—and then caught sight of Feronantus being unhorsed by a broad Mongol wielding a long pole, festooned with a plethora of horsehair braids. As he watched, the broad Mongol caught up with a pony laboring under the weight of its rider, a man wearing plum-colored clothing, and in a maneuver that bespoke a life spent on horseback, the pony lost its rider to the other horse.

The *Khagan*, Raphael realized.

Ignoring the other pair of Mongol riders nearby, he kicked his mount toward the fleeing horse. They had to catch the *Khagan* before he managed to reach the vale leading out of the valley.

Something kicked him in the ribs, and he pitched forward across the horn of his saddle. He knew, without contorting himself to check, that he had just been hit with an arrow. A second arrow passed through the maille on his shoulder, grazing his neck, and he cursed his foolishness.

He shouldn't have turned his back on the Mongols. He had forgotten their skill with bows. But he couldn't turn back now. He had to keep riding. He had to catch the *Khagan*...

* * *

Yasper, his ears still ringing, slid down the hillside on his rump. The second explosion had scattered the horses, and the remaining Mongols were either wounded or dazed. A few horses were trotting aimlessly about the floor of the valley. If he could catch one, he could go find the others. Maybe even lend a hand.

He drew up several paces short of the valley floor as he heard the sound of a horse approaching. As he crouched beside a flattened rock, the horse came into view, burdened by a pair of riders. He recognized the one wearing the fanciful outfit, and as he watched, they leaped off their weary horse. He couldn't help but marvel at how quickly and effortlessly they caught two of the other horses, leaped into their saddles, and galloped off again.

Yasper stared after the fleeing pair, realizing he had just let the *Khagan* slip through his fingers.

Scrambling to his feet, he started toward the other horses and stopped as he realized he was about to run through a wide smear of gore. Gulping back his queasy stomach, he diverted his course, skirting the glistening patch of blood and body parts.

Some of the other Mongols were moving toward the horses too. The sight of the *Khagan* had broken their confusion. Yasper was going to have some competition for a steed.

* * *

Eleázar saw the huge Mongol unhorse Feronantus, and he mentally clucked his tongue at the elder warrior's clumsiness. The Mongol had battered the Shield-Brethren with the horsehair lance he carried, the sort of clumsy buffeting employed by an initiate who knew little about fighting from horseback, and Feronantus should have been able to stay in the saddle. Eleázar squeezed his horse with his knees, guiding the animal toward the fallen Shield-Brethren master.

A mounted Mongol warrior charged toward him, bow drawn, and Eleázar raised his shield to block the horseman's arrow. He felt the arrow hit his shield, and then the Mongol rider was behind him. Twisting in his saddle, Eleázar caught the second arrow in his shield too. The Mongols were really good at shooting their bows from horseback, and he had seen them twist their bodies and shoot arrows behind them.

He swept his shield around, in time to intercept a Mongol sword. He had seen the second rider coming, and knew the pair had been setting him up for a trap. The archer had wanted Eleázar to pay attention to him, so that he wouldn't notice the other rider coming. Eleázar wasn't that sort of fool, and he shoved his shield hard at the oncoming rider, bashing the warrior right out of his saddle.

He circled Feronantus, putting himself between the unhorsed knight and a trio of approaching Mongols. "Get on your horse, old man," he shouted.

Feronantus shouted something in return, but his words were lost in the battlefield noise. Eleázar took several more arrows in his shield, and kneed his horse toward the three archers. They felt they were far enough away for another volley, and Eleázar grinned as he spotted Percival coming from their rear. *We know how to distract our enemies too*, he thought, holding his shield ready as if he were trying to hide behind it as he charged. Percival broke through them, catching one in the back of the skull with his mace and slicing the throat of another with a backhanded swing of his sword.

The third, distracted by the sudden death of his companions, released his arrow too early, and it flew harmlessly past Eleázar's head. He thrust with his sword as his horse galloped past, feeling the blade slide up the man's leather armor and catch momentarily on the archer's jaw. And then it kept moving, opening up the man's throat.

"The *Khagan* has fled," Percival shouted at him. "Waste no more time on this field." He pointed toward the end of the valley. Eleázar wheeled his horse around and slapped the flat of his blade against his horse's rump. The animal started, recovering quickly and running hard toward the end of the valley. There were still scattered groups of Mongols, but they looked unorganized. Percival and Vera could take care of them.

As he rode, body moving in concert with his horse's steady gallop, the occasional Mongol arrow would come his way. Most of them fell short, but a few struck his maille, failing to do much more than get tangled in the chain. Eleázar had lived through a barrage of Mongol arrows before, at the river crossing battle. He laughed. *That had been a battle*, he thought.

He approached the narrow vale where the alchemist had planned his ambush, and he spotted the wreckage of broken stone and—his stomach tightened at the sight of the carnage wreaked by Yasper's incendiaries. The route narrowed, and on the left side of the cleft, he spotted a number of unclaimed ponies and a few scattered Mongols.

And one man in Western armor who appeared to be in a losing wrestling match with a Mongol.

Yasper.

Several Mongols turned toward Eleázar, raising their bows, and he goaded his horse, trying to eke more speed out of the animal. Trying to get close enough to bring his weapons to bear. The horse was flagging already; he had ridden it too hard. The Mongols loosed arrows, and his horse stumbled.

It had been bound to happen. Eventually, one of the Mongols would shoot an arrow at his horse instead of him; given how futile their arrows were against Western maille, he was somewhat surprised it had taken them this long to change their tactics. As his horse stumbled again, its lungs laboring, he kicked his feet out of his stirrups and jumped. The horse tripped, plowing headfirst into the ground, but he was no longer in the saddle.

Eleázar hit the ground, the impact jarring his sword out of his hand, and he rolled, managing to hold on to his shield. As he came out of his roll, he hurled his shield at the Mongols. It was a clumsy missile, but it caused the archers to scatter out of the way. Eleázar darted back to his dying horse, and grabbed his two-handed sword, which was strapped along the horse's flank.

Whirling the long blade in continuous circles, he charged the archers. One managed to shoot an arrow, and he felt it strike his shoulder, the point tangling in his maille. He cut the first man in half, the second stumbled back enough that Eleázar only managed a deep slice across the front of the man's hip, and the third one turned and ran before Eleázar's whirling sword could cut him down.

Yasper was on the ground, trying to shove off the Mongol who was trying to bury a knife in the alchemist's chest. Eleázar came up behind the struggling pair, and the tip of his two-handed sword caught the Mongol in the side, under the arm, and the blade sliced right through to the spine. The blade caught on bone, but the force of Eleázar's swing was enough to lift the man bodily off the supine alchemist. Eleázar shook his sword, an expert twitch of his hands, and the blade came free of the nearly severed Mongol, who fell a short distance and then sprawled on the ground, bleeding out in a few seconds.

"Get up, runt," Eleázar laughed. "This is no time for napping."

Yasper scrambled to his feet. His face was dark with soot and dirt, blood from a gash across his forehead a long smear across his face. "The *Khagan*," Yasper gasped. "I saw him ride past."

"Aye," Eleázar said. "So I have heard." He nodded toward one of the wandering ponies. "Catch yourself a horse," he said. "Go after him."

"What about you?" Yasper said.

Eleázar laughed again. "Me? On one of those tiny little horses?" He shook his head, glancing around the passage out of the valley. "I will stay here for the time being," he said.

"I'll keep the stragglers busy." He reached over and yanked the Mongol arrow out of his maille.

They both turned as they heard a pair of horses approaching. The riders wore maille and the red rose of the Shield-Brethren. Yasper pointed in the direction the *Khagan* had fled, and the horsemen thundered past. Raphael and Feronantus.

"I should be going then," Yasper said.

"Aye, you should," Eleázar replied.

"May the Virgin watch over you." Yasper offered his hand to the Spaniard.

"May the Virgin watch over you as well, little alchemist," Eleázar said, clasping Yasper's hand firmly. "It has been good to ride with you."

"I hope we'll do it again," Yasper said.

"Aye. Me too," Eleázar said. "Now, go!"

Yasper nodded and ran toward one of the wandering Mongol ponies. Eleázar turned toward the valley of the cave bear. Three of the company were going after the *Khagan*. It fell upon him now to make sure none of the surviving Mongols followed.

He laughed, swinging his two-handed sword as he moved into position.

They weren't getting past him.

CAST OUT

ATHER RODRIGO SEEMED to hear Ferenc's desperate plea. The priest relaxed, his hands slackening on Ocyrhoe's neck. The girl took a huge, loud draw of breath and was about to let it out when a spasm shook Father Rodrigo's body. His hands tightened again around her throat; she fought at his grip with furious desperation. Ferenc wrenched Rodrigo's neck more, until he felt it reach its limit.

Father Rodrigo bellowed with pain as he struggled against Ferenc's grip, but Ferenc's hands continued to squeeze. Ocyrhoe's face turned purple, her tongue protruding from her mouth.

"Stop it, Rodrigo. Rodrigo Bendrito!" Ferenc begged. "Father Rodrigo Bendrito! Listen to me!" He felt tears start from his eyes.

It was unfair to have this choice forced upon him. He and the priest had survived Mohi; they had traveled together for so long. He had built fires to warm the man's body when the warmth of the fevers had fled; he had foraged for tiny streams within rocky clefts in the high mountains for cool water to cool Father Rodrigo's burning skin. He had brought the priest to Rome so that his message— the last shred of his faith that had kept him alive throughout their journey—could be delivered. Once in Rome, a land as foreign and strange as any he could possibly imagine, he had found someone

who could communicate with him. She used the same finger language as his mother, and almost instantly, this tiny girl had become
so important to him.

And now he had to choose between them.

This is what was, his mother had told him, showing him the old
roots. *This is what will be.* She patted the soil where she had recently
planted the seeds. *What grows is what we remember, what we bind ourselves to.*

It is the choices we make.

Father Rodrigo continued to strain in Ferenc's grip, and
from some unearthly source of dreadful strength, he began lifting
Ocyrhoe's thin body off the ground.

"Stop it!" Ferenc was screaming now, his lips against the priest's
ear. "You saved my life at Mohi; let me save yours now! Put her down!
Let her go! *Rodrigo!*"

Father Rodrigo shouted, his voice an octave lower than his normal speaking voice; Ferenc almost expected a demon to slink out of
his mouth. Ocyrhoe's eyes began to roll up.

"Stop it! You are *killing* her!" Ferenc screamed. "Take the Grail
and go!"

"She is the Devil; she must die, or she will follow me forever!"
Rodrigo shouted, again in a demonically thundering bass.

Ferenc's body convulsed with sobs. There was no time, no time
to think this through, no time to try some other way. Muttering rapid
prayers for forgiveness, he made his choice. Closing his eyes as if that
somehow made a difference, he shot his left arm forward and snapped his
right arm back, twisting Rodrigo's head at an impossible angle over his
right shoulder. Immediately the priest gasped and shuddered, releasing
Ocyrhoe. When Ferenc relaxed his arms, Father Rodrigo made a tiny
sound, almost like a sigh of relief, and collapsed at Ferenc's feet.

Ocyrhoe's terrified coughs and gasps were so loud and painful that Ferenc did not realize for a moment he was gasping

too; he turned away and vomited into the grass, then fell to his knees beside Father Rodrigo's now lifeless body, sobbing like an orphaned child.

* * *

An unruly mob swarmed the streets of Rome. As far as Cardinal Fieschi could tell, the mob was leaderless—agitated citizens with no clear purpose or direction. By the time his carriage reached the Vatican, he was certain the swarm of citizenry milling about the streets was simply there to delay his return. Yet another obstacle he had to endure.

His first stop had been the Orsini estate, where he learned that the Senator had been summoned to the Vatican—an unwelcome piece of news, for who, other than himself, would summon the Senator? The interminable ride through the crowded streets of Rome did little to dispel his apprehension.

He dismounted quickly from the carriage, angrily rejecting the ostiarius's offer of a helpful hand. "Senator Orsini," he snapped. "Is he still here?"

"I believe so," the porter replied. "He asked to be taken to the main receiving chamber."

"And the other cardinals?"

"They are preparing to announce the new Pope," the ostiarius said.

"And who is the new Pope?" Fieschi asked, secretly fearing that some other reversal had occurred in the time he had been absent.

"Celestine IV," a woman's voice provided.

Léna, the Binder from Frederick's camp, stood on the broad steps. She descended to his level and offered him a respectful bow. "Cardinal Fieschi," she said. "I had hoped to meet you before I departed."

"What do you want?" Fieschi snarled.

"How was your visit with the Holy Roman Emperor?" Léna asked, oblivious to his agitation. "I don't see the girl with you. Were you able to successfully negotiate the return of your missing priest?"

Fieschi grabbed the front of Léna's cloak and drew her to him. "I know you are working with the Emperor, Binder, in a way that violates your precepts."

Léna remained unruffled. Up close, he could see there was no fear in her eyes. Only a steadiness of resolve that gave him pause. "You know nothing about me or my sisters, Cardinal Fieschi," she said quietly. Her eyes flicked down at his clenched fists. "Your hands, Your Eminence," she pointed out. "Are you sure you want to dirty them again? So soon after the last time?"

Fieschi released her, a very un-cardinal-like oath threatening to spill out of his mouth. "You are not welcome here," he said, forcing the profane words aside. "You and your sisters. If I see any of you or hear word that you are in my city, you will be marked as spies and treated accordingly."

"*Your* city?" Léna noted.

"Yes," Fieschi snapped. "My city." He gestured at the buildings around them, especially the rounded dome of St. Peter's Basilica. "My church."

"Of course it is," Léna said, a mixture of admiration and revulsion in her voice. "I will be sure to tell my sisters they are no longer welcome here. When they are released from wherever the Senator has them imprisoned, that is." She offered the cardinal a hard smile. "It would be disappointing if we were not allowed the freedom to meet your demand that the Binders quit Rome."

"Take them," Fieschi said. "Take all of them with you. I left one with the Emperor already."

"Yes," Léna said. "Good. I appreciate you taking her to Frederick. That was very helpful."

"Helpful?" Fieschi choked, instantly disliking the idea that he had been, in any way, helpful to this woman.

Léna reached up and extracted a tiny chain from beneath her cloak. She closed her hand over whatever was suspended from the end of the silver loop and broke the chain with a sharp jerk of her hand. She laid her still-closed hand over her heart. "Cardinal Sinibaldo Fieschi, I am bound to you with a message."

"What nonsense is this?" Fieschi sputtered.

"A message from Pope Gregory IX," she finished. She opened her hand and held it out to him. Resting on her palm was a small gold ring. A Greek letter, broken in half, was stamped on its surface. "He wanted this ring delivered to his *successor*."

His heart pounding, Fieschi reached for the ring, but Léna closed her hand suddenly.

"Thus delivered of my message, I am like the fox," she said, "unbound here and everywhere. Do you agree, Cardinal Fieschi? I will deliver your late Pope's message because that is what a Binder does, but in doing so, I am freed. Unencumbered by all."

"Yes," Cardinal Fieschi said. "Yes. Give it to me."

Léna closed her eyes briefly and then opened her hand. "And so it is done," she said softly. The ring fell into Fieschi's outstretched hand, and he closed his fingers quickly, before she changed her mind.

"Ho, porter," she called to the ostiarius standing nearby. "Is that carriage available?"

"My apologies, Lady," the priest said. "It belongs to the Church."

"Of course it does," she said. "But I am sure the Church would put it at my disposal, wouldn't it, Cardinal Fieschi?"

He started at the sound of her voice. The ring was heavy in his hand, and he wanted to look at it. He wanted to put it on.

But not in *her* presence.

"What?" he said. "Oh, yes. The carriage." He waved his other hand at the ostiarius. "Let her have it. Get her out of my sight. *Out of Rome.*"

Léna curtsied, and the ostiarius hurried to assist her aboard the carriage. As the driver snapped his whip at the horses, Fieschi turned away and hurried up the steps. When he reached the top and passed into the shadow of the broad arch of the doorway, he opened his hand and looked at the ring.

The sigil was two *fasces*—the staves carried by Roman legates in the time before the Church—but they had been bent so that they appeared to form halves of a sundered omega. The ring had been given to him and not to Castiglione. Gregory IX's successor. The one who would truly carry on in the spirit of the previous Pope.

Celestine IV will not rule long, Fieschi thought. The ring fit snugly on the small finger of his right hand. *And then it will be my turn*

He closed his hand and looked at the ring.

My church.

* * *

The sight of Father Rodrigo's body was horrible, made more so by how his death had come to pass. His eyes remained open, and Ocyrhoe couldn't bear passing in front of them. She felt like they were still watching her, like part of him was still aware inside the sprawled body. She didn't know which part of him it was—the befuddled Father Rodrigo who had been kind to her, or the monster that had he had become in the end. She didn't understand how the transformation had happened, and thus, wasn't entirely sure that whatever it was that had possessed Father Rodrigo couldn't animate his dead body.

Ferenc rocked and forth on his knees, weeping profusely, and she didn't know how to console him. What could she say to him?

That the priest had left him no choice? She would have died if Ferenc hadn't acted, and with each painful breath, she was glad he made the choice he had.

The satchel lay nearby, forgotten, as did the cup. Using the satchel, she scooped up the lackluster cup and closed the bag tight around it. The cup no longer glowed, and she put the idea out of her mind that it had taken on a dull rose tint.

The Emperor had only asked that the priest and the cup be separated, and they had in the most brutal way possible. But what was she supposed to do with it now? Take it back to the Emperor?

The cardinal would be sending men out to search for Ferenc and Father Rodrigo. She had had a few hours' head start on the search parties, but the longer she stood here, the closer the men of Rome would get.

I can't go back, she realized. This is what Léna meant for her to do. The Binder had told her she was ready to leave the city, that she had the skills to survive outside the walls that had been her home. Ocyrhoe didn't understand how Léna could have anticipated this series of events, but somehow the Binder had known.

What had Léna called her when they had first met? An *orba matre*. Ocyrhoe didn't know what that meant, but as she furiously thought about what she was supposed to do, she realized Léna had been speaking from personal experience. She and Léna were the same, albeit at different stages of their lives. With that insight came the understanding that Léna would have never asked anything of Ocyrhoe that she wouldn't have been willing to do herself.

Ocyrhoe wasn't alone. There was an unassailable connection between her and the other woman. They were, in fact, bound to one another. "Unencumbered by all," Ocyrhoe whispered, and shivered as she felt the words were being spoken elsewhere at the same moment.

She knew what she had to do.

She touched Ferenc lightly, and he spooked at her touch. He looked at her, his face puffy and his eyes red from crying, and her heart ached at the sight of his suffering. How she wished she could ease it. Using soothing words and a light touch, she talked to him, explaining what had to be done.

They didn't have the tools to bury the priest's body, and Father Rodrigo deserved better than to be dragged into the hills by scavengers. His body needed to go back to Rome, and someone needed to go with it. Someone like Ferenc.

Eventually, he nodded, understanding what she wasn't telling him, and he rose from his kneeling position and set about taking care of the priest's body. Moving dead weight was much harder than she imagined it could be, but between them they got Father Rodrigo's body across the saddle of one of the two horses Frederick had given them.

Ferenc helped her to mount her own horse, and once she was in the saddle she put the satchel carefully into one of her saddlebags and made sure the flap was securely tied down. She looked down at Ferenc. "My friend..." Her voice was but a whisper, the bruised muscles of her neck twitching with a new dismay. She didn't want to say good-bye...

She touched her waist and pointed to his, indicating that he should give her his knife. Blinking back tears, he complied, unsure of what she intended to do. She felt in her tangled hair for the braided piece, the one with the knots he had recognized when they had first met. She separated the strand, and cut it with a quick jerk of his knife.

He accepted her gift, kissing the back of her hand as he did, and he did not try to stop the tears from streaming down his cheeks. He shook his head when she tried to give back the knife, offering her the sheath as well.

"Okay," she said, pressing the sheathed knife to her lips. "It will keep me safe."

Ferenc nodded, a brave expression on his face, and then he turned and leaped up onto the third mount with a nimbleness that amazed her. With a final sad smile, he leaned over and gathered the reins of the horse that carried Father Rodrigo. He clicked to the horses and they began a slow walk. Back toward the Emperor's camp. Back toward Rome.

She watched them for a moment, until the sight of them became too much to bear, and she turned her gaze in the opposite direction. She had absolutely no idea where the road led. That part of her mind that had, in Rome, been an exquisitely detailed, crowded map was now blank parchment. Fresh and unmarked, waiting to reveal itself to her.

And she knew it would.

She pressed her heels against her horse's side, nudging him forward on the unknown road.

the death
of a boy

T HE SKY ABOVE Hünern was alight with purple, gold, red, and orange—the sort of sunset that would cause a bard to spontaneously break out into song. But the beauty of the sun was lost on Hans. He wandered through the ruins of the Mongol camp as if in a dream. The painted sky was as unreal to him as the whimpering cries of the wounded and dying.

The scavengers of Hünern were beginning to converge, the bravest had already crept through the open gate and begun looting the bodies of the dead Mongols. Others would follow, timorous rodents that would strip the tents clean. In the wake of the battle, there would be a period of lawlessness as the people of Hünern came to pillage the Mongol camp. There was no reason to stand in the way of this restitution. The survivors had lost everything, and what wealth they could scavenge from the camp was poor compensation.

He still felt nothing. In the brief instances when he blinked, he saw Tegusgal's panicked face. The Mongol's eyes large and round before Hans had driven the dagger into the left one. The sound the man had made as the steel point went through the eye and into his brain. The way his body had bucked and quivered as the life left him.

Hans never wanted to close his eyes again.

The knights of the various orders were collecting the bodies of their fallen comrades, and Hans saw a group of Shield-Brethren gathered around a row of supine figures. He didn't know where else to go. The Rats, who had come to his aid, pelting the Mongol commander with rocks, had kept their distance after Tegusgal died, their dirty faces pinched and stretched with horrific expressions. Throwing rocks at a hated enemy was a childish act, the defiance of the innocent. Killing a man was something else entirely. Hans was no longer one of them, and they had fled when he had tried to reach out to them.

He was covered in blood, very little of it his, and as he wandered toward the group of Shield-Brethren, he saw how he looked more like the battle-weary knights than like the dirty urchins of Hünern.

The Shield-Brethren dead were laid side by side, arranged as naturally as they could be, their longswords laid across the bodies. Hans counted them slowly—fifteen in all—marking each face in his mind, and when he looked upon the peaceful features of the body at the end of the row, his body shook and he started to cry.

Several of the knights hovered awkwardly nearby, and one finally touched Hans lightly on the shoulder. "He was the best of us," the man said gruffly. His own face was streaked with dried tears.

The words made little sense to Hans. Had they not said the same of Andreas? Why did the best keep dying? Why were they—the worst, the unworthy, the frightened ones—why were they allowed to live? He drew in a long, shuddering breath and took a few tentative steps closer to Rutger's body. The quartermaster's hands, the left wrapped with a filthy cloth, were clasped over the hilt of a longsword, and his brow was slightly creased as if there were unspoken words still trapped inside his skull. Unlike the ones next to him, his body did not have an apparent fatal wound.

"Why are you gone?" Hans whispered as he collapsed next to Rutger's body.

"It happens," the gruff one said. "Sometimes she claims them even though they have not suffered grievous wounds."

Hans looked over his shoulder at the knight. "That isn't fair," he said.

"Little is, boy," the man said. "That is why we grieve. Later, we will celebrate that it wasn't our turn." He shrugged as if that was all the explanation anyone would ever require.

Beyond the knight, Hans spotted a group of men approaching. One of the other knights saw the approaching men as well, and his hand fell to his sword for a moment. Of the approaching group, two were wearing the colors of the Shield-Brethren, and Hans recognized them: Styg and Eilif. With them were Kim, Zug, and another freed prisoner.

"There you are," Styg said as he reached the row of bodies. "When we heard Maks had fallen in battle, we did not know what happened to you. Where have you been?"

Hans shook his head. He did not want to say the Mongol commander's name out loud.

Kim pushed past the others and rushed to Hans's side. He knelt and put his hands on the young boy's shoulders. Kim's face was dirty and bloody, and Hans flinched as he looked in the Flower Knight's eyes and saw a flickering reminder of what he had done.

"It's okay," Kim said, nodding slowly. "Did you have any choice?"

Hans shook his head.

"Then you did the right thing," Kim said.

"Te...Tegusgal," Hans stammered. He started to cry again.

Kim wrapped his arms around the boy and squeezed him tight. "You most certainly did the right thing," he said. There was a note of pride in his voice, and Hans clung to that sentiment as firmly as he held on to the Flower Knight.

Ōgedei's Legacy

THEY REACHED A rocky spur that sliced through the forest like a ragged cut left by a dull sword. Over the years, a stream had dug a track along the base of the rocky shelf, and it held water now, though it was little more than a trickle. On their right, the forest was dense, filled with grassy hillocks and tightly bunched clumps of alder trees. It wasn't the easiest terrain for their single horse (weighed down with both Cnán and the Chinese woman, Lian), though the lack of trees made it easier to see and avoid the crevasses and gaps in the rock.

They moved quickly across the open terrain, and Cnán kept her horse close to the tree line where the ground was safer.

Sound carried well along the shelf, caught between the trees and the rocks, and they heard the horses coming a while before they spotted them. Haakon and Krasniy made no move to hide themselves. Cnán's heart beat faster, and she tried to not let her apprehension pass to her horse. The echoes tripped over each other, confounding the number of animals approaching, and Cnán doubted the riders approaching were friendly.

Haakon and Krasniy each had a sword, and Krasniy had managed to pick up a spear as well on their way out of the camp, but neither wore any armor. They weren't very well equipped to stand against a host of any size.

The riders came into view, and both parties paused, catching sight of one another. Cnán peered at the pair facing them, noting they were Mongolian and that one—the broader one—appeared to be injured. The other she recognized after a moment as the *Khagan* himself.

"Ögedei," Haakon called out, having recognized the man in plum too. He raised his hand and beckoned, waving the *Khagan* toward him.

The broad Mongol kneed his horse forward, lowering the tall pole he carried until it was pointed at the pair of Westerners like a lance. The horsehair braids danced as his horse charged.

Krasniy laughed, a rolling sound that came deep from his belly. He motioned Haakon to stand aside as he stepped forward, raising his spear.

* * *

At the mouth of the valley, Ögedei and Namkhai had stopped for fresher mounts, taking them from the scattered *Torguud* who appeared to have been ambushed. Namkhai urged Ögedei to keep riding, and while a part of him was angered by the idea of fleeing, prudence won out and he followed Namkhai. The *Torguud*'s responsibility was to protect him, and leaving them behind to fight the assassins who had sprung out of the woods was the right thing to do.

Ögedei followed Namkhai through the woods, retracing the route they had taken the day before. The clearing near the river where they had camped flashed past, and then Namkhai turned north, heading up a slow incline toward rockier terrain. For a while, he simply focused on Namkhai's broad back and the fluttering horsehair braids of the Spirit Banner, letting his horse run at its own pace.

And then Namkhai slowed his horse, cutting to the side, and Ögedei looked ahead. He saw a horse carrying two riders and a pair of men, standing in the open. He squinted at them, knowing he knew who the men were, but unable to comprehend why he was meeting them on this trackless rock. "Who—?" he began, and then one of the pair called out his name.

With a shout, Namkhai urged his horse forward, couching the Spirit Banner like a long spear, leaving Ögedei to puzzle out the presence of men whom he thought were caged back at the camp. *How had they gotten out?* he wondered. *Why were they here?*

The giant, the red-haired one who had fought like a crazed bear in the gladiatorial matches, carried a spear, and as Namkhai charged, the giant trotted forward, his arm moving back for a long throw. Namkhai suddenly changed his tactic, realizing the giant's target, and he swept the Spirit Banner to the side. With a final spurt of speed, the giant lunged forward, releasing the spear in an over-handed throw. A second later, the shaft of the Spirit Banner slammed into his chest and hurled him off his feet.

Ögedei's attention snapped to the flying spear. The giant hadn't thrown it at Namkhai. He had hurled it, like it weighed not much more than an arrow, past Namkhai.

Ögedei was the target.

He jerked his horse's head to the side, pounding his feet against its barrel to get it to move. It jerked its head back, snorting at the biting pain he was inflicting by pulling so hard on the reins, and it danced angrily, refusing to obey. The spear arced down, and Ögedei hurled himself out of the saddle, and as he hit the ground hard, painfully scrapping his palms on the rock, he heard the heavy sound of impact. His horse screamed, and he rolled away as it collapsed, thrashing in agony.

The other man, the young Northerner who had stood in the gladiator ring with the fish gutter—the *boy* who had eyeballed him fiercely, thinking quite seriously about throwing the knife—was running at him. He had a sword, and that same look was plain on his face.

He wasn't going to stop this time.

* * *

As soon as Krasniy released the spear, Haakon realized the sacrifice the giant had made for him. He started sprinting, sword in hand.

The thrown spear hit the *Khagan*'s horse and the *Khagan* fell from his saddle as the horse went down, its legs thrashing. The *Khagan* hit the ground roughly, but got to his feet—sword drawn—in time to meet Haakon's first attack.

He launched a two-handed downward stroke at the *Khagan*'s head. Ögedei was dazed from his fall, and he did get his sword up in time, but only just. Haakon's blow bent Ögedei's arm, and the *Khagan* threw his head back to keep from getting hit by his own blade.

Ögedei surged forward, pushing against Haakon's blade, and Haakon batted the underpowered swing aside. He was fighting with one of the curved Mongolian swords, and they didn't have the same point as a Western longsword. The curved end of his blade slid off the *Khagan*'s jacket, slicing through the fur-lined material but failing to penetrate the leather jerkin underneath. He turned his wrists, rotating the sharp edge of the blade toward the *Khagan*'s bare neck, and pulled the weapon back in a cutting motion.

Ögedei jerked his head aside and got his blade underneath Haakon's enough to keep his throat from getting cut. He lashed out with an attack of his own, his blade twisting like an angry serpent, and Haakon caught it between quillons and blade. Ögedei lifted his hands, shoving his blade, and Haakon gasped as the curved edge slid over the base of his hand, slicing his flesh.

Haakon retreated, berating himself for neglecting to remember the differences—once again—between the blade he was fighting with and the one he had trained with. *It doesn't have a point*, he castigated himself. *It is the edge I have to think about.*

Ögedei, seeing the blood running across Haakon's hand, came at him again, swinging his sword in looping, whirling attacks. Ögedei was swinging his sword hard too; each time Haakon rebuffed his attack, he felt the shock of contact in his hand.

His grip was getting slippery.

Ögedei wasn't trying to hit him. The *Khagan* was trying to overtax his wounded hand. If there was enough blood, Haakon might lose control of his weapon.

* * *

The broad Mongol thundered past, and Cnán felt Lian shrink, pressing herself against Cnán's back in an effort to make herself small. As the Mongol brought his horse around, Krasniy shouted at them to get off the rock plateau. Cnán fumbled with the reins of the horse, trying to get the animal's head turned in the right direction. Krasniy rushed in front of her horse, spooking the animal further, and she spat a furious curse at him.

The Mongol rider was coming back, the long horsehair banner lowered again. Krasniy stood his ground, grinning like a demon, and as the Mongol closed in, Krasniy raised his sword and hurled it one-handed.

Cnán could not believe how eager the man was to throw things. *Though*, she thought, watching the sword flip end over end, *given his aim, it's a good strategy.*

The sword hit the Mongol's horse in the head, causing the animal to veer and stumble. The Mongol fought to control his mount, which meant he wasn't paying attention to his target. His lance missed, and Krasniy jumped at the horse as it half galloped, half stumbled past, unhorsing the big Mongol. They hit the ground, flailing at each other in a way that spoke of extensive wrestling experience. They looked like two bears fighting for territorial dominance.

"Look," Lian shouted in her ear, and Cnán followed her pointed finger.

There were more riders approaching, from the direction that the *Khagan* and his bodyguard had come. Sunlight glinted off maille and Cnán's heart leaped. She snapped her reins, and Lian held on as the horse started to run toward the two Shield-Brethren knights.

* * *

As the *Khagan* swept his sword around for another swing, Haakon lunged forward, slapping his sword at the *Khagan*'s blade before it could complete its revolution. He followed through, reaching over and grabbing at the end of the pommel of the *Khagan*'s sword. He made contact, then twisted and shoved his body forward, angling his blade down. He thrust his fist forward, the hilt of his weapon clenched as tightly as he could manage with a palm slippery with blood, and he connected with the *Khagan*'s chin.

Ögedei's head snapped up and his knees trembled. Haakon felt the *Khagan*'s grip loosen, and he yanked the sword out of Ögedei's hand. Though Taran had done it to him so many times, he was momentarily surprised that the technique actually worked. For a second he had both swords.

But then Ögedei recovered from the chin punch and bulled into him, knocking him off balance. Haakon stumbled, caught his foot on a protruding knob of rock, and fell on his ass. He tried to hang on to both swords, but lost one, and his head bounced off another rock before he came to a rest. He scrambled to his feet, trying to get his sword pointed at his enemy.

Who was standing still, looking at something behind Haakon. A horse nickered and he heard the *chingle* of maille.

Trying to keep an eye on the *Khagan*, he glanced over his shoulder and shouted with surprise at the sight of a pair of Shield-Brethren knights. He recognized both immediately. "Feronantus! Raphael!" Both were haggard; Feronantus's beard was patchy and ragged, and Raphael leaned awkwardly forward in his saddle.

"Ho, Haakon," Raphael said, waving a hand, "you should keep an eye on your friend there."

Haakon whirled back, raising his sword to keep the *Khagan* at bay. Ögedei had come a few steps closer, but he paused at the sight of Haakon's ready weapon, raising his hands so that Haakon could see that he was unarmed.

Feronantus was looking farther down the valley, and Haakon spared a quick glance over his shoulder. Cnán's horse was galloping toward them, and beyond, Feronantus could see Krasniy and Ögedei's man locked in a furious wrestling match.

"Well, young Haakon," Feronantus said absently. "We have ridden far, only to find that you have reached our goal before us."

Raphael let loose a bleak laugh. "All this way and we get to watch the youngster."

"Do you know who this man is?" Feronantus asked.

"Aye," Haakon said. "He is Ögedei Khan, the *Khagan* of the Mongol Empire."

"Then kill him quickly," Feronantus said. "We have very little time." He spurred his horse, passing Cnán who was slowing her own mount as she reached them. For a moment, there were too many moving bodies, and Haakon realized he was watching the wrong one. He heard Raphael's shout almost too late.

He pulled his sword arm in, dropping his weapon across his body, as he danced back across the rocky ground. He heard Ögedei grunt and he felt the cold touch of a knife slide across his back. He twisted away from the blade, wrenching his arm around. His blade hit Ögedei, but the edge was turned the wrong way, and he only battered Ögedei on the side of the head.

Ögedei grabbed his shoulder and tried to keep him from getting away. The knife disappeared and Haakon knew it was coming back. As long as the *Khagan* had a hand on him, it was going to be very hard to use his sword effectively. He grabbed the blade with his left hand, pinching it tightly between his fingers, and using only a tiny span at the base of the weapon, he tried to draw the weapon across the side of Ögedei's head.

He felt the blade cut through fur and leather, heard Ögedei roar in pain, and then cried out himself as the *Khagan*'s knife went deep into his hip. He slashed with his sword again, snapping his right hand out to finish the cut with a pommel strike, and this time he felt something break beneath the metal of his hilt.

They separated, both stumbling and falling to their knees. The *Khagan* was bleeding profusely from two places on his head, and Haakon's vision went white as he accidentally bumped his elbow against the hilt of the *Khagan*'s dagger protruding from his hip. The *Khagan* shook his head, and when he looked at Haakon, his face was ugly with blood, his left eye already swelling closed.

Sparing a thought to the Virgin, Haakon let go of his sword and grabbed at the dagger stuck in his hip. He howled as he pulled it free, the pain roaring up through his gut and chest. The *Khagan* raised his hands as Haakon lunged, beating ineffectively at Haakon with a half-closed fist.

Haakon reached over the outstretched arm, and plunged the *Khagan*'s own dagger into Ögedei's neck.

***

Ögedei went away for a moment. He had been fighting the Northerner with his father's knife, trying to take advantage of the boy's lack of focus, but something had gone wrong. While his eyes were closed, he tried to remember what had happened, but all that he remembered was a wave of darkness, like a flock of ravens, blotting out everything.

The left side of his face alternated between hot and cold, and whenever it switched, his skin felt slick and damp. He thought he heard a stream running nearby, but when he swallowed, the sound vanished, as if the water were suddenly drawn into a sucking hole in the ground.

Had he been dreaming of flying? That made little sense, for he wasn't a bird. He was a horse, a four-legged beast of the steppe. All he wanted to do was run and run and run. Run all the way to the sea, with his brothers and sisters at his side. All of their manes streaming behind them in the wind. All he wanted was to run...

He coughed, and the pain was so fierce, he let the ravens take him away for a little while. When he came back, there was someone else there with him. A pale-haired spirit. He tried to tell the spirit what was wrong with him, but the words he spoke were all wrong. *Tolui...Tolui...Who was this* Tolui? *Was that the spirit's name?*

The spirit raised a hand, and when he saw the blood, he screamed. He howled and screeched, and when there was nothing left but a hoarse whimper, Ögedei remembered where he was. He hadn't been flying at all.

He turned his head—slowly, for the pain stabbing down along his left side—and blinked his right eye heavily at the blurry figure squatting over him. His hands twitched, fumbling for his knife, but he couldn't find it. Where had it gone? He had just had it...

The boy was talking to him. "Lie still," he said.

Why should he lie still? He was Khan of Khans. He was...cold.

He tried to tell the boy this, but when he opened his mouth, he felt like nothing came out but water. Thick, foultasting water. It ran down his chin, and he coughed as it threatened to fill his mouth.

The ravens came again, and he spent some time wandering in their wake, looking for something. What was it?

His father's knife.

He shouldn't lose it. It was important. Genghis had given it to him during his first hunt, when he had shot the deer. He had used it to dress the animal.

There had been so much blood.

One of his father's men had helped him carry the meat back to camp. What had that man's name been? *Tolui?*

No, Tolui was someone else. Someone he needed to remember. Someone important to him. *Tolui?* he called out, but Tolui didn't answer.

Tolui hadn't answered for many years.

He was gone. So was his father.

He could never be like his father. He had always known he would fail to be as great a man as Genghis Khan. No one could. Genghis stopped being a man the instant his spirit left his body. He was a ghost that grew more powerful every year as those who thought they knew him told stories that were little more than their own wishful thinking. They made him a ghost, yet they expected his son to be stronger and braver. They expected more because they could not face the darkness; they were afraid to admit they did understand Genghis's vision.

They did not know what to do with his legacy. They dreamed—or thought they dreamed—of the endless sea of horses, and they did not know the meaning of such a vision. They thrust the Spirit Banner into the hands of the sons of Genghis Khan and begged them to be more than their father. They begged *him* to keep the promise they imagined Genghis had made.

But they couldn't face the idea that Genghis had made no promise to them. The only love Genghis had ever had was for his family—his wives and his sons. They were all that mattered. They were his true legacy.

Ögedei opened his eyes once more. The Northerner was still there.

"The sea," Ögedei croaked, and the boy leaned closer. Ögedei remembered the dream he had had, of riding a horse away from the heart of the empire, away from the legacy of his father. Riding until he crossed the entire world and reached the western sea. "All I ever wanted was to see the sea," he sighed.

The boy nodded. "Aye," he said. "I have seen it."

"Tell me," Ögedei said.

The boy did, using words that Ögedei did not understand. But it didn't matter. He could read the boy's face well enough. It was all he could see anyway. The ravens had blotted out the rest of the sky. It was getting colder. Like the sea the boy was talking about. Ögedei closed his eyes, and in the fading twilight of his life, saw the horses again. Running endlessly across the grass of the steppes, running all the way to the end of the world where the sea met the sky.

"You have seen more of the world than I," Ögedei said just before he died.

epilogue:
a tree has many
branches

ITH CNÁN'S HELP, Raphael dressed the knife wound on Haakon's hip. Raphael moved stiffly, and Haakon eventually saw why. A tiny stub of a broken arrow protruded from Raphael's back. When Raphael finished with Haakon, Cnán said something about the arrow.

"It's fine," Raphael said.

"It doesn't *look* fine," she argued.

"It'll keep," Raphael said, rolling up his medical kit. "I have to take my maille off to get to the rest of it, and there isn't time." He stood, trying to hide how stiff he was, and his gaze wandered down the narrow valley. "Where is Feronantus?" he asked.

Haakon, Cnán, and the Chinese woman all looked as well. All they could see was a single horse, cropping the tiny tufts of hardy grass, and a pair of bodies, still tangled together, but unmoving. Of the leader of the Shield-Brethren company there was no sign.

"God damn him," Raphael swore. "He left us."

"What?" Cnán said.

"He had a plan, remember?" Raphael said savagely. "It just didn't include the rest of us." He stalked back to his horse. "Haakon," he called. "That horse over there. It's yours."

Haakon looked down at the still body of the *Khagan*. "What about him?" he said. "We can't just leave him."

"We can and will," Raphael said as he swung painfully up into his saddle. He nodded toward the dead body of the *Khagan*'s horse. "It is a hunting accident. Nothing more. As long as we are not here when the Mongols come." He snapped his reins and his horse trotted away.

Cnán and the other woman got back on their horse as well, and the Binder motioned for Haakon to follow them. He hesitated, looking back and forth between the dead body of the *Khagan* and his friends.

Haakon limped over to the body and pulled the *Khagan*'s knife free. *No one was going to think* hunting accident *with the knife sticking out of his neck,* he rationalized. He wiped the blade clean on his own ragged trousers and retrieved the sheath from Ögedei's belt. He felt like he should cover the body or something, but there was no cloth available and so he settled for making sure the *Khagan*'s right eye was closed. The left had swollen shut.

He picked up his sword, even though the *Khagan*'s looked to be a finer blade. He was already keeping the knife. Taking the sword too was tantamount to robbing from the dead.

The knife, he told himself, was a spoil of war. A testament to what had been done.

Painfully, he jogged down the valley until he reached the bodies of Krasniy and the *Torguud* captain. There was a lot of blood on both men, and it was hard to tell who had died first, but neither had given up. He stopped a moment to offer a prayer to the Virgin for the red-haired giant who had been his only friend in this strange land.

He turned, whistling lightly at the *Torguud* captain's pony. It pricked up its ears and regarded him warily. He limped toward it slowly, talking calmly to it. Assuring it he was friendly.

And then he stopped, casting around for something that should have been lying on the ground nearby. He raised his arm and called out to Raphael and Cnán, who circled back.

"It's missing," he said when they rode up.

"What is?" Raphael asked.

"The lance that the *Torguud* captain was carrying," He said.

Cnán looked around too and nodded. "Haakon's right. The *Khagan*'s bodyguard was carrying a banner. There were streamers attached to it, made from hair. Horsehair, I think."

Lian spoke up from behind Cnán. "Spirit Banner," she said in the Mongol tongue.

"What did she say?" Raphael demanded.

"She said it was a Spirit Banner," Haakon translated.

"The symbol of the Mongol Empire," Cnán supplied. "It belonged to Genghis Khan, Ögedei's father."

"Is he the one who first built the empire?" Raphael asked.

"Aye, he was. He united the clans."

"Of course he did," Raphael said with a heavy sigh. He shook his head. "Feronantus has it."

"Why?" Cnán asked.

"You were there," Raphael said. "At the *Kinyen* when Istvan spouted his nonsense about the All-Father."

"All-Father?" Haakon asked. "The Norse All-Father? What are you talking about?"

"Yggdrasil," Raphael said. "Ragnarök." His eyes were bright, filled with tears. "Surely you know the stories, Haakon."

* * *

They did not want to talk to him, but Kristaps was persistent. His mood and the alacrity with which his hand fell to the hilt of his sword helped, and finally he found a young Hospitaller who was willing to tell him what had happened at the bridge. He did not believe the story at first, but in the absence of any other evidence, it became the story he would tell.

The Livonians left Hünern at dawn, Kristaps at their head. They had lost half of their knights in the final battle with the Mongols—their losses were commensurate with the losses suffered by the other orders—and the company that rode south, following the river, was somber. They had survived, but the cost of their survival had been great.

It was nothing compared to Schaulen, he wanted to tell them. What had been accomplished at Hünern was a victory that the West would celebrate for generations. The battles at Legnica and Mohi had been disastrous blows to the West, and the blight of those tragedies would never truly be wiped away from the history of Christendom, but the fight at Hünern was a victory against all odds. It was a rallying cry for the rest of Christendom. The Mongol host was still on the verge of the West, and their numbers were undiminished by the loss of men at Hünern, but the horde had been bloodied.

The victory at Hünern was a symbol of hope. Evil could be vanquished by Good.

But for Kristaps, when he and his men discovered Dietrich's horse calmly grazing along the riverbank, some miles downstream from the shantytown, he knew Hünern was nothing more than a betrayal.

At Schaulen, they had been destroyed by Volquin's hubris. He would never say as much to his men, but Kristaps knew the fault lay with the previous *Heermeister*. Volquin had led the men to the river; he had failed to recognize the danger of the terrain. He had been overconfident and had thought the pagans were too frightened of the Livonian Sword Brothers to band together effectively. He had underestimated what fear could make men do.

Dietrich had made that same mistake, but it was the other orders who had betrayed him.

"We ride for Rome," he told his men after Dietrich's horse had been retrieved.

I will destroy all of them, he vowed.

* * *

The warm sun slanted brightly through the opened face of the tent; the other three walls were drawn down, both to block the wind and to dampen the constant noise of the tent city being dismantled around them. Already half of the troops were on their way back to Germany. Frederick had ordered his pavilion to be the last one struck. He was engaged in a favorite pastime: playing chess.

It would be more fun, of course, if he actually had an opponent, but Cardinal Fieschi hadn't responded yet to his latest request for a visit. Sadly enough, he doubted the cardinal would be responding to any request from the Holy Roman Empire in the near future.

Frederick fingered a ginger curl near his temple, squinting at the board. He had never played against himself before, and the game had taken on an interesting perspective when he knew all the moves he was going to make.

A shadow crossed the board and he looked up, hoping that the cardinal had decided to visit after all. A broad smile creased his face when he saw who it was instead. "Good afternoon, Léna," he said. "You have arrived in the nick of time. I have not been able to figure out how to lure myself into exposing my queen."

The Binder approached the table and sat down on the camp stool opposite him. "Good afternoon, Your Majesty," she responded. She put her hand over the queen on her side—the black one—and the links of a silver chain spilled out of her palm, draping around the shoulders of the chess piece.

Frederick stared at the silver chain. Its links had been separated in one spot. "You delivered your message," he said somewhat curtly.

"I did," she said.

"I was hoping you wouldn't".

She put her head to one side, gazing with a look normally reserved for recalcitrant children. Frederick sighed. "I don't understand why you had to actually *help* the cardinal. It's only going to give him an incentive to act outrageously, which is only going to make him more dangerous. Especially if he decides to follow through with his threat of becoming Pope."

"He will," Léna said. She moved a black rook, taking one of the white pawns. "Besides, would you have trusted me, as a Binder, if I failed to deliver that message?"

Frederick grunted in reply, staring at the board. He fingered a knight, debating whether he should take the rook that Léna had just exposed. It was a trap, he suspected, and he tried to extrapolate the possible responses.

"You should have more faith," Léna said with a smile.

Frederick snorted. "That is easy for you to say." He decided against moving his knight and shoved a pawn forward instead. It wasn't threatening her rook directly, but in another move, it could.

"You sent the girl after the priest," Léna pointed out.

"I did, though it ran counter to every fiber of my being."

"Such is the nature of faith," Léna countered.

"It isn't something I wish to make a habit of," he said.

"I shall try not to ask Your Majesty to make such sacrifices too often," she demurred, moving a pawn to protect her rook.

"She'll be hunted," Frederick said, sounding regretful. He moved one of his bishops. "By everyone, from champions to madmen, saints to villains. And once your kin-sisters find out she went rogue, they won't shelter her. She's going to be entirely on her own."

Léna sobered. "I am aware of that, and I regret it. There was no other way."

"Your kin-sisters won't be pleased if they learn of your hand in this, either."

Léna stiffened very slightly, but recovered quickly enough. She reached for the pawn in front of her queen, advancing it toward Frederick's side of the board. "He freed me," she said. "When I gave him the ring."

"What do you mean?" Frederick asked.

"In return for the ring, I asked him to set me free. *Unencumbered by all.*"

Frederick shook his head. "You are out of your fucking mind, woman," he said.

She got up from her stool and came around to his side of the table, kneeling beside him so that her head was slightly lower than his. "I had to if I am going to help you." She dipped her head slightly. "You won't tell my sisters, will you?"

Frederick looked at her and grinned. "Not I. My lips are sealed."

Léna smiled. "I know," she said, and leaned forward to kiss him.

* * *

At night, when the sky was filled with stars, she would be tempted to unwrap the bundle in her satchel. But, more often than not, she resisted the urge.

Instead, she would wrap her thin blankets more tightly around her narrow shoulders and try to make herself more comfortable on the hard ground. It had taken some time for her to get used to sleeping out in the open, but she was making the adjustment. It was a matter of practice.

Like so many things she had been forced to learn since she had fled Rome.

Ocyrhoe didn't know where she was going. That much had been true when she had said good-bye to Ferenc. She had never been outside the walls of the city that had raised her. The world was a vast blankness to her, an empty map that had only one landmark, and she was moving farther and farther away from that spot on the map.

When the nights were especially cold and when the sky was too vast and bright with stars, she would relent and retrieve the cup from her satchel. She would hug it against her chest, the gold slowly warming against her body. The idea of selling it or throwing it into a crevice or a river never crossed her mind.

If she spit in it, it would catch the light of the stars. She would wrap her blankets over her head, blocking out all the light except for the glow coming from the cup.

She tried very hard not to rely on the cup's light or warmth to feel safe, but the nights when she feel asleep hugging the Grail were the nights she was without fear or anxiety. Those were the nights when she knew what she had to do.

* * *

From a vantage point near the top of a narrow ridge, Gansukh watched the *Skjaldbrædur* ride west. There were seven of them, including the young Northerner. There were three women in the group, one of whom was Lian.

He didn't know why she was with them, though a number of ugly reasons had flitted through his head more than once since they had picked up the *Skjaldbrædur* trail.

The black-haired man who had been one of the two archers on the day the *Khagan* died was not among the seven, and Gansukh continued to puzzle over that man's absence—as well as the absence of the other one, the grizzled veteran who led them. His body had not been accounted for either.

They had left two behind: the tall archer whom he and Alchiq had brought down, and another one—the wielder of the immense sword. Gansukh couldn't believe such a blade could actually be swung, but the presence of several legless ponies near the man's body had suggested otherwise.

The *Skjaldbrœður* made little effort to hide themselves as they rode, and Gansukh wondered if it was arrogance that allowed them to think themselves invisible and invincible to any roving group of Mongol tribesmen or simply that they did not know where they were going. West was easy enough; they followed the track of the sun across the sky, reorienting themselves in the afternoon.

They were going home. They had accomplished what they came to do.

Having satisfied his curiosity as to the location and condition of the *Skjaldbrœður* party, he climbed over the ridge and returned to his horse. He had shot several rabbits, and his stomach grumbled noisily at the thought of fresh meat for dinner. He rode north, losing himself in the endless grasslands of the steppe, until he reached the narrow stream. He followed it awhile, fording it at a place where it bent back on itself.

The camp was on the lee of a small rise, sheltered from the wind. His horse nickered as he approached, and he heard an answering call from the other horse.

Alchiq looked up from where he sat beside the fire, his leather jerkin in his lap, needle and thread in his hand.

Gansukh tossed the rabbits on the ground. "Still heading west," he reported as he slid off his horse and went about taking off the saddle.

Alchiq nodded as he tied his thread, biting it off, and packed up his sewing kit. "Is *she* still with them?"

Gansukh began brushing his horse down. "She is."

"Still think she didn't betray us?"

And when Gansukh didn't reply, Alchiq chuckled and began dressing the rabbits. "They'll lead us to it," he said. "And when we find the Spirit Banner, you can do whatever you like."

here ends
the mongoliad:
book three

The Mongoliad

CAST OF CHARACTERS

onghwe khan

A bored son of the *Khagan*, Onghwe finds little thrill in simple conquest. He participates in the expansion of the Mongolian Empire only inasmuch as it allows him to increase his menagerie of martial warriors—the gladiators who fight in his Circus of Swords.

teguscal

Captain of Onghwe Khan's guard, Tegusgal is in charge of keeping
an eye on the Khan's gladiators, ensuring that their aggression is
played out in the arena and not in a plot to escape.

Ashiq Temür

Tegusgal's second in command, Ashiq Temür believes that girth is a
physical demonstration of power.

MADHUKAR

A fighter from the Indian subcontinent, Madhukar likes to use anything he can get his hands on for a weapon. Once, the rumors go, he tore a tree out of the ground and used it to knock Mongol warriors off their horses.

Lakshaman

A Malaysian fighter, Lakshaman wields twin knives with deadly efficiency.

RICCARDO ANNIBALDI

A cardinal of the Holy Roman Church, Riccardo Annibaldi was
never Pope himself, but he remained close to St. Peter's throne by
virtue of his extensive family relations.

ROMANO BONAVENTURA

A cardinal of the Holy Roman Church, Romano Bonaventura was
a shrewd negotiator who was well-positioned to become the next
Pope during the *sede vacante* election of 1241. Until Father Rodrigo
showed up...

GOFFREDO CASTIGLIONE

Bishop of Sabina, Goffredo Castiglione was a quiet man, known for
the strength of his piety. During the *sede vacante* election of 1241, he
was a calm center to which the other cardinals gravitated.

STEFANO DE NORMANDIS
DEI CONTI

A cardinal of the Holy Roman Church, Stefano de Normandis dei
Conti was the nephew of Pope Innocent III.

TOMMASO DA CAPUA

A cardinal of the Holy Roman Church, Tommaso da Capua was
also a gifted musician. He wrote a number of hymns to the Blessed
Virgin.

RINALDO DE SEGNI

A cardinal of the Holy Roman Church, Rinaldo de Segni was a
well-connected man. His family provided the Church with two
popes, and he was Cardinal Ugolino Conti de Segni's assistant
before the cardinal became Pope Gregory IX.

GIL TORRES

A cardinal of the Holy Roman Church, Gil Torres was useful to
several popes on the strength of his diplomatic skills and his ability
to negotiate settlements.

FREDERICK II

The Holy Roman Emperor, Frederick II was a foulmouthed, over-
educated, enlightened ruler. He did not mind when his chroniclers
used the Latin term *stupor mundi*—wonder of the world—when
describing him.

LÉNA

A Binder of indeterminate Italian background, Léna is working
in concert with Frederick II to bring about a rational and peaceful
resolution to the *sede vacante* in Rome.

TOREÇENE

Ögedei Khan's first wife. Proud of her position in the *Khagan*'s
court, she tolerates the other wives to some degree, while plotting
ways in which she can get her son, Guyuk, elevated to *Khagan*.

JACHIN

Ögedei Khan's second wife. Pampered from birth, she was married
to the *Khagan* as soon as she reached a proper age. She accompanies
the *Khagan* on his trip to Burqan-qaldun.

NAMKHAI

The *Khagan*'s wrestling champion. Eventually, he becomes the captain of the *Torguud*, the *Khagan*'s elite guard.

alchiq

Known by the party from the West as "Graymane," Alchiq is an old
friend of Ögedei Khan. Exiled by Master Chucai for facilitating
the *Khagan*'s drinking, Alchiq returns to warn the *Khagan* of the
approaching party of Shield-Brethren assassins.

acknowledgments

ERIK BEAR

Thanks to my family, to my friends, and to everyone who's fought alongside me on this book both metaphorically and literally. Thanks to all the other writers, especially Mark, for working harder than any one person should. Thanks to my dad and my grandpa, for guiding me down the path of writing.

GREG BEAR

It's been terrific working with all of these fine writers, clashing steel in the mornings under Neal's guidance, then quaffing coffee and breakfasting out of pink boxes of muffins while plotting at a mad pace...watching Mark outline and organize chapters on our blackboard while Joe and Cooper paced and swung and flashed their blades, shooting ideas back and forth with Neal across our writers' table, talking across the continent with Nicole (and wickedly offering her virtual muffins), collaborating with son Erik on both fight strategies and chapters...while we all ventured on foot and horseback through untold carnage and across wide plains of rippling grass, straight into the fabulous territories of Harold Lamb, Talbot Mundy, and Robert E. Howard. Thanks to all for the amazing experience!

JOSEPH BRASSEY

To Neal Stephenson, who gave me my shot, I hope I've made you proud. To Mark Teppo, who beat my prose with a stick until it was pretty. To Greg, Erik, Cooper, Nicole, and everyone else at Subutai. To Tinker, who taught me to always add violence and put my feet on the path. To Ken and Rob at Fort Lewis, for opening my mind to new possibilities. To my lovely wife and my patient parents, who have always supported me. To my little sister and every friend I've had along the way who believed this could happen. Dreams come true. This is for you.

NICOLE GALLAND

Much gratitude to Mark, Neal, Greg, Cooper, Joe, and Erik for the lively trip we've all taken together—especially for keeping the Skype signal open over the miles, even with all those crickets. A special thank-you to Liz Darhansoff. And a nod to everyone involved in the brief, ineffable existence of E.D. DeBirmingham.

COOPER MOO

Heartfelt thanks to my family for their support: my wife, Mary; our children Keagan, Connor, and Haven; and my parents, Jan and Greg Moo. A debt of gratitude is owed every member of the writing team, particularly Neal for his leadership and Mark for his editorial guidance. I raise a bowl of *airag* to you all!

NEAL STEPHENSON

Thanks to Mark Teppo, the centripetal force.

MARK TEPPO

This project began when someone asked that eternal question that every storyteller loves to hear: "So what happened next?" I don't think any of us realized the full scope of what Foreworld would be (and it is still very much in its infancy), but I am exceptionally grateful to have had this creative team—Erik, Greg, Cooper, Nicole, Joseph, and Neal—during this journey. I'd also like to thank Karen Laur, Jason Norgaar, and Neal Von Flue for the character portraits they provided, as well as the entire mongoliad.com community that ventured into the shiny future with us. Jeremy Bornstein and Lenny Raymond took care of us in that eternally unrecognized way that infrastructure people do; thank you, gentlemen. Fleetwood Robbins provided a keen editorial eye, offering a great perspective on the final arrangement of these words. Also, a nod to Emm, whose constant and unflagging support matters. So very much.

Tinker Pierce, Gus Trim, and Guy Windsor provided a great deal of useful insight and instruction as to the Western martial arts. Additionally, Ellis Amdur and Aaron Fields offered fantastic commentary on all matters relating to the martial arts of thirteenth-century Japan. These five gentlemen are true scholars in their fields, and any creative license taken with the arts they study is entirely our own.

about the authors

Neal Stephenson is primarily a fiction author and has received several awards for his works in speculative fiction. His more popular books include *Snow Crash*, *The Diamond Age*, *Cryptonomicon*, *The Baroque Cycle*, and *Anathem*.

Greg Bear is the author of more than thirty books, spanning the thriller, science fiction, and fantasy genres, including *Blood Music*, *Eon*, *The Forge of God*, *Darwin's Radio*, *City at the End of Time*, and *Hull Zero Three*. His books have won numerous international prizes, have been translated into more than twenty-two languages, and have sold millions of copies worldwide.

Nicole Galland is the author of *I, Iago*, as well as *The Fool's Tale*, *Revenge of the Rose*, and *Crossed: A Tale of the Fourth Crusade*. An award-winning screenwriter, she is married to actor Billy Meleady and, unlike all her handsome and talented cowriters, spends no time at all hitting people with sticks in Seattle.

Mark Teppo is the author of the Codex of Souls urban fantasy series, the hypertext dream narrative *The Potemkin Mosaic*, and the eco-thriller *Earth Thirst*.

Joseph Brassey lives in the Pacific Northwest with his wife and two cats. He teaches medieval fighting techniques to members of the armed forces. *The Mongoliad* is his first published fiction.

Erik Bear lives and writes in Seattle, Washington. He has written for a bestselling video game and is currently working on several comic book series.

Cooper Moo spent five minutes in Mongolia in 1986 before he had to get back on the train—he never expected to be channeling Mongolian warriors. In 2007 Cooper fought a Chinese longsword instructor on a Hong Kong rooftop—he never thought the experience would help him write battle scenes. In addition to being a member of *The Mongoliad* writing team, Cooper has written articles for various magazines. His autobiographical piece "Growing Up Black and White," published in the *Seattle Weekly*, was awarded Social Issues Reporting Article of the Year by the Society of Professional Journalists. He lives in Issaquah, Washington, with his wife, three children, and numerous bladed weapons.